To Shawn
From Grandpa
CHRISTMAS SEAL GREETINGS • 1986

Storytime

SEVENTY STORIES
SELECTED BY THE EDITORS OF
READER'S DIGEST
CONDENSED BOOKS

The Reader's Digest Association
Pleasantville, New York
Cape Town, Hong Kong, London,
Montreal, Sydney

The following selections appear in condensed form:

Two Logs Crossing, Hats for Horses,
The Three Travellers, Being a Public Character,
The Tale of the Lazy People, A Look at the Grand Champ,
Tony Beaver, The Chimaera.

The following are excerpts from longer works:

The Ghost in the Attic, Kildee House,
Roof Sitter, A Lemon and a Star, Pecos Bill,
Call This Land Home, The Doughnuts, Nonsense, Tom and the Dude,
Mama and the Graduation Present, Stormy Place, Blue Willow,
Spurs for Antonia, Reggie's No-Good Bird, Byng Takes a Hand,
Caddie Woodlawn and the Indians.

Second Printing

Library of Congress Cataloging in Publication Data
Main entry under title:

Storytime : adventures in reading for young people:
seventy stories / selected by the editors of Reader's Digest condensed books.
— 1st ed. — Pleasantville, N.Y. : Reader's Digest Association, c1982.
445 p. : col. ill. ; 27 cm.
Summary: A collection of seventy stories
from the United States and other countries.
ISBN 0-89577-145-4

1. Children's stories [1. Short stories] I. Reader's digest condensed books.
PZ5.S8926 1982 [Fic]—dc19 82-80898
AACR 2 MARC
Library of Congress AC

Printed in the United States of America

Contents

The editors wish to
express warm thanks to the following artists
for their contributions to this volume:

Angela Adams, Patience Brewster,
Gwen Connelly, Jon Goodell, Friso Henstra,
Marion Krupp, Ron LeHew, Robert McCloskey,
Leslie Morrill, Jerry Pinkney, Larry Raymond,
Arvis Stewart, Pat Traub

Storytime

The Ghost in the Attic

by Eleanor Estes

The four Moffat children had suffered a lot from Peter the bully. On Halloween they intended to even the score.

Jane came skipping up the street. What a good day it had been so far! And it was going to be even better, of that she was sure. It had been a good day in school because the drawing teacher, Miss Partridge, who visited every class in town once in the fall, once in the winter, and once in the spring, had paid her autumn visit that day.

Jane was nine. Everyone in her class had drawn an autumn leaf. Everyone in her little brother Rufus', a pumpkin. Everyone in her big brother Joe's, an apple. All the children in the grammar schools came home with a drawing fluttering in the wind—a drawing of a pumpkin, an apple, or an autumn leaf. It is true that sometimes the children grew tired of drawing leaves, pumpkins, and apples. However, Miss Partridge never thought of letting them draw anything else.

Still, no matter what they had to draw, the children loved the day of Miss Partridge's visit: first, because all studies would be swept aside for the sake of autumn leaves and pumpkins; second, because Miss Partridge was so amiable. She was always smiling, always. The children called her the smiley teacher. No one had ever seen her frown or heard her speak a cross word.

So today they had had a visit from the smiley teacher! And as soon as the drawing lesson was over and the best autumn leaf drawings had been placed around the room on exhibition, Miss Partridge had produced thirty-eight orange lollipops, one for everyone in the class, and said that now they would play games, have stories, and go home fifteen minutes early.

Why all these good things in one day? Because today was Halloween!

Jane shivered as she thought of the

stories Miss Partridge had told with the shades lowered. One about a golden arm and one dreadful one about stairs and something creeping up them. Then they'd played some good rough games and left early.

Jane scuffled through the dry crackling leaves in the gutter, holding her drawing carefully in one hand for Mama. She skipped through the gate, skipped as fast as she could around the house to the back door with Catherine-the-cat racing after her. She burst into the kitchen that today smelled of hot gingerbread and ran into the front room, where Mrs. Shoemaker was trying on a white satin gown.

Mama, who was the finest dressmaker in town, had her mouth full of pins, but she stopped pulling the gown down over Mrs. Shoemaker's fuzzy yellow hair long enough to look admiringly at the drawing of the autumn leaf. It would be put away later with all the apples, pumpkins, and autumn leaves in the box where Mama kept these things. She nodded her head up and down when Jane said, "May I have a piece of gingerbread?"

Jane grabbed the gingerbread and ran out to join Rufus and Joe in the barn.

"Are you gettin' ready for tonight?" she asked.

"You bet," said Joe. "We're goin' to make a ghost and put it in the attic to scare Peter Frost."

"When?"

"Tonight."

Jane sucked her breath in between her teeth. Ooh! Think of a ghost in the attic!

"Are you sure Peter Frost will come?"

"Oh, sure," said Joe. "He said to me, 'Ghosts! Ha-ha! Ghosts! No such thing!' And I said to him, 'Sure, in our attic there's a ghost.' "

"What did he say to that?" asked Jane.

"He said, 'Ghost, nothin'!' And I said, 'All right, if you don't believe me, come on over to our house at eight o'clock' and we'd show him."

"Well, we better get busy," said Rufus energetically. "What do we do first?"

"First we have to carve the head. This ghost is going to have a pumpkin head." Joe went to a dark corner of the barn and fetched a beautiful pumpkin. The three of them set to work digging out a most startling face. And as they worked, they reviewed their grudges against Peter Frost, who lived across the street and was always tormenting them.

"Remember that time he made Rufus fall off the hitchin' post?"

"Remember that time he told Jane to put her mouth up against the hole in the fence and he would give her a piece of candy and he gave her a mouthful of sand instead?"

Remember? Indeed they remembered all these insults and a great many others. Something just had to be done to settle the account. They worked harder and faster than they'd ever worked before.

After a while Rufus said, "I know what. We can use my teeth in this head."

"Oh, fine," said Joe. "Where are they?"

Without answering, Rufus climbed to the loft. He found the secret hiding place under the beams where he kept some of his treasures. Here was the old tin Prince Albert tobacco box where he kept his collection of teeth. Safe apparently and quite full too. He looked at them lovingly. Some of the teeth were quite small. These were Rufus' own. But most of the collection he had found under the front-room window. Dr. Witty, who had lived in their house before the Moffats, was a dentist. Apparently every time he pulled out a tooth, he had just tossed it out the window. The first tooth Rufus had found one day when he was digging a hole, hoping to get a peep into China. It had filled him with the most amazed delight. In excitement he had rushed in to show it to Mama, thinking she would be as interested as he was. On the contrary, she hadn't been at all pleased about it and had said, "Throw that nasty thing away." He didn't show her his finds after that, but stored them privately in his Prince Albert box.

"Well, what are you doin' up there?" called Jane.

"Comin'," said Rufus, carefully putting them back in the box. Making his way down the ladder with the box, he poured them out between Jane and Joe.

They looked at the teeth admiringly.

"Gee, those are swell," said Jane. "Look at that one, will you?" she said, pointing to an enormous one.

"Yeh," agreed Rufus, looking at it with pride. "Old Natby the blacksmith gave me that one. He said he'd been shoein' an old mare one day and that tooth fell out of her mouth. He said it was the biggest he'd ever seen."

They stuck the teeth in the pumpkin head and at last it was finished. They looked at their work with satisfaction. Phew! It looked gruesome, particularly with that old mare's tooth hanging over its lower lip. Twilight was approaching and they had difficulty in seeing clearly. As it grew darker, they automatically lowered their voices. Now they were talking in whispers, putting the finishing touches on their plan for the night. They began to feel a creepy uneasiness. Their own ideas scared them and sent prickles up and down their spines. They jumped when Sylvie, who was fifteen, came to the kitchen door and called them to supper; then they tore from the barn as though all the hobyahs, pookas, and goblins in the world were at their heels.

The light from the kitchen spread a warm welcome to them. From up and down the street they could hear the different whistles and calls that summoned the other children in the block home to their dinners. Pookas, hobyahs, and goblins fled . . . temporarily. The five Moffats sat down around the kitchen table. As they ate, the oil lamp in the middle of the table sputtered and sent little curls of black smoke to the top of the glass chimney.

"A wind is rising," said Mama.

The children exchanged pleased glances. A wind! So much the better.

Jane whispered to Sylvie, "Have you had a chance to bring the Madame upstairs?" Madame was a bust. She served as a model when the ladies Mama sewed for could not come to try on. Madame-the-bust was to be the ghost this night.

"Not yet," Sylvie whispered back. "There's plenty of time."

"Plenty of time!" echoed Jane impatiently. "Supposin' Peter Frost comes before everything's ready?" She couldn't eat another bite. Rufus had finished too. Finally the others put down their spoons. Dinner was over.

"Now," said Mama, "I see no reason, even if it is Halloween, why I shouldn't leave you four children. Mrs. Pudge wants me to talk over plans for her silver wedding anniversary dress, so I think I'll go tonight. Now don't be gallivanting through the streets after eight o'clock. And, Joey, please tie the garbage pail to the back porch, or some of those street hoodlums will be trying to tie it to the lamppost. And see that the rake and anything else that's movable is locked in the barn. I won't be very late." Then she put on the black velvet hat with the blue violets that matched her eyes and went out.

How still and empty the house suddenly became without Mama in it! Inside, not a sound except the ticking of the clock in the sitting room and the creaking of the cane rocking chair that no one was sitting in. Outside, the wind rustled in the trees and a dog that sounded miles away howled mournfully. The children sat hushed and motionless. Suddenly a hot coal fell in the grate. Catherine-the-cat jumped from her place under the stove, arched her back, and bristled her tail. The children broke into screams of laughter and the house became friendly again.

"Well," said Sylvie, "we'd better hurry. First the pumpkin. Who'll get that?"

Who indeed? Who would go out in that dark barn and get the pumpkin head? No one answered, so Joe and Jane were sent.

"We'll stand in the door," said Sylvie.

Breathlessly, Joe and Jane tore to the barn, snatched up the fierce-looking pumpkin head, and tore back into the warm kitchen.

"Now the Madame," said Sylvie, solemnly lighting the smallest oil lamp and leading the way into the front room. Catherine-the-cat leaped ahead of her, wagging her tail restlessly. What was the matter with Catherine tonight, anyway? She kept meowing and meowing and following them all around. Sylvie set the lamp carefully on the table. Catherine-the-cat sat in the shadow. Her yellow eyes shone with a knowing gleam.

"Look at Catherine," said Jane. "She's watchin' us and watchin' us."

"Let her watch," said Sylvie as she carefully removed Mrs. Shoemaker's white satin gown from Madame-the-bust. Then she grasped Madame tightly in her arms.

"You carry the pumpkin, Joe. And Rufus, you bring your scooter. Jane can carry some sheets."

Slowly the procession made its way out of the front room, into the hall, and up the stairs to the second floor. Joe led the way with his pocket flashlight. From the hall upstairs, a stepladder led to the attic, which did not have a regular door but a hatch, which Joe had to push up with his shoulders. It fell open with a groan and the strange musty smell of the attic greeted them. Joe set the head on the floor and flashed the light down the stepladder so the others could see to climb up.

Sylvie hoisted Madame up before her and climbed in. Then Rufus handed up his scooter and hoisted himself in. As Jane was making her way up, Catherine-the-cat leaped past her and disappeared into the dark recesses of the attic. Jane bit her tongue but managed to keep from screaming.

The four Moffats stood around the entrance, the nearest point to the kitchen, to safety. Joe's tiny flashlight scarcely penetrated the darkness of the attic. But they knew what was up here all right without seeing. Dr. Witty had had many different hobbies. Collecting and stuffing wild animals and birds was one of them. He stored these in the attic. In one corner was a stuffed owl. In another a stuffed wildcat. And all around were a great many little stuffed partridges and quail. The four children shivered, partly from cold, partly from excitement.

"Oh, let's hurry and get out of this place," said Jane.

They placed the scooter in the corner by the owl. Then they put Madame on the scooter, put the pumpkin head with its ominous, gaping mouth on her headless neck, and draped the sheets about her. They tied one end of the rope to the scooter and made a loop in the other end in order to be able to pull the ghost around easily. The end of the rope with the loop they placed near the hatchway.

"All right," said Sylvie. "Now let's see how she looks."

They went to the head of the ladder. Joe flashed his light on Madame—who was Madame-the-bust no longer, but Madame-the-ghost!

"Phew!" he whistled.

"Boy, oh, boy!" said Rufus.

"Oh"—Jane shivered—"come on."

As fast as they could, they pushed the hatch back in place and hurried helter-skelter to the kitchen, where they warmed their hands over the kitchen fire.

"Boy, oh, boy!" said Rufus again. "What a ghost!"

Then they all put on the most fearful masks that Sylvie had made for them. And just in the nick of time, for Peter Frost was stamping on the back porch.

"Hey there, Moffats," he said witheringly. "Where's your old ghost, then?"

Oh, his arrogance was insufferable.

"Don't worry," said Sylvie, "you'll see her all right. But you must be quiet."

"Haw-haw," jeered Peter Frost.

But he stopped short, for out of the night came a long-drawn howl, a howl of reproach.

Sylvie, Joe, Jane, and Rufus had the same thought. Catherine-the-cat! They had forgotten her up there with the ghost. But Peter Frost! Why, he knew nothing of that, of course, and although he was inclined to toss the matter lightly aside, still he blanched visibly when again from some mysterious dark recess of the house came the same wild howl.

The four Moffats knew when to be silent and they were silent now. So was Peter Frost. So was the whole house. It was so silent it began to speak with a thousand voices. When Mama's rocking chair creaked, Peter Frost looked at it as though he expected to see the ghost sitting right in it. Somewhere a shutter came unfastened and banged against the house with persistent regularity. The clock in the sitting room ticked slowly, painfully, as though it had a lump in its throat, then stopped altogether. Even the Moffats began to feel scared, particularly Rufus. He began to think this whole business on a par with G-R-I-N-D your bones in "Jack and the Beanstalk."

Peter Frost swallowed his breath with a great gulp and said in a voice a trifle less jeering, "Well, what're we waitin' for? I want to see yer old ghost."

"Very well, then," said the four Moffats in solemn voices. "Follow us."

Again they left the warm safety of the kitchen, mounted the inky black stairs to the second floor, each one holding to the belt of the one in front. When they reached the stepladder, they paused a moment to count heads.

"Now we go up the stepladder," said Joe in a hoarse whisper. "I'll push open the hatch."

Cautiously the five mounted the stepladder. It seemed to lead to a never ending pit of darkness.

"Why don't you turn on your flashlight?" asked Peter Frost, doing his best to sound carefree and easy.

"And scare away the ghost, I suppose," snorted Joe. "You know, a ghost isn't comin' out where there's a light and all this many people. That is, unless there's a certain one around it happens to be interested in."

Another howl interrupted Joe's words. This sounded so close to them now that the four Moffats were afraid Peter Frost would recognize the voice of Catherine-the-cat. But he didn't. He began to shake violently, making the stepladder they were standing on shiver and creak.

Joe pushed the hatch up with his shoulders. It fell open with a groan, just as it had done before. They all climbed in and stood on the attic floor. Except for a pale glow from the light below, the attic was in the thickest blackness. For a moment they stood there in silence. Then suddenly Joe flashed his light into the corner of the attic. It fell for a second on the stuffed wildcat.

Peter Frost started but said not a word.

Then swiftly Joe flashed the light in the other corner. The stuffed owl stared at them broodingly.

But Peter Frost said nothing.

And then Joe flashed his light on Madame-the-ghost herself. There she was, lurking in the corner, her orange head gaping horribly. All the children gasped, but still Peter Frost said nothing. All of a sudden, without any warning whatsoever, Madame-the-ghost started careening madly toward them. And dragging heavy chains behind her too, from the sound.

Jane called out in a shrill voice, "Peter Frost! Peter Frost! E-e-e-e-e-e-e-e-e-e!"

Joe flashed his light on and off rapidly. Madame-the-ghost dashed wildly around and around the attic. The same howl rent the air! The shutters banged. Then Peter Frost let out a roar of terror. That *thing* was after *him*. He tore around the attic room, roaring like a bull. And the ghost, dragging its horrible chains, tore after him.

"Let me go," he bellowed. But he couldn't find the hatch. Around and around the attic he stumbled, kicking over stuffed partridges and quail. Finally he tripped over the wildcat and sprawled on the floor. Joe flashed his light on them for a second, and when Peter Frost saw that he was sitting on the wildcat, he let out another piercing yell and leaped to his feet. He had seen now where the hatch was, and he meant to escape before that ghost could catch up with him. Again he tripped and was down once more, this time with the ghost right on top of him. She would smother him with those ghastly robes of hers.

"She's got me! She's got me!" he roared.

Frantically he shook himself free of the ghost, and in wild leaps he made again for the hatch.

But now Rufus and Jane too had stood all they could of this nerve-racking business. They both began howling with fright and screaming, "Mama, Mama!" What with Peter Frost's yelling, Catherine-the-cat's yowling, the screams of Rufus and Jane, Sylvie herself began laughing hysterically and the place sounded like bedlam. To make matters worse, the battery of Joe's flashlight gave out, so there was no way of turning on the blessed light and showing everyone there was no real ghost.

No, the ghost was real enough to Peter Frost, and as he finally reached the hatch and clattered down the ladder he thought he could still feel its cold breath on his neck and cheeks. The four Moffats followed after him, half tumbling, half sliding, until they reached the kitchen. Peter Frost tore out the back door with a bang and left the four of them there in the kitchen, breathless and sobbing and laughing all at once.

"Phew," gasped Joe. "Some ghost, I'll say!"

" 'Twas real, then?" said Rufus, getting ready to howl again.

"Of course not, silly," said Joe, whose courage had returned. "Come on, though. We've got to get the things down. Mama'll be home in a minute. Sylvie better carry the little lamp."

Rufus and Jane did not want to go back into that attic. They'd had enough of ghosts and goblins. But neither did they want to stay down in the kitchen alone. So up to the attic the four went once more. And with all the light made from the little lamp Rufus could see there wasn't any real ghost at all. Just Madame and the pumpkin head he'd stuck his own teeth into and his own scooter that Catherine-the-cat, caught in the loop of the rope, was dragging around and around.

Swiftly Sylvie unloosened the cat. She gave them all a triumphant leer and leaped down the hatch with short meows. Next they dismantled the ghost and returned Madame to the front room, where Sylvie dressed her again in Mrs. Shoemaker's new dress. The pumpkin head had received many bad cracks, but they put it in the sitting-room window with a candle lighted inside of it, where it looked quite jolly and altogether harmless.

Then they sat down to talk the evening over. They agreed the ghost had been a success.

"That'll teach him to be always tormentin' the life outta us," said Jane with a yawn.

"Sh-h-h," warned Sylvie. "Here comes Mama."

Mama came in the door. She took off her hat and wiped the tears that the wind had put there from her eyes.

"Goodness," she said. "The witches certainly must be out tonight all right. I just passed Peter Frost racing like sixty up the street. He muttered some gibberish about a ghost being after him. And look at Catherine! She looks as though she's preparing for a wild night. And . . . why, for goodness' sakes! Will you look here, please?" Mama's voice went on from the front room, where she had gone to hang her hat. "Just look here! Mrs. Shoemaker's dress is turned completely around. The hobgoblins must have done it." (Here Rufus smothered his laughter in his brown chubby fist.) "Well, well . . ." she continued, "let's bob for apples. . . ."

How the Rhinoceros Got His Skin

by Rudyard Kipling

Once long ago, on an island in the Red Sea, the Rhino was too greedy for his own good.

Once upon a time, on an uninhabited island on the shores of the Red Sea, there lived a Parsee from whose hat the rays of the sun were reflected in more than oriental splendor. And the Parsee lived by the Red Sea with nothing but his hat and his knife and a cooking stove of the kind that you must particularly never touch. And one day he took flour and water and currants and plums and sugar and things, and made himself one cake, which was two feet across and three feet thick. It was indeed a Superior Comestible (*that's* magic), and he put it on the stove because *he* was allowed to cook on that stove, and he baked it and he baked it till it was all done brown and smelled most sentimental. But just as he was going to eat it there came down to the beach from the Altogether Uninhabited Interior one Rhinoceros, with a horn on his nose, two piggy eyes, and few manners. In those days the Rhinoceros' skin fitted him quite tight. There were no wrinkles in it anywhere. He looked exactly like a Noah's Ark Rhinoceros, but of course much bigger.

All the same, he had no manners then, and he has no manners now, and he never will have any manners. He said, "How!"

and the Parsee left that cake and climbed to the top of a palm tree with nothing on but his hat, from which the rays of the sun were always reflected in more than oriental splendor.

And the Rhinoceros upset the oil stove with his nose, and the cake rolled on the sand, and he spiked that cake on the horn of his nose, and he ate it, and he went away, waving his tail, to the desolate and Exclusively Uninhabited Interior, which abuts on the islands of Mazanderan, Socotra, and the Promontories of the Larger Equinox. Then the Parsee came down from his palm tree and put the stove on its legs and recited the following *Sloka*, which, as you have not heard, I will now proceed to relate:

Them that takes cakes
Which the Parsee man bakes
Makes dreadful mistakes.

And there was a great deal more in that than you would think.

Because, five weeks later, there was a heat wave in the Red Sea, and everybody took off all the clothes they had. The Parsee took off his hat; but the Rhinoceros took off his skin and carried it over his shoulder as he came down to the beach to bathe. In those days it buttoned underneath with three buttons and looked like a raincoat. He said nothing whatever about the Parsee's cake, because he had eaten it all; and he never had any manners, then, since, or henceforward. He waddled straight into the water and blew bubbles through his nose, leaving his skin on the beach.

Presently the Parsee came by and found the skin, and he smiled one smile that ran all around his face two times. Then he danced three times around the skin and rubbed his hands. Then he went to his camp and filled his hat with cake crumbs, for the Parsee never ate anything but cake, and never swept out his camp. He took that skin, and he shook that skin, and he scrubbed that skin, and he rubbed that skin just as full of old, dry, stale, tickly cake crumbs and some burned currants as ever it could *possibly* hold. Then he climbed to the top of his palm tree and waited for the Rhinoceros to come out of the water and put it on.

And the Rhinoceros did. He buttoned it up with the three buttons, and it tickled like cake crumbs in bed. Then he wanted to scratch, but that made it worse; and then he lay down on the sands and rolled and rolled and rolled, and every time he rolled, the cake crumbs tickled him worse and worse and worse. Then he ran to the palm tree and rubbed and rubbed and rubbed himself against it. He rubbed so much and so hard that he rubbed his skin into a great fold over his shoulders, and another fold underneath, where the buttons used to be (but he rubbed the buttons off), and he rubbed some more folds over his legs. And it spoiled his temper, but it didn't make the least difference to the cake crumbs. They were inside his skin and they tickled. So he went home, very angry indeed and horribly scratchy; and from that day to this every rhinoceros has great folds in his skin and a very bad temper, all on account of the cake crumbs inside.

But the Parsee came down from his palm tree, wearing his hat, from which the rays of the sun were reflected in more than oriental splendor, packed up his cooking stove, and went away in the direction of Orotavo, Amygdala, the Upland Meadows of Anantarivo, and the Marshes of Sonaput.

The Crab that Played with the Sea

by Rudyard Kipling

In the Time of the Very Beginnings, there were no tides, and the Sea stayed where it belonged.

Before the High and Far-off Times, O my Best Beloved, came the Time of the Very Beginnings; and that was in the days when the Eldest Magician was getting Things ready. First he got the Earth ready; then he got the Sea ready; and then he told all the Animals that they could come out and play. And the Animals said, "O Eldest Magician, what shall we play at?" and he said, "I will show you." He took the Elephant—All-the-Elephant-there-was—and said, "Play at being an Elephant," and All-the-Elephant-there-was played. He took the Beaver—All-the-Beaver-there-was—and said, "Play at being a Beaver," and All-the-Beaver-there-was played. He took the Cow—All-the-Cow-there-was—and said, "Play at being a Cow," and All-the-Cow-there-was played. He took the Turtle—All-the-Turtle-there-was—and said, "Play at being a Turtle," and All-the-Turtle-there-was played. One by one he took all the beasts and birds and fishes and told them what to play at.

But toward evening, when people and things grow restless and tired, there came up the Man (with his own little girl-daughter?)—yes, with his own best-beloved little girl-daughter sitting upon his shoulder, and he said, "What is this play, Eldest Magician?" And the Eldest Magician said, "Ho, Son of Adam, this is the play of the Very Beginning; but you are too wise for this play." And the Man saluted and said, "Yes, I am too wise for this play; but see that you make all the Animals obedient to me."

Now, while the two were talking together, Pau Amma the Crab, who was next in the game, scuttled off sideways and stepped into the Sea, saying to himself, I will play my play alone in the deep waters, and I will never be obedient to this son of Adam. Nobody saw him go away except the little girl-daughter where she leaned on the Man's shoulder. And the play went on till there were no more Animals left without orders; and the Eldest Magician wiped the fine dust off his hands and walked about the world to see how the Animals were playing.

He went north, Best Beloved, and he found All-the-Elephant-there-was digging with his tusks and stamping with his feet in the nice new clean earth that had been made ready for him.

"*Kun?*" said All-the-Elephant-there-was, meaning, Is this right?

"*Payah kun,*" said the Eldest Magician, meaning, That is quite right; and he breathed upon the great rocks and lumps of earth that All-the-Elephant-there-was had thrown up, and they became the great Himalayan Mountains, and you can look them out on the map.

He went east, and he found All-the-Cow-there-was feeding in the field that had been made ready for her, and she licked her tongue around a whole forest at a time, and swallowed it and sat down to chew her cud.

"*Kun?*" said All-the-Cow-there-was.

"*Payah kun,*" said the Eldest Magician; and he breathed upon the bare patch where she had eaten, and upon the place where she had sat down, and one became the great Indian Desert, and the other became the Desert of Sahara, and you can look them out on the map.

He went west, and he found All-the-Beaver-there-was making a beaver dam across the mouths of broad rivers that had been got ready for him.

"*Kun?*" said All-the-Beaver-there-was.

"*Payah kun,*" said the Eldest Magician; and he breathed upon the fallen trees and the still water, and they became the Everglades in Florida, and you may look them out on the map.

Then he went south and found All-the-Turtle-there-was scratching with his flippers in the sand that had been got ready for him, and the sand and the rocks whirled through the air and fell far off into the sea.

"*Kun?*" said All-the-Turtle-there-was.

"*Payah kun,*" said the Eldest Magician; and he breathed upon the sand and the rocks, where they had fallen in the Sea, and they became the most beautiful islands of Borneo, Celebes, Sumatra, Java, and the rest of the Malay Archipelago, and you can look *them* out on the map!

By and by the Eldest Magician met the Man on the banks of the Perak River, and said, "Ho! Son of Adam, are all the Animals obedient to you?"

"Yes," said the Man.

"Is all the Earth obedient to you?"

"Yes," said the Man.

"Is all the Sea obedient to you?"

"No," said the Man. "Once a day and once a night the Sea runs up the Perak River and drives the sweet water back into the forest, so that my house is made wet; once a day and once a night it runs down the river and draws all the water after it, so that there is nothing left but mud, and my canoe is upset. Is that the play you told it to play?"

"No," said the Eldest Magician. "That is a new and a bad play."

"Look!" said the Man, and as he spoke the great Sea came up the mouth of the Perak River, driving the river backward till it overflowed all the dark forests for miles and miles, and flooded the Man's house.

"This is wrong. Launch your canoe and we will find out who is playing with the Sea," said the Eldest Magician. They stepped into the canoe; the little girl-daughter came with them; and the Man took his kris—a curving, wavy dagger with a blade like a flame—and they pushed out on the Perak River.

Then the Sea began to run back and back, and the canoe was sucked out of the mouth of the Perak River, past Selangor, past Malacca, past Singapore, out and out to the Island of Bintang, as though it had been pulled by a string.

Then the Eldest Magician stood up and shouted, "Ho! Beasts, birds, and fishes, that I took between my hands at the Very Beginning and taught the play that you should play, which one of you is playing with the Sea?"

Then all the beasts, birds, and fishes said together, "Eldest Magician, we play the play that you taught us to play—we and our children's children. But not one of us plays with the Sea."

Then the Moon rose big and full over the water, and the Eldest Magician said to the hunchbacked old man who sits in the Moon spinning a fishing line with which he hopes one day to catch the world, "Ho! Fisher of the Moon, are you playing with the Sea?"

"No," said the Fisherman. "I am spinning a line with which I shall someday catch the world; but I do not play with the Sea." He went on spinning his line.

Now there is also a Rat up in the Moon who always bites the old Fisherman's line as fast as it is made, and the Eldest Magician said to him, "Ho! Rat of the Moon, are *you* playing with the Sea?"

And the Rat said, "I am too busy biting through the line that this old Fisherman is spinning. I do not play with the Sea." And he went on biting the line.

Then the little girl-daughter put up her little soft brown arms with the beautiful white shell bracelets and said, "O Eldest Magician! When my father here talked to you at the Very Beginning, and I leaned upon his shoulder while the beasts were being taught their plays, one beast went away naughtily into the Sea before you had taught him his play."

And the Eldest Magician said, "How wise are little children who see and are silent! What was the beast like?"

And the little girl-daughter said, "He was round and he was flat; and his eyes grew upon stalks; and he walked sideways like this; and he was covered with strong armor upon his back."

And the Eldest Magician said, "How wise are little children who speak truth! Now I know where Pau Amma went. Give me the paddle!"

So he took the paddle; but there was no need to paddle, for the water flowed steadily past all the islands till they came to the place called Pusat Tasek—The Heart of the Sea—where the great hollow is that leads down to the heart of the world, and in that hollow grows the Wonderful Tree, Pauh Janggi, that bears the magic twin nuts. Then the Eldest Magician slid his arm up to the shoulder through the deep warm water, and under the roots of the Wonderful Tree he touched the broad back of Pau Amma the Crab. And Pau Amma settled down at the touch, and all the Sea rose up as water rises in a basin when you put your hand into it.

"Ah!" said the Eldest Magician. "Now I know who has been playing with the Sea"; and he called out, "What are you doing, Pau Amma?"

And Pau Amma, deep down below, answered, "Once a day and once a night I go out to look for food. Once a day and once a night I return. Leave me alone."

Then the Eldest Magician said, "Listen, Pau Amma. When you go out from your cave the waters of the Sea pour down into the Pusat Tasek, and all the beaches of all the islands are left bare, and the little fish die, and Raja Moyang Kaban, the King of the Elephants, his legs are made muddy. When you come back and sit in Pusat Tasek, the waters of the Sea rise, and half the little islands are drowned, and the Man's house is flooded, and Raja Abdullah, the King of the Crocodiles, his mouth is filled with the salt water."

Then Pau Amma, deep down below, laughed and said, "I did not know I was so important. Henceforward I will go out seven times a day, and the waters shall never be still."

And the Eldest Magician said, "I cannot make you play the play you were meant to play, Pau Amma, because you escaped me at the Very Beginning; but if you are not afraid, come up and we will talk about it."

"I am not afraid," said Pau Amma, and he rose to the top of the Sea in the moonlight.

There was nobody in the world so big as Pau Amma—for he was the King Crab of all Crabs. Not a common Crab, but a King Crab. One side of his great shell touched

the beach at Sarawak; the other touched the beach at Pahang; and he was taller than the smoke of three volcanoes. As he rose up through the branches of the Wonderful Tree he tore off one of the great twin fruits—the magic double-kerneled nuts that make people young—and the little girl-daughter saw it bobbing alongside the canoe, and pulled it in and began to pick out the soft eyes of it with her little golden scissors.

"Now," said the Eldest Magician, "make a Magic, Pau Amma, to show that you are really important."

Pau Amma rolled his eyes and waved his legs, but he could only stir up the Sea, because, though he was a King Crab, he was nothing more than a Crab, and the Eldest Magician laughed.

"You are not so important after all, Pau Amma," he said. "Now, let *me* try," and he made a Magic with his left hand—with just the little finger of his left hand—and, lo and behold, Best Beloved, Pau Amma's hard, blue-green-black shell fell off him as a husk falls off a coconut, and Pau Amma was left all soft—soft as the little crabs that you sometimes find on the beach, Best Beloved.

"Indeed, you are very important," said the Eldest Magician. "Shall I ask the Man here to cut you with his kris? Shall I send for Raja Moyang Kaban, the King of the Elephants, to pierce you with his tusks, or shall I call Raja Abdullah, the King of the Crocodiles, to bite you?"

And Pau Amma said, "I am ashamed! Give me back my hard shell and let me go back to Pusat Tasek, and I will only stir out once a day and once a night to get my food."

And the Eldest Magician said, "No, Pau Amma, I will *not* give you back your shell, for you will grow bigger and prouder and stronger, and perhaps you will forget your promise, and you will play with the Sea once more."

Then Pau Amma said, "What shall I do? I am so big that I can only hide in Pusat Tasek, and if I go anywhere else, all soft as I am now, the sharks and the dogfish will eat me. And if I go to Pusat Tasek, all soft as I am now, though I may be safe, I can never stir out to get my food, and so I shall die." Then he waved his legs and lamented.

"Listen, Pau Amma," said the Eldest Magician. "I cannot make you play the play you were meant to play, because you escaped me at the Very Beginning; but if you choose, I can make every stone and every hole and every bunch of weed in all the seas a safe Pusat Tasek for you and your children for always."

Then Pau Amma said, "That is good, but I do not choose yet. Look! There is the Man who talked to you at the Very Beginning. If he had not taken up your attention, I should not have grown tired of waiting and run away, and all this would never have happened. What will *he* do for me?"

And the Man said, "If you choose, I will make a Magic, so that both the deep water and the dry ground will be a home for you and your children—so that you shall be able to hide on the land and in the seas."

And Pau Amma said, "I do not choose yet. Look! There is the girl who saw me running away at the Very Beginning. If she had spoken then, the Eldest Magician would have called me back, and all this would never have happened. What will *she* do for me?"

And the little girl-daughter said, "This is a good nut that I am eating. If you choose, I will make a Magic and I will give you this pair of scissors, very sharp and strong, so that you and your children can eat coconuts like this all day long when you come up from the Sea to the land; or you can dig a Pusat Tasek for yourself with the scissors that belong to you when there is no stone or hole nearby; and when the earth is too hard, by the help of these same scissors you can run up a tree."

And Pau Amma said, "I do not choose yet, for, all soft as I am, these gifts would not help me. Give me back my shell, O Eldest Magician, and then I will play your play."

And the Eldest Magician said, "I will give it back, Pau Amma, for eleven months of the year; but on the twelfth month of every year it shall grow soft again, to remind you and all your children that I can make Magics, and to keep you humble, Pau Amma; for I see that if you can run both under the water and on land, you will grow too bold; and if you can climb trees and crack nuts and dig holes with your scissors, you will grow too greedy, Pau Amma."

Then Pau Amma thought a little and said, "I have made my choice. I will take all the gifts."

Then the Eldest Magician made a Magic with the right hand, with all five fingers of his right hand, and lo and behold, Best Beloved, Pau Amma grew smaller and smaller and smaller, till at last there was only a little green crab swimming in the water alongside the canoe, crying in a very small voice, "Give me the scissors!"

And the girl-daughter picked him up on the palm of her little brown hand, and sat him in the bottom of the canoe and gave him her scissors, and he waved them in his little arms, and opened them and shut them and snapped them, and said, "I can eat nuts. I can crack shells. I can dig holes. I can climb trees. I can breathe in the dry air, and I can find a safe Pusat Tasek under every stone. I did not know I was so important. *Kun?*" (Is this right?)

"*Payah kun,*" said the Eldest Magician, and he laughed and gave him his blessing; and Pau Amma scuttled over the side of the canoe into the water; and he was so tiny that he could have hidden under the shadow of a dry leaf on land or of a dead shell at the bottom of the sea.

"Was that well done?" said the Eldest Magician.

"Yes," said the Man. "But now we must go back to Perak, and that is a weary way to paddle. If we had waited till Pau Amma had gone out of Pusat Tasek and come home, the water would have carried us there by itself."

"You are lazy," said the Eldest Magician. "So your children shall be lazy. They shall be the laziest people in the world. They shall be called the Malazy—the lazy people"; and he held up his finger to the Moon and said, "O Fisherman, here is the Man too lazy to row home. Pull his canoe home with your line, Fisherman."

"No," said the Man. "If I am to be lazy all my days, let the Sea work for me twice a day forever. That will save paddling."

And the Eldest Magician laughed and said, "*Payah kun.*" (That is right.)

And the Rat of the Moon stopped biting the line; and the Fisherman let his line down till it touched the Sea, and he pulled the whole deep Sea along, past the Island of Bintang, past Singapore, past Malacca, past Selangor, till the canoe whirled into the Perak River again.

"*Kun?*" said the Fisherman of the Moon.

"Payah kun," said the Eldest Magician. "See now that you pull the Sea twice a day and twice a night forever, so that the Malazy fishermen may be saved paddling. But be careful not to do it too hard, or I shall make a Magic on you as I did to Pau Amma."

Then they all went up the Perak River and went to bed, Best Beloved.

Now listen and attend!

From that day to this the Moon has always pulled the Sea up and down and made what we call tides. Sometimes the Fisher of the Sea pulls a little too hard, and then we get spring tides; and sometimes he pulls a little too softly, and then we get what are called neap tides; but nearly always he is careful, because of the Eldest Magician.

And Pau Amma? You can see when you go to the beach how all Pau Amma's babies make little Pusat Taseks for themselves under every stone and bunch of weed on the sands; you can see them waving their little scissors; and in some parts of the world they truly live on the dry land and run up the palm trees and eat coconuts, exactly as the girl-daughter promised. But once a year all Pau Ammas must shake off their hard armor and be soft—to remind them of what the Eldest Magician could do. And so it isn't fair to kill or hunt Pau Amma's babies just because old Pau Amma was stupidly rude a very long time ago.

Oh yes! And Pau Amma's babies hate being taken out of their little Pusat Taseks and brought home in pickle bottles. That is why they nip you with their scissors, and it serves you right!

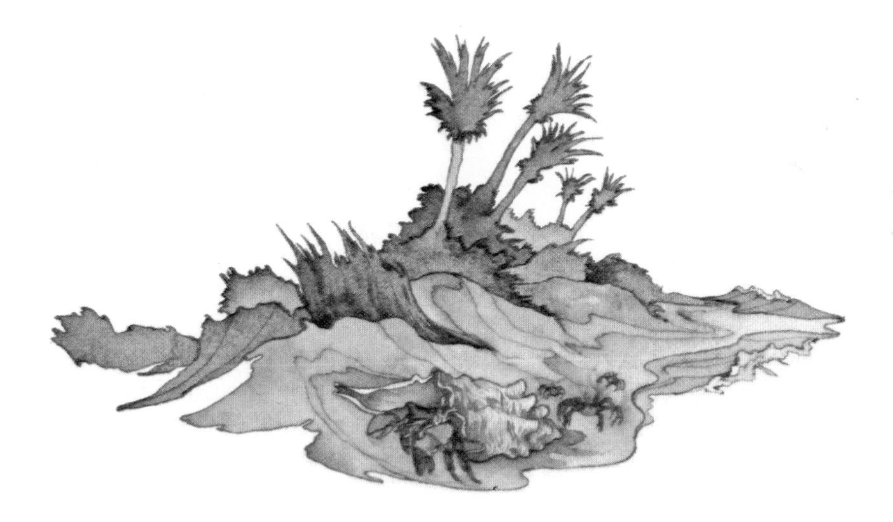

Impunity Jane

by Rumer Godden

No doll as spunky as Jane
could be happy shut up in a doll's house.
Gideon could save her—but Gideon was a thief.

Once there was a little doll who belonged in a pocket. That was what *she* thought. Everyone else thought she belonged in a doll's house. They put her in one, but, as you will see, she ended up in a pocket.

She was four inches high and made of thick china; her arms and legs were joined to her with loops of strong wire; she had painted blue eyes, a red mouth, rosy cheeks, and painted shoes and socks; the shoes were brown, the socks white with blue edges. Her wig of yellow hair was stuck on with strong firm glue. She had no clothes, but written in the middle of her back with a pencil was

5½ d

This was in London, England, many years ago, when the streets were lighted with gas and boys wore sailor suits and girls had many heavy petticoats. The little doll was in a toy shop. She sat on the counter near a skipping rope, a telescope, and a sailing ship; she was quite at home among these adventurous toys.

Into the toy shop came an old lady and a little girl.

"Grandma?" said the little girl.

"What is it, Effie?" asked the old lady.

"That little doll would just go in my doll's house!" said Effie.

"But I don't want to go in a doll's house," said the little doll. "I want to be a skipping rope and dance out into the world, or a sailing ship and go to sea, or a telescope and see the stars!" But she was only a little fivepence-halfpenny doll and in a moment she was sold.

The shopwoman was about to wrap her up when the old lady said, "Don't put her in paper. She can go in my pocket."

"Won't she hurt?" said Effie.

"This little doll is very strongly made," said the shopwoman. "Why, you could drop her with impunity."

"I know 'imp,' " said Effie. "That's a naughty little magic person. But what is impunity?"

"Impunity means escaping without hurt," said the old lady.

"That is what I am going to do forever and ever," said the little doll, and she decided that it should be her name. "Imp-imp-impunity," she sang.

Effie called her Jane; afterward, other children called her Ann or Polly or Belinda, but that did not matter; her name was Impunity Jane.

She went in Grandma's pocket.

Impunity Jane's eyes were so small that she could see through the weave of the pocket. As Effie and Grandma walked home, she saw the bright daylight and sun; she saw trees and grass and the people on the pavements; she saw horses trotting (in those days there were horse buses and carriages, not cars). "Oh, I wish I were a little horse!" cried Impunity Jane.

It was twelve o'clock and the bells were chiming from the church steeples. Impunity Jane heard them, and bicycle bells as well. "Oh, I wish I were a bell!" cried Impunity Jane.

In the barracks a soldier was blowing a bugle; it sounded so brave and exciting that it seemed to ring right through her. "A bugle, a horse, a bell—oh, I want to be everything!" cried Impunity Jane.

But she was only a doll; she was taken out of Grandma's pocket, put into Effie's doll's house, and made to sit on a bead cushion. Have you ever had to sit on a bead cushion? They are hard and cold, and, to a little doll, the beads are as big as pebbles.

There she sat. "I want to go in a pocket, a pocket, a pocket," wished Impunity Jane, but nobody heard.

Dolls, of course, cannot talk. They can only make wishes that some people can feel.

A doll's house by itself is just a thing, like a cupboard full of china or a silent music box; it can live only if it is used and played. Some children are not good at playing; Effie was one. She liked pressing flowers. She did not feel Impunity Jane wishing in the doll's house.

"I want to go out in a pocket," wished Impunity Jane.

Effie did not feel a thing!

Presently Effie grew up, and another child, Elizabeth, had the doll's house. There were changes in the nursery; the old oil lamp and the candles were taken away, and there was gaslight, like that in the streets. Elizabeth's nurse did not wear a high cap, as Effie's nurse had, and Elizabeth's dresses were shorter than Effie's had been; nor did Elizabeth wear so many petticoats.

Elizabeth liked sewing doll clothes; she made clothes for Impunity Jane, but the stitches, to a little doll, were like carving knives. Elizabeth made a dress and a tiny muff. The dress was white with blue sprigs, the muff was cotton wool. Impunity Jane would have liked to wear it as a hat; it could have been like that soldier's cap—and far off she seemed to hear the bugle—but, no, it was a muff. After she was dressed, Elizabeth put her carefully back on the bead cushion.

Through the doll's house window Impunity Jane could see Elizabeth's brother playing with his clockwork railway under the table; around and around whirred the shining fast train. "Oh, I wish I were a train!" said Impunity Jane.

The years went by; Elizabeth grew up and Ethel had the doll's house. Now the nursery (and the street outside) had electric lights, and there was an electric stove; the old high fender where Effie's and Elizabeth's socks and shirts used to dry was taken away. Ethel did not have any petticoats at all; she wore a jersey and skirt and knickers to match.

Ethel liked lessons. She bought a school set with her pocket money, little doll books and a doll blackboard; she taught Impunity Jane reading and writing and arithmetic, and how to draw a thimble and a blackberry and how to sing a scale.

Through the open door Impunity Jane could see Ethel's brother run off down the stairs and take his hoop.

"Do re mi fa so la ti do," sang Ethel.

"Fa! Fa!" said Impunity Jane.

After Ethel there was Ellen, who kept the doll's house shut.

Ellen wore gray flannel shorts and her curls were tied up in a ponytail. She went to a day school, and if her mother went out in the evening, she had a sitter.

Ellen was too busy to play; she listened to the radio or stayed for hours in the living room, looking at television.

Impunity Jane had now sat on the bead cushion for more than fifty years. "Take me out," she would wish into Ellen as hard as she could. Impunity Jane nearly cracked with wishing.

Ellen felt nothing at all.

Then one day Ellen's mother said, "Ellen, you had better get out all your toys. Your cousin Gideon is coming to tea."

Ellen pouted and was cross because she did not like boys, and she had to open the doll's house and dust its furniture and carpets. Everything was thick with dust, even Impunity Jane. She had felt it settling on her, and it made her miserable. The clothes with the big stitches, the lessons, had been better than dust.

"Gideon! Gideon! What a silly name!" said Ellen.

To Impunity Jane it did not sound silly. "G-G-G"—the sound was hard and gay, and she seemed to hear the bugle again, brave and exciting.

Gideon was a boy of seven with brown eyes and curly hair. When he laughed his nose had small wrinkles at the sides, and when he was very pleased—or frightened or ashamed—his cheeks grew red.

From the first moment he came into the nursery he was interested in the doll's house. "Let me play with it," he said, and he bent down and looked into the rooms.

"You can move the furniture about and put out the cups and saucers, as long as you put them all back," said Ellen.

"*That's* not playing!" said Gideon. "Can't we put the doll's house up a tree?"

"A tree? Why, the birds might nest in it!" said Ellen.

"Do you think they would?" asked Gideon, and he laughed with pleasure. "Think of robins and wrens sitting on the tables and chairs!"

Impunity Jane laughed too.

"Let's put it on a raft and float it on the river," said Gideon.

"Don't be silly," said Ellen. "It might be swept away and go right out to sea."

"Then fishes could come into it," said Gideon.

"Fishes!"

Impunity Jane became excited, but Ellen still said, "No."

Gideon looked at Impunity Jane on the bead cushion. "Does that little doll just sit there doing nothing?" he asked.

"What could she do?" asked Ellen.

Gideon did not answer, but he looked at Impunity Jane with his bright brown eyes; they twinkled, and suddenly Impunity Jane knew she could make Gideon feel. "Rescue me," wished Impunity Jane as hard as she could. "Gideon, rescue me. Don't leave me here, here where Effie and Elizabeth and Ethel and Ellen have kept me so long. Gideon! *Gideon!*"

But Gideon was tired of Ellen and the nursery. "I think I'll take a ball out into the garden," he said.

"Gideon! Gideon, I shall crack!" cried Impunity Jane. *"Gideon! G-i-d-e-o-n!"*

Gideon stopped and looked at Impunity Jane; then he looked around at Ellen. Ellen was eating cherries from a plate; she ought to have shared them with Gideon, but she had gobbled most of them up; now she was counting the pits. "Tinker, tailor, soldier, sailor," counted Ellen.

"Gideon, Gideon," wished Impunity Jane.

"Rich man, poor man, beggar man"—and just as Ellen said "thief," Gideon, his cheeks red, slid his hand into the doll's house, picked up Impunity Jane, and put her into his pocket.

Ages and ages ago Impunity Jane had been in Grandma's pocket, but Grandma's pocket was nothing to Gideon's. To begin with, Gideon's pockets often had real holes in them, and Impunity Jane could put her head right through them into the world. Sometimes she had to hold on to the edges to avoid falling out altogether, but she was not afraid.

"I'm Imp-imp-impunity," she sang.

Grandma had not run, and oh, the feeling of running, spinning through the air! Grandma had not skated, or ridden on a scooter. "I can skate and I can scoot," said Impunity Jane.

Grandma had not swung; Gideon went on the swings in the park, and Impunity Jane went too, high and higher, high in the air.

Grandma had not climbed trees; Gideon climbed, to the very top, and there he took Impunity Jane out of his pocket and sat her on one of the boughs; she could see far over houses and steeples and trees, and feel the bough moving in the wind. "I feel the wind. I feel the wind!" cried Impunity Jane.

In Grandma's pocket there had been only Impunity Jane and a folded white handkerchief that smelled of lavender water. In Gideon's pockets were all kinds of things. Impunity Jane never knew what she would find there—string and corks, candy and candy wrappers, nuts, baseball cards, an important message, a knife with a broken handle, some useful screws and tacks, a bit of pencil, and, for a long time, a little brown snail.

The snail had a polished brown shell with smoke-curl markings. Gideon used to take her out and put her down to eat on the grass; then a head with two horns like a little cow's came out at one side of the shell and a small curved tail at the other; the tail left a smeary silvery trail like glue; it made the inside of Gideon's pocket beautifully sticky. Gideon called the snail Ann Rushout because of the slow way she put out her horns.

"I once had a chestnut as a pretend snail," said Gideon, "but a real snail's much better."

Impunity Jane thought so too.

But in all this happiness there was a worry. It worried Gideon, and so, of course, it worried Impunity Jane. (If dolls can make you feel, you make them feel as well.)

The worry was this. Gideon was a boy, and boys do not have dolls, not even in their pockets.

"They would call me sissy," said Gideon, and his cheeks grew red.

On the corner of the street a gang of boys used to meet; they met in the park as well. The leader of the gang was Joe McCallaghan. Joe McCallaghan had brown hair that was stiff as a brush, a turned-up nose, freckles, and gray eyes. He wore a green wolf cub jersey and a belt bristling with knives; he had every kind of knife, and he had bows and arrows, an air gun, a space helmet, and a bicycle with a dual brake control, a lamp, and a bell. He was nine years old and Gideon only seven, but "he quite likes me," said Gideon.

Once Gideon had a new catapult, and Joe McCallaghan took it into his hand to look at it. Gideon trembled while Joe McCallaghan stretched the catapult, twanged it, and handed it back. "Decent weapon," said Joe McCallaghan. Gideon would have said, "Jolly wizard!" But how ordinary that sounded now! "Decent weapon, decent weapon," said Gideon over and over again.

Impunity Jane heard him and her china seemed to grow cold. Suppose Joe McCallaghan, or one of the gang, should find out what Gideon had in his pocket?

"I should die," said Gideon.

"But I don't look like a proper doll," Impunity Jane tried to say.

That was true. The white dress with the sprigs had been so smeared by Ann Rushout that Gideon had taken it off and thrown it away. Impunity Jane no longer had dresses with stitches like knives; her dresses had no stitches at all. Gideon dressed her in a leaf, or some feathers, or a piece of rag; sometimes he buttoned the rag with a berry. If you can imagine a dirty little Gypsy doll, that is how Impunity Jane looked now.

"I'm not a proper doll," she pleaded, but Gideon did not hear.

"Gideon, will you mail this letter for me?" his mother asked one afternoon.

Gideon took the letter and ran downstairs and out into the street. Ann Rushout lay curled in her shell, but Impunity Jane put her head out through a brand-new hole. Gideon scuffed up the dust with the toes of his new shoes, and Impunity Jane admired the puffs and the rainbow specks of it in the sun (you look at dust in the sun), and so they came to the mailbox.

Gideon stood on tiptoe, and had just posted the letter when—"Hands up!" said Joe McCallaghan. He stepped out from behind the mailbox, and the gang came from around the corner where they had been hiding.

Gideon was surrounded.

Impunity Jane could feel his heart beating in big jerks. She felt cold and stiff. Even Ann Rushout woke up and put out her two little horns.

"Search him," said Joe McCallaghan to a boy called Puggy.

Impunity Jane slid quickly to the bottom of Gideon's pocket and lay there under Ann Rushout, the cork, the candy, the pencil, and the string.

Puggy ran his hands over Gideon like a policeman and then searched his pockets. The first thing he found was Ann Rushout. "A snail. Ugh!" said Puggy, and nearly dropped her.

"It's a beautiful snail," said Joe McCallaghan, and the gang looked at Gideon with more respect.

Puggy brought out the cork, the candy—Joe McCallaghan tried one through the paper with his teeth and handed it back—the pencil, a lucky sixpence, the knife—"Broken," said Puggy scornfully, and Gideon grew red. Puggy brought out the string. Then Impunity Jane felt his fingers close around her, and out she came into the light of day.

Gideon's cheeks had been red; now they went dark, dark crimson. Impunity Jane lay stiffly as Puggy handed her to

Joe McCallaghan; the berry she had been wearing broke off and rolled in the gutter.

"A doll!" exclaimed Joe McCallaghan in disgust.

"Sissy!" said Puggy. "Sissy!"

"Sissy got a dolly," the gang jeered, and waited to see what Joe McCallaghan would do.

"You're a sissy," said Joe McCallaghan to Gideon, as if he were disappointed.

Impunity Jane lay stiffly in his hand. "I'm Imp-imp-impunity," she tried to sing, but no words came.

Then Gideon said something he did not know he could say. He did not know how he thought of it; it might have come out of the air, the sky, the pavement, but amazingly it came out of Gideon himself. "I'm not a sissy," said Gideon. "She isn't a doll, she's a model. I use her in my model train."

"A model?" said Joe McCallaghan, and looked at Impunity Jane again.

"Will he throw me in the gutter like the berry?" thought Impunity Jane. "Will he put me down and tread on me? Break me with his heel?"

"A model," said Gideon firmly. "She can be a fireman or a porter or a driver or a sailor," he added.

"A sailor?" said Joe McCallaghan, and he looked at Impunity Jane again. "I wonder if she would go in my model yacht," he said. "I had a lead sailor, but he fell overboard."

"She wouldn't fall overboard," said Gideon.

Joe McCallaghan looked at her again. "Mind if I take her to the pond?" he said over his shoulder to Gideon.

Now began such a life for Impunity Jane. She, a little pocket doll, was one of a gang of boys! Because of her, Gideon was allowed to be in the gang too. "It's only fair," said Joe McCallaghan, whom we can now call Joe, "it's only fair, if we use her, to let him in."

Can you imagine how it feels, if you are a little doll, to sit on the deck of a yacht and go splashing across a pond? You are sent off with a hard push among ducks as big as icebergs, over ripples as big as waves. Most people would have been afraid and fallen overboard, like the lead sailor, but "Imp-imp-impunity," sang Impunity Jane, and reached the far side wet but perfectly safe.

She went up in airplanes. Once she was nearly lost when she was tied to a balloon; she might have floated over to France, but Gideon and Joe ran and ran, and at last they caught her in a garden square, where they had to climb the railings and were caught themselves by an old lady, who said she would complain to the police. When they explained that Impunity Jane was being carried off to France, the old lady understood and let them off.

The gang used Impunity Jane for many things: she lived in igloos and wigwams, ranch houses, forts, and rocket ships. Once she was put on a catherine wheel until Joe thought her hair might catch fire and took her off, but she saw the lovely bright fireworks go blazing around in a shower of bangs and sparks.

She was with Joe and Gideon when they ran away to sea, and with them when they came back again because it was time for dinner. "Better wait till after Christmas," said Joe. Gideon agreed—he was getting a bicycle for Christmas—but Impunity Jane was sorry; she wanted to see the sea.

Next day she was happy again because they started digging a hole through to Australia, and she wanted to see Australia. When they pretended the hole was a gold mine, she was happy to see the gold, and when the gold mine was a cave and they wanted a fossilized mouse, she was ready to be a fossilized mouse.

"I say, will you sell her?" Joe asked Gideon.

Gideon shook his head, though it made him red to do it. "You can borrow her when you want to," he said. "But she's mine."

But Impunity Jane was not Gideon's; she was Ellen's.

The gang was a very honorable gang. "One finger wet, one finger dry," they said, and drew them across their throats; that meant they would not tell a lie. Gideon knew that even without fingers they would never, never steal, and he, Gideon, had stolen Impunity Jane.

She and Gideon remembered what Ellen had said as she counted cherry pits. (Do you remember?) "Rich man, poor man, beggar man, thief," said Ellen.

"Thief! Thief!"

Sometimes, to Gideon, Impunity Jane felt as heavy as lead in his pocket; sometimes Impunity Jane felt as heavy and cold as lead herself. "I'm a thief!" said Gideon, and grew red.

Impunity Jane could not bear Gideon to be unhappy. All night she lay awake in his pajama pocket. "What shall I do?" asked Impunity Jane. She asked Ann Rushout. Ann Rushout said nothing, but in the end the answer came. Perhaps it came out of the night, or Ann's shell, or out of Gideon's pocket, or even out of Impunity Jane herself. The answer was very cruel. It said, "You must wish Gideon to put you back."

"Back? In the doll's house?" said Impunity Jane. "Back, with Ellen, Ellen who kept it shut?" And she said slowly, "Ellen was worse than Ethel or Elizabeth or Effie. I can't go back," said Impunity Jane. "I can't!" But, from far off, she seemed to hear the bugle telling her to be brave, and she knew she must wish, "Gideon, put me back."

She wanted to say, "Gideon, hold me tightly," but she said, "Gideon, put me back."

So Gideon went back to Ellen's house with Impunity Jane in his pocket. He meant to edge around the nursery door while his mother talked to Ellen's mother, then open the doll's house, and slip Impunity Jane inside and onto the bead cushion. He went upstairs, opened the nursery door, and took Impunity Jane in his hand.

It was the last minute. "No more pockets," said Impunity Jane. "No more running and skating and swinging in the air. No more igloos and ripples. No rags and berries for dresses. No more Ann Rushout. No more warm dirty fingers. No more feeling the wind. No more Joe, no gang, not even Puggy. No more . . . Gideon!" cried Impunity Jane—and she cracked.

But what was happening in Ellen's nursery? The doll's house was not in its place—it was on the table with a great many other toys. Ellen was sorting them and doing them up in parcels.

"I'm going to give all my toys away," said Ellen with a toss of her head. "I'm too old to play with them anymore. I'm going to boarding school. Wouldn't you like to go to boarding school?" she said to Gideon.

"No," said Gideon.

"Of course, you're still a *little* boy," said Ellen. "You still like toys."

"Yes," said Gideon, and his fingers tightened on Impunity Jane.

"Would you like a toy?" asked Ellen, who was polishing a music box.

"Yes," said Gideon.

"What would you like?" asked Ellen.

"Please," said Gideon. His cheeks were bright red. "Please"—and he gulped—"could I have"—gulp—"the pocket doll"—gulp—"from the doll's house?"

"Take her," said Ellen without looking up.

Gideon has a bicycle now. Impunity Jane rides on it with him. Sometimes she is tied to the handlebars, but sometimes Gideon keeps her where she likes to be best of all, in his pocket. Now Impunity Jane is not only his model, she is his mascot, which means she brings him luck.

The crack was mended with china cement by Gideon's mother.

Ellen went to boarding school.

As for the doll's house, it was given away.

As for the bead cushion, it was lost.

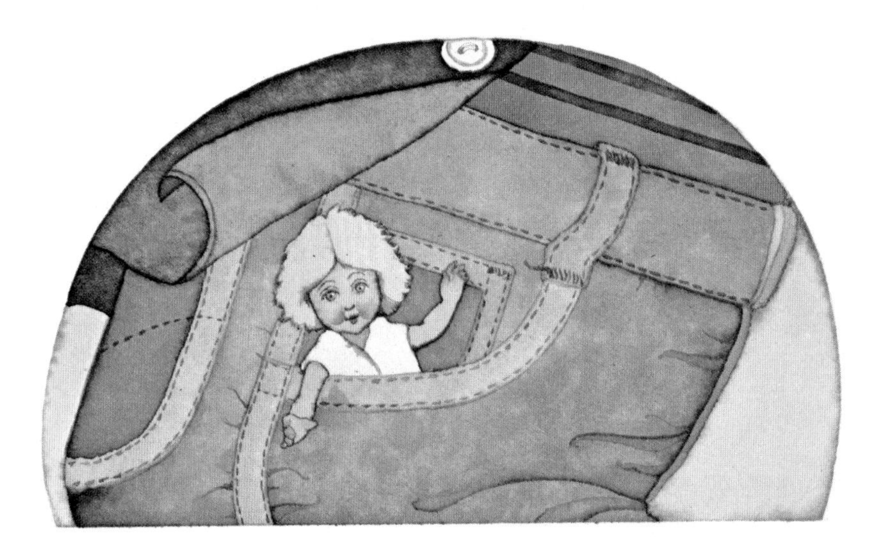

Kildee House

by Rutherford Montgomery

An unsociable man and an equally unsociable raccoon call the same redwood tree home.

Jerome Kildee had built himself a house on the mountainside. It was an odd house, because Jerome Kildee was an odd man. He built his house under a giant redwood tree on Windy Point. At the time he built his house most folks did not build on knobs high on a mountainside, even the round-topped, wooded mountains of the Pacific Coast range.

What the neighbors said or what they thought was of no concern to Jerome. The day he walked out on Windy Point, and looked up at the giant redwood towering into the sky, and stood savoring the deep silence, he knew he was going to stay. When he turned from the great tree and looked down over the green ridges, the smoky valley, into the gray-white haze of the Pacific, he smiled. This was a land of silence, the place for a silent man.

The house Jerome built was not as wide as the redwood; to have made it so wide would have been a waste of space, because Jerome did not need that much room. He toted the biggest window he could buy to the cabin, and set it in the wall that faced a panorama of ridges and valleys. The window was as high as the wall; it was one wall as far across as the door. It had been made to be a plate-glass window for a store.

The back wall was the redwood trunk. It made an odd house, one wall curving inward and finished with shaggy redwood bark. Jerome rented a horse and packed Monterey stone up for a fireplace. The fireplace was a thing of beauty. It filled one end of the room. The cream Monterey stone, traced through with threads of red, was carefully fitted and matched for grain; the hearth was wide, and the mantel was inlaid with chips of abalone shell. It was the last piece of stonework Jerome planned to make, and he made it a masterpiece. In a recess back of the last slab of stone he tucked away the tools of his trade and sealed them into the wall. Jerome Kildee, maker of fine monuments, was no more. There remained only Jerome Kildee, philosopher, a silent little man, seeking to become a part of a silent mountain.

Jerome Kildee did not work. He owned the hundred acres of woods and hillside around him, but he did not clear any of it. He bought all of his food, and he had stove and fireplace wood hauled up and stacked outside his door, even though he had a good supply of oak growing close to his cabin.

He had no near neighbors, nor would he ever have any, because he had built in the exact center of his hundred acres. He had gone through life silent, unable to talk to people, expecting them to leave him to his own thoughts.

But Jerome Kildee found he was not

without friends. He had a host of them and he didn't have to talk to them to keep their friendship. In fact, his silence helped to keep them friendly. They were all interested in him, a new experience for Jerome, and he was interested in them. Jerome found that they were not unlike the people back where he had operated his monument shop. They were willing to take advantage of him, they were selfish, and some of them were thieves, like the pack rats who packed off anything they could carry, regardless of whether or not they could use it.

He soon learned that none of the raccoons could be trusted inside the cabin. They unscrewed the caps off the catsup bottles as easily as he could do it; they unlatched cupboard doors or opened them if there was a knob on them. One old raccoon, who was the neighborhood grouch, lived in a hole in the trunk of his redwood tree. Old Grouch had refused to move when Jerome built his house. He considered the redwood tree his tree. And he made it very clear that Jerome was trespassing.

The pair of spotted skunks who set up housekeeping under his floor were folks of a different sort from the raccoons. They were not dull-witted stinkers such as Jerome had known in his boyhood, dumb fellows who for ages had been depending upon poison gas instead of their wits for protection. These little spotted skunks carried guns but seldom used them. They were as smart as the raccoons, and about as curious. They had a real sense of humor and were always playing pranks on the raccoons. With them around, Jerome always had to get down on his hands and knees and explore the chimney of his fireplace before he built a fire. The skunks liked the fireplace and would gladly have traded it for their nest under the floor. They were not big stinkers like the swamp skunks, so Jerome could always fish them out of the chimney with his broom.

Jerome would probably have been crowded out of his house by the assortment of mice that found it and the fine bark wall of the redwood to their liking if it had not been for the spotted skunks. The skunks had large appetites, so they kept the mouse population on an even keel.

Two big wood mice lived in a bark nest back of a knot in the tree trunk. They furnished dinners for the spotted skunks with a regularity that should have become monotonous. How they could go on having big families, nursing them to a size to go out into the world, only to have them gobbled up one at a time as they left the nest, was more than Jerome could understand.

There was another pair of mice who lived under his bed in a box of old letters, which they made good use of without snooping into the contents or trying to figure out why Jerome had tied them in bundles. They chewed up all of the letters except those written in indelible pencil. This removed from Jerome's life any desire to brood over the past.

Jerome's wooded acres harbored many black-tailed deer and many gray foxes and possums. The foxes never made friends, and the possums ignored him because he never kept chickens. They had no bump of curiosity to draw them to his house. He saw them often and had a nodding acquaintance with them, so to speak. The blacktails visited his garbage pit regularly. The does often brought their fawns into his yard. But they did not bother much with him because he did not grow a garden or set out young fruit trees. He was about like any other dweller on the wooded mountain: he just lived there.

It was during the second year that Old Grouch turned the head of a dainty little raccoon miss. Like many another lass before her, she fell in love with a good-for-nothing. Old Grouch brought her to his nest in the redwood. It was high up on the tree, where a burl formed a deep pocket. Old Grouch had learned that a redwood tree was a safe haven. When coon dogs chased him, followed by yelling humans, all he had to do was shinny up the giant tree. The hunters could not shake him out or climb the tree. Of course after Jerome came, the coon dogs and the hunters stayed away.

Old Grouch brought his bride home in January during the heavy rains. In April she presented him a family. Like many another good-for-nothing, Old Grouch failed to provide for his family, though he did share the nest with them, taking the dry side and grabbing any of the food his bride rustled that suited his taste. Jerome couldn't climb the tree to look into the nest, but he heard the babies and listened to the family chitchat over them.

Old Grouch mildly irritated Jerome. He was smug and fat, always ready to march into the cabin and demand part of Jerome's fried egg or lamb chop, but always staying outside unless there was food. Any friendly advance was met with a snarl or a snapping of white fangs. He was a surly fellow, but Jerome admired the way he had with the ladies.

His wife was of a different sort. She was friendly and thankful to Jerome for bits of food he gave her. She visited the cabin while he was in it, and not just when it was mealtime. She would have taken over his larder if he had allowed it. Her willingness to shift Old Grouch's responsibility for the family to him gave Jerome a problem. He was forced to invent new catches for his cupboard doors, and to fashion latches for his pull drawers.

Outwitting the slim little bride was no easy matter. With feminine wile she made up to Jerome, letting him stroke her head and scratch around her ears, smiling coyly up at him as he sat in his padded chair, but raiding his cupboard as sure as he went for a walk. Jerome fixed inside catches for the doors, worked by wires that went up through the inside of the cupboard and were pulled by strings dangling from the ceiling, well out of reach of a raccoon. The pull drawers became pop-out drawers, worked by wires with strings attached to them. Jerome's house was well decorated with strings hanging from the ceiling. A large button dangled at the end of each string like a black spider.

When Jerome wanted an egg for breakfast he pulled a string, and open popped a drawer exposing the egg carton. Then Jerome always had to take out two eggs because the minute the door popped open in popped Mrs. Grouch, and Jerome had to split fifty-fifty with her. He could have closed and barred the door, but then he would have had to sit by the big window eating his egg with Mrs. Grouch's furry bangs pressed against the plate glass, her bright eyes watching every bite he took, her little tongue dripping hungrily.

The rains lasted a long time that spring, keeping on until June. Mrs. Grouch stood the home her old man had provided for her as long as she could. The babies were growing and taking up more room, the roof leaked, and Old Grouch always took the dry side. One afternoon while Jerome was tramping in the woods, snug in oilskins and rubber boots, she moved her babies into the house. Helping herself to the stuffing in his mattress, she made a nest in the oven. She had long ago learned how to open the oven door. The smell of the oven pleased her. It had a faint food smell that was elegant. She could feed her babies and lick the oven walls, nibbling bits of burned meat as she came to them.

Jerome discovered the family at once, because the oven door was open. He did not scold about the mattress when she showed him her brood of silky raccoons. But he was hungry and this was Saturday afternoon. Jerome always fixed a beef roast for Saturday supper. Once a week the mailman left the meat in his mailbox at the foot of the hill. Jerome got a wooden box and put it in a corner, then he moved the family into it. Mrs. Grouch was miffed, but she accepted the change with a sly smile. Later she would slip her family back into the oven.

Old Grouch stamped up on the porch and seated himself in the open doorway. He scolded his wife in proper style; he glared at Jerome and tossed a few nasty cracks at him. Between growls he kept sniffing the roast cooking in the oven and shaking his fur to get the raindrops off it. With a final warning to his wife, he turned about, climbed the redwood trunk, and got into his nest. The wind was from the north, and his wife was not there to keep the rain off his back. He stayed in the nest for half an hour, then he climbed back down the tree trunk and walked to the door. Jerome grinned at him. He was cutting the roast. He sliced off a piece and laid it on a saucer. He set the saucer on the floor.

Old Grouch looked at the saucer. This was dangerous business. Going into a cabin was like stepping into a box trap. But he was wet and cold; his wife had walked out on him. He needed food and warmth. Ruffling his scruff, he walked into the house. He paused at the saucer and sniffed the good smell of the roast. He took a bite. When Mrs. Grouch scurried across the floor to share with him, he caught up the piece of meat in his forepaws. He sat up and glowered at her. Then he began munching the roast. His wife sniffed eagerly. She looked up at Jerome. He handed her a slice of meat. She took it and seated herself beside her husband. They sat there eating very much like humans, using their small hands to tear bits of meat from the large pieces, then stuffing the bits into their mouths.

By the time Jerome had finished his supper, Old Grouch had made up his mind. He had marched to the door three times, and each time the cold rain had spattered into his face. He knew his wife and babies were going to sleep warm and

dry inside the cabin. She had already returned to the box, where she sat with her small black eyes just above the edge. Old Grouch felt he could do with some more roast, too. He was still a bit hungry. He would stay in the cabin.

After the dishes were washed, Jerome lighted his pipe. He was faced with a new problem. He had been trying for weeks to get Old Grouch into the cabin. Now that the old fellow and his family had moved in, he dared not close the door. If he closed the door, it was hard to say what Old Grouch would do. Jerome was sure it would be pretty wild.

But the night air was growing chilly. The wind was blowing into the room, wet and cold. Even if he did chase Old Grouch out into the rain, he couldn't put Mrs. Grouch and the babies out. Jerome got to his feet. Old Grouch took one look at Jerome towering above him, then scuttled out into the night.

Jerome set the gasoline mantle lamp on the table so the white light would flood the door. He got his tool chest from under the bed. Mrs. Grouch kept her eyes just above the edge of the box. Jerome cut a small door in the bottom of his big door. He swung the small door by butterfly hinges and bored three holes in it.

Jerome had never been able to make friends; it might be that the little door would change that. He took the lamp and examined the chimney of his fireplace. The little skunks were not sleeping on the damper, so he lighted the fire he had laid earlier in the day. Pulling his padded chair up to the fireplace, he set his tobacco jar on the chair arm. As an afterthought he got a saucer and stacked a few squares of roast on it. He set the saucer on the floor beside the chair.

Jerome puffed slowly on his pipe. He watched the red tongues of flame lick around the logs in the fireplace. The warmth made him feel drowsy. He was on his second pipe when Old Grouch solved the mystery of the little door. He had peeped in through the three holes and discovered that Jerome had turned out the gasoline lamp, that his wife was snug and dry in the box with the babies. He sniffed and caught the rich smell of roast beef. He was wet and cold. He eased through the little door just as his wife hopped from the box, carrying one of the babies. She had her teeth set in the scruff. Shaking the water from his fur, he watched her put the youngster into the oven. He scowled at her, but he didn't make a sound. The warmth of the fireplace and the smell of the roast drew him. He moved warily toward the fire. His experience with men had made him wary. But he was cold and he had an idea he could eat some more. Seating himself in the deep shadows near the chair, he stretched his snout toward the dish. He kept his eyes on Jerome. When Jerome did not move, Old Grouch eased forward and picked up a piece of meat. He sat up and began munching it.

Mrs. Grouch had finished transferring her babies to the oven. She sat on the door for a while, watching the two males at the fireplace. Shaking her head, she turned her back upon them and curled up with her brood.

Jerome had never been able to talk with people. He had always known he was missing a great deal, but he had never been able to say the weather was nice or that the weather was bad when people came into his shop. He set his pipe on the arm of the chair and tossed another log on the fire. Old Grouch ducked into a patch of deep shadow, but he came out again and got another piece of meat. The warmth of the fire was beating against his fur. He felt contented and happy. Jerome leaned back and spoke out loud. The sound of his voice startled even himself. Old Grouch, now gorged with roast and sleepy from the heat, toppled off the hearth and had to make quite an effort to right himself. Mrs. Grouch thrust her head out of the oven and stared at Jerome wildly. If it had not been for her babies, she would have fled into the night.

"When I came up here I was licked," Jerome had said. It was as though a stranger had spoken to him; he heard his own voice so seldom. He felt called upon to answer the stranger.

"And were you licked?"

Old Grouch batted his eyes fearfully. He looked all around the room but saw no human being except Jerome, whom he had ceased to consider a man because Jerome never shouted or whistled or talked at all.

"I've spent a lifetime carving cherubs and angels on tombstones. I've cut many a nice sentiment on a gravestone, but never was able to recite a single line before company." Jerome pointed his pipestem toward the fire. "It's a sad business, dealing with sad people, and not being able to say a word to comfort them."

Old Grouch braced himself and let his stomach ease down until he was resting comfortably. The fire was very nice. Jerome smiled down at him. Old Grouch looked like a small bandit, with the black patches that circled his eyes and extended along his cheeks like black bands making a perfect mask against the lighter coloring of his fur. He cocked his head. He was in a mellow mood. His stomach was full to bursting; his furry hide was warm. He felt like singing.

He started out with a soft "*Shur-r-r-r,*" then went into a deeper note, a long-drawn, tremulous "*Whoo-oo-oo,*" not unlike the call of a screech owl, only softer and sweeter, much more mellow. Jerome's smile widened. He had never dared venture a note himself. In all of the hundreds of times he had sat alone in his pew in church he had never dared open his mouth and sing.

"I have missed much," he said.

"*Whoo-oo-oo,*" Old Grouch sang, his head swaying sleepily.

From the oven door came an answering trill. Never had Mrs. Grouch heard her

husband put so much tenderness, so much romance into his song. It touched her deeply, so deeply she closed her eyes and sang back to him. Jerome laid down his pipe.

Turning to catch the high soprano from the oven, Jerome noticed that the little door was bobbing back and forth. He fixed his attention upon it. A small head with black shoe-button eyes appeared. The head moved into the room, followed by a slim body. A moment later another slim body moved through the door. Two tall white plumes lifted. The little spotted skunks had come visiting. Papa waved his plume and stamped his feet; Mama waved her plume and stamped her feet. Like a good host, Jerome arose from his chair. Instantly the two little skunks vanished through the door. Jerome filled a saucer with canned milk and set it near the door, then he went back to his chair.

Almost at once the little door opened and the skunks marched in. They sat down and began lapping eagerly. When Mrs. Grouch hopped off the oven door and started toward the saucer, Papa elevated his plume and stamped his forefeet. He rushed at her, did a handstand, flipped his hind feet down again, then stamped some more. Mrs. Grouch knew what that meant, as did every living thing in the woods. She hastily retreated to the oven door. Papa went back to his milk.

Jerome leaned back in his chair. Old Grouch was in full voice now; his *whoo-oo-oo* was deep and bell-like. Jerome tried an experimental note himself. He was amazed at its quality. It was a baritone note, with feeling and depth in it. But it sent Mrs. Grouch scrambling back into the oven. Old Grouch was not startled though. He just sat, and swayed back and forth, and sang. He seemed to have caught the fine flavor of Jerome's baritone. Jerome tried a few more notes. Mrs. Grouch stayed in the oven; the spotted skunks returned to their home under the floor.

Old Grouch picked up the last square of roast and ate it slowly. When he swallowed it his stomach bulged bigger. He cocked an eye at Jerome. Jerome tried a few hymns he remembered. Old Grouch joined in. He had only one song, but it blended well with any hymn.

After a bit Jerome began to feel sleepy. He was sleepy and he was happy. He leaned back and closed his eyes. Old Grouch yawned. He ambled toward the oven door. After two tries he managed to hop up on the door. Easing into the oven, he curled up with his family. Jerome sighed deeply. Here among friends he could talk about things he had always wanted to talk about, and he could sing when he felt like it. He got to his feet and took his flannel nightgown from its hook. He smiled as he got ready for bed.

A Strange Wild Song

by Lewis Carroll

He thought he saw a Buffalo
Upon the chimneypiece;
He looked again, and found it was
His Sister's Husband's Niece.
"Unless you leave this house," he said,
"I'll send for the Police."

He thought he saw a Rattlesnake
That questioned him in Greek;
He looked again, and found it was
The Middle of Next Week.
"The one thing I regret," he said,
"Is that it cannot speak!"

He thought he saw a Banker's Clerk
Descending from the bus;
He looked again, and found it was
A Hippopotamus.
"If this should stay to dine," he said,
"There won't be much for us!"

He thought he saw a Kangaroo
That worked a coffee mill;
He looked again, and found it was
A Vegetable Pill.
"Were I to swallow this," he said,
"I should be very ill."

He thought he saw a Coach and Four
That stood beside his bed;
He looked again, and found it was
A Bear without a Head.
"Poor thing," he said, "poor silly thing!
It's waiting to be fed!"

He thought he saw an Albatross
That fluttered round the Lamp;
He looked again, and found it was
A Penny Postage Stamp.
"You'd best be getting home," he said;
"The nights are very damp!"

He thought he saw a Garden Door
That opened with a key;
He looked again, and found it was
A Double Rule of Three.
"And all its mystery," he said,
"Is clear as day to me!"

The Three Little Pigs and the Ogre

by Howard Pyle

Those who venture far from the safety of the barnyard had better be supplied with a good bag of tricks.

There were three nice, fat little pigs. The first was small, the second was smaller, and the third was the smallest of all. These three little pigs thought of going out into the woods to gather acorns, for there were better acorns there than here.

"There's a great ogre who lives over yonder in the woods," says the barnyard cock.

"He will eat you up, body and bones," says the speckled hen.

"And there will be an end of you," says the black drake.

"If folks only knew what was good for them, they would stay at home and make the best of what they had there," said the old gray goose who laid eggs under the barn, and who had never gone out into the world or had a peep of it beyond the garden gate.

But no, the little pigs would go out into the world, whether or no. "For," said they, "if we stay at home because folks shake their heads, we will never get the best acorns that are to be had." There was more than one barleycorn of truth in that chaff, I can tell you.

So out into the woods they went.

They hunted for acorns here and they hunted for acorns there, and by and by whom should the smallest of all the little pigs meet but the great, wicked ogre himself.

"Aha!" says the great, wicked ogre. "It is a nice, plump little pig that I have been wanting for my supper this many a day past. So you may just come along with me now."

"Oh, Master Ogre," squeaked the smallest of the little pigs in the smallest of voices. "Oh, Master Ogre, don't eat me! There's a bigger pig back of me, and he will be along presently."

So the ogre let the smallest of the little pigs go, for he would rather have a larger pig if he could get it.

By and by came the second little pig. "Aha!" says the great, wicked ogre. "I have been wanting just such a little pig as you for my supper for this many a day past. So you may just come along with me now."

"Oh, Master Ogre," said the middle-size pig in his middle-size voice, "don't take me for your supper; there's a bigger pig than I am coming along presently. Just wait for him."

Well, the ogre was satisfied to do that; so he waited, and by and by, sure enough, came the largest of the little pigs.

"And now," says the great, wicked ogre, "I will wait no longer, for you are just the pig I want for my supper, and so you may march along with me."

But the largest of the little pigs had his wits about him, I can tell you. "Oh, very well," says he. "If I am the shoe that fits, there is no use in hunting for another; only, have you a roasted apple to put in my mouth when I am cooked? For no one ever heard of a little pig brought on the table without a roast apple in its mouth."

No, the ogre had no roasted apple.

Dear, dear! That was a great pity. If he would wait for a little while, the largest of the little pigs would run home and fetch one, and then things would be as they should.

Yes, the ogre was satisfied with that. So off ran the little pig, and the ogre sat down on a stone and waited for him.

Well, he waited and he waited and he waited and he waited, but not a tip of a hair of the little pig did he see that day, as you can guess without my telling you.

And the great, wicked ogre is not the only one who has gone without either pig or roast apple, because when he could get the one he would not take it without the other.

"And now," says the cock and the speckled hen and the black drake and the old gray goose who laid her eggs under the barn, and had never been out into the world beyond the garden gate—"and now perhaps you will run out into the world and among ogres no more. Are there not good enough acorns at home?"

Perhaps there were, but that was not what the three little pigs thought. "See, now," said the smallest of the three little pigs, "if one is afraid of the water, one will never catch any fish. I, for one, am going out into the woods to get a few acorns."

So out into the woods he went, and there he found all of the acorns that he wanted. But on his way home, whom should he meet but the great, wicked ogre.

"Aha!" says the ogre. "And is that you?"

Oh, yes, it was nobody else; but had the ogre come across three fellows tramping about in the woods down yonder?

No, the ogre had met nobody in the woods that day.

"Dear, dear," says the smallest little pig, "but that is a pity, for those three fellows were three wicked robbers, and they have just hidden a meal bag full of money in that hole up in the big tree yonder."

You can guess how the ogre pricked up his ears at this, and how he stared till his eyes were as big as saucers.

"Just wait," said he to the smallest little pig, "and I will be down again in a minute." So he laid his jacket to one side and up the tree he climbed, for he wanted to find that bag of money, and he meant to have it.

"Do you find the hole?" says the smallest of the little pigs.

Yes, the ogre had found the hole.

"And do you find the money?" says the smallest of the little pigs.

No, the ogre could find no money.

"Then good-by," says the smallest of the little pigs, and off he trotted home, leaving the ogre to climb down the tree again as he chose.

"And now, at least, you will go out into the woods no more," says the cock, the speckled hen, the black drake, and the gray goose.

Oh, well, there was no telling what the three little pigs would do yet; they would have to wait and see.

One day it was the middle-size little pig who would go out into the woods, for he also had a mind to taste the acorns there.

So out into the woods the middle-size little pig went, and there he had all the acorns that he wanted.

But by and by the ogre came along. "Aha!" says he. "Now I have you for sure and certain."

But the middle-size little pig just stood and looked with all of his might and main at a great rock right in front of him. "Sh-h-h-h-h!" says he. "I am not to be talked to or bothered now!"

Hoity-toity! Here was a pretty song, to be sure! And why was the middle-size pig not to be talked to? That was what the ogre should like to know.

Oh, the middle-size little pig was looking at what was going on under the great rock, for he could see the little folk brewing more beer than thirty-seven men could drink.

So! Why, the ogre would like to see that for himself.

"Very well," says the middle-size little pig, "there is nothing easier than to learn that trick! Just take a handful of leaves from yonder bush and rub them over your eyes, and then shut them tight and count fifty."

Well, the ogre would have a try at that. So he gathered a handful of the leaves and rubbed them over his eyes, just as the middle-size pig had said.

"And now are you ready?" said the middle-size little pig.

Yes, the ogre was ready.

"Then shut your eyes and count," said the middle-size little pig.

So the ogre shut them as tightly as he could and began to count, "One, two, three, four, five," and so on; and while he was counting, why, the little pig was running away home again.

By and by the ogre bawled out "*Fifty!!!*" and opened his eyes, for he was done. Then he saw not more, but less, than he had seen before, for the little pig was not there.

And now it was the largest of the three little pigs who began to talk about going out into the woods to look for acorns.

"You had better stay at home and take things as they come. The crock that goes often to the well gets broken at last." That was what the cock, the speckled hen, the black drake, and the gray goose said, and they thought themselves very wise to talk as they did.

But no. The little pig wanted to go out into the woods, and into the woods the little pig would go, ogre or no ogre.

After he had eaten all of the acorns that he wanted he began to think of going home again, but just then the ogre came stumping along. "Aha!" says he. "We have met again, have we?"

"Yes," said the largest of the three little pigs, "we have. And I want to say that I could find no roast apple at home, and so I did not come back again."

Yes, yes, that was all very fine; but they should have a settling of old scores now. The largest of the three little pigs might just come along home with the ogre, and tomorrow he should be made into sausages; for there was to be no trickery this time, so there was an end of the matter.

Come, come! The ogre must not be too testy. There was such a thing as having too much pepper in the pudding—that was what the largest of the little pigs said. If it was sausages that the ogre was after, maybe the pig could help him. Over home at the farm yonder was a storehouse filled with more sausages and good things than two men could count. There was a window where the ogre could just squeeze through. Only he must promise to eat what he wanted and to carry nothing away with him.

Well, the ogre promised to eat all he wanted in the storehouse, and then off they went together.

Soon they came to the storehouse at the farm, and there, sure enough, was a window, and it was *just* large enough for the ogre to squeeze through without a button to spare in the size.

Dear, dear! How the ogre did stuff himself with the sausages and puddings and other good things in the storehouse.

By and by the little pig bawled out as loud as he could, "*Have you had enough yet?*"

"Hush-sh-sh-sh-sh-sh-sh!" says the ogre. "Don't talk so loud, or you'll be rousing the folks and having them about our ears like a hive of bees."

"No," bawled the little pig, louder than before, "but tell me, *have* you had enough yet?"

"Yes, yes," says the ogre, "I have had almost enough, only do be still about it!"

"Very well!" bawled the little pig, as loud as he could. "If you have had enough, and if you have eaten all of the sausages and all of the puddings you can stuff into yourself, it is about time that you were going, for here come the farmer and two of his men to see what all the stir is about."

And, sure enough, the farmer and his men were coming as fast as they could lay foot to the ground.

But when the ogre heard them coming, he felt sure that it was time he was starting home again, and so he tried to get out of the same window that he had gotten in a little while before. But he had stuffed himself with so much of the good things that he had swelled like everything, and there he stuck in the storehouse window like a cork in a bottle, and could budge neither one way nor the other; and that was a pretty pickle for him to be in.

"Oho!" says the farmer. "You were after my sausages and my puddings, were you? Then you will come no more."

And that was so; when the farmer and his men were done with the ogre, he never went into the woods again, for he could not.

As for the three little pigs, they trotted away into the woods every day of their lives, for there was nobody now to stop them from gathering all the acorns they wanted.

Now, don't you believe folks when they say that this is *all* stuff and nonsense that I have been telling you; for if you turn it upside down and look in the bottom of it, you will find that there is more than one grain of truth there; that is if you care to scratch among the chaff for it. And that is the end of this story.

Two Logs Crossing

by Walter D. Edmonds

John needed a lot of courage to ask the judge for money but even more to do what the judge asked of him.

Nobody in High Falls had ever put much stock in the Haskell family. They were poor, even in a backwoods settlement like High Falls, where living came hard. People said that the Haskells were shiftless. "They don't get anywhere," they said. Charley Haskell had never stuck to anything, and now it looked as if his son John was going to turn out the same way.

He was getting tall for his age. He had outgrown his shirt and his hair needed cutting, but now, as he came along the village road with a string of trout slapping against his bare legs, it didn't occur to him that people might disapprove of him. He had been up the Moose River for two days, fishing the runs below the clefts, and the fish in his string were big ones. When he noticed the people eyeing him, he thought it was because they felt envious of anybody who could bring in fish that size, and he let them slap a little harder against his legs as he approached the store.

There wasn't anything to take him into the store, so he kept on toward home, figuring that he would get there in time for his mother to use some of the fish for dinner. He passed the last house, and then the road began to peter out until it was no more than a track in the grass along the riverbank.

The Haskell place stood at the end of it, and the house and barn had a kind of miserable, tumbledown look, even for a poor town like High Falls. About their only advantage was that from the yard you could see over the river between them to Judge Doane's place—if that was an advantage when the roof leaked and the pig fence broke and let the pig into the woods. But John didn't take notice of the looks of the place. His two sisters were on the porch as he came up, and he held up his fish for them to see; and when Lissa, who was the next oldest to him, said their mother had been wondering when he would get back, he hung his pole under the porch roof and went inside to the kitchen, where their mother was getting dinner.

The brush had been allowed to grow close up to the windows, so the kitchen was kind of a dark room, but with the fire going it seemed all right to John, and he was glad to be home. He slapped the fish on the board beside the dishpan and said that the biggest would go all of three pounds. His mother said they were fine fish and called Lissa in to help fix them.

Lissa kept swinging one or the other of her braids back over her shoulder to keep it out of the way. She was getting almost womanish-looking, John thought, as he sat down beside the table to watch his mother cook dinner. Then his brother Morris came into the house to see his fish and ask questions of where he'd got them. Morris said he wanted to be taken along next time, and John said he would take him when he got big enough to walk the ten miles without sitting down to rest every ten minutes, just the way John's father used to tell him when he was Morris' age.

Then his younger sister Mary brought in a load of wood in her plump arms and dumped it in the woodbox; and the baby, Nat, woke up and started yelling in the ground-floor bedroom; and the cat came out of the bedroom with his tail up and walked through the kitchen without even noticing the fish and went outdoors.

Sitting there with all this business going on around him, John thought his father must have felt the same way at times. It gave him a pleased feeling, like being the head of the family. And then he noticed that his mother was watching him, and he had a disturbing idea that there was something she expected of him.

"John," she said. "After dinner I want to have a talk with you."

When Charley Haskell had died that spring, he had left his widow with six children, the four-room house and the rickety barn, the old cow, and a dollar owing from Judge Doane for the sale of a calf.

Mrs. Haskell was a plain, honest, and fairly easygoing woman. She worked hard enough in the house to keep it and the children's clothes pretty clean, but for outside things she had depended on her husband. And for a few weeks after his death she had gone on in her old way, letting things ride. But now she had seen that wasn't going to be enough for the family to get along on, and when John came back she knew she would have to have a talk with him.

John was the oldest boy. Morris, who was seven, was the next. In between were the two girls. Mrs. Haskell told John, therefore, that it was up to him to take his father's place toward his brothers and sisters. They looked to him for support, she said, and she depended on him. Then she kissed him a little tearfully, wiped her cheeks with her apron, and took up her existence again exactly where she had left it off when her husband died.

The sight of her unexpected tears sobered John. He went out of the kitchen and stood awhile on the porch. He looked across the yard, where the brown hen and her chicks were pecking around in the pigweed, and then he went out to look at the corn patch.

He found it full of weeds. It was an unusual thing for him to get the hoe without being told to, but he did, and after he had cleaned the first row, he found that it looked much better when you could see the corn. By the time he came in to supper that night, he had a quarter of the field hoed. He called his mother and sisters out to see what he had done and listened with pride as they said it looked nice.

It was while his mother was looking at the corn that she remembered that they had never collected the dollar from the judge for the calf. She told John that he had better get it that evening.

John said quickly, "I couldn't do that, Ma."

But Mrs. Haskell said he would have

to. "You're the man of the family now," she said. "It's up to you to tend to the business."

John was frightened at the idea of going to the judge's house. In 1830, compared with the small houses in the village, the judge's big stone house across the river was like a palace. John had never seen the inside of it, but he had seen the lace curtains at the windows and, when he went by at night, the oil lamps—two or even three of them in the same room, for Judge Doane was the great man of the district. He owned a vast amount of timberland and held mortgages on most of the farms and had been a representative of the county in the state legislature.

John's mother had brushed his coat for him, but even so it looked very shabby and frayed and outgrown as he knocked on the front door and asked the hired girl if he could see the judge. He had the feeling that it was an impertinence to ask a person like the judge to pay a dollar, even when he owed it to you. He thought that probably the judge would have him thrown out of the house. But his mother had said they needed the dollar for flour and that at least he had to try to get it.

The hired girl left John standing in a big front hall and disappeared down the long passage that led toward the back of the house. After a while she returned, led him to the judge's office, opened the door, and closed it behind him. John stood with his back to it, holding his hat in both hands—a lanky, overgrown boy, with a thin, rather pale face and brown frightened eyes. He looked like someone made of splinters.

The judge's light blue eyes looked cold under the heavy black brows, and he regarded John for a full minute before he said, "Hello, John. What do you want with me?"

But his voice sounded not unfriendly, so John managed, after a couple of attempts, to say that he had come for the dollar for the calf.

"Oh yes," said the judge. "I'd forgotten about that. I'm sorry."

He heaved himself up from his leather armchair and went to his writing desk and took one end of his gold watch chain from the pocket of his well-filled, speckled waistcoat, and unlocked a drawer. While his back was turned, John was able to see the room, with the impressive lace curtains at the windows, the silver plate hung on the chimneypiece, and the fire on the hearth, where the judge burned wood just for the sake of seeing it burn.

The judge relocked the drawer, replaced the key in his pocket, and handed John a dollar bill. He was a heavy man, and standing close like that, he seemed to loom over John, but in a moment he went back to his chair and told the boy to sit down. John did so, on the edge of the nearest chair.

"How are you making out?" asked the judge.

"All right, I guess," answered John. "I wouldn't have bothered you for this, only we had to have it for flour."

"That's all right," said the judge slowly. "I should have remembered it. I didn't think of it because your father owed me money anyway."

"I didn't know that," said John. He couldn't think of anything to say. He only looked at the judge and wondered how his father had had the nerve to borrow money from a man like him.

The judge made an impressive figure before his fire. He was a massive man, with a red face, strong white hair, and uncompromising eyes. He was looking at John, too, rather curiously.

He nodded after a while and said, "He owed me forty dollars."

That was what John had wanted to know, but he was so shocked at the amount of it that all he could do was to repeat, "I didn't know that, sir."

"No," said the judge, "probably not. He was a kind of cousin of my wife's, but we neither of us said much about it. And after Mrs. Doane died he didn't come around much." His brows drew bushily together and he stared into the fire. "How old are you, son?" he asked.

John replied that he was sixteen.

The judge went on to ask about the family, the age of each child, and what Charley Haskell had got planted that spring. John answered all the questions, and as he did he felt a little more confidence. It seemed odd that anyone living in the High Falls settlement could know so little about anyone else. Why, he knew a lot more about the judge than the judge did about him. He told how high the corn stood. He said, "It stands as high as any I've seen around here, excepting yours, Judge. And now I've started looking out for it, maybe it will catch up."

The judge said, "Hoeing is the best garden fertilizer in the world. And sweat is the next best thing to money."

"Yes, sir," said John. It made him feel proud that he had hoed so much of his corn that day. Tomorrow he'd really get after the piece.

"You can't live on potatoes and corn, though," said the judge. "What are you going to do?"

John was awed to be talking so familiarly to a man half the town was scared of; a man, it was said, who had even talked out in the legislature down in Albany. But his face wrinkled and he managed to grin. "Work, I guess, sir."

The judge grunted then, and stood up. "You do that and you'll take care of your family all right. Maybe you'll even pay back the forty dollars your father owed me." He held out his hand, which John hardly dared take. "When do you suppose that'll be?"

John got white. "I don't know, sir."

The judge smiled. "I like that a lot better than easy promises, John." He walked beside him into the hall, his meaty hand on John's shoulder. "Good luck to you," he said from the front door.

During the summer John managed to get work from time to time, hiring out for as much as forty cents a day. At first he didn't have much luck getting jobs, for though he was a good deal stronger than he appeared to be, and worked hard, people remembered his father's prejudice against work and preferred getting other help when they could. Besides, in the 1830s there weren't many people in High Falls who could afford to hire help. So, by working in the evenings and on Sundays also, John had ample time to take care of their corn and potatoes and the other vegetables he had planted late.

It used to puzzle him how his father had ever been able to take life so easily. He himself hardly ever found time to go fishing that summer. And once or twice when he did have the time, he thought of the forty dollars he owed Judge Doane and he went out and looked for work instead. He even found occasional jobs at Greig, up the river, and walked the five miles back and forth every morning and evening.

Little by little, the forty dollars became an obsession with John, and while at first he had given all his earnings to his mother to spend, he now began to save out a few pennies here and there. When, at the end of August, he had saved out his first complete dollar and held it all at once in his hand, he realized that someday he might pay off the debt; and from there his mind went further, and he began to see that it was even possible that someday he would be able to build a decent house for his mother. Perhaps he'd have his own place, too, and get married; and when the settlement became a town, as they said it would, perhaps he might even get elected to the town board.

By the middle of October, John had saved up enough money to see the family through the winter, as he calculated it, for besides his secret bit, he had persuaded his mother to lay by some of what he gave her. Further, she had been moved by the sight of a decent garden to preserve some beans and also some berries that the girls had gathered. The potato piece had yielded forty bushels; and the corn, which John had sold, had brought in a few dollars more.

The day before he finished cutting the winter wood supply, John counted up his money and decided he would make a five-dollar payment on the forty-dollar debt to the judge that night.

He went up to the big house when he felt sure that the judge would have finished his supper; and he had the same business of knocking and waiting in the hall while the hired girl took his name in. He found the judge sitting as he had found him the first time.

"Sit down, John," said the judge, "and tell me what I can do for you."

John obviously did not know how to begin his business properly, so the judge, after watching him under his brows for a moment, continued in his gruff voice, "I may as well tell you I've kind of kept my eye on you this summer, John. I like the way you've taken hold. I'm willing to admit, too, that I was surprised. And I'll be glad to help you out."

John flushed right up to his hair. "I didn't come to ask for anything, Judge." He fished in his pocket and pulled out his coins. His hands were stiffly clumsy. Some of the coins fell to the floor and one rolled musically all the way under the desk. As he went on his knees to retrieve it, John wished he had had the sense to tie them up, instead of jingling them loosely in his pocket all the way. He couldn't bear to look at the judge when he handed him the coins.

The boy said, "I wanted to pay something back on that forty dollars, sir. It's only five dollars." The judge cupped his two hands. "Maybe you'd better count it, sir." It didn't look like so much in the judge's hands.

The judge said, "Quite right, John," and counted up the money. Then he went to his desk, put the money in a drawer, and wrote out a receipt, which he gave to John.

"Yes, sir," said John, wondering what it was.

The judge looked grave. "That's a receipt. It says you've paid me back five dollars." He shook hands. "What are you going to do this winter, John?"

"I don't know, sir. I tried to get a job from Brown at the hotel, splitting firewood, but he's hired Ance instead. Mr. Freel's got all the help he needs at the tannery." Those were about the only winter jobs a man could hope to find in High Falls.

The judge nodded and said, "I'd offer you something, if it didn't mean getting rid of someone else, John. I couldn't rightly do that."

"No, sir," John said, and started home.

Somehow, he felt so happy all the way home that when he reached the house and found his mother sitting up in the kitchen, he couldn't help telling her the whole business. He blurted it all out, the way he had saved a little now and then until he had actually got five dollars. Then he showed her the receipt.

His mother didn't say a word as she looked at the receipt, but her head gradually bent farther and farther forward and all at once she started crying. John could not understand at first. He thought it might be because she was happy. But she did not cry like a happy person. Finally she lifted her face to him.

"Oh, John, why did you do that?"

"I wanted to pay off that debt Pa laid up," he said uneasily. "Ain't that all right?"

"I guess it is, John. But why didn't you tell me first?"

"I kind of wanted to surprise you," he mumbled. "I didn't mean for to make you feel bad, Ma."

"It ain't that, John."

"But ain't I give you enough?"

"I didn't tell you either," she said, almost smiling. Then she started crying again. "I'm going to have another baby, John."

"Baby," said John. "Gee, Ma, I didn't know."

She went right on crying.

"But ain't we got enough?" he demanded.

"Oh yes. You've done fine, John. But the way you've been working has made me feel kind of better. I got to thinking people talked to us different now. I never thought about that before. Sure," she went on, lifting her face. "I'll be all right now. Only when you showed me that about the five dollars, it made me think I could have had a baby that wasn't on the town. I've never had. I don't want to say anything against your father. I loved him. But I never realized before what it would be like to have a baby not on the town. You see," she finished, quite dry-eyed now, "five dollars would have paid Dr. Slocum and Mrs. Legrand. Two for him and three for her."

Even so, John did not quite understand his mother, except to see that he had taken something desperately precious from her. As he thought it over during the next two or three days, he felt all torn up in his chest. He began to see that by starting to be respectable, he had done more than just work for himself. He had done something to his mother, too. And now, by paying the judge that extra money, he had put her back where she used to be. It did not seem logical, but that was how it was.

Perhaps he would have fallen back then and there to his old ways of letting the world slide, if he hadn't met Seth one evening at the blacksmith's, where he had gone to get the big cook kettle mended. Seth was having Jorgen do some work on a few of his beaver traps.

Seth was an Indian. In summer he worked in the sawmills, when it occurred to him to do so, but in the winter he went into the north woods. People distrusted Seth. They did not like the way he smelled. Even in the forge you could smell him, greasy sweet, through his thick tobacco smoke.

Seth said he was planning to go north in about two weeks. He was late, but the winter looked slow. He thought the furs would be coming up pretty quick, though. Better than last year. Last year he had cleared only two hundred dollars.

Two hundred dollars, thought John. He wondered how a man like Seth could spend all that.

He turned shyly to the Indian. "How much does a man need to get traps and food for the winter?" he asked.

The Indian turned his brown face. He wasn't amused, or he did not show it if he was.

"Seventy-five dollar, maybe. You got a gun?"

John nodded. Seventy-five dollars, he thought. He knew only one person who could stake him that much.

The Indian asked, "You going?"

"Maybe," said John.

"You come wit' me. Good range over mine. Plenty room us both. I help you make a cabin."

"I'll see."

It was almost ten thirty at night when John reached the judge's house. He had made up his mind he would ask the judge, if there was a downstairs light still on when he got there.

The house was dark on the town side, but when John went around to the office window, his heart contracted to see that the judge was still up. He tapped on the window. The judge did not start. He got slowly up and came to the window and opened it to the frosty night. When he saw the boy's white face and large eyes, he said harshly, "What do you want?"

"Please, Judge," said John, "could I talk to you?"

"It's late," said the judge, staring with his cold blue eyes for a while. Then he shut the window and presently opened the front door. He was looking a little less threatening by then, but he wasn't looking friendly.

"Be as quick as you can," he said, when they were back in the office.

John was as pale as a person could be. His tongue stuttered. "I—I wanted to ask you something, Judge. But if you don't like it, say so plain. It's about me and getting to trap this winter on account of that five dollars I paid you." He couldn't think decently straight.

The judge barked at him, "Talk plain, boy. Begin at the beginning. What's the five dollars got to do with it?"

John began to talk. He repeated what had happened with his mother, how she felt, how odd it seemed to him, but there it was. The judge began to sit less stiffly. He even nodded. "Women are the limit," he observed. "You want to take back that money?"

"No, no, *I* don't," John said desperately. "But people don't like giving me work yet, and I want Ma to feel respectable. I thought if you could make me a stake to go trapping—"

"How much?"

"Seth said seventy-five dollars," the boy almost whispered. "But I guess I could get along with fifty. I'd get the traps and some powder and ball, and I could go light on the food. I don't eat a great lot and I'm a handy shot, Judge."

"Seventy-five dollars," said the judge. "You're asking me to lend that much to a boy, just like that?" His red face was particularly heavy-looking.

"I'd make it on fifty," said John. "But it was just an idea. If you don't think it's all right, I won't bother you anymore."

"Then you want the five back, too, I suppose—makes it forty again. Forty and seventy-five is a hundred and fifteen."

"It would be ninety dollars, wouldn't it, if you give me fifty?"

"Shut up," barked the judge. "If I'm going to stake you, I'll do it so I'll have a chance of getting my money back. It won't pay me to send you in with so little you'll starve to death before spring, will it?"

John could only gape.

"How about this Seth?" asked the judge. "He's a drunken brute. Can you trust him?"

"I've met him in the woods," said John. "He's always been nice to me."

The judge grumbled. He rose and took five dollars from his desk and gave it to John.

"You bring me back that receipt tomorrow night," was all he said.

When John gave the money to his mother, it made her so happy that he felt wicked to feel so miserable himself. It seemed as if all his summer's work had been burned with one spark. And he was frightened to go next night to the judge's house. But he went.

The judge kept him only a moment. He took the receipt and gave John another paper. "Put a cross in the right-hand bottom corner," he directed; and when John had done so, "That is a receipt for seventy-five dollars. Here's the money. Don't lose it going home."

He walked to the door with John and shook hands. "Good luck. Come here next spring as soon as you get back."

"Thanks," was all John could say.

The judge made a harsh noise in his throat and fished a chew from his pocket. "Good-by," he said.

John got Seth to help select his outfit. The Indian enjoyed doing that. John felt so proud over his new traps, his powder flask and bullet pouch, and his big basket of provisions; and he felt so grateful to the Indian that he offered to buy him a drink out of the two-shilling bit he had left.

"No drink," said the Indian. "Next spring, oh yes."

He shared his canoe with John up the Moose River, and they spent two weeks getting into Seth's range. They dumped his stuff in the little log cabin and moved over the range together to the one Seth had selected for John. There they laid up a small cabin, just like the Indian's, and built a chimney. They had trouble finding clay to seal the cracks, for by then the frost was hard and snow coming regularly each afternoon.

Then Seth took John with him while he laid out his own lines, and after two days went with John, showing him what to start on. After that the Indian spent all his spare time making John snowshoes. He finished them just before the first heavy snow.

John learned a great deal from Seth that fall. First of all he learned that an Indian in the woods is a very different person from an Indian imitating white men. He had always liked Seth, but he had never suspected his generosity and good humor.

Seth seemed to understand how lonely it could get for a boy living by himself, and during the entire winter he never failed to pay John a weekly visit and ask him back to his cabin in return.

John never figured out which was the best part of that exchange of visits—the sight of Seth coming down the brook shore on a Saturday afternoon, or his own trip the next day over the trail between the cabins. In one way he liked this second part better, for it meant that when he got to Seth's he had nothing to do but sit down and be fed.

It was a six-mile walk that took John up along his own creek for a mile and a half to a low pass between two mountains. Then there was a beech ridge where the bucks had scarred the trees with their horns and fought long battles in the fall. From this ridge the trail went down into an alder swamp. After that John climbed another ridge and picked up a small brook on the far side that led him down a long easy grade to the small lake on which Seth's cabin stood. And when he came out on the ice, John would see the smoke rising from the fringe of cedars.

The cabin itself was hidden under the trees, but when he yelped he would hear Seth's yell in return, high-pitched and far carrying and a little wild sounding, especially when the echo came back off the ridge where the pines towered. Then, presently, he would see Seth, brown and shapeless in his old coat, come out on the ice, lifting his arm in greeting as John approached, grinning around the stem of his old pipe, and taking it out long enough to say, "How, John?" before they shook hands. Then they would go into the cabin, which seemed solid with heat and tobacco smoke and the smell of cured pelts and the steam from the kettle of broth that Seth had on the fire.

Seth was always making broth of some kind—it might have a rabbit in it, or black squirrel, or partridges or even odds and ends, like muskrat, that John would have found it hard to like if he had known of them beforehand. Generally, though, it was a mixture of a good many things and thick and strong, and after his walk through the cold it tasted good to John.

He would admire it, giving Seth great pleasure, and the old Indian would sit back and beam, his broad face suddenly squeezed into innumerable fine wrinkles.

Afterward they would look at some of Seth's pelts and talk about their traplines and wonder how much money they had made, until it was time for John to start back.

At first he had arranged his visits so that he could get started before dark, but as the winter went on he became so familiar with his route that he often tackled it after sunset. His snowshoes had packed a hard footing it was easy to follow, even in the dark. The snow had a faint luminance to shape the trees. The night would be full of frost sounds, or he would hear a fox barking on the high slopes, or an owl would hoot him over the pass, and he would occasionally see its dim shape, noiseless as a snowflake in its passing, a dark blot against the stars. The owl lived there all winter and seemed to feel a kind of familiarity toward the boy—as if it looked for his coming. After he got over the first eerie sense of being followed by the disembodied, invisible voice, John came to look for the owl in his turn.

Occasionally he would pick up the sound of his own brook, muffled under the deep snow, and hollow-voiced, where it made small falls between big rocks. This sound of running water came and went beside him until he reached his own cabin under the thick stand of spruce. He would feel his way in and stir up his fire, climb into his bunk and pull his blanket over him, thinking it would be a full week now before he would hear Seth's yell echoing down from the pass and he in turn would go out and wait for the brown figure to come down along the brook.

But that was for the end of the week. Every day John would run one or other of his traplines. These lines would keep him out till dark, walking hard all the way, when he wasn't resetting his traps.

It never occurred to him to worry about anything happening to him, and he was lucky. He didn't get sick, except for one heavy cold and that came near the end of the week, and Seth showed up to look out for him. Seth rigged blankets over a kettle to make what he called a steam lodge. He made John sit naked under the tent of blankets while he dropped hot stones into the kettle until the steam had the boy pouring sweat. Then the Indian took him out in the snow and rubbed his bare skin with it and dressed him and put him in his bunk and covered him. After that he made him an infusion of some tree bark and roots that tasted bitter, and John went to sleep suddenly, his last sight being one of Seth sitting on the floor before the fire, poking wood into it, and smoking his pipe.

Once in a while Seth would give a day to go over one of John's traplines with him, showing him how to reset this or

that trap; whereabouts at the top of a slide to set for otter; how to bait for marten; the best way to make deadfalls. John learned how to build pens for beaver under the ice and sink fresh twigs for bait, and when the younger beaver swam in, to drop the closing pole and let them drown.

There were days, of course, when John came in without a single skin, but generally he had something to keep him busy in the evenings. And sometimes he would work by the firelight until he fell asleep and the cold woke him later, when the fire was just a handful of embers. It was lonesome for a boy then, and one night he was so cold and stiff it hardly seemed worth trying to move and he let his eyes close again. But suddenly he came wide awake in a kind of panic and found himself standing up. He never knew what waked him; but years afterward, when he was an old man, he told one of his grandchildren that every man, at least once in his life anyway, comes close to death, and maybe that was the time.

It was hard work running traplines. It was hard work just to live alone in the woods and keep working, even when you had a friend only six miles cross-country. But John did well. Early in March his bale of furs had mounted up so that he had Seth make a special trip over and appraise them. The Indian said that John had more than two hundred dollars' worth. It would depend on the market. By the end of the month he might have two hundred and fifty dollars' worth.

John dug into his flour and made soda biscuits for the Indian. They ate them with a little sugar he had left, and Seth spent the night in celebration. They talked a long time about how John would be fixed up to pay off the judge, not only the stake but also the debt, and even have some money to start the summer on. Next winter he would make a clear profit. He would put money in the bank.

Seth did not understand what you put money in the bank for—not even when John explained that it was by saving money and laying it up against the future that a man got rich like the judge. Seth agreed that it was a wonderful thing to have a house like the judge's and hire help; but he still did not see the point of having money you did not use up. Besides, as he said, the judge didn't like him. "Don't like Indian. Don't like me drunken brute."

"That's it," John said. "You spend your money on likker, Seth. Then you haven't got anything at all."

For a few minutes Seth looked both enlightened and sad. But then he smiled at John. "I lose money," he said. "Well, maybe I get some more."

It came to John then that the future meant nothing to Seth. He worked and made money and drank it up and worked again, but it all meant nothing. He was just passing his time that way. It didn't bother John much, though. Seth was a good friend.

The snow went down quickly. When he woke one morning, John was aware of a faint ticking sound all through the woods. He went out of his cabin and looked around, but there was nothing to see. Later, however, the drip from the branches began to dent the snow in the black part of the spruce woods. Seth said maybe it was the frost working out of the trees, or the first creeping of sap. It came every spring. You didn't know. Maybe it was the little people under the earth getting ready to push the grass up.

Whatever it was, John began to get

restless. He was eager now to leave. He wanted to show his furs; he wanted to sell them, he told Seth, on a young market. Seth nodded. He knew how John felt, and he agreed that if John went now, there was a chance he could get across the Moose River somewhere on the ice. So he came over to help John pack his furs and traps. They had a big feed on about the last of John's grub.

In the morning the boy set out. The Indian walked with him to the end of his own south line and shook hands.

"You one good boy, John," he said unexpectedly. "You come again next year."

"I will sure," promised John. "Thanks for all you've done for me, Seth. Without you, I wouldn't have done this." He hitched the heavy pack up on his shoulders. "I guess next the judge, you're about the best friend I ever had."

The Indian's face wrinkled all over beneath his battered hat. He held John's hand and said, "Now listen to Seth. *If creeks open, you cut two logs crossing.* You mind Seth. You cut two logs. One log roll. Two logs safe crossing water."

"Yes, sure," agreed John. He wanted to get away. The sun was well up by now.

"By," said Seth.

John walked hard. He felt strong that morning. He felt like a grown man. The weight of the pack, galling his shoulders, was a pleasure to carry.

Every time he eased it one way or another, he thought about what it was going to mean. He thought about coming home and telling his mother. He would buy her a new dress. He would make a purchase of some calico for his sisters. Make a purchase, when you said it that way, was quite a word. He'd never even thought of it before.

He would see the judge. He imagined himself walking into the judge's office and dropping the pack on the floor and looking the judge in the eye. He realized that this almost meant more to him even than doing things for his family.

He remembered the way he had started the winter. He had asked Seth to estimate the worth of each first pelt. When they had figured up to forty dollars, he had made a bundle of them. They were still packed together in the bottom of the pack. It seemed to him that getting that first forty dollars' worth was twice as much of a job as all the rest afterward had been.

The snow was a little slushy here and there, but it held up well in the big woods and John made pretty good time. Nights he set himself up a lean-to of cedar and balsam branches, and sitting before his small fire, he would think ahead a few years. He could see himself someday, pretty near like the judge. He even figured on teaching himself to read and write, write his own name anyway. No matter how you looked at it, you couldn't make a cross seem like John Haskell, written out in full, with big and little letters in it.

Mornings, he started with the first gray light, when the mist was like a twilight on the water and the deer moused along the runways and eyed him, curious as chipmunks. He walked south down the slopes of the hills, across the shadows of the sunrise, when the snow became full of color and the hills ahead wore a bloody purple shadow on their northern faces.

John had grown taller during the winter, and he seemed even lankier, but his eyes were still the boy's eyes of a year ago.

He crossed the Moose River on the ice

just at dusk one evening. The snow had been a good deal softer that day and his legs ached and the pack weighed down a bit harder than usual. But though the ice had been treacherous close to shore, he had found a crossing place easily enough.

That night, however, as he lay in his lean-to, he heard the river ice begin to work. It went out in the morning with a grinding roar and built a jam half a mile below his camp.

He saw it with a gay heart as he set out after breakfast. It seemed to him the most providential thing he ever had heard of. If he had waited another day before starting, he would have found the river open and he would have had to go back to Seth's cabin and wait till the Indian was ready to come out. But as it was now, he would have only creeks to cross.

There were a good many of them, and most of them were opening. But he found places to cross them, and he had no trouble till afternoon, when he found some running full. They were high with black snow water, several of them so high that he had to go upstream almost a mile to find a place where he could fell a bridge across.

Each time he dropped two logs and went over easily enough. But each time the delay chafed him a little more. By late afternoon, when he was only a few miles from High Falls and began to recognize his landmarks, he came to what he knew was the last creek.

It was a strong stream, with a great force of water, and it was boiling full. Where John happened on it, it began a slide down the steep bank for the river, with one bend and then a straight chute. But it was narrow there, and beside where he stood grew a straight hemlock, long enough to reach across.

Hardly stopping to unload his pack, John set to work with his axe. The tree fell nicely, just above the water. There was no other tree close by, but John thought about that only for a moment. It was the last creek, he was almost home, and his heart was set on getting there that night. Besides, he had had no trouble on the other crossings. He was surefooted and in every case he had run across one log.

He gave the tree a kick, but it lay steady, and suddenly he made up his mind to forget what Seth had said. He could get over easy enough and see the judge that evening.

With his furs on his back, his axe in one hand and his gun in the other, he stepped out on the log. It felt solid as stone under his feet and he went along at a steady pace. The race of water just under the bark meant nothing to John. His head was quite clear and his eyes already were on the other side.

It was just when he was halfway over that the log rolled without any warning and pitched John into the creek.

The water took hold of him and lugged him straight down and rolled him over and over like a dead pig. He dropped his gun and axe at the first roll and instinctively tugged at the traps, which weighted him so. As he struggled to the top, he felt the fur pack slip off. He made a desperate grab for it, but it went away. When he finally washed up on the bend and crawled out on the snow, he hadn't a thing left but his life.

That seemed worthless to him as he lay there on the snow. He could not even cry about it.

He lay there for perhaps half an hour,

while the dusk came in on the river. Finally he was able to get to his feet and searched downstream, poking with a stick along the bottom, although he knew it was hopeless. The creek ran like a millrace down the slope for the river, and the chances were a hundred to one that the traps, as well as the furs, had been taken by the strength of water and the slide all the way down to the river. But John continued his search till nearly dark before he gave up.

By the time he reached High Falls, John had managed to get back just enough of his courage to go straight to the judge. It was very late, but the office light was still burning, and John knocked and went in. He stood on the hearth, shivering and dripping, but fairly erect, and in a flat, low voice, told the judge exactly what had happened, even to Seth's parting admonition.

The judge said never a word till the boy was done. He merely sat studying him from under his bushy brows. Then he stood up and fetched a glass of hot water with some whiskey in it and gave it to him.

Though the drink seemed to bring back a little life, it only made John more miserable. He waited like a wavering ghost for the judge to have his say.

But the judge only advised in his heavy voice: "You'd better go on home. I understand you have a new sister. You'd better start hunting work tomorrow." His voice became gruffer. "Everybody has to learn things. It's been bad luck for us both that you had to learn it like this."

John went home. All he could remember was that the judge had said it was bad luck for them both. It seemed to him that was a very kind thing for the judge to say.

John did not see anything of the judge that summer. He worked hard, planting corn and potatoes and the garden, and later he managed to hire himself out. He seemed to get jobs more easily that summer. But his family seemed to need more money. People had been impressed by Mrs. Haskell's having the doctor and

Mrs. Legrand for her lying-in, and now and then they visited a little, and that meant extra money for food and tea. By working hard, though, John found himself in the fall about where he had been the preceding year.

He had put in a bid with the tannery for winter work and had had the job promised to him. Two days before he would have started, however, the judge sent word for him to come to the big house.

The judge made him sit down. "John," he said, "you've kept your courage up when it must have been blamed hard. I've been thinking about you and me. I think the best thing for us both, the best way I can get my money back, is to give you another stake, if you're willing to go."

John felt that he was much nearer crying than he had been when he lost his furs. He hardly found the voice to say that he would go.

For some reason that John never understood, Seth had decided to move west in the state, so the boy had to go into the woods alone. The idea worried his mother, but he told her that in a way it would be better for him. He would be able to use Seth's cabin and work both their ranges.

But on the second day of his trip in, lying alone by his campfire, with all the miles of woods he still had to travel, he knew that it wasn't better for him; and when at last he reached the little lake and saw Seth's cabin, he would have swapped both their ranges together for a sight of the broad brown face and the shapeless figure coming along the shore with the deceptive stride, which, like a bear's, seemed slow and shuffling but which carried him along so quickly.

He settled into Seth's cabin because it was better than his own; but there were times during that winter when he would start up because he thought he heard Seth's wild-sounding yell echoing off the pine ridge, and he would go outdoors in the darkness to listen. All through the winter, he never quite got rid of the notion that somehow Seth was going to turn up; but he never did. John never saw him again as long as he lived, but he never forgot him.

The cabin had been shut up tight. Porcupines had whittled here and there around the outside, but there was little to interest them. Seth had left the ground around his cabin looking as if he had never been there. The inside of the cabin might appear to be inhabited by a pack rat, for the litter that jumbled it. But the woods Seth never spoiled the way a white man would; even John, who had picked up habits from the Indian, never learned the full art of it. Seth could spend the night and move on in the morning, and only an Indian would have known a man had slept there. It was so around his cabin.

John laid his lines out early, and when the freeze came he was ready to start trapping. He followed two of the Indian's lines and laid out two new ones on his own, and after a month or so these two began to earn as well as the two others. He kept learning more and more about animals, and now and then, when he did well, he would think that Seth might have said, "Good!" the way he used to, and he could almost hear the quick laughter.

The hardest part of living alone was the Sundays without company. It was then that he realized how much Seth had done for him. The storekeeper had given him an almanac, and every night before John sat down to supper, he checked off the day. That was the first reading he did, learning the look of the days of the week in print. He spent long hours puzzling over the other words and symbols and studying the picture at the head of each month. For December there was a picture of a family sitting down to dinner at a table with a white cloth, and John sometimes fancied himself as sitting in the place of the man. When things got too lonesome, he would get out that picture and think about it.

There were deep snows in February, but after the crust formed, John suddenly had a run of luck with his traps, better than anything he had had the year before, so that sometimes it was past midnight before he had finished cleaning the skins. But even so, he stayed right through to the end of the season, and then his pack was so heavy that he had to leave his traps behind.

The morning he decided to go, there was a mist over the ice on the lake and the trees were like clouds in it. Somewhere back in the woods he heard a deer flounder in the heavy snow.

Then in the ensuing complete silence, he seemed to hear Seth's voice: "You mind Seth. *You cut two logs crossing.*" But John didn't need to be told.

The Moose River was open when he reached it, so he had to build himself a raft. He spent a full day working at it. And from that point on he took plenty of time when he came to the creeks, and dropped two logs over them and made a trial trip over and back without his fur packs. It took him three days longer to come out of the woods than it had the year before, but he brought his furs with him.

The judge saw to it that he got good prices; and when the dealer was done with the buying, John was able to pay the judge for both stakes and for the forty-dollar loan as well. The year after that he made a clear profit for himself.

John did well in the world. He found time to learn to read and write and handle figures. From time to time he visited the judge, and he found that the judge was not a person that anyone needed to be afraid of. When the judge died, in John's thirtieth year, John was owner of Freel's tannery and one of the leading men in High Falls.

Going to the judge's house that day, to help settle the affairs, he thought of how scared he had been the first time he went to visit and, strangely, he remembered Seth. Without the two of them, he might never have got started in life.

It is a simple story, this of John Haskell's, but it is not quite done. When the judge's will was read that afternoon in the big house, it was found that the judge had left the house to John, together with a good share of his timberland. There was also a sealed letter for John.

That night in his own home, John opened the letter. It was dated the same day that John had received the money for his first pack of furs and paid the judge. It was just a few lines long and it contained forty dollars in bills.

Dear John,

Here is the forty dollars, and I am making you a confession with it. I liked your looks when you came to me that first time. I thought you had the stuff in you. It was a dirty thing to do in a way, but I wanted to make sure of you. I never liked your father and I would never have lent him a cent. I invented that debt.

Good luck, John.

Hats for Horses

by Margery Williams Bianco

No ladies wanted Miss Minnegan's flowered and feathered bonnets anymore. So she put her talents to a most unexpected new use.

For years Miss Minnegan has kept the tiny millinery store next door to the barber's. It is such a tiny little store that you wouldn't really know it was a store at all, except for the two or three hats neatly arranged in the front window, and the bell above the door that goes dingle-dingle whenever anyone turns the handle, which is very seldom. Just inside the window, where you can read it clearly through the glass, is a card on which is printed in small lettering:

MISS MINNEGAN
MILLINERY PARLORS

In the old days when elderly ladies still wore bonnets, and when young ladies wore beautiful hats like flower gardens, with roses and violets and poppies, and even cherries and sheaves of oats on them, and wonderful bows of ribbon stiffened with wire, Miss Minnegan used to do a very good business. There was no one who could tie a bow like Miss Minnegan, or arrange a spray of roses with such elegant effect, and when it came to bonnets, no one in the world could beat her. With bits of draped velvet, and pansies, and curled feathers and jet dingle-dangles, she could turn out a bonnet that everyone would stare at in envy as you walked down the street.

But bonnets, alas, went out of fashion. All those loops of wire and ends of velvet and nodding plumes and jet aigrettes went into a big cardboard box on Miss Minnegan's top shelf to await the time when, as she fondly hoped, people would return to sensible ideas once more. Hats still remained, and with hats she could still work wonders. But by and by the fashion in hats changed too. No one wanted flowers or feathers or big bows of ribbon any longer. All they wanted were miserable little felt things pulled down tight on their heads, with no trimming at all.

If her customers wanted hats like that, Miss Minnegan said to herself, they could go and buy them at Mr. Porium's new dry-goods store just across the way. And that, of course, was just what the customers did do. So that trade became slacker and slacker, and the little front doorbell ceased to go dingle-dingle at all, and there was Miss Minnegan left sitting among her sprays of roses and yards of ribbon, with her scissors idle beside her, wondering what the world was coming to.

It was then that she wrote out the little sign, MILLINERY PARLORS, and set it in her front window—for up to that time there had never been any need for Miss Minnegan to put out a sign. Everyone had always known where she lived, and everyone had always come to her whenever they wanted a new hat made or an old one fixed over. But now even the little card, and the few new-fashioned hats that Miss Minnegan bought, very unwillingly, and arranged beside it in her front window, brought scarcely a customer to her door.

In fact, her only visitors were little girls who wanted a yard of ribbon or a scrap of silk to make a doll's frock with, and who knew that Miss Minnegan would let them rummage through her drawers and boxes till they found just what they wanted, and would charge them very little for it.

Now Miss Minnegan's shop was right at the end of the street, away from all the bustle and traffic, and with a cool shady space before it where the old town watering trough stood. For years there had been talk of doing away with the old watering trough, now that there were so few horses on the road to use it, but it was a landmark, so there it still stood, deep and cool, with a trickle of fresh water always running from the iron pipe above. Little boys sailed paper boats in it and splashed one another on their way home from school, and the sparrows used it for their morning bathtub, and once in a while some farmer who still drove a wagon or old-fashioned buggy would pull up there to give his horse a drink.

One hot summer day, when Miss Minnegan was standing idle at her doorway, an old farmer drove by in his wagon, with a friendly-looking sorrel horse between the shafts. He climbed down and mopped his forehead, and began to splash water over his horse's nose and feet before he let him drink. And while he was mopping and splashing, he looked up and nodded to Miss Minnegan.

"It's a hot day!" he said.

"It is indeed," chirped Miss Minnegan. "And your horse looks very warm too."

"That's the sun, blazing down on the road," said the farmer. "It's very hard on horses, a sun like this. I fixed some leaves over his head to try and keep him cool a bit, but they dropped off along the road. Years ago I remember seeing in some newspaper how they was selling hats for horses, to keep the sun off their heads, but I've asked here and there, and it seems they don't make 'em anymore. I guess horses has gone out of fashion. It's all cars nowadays, and I'll say this for cars, that they ain't liable to sunstroke!"

Then and there, just like a bolt from the blue, as Miss Minnegan said after, the idea came to her. Hats for horses! Why, of course! Horses didn't care about fashions. What a horse needed was a real sensible hat.

"Are you going to be long in town?" she asked the farmer.

"Why, about a half hour or so," he answered, while the sorrel horse stretched his neck and began to suck up the water in long, thirsty gulps. "Just long enough to buy my feed and groceries and to give old Tom here a rest. Why?"

"Because if you really don't mind waiting," said Miss Minnegan, all of a fluster, "I'm sure I can make a hat for your horse that will be just the thing he'd like!"

"Well, now, ma'am, I'd certainly be grateful, and so would he," said the farmer. "If it won't be putting you to too much trouble!"

"No trouble in the world!" cried Miss Minnegan. And she fairly hopped back into her little parlor and began pulling open drawers, and dragging down cardboard boxes, and all the time murmuring to herself, "Now I'm sure—I'm *sure*—I've got the very thing!"

And so she had; for Miss Minnegan was a thrifty person, and never threw anything away that might be useful later. Long ago, when big hats went out of fashion, she had put aside a whole stock of flat, floppy straw shapes, the kind that in those old days used to be trimmed so becomingly with bunches of oats and red silk poppies. Out she dragged the biggest one, and after considering it a moment, and running to the door to get another good look at the sorrel horse's head as he nodded there comfortably in the shade, she took her scissors and snipped out two holes, one for each of his ears, and bound the holes with red braid, so that the straw edges wouldn't tickle him. And she sewed red braid all around the brim too, with two plaited braid strings to tie under his chin, and by the time the farmer came back again there was a splendid hat for his horse, cool and shady and just an exact fit. And very grand the old sorrel looked in it, with his wise, gentle eyes staring down his nose and his two ears sticking out so perkily on top.

"That's what I call a fine hat, ma'am," the farmer said as he stood off and looked at it admiringly. "Practical too! What's more, when all the folks out our way see that hat, they won't know rest nor peace till their horses have hats just like it. And *that*," he ended as he climbed back on the wagon seat, "I'll guarantee, or my name's not John Dover!"

Farmer Dover was right. No sooner did they see that hat than everyone who owned a horse—and there were still quite a number of them round about—wanted a hat like it, and came hurrying to Miss Minnegan to beg her to make one. Very soon her stock of fine Florentine straws and Leghorns was all used up, and she had to fall back on braiding the hats herself, which she was quite clever at doing. And as she braided and stitched and snipped away so happily, she said to herself over and over, "Hats for horses! Hats for horses! If people won't wear my hats, horses will!"

And at fifty cents a hat, she soon had quite a little store of money tucked away in the savings bank.

Only one thing worried her. All the hats that she made were quite plain; serviceable, but not in any sense ornamental, except for a little twist of braid or quirk of ribbon that she couldn't help adding, just to give them an air.

Feathers or velvet . . . she thought. Of course that might not be quite suitable. But a bunch of oats, now, or a few poppies or roses . . . Surely oats would be becoming to any horse!

And she would tuck a tiny spray in,

here or there, just to see the effect, and then reluctantly take it out again. Because, for some strange reason, the farmers all seemed to feel that their horses' hats should be quite plain.

"If I could make just *one* good-looking hat," said Miss Minnegan, "just to show what I can do, then I wouldn't mind going back to the plain ones again."

June and July passed, and the time drew near for the county fair. The county fair is a great event. Not only do the farmers send their horses and cows, their turkeys and chickens and pigs, to compete for the prizes and blue ribbons, but the farmers' wives bring their finest vegetables, cakes, preserves in shining jars, and—if they are clever enough to be able to make such things—their pieced quilts, hooked rugs, embroidery, and fine handwork of every kind. In fact, everyone who has made anything at all that he or she can take a pride in sends it to the county fair to be duly admired and praised.

Now among the many horses, brown and sorrel and gray and black, that Miss Minnegan had made hats for during the past few weeks was an old white mare that belonged to a boy named Billy Jones. Ever since Billy's father died, Billy and his mother had kept the little farm, just a few miles out of town, where they had always lived. Billy's mother raised chickens and vegetables, and Billy himself, though he was only thirteen, did all the farm work, and between them they managed to make both ends meet.

Billy took as much care of his two pigs and his one spotted cow and his old white mare as though they were the most priceless animals in the world, and of them all, Fanny, the mare, was his special pride.

He had bought her very cheaply from a neighboring farmer who, seeing that Fanny was long past her best days, was willing enough to trade her to his young friend for a very few dollars, and the agreement that Billy should give him so many days' work a month till the horse was paid for.

Fanny was a sorry-looking creature when Billy first led her home. Her mane was ragged, her coat unkempt, and her bones fairly stuck out till she looked more like a hat rack than a horse. But there was plenty of strength in her yet, and by the time Billy had fed her and groomed her and combed her for a few months, she began to look very different indeed; so much so that the farmer, every time he met Billy on the road driving his mother in or out of town with her eggs and vegetables, would joke about it and declare that he'd made a bad bargain after all, and the horse was worth a hundred dollars instead of ten!

Every time Billy drove into town he would stop by the watering trough near Miss Minnegan's Millinery Parlors, and Miss Minnegan would always drop her work and come out to have a chat, and ask how Fanny was getting along, and perhaps give her a crust or two of bread or a lump of sugar.

One day while Billy was waiting for Fanny to drink, and scooping up the water in his hands to splash it over her dusty tired hoofs, as he always did, a man who was passing stopped to say, "That's a fine horse you've got!"

"Indeed she is," returned Billy proudly.

"Why, if *I* had a horse like that," the man went on, "I'd show her at the county fair, that I would!"

Now the man was only joking, for he knew Fanny's story, and instead of looking at the old horse's sleek coat and carefully groomed mane he was looking at her knobbly knees, and at the rickety buckboard and shabby harness, all patched up with string and rope, which was all that Billy could afford.

But Billy thought he was in earnest, and the idea took hold of him: Why not take Fanny to the county fair? The only thing that worried him was the question of what she should wear. For all the other horses, he knew, would be decked out in their very best bridles and trappings, with shiny leather and ribbons and whatnot, while poor Fanny hadn't even a decent-looking halter.

All at once he thought of Miss Minnegan. Long ago Miss Minnegan had given Fanny a hat, but Fanny had worn it all summer, working in the fields, and what with the sun and the wind and an occasional thundershower as well, it was pretty limp and shabby by now. But a new hat! Surely with a new hat Fanny would look grand!

Miss Minnegan was delighted at the idea.

"A hat?" she said. "Indeed she shall have a hat, and the best I can make! She shall have such a hat," said Miss Minnegan solemnly, "as will make every other horse at the fair green with envy!"

"But it will cost a lot of money," said Billy doubtfully.

"Leave that to me," returned Miss Minnegan. "Haven't I everything ready, here in the house? For the longest while," she said, "I've wanted to make a really beautiful hat for a horse, and now, between you and me, Billy, we'll show everyone just how fine a horse can look!"

So she thought and she studied, and looked at Fanny long and carefully, full face and sideways and even from the back, just as she used to study her customers in the old days, pursing up her lips and wrinkling her forehead, with her head a bit on one side; and when she had thought it all out she took her scissors and her thimble and she set to work.

Right at the bottom of one of Miss Minnegan's cardboard boxes, laid away in tissue paper, was one hat that she had always kept for some very special occasion. It was a finely braided straw, soft and floppy, with an edge like lace. Miss Minnegan took it out and pressed it and smoothed it, and having carefully measured with her tape measure, she snipped the two holes, just at the right distance, for Fanny's ears.

That was only the beginning!

For two whole days and one night Miss Minnegan sat in her little parlor, and snipped and sewed and pondered, humming to herself as she worked, and when she had finished . . .

Well, no one, certainly, had ever seen such a hat before!

The day of the county fair dawned clear and perfect. The sun beat down on the fairgrounds. Everyone was there, dressed in their best. The judges went their rounds, very solemn and important, puffing a little with the heat, and they judged this and they judged that, and they hung the blue and the red and the green ribbons where they deserved to hang.

In the afternoon they judged the horses. Class after class was shown, the saddle horses and the ponies and the farm horses too, and even one small gray donkey with blue rosettes in his ears. And then the onlookers fidgeted, and looked at the very last line on their programs. It read:

CLASS 77. HORSES WITH HATS

There was only one entry.

Everyone stared. All the people in the seats craned their necks. And there, stepping slowly and with great dignity across the turf, came old Fanny.

Her coat had been groomed till it shone. Her mane and tail had been combed and brushed till every hair stood out glistening. Her clumsy old hoofs had been blacked and polished. And on her head was Miss Minnegan's hat.

What a hat it was! It had a bunch of oats on one side and a bunch of poppies on the other, and a beautiful trailing spray of cornflowers that hung gracefully down to nestle against Fanny's mane. And under her chin, tied smartly on one side, was an elegant bow of wide satin ribbon with floating ends.

On she came, stepping carefully, holding her head proudly up and glancing right and left with her big rolling eyes. She looked just as if she knew that she was the grandest and most elegantly dressed horse in the whole fair, and so she was. Right up to the judges' stand she stepped, and there she stood waiting, breathing a little heavily from excitement and switching her tail coquettishly from side to side.

A big cheer broke out from the crowd. Fanny looked around, but it didn't disturb her. She knew that she deserved it.

There was a whispered consultation, and then the judge cleared his throat.

"The prize for this entry," he announced, "is awarded unanimously to Mr. William Jones and Miss Elvira Minnegan."

He paused, and the people cheered again.

"I also have great pleasure," he continued, "in announcing that the further prize, of twenty dollars, is awarded to Miss Elvira Minnegan and Mr. William Jones, for the most original exhibit in the fair!"

Then Billy and Miss Minnegan walked up side by side to the judges' stand and bowed and shook hands, and received their prize, while a pretty young lady stepped down and pinned two ribbons, a red and a green, one on each side of Fanny's hat. And there was more cheering, and Billy looked very proud, and Miss Minnegan looked very happy and flustered, and they shook hands with one another again.

But when they came to look at Fanny, lo and behold, she had chosen the very moment when their backs were turned to stretch out her long pink tongue and curl it around till she caught hold of the dangling bunch of oats and poppies on her hat, and there she was, calmly munching them up!

It was clear to see that, in her opinion, that hat had already done its duty.

The Most Precious Possession

by Domenico Vittorini

Two wealthy Italian gentlemen learn a new way to value gifts.

There was a time when Italian traders and explorers, finding the way to the East blocked by the Turks, turned west in their search for new lands to trade with—a search that led to the discovery of the New World.

In those days there lived in Florence a merchant by the name of Ansaldo. He belonged to the Ormanini family, known not only for its wealth but for the daring and cunning of its young men. It happened that on one of his trips in search of adventure and trade, Ansaldo ventured beyond the Strait of Gibraltar and, after battling a furious storm, landed on one of the Canary Islands.

The king of the island welcomed him cordially, for the Florentines were well known to him. He ordered a magnificent banquet to be served in the sumptuous hall, resplendent with mirrors and gold, in which he had received Ansaldo.

When it was time to serve the meal, Ansaldo noticed with surprise that a small army of youths, carrying long, stout sticks, entered and lined up against the walls of the banquet hall. As each guest sat down, one of the youths took up a place directly behind him, the stick held in readiness to strike.

Ansaldo wondered what all this meant, and racked his brain for some clue to these odd goings-on. He didn't have long to wait. Suddenly a horde of huge, ferocious rats poured into the hall and threw themselves upon the food that was being served. Pandemonium broke loose as the boys darted here and there, wielding the sticks.

For many years the Florentines had enjoyed the reputation of being the cleverest people on earth, able to cope with any situation. Ansaldo saw a chance to uphold the tradition. He asked the king's permission to go back to his ship, and returned shortly with two big Persian cats. These animals were much admired and loved by the Florentines and Venetians, who had first seen them in the East and who had brought many of them back to Italy. Ever since, one or two cats always completed the crew of a ship when it set out on a long journey.

Ansaldo let the cats go, and before long the entire hall was cleared of the revolting and destructive rats.

The astonished and delighted king thought he was witnessing a miracle. He could not find words enough to thank Ansaldo, whom he hailed as the savior of the island, and when Ansaldo made him a present of the cats, his gratitude knew no bounds.

After a pleasant visit, Ansaldo made ready to sail for home. The king accompanied him to his ship, and there he showered him with rich and rare gifts, much gold and silver, and many precious stones of all kinds and colors—rubies, topazes, and diamonds.

Ansaldo was overwhelmed not only by these costly gifts but by the king's gratitude and the praises he heaped upon him and on the cats. As for the latter, they were regarded with awe by all the islanders and as their greatest treasure by the king and the entire royal household.

When Ansaldo returned home, he regaled his friends with the account of his strange adventure. There was among them a certain Giocondo de' Fifanti, who was as rich in envy as he was poor in intelligence. He thought, If the island king gave Ansaldo all these magnificent gifts for two mangy cats, what will he not give me if I present him with the most beautiful and precious things that our city of Florence has to offer? No sooner said than done. He purchased lovely belts, necklaces, bracelets studded with diamonds, luxurious garments, and many other expensive gifts and took ship for the now famous Canary Islands.

After an uneventful crossing he arrived in port and hastened to the royal palace. He was received with more pomp than was Ansaldo. The king was greatly touched by the splendor of Giocondo's gifts and wanted to be equally generous. He held a long consultation with his people and then informed Giocondo happily that they had decided to share with the visitor their most precious possession. Giocondo could hardly contain his curiosity. However, the day of departure finally arrived and found Giocondo on his ship, impatiently awaiting the visit of the king. Before long, the king, accompanied by the entire royal household and half the islanders, approached the ship. The king himself carried the precious gift on a silken cushion. With great pride he put the cushion into Giocondo's outstretched greedy hands. Giocondo was speechless. On the cushion, curled up in sleepy, furry balls, were two of the kittens that had been born to the Persian cats Ansaldo had left on the island.

The old story does not go on to say whether Giocondo, on his return to Florence, ever regaled his friends with the tale of *his* adventure!

March and the Shepherd

by Domenico Vittorini

Once the month of March had only thirty days.
This old Italian tale tells why another day was added.

One morning, in the very beginning of spring, a shepherd led his sheep to graze, and on the way he met March.

"Good morning," said March. "Where are you going to take your sheep to graze today?"

"Well, March, today I am going to the mountains."

"Fine, Shepherd. That's a good idea. Good luck." But to himself March said, Here's where I have some fun, for today I'm going to fix you.

And that day in the mountains the rain came down in buckets; it was a veritable deluge. The shepherd, however, had watched March's face very carefully and noticed a mischievous look on it. So, instead of going to the mountains, he had remained in the plains. In the evening, returning home, he met March again.

"Well, Shepherd, how did it go today?"

"It couldn't have been better. I changed my mind and went to the plains. A very beautiful day. Such a lovely warm sun."

"Really? I'm glad to hear it," said March, but he bit his lip in vexation. "Where are you going tomorrow?"

"Tomorrow I'm going to the plains too.

With this fine weather, I would be crazy if I went to the mountains."

"Oh, really? Fine! Farewell."

And they parted.

But the shepherd didn't go to the plains again; he went to the mountains. And on the plains March brought rain and wind and hail—a punishment indeed from heaven. In the evening he met the shepherd homeward bound.

"Good evening, Shepherd. How did it go today?"

"Very well indeed. Do you know, I changed my mind again and went to the mountains after all. It was heavenly there. What a day! What a sky! What a sun!"

"I'm really happy to hear it, Shepherd. And where are you going tomorrow?"

"Well, tomorrow I'm going to the plains. I see dark clouds over the mountains. I wouldn't want to find myself too far from home."

To make a long story short, whenever the shepherd met March, he always told him the opposite of what he planned to do the next day, so March was never able to catch him. The end of the month came and on the last day, the thirtieth, March said to the shepherd, "Well, Shepherd, how is everything?"

"Things couldn't be any better. This is the end of the month and I'm out of danger. There's nothing to fear now; I can begin to sleep peacefully."

"That's true," said March. "And where are you going tomorrow?"

The shepherd, certain that he had nothing to fear, told March the truth. "Tomorrow," he said, "I shall go to the plains. The distance is shorter and the work less hard."

"Fine. Farewell."

March hastened to the home of his cousin April and told her the whole story. "I want you to lend me at least one day," he said. "I am determined to catch this shepherd." Gentle April was unwilling, but March coaxed so hard that finally she consented.

The following morning the shepherd set off for the plains. No sooner had his flock scattered than there arose a storm that chilled his very heart. The sharp wind howled and growled; snow fell in thick icy flakes; hail pelted down. It was all the shepherd could do to get his sheep back into the fold.

That evening as the shepherd huddled in a corner of his hearth, silent and melancholy, March paid him a visit.

"Good evening, Shepherd," he said.

"Good evening, March."

"How did it go today?"

"I'd rather not talk about it," said the shepherd. "I can't understand what happened. Not even in the middle of January have I ever seen a storm like the one on the plains today. It seemed as if all the devils had broken loose from hell. Today I had enough rough weather to last me the whole year. And, oh, my poor sheep!"

Then at last was March satisfied.

And from that time on March has had thirty-one days, because, as it is said in Tuscany, the rascal never returned to April the day he borrowed from her.

Jug of Silver

by Truman Capote

The jug in the drugstore was filled with money. The person who guessed how much would win it all. But could Appleseed, who really needed it, come up with the answer?

After school I used to work in the Valhalla drugstore. It was owned by my uncle, Mr. Ed Marshall. I call him Mr. Marshall because everybody, including his wife, called him Mr. Marshall. Nevertheless he was a nice man.

This drugstore was maybe old-fashioned, but it was large and dark and cool; during summer months there was no pleasanter place in town. At the left, as you entered, was a tobacco-magazine counter behind which, as a rule, sat Mr. Marshall, a squat, square-faced, pink-fleshed man with looping, manly white mustaches.

Beyond this counter stood the beautiful soda fountain. It was very antique and made of fine yellowed marble, smooth to the touch but without a trace of cheap glaze. Mr. Marshall bought it at an auction in New Orleans in 1910 and was plainly proud of it. When you sat on the high, delicate stools and looked across the fountain you could see yourself reflected softly, as though by candlelight, in a row of ancient mahogany-framed mirrors. All general merchandise was displayed in glass-doored, curiolike cabinets that were locked with brass keys. There was always in the air the smell of syrup and nutmeg and other delicacies.

The Valhalla was the gathering place of Wachata County till a certain Rufus McPherson came to town and opened a second drugstore directly across the courthouse square. This old Rufus McPherson was a villain; that is, he took away my uncle's trade. He installed fancy equipment such as electric fans and colored lights; he provided curb service and made grilled-cheese sandwiches to order. Naturally, though some remained devoted to Mr. Marshall, most folks couldn't resist Rufus McPherson.

For a while, Mr. Marshall chose to ignore him; if you were to mention McPherson's name, he would sort of snort, finger his mustaches and look the other way. But you could tell he was mad. And getting madder. Then one day toward the middle of October I strolled into the Valhalla to find him sitting at the fountain, playing dominoes and drinking wine with Hamurabi.

Hamurabi was an Egyptian and some kind of dentist, though he didn't do much business as the people hereabouts have unusually strong teeth, due to an element in the water. He spent a great deal of his time loafing around the Valhalla and was my uncle's chief buddy. He was a handsome figure of a man, this Hamurabi, being dark-skinned and nearly seven feet tall; the matrons of the town kept their daughters under lock and key and gave him the eye themselves. He had no foreign accent whatsoever, and it was always my opinion that he wasn't any more Egyptian than the man in the moon.

Anyway, there they were swigging red Italian wine from a gallon jug. It was a troubling sight, for Mr. Marshall was a renowned teetotaler. So naturally, I thought, Oh, golly, Rufus McPherson has finally got his goat. That was not the case, however.

"Here, son," said Mr. Marshall, "come have a glass of wine."

"Sure," said Hamurabi, "help us finish it up. It's store bought, so we can't waste it."

Much later, when the jug was dry, Mr. Marshall picked it up and said, "Now we shall see!" And with that disappeared out into the afternoon.

"Where's he off to?" I asked.

"Ah," was all Hamurabi would say. He liked to devil me.

A half hour passed before my uncle returned. He was stooped and grunting under the load he carried. He set the jug atop the fountain and stepped back, smiling and rubbing his hands together. "Well, what do you think?"

"Ah," purred Hamurabi.

"Gee . . ." I said.

It was the same wine jug, God knows, but there was a wonderful difference; for now it was crammed to the brim with nickels and dimes that shone dully through the thick glass.

"Pretty, eh?" said my uncle. "Had it done over at the First National. Couldn't get in anything bigger-sized than a nickel. Still, there's lotsa money in there, let me tell you."

"But what's the point, Mr. Marshall?" I said. "I mean, what's the idea?"

Mr. Marshall's smile deepened to a grin. "This here's a jug of silver, you might say—"

"The pot at the end of the rainbow," interrupted Hamurabi.

"And the idea, as you call it, is for folks

to guess how much money is in there. For instance, say you buy a quarter's worth of stuff—well, then you get to take a chance. The more you buy, the more chances you get. And I'll keep all guesses in a ledger till Christmas Eve, at which time whoever comes closest to the right amount will get the whole shebang."

Hamurabi nodded solemnly. "He's playing Santa Claus—a mighty crafty Santa Claus," he said. "I'm going home and write a book: *The Skillful Murder of Rufus McPherson.*" To tell the truth, he sometimes did write stories and send them out to the magazines. They always came back.

It was surprising, really like a miracle, how Wachata County took to the jug. Why, the Valhalla hadn't done so much business since Stationmaster Tully, poor soul, went stark raving mad and claimed to have discovered oil back of the depot, causing the town to be overrun with wildcat prospectors. Even the pool-hall bums who never spent a cent on anything not connected with whiskey or women took to investing their spare cash in milk shakes. A few elderly ladies publicly disapproved of Mr. Marshall's enterprise as a kind of gambling, but they didn't start any trouble and some even found occasion to visit us and hazard a guess. The school kids were crazy about the whole thing, and I was very popular because they figured I knew the answer.

"I'll tell you why all this is," said Hamurabi, lighting one of the Egyptian cigarettes he bought by mail from a concern in New York City. "It's not for the reason you may imagine; not, in other words, avidity. No. It's the mystery that's enchanting. Now you look at those nickels and dimes and what do you think, Ah, *so* much! No, no. You think, Ah, *how* much? And that's a profound question, indeed. It can mean different things to different people. Understand?"

And oh, was Rufus McPherson wild! When you're in trade, you count on Christmas to make up a large share of your yearly profit, and he was hard pressed to find a customer. So he tried to imitate the jug; but being such a stingy man he filled his with pennies. He also wrote a letter to the editor of *The Banner*, our weekly paper, in which he said that Mr. Marshall ought to be "tarred and feathered and strung up for turning innocent little children into confirmed gamblers and sending them down the path to hell!" You can imagine what kind of laughingstock he was. Nobody had anything for McPherson but scorn. And so by the middle of November he just stood on the sidewalk outside his store and gazed bitterly at the festivities across the square.

At about this time Appleseed and sister made their first appearance.

He was a stranger in town. At least no one could recall ever having seen him before. He said he lived on a farm a mile past Indian Branches; told us his mother weighed only seventy-four pounds and that he had an older brother who would play the fiddle at anybody's wedding for fifty cents. He claimed that Appleseed was the only name he had and that he was twelve years old. But his sister, Middy, said he was eight. His hair was straight and dark yellow. He had a tight, weather-tanned little face with anxious green eyes that had a very wise and knowing look. He was small and puny and high-strung; and he wore always the same outfit: a red sweater, blue denim britches, and a pair of man-size boots that went *clop-clop* with every step.

It was raining that first time he came into the Valhalla; his hair was plastered around his head like a cap, and his boots were caked with red mud from the country roads. Middy trailed behind as he swaggered like a cowboy up to the fountain, where I was wiping some glasses.

"I hear tell you folks got a bottle fulla money you fixin' to give 'way," he said, looking me square in the eye. "Seein' as you-all are givin' it away, we'd be obliged iffen you'd give it to us. Name's Appleseed, and this here's my sister, Middy."

Middy was a sad, sad-looking kid. She was a good bit taller and older-looking than her brother: a regular bean pole. She had tow-colored hair that was chopped short, and a pale, pitiful little face. She wore a faded cotton dress that came way up above her bony knees. There was something wrong with her teeth, and she tried to conceal this by keeping her lips primly pursed like an old lady.

"Sorry," I said, "but you'll have to talk with Mr. Marshall."

So sure enough he did. I could hear my uncle explaining what he would have to do to win the jug. Appleseed listened attentively, nodding now and then. Presently he came back and stood in front of the jug and, touching it lightly with his hand, said, "Ain't it a pretty thing, Middy?"

Middy said, "Is they gonna give it to us?"

"Naw. What you gotta do, you gotta guess how much money's inside there. And you gotta buy two bits' worth so's even to get a chance."

"Huh, we ain't got no two bits. Where you 'spec we gonna get us two bits?"

Appleseed frowned and rubbed his chin. "That'll be the easy part, just leave it to me. The only worrisome thing is, I can't just take a chance and guess. . . . I gotta *know*."

Well, a few days later they showed up again. Appleseed perched on a stool at the fountain and boldly asked for two glasses of water, one for him and one for Middy. It was on this occasion that he gave out the information about his family: ". . . Then there's Papa Daddy, that's my mama's papa, who's a Cajun, an' on accounta that he don't speak English good. My brother, the one what plays the fiddle, he's been in jail three times. . . . It's on accounta him we had to pick up and leave Louisiana. He cut a fella bad in a razor fight over a woman ten years older'n him. She had yellow hair."

Middy, lingering in the background, said nervously, "You oughtn't to be tellin' our personal private fam'ly business thataway, Appleseed."

"Hush now, Middy," he said, and she hushed. "She's a good little gal," he added, turning to pat her head, "but you can't let her get away with much. You go look at the picture books, honey, and stop frettin' with your teeth. Appleseed here's got some figurin' to do."

This figuring meant staring hard at the jug, as if his eyes were trying to eat it up. With his chin cupped in his hand, he studied it for a long period, not batting his eyelids once. "A lady in Louisiana told me I could see things other folks couldn't see 'cause I was born with a caul on my head."

"It's a cinch you aren't going to see how much there is," I told him. "Why don't you just let a number pop into your head, and maybe that'll be the right one."

"Uh-uh," he said. "Too darn risky. Me, I can't take no sucha chance. Now, the way I got it figured, there ain't but one surefire thing and that's to count every nickel and dime."

"Count!"

"Count what?" asked Hamurabi, who had just moseyed inside and was settling himself at the fountain.

"This kid says he's going to count how much is in the jug," I explained.

Hamurabi looked at Appleseed with interest. "How do you plan to do that, son?"

"Oh, by countin'," said Appleseed matter-of-factly.

Hamurabi laughed. "You better have X-ray eyes, son, that's all I can say."

"Oh, no. All you gotta do is be born with a caul on your head. A lady in Louisiana told me so. She was a witch; she loved me and when my ma wouldn't give me to her she put a hex on her and now my ma don't weigh but seventy-four pounds."

"Ve-ry in-ter-esting," was Hamurabi's comment as he gave Appleseed a queer glance.

Middy sauntered up, clutching a copy of *Screen Secrets*. She pointed out a certain photo to Appleseed and said, "Ain't she the nicest-lookin' lady? Now you see, Appleseed, you see how pretty her teeth are? Not a one outa joint."

"Well, don't you fret none," he said.

After they left, Hamurabi ordered a bottle of orange Nehi and drank it slowly, while smoking a cigarette. "Do you think maybe that kid's okay upstairs?" he asked presently in a puzzled voice.

Small towns are best for spending Christmas, I think. They catch the mood quicker and change and come alive under its spell. By the first week in December housedoors were decorated with wreaths, and store windows were flashy with red paper bells and snowflakes of glittering isinglass. The kids hiked out into the woods and came back dragging spicy evergreen trees. Already the women were busy baking fruitcakes, unsealing jars of mincemeat and opening bottles of blackberry and scuppernong wine. In the courthouse square a huge tree was trimmed with silver tinsel and colored electric bulbs that were lighted up at sunset. Late of an afternoon you could hear the choir in the Presbyterian church practicing carols for their annual pageant. All over town the japonicas were in full bloom.

The only person who appeared not the least touched by this heartwarming atmosphere was Appleseed. He went about his declared business of counting the jug money with great, persistent care. Every day now he came to the Valhalla and concentrated on the jug, scowling and mumbling to himself. At first we were all fascinated, but after a while it got tiresome and nobody paid him any mind whatsoever. He never bought anything, apparently having never been able to raise the two bits. Sometimes he'd talk to Hamurabi, who had taken a tender interest in him and occasionally stood treat to a jawbreaker or a penny's worth of licorice.

"Do you still think he's nuts?" I asked.

"I'm not so sure," said Hamurabi. "But I'll let you know. He doesn't eat enough. I'm going to take him over to the Rainbow Café and buy him a plate of barbecue."

"He'd appreciate it more if you'd give him a quarter."

"No. A dish of barbecue is what he needs. Besides, it would be better if he never was to make a guess. A high-strung kid like that, so unusual, I wouldn't want to be the one responsible if he lost. Say, it would be pitiful."

I'll admit that at the time Appleseed struck me as being just funny. Mr. Marshall felt sorry for him, and the kids tried to tease him, but had to give it up when he refused to respond. There you could see him plain as day sitting at the fountain with his forehead puckered and his eyes fixed forever on that jug. Yet he was so withdrawn you sometimes had this awful creepy feeling that, well, maybe he didn't exist. And when you were pretty much convinced of this he'd wake up and say something like, "You know, I hope a 1913 buffalo nickel's in there. A fella was tellin' me he saw where a 1913 buffalo nickel's worth fifty dollars." Or, "Middy's gonna be a big lady in the picture shows. They make lotsa money, the ladies in the picture shows do, and then we ain't gonna never eat another collard green as long as we live. Only Middy says she can't be in the picture shows 'less her teeth look good."

Middy didn't always tag along with her brother. On those occasions when she didn't come, Appleseed wasn't himself; he acted shy and left soon.

Hamurabi kept his promise and stood treat to a dish of barbecue at the café. "Mr. Hamurabi's nice, all right," said Appleseed afterward, "but he's got peculiar notions. Has a notion that if he lived in this place named Egypt he'd be a king or somethin'."

And Hamurabi said, "That kid has the most touching faith. It's a beautiful thing to see. But I'm beginning to despise the whole business." He gestured toward the jug. "Hope of this kind is a cruel thing to give anybody, and I'm damned sorry I was ever a party to it."

Around the Valhalla the most popular pastime was deciding what you would buy if you won the jug. Among those who participated were Solomon Katz, Phoebe Jones, Carl Kuhnhardt, Puly Simmons, Addie Foxcroft, Marvin Finkle, Trudy Edwards and a colored man named Erskine Washington. And these were some of their answers: a trip to and a permanent wave in Birmingham, a secondhand piano, a Shetland pony, a gold bracelet, a set of *Rover Boys* books and a life insurance policy.

Once Mr. Marshall asked Appleseed what he would get. "It's a secret," was the reply, and no amount of prying could make him tell. We took it for granted that whatever it was, he wanted it real bad.

Honest winter, as a rule, doesn't settle on our part of the country till late January, and then is mild, lasting only a short time. But in the year of which I write we were blessed with a singular cold spell the week before Christmas. Some still talk of it, for it was so terrible: water pipes froze solid; many folks had to spend the days in bed snuggled under their quilts, having neglected to lay in enough kindling for the fireplace; the sky turned that strange dull gray as it does just before a storm, and the sun was pale as a waning moon. There was a sharp wind; the old dried-up leaves of last fall fell on the icy ground, and the evergreen tree in the courthouse square was twice stripped of its Christmas finery. When you breathed, your breath made smoky clouds. Down by the silk mill where the very poor people lived, the families huddled together in the dark at night and told tales to keep their minds off the cold. Out in the country the farmers covered their delicate plants with gunnysacks and prayed; some took advantage of the weather to slaughter their hogs and bring the fresh sausage to town. Mr. R. C. Judkins, our town drunk, outfitted himself in a red cheesecloth suit and played Santa Claus at the five-'n'-dime. Mr. R. C. Judkins was the father of a big family, so everybody was happy to see him sober enough to earn a dollar. There were several church socials, at one of which Mr. Marshall came face to face with Rufus McPherson. Bitter words were passed, but not a blow was struck.

Now, as has been mentioned, Appleseed lived on a farm a mile below Indian Branches; this would be approximately three miles from town, a mighty long and lonesome walk. Still, despite the cold, he came every day to the Valhalla and stayed till closing time, which, as the days had grown short, was after nightfall. Once in a while he'd catch a ride partway home with the foreman from the silk mill, but not often. He looked tired, and there were worry lines about his mouth. He was always cold and shivered a lot. I don't think he wore any warm drawers underneath his red sweater and blue britches.

It was three days before Christmas when out of the clear sky he announced, "Well, I'm finished. I mean I know how much is in the bottle." He claimed this with such grave, solemn sureness it was hard to doubt him.

"Why, say now, son, hold on," said Hamurabi, who was present. "You can't

know anything of the sort. It's wrong to think so; you're just heading to get yourself hurt."

"You don't need to preach to me, Mr. Hamurabi. I know what I'm up to. A lady in Louisiana, she told me—"

"Yes, yes, yes—but you got to forget that. If it were me, I'd go home and stay put and forget about this damned jug."

"My brother's gonna play the fiddle at a wedding over in Cherokee City tonight and he's gonna give me the two bits," said Appleseed stubbornly. "Tomorrow I'll take my chance."

So the next day I felt kind of excited when Appleseed and Middy arrived. Sure enough, he had his quarter; it was tied for safekeeping in the corner of a red bandanna.

The two of them wandered hand in hand among the showcases, holding a whispery consultation as to what to purchase. They decided finally on a thimble-size bottle of gardenia cologne, which Middy promptly opened and partly emptied on her hair. "It smells like . . . Oh, darlin' Mary, I ain't never smelled nothin' as sweet. Here, Appleseed, honey, let me douse some on your hair." But he wouldn't let her.

Mr. Marshall got out the ledger in which he kept his records, while Appleseed strolled over to the fountain and cupped the jug between his hands, stroking it gently. His eyes were bright and his cheeks flushed from excitement. Several persons who were in the drugstore at that moment crowded close. Middy stood in the background quietly scratching her leg and smelling the cologne. Hamurabi wasn't there.

Mr. Marshall licked the point of his pencil and smiled. "Okay, son, what do you say?"

Appleseed took a deep breath. "Seventy-seven dollars and thirty-five cents," he blurted.

In picking such an uneven sum he showed originality, for the run-of-the-mill guess was a plain round figure. Mr. Marshall repeated the amount solemnly as he copied it down.

"When'll I know if I won?"

"Christmas Eve," someone said.

"That's tomorrow, huh?"

"Why, so it is," Mr. Marshall said, not surprised. "Come at four o'clock."

During the night the thermometer dropped even lower, and toward dawn there was one of those swift, summerlike rainstorms, so that the following day was bright and frozen. The town was like a picture postcard of a northern scene, what with icicles sparkling whitely on the trees and frost flowers coating all windowpanes. Mr. R. C. Judkins rose early and, for no clear reason, tramped the streets ringing a supper bell, stopping now and then to take a swig of whiskey from a pint that he kept in his hip pocket. As the day was windless, smoke climbed lazily from various chimneys straightway to the still, frozen sky. By midmorning the Presbyterian choir was in full swing; and the town kids (wearing horror masks, as at Halloween) were chasing one another around and around the square, kicking up an awful fuss.

Hamurabi dropped by at noon to help us fix up the Valhalla. He brought along a fat sack of satsumas, and together we ate every last one, tossing the hulls into a newly installed potbellied stove (a present from Mr. Marshall to himself), which stood in the middle of the room. Then my uncle took the jug off the fountain, polished and placed it on a prominently situated table. He was no help after that whatsoever, for he squatted in a chair and spent his time tying and retying a tacky green ribbon around the jug. So Hamurabi and I had the rest to do alone. We swept the floor and washed the mirrors and dusted the cabinets and strung streamers of red and green crepe paper from wall to wall. When we were finished, it looked very fine and elegant.

But Hamurabi gazed sadly at our work and said, "Well, I think I better be getting along now."

"Aren't you going to stay?" asked Mr. Marshall, shocked.

"No, oh, no," said Hamurabi, shaking his head slowly. "I don't want to see that kid's face. This is Christmas and I mean to have a rip-roaring time. And I couldn't, not with something like that on my conscience. Hell, I wouldn't sleep."

"Suit yourself," said Mr. Marshall. And he shrugged, but you could see he was really hurt. "Life's like that—and besides, who knows, he might win."

Hamurabi sighed gloomily. "What's his guess?"

"Seventy-seven dollars and thirty-five cents," I said.

"Now I ask you, isn't that fantastic?" said Hamurabi. He slumped in a chair next to Mr. Marshall and crossed his legs and lit a cigarette. "If you got any Baby Ruths, I think I'd like one; my mouth tastes sour."

As the afternoon wore on, the three of us sat around the table feeling terribly blue. No one said hardly a word, and as the kids had deserted the square, the only sound was the clock tolling the hour in the courthouse steeple. The Valhalla was closed to business, but people kept passing by and peeking in the window. At three o'clock Mr. Marshall told me to unlock the door.

Within twenty minutes the place was jam full; everyone was wearing his Sunday best, and the air smelled sweet, for most of the little silk-mill girls had scented themselves with vanilla flavoring. They scrunched up against the walls, perched on the fountain, squeezed in wherever they could; soon the crowd had spread to the sidewalk and stretched into the road. The square was lined with team-drawn wagons and Model T Fords that had carted farmers and their families into town. There was much laughter and shouting and joking—several outraged ladies complained of the cursing and the rough, shoving ways of the younger men, but nobody left. At the side entrance a gang of colored folks had formed and were having the most fun of all. Everybody was making the best of a good thing. It's usually so quiet around here; nothing much ever happens. It's safe to say that nearly all of Wachata County was present but invalids and Rufus McPherson. I looked around for Appleseed but didn't see him anywhere.

Mr. Marshall harumphed, and clapped for attention. When things quieted down and the atmosphere was properly tense, he raised his voice like an auctioneer and called, "Now listen, everybody, in this here envelope you see in my hand"—he held a manila envelope above his head—"well, in it's the *answer*—which nobody but God and the First National Bank knows up to now, ha-ha. And in this book"—he held up the ledger with his free hand—"I've got written down what you folks guessed. Are there any questions?" All was silence. "Fine. Now, if we could have a volunteer . . ."

Not a living soul budged an inch; it was as if an awful shyness had overcome the crowd, and even those who were ordinarily natural-born show-offs shuffled their feet, ashamed. Then a voice, Appleseed's, hollered, "Lemme by. . . . Outa the way, please, ma'am." Trotting along behind as he pushed forward were Middy and a lanky, sleepy-eyed fellow who was evidently the fiddling brother. Appleseed was dressed the same as usual, but his face was scrubbed rosy clean, his boots polished and his hair slicked back skin tight with Stacomb. "Did we get here in time?" he panted.

But Mr. Marshall said, "So you want to be our volunteer?"

Appleseed looked bewildered, then nodded vigorously.

"Does anybody have an objection to this young man?"

Still there was dead quiet. Mr. Marshall handed the envelope to Appleseed, who accepted it calmly. He chewed his underlip while studying it a moment before ripping the flap.

In all that congregation there was no sound except an occasional cough and the soft tinkling of Mr. R. C. Judkins' supper bell. Hamurabi was leaning against the fountain, staring up at the ceiling; Middy was gazing blankly over her brother's shoulder, and when he started to tear open the envelope she let out a pained little gasp.

Appleseed withdrew a slip of pink paper and, holding it as though it was very fragile, muttered to himself whatever was written there. Suddenly his face paled and tears glistened in his eyes.

"Hey, speak up, boy," someone hollered.

Hamurabi stepped forward and all but snatched the slip away. He cleared his throat and commenced to read when his expression changed most comically. "Well, Mother o' God . . ." he said.

"Louder! Louder!" an angry chorus demanded.

"Buncha crooks!" yelled Mr. R. C. Judkins, who had a snootful by this time. "I smell a rat and he smells to high heaven!" Whereupon a cyclone of catcalls and whistling rent the air.

Appleseed's brother whirled around and shook his fist. "Shuddup, shuddup 'fore I bust every one a your damn heads together so's you got knots the size a muskmelons, hear me?"

"Citizens," cried Mayor Mawes, "citizens—I say, this is Christmas. . . . I say . . ."

And Mr. Marshall hopped up on a chair and clapped and stamped till a minimum of order was restored. It might as well be noted here that we later found out Rufus McPherson had paid Mr. R. C. Judkins to start the rumpus. Anyway, when the outbreak was quelled, who should be in possession of the slip but me . . . don't ask how.

Without thinking, I shouted, "Seventy-seven dollars and thirty-five cents." Naturally, due to the excitement, I didn't at first catch the meaning; it was just a number. Then Appleseed's brother let forth with his whooping yell, and so I understood. The name of the winner spread quickly, and the awed, murmuring whispers were like a rainstorm.

Oh, Appleseed himself was a sorry sight. He was crying as though he was mortally wounded, but when Hamurabi lifted him onto his shoulders so the crowd could get a gander, he dried his eyes with the cuffs of his sweater and began grinning. Mr. R. C. Judkins yelled, "Gyp! Lousy gyp!" but was drowned out by a deafening round of applause.

Middy grabbed my arm. "My teeth," she squealed. "Now I'm gonna get my teeth."

"Teeth?" said I, kind of dazed.

"The false kind," says she. "That's what we're gonna get us with the money—a lovely set of white false teeth."

But at that moment my sole interest was in how Appleseed had known. "Hey, tell me," I said desperately, "tell me, how in God's name did he know there was just exactly seventy-seven dollars and thirty-five cents?"

Middy gave me this *look*. "Why, I thought he told you," she said, real serious. "He counted."

"Yes, but how—how?"

"Gee, don't you even know how to count?"

"But is that all he did?"

"Well," she said, following a thoughtful pause, "he did do a little praying too." She started to dart off, then turned back and called, "Besides, he was born with a caul on his head."

And that's the nearest anybody ever came to solving the mystery. Thereafter, if you were to ask Appleseed "How come?" he would smile strangely and change the subject. Many years later he and his family moved to somewhere in Florida and were never heard from again.

But in our town his legend flourishes still; and, till his death a year ago last April, Mr. Marshall was invited each Christmas Day to tell the story of Appleseed to the Baptist Bible class. Hamurabi once typed up an account and mailed it around to various magazines. It was never printed. One editor wrote back and said that "if the little girl really turned out to be a movie star, then there might be something to your story." But that's not what happened, so why should you lie?

When Shlemiel Went to Warsaw

by Isaac Bashevis Singer

Maybe Shlemiel had found a second village just like his own. Maybe he had gone crazy. Maybe he wasn't Shlemiel at all. Mrs. Shlemiel and the village Elders wondered. And so will you.

Though Shlemiel was a lazybones and a sleepyhead and hated to move, he always daydreamed of taking a trip. He had heard many stories about faraway countries, huge deserts, deep oceans, and high mountains, and often discussed with Mrs. Shlemiel his great wish to go on a long journey. Mrs. Shlemiel would reply, "Long journeys are not for a Shlemiel. You better stay home and mind the children while I go to market to sell my vegetables." Yet Shlemiel could not bring himself to give up his dream of seeing the world and its wonders.

A recent visitor to Chelm had told Shlemiel marvelous things about the city of Warsaw. How beautiful the streets were, how high the buildings and luxurious the stores. Shlemiel decided once and for all that he must see this great city for himself. He knew that one had to prepare for a journey. But what was there for him to take? He had nothing but the old clothes he wore. One morning, after Mrs. Shlemiel left for the market, he told the older boys to mind the younger children. Then he took a few slices of bread, an onion, and a clove of garlic, put them in a kerchief, tied it into a bundle, and started for Warsaw on foot.

There was a street in Chelm called Warsaw Street and Shlemiel believed that it led directly to Warsaw. While still in the village, he was stopped by several neighbors who asked him where he was going. Shlemiel told them that he was on his way to Warsaw.

"What will you do in Warsaw?" they asked him.

Shlemiel replied, "What do I do in Chelm? Nothing."

He soon reached the outskirts of town. He walked slowly because the soles of his boots were worn through. Soon the houses and stores gave way to pastures and fields. He passed a peasant driving an ox-drawn plow. After several hours of walking, Shlemiel grew tired. He was so weary that he wasn't even hungry. He lay down on the grass near the roadside for a nap, but before he fell asleep he thought, When I wake up, I may not remember which is the way to Warsaw and which leads back to Chelm. After pondering a moment, he removed his boots and set them down beside him with the toes pointing toward Warsaw and the heels toward Chelm. He soon fell asleep and dreamed that he was a baker baking onion rolls with poppy seeds. Customers came to buy them, and Shlemiel said, "These onion rolls are not for sale."

"Then why do you bake them?"

"They are for my wife, my children, and for me."

Later he dreamed that he was the king of Chelm. Once a year, instead of taxes, each citizen brought him a pot of strawberry jam. Shlemiel sat on a golden throne and nearby sat Mrs. Shlemiel, the queen, and his children, the princes and princesses. They were all eating onion rolls and spooning up big portions of strawberry jam. A carriage arrived and took the royal family to Warsaw, America, and to the River Sambation, which spurts out stones the week long and rests on the Sabbath.

Near the road, a short distance from where Shlemiel slept, was a smithy. The blacksmith happened to come out just in time to see Shlemiel carefully placing his boots at his side with the toes facing in the direction of Warsaw. The blacksmith was a prankster, and as soon as Shlemiel was sound asleep he tiptoed over and turned the boots around. When Shlemiel awoke, he felt rested but hungry. He got out a slice of bread, rubbed it with garlic, and took a bite of onion. Then he pulled his boots on and continued on his way.

He walked along and everything looked strangely familiar. He recognized houses that he had seen before. It seemed to him that he knew the people he met. Could it be that he had already reached another town? Shlemiel wondered. And why was it so similar to Chelm? He stopped a passerby and asked the name of the town. "Chelm," the man replied.

Shlemiel was astonished. How was this possible? He had walked away from Chelm. How could he have arrived back there? He began to rub his forehead and soon found the answer to the riddle. There were two Chelms and he had reached the second one.

Still it seemed very odd that the streets, the houses, the people were so similar to those in the Chelm he had left behind. Shlemiel puzzled over this fact until he suddenly remembered something he had learned in school: "The earth is the same everywhere." And so why shouldn't the second Chelm be exactly like the first one? This discovery gave Shlemiel great satisfaction. He wondered if there was a street here like his street and a house on it like the one he lived in. And indeed he soon arrived at an identical street and house. Evening had fallen. He opened the door and to his amazement saw a second Mrs. Shlemiel with children just like his. Everything was exactly the same as in his own household. Even the cat seemed the same. Mrs. Shlemiel at once began to scold him.

"Shlemiel, where did you go? You left the house alone. And what have you there in that bundle?"

The children all ran to him and cried, "Papa, where have you been?"

Shlemiel paused a moment and then he said, "Mrs. Shlemiel, I'm not your husband. Children, I'm not your papa."

"Have you lost your mind?" Mrs. Shlemiel screamed.

"I am Shlemiel of Chelm One and this is Chelm Two."

Mrs. Shlemiel clapped her hands so hard that the chickens sleeping under the stove awoke in fright and flew out all over the room.

"Children, your father has gone crazy," she wailed. She immediately sent one of the boys for Gimpel, the healer. All the neighbors came crowding in. Shlemiel stood in the middle of the room and proclaimed, "It's true, you all look like the people in my town, but you are not the same. I come from Chelm One and you live in Chelm Two."

"Shlemiel, what's the matter with you?" someone cried. "You're in your own house, with your own wife and children, your own neighbors and friends."

"No, you don't understand. I come from Chelm One. I was on my way to Warsaw, and between Chelm One and Warsaw there is a Chelm Two. And that is where I am."

"What are you talking about? We all know you and you know all of us. Don't you recognize your chickens?"

"No, I'm not in my town," Shlemiel insisted. "But," he continued, "Chelm Two does have the same people and the same houses as Chelm One, and that is

why you are mistaken. Tomorrow I will continue on to Warsaw."

"In that case, where is my husband?" Mrs. Shlemiel inquired in a rage, and she proceeded to berate Shlemiel with all the curses she could think of.

"How should I know where your husband is?" Shlemiel replied.

Some of the neighbors could not help laughing; others pitied the family. Gimpel, the healer, announced that he knew of no remedy for such an illness. After some time, everybody went home.

Mrs. Shlemiel had cooked noodles and beans that evening, a dish that Shlemiel liked especially. She said to him, "You may be mad, but even a madman has to eat."

"Why should you feed a stranger?" Shlemiel asked.

"As a matter of fact, an ox like you should eat straw, not noodles and beans. Sit down and be quiet. Maybe some food and rest will bring you back to your senses."

"Mrs. Shlemiel, you're a good woman. My wife wouldn't feed a stranger. It would seem that there is some small difference between the two Chelms."

The noodles and beans smelled so good that Shlemiel needed no further coaxing. He sat down, and as he ate he spoke to the children.

"My dear children, I live in a house that looks exactly like this one. I have a wife and she is as like your mother as two peas are like each other. My children resemble you as drops of water resemble one another."

The younger children laughed; the older ones began to cry. Mrs. Shlemiel said, "As if being a Shlemiel wasn't enough, he had to go crazy in addition. What am I going to do now? I won't be able to leave the children with him when I go to market. Who knows what a madman may do?" She clasped her head in her hands and cried out, "God in heaven, what have I done to deserve this?"

Nevertheless, she made up a fresh bed for Shlemiel; and even though he had napped during the day, near the smithy, the moment his head touched the pillow he fell fast asleep and was soon snoring loudly. He again dreamed that he was the king of Chelm and that his wife, the queen, had fried for him a huge panful of blintzes. Some were filled with cheese, others with blueberries or cherries, and all were sprinkled with sugar and cinnamon and were drowning in sour cream. Shlemiel ate twenty blintzes all at once and hid the remainder in his crown for later. In the morning, when Shlemiel awoke, the house was filled with townspeople. Mrs. Shlemiel stood in their midst, her eyes red with weeping. Shlemiel was about to scold his wife for letting so many strangers into the house, but then he remembered that he himself was a stranger here. At home he would have gotten up, washed, and dressed. Now in front of all these people he was at a loss as to what to do. As always when he was embarrassed, he began to scratch his head and pull at his beard. Finally, overcoming his bashfulness, he decided to get up. He threw off the covers and put his bare feet on the floor. "Don't let him run away," Mrs. Shlemiel screamed. "He'll disappear and I'll be a deserted wife, without a Shlemiel."

At this point Baruch, the baker, interrupted. "Let's take him to the Elders. They'll know what to do."

"That's right! Let's take him to the Elders," everybody agreed.

Although Shlemiel insisted that since

he lived in Chelm One, the local Elders had no power over him, several of the strong young men helped him into his pants, his boots, his coat and cap and escorted him to the house of Gronam the Ox. The Elders, who had already heard of the matter, had gathered early in the morning to consider what was to be done.

As the crowd came in, one of the Elders, Dopey Lekisch, was saying, "Maybe there really are two Chelms."

"If there are two, then why can't there be three, four, or even a hundred Chelms?" Sender Donkey interrupted.

"And even if there are a hundred Chelms, must there be a Shlemiel in each one of them?" argued Shmendrick Numskull.

Gronam the Ox, the head Elder, listened to all the arguments but was not yet prepared to express an opinion. However, his wrinkled, bulging forehead indicated that he was deep in thought. It was Gronam the Ox who questioned Shlemiel. Shlemiel related everything that had happened to him, and when he finished, Gronam asked, "Do you recognize me?"

"Surely. You are wise Gronam the Ox."

"And in your Chelm is there also a Gronam the Ox?"

"Yes, there is a Gronam the Ox and he looks exactly like you."

"Isn't it possible that you could have turned around and come back to Chelm?" Gronam inquired.

"Why should I turn around? I'm not a windmill," Shlemiel replied.

"In that case, you are not this Mrs. Shlemiel's husband."

"No, I'm not."

"Then Mrs. Shlemiel's husband, the real Shlemiel, must have left the day you came."

"It would seem so."

"Then he'll probably come back."

"Probably."

"In that case, you must wait until he returns. Then we'll know who is who."

"Dear Elders, my Shlemiel has come back," screamed Mrs. Shlemiel. "I don't need two Shlemiels. One is more than enough."

"Whoever he is, he may not live in your house until everything is made clear," Gronam insisted.

"Where shall I live?" Shlemiel asked.

"In the poorhouse."

"What will I do in the poorhouse?"

"What do you do at home?"

"Good God, who will take care of my children when I go to market?" moaned Mrs. Shlemiel. "Besides, I want a husband. Even a Shlemiel is better than no husband at all."

"Are we to blame that your husband left you and went to Warsaw?" Gronam asked. "Wait until he comes home."

Mrs. Shlemiel wept bitterly and the children cried too. Shlemiel said, "How strange. My own wife always scolded me. My children talked back to me. And here a strange woman and strange children want me to live with them. It looks to me as if Chelm Two is actually better than Chelm One."

"Just a moment. I think I have an idea," interrupted Gronam.

"What is your idea?" Zeinvel Ninny inquired.

"Since we decided to send Shlemiel to the poorhouse, the town will have to hire someone to take care of Mrs. Shlemiel's children so she can go to market. Why not hire Shlemiel for that? It's true, he is not Mrs. Shlemiel's husband or the children's father. But he is so much like the real Shlemiel that the children will feel at home with him."

"What a wonderful idea!" cried Feyvel Thickwit.

"Only King Solomon could have thought of such a wise solution," agreed Treitel the Fool.

"Such a clever way out of this dilemma could only have been thought of in our Chelm," chimed in Shmendrick Numskull.

"How much do you want to be paid to take care of Mrs. Shlemiel's children?" asked Gronam.

For a moment Shlemiel stood there completely bewildered. Then he said, "Three groschen a day."

"Idiot, moron, ass!" screamed Mrs. Shlemiel. "What are three groschen nowadays? You shouldn't do it for less than six a day." She ran over to Shlemiel and pinched him on the arm. Shlemiel winced and cried out, "She pinches just like my wife."

The Elders held a consultation among themselves. The town budget was very limited. Finally Gronam announced, "Three groschen may be too little, but six groschen a day is definitely too much, especially for a stranger. We will compromise and pay you five groschen a day. Shlemiel, do you accept?"

"Yes, but how long am I to keep this job?"

"Until the real Shlemiel comes home."

Gronam's decision was soon known throughout Chelm and the town admired his great wisdom and that of all the Elders of Chelm.

At first, Shlemiel tried to keep for himself the five groschen the town paid him.

"If I'm not your husband, I don't have to support you," he told Mrs. Shlemiel.

"In that case, since I'm not your wife, I don't have to cook for you, darn your socks, or patch your clothes."

And so, of course, Shlemiel turned over his pay to her. It was the first time that Mrs. Shlemiel had ever gotten any money for the household from Shlemiel. Now when she was in a good mood, she would say to him, "What a pity you didn't decide to go to Warsaw ten years ago."

"Don't you ever miss your husband?" Shlemiel would ask.

"And what about you? Don't you miss your wife?" Mrs. Shlemiel would ask.

And both would admit that they were quite happy with matters as they stood.

Years passed and no Shlemiel returned to Chelm. The Elders had many explanations for this. Zeinvel Ninny believed that Shlemiel had crossed the black mountains and had been eaten alive by the cannibals who live there. Dopey Lekisch thought that Shlemiel most probably had come to the Castle of Asmodeus, where he had been forced to marry a demon princess. Shmendrick Numskull came to the conclusion that Shlemiel had reached the edge of the world and had fallen off. There were many other theories. For example, that the real Shlemiel had lost his memory and had simply forgotten that he was Shlemiel.

Gronam did not like to impose his theories on other people; however, he was convinced that Shlemiel had gone to the other Chelm, where he had had exactly the same experience as the Shlemiel in this Chelm. He had been hired by the local community and was taking care of the other Mrs. Shlemiel's children for a wage of five groschen a day.

As for Shlemiel himself, he no longer knew what to think. The children were growing up and soon would be able to take care of themselves. Sometimes Shlemiel would sit and ponder. Where is the other Shlemiel? When will he come home? What is my real wife doing? Is she waiting for me, or has she got herself another Shlemiel? These were questions that he could not answer.

Every now and then Shlemiel would still get the desire to go traveling, but he could not bring himself to start out. What was the point of going on a trip if it led nowhere? Often, as he sat alone puzzling over the strange ways of the world, he would become more and more confused and begin humming to himself:

"Those who leave Chelm
End up in Chelm.
Those who remain in Chelm
Are certainly in Chelm.
All roads lead to Chelm.
All the world is one big Chelm."

Shrewd Todie & Lyzer the Miser

by Isaac Bashevis Singer

Strange things can happen
when greed overpowers even common sense.

In a village somewhere in the Ukraine there lived a poor man called Todie. Todie had a wife, Shaindel, and seven children, but he could never earn enough to feed them properly. He tried many trades and failed in all of them. It was said of Todie that if he decided to deal in candles, the sun would never set. He was nicknamed Shrewd Todie because whenever he managed to make some money, it was always by trickery.

This winter was an especially cold one. The snowfall was heavy and Todie had no money to buy wood for the stove. His seven children stayed in bed all day to keep warm. When the frost burns outside, hunger is stronger than ever, but Shaindel's larder was empty. She reproached Todie bitterly, wailing, "If you can't feed your wife and children, I will go to the rabbi and get a divorce."

"And what will you do with it, eat it?" Todie retorted.

In the same village there lived a rich man called Lyzer. Because of his stinginess he was known as Lyzer the Miser. He permitted his wife to bake bread only once in four weeks because he had discovered that fresh bread is eaten up more quickly than stale.

Todie had more than once gone to Lyzer for a loan of a few guldens, but Lyzer had always replied, "I sleep better when the money lies in my strongbox rather than in your pocket."

Lyzer had a goat, but he never fed her. The goat had learned to visit the houses of the neighbors, who pitied her and gave her potato peelings. Sometimes, when there were not enough peelings, she would gnaw on the old straw of the thatched roofs. She also had a liking for tree bark. Nevertheless, each year the goat gave birth to a kid. Lyzer milked her but, miser that he was, did not drink the milk himself. Instead he sold it to others.

Todie decided that he would take revenge on Lyzer and at the same time make some much needed money for himself.

One day, as Lyzer was sitting on a box eating borscht and dry bread (he used his chairs only on holidays so that the upholstery would not wear out), the door opened and Todie came in.

"Reb Lyzer," he said, "I would like to ask you a favor. My oldest daughter, Basha, is already fifteen and she's about to become engaged. A young man is coming from Janev to look her over. My cutlery is tin, and my wife is ashamed to ask the young man to eat soup with a tin spoon. Would you lend me one of your silver spoons? I give you my holy word that I will return it to you tomorrow."

Lyzer knew that Todie would not dare to break a holy oath and he lent him the spoon.

No young man came to see Basha that evening. As usual, the girl walked around barefoot and in rags, and the silver spoon lay hidden under Todie's shirt. In the early years of his marriage Todie had possessed a set of silver tableware himself. He had long since sold it all, with the exception of three silver teaspoons that were used only on Passover.

The following day, as Lyzer, his feet bare (in order to save his shoes), sat on his box eating borscht and dry bread, Todie returned.

"Here is the spoon I borrowed yesterday," he said, placing it on the table together with one of his own teaspoons.

"What is the teaspoon for?" Lyzer asked.

And Todie said, "Your tablespoon gave birth to a teaspoon. It is her child. Since I am an honest man, I'm returning both mother and child to you."

Lyzer looked at Todie in astonishment. He had never heard of a silver spoon giving birth to another. Nevertheless, his greed overcame his doubt and he happily accepted both spoons. Such an unexpected piece of good fortune! He was overjoyed that he had loaned Todie the spoon.

A few days later, as Lyzer (without his coat, to save it) was again sitting on his box eating borscht with dry bread, the door opened and Todie appeared.

"The young man from Janev did not please Basha because he had donkey ears, but this evening another young man is coming to look her over. Shaindel is cooking soup for him, but she's ashamed to serve him with a tin spoon. Would you lend me—"

Before Todie could finish the sentence, Lyzer interrupted. "You want to borrow a silver spoon? Take it with pleasure."

The following day Todie once more returned the spoon and with it one of his own silver teaspoons. He again explained that during the night the large spoon had given birth to a small one and in all good conscience he was bringing back the mother and newborn baby. As for the young man who had come to look Basha over, she hadn't liked him either, because his nose was so long that it reached to his chin. Needless to say that Lyzer the Miser was overjoyed.

Exactly the same thing happened a third time. Todie related that this time his daughter had rejected her suitor because he stammered. He also reported that Lyzer's silver spoon had again given birth to a baby spoon.

"Does it ever happen that a spoon has twins?" Lyzer inquired.

Todie thought it over for a moment. "Why not? I've even heard of a case where a spoon had triplets."

Almost a week passed by and Todie did not go to see Lyzer. But on Friday morning, as Lyzer (in his underdrawers to save his pants) sat on his box eating borscht and dry bread, Todie came in and said, "Good day to you, Reb Lyzer."

"A good morning and many more to you," Lyzer replied in his friendliest manner. "Did you perhaps come to borrow a silver spoon? If so, help yourself."

"Today I have a very special favor to ask. This evening a young man from the big city of Lublin is coming to look Basha over. He is the son of a rich man and I'm told he is clever and handsome as well. Not only do I need a silver spoon, but since he will remain with us over the Sabbath I need a pair of silver candlesticks, because mine are brass and my wife is ashamed to place them on the Sabbath table. Would you lend me your candlesticks? Immediately after the Sabbath, I will return them to you."

Silver candlesticks are of great value, and Lyzer the Miser hesitated. But remembering his good fortune with the spoons, he said, "I have eight silver candlesticks in my house. Take them all. I know you will return them to me just as you say. And if it should happen that any of them give birth, I have no doubt that you will be as honest as you have been in the past."

"Certainly," Todie said. "Let's hope for the best."

The silver spoon Todie hid beneath his shirt as usual. But taking the candlesticks, he went directly to a merchant, sold them for a considerable sum, and brought the money to Shaindel. When Shaindel saw so much money, she demanded to know where he had gotten such a treasure.

"When I went out, a cow flew over our roof and dropped a dozen silver eggs," Todie replied. "I sold them and here is the money."

"I have never heard of a cow flying over a roof and laying silver eggs," Shaindel said doubtingly.

"There is always a first time," Todie answered. "If you don't want the money, give it back to me."

"There'll be no talk about giving it back," Shaindel said. She knew that her husband was full of cunning and tricks—but when the children are hungry and the larder is empty, it is better not to ask too many questions. Shaindel went to the marketplace and bought meat, fish, white flour, and even some nuts and raisins for a pudding. And since a lot of money still remained, she bought shoes and clothes for the children.

It was a very gay Sabbath in Todie's house. The boys sang and the girls danced. When the children asked their father where he had gotten the money, he replied, "It is forbidden to mention money during the Sabbath."

Sunday, as Lyzer (barefoot and almost naked to save his clothes) sat on his box finishing up a dry crust of bread with borscht, Todie arrived and, handing him his silver spoon, said, "It's too bad. This time your spoon did not give birth to a baby."

"What about the candlesticks?" Lyzer inquired anxiously.

Todie sighed deeply. "The candlesticks died."

Lyzer got up from his box so hastily that he overturned his plate of borscht.

"You fool! How can candlesticks die?" he screamed.

"If spoons can give birth, candlesticks can die."

Lyzer raised a great hue and cry and had Todie called before the rabbi. When the rabbi heard both sides of the story, he burst out laughing. "It serves you right," he said to Lyzer. "If you hadn't chosen to believe that spoons give birth, now you would not be forced to believe that your candlesticks died."

"But it's all nonsense," Lyzer objected.

"Did you not expect the candlesticks to give birth to other candlesticks?" the rabbi said admonishingly. "If you accept nonsense when it brings you profit, you must also accept nonsense when it brings you loss." And he dismissed the case.

The following day, when Lyzer the Miser's wife brought him his borscht and dry bread, Lyzer said to her, "I will eat only the bread. Borscht is too expensive a food, even without sour cream."

The story of the silver spoons that gave birth and the candlesticks that died spread quickly through the town. All the people enjoyed Todie's victory and Lyzer the Miser's defeat. The shoemaker's and tailor's apprentices, as was their custom whenever there was an important happening, made up a song about it:

Lyzer, put your grief aside.
What if your candlesticks have died?
You're the richest man on earth
With silver spoons that can give birth
And silver eggs as living proof
Of flying cows above your roof.
Don't sit there eating crusts of bread—
To silver grandsons look ahead.

However, time passed and Lyzer's silver spoons never gave birth again.

Roof Sitter

by Frances Eisenberg

Sarah Blevins was a tall, skinny girl who thought she knew how to manage children. Then she met Joe.

From the very beginning there were two things wrong with my brother, Joe. He was shy and he was stubborn. This is the way he did. If somebody tried to make him not shy, then he got stubborn. Like the time when he was only four years old and he was supposed to be a butterfly in the Sunday school entertainment, and Miss Wilson tried and tried to push Joe out on the stage and make him flutter his wings, but he lay down on the floor and wouldn't get up no matter how much the other butterflies stepped on him.

And when he started to kindergarten and his teacher kept asking him to come up in front and tell the other children about his pets, Joe ran out of the room and hid downstairs in the boys' toilet until they had to call the janitor to get him out.

My mother had tried her best to make Joe not like he was, but when he was six years old she had to give up. She said she hoped he would outgrow it. And she asked Joe's teacher please not to try to draw Joe out anymore. So after that everybody left him alone.

One morning in June just after school was out we got a telegram from Nashville saying that my father's aunt Sadie was in a dying condition, and for my parents to come quick. At first my mother didn't know what to do, because she knew they wouldn't want children there, and there wasn't anybody to leave us with. But she thought awhile, and then all of a sudden she said, "Sarah Blevins."

"Who is that?" I asked.

"She is a college student," said my mother. "She is Mrs. White down the street's niece, and she is staying with her and earning her way through college by taking care of children and things like that this summer."

So my mother hurried down to Mrs. White's house, and I went too, and Mrs. White said that Sarah Blevins would be glad to take care of us. "She is very good with children," Mrs. White said. "She has had some courses in child training at the university and she knows all about children."

Then Mrs. White called Sarah Blevins out and she was a tall skinny girl with glasses on and a serious look. She told my mother that she would be glad to stay with us, and would give us the best of care. "How old are these children?" Sarah Blevins asked, looking at me, and stretching her mouth a little like a smile.

"This is Helen," my mother said. "She is nine. And Joe, her little brother, is six."

"Oh, that's very fortunate," Sarah Blevins said, "because I have just finished a course at the university in the child from six to twelve years, and that includes both of your children."

"Yes," my mother said. "But please be careful with little Joe. He is a very shy child and doesn't like to be noticed. As long as he's left alone, though, he's very nice."

Sarah Blevins looked interested. "I will try to adjust your little boy," she said. "I have done a lot of fieldwork on problem children."

My mother looked worried. "Oh, there's nothing wrong with Joe," she said. "He's just a little young for his age."

"I'm sure we'll get along splendidly," said Sarah Blevins, stretching her mouth at me again. She went into her aunt's house and came out with her clothes in a little black bag, and we all hurried back to our house because my mother had to meet my father in town and catch the one-o'clock train.

When we got to our yard Joe was playing under the sweet gum tree. He had some rocks and little sticks, and when he saw Sarah Blevins he stared at her for a minute and then went on playing.

"This is Joe," said my mother in a hurry. "Joey, this is Sarah Blevins. She is going to take care of you while Mother is gone, and you must be a good little boy and do what she says." Then my mother went into the house to get ready.

Joe stared at Sarah Blevins again, and then he began to hammer a stick into the ground with a rock. Sarah Blevins went over to Joe and held out her hand. "How do you do, Joe," she said.

Joe began to look nervous. He twisted his head around so he couldn't see her, but she kept on holding her hand out for him to shake. When she saw he wasn't going to shake hands with her, finally she put her hand down. She looked at the sticks and the rocks he was playing with.

"Oh, a house," she said. "Joe is building a nice house. Who will live in your house when it is built? Is it a fairy house? Will a tiny fairy live in it?"

Joe put his arm up and hid his face. Then he went over and stood behind a bush where Sarah Blevins couldn't see him.

"He doesn't like for people to talk to him," I told Sarah Blevins. "Just the family. He's shy of people."

Sarah Blevins looked a little mad. "Yes, but that's very wrong to encourage him in it," she said. "That way he'll get conditioned and then it will be hopeless. He should be drawn out."

"He doesn't like to be drawn out," I told her. "That just makes him worse."

"Not if it's done right," she said. She began to pretend that she didn't know where Joe was. "There was a little boy here a minute ago," she said. "Where did he go? Maybe he had on a pair of magic shoes, or maybe he changed into a flower or a butterfly?"

Just then my mother came out of the house. She kissed me good-by. "Joe is behind the bush," I told her.

My mother went over and kissed him good-by. "Be a good boy," she told him. "Good-by," she said to Sarah Blevins. "I know you're going to be fine with the children. Just take charge of things, and order what you need from the grocery. We'll be back by Wednesday at least."

Then she got into the taxi and rode away.

Sarah Blevins stood still a minute, then she said, "I will just leave your little brother alone for the time being." And she took her bag and we went into the house and I showed her where to put her things.

After a while, when she had looked in the icebox to see what food there was, she got a piece of notepaper and began to write on it. She told me she was writing out what I should do every hour of the day and beginning tomorrow I must do exactly what it said. She stuck the paper on the kitchen door with some thumbtacks.

"Now you must take care of everything for a few minutes," she said. "I am going to run down to the grocery store and get some celery. Your little brother seems to be lacking in iron."

While she was gone I went out and hunted for Joe. He was digging holes in the backyard.

"Is she gone yet?" he asked. I knew he meant Sarah Blevins.

"She is gone, but she is coming back in a minute," I told him. "She has gone to get something for you to eat to give you iron."

"I don't want iron," Joe said.

"But listen, Joe," I told him. "She is supposed to take care of us, and we are supposed to mind her while Mother and Father are away. So don't be stubborn. Do what she says, and maybe they will bring us something nice."

"I don't like her," Joe said.

I didn't know what else to say to Joe. I could see that he was going to be stubborn, but I didn't know how to make him not be.

Pretty soon I could hear Sarah Blevins in the kitchen fixing the supper, and after a while she called us in to eat it.

It was mostly lamb chops and celery and carrots with nothing for dessert. All through supper Sarah Blevins talked to Joe. She asked him things like did he like furry kittens, and did he ever see a brownie, and things like that. Joe would take a bite of whatever it was, and then he would put his head under the table to chew it so he wouldn't have to look at Sarah Blevins. And just as soon as he got through eating he went into the living room and turned on the radio to the "Krunchy Krispy Kiddies" hour and I went in there too, and we listened to it.

It had got to the place where the twins had sailed to the moon in their rocket ship and found the palace of King Zoozag, the moon king. While the twins were looking around for the moon pearl, King Zoozag's magician had caught them and locked them up in a dungeon with a ceiling that kept coming down closer and closer to crush the twins to pieces. It was very exciting. The roof was just above their heads and you could hear it giving awful creaks, and you could hear the king laughing an awful laugh, ha-ha-ha-ha, when all of a sudden Sarah Blevins came rushing in there looking like she was going to faint. She ran over and turned off the radio.

"My goodness," she said. She sat down in a chair and got her breath. "No wonder your little brother has got a complex if your mother lets him listen to such things as that. Especially at night.

"Now," she went on in a cheerful voice. "Let's tell stories. Shall we? First I'll tell a story, then Helen will tell one and then Joe will. Or maybe Joe would tell his first."

Joe looked at her for just a minute, and then he shook his head. But Sarah Blevins paid no attention to that. "Joe's going to tell us a story, Helen," she said. "Won't that be nice? I wish Joe would tell us a story about a little white rabbit. Don't you?"

"Yes, but he won't," I told her. "He doesn't like to talk before people."

"Oh, yes, Joe will. I know he will," Sarah Blevins said. She gave me a kind of a mad look. "Joe will tell us a story."

Joe put his head down in a corner of the chair and pulled a cushion over it.

"You see," I said. "He won't."

"Shhhh," hissed Sarah Blevins, frowning at me. "Yes he will," she said out loud. "Just as soon as he thinks awhile. Let's be quiet and let him think. Oh, what a nice story Joe is going to tell us."

For a little while we were quiet and Joe didn't take his head out.

"Now," Sarah Blevins said finally. "Now I think Joe is ready to begin. But where is Joe?" she asked in a surprised voice. "Why, he was here just a minute ago. Where can he be? Is he behind the radio?" She went over and looked. "No, he's not there. Is he behind the door? No." Then she went over to the chair where Joe was and lifted up the cushion. "Why, *here* he is."

But before she could say anything else Joe slid out of the chair and ran upstairs.

"I guess he's going to hide in the bathroom," I told Sarah Blevins. "Sometimes he does that when ladies bother him, because they can't go in there after him."

Sarah went to the foot of the stairs. "Joe's sleepy," she said in a loud voice. "I guess he wants to go to bed. He will tell us a story tomorrow. Good night, Joe."

Then she came back and sat down in the living room. "Helen," she said, "you must keep quiet when I'm talking to Joe. What's wrong with him is that he's heard people say he's shy so much that he thinks he is shy. So he acts shy. He isn't really shy, he only thinks he is. When he withdraws like this you must pretend it's just a game he's playing, or you must explain it to him like I did just now and make it reasonable. Do you understand?"

"I don't know if I do or not," I said.

"Well, it doesn't matter. Just so you keep quiet and let me manage your little brother my own way. By the time your mother comes back I'll have him adjusted. But you must cooperate."

"All right," I told her. Because it would be nice and my mother would be glad if she got home and Joe was talking to people and not running from them anymore, and not being stubborn, and singing little songs when they asked him to, and making speeches and things like that. So I would do like Sarah Blevins said, and be quiet and pretend I didn't know why he was hiding.

The next morning we had breakfast and I looked on the notepaper to see what I was supposed to do. I was supposed to do Household Tasks for a half an hour. Sarah Blevins told me to go upstairs and make up my bed and then come down and play outdoors until lunch. So I went up and I began to clean up the bedroom, and I looked out of the window and saw Joe playing in the front yard. He had some marbles and he was putting them in a row on the grass.

Pretty soon I saw Sarah Blevins coming out there and she had some papers in her hands. "Hello, Joe," she said. She sat down on the grass beside him.

"May I play with you?" she asked, stretching her mouth into a smile at him.

Joe looked down and began to pick up the marbles one at a time.

"Would you like to play a game that I have here?" Sarah Blevins said. She put one of the papers down on the grass. "It's a game with pictures. Look. It's fun. Do you want to play it with me?"

Joe began to shake his head. He began to slide away from her a little toward the bush.

"See the little girl in the picture," Sarah Blevins told him, holding it up. "She is rolling a hoop. But something is missing. Can you take the red pencil and put in what is missing?"

Joe kept shaking his head and Sarah kept holding out the pencil to him. Finally Joe got up and ran to the bush and hid behind it. But Sarah went over there too and sat down. "It's nicer over here, isn't it, Joe?" she said. "Let's don't play that game, then; let's play another one. Listen."

She took another piece of paper and began to read off of it. "*The sun was shining on the sea, shining with all his might.* Can you say that, Joe? Listen: *The sun was shining on the sea, shining with all his might.* Now you say it."

But Joe began to look more nervous than ever, and he went around to the other side of the bush, and Sarah followed him around there. She kept on talking. "This is fun, isn't it, Joe?" she said. "It's like a game I know called follow the leader. Did you ever play that game?"

Joe began to look kind of wild. He looked for another place to hide. There wasn't any.

He ran toward the front porch, but I guess he thought that wouldn't be any good, and all of a sudden he started climbing up the rose trellis. There weren't many roses on it, and it was kind of like a ladder.

This time Sarah did not follow him. But anyway he climbed higher until he got up to the porch roof, and then he crawled up on it and sat there and looked down at Sarah Blevins.

I spread up the bed in a hurry and went on downstairs and out into the yard. I wanted to see what Sarah was going to do next to adjust Joe.

Sarah was standing there on the ground looking up at the roof. Her face was red and she looked sort of mad, but she laughed and said to me, "Did you see Joe go up the trellis? He's playing that he's

a little squirrel, I guess. Did you see him climb?"

"Yes," I said. I was not going to say anything else, because I was supposed to cooperate with her and keep quiet.

"I wonder how a little squirrel comes down off a roof," Sarah Blevins said. "Can you show us, Joe?"

We waited about ten minutes, but Joe did not come down. He went over and sat down behind the chimney.

Then I forgot. "We could get the stepladder and get him down that way," I told Sarah. She gave me an awful mad look.

"Be quiet," she said under her breath. Then she said in a loud voice, "Why, we don't want to get a little squirrel down with a ladder. He will come down himself in a little while to get some nuts."

"Or maybe he thinks he's a bird," I said.

But Sarah Blevins didn't pay any attention to me. "I'm going to fix your lunch now, and when I get back I wouldn't be surprised if Joe is on the ground playing with you, Helen," she said. "Being a squirrel is fun, but after all it's nicer to be a little boy, isn't it?" And she took the papers and things and went into the house.

I sat down on the ground and looked up at Joe.

After a while I said, "Sarah Blevins has gone inside now, Joe. Why don't you come down off of the roof and surprise her?"

Joe got out from behind the chimney. "No," he said. After a minute he asked, "When is she going home?"

"Maybe not till next Wednesday," I said. "So come on down and do what she says. We're supposed to."

"I'll come down next Wednesday," Joe said.

I could see that he was going to be stubborn and not come down off of the roof, and then Sarah Blevins couldn't adjust him before Mother came back. I didn't know what to do, so I just sat there and tried to think of something.

After a while some children from the next block came skating along the sidewalk. "What are you doing, Helen?" they asked.

"Nothing," I told them. "Only sitting here waiting for my little brother, Joe, to come down off of the roof."

They came up in the yard and looked up at Joe's face, which was sticking over.

"What is he doing up there?" they asked.

"Just waiting. He's going to sit there until next Wednesday."

Just then an automobile with two men in it came driving slowly along the street. The men looked out at us and stopped the car. A fat one stuck his head out of the window. "Hey, kids," he said. "Having a big time with school out and everything?"

"Yes sir," we said.

"Well then, how would you like to have your pictures on the kiddies' vacation page of the *Morning Journal* so all the other kids all over the city can see what fun you're having? Would you like that?"

"Yes sir," we told him.

So they got out of the car and the thin one had a camera. The fat one told us to stand in a row with our hands on each other's shoulders and pretend that we were skating. One of the other children said, "Hey, mister, can Joe be in the picture?"

"Sure, sure," the fat man said. "Who is Joe, your dog?"

"No," I told him. "He's my little brother. He's up there." I pointed up at the roof.

"Sure, Joe can be in it," the fat man said. "Hold everything, Bill," he said to the man with the camera. "Come on down, Joe," he said.

"He can't be in the picture if he has to come down to be in it," I told the man. "He's going to stay up there all the rest of this week and some more too."

"Ha-ha," laughed the fat man. "That's a new one. All over town they're sitting in trees, but he's the first roof sitter. Well, we wouldn't want Joe to spoil his record, so we'll take a picture of him from the ground. The rest of you can stand around and be looking up at Joe."

So we all stood around and pointed up at the roof, and the cameraman clicked the picture so quick that Joe couldn't hide his face or do anything about it. Then the fat man asked us our names and how old we were, what grades at school we were in, and then they got in their car and drove away. And the children from the next block hurried home to tell their mothers about having their pictures taken. And just then Sarah Blevins came to the door and said lunch was ready. "We have peanut butter sandwiches, Helen," she said. "Maybe Joe will come down and get some."

But he didn't. I went in and sat down at the table.

"A man took our pictures," I told Sarah Blevins.

But she didn't pay any attention. I guess she was thinking what to do next to adjust Joe. When we finished lunch she said we would just let Joe alone until he got hungry, and she put the dishes in to soak and sat down and began to read a magazine.

I went outside and stayed in the front yard. So the afternoon went by and it was beginning to get dark, and after a while it was really dark, and still Joe was on the roof. I went in the house to see if supper was ready and to ask Sarah Blevins what she was going to do.

"It's dark," I said, "and Joe is still up on the roof."

"Go out and tell him that supper is ready," said Sarah Blevins. "But don't tell him to come down. He must decide that for himself. He must make up his own mind what he is going to do. If I make him come down now, everything will be ruined."

So I went out and told Joe supper was ready. "Don't you want any?" I asked him.

His voice sounded very weak and far away. "No," he said.

"Are you going to sleep up there?" I asked him.

"Yes," he said, and he sounded scared and stubborn at the same time.

I went back and told Sarah Blevins. "Very well," she said.

So we ate supper and it was bedtime, and I went upstairs. I went to the window of my mother and father's bedroom. The moon was shining and I could look down on the porch roof and see Joe, sitting up close to the chimney.

"Are you awake, Joe?" I asked him.

"Yes," his voice came up.

"Good night, then," I said. I went to bed and I felt awful. I thought well anyway he can't roll off, because the roof is wide and flat, but it would be hard and maybe he would be hungry. So after a while I got two pillows and a blanket, and I went to the window and dropped them down to Joe. I didn't care if I had promised Sarah to cooperate. I knew my mother wouldn't want Joe to sleep out of doors without a blanket. "Do you want something to eat, Joe?" I asked him, low so Sarah wouldn't hear.

"Yes," he said. "I want a peanut butter sandwich and some crackers."

So I went into the kitchen and when I went past the living room I told Sarah Blevins I was going for a glass of milk, and I got some peanut butter sandwiches and a whole box of crackers, and I went back up to the window and let them down to Joe by a string.

"But you oughtn't to be so stubborn, Joe," I told him while he was eating them. "You ought to mind people better, or something awful might happen to you."

"I don't care," Joe said. He was fixing the blanket and the pillows. He lay down on them and went to sleep.

The next morning Joe was still on the roof. We talked to him from the upstairs window, but he turned his back because Sarah was there. "Your little brother is a very strange case," Sarah Blevins said to me. She told me to get a bottle of milk and let it down to him, because we couldn't have him starving. And she would think of what to do next.

About ten o'clock people began to drive

past the house, and they would go slow and point up to our roof. A few of them stopped their cars and got out and came up on the sidewalk and looked. "Little girl," they said to me, "is this where the little boy lives that's sitting on the roof, that his picture was in the *Journal* this morning?"

I went and got the paper, and there we all were on the vacation page, and under the picture it said, "Out to establish new record," and "Little Joe Marsden, six, 342 Cedar Street, has joined the ranks of marathon sitters and declares that he will stay on his roof until next Wednesday afternoon."

You couldn't see much of Joe in the picture, only his head. But the rest of us were plain. I ran and showed the paper to Sarah Blevins. "Look!" I said. "Joe got his picture in the paper, and look out in the street at all the people."

Sarah looked and she turned sort of pale. "I'm going out there and try one more time," she said. "This is the last straw."

"You mean you're not going to try to adjust him anymore?" I asked her, following her out into the yard, but she didn't answer me.

She looked up at him from the sidewalk. She changed her voice from mad to sweet. "Helen, do you believe in magic?" she said to me. "I do. I'm going to close my eyes and count to ten, and when I open them I believe Joe will be down off of the roof, standing right here on the grass." Then she shut her eyes and began to count.

By now several cars were parked in front of the house and something funny seemed to happen to Joe. He looked down and saw the people looking up at him and all of a sudden instead of hiding from them he began to jump up and down on the roof and yell at Sarah. "This is my house. Let me alone." And then he called her a bad name. "Go home, old jackass," he said.

Sarah opened her mouth and looked surprised. I guess she was surprised that Joe could talk. He had not said anything before her until now.

Some of the people began to laugh. "That's telling her," they said.

Twice Sarah started to climb the trellis so she could talk to Joe better, but both times he said, "Let me alone," and looked like he was going to jump. So Sarah had to get down, and she went over and talked to a woman. She told her that in all the time she had worked with children she had never in her life seen one as stubborn as Joe. But she said if everyone had just let him alone, she could have had him adjusted, but now everything was spoiled.

But nobody paid much attention to her, because now Joe had turned out to be famous, because he was the only roof sitter in town, and nobody cared what Sarah thought.

The more people stopped and looked up at Joe the more I got proud of him and I would tell everybody I was his sister and that he had stayed up there all day and all night and was going to stay on until Wednesday, and about three o'clock some newsreel cameramen that were in town for something else took some pictures of Joe for the movies.

It was just after this that my mother and father came home. When they got out of the taxi my mother saw the people standing there and she began to look scared. "What is it?" she said. "What's happened?"

"Look, Mother. Look, Papa," I yelled, pointing up to the roof. "Joe's up there.

He's been up there nearly two days. He had his picture in the paper, and the people have been coming to see him all day. He's famous now."

Then Sarah Blevins ran over and began talking fast, and she was really crying. She kept saying how she had tried to adjust Joe, and then these people began to come and notice him, and everything was spoiled.

"And he called her a jackass," I said. "And this is the stubbornest he ever was in his life. But now he's not so shy anymore. He didn't hide from the people. Aren't you glad Joe's going to be in the movies and everybody will get to see him?"

But my mother didn't seem to be glad. She stood there looking mad and disgusted. "I ought never to have gone off in the first place," she said.

"Joe, you ought not to have done that," my father told him. "You ought to know better." Just then he saw the roses that had been stepped on and smashed on Joey's way up and he gave a mad sound. "I've a good notion to come up there on that roof and blister you good," he said.

But when Joe saw that Sarah was leaving he came down by himself. And Sarah went away with her little black bag, and she said she was so nervous she didn't know what she was doing. All the people went away, and that was the end of Joe being a roof sitter. He had to eat his supper and go to bed, even if it wasn't dark, and he couldn't have any of the box of candy they had brought from Nashville, where they had left and come home because my father's aunt Sadie had turned out not to be so sick after all.

But Joe was famous for several days and all over town children began sitting on roofs, trying to break the record. One of them, a little girl named Gladys Potts, sat on her garage roof for ninety-three hours, but a storm came up, and she had to come down.

Still, it seemed that all the attention he had got did not quite adjust Joe, because later when they asked him to be in a Sunday school play he said he wouldn't, and he didn't. Not even when they promised to give him some bananas afterward.

Mighty Mikko

by Parker Fillmore

Young Mikko's inheritance was only three animal traps, but they yielded a truly royal catch. A tale from Finland.

There was once an old woodsman and his wife who had an only son named Mikko. As the mother lay dying the young man wept bitterly.

"When you are gone, my dear mother," he said, "there will be no one left to think of me."

The poor woman comforted him as best she could, and said to him, "You will still have your father."

Shortly after the woman's death, the old man, too, was taken ill.

Now, indeed, I shall be left desolate and alone, Mikko thought, as he sat at his father's bedside and saw him grow weaker and weaker.

"My boy," the old man said just before he died, "I have nothing to leave you but the three snares with which these many years I have caught wild animals. Those snares now belong to you. When I am dead, go into the woods, and if you find a wild creature caught in any of them, free it gently and bring it home alive."

After his father's death, Mikko remembered the snares and went out to the woods to see them. The first was empty and also the second, but in the third he found a little red Fox. He carefully lifted the spring that had shut down on one of the Fox's feet and then carried the little creature home in his arms. He shared his supper with it, and when he lay down to sleep the Fox curled up at his feet. They lived together some time until they became close friends.

"Mikko," said the Fox one day, "why are you so sad?"

"Because I'm lonely."

"Pooh!" said the Fox. "That's no way for a young man to talk! You ought to get married! Then you wouldn't feel lonely!"

"Married!" Mikko repeated. "How can I get married? I can't marry a poor girl because I'm too poor myself, and a rich girl wouldn't marry me."

"Nonsense!" said the Fox. "You're a fine well-set-up young man and you're kind and gentle. What more could a princess ask?"

Mikko laughed to think of a princess wanting him for a husband.

"I mean what I say!" the Fox insisted. "Take our own Princess now. What would you think of marrying her?"

Mikko laughed louder than before.

"I have heard," he said, "that she is the most beautiful princess in the world! Any man would be happy to marry her!"

"Very well," the Fox said. "If you feel that way about her, then I'll arrange the wedding for you."

With that the little Fox actually did trot off to the royal castle and gain audience with the King.

"My master sends you greetings," the Fox said, "and he begs you to loan him your bushel measure."

"My bushel measure!" the King repeated in surprise. "Who is your master and why does he want to borrow my bushel measure?"

"Ssh!" the Fox whispered, as though he didn't want the courtiers to hear what he was saying. Then slipping up quite close to the King he murmured in his ear, "Surely you have heard of Mikko, haven't you? Mighty Mikko, as he's called."

The King had never heard of any Mikko who was known as Mighty Mikko, but thinking that perhaps he should have heard of him, he shook his head and murmured, "Hm! Mikko! Mighty Mikko! Oh, to be sure! Yes, yes, of course!"

"My master is about to start off on a journey and he needs a bushel measure for a very particular reason."

"I understand! I understand!" the King said, although he didn't understand at all, and he gave orders that the bushel measure that they used in the storeroom of the castle be brought in and given to the Fox.

The Fox carried off the measure and hid it in the woods. Then he scurried about to all sorts of little out-of-the-way nooks and crannies where people had hidden their savings and he dug up a gold piece here and a silver piece there until he had a handful. Then he went back to the woods and stuck the various coins in the cracks of the measure. The next day he returned to the King.

"My master, Mighty Mikko," he said, "sends you thanks, O King, for the use of your bushel measure."

The King held out his hand, and when the Fox gave him the measure he peeped inside to see if by chance it contained any trace of what had recently been measured. His eye of course at once caught the glint of the gold and silver coins lodged in the cracks.

"Ah!" he said, thinking Mikko must be a very mighty lord indeed to be so careless of his wealth. "I should like to meet your master. Won't you and he come and visit me?"

This was what the Fox wanted the King to say, but he pretended to hesitate.

"I thank Your Majesty for the kind invitation," he said, "but I fear my master can't accept it just now. He wants to get married soon and we are about to start off on a long journey to inspect a number of foreign princesses."

This made the King all the more anxious to have Mikko visit him at once, for he thought that if Mikko should see his daughter before he saw those foreign princesses, he might fall in love with her and marry her. So he said to the Fox, "My dear fellow, you must prevail on your master to make me a visit before he starts out on his travels! You will, won't you?"

The Fox looked this way and that, as if he were too embarrassed to speak.

"Your Majesty," he said at last, "I pray you pardon my frankness. The truth is you are not rich enough to entertain my master and your castle isn't big enough to house the immense retinue that always attends him."

The King, who by this time was frantic to see Mikko, lost his head completely.

"My dear Fox," he said, "I'll give you anything in the world if you prevail upon your master to visit me at once! Couldn't you suggest to him that he travel with a modest retinue this time?"

The Fox shook his head.

"No. His rule is either to travel with a great retinue or to go on foot disguised as a poor woodsman attended only by me."

"Couldn't you prevail on him to come to me disguised as a poor woodsman?" the King begged. "Once he was here, I could place gorgeous clothes at his disposal."

But still the Fox shook his head.

"I fear Your Majesty's wardrobe doesn't contain the kind of clothes my master is accustomed to."

"I assure you I've got some very good clothes," the King said. "Come along this minute and we'll go through them and I'm sure you'll find some that your master would wear."

So they went to a room that was like a big wardrobe, with hundreds and hundreds of hooks upon which were hung hundreds of coats and breeches and embroidered shirts. The King ordered his attendants to take down the costumes one by one and place them before the Fox.

They began with the plainer clothes.

"Good enough for most people," the Fox said, "but not for my master."

Then they took down garments of a finer grade.

"I'm afraid you're going to all this trouble for nothing," the Fox said. "Frankly now, don't you realize that my master couldn't possibly put on any of these things?"

The King, who had hoped to keep for his own use his most gorgeous clothes of all, now ordered these to be shown.

The Fox looked at them sideways, sniffed them critically, and at last said, "Well, perhaps my master would consent to wear these for a few days. They are not what he is accustomed to wear, but I will say this for him—he is not proud."

The King was overjoyed.

"Very well, my dear Fox. I'll have the guest chambers put in readiness for your master's visit and I'll have all these, my finest clothes, laid out for him. You won't disappoint me, will you?"

"I'll do my best," the Fox promised.

With that he bade the King a civil good-day and ran home to Mikko.

The next day as the Princess was peeping out of an upper window of the castle, she saw a young woodsman approaching accompanied by a Fox. He was a fine stalwart youth, and the Princess, who knew from the presence of the Fox that he must be Mikko, gave a long sigh and confided to her serving maid, "I think I could fall in love with that young man if he really were only a woodsman!"

Later, when she saw him arrayed in her father's finest clothes—which looked so well on Mikko that no one even recognized them as the King's—she lost her heart completely, and when Mikko was presented to her she blushed and trem-

bled just as any ordinary girl might before a handsome young man.

All the court was equally delighted with Mikko. The ladies went into ecstasies over his modest manners, his fine figure, and the gorgeousness of his clothes, and the old graybeard councillors, nodding their heads in approval, said to each other, "Nothing of the coxcomb about this young fellow! In spite of his great wealth, see how politely he listens to us when we talk!"

The next day the Fox went privately to the King, and said, "My master is a man of few words and quick judgment. He bids me tell you that your daughter, the Princess, pleases him mightily and that, with your approval, he will make his addresses to her at once."

The King was greatly agitated and began, "My dear Fox—"

But the Fox interrupted him to say, "Think the matter over carefully and give me your decision tomorrow."

So the King consulted with the Princess and with his councillors and in a short time the marriage was arranged and the wedding ceremony actually performed!

"Didn't I tell you so?" the Fox said, when he and Mikko were alone after the wedding.

"Yes," Mikko acknowledged, "you did promise that I should marry the Princess. But, tell me, now that I am married, what am I to do? I can't live on here forever with my wife."

"Put your mind at rest," the Fox said. "I've thought of everything. Just do as I tell you and you'll have nothing to regret. Tonight say to the King, 'It is now only fitting that you should visit me and see for yourself the sort of castle over which your daughter is hereafter to be mistress!' "

When Mikko said this to the King, the King was overjoyed, for now that the marriage had actually taken place he was wondering whether he hadn't perhaps been a little hasty. Mikko's words reassured him and he eagerly accepted the invitation.

On the morrow the Fox said to Mikko, "Now I'll run on ahead and get things ready for you."

"But where are you going?" Mikko said, frightened at the thought of being deserted by his little friend.

The Fox drew Mikko aside and whispered softly, "A few days' march from here there is a very gorgeous castle belonging to a wicked old dragon who is known as the Worm. I think the Worm's castle would just about suit you."

"I'm sure it would," Mikko agreed. "But how are we to get it away from the Worm?"

"Trust me," the Fox said. "All you need do is this: lead the King and his courtiers along the main highway until by noon tomorrow you reach a crossroads. Turn there to the left and go straight on until you see the tower of the Worm's castle. If you meet any men by the wayside, shepherds or the like, ask them whose men they are and show no surprise at their answer. So now, dear master, farewell until we meet again at your beautiful castle."

The little Fox trotted off at a smart pace, and Mikko and the Princess and the King, attended by the whole court, followed in more leisurely fashion.

The little Fox, when he had left the main highway at the crossroads, soon met ten woodsmen with axes over their shoulders. They were all dressed in blue smocks of the same cut.

"Good day," the Fox said politely. "Whose men are you?"

"Our master is known as the Worm," the woodsmen told him.

"My poor, poor lads!" the Fox said, shaking his head sadly.

"What's the matter?" the woodsmen asked.

For a few moments the Fox pretended to be too overcome with emotion to speak. Then he said, "My poor lads, don't you know that the King is coming with a great force to destroy the Worm and all his people?"

The woodsmen were simple fellows and this news threw them into great consternation.

"Is there no way for us to escape?" they asked.

The Fox put his paw to his head and thought.

"Well," he said at last, "there is one way you might escape and that is by telling everyone who asks you that you are the Mighty Mikko's men. But if you value your lives, never again say that your master is the Worm."

"We are Mighty Mikko's men!" the woodsmen at once began repeating over and over. "We are Mighty Mikko's men!"

A little farther on the road, the Fox met twenty grooms, dressed in the same blue smocks, who were tending a hundred beautiful horses. The Fox talked to the twenty grooms as he had talked to the woodsmen, and before he left them they, too, were shouting, "We are Mighty Mikko's men!"

Next the Fox came to a huge flock of a thousand sheep tended by thirty shepherds all dressed in the Worm's blue smocks. He stopped and talked to them until he had them roaring out, "We are Mighty Mikko's men!"

Then the Fox trotted on until he reached the castle of the Worm. He found the Worm himself inside lolling lazily about. He was a huge dragon and had been a great warrior in his day. In fact his castle and his lands and his servants and his possessions had all been won in battle. But now for many years no one had cared to fight him and he had grown fat and lazy.

"Good day," the Fox said, pretending to be very breathless and frightened. "You're the Worm, aren't you?"

"Yes," the dragon said boastfully. "I am the great Worm!"

The Fox pretended to grow more agitated.

"My poor fellow," he said, "I am sorry for you! But of course none of us can expect to live forever. Well, I must hurry along. I thought I would just stop and say good-by."

Made uneasy by the Fox's words, the Worm cried out, "Wait just a minute! What's the matter?"

The Fox was already at the door, but at the Worm's entreaty he paused and said over his shoulder, "Why, my poor fellow, you surely know, don't you, that the King with a great force is coming to destroy you and all your people?"

"What!" the Worm gasped, turning a sickly green with fright. He knew he was fat and helpless and could never again fight as in the years gone by.

"Don't go just yet!" he begged the Fox. "When is the King coming?"

"He's on the highway now! That's why I must be going! Good-by!"

"My dear Fox, stay just a moment and I'll reward you richly! Help me to hide so that the King won't find me! What about the shed where the linen is stored? I could crawl under the linen, and then if you locked the door from the outside, the King could never find me."

"Very well," the Fox agreed, "but we must hurry!"

So they ran outside to the shed where the linen was kept, and the Worm hid himself under the linen. The Fox then locked the door and set fire to the shed. Soon there was nothing left of that wicked old dragon, the Worm, but a handful of ashes.

The Fox now called together the dragon's household and talked them over to Mikko as he had the woodsmen and the grooms and the shepherds.

Meanwhile the King and his party were slowly covering the ground over which the Fox had sped so quickly. When they came to the ten woodsmen in blue smocks, the King said, "I wonder whose woodsmen those are."

One of his attendants asked the woodsmen, and the ten of them shouted out at the top of their voices, "We are Mighty Mikko's men!"

Mikko said nothing and the King and all the court were impressed anew with his modesty.

A little farther on they met the twenty grooms with their hundred prancing horses. When the grooms were questioned, they answered with a shout, "We are Mighty Mikko's men!"

The Fox certainly spoke the truth, the King thought to himself, when he told me of Mikko's riches!

A little later the thirty shepherds when they were questioned made answer in a chorus that was deafening to hear, "We are Mighty Mikko's men!"

The sight of the thousand sheep that belonged to his son-in-law made the King feel poor and humble by comparison, and the courtiers whispered among themselves, "For all his simple manner, Mighty Mikko must be a richer, more powerful lord than the King himself! In fact, it is only a very great lord indeed who could be so simple!"

At last they reached the castle, which from the blue-smocked soldiers that guarded the gateway they knew to be Mikko's. The Fox came out to welcome the King's party. Behind him in two rows stood all the household servants. These, at a signal from the Fox, cried out in one voice, "We are Mighty Mikko's men!"

Then Mikko, in the same simple manner that he would have used in his father's mean little hut in the woods, bade the King and his followers welcome and they all entered the castle, where they found a great feast prepared and waiting.

The King stayed on for several days, and the more he saw of Mikko the better pleased he was that he had him for a son-in-law.

When he was leaving he said to Mikko, "Your castle is so much grander than mine that I hesitate ever asking you back for a visit."

But Mikko reassured the King by saying earnestly, "My dear father-in-law, when first I entered your castle I thought it was the most beautiful castle in the world!"

The King was flattered and the courtiers whispered among themselves, "How affable to say that, knowing very well how much grander his own castle is!"

When the King and his followers were safely gone, the little red Fox came to Mikko and said, "Now, my master, you have no reason to feel sad and lonely. You are lord of the most beautiful castle in the world and you have for wife a sweet and lovely Princess. You have no longer any need of me, so I am going to bid you farewell."

Mikko thanked the little Fox for all he had done and the little Fox trotted off to the woods.

So you see that Mikko's poor old father, although he had no wealth to leave his son, was really the cause of all Mikko's good fortune, for it was he who told Mikko in the first place to carry home alive anything he might find caught in the snares.

Osmo's Share

by Parker Fillmore

In this tale from Finland,
you'll read about Osmo the Bear,
who knew how to plant—but not how to harvest.

One day Osmo the Bear came to a clearing where a Man was plowing.

"Good day," the Bear said. "What are you doing?"

"I'm plowing," the Man answered. "After I finish plowing I'm going to harrow and then plant the field, half in wheat and half in turnips."

Yum! Yum! Osmo thought to himself. Good food, that—wheat and turnips!

Aloud he said, "I know how to plow and harrow. What do you say to my helping you?"

"If you will help me," the Man said, "I will gladly share the harvest with you."

So Osmo set to work and between them they soon had the field plowed, harrowed, and planted.

When autumn came they went to get their crops.

At the turnip field the Man said, "Now what do you want as your share—the part that grows above the ground or the part that grows below?"

Osmo the Bear, seeing how green and luxuriant the turnip tops were, said, "Give me the part that grows above ground."

After they had harvested the turnips, they went on to the wheat field, where the Man put the same question.

The wheat stocks were all dry and shriveled. Osmo looked at them wisely and said, "This time you better give me the part that grows under the ground."

The Man laughed in his sleeve and agreed.

One day the following winter the two met and the Man invited the Bear to dinner. Osmo, who was very hungry, accepted the invitation gladly.

First they had baked turnips.

"Oh, but these are good!" Osmo said. "I've never tasted anything better! What are they?"

"Why," the Man said, "they're the turnips from that field that you and I planted together."

The Bear was greatly surprised.

Then they had some freshly baked bread.

"How good! How good!" Osmo exclaimed. "What is it?"

"Just plain bread," the Man said, "baked from the wheat that you and I planted together."

Osmo was more surprised than ever.

"Why, do you know," he said, "my turnips and my bread don't taste a bit like this!"

The Man burst out laughing and Osmo wondered why.

The Princess and the Vagabone

by Ruth Sawyer

The Princess was fair of face, but so fearfully sharp of tongue that her despairing father gave her away to a suitor she was not quite prepared for.

Once, in the golden time, when an Irish king sat in every province and plenty covered the land, there lived in Connaught a grand old king with one daughter. She was as tall and slender as the reeds that grow by Lough Erne, and her face was the fairest in seven counties. This was more the pity, for the temper she had did not match it at all, at all; it was the blackest and ugliest that ever fell to the birthlot of a princess. She was proud, she was haughty; her tongue had the length and the sharpness of the thorns on a *sidheog* bush; and from the day she was born till long after she was a woman grown she was never heard to say a kind word or known to do a kind deed to a living creature.

As each year passed, the King would think to himself, 'Tis the New Year will see her better. But it was worse instead of better she grew, until one day the King found himself at the end of his patience, and he groaned aloud as he sat alone, drinking his poteen.

"Faith, another man shall have her for the next eighteen years, for, by my soul, I've had my fill of her!"

So it came about that the King sent word to the nobles of the neighboring provinces that whosoever would win the consent of his daughter in marriage should have half of his kingdom and the whole of his blessing. On the day that she was eighteen they came: a wonderful procession of earls, dukes, princes, and kings, riding up to the castle gate, acourting. The air was filled with the ring of the silver trappings on their horses, and the courtyard was gay with the colors of the long cloaks they wore. The King made each welcome according to his rank; and then he sent a servingman to his daughter, bidding her come and choose her suitor, the time being ripe for her to marry. It was a courteous message that the King sent, but the Princess heard little of it. She flew into the hall on the heels of the servingman, like a chicken hawk after a bantam cock. Her eyes burned with anger, while she stamped her foot until the rafters rang with the noise of it.

"So, ye will be giving me away for the asking—to any one of these blithering fools who has a rag to his back or a castle to his name?"

The King was ashamed that they should all hear how sharp was her tongue; moreover, he was fearsome lest they should take to their heels and leave him with a shrew on his hands for another eighteen years. He was hard at work piecing together a speech when the Princess strode past him, on to the first suitor in the line.

"At any rate, I'll not be choosing ye, ye long-legged corncrake," and she gave him a sound kick as she went on to the next. He was a large man with a shaggy beard; and, seeing how the first suitor had fared, he tried a wee bit of a smile on her while his hand went out coaxingly. She sprang at him, digging the two of her hands deep in his beard, and then she wagged his foolish head back and forth, screaming, "Take that, and that, and that, ye old whiskered rascal!"

It was a miracle that any beard was left on his face the way that she pulled it. But she let him go free at last, and turned to a thin, sharp-faced prince with a monstrous long nose. The nose took her fancy, and she gave it a tweak, telling the prince to take himself home before he did any damage with it. The next one she called "pudding face" and slapped his fat cheeks until they were purple, and the poor lad groaned with the sting of it.

"Go back to your trough, for I'll not marry a grunter, i' faith," said she.

She moved swiftly down the line. It came to the mind of many of the suitors that they would be doing a wise thing if they betook themselves off before their turn came; as many of them as were not fastened to the floor with fear started away. There happened to be a fat, crooked-legged prince from Leinster just making for the door when the Princess looked around. In a trice she reached out for the tongs that stood on the hearth nearby, and she laid it across his shoulders, sending him spinning into the yard.

"Take that, ye old gander, and good riddance to ye!" she cried after him.

It was then that she saw looking at her a great towering giant of a man; and his eyes burned through hers, deep down into her soul. He could have picked her up with a single hand and thrown her after the gander; and she knew it and yet she felt no fear. Not a mortal fault could she have found with him, not if she had tried for a hundred years. The two of them stood facing each other, glaring, as if each would spring at the other's throat the next moment; but all the while the Princess was thinking, and thinking how handsome he was, from the top of his curling black hair, down the seven feet of him, to the golden clasps on his shoes.

Like a breath of wind on smoldering turf, her liking for him set her anger fierce burning again. She gave him a sound cuff on the ear, then turned, and with a sob she went flying from the room, the servingmen scattering before her.

And the King? Faith, he was dumb with rage. But when he saw the blow that his daughter had given to the finest gentleman in all of Ireland, he went after her as if he had been two million constables on the trail of robbers.

"Ye are a disgrace and a shame to me," said he, catching up with her and holding firmly to her two hands; "and what's more, ye are a disgrace and a blemish to my castle and my kingdom; I'll not keep ye in it a day longer. The first traveling vagabone who comes begging at the door shall have ye for his wife."

"Will he?" And the Princess tossed her head in the King's face and went to her chamber.

The next morning a poor singing vagabone came to the castle to sell a song for a penny or a morsel of bread. The song was sweet that he sang, and the Princess listened as Oona, the tirewoman, was winding strands of her long black hair with golden thread.

"The gay young wren sang over the moor.
'I'll build me a nest,' sang he.
''Twill have a thatch and a wee latched door,
For the wind blows cold from the sea.
And I'll let no one but my true love in,
For she is the mate for me,'
Sang the gay young wren.

"The wee brown wren by the hedgerow cried,
'I'll wait for him here,' cried she.
'For the way is far and the world is wide,
And he might miss the way to me.
Long is the time when the heart is shut,
But I'll open to none save he,'
Sang the wee brown wren."

A strange throb came to the heart of the Princess when the song was done. She pulled her hair free from the hands of the tirewoman.

"Get silver," she said. "I would throw it to him." And when she saw the wonderment grow in Oona's face, she added, "The song pleased me. Can I not pay for what I like without having ye look at me as if ye feared my wits had flown? Go, get the silver!"

But when she pushed open the grating and leaned far out to throw it, the vagabone had gone.

For the King had heard the song as well as the Princess. His rage was still with him, and when he saw who it was, he lost no time, but called him quickly inside.

"Ye are as fine a vagabone as I could wish for," he said. "Maybe ye are not knowing it, but ye are a bridegroom this day." And the King went on to tell him the whole tale. The tale being finished, he sent ten strong men to bring the Princess down.

A king's word was law in those days. The vagabone knew this; and, what's more, he knew he must marry the Princess, whether he liked it or no. The vagabone had great height, but he stooped so that it shortened the length of him. His hair was long, and it fell, uncombed and matted, about his shoulders. His brogues were patched, his hose were sadly worn, and with his rags he was the sorriest cut of a man that a maid ever laid her two eyes on. When the Princess came, she was dressed in a gown of gold, with jewels hanging from every thread of it, and her cap was caught with a jeweled brooch. She looked as beautiful as a May morning—with a thundercloud rising back of the hills; and the vagabone held his breath for a moment, watching her. Then he pulled the King gently by the arm.

"I'll not have a wife that looks grander than myself. If I marry your daughter, I must marry her in rags—the same as my own."

The King agreed 'twas a good idea, and sent for the worst dress of rags in the whole countryside. The rags were fetched, the Princess dressed, the priest brought, and the two of them married; and, though she cried and she kicked and she cuffed and she prayed, she was the vagabone's wife.

"Now take her, and good luck go with ye," said the King. Then his eyes fell on the tongs by the hearth. "Here, take these along—they may come in handy on the road."

Out of the castle gate and into the country that lay beyond went the Princess and the vagabone. The sky was blue over their heads and the air was full of spring; each wee creature that passed them on the road seemed bursting with the joy of it. There was naught but anger in the Princess' heart, however; and what was in the heart of the vagabone I cannot be telling. This I know, that he sang the "Song of the Wren" as they went. Often and often the Princess turned back on the road or sat down, swearing she would go no farther; and often and often did she feel the weight of the tongs across her shoulders that day.

At noon the two sat down by the cross-roads to rest.

"I am hungry," said the Princess. "Not a morsel of food have I tasted this day. Ye will go get me some."

"Not I, my dear," said the vagabone. "Ye will go beg for yourself."

"Never," said the Princess.

"Then ye'll go hungry," said the vagabone; and that was all. He lighted his pipe and went to sleep with one eye open and the tongs under him.

One, two, three hours passed, and the sun hung low in the sky. The Princess sat there until hunger drove her to her feet. She rose wearily and stumbled to the road. It might have been the sound of wheels that had started her, I cannot be telling; but as she reached the road a great coach drawn by six black horses came galloping up. The Princess made a sign for it to stop; though she was in rags, yet she was still so beautiful that the coachman drew in the horses and asked her what she was wanting.

"I am near to starving." And as she spoke, the tears started to her eyes, while a new soft note crept into her voice. "Do ye think your master could spare me a bit of food—or a shilling?" And the hand that had been used to strike went out for the first time to beg.

It was a prince who rode inside the coach that day, and he heard her. Reaching out a fine, big hamper through the window, he told her she was hearty welcome to whatever she found in it, along with his blessing. But as she put up her arms for it, just, she looked—and saw that the prince was none other than the fat suitor whose face she had slapped on the day before. Then anger came back to her again, for the shame of begging from him. She emptied the hamper—chicken pasty, jam, currant bread, and all—on top of his head, peering through the window, and threw the empty basket at the coachman. Away drove the coach; away ran the Princess, and threw herself, sobbing, on the ground, near the vagabone.

"'Twas a good dinner that ye lost," said the vagabone; and that was all.

That night they reached a wee scrap of a cabin on the side of a hill. The vagabone climbed the steps and opened the door. "Here we are at home, my dear," said he.

"What kind of a home do ye call this?" And the Princess stamped her foot. "Faith, I'll not live in it."

"Then ye can live outside; it's all the same to me." The vagabone went in and closed the door after him; and in a moment he was whistling merrily the song of the wee brown wren.

The Princess sat down on the ground and nursed her poor tired knees. She had walked many a mile that day, with a heavy heart and an empty stomach. The night came down, black as a raven's wing; the dew fell, heavy as rain, wetting the rags and chilling the Princess to the marrow. The wind blew fresh from the sea, and the wolves began their howling in the woods nearby; and at last, what with the cold and the fear and the loneliness of it, she could bear it no longer, and she crept softly up to the cabin and went in.

"There's the creepie stool by the fire waiting for ye," said the vagabone; and that was all. But late in the night he lifted her from the chimney corner where she had dropped asleep and laid her gently on the bed, which was freshly made and clean. And he sat by the hearth till dawn, keeping the turf piled high on the fire, so that cold would not waken her. Once he left the hearth; coming to the bedside, he stood a moment to watch her while she slept, and he stooped and kissed the palm of her hand that lay there like a half-closed lough lily.

Next morning the first thing the Princess asked was where was the breakfast, and where were the servants to wait on her, and where were some decent clothes.

"Your servants are your own two hands, and they will serve ye well when ye teach them how," was his answer.

"I'll have neither breakfast nor clothes if I have to be getting them myself. And shame on ye for treating a wife so."

"Have your own way, my dear," he said, and left her, to go out on the bogs and cut turf.

That night the Princess hung the kettle and made stirabout and griddle bread for the two of them.

"'Tis the best I have tasted since I was a lad and my mother made the baking," said the vagabone; and that was all. But often and often his lips touched the braids of her hair as she passed him in the dark; and again he sat through the night, keeping the fire and mending her wee leather brogues, that they might be whole against the morrow.

Next day he brought some willow twigs and showed her how to weave them into creels to sell on coming market day. But the twigs cut her fingers until they bled, and the Princess cried, making the vagabone white with rage. Never had she seen such a rage in another creature. He threw the willow twigs about the cabin, making them whirl and eddy like leaves before an autumn wind; he stamped upon the half-made creel, crushing it to pulp under his feet; and catching up the table, he tore it to splinters, throwing the fragments into the fire, where they blazed.

"By Saint Patrick, 'tis a bad bargain that ye are! I will take ye this day to the castle in the next county, where I hear they are needing a scullery maid; and there I'll apprentice ye to the King's cook."

"I will not go," said the Princess; but even as she spoke, fear showed in her eyes and her knees began shaking under her.

"Aye, but ye will, my dear." And the vagabone took up the tongs quietly from the hearth.

For a month the Princess worked in the castle of the King, and all that time she never saw the vagabone. Often and often she said to herself, fiercely, that she was well rid of him; but often, as she sat alone after her work in the cool of the night, she would wish for the song of the wee brown wren, while a new loneliness crept deeper and deeper into her heart.

She worked hard about the kitchen, and as she scrubbed the pots and turned the spit and cleaned the floor with fresh white sand she listened to the wonderful tales the other servants had to tell of the King. They had it that he was the handsomest, aye, and the strongest, king in all of Ireland; and every man and child and little creature in his kingdom worshipped him. And after the tales were told, the Princess would say to herself, "If I had not been so proud and free with my tongue, I might have married such a king, and ruled his kingdom with him, learning kindness."

Now it happened one day that the Princess was told to be unusually spry and careful about her work; and there was a monstrous deal of it to be done: cakes to be iced and puddings to be boiled, fat ducks to be roasted, and a whole suckling pig put on the spit to turn.

"What's the meaning of all this?" asked the Princess.

"Ochone, ye poor feebleminded girl!" And the cook looked at her pityingly. "Haven't ye heard the King is to be married this day to the fairest princess in seven counties?"

Once that was I, thought the Princess, and she sighed.

"What makes ye sigh?" asked the cook.

"I was wishing, just, that I could be having a peep at her and the King."

"Faith, that's possible. Do your work

well, and maybe I can put ye where ye can see without being seen."

So it came about, at the end of the day, when the feast was ready and the guests come, that the Princess was hidden behind the broidered curtains in the great hall. There, where no one could see her, she watched the hundreds upon hundreds of fair ladies and fine noblemen in their silken dresses and shining coats, all silver and gold, march back and forth across the hall, laughing and talking and making merry among themselves. Then the pipers began to play, and everybody was still. From the farthest end of the hall came two and twenty lads in white and gold; and these were followed by two and twenty pipers in green and gold, and two and twenty bowmen in saffron and gold, and, last of all, the King.

A scream, a wee wisp of a cry, broke from the Princess, and she would have fallen had she not caught one of the curtains. For the King was tall and strong and beautiful; and from the top of his curling black hair down the seven feet of him to the golden clasps of his shoes he was every whit as handsome as he had been that day when she had cuffed him in her father's castle.

The King heard the cry and stopped the pipers. "I think," said he, "there's a scullery maid behind the curtains. Someone fetch her to me."

A hundred hands pulled the Princess out; a hundred more pushed her across the hall to the feet of the King, and held her there, fearing lest she escape. "What were ye doing there?" the King asked.

"Looking at ye, and wishing I had the

undoing of things I have done." And the Princess hung her head and sobbed piteously.

"Nay, sweetheart, things are best as they are." And there came a look into the King's eyes that blinded those watching, so that they turned away and left the two alone.

"Heart of mine," he went on softly, "are ye not knowing me?"

"Ye are putting more shame on me because of my evil tongue and the blow my hand gave ye that day."

"I' faith, it is not so. Look at me."

Slowly the eyes of the Princess looked into the eyes of the King. For a moment she could not be reading them; she was as a child who pores over a strange tale after the light fades and it has grown too dark to see. But bit by bit the meaning of it came to her, and her heart grew glad with the wonder of it. Out went her arms to him with the cry of loneliness that had been hers so long.

"I never dreamed that it was ye, never once."

"Can ye ever love and forgive?" asked the King.

"Hush ye!" and the Princess laid her finger on his lips.

The tirewomen were called and she was led away. Her rags were changed for a dress that was spun from gold and woven with pearls, and her beauty shone about her like a great light. They were married again that night, for none of the guests were knowing of the first wedding.

Late o' that night a singing vagabone came under the Princess' window, and very softly the words of his song came to her:

"The gay young wren sang over the
moor.
'I'll build me a nest,' sang he.
''Twill have a thatch and a wee latched
door,
For the wind blows cold from the
sea.
And I'll let no one but my true love in,
For she is the mate for me,'
Sang the gay young wren.

"The wee brown wren by the hedgerow
cried,
'I'll wait for him here,' cried she.
'For the way is far and the world is
wide,
And he might miss the way to me.
Long is the time when the heart is
shut,
But I'll open to none save he,'
Sang the wee brown wren."

The grating opened slowly; the Princess leaned far out, her eyes like stars in the night, and when she spoke there was naught but gentleness and love in her voice.

"Here is the silver I would have thrown ye on a day long gone by. Shall I throw it now, or will ye come for it?"

And that was how a princess of Connaught was won by a king who was a vagabone.

The Scotty Who Knew Too Much

by James Thurber

When a cocky city dog picks fights in the country, he finds out a few things.

Several summers ago there was a Scotty who went to the country for a visit. He decided that all the farm dogs were cowards, because they were afraid of a certain animal that had a white stripe down its back. "You are a pussycat and I can lick you," the Scotty said to the farm dog who lived in the house where the Scotty was visiting. "I can lick the little animal with the white stripe, too. Show him to me." "Don't you want to ask any questions about him?" said the farm dog. "Naw," said the Scotty. "*You* ask the questions."

So the farm dog took the Scotty into the woods and showed him the white-striped animal and the Scotty closed in on him, growling and slashing. It was all over in a moment and the Scotty lay on his back. When he came to, the farm dog said, "What happened?" "He threw vitriol," said the Scotty, "but he never laid a glove on me."

A few days later the farm dog told the Scotty there was another animal all the farm dogs were afraid of. "Lead me to him," said the Scotty. "I can lick anything that doesn't wear horseshoes." "Don't you want to ask any questions about him?" said the farm dog. "Naw," said the Scotty. "Just show me where he hangs out." So the farm dog led him to a place in the woods and pointed out the little animal when he came along. "A clown," said the Scotty, "a pushover," and he closed in, leading with his left and exhibiting some mighty fancy footwork. In less than a second the Scotty was flat on his back, and when he woke up the farm dog was pulling quills out of him. "What happened?" said the farm dog. "He pulled a knife on me," said the Scotty, "but at least I have learned how you fight out here in the country, and now I am going to beat *you* up." So he closed in on the farm dog, holding his nose with one front paw to ward off the vitriol and covering his eyes with the other front paw to keep out the knives. The Scotty couldn't see his opponent and he couldn't smell his opponent and he was so badly beaten that he had to be taken back to the city and put in a nursing home.

Moral: *It is better to ask some of the questions than to know all the answers.*

Oliver and the Other Ostriches

by James Thurber

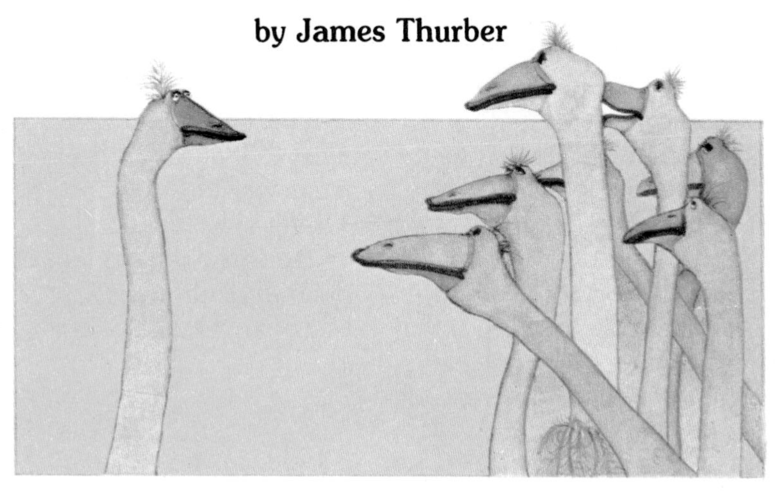

Big birds can make big mistakes.

An austere ostrich of awesome authority was lecturing younger ostriches one day on the superiority of their species to all other species. "We were known to the Romans, or, rather, the Romans were known to us," he said. "They called us *avis struthio*, and we called them Romans. The Greeks called us *strouthion*, which means 'truthful one,' or, if it doesn't, it should. We are the biggest birds, and therefore the best."

All his listeners cried, "Hear! Hear!" except a thoughtful one named Oliver. "We can't fly backward like the hummingbird," he said aloud.

"The hummingbird is losing ground," said the old ostrich. "We are going places, we are moving forward."

"Hear! Hear!" cried all the other ostriches except Oliver.

"We lay the biggest eggs and therefore the best eggs," continued the old lecturer.

"The robin's eggs are prettier," said Oliver.

"Robins' eggs produce nothing but robins," said the old ostrich. "Robins are lawn-bound worm addicts."

"Hear! Hear!" cried all the other ostriches except Oliver.

"We get along on four toes, whereas Man needs ten," the elderly instructor reminded his class.

"But Man can fly sitting down, and we can't fly at all," commented Oliver.

The old ostrich glared at him severely, first with one eye and then the other. "Man is flying too fast for a world that is round," he said. "Soon he will catch up with himself, in a great rear-end collision, and Man will never know that what hit Man from behind was Man."

"Hear! Hear!" cried all the other ostriches except Oliver.

"We can make ourselves invisible in time of peril by sticking our heads in the sand," ranted the lecturer. "Nobody else can do that."

"How do we know we can't be seen if we can't see?" demanded Oliver.

"Sophistry!" cried the old ostrich, and all the other ostriches except Oliver cried "Sophistry!" not knowing what it meant.

Just then the master and the class heard a strange alarming sound, a sound like thunder growing close and growing closer. It was not the thunder of weather, though, but the thunder of a vast herd of rogue elephants in full stampede, frightened by nothing, fleeing nowhere. The old ostrich and all the other ostriches except Oliver quickly stuck their heads in the sand. Oliver took refuge behind a large nearby rock until the storm of beasts had passed, and when he came out he beheld a sea of sand and bones and feathers—all that was left of the old teacher and his disciples. Just to be sure, however, Oliver called the roll, but there was no answer until he came to his own name. "Oliver," he said.

"Here! Here!" said Oliver, and that was the only sound there was on the desert except for a faint, final rumble of thunder on the horizon.

Moral: *Thou shalt not build thy house, nor yet thy faith, upon the sand.*

Cowpony's Prize

by Lavinia R. Davis

Patsy's beloved cowpony won no prizes in the show-ring, but on a rough woodland trail, in the dark of night, it was another story.

Spike was a very small cowpony with a velvety nose and long ears. He had been sent east as a birthday present for Patsy Cameron because he was no longer needed on her uncle's ranch. Patsy fell in love with him the very first moment she saw him. He was so small and sturdy and dependable that you just couldn't help loving him.

"Let me try him," she pleaded with her brother, who had ridden him home from the station.

"Go as far as you like," said Jack condescendingly. Jack had been hunting for the past two years, and as a member of the Middletown Hunt, he looked down on cowponies. "He's not very exciting."

But Patsy was so busy trotting Spike up and down the drive that she never heard. "He's nicer than any horse I've ever ridden."

"Oh, well," said Jack. "Everybody thinks the first horse they own is perfect."

"But he *is* perfect," said Patsy. "You just wait until the horse show. Then you'll see."

Jack laughed good-naturedly. "You'll have to work some if you want to turn him into a show horse. And even if you do train him perfectly, somebody might mistake him for a donkey. Just look at his ears!"

Patsy said nothing but stroked Spike's soft gray nose. "Don't listen," she whispered, riding him toward the stable.

Jack's hunter, Tipperary, looked up and snorted as she led Spike into his new home. "Just you keep quiet, Tip," she said, slipping a halter over Spike's wise old head. "Just because you have a few horse-show ribbons hung over your stall doesn't mean that you're the only person in the stable. Spike may have something to show for himself, too, one of these days."

But Jack's advice was good, Patsy knew, and the very next day she began to train Spike to be a show horse. It wasn't that his manners weren't good already, but they were more suited to the ranch than the show-ring. Cantering from a walk, for instance, had been quite left out of his education. And then he was too anxious to start off the minute you got in the saddle, and he had never been taught to sidestep or to back.

"Now," Patsy would say as he walked calmly along, his ears flapping. "Now, canter." But generally Spike would trot instead, and not break into his loping canter until he felt like it. Then Patsy would pull him up and comfort herself with the thought that the horse show was a long way off.

Each day she would finish the performance by making Spike ride herd on the two cows and the old farm horse that had to be brought in from the south pasture.

"What's the idea?" asked Jack when he saw Patsy and Spike at work. "They won't make you do that in a horse show!"

"No," said Patsy, "but I don't want him to forget the things he was really meant for."

But the summer went all too quickly, and soon it was the last day of the Middletown Horse Show and Patsy was riding Spike in the class for useful road hacks. Jack said that this was the class in which performance counted most and appearance least.

If only he behaves perfectly, maybe they won't notice his looks, Patsy thought, as Spike and eleven other horses trotted briskly around the judges' stand.

"Walk, please," came the order from the middle of the ring.

Patsy pulled Spike down to a walk. Now, it's coming, she thought. Now, it's coming! Oh! Please, Spike, be a good boy and canter nicely.

"Canter, please!" came the command.

Gently Patsy guided Spike to a corner of the ring, pulled slightly on the left rein, and urged him forward with her right foot. In another moment he was breaking into a nice, even canter.

Patsy breathed a sigh of relief. "Good boy," she murmured. "Good boy."

The months of training were being rewarded. Spike was behaving perfectly!

Soon the judges ordered all the horses into the middle of the ring. Patsy held her head high with pride as Spike stood stock-still, the way she had taught him. But when the judges called out the numbers of the four prizewinners, Spike was not among them.

"Never you mind," Patsy whispered to Spike consolingly as they followed the other losers out of the ring. "You did the best you could and I think you were splendid." But as she and Spike came slowly out of the ring, she was rather glad that Jack was watching the hunter trials in another part of the grounds.

"I'm sorry we didn't win something," she whispered as she sponged down Spike. "Just so that you could have a ribbon to show Tipperary." Spike nuzzled her pocket for sugar. "Go along," she laughed. "You act as if you didn't care."

When she had rubbed Spike down, Patsy went out to see the rest of the horse show. It was all exciting, even seeing the horses being walked up and down before going into the ring. There were brown horses and gray horses, chestnuts and bays. Hunters being limbered up for the jumping classes and ponies being walked on leading straps. Everywhere horses were walking and trotting, whinnying and shying, and showing off their manners to admiring onlookers.

She watched Cecily Prentice's mare, Holiday, trot mincingly past, her small head held high in the air. She is beautiful,

Patsy thought admiringly. But I don't believe she's as useful as Spike.

"Hello, Cecily," she called. "Congratulations on winning the road-hack class."

"Well, there wasn't much competition," the other girl laughed. "You don't really think that cowpony of yours is a show horse now, do you?"

"No, I don't think he's a show horse," Patsy said, "but I do think he's a useful road hack"—besides being the sweetest pet in the whole world, she added to herself.

"Say, Patsy!" Cecily said as she trotted toward her again. "I've got an extra space in the van that's taking my horses home. Don't you want to send Spike along? He won't be any trouble at all and we can drop him on the way."

"No, thanks." Patsy was polite but firm. "He might get kicked."

"Oh, don't be silly. I'm sending all three of my horses. Claude'll be right on the van to take care of them."

It was a long way home, but Patsy never hesitated. "No, thanks," she said again. "I think I'll ride Spike home. He's used to long rides. And besides," she added, grinning, "out in Wyoming where he comes from they don't cart useful horses around in vans."

An hour or so later Patsy was riding Spike home along a deserted country road. "I'm glad I didn't let you go in Cecily's van," she decided, patting the pony's wet sides. "It was nice of her, but Jack says horses often get hurt that way, and what's more, a van's no place for a respectable cowpony."

It was hot riding and the lonely road seemed endless. Spike was tired and his long ears hung forward sadly. We won't be home until late, Patsy realized. I wish I'd waited and brought you home tomorrow with Jack. She patted the pony's neck and then held on with both hands as he pulled abruptly into the gutter to let a large truck roar by. "Good boy," she applauded, rubbing the dust out of her eyes. "Any other horse would have shied with a great thing like that going by. That must be Cecily's van. I guess they came this way to miss the traffic."

It was growing darker now. There was a crackling noise in the woods that made Patsy jump. Nervously she remembered the story of the tiger that had once escaped from the county zoo. Suppose there were some such hidden danger behind those shadows? The noise continued. "Come on, boy," Patsy murmured, urging Spike into a trot. "This road is too lonely for fun."

They went through a dark stretch of wood and then, at the top of a long hill, Patsy pulled Spike down to a walk. "Easy, boy," she said. "You walk down to the bridge. We've still got a long way before we get home."

Through the dusk, she looked toward the tiny wooden bridge that led over the brook at the bottom of the hill. They ought to build a new bridge over that creek, she thought. This one's so old the wood's all rotten. She looked forward as Spike made his way slowly down the hill. "Whew," Patsy whistled as the bridge came into clear view. "Something's happened. A truck's gone right through the planking."

Sure enough, at the bottom of the hill a large red van was half in and half out of the water. A Negro groom was trying to quiet two excited horses that were tied to a nearby tree.

"Claude," she called, suddenly recognizing him. "Claude, are you hurt? Whatever happened?"

"De truck done busted through de bridge, Miss Patsy." The man winced with pain as he spoke. "And I was battered up somethin' awful and Dixie Boy here strained his shoulder and Vixen scraped both her knees. But Holiday, she done run away. She done be quite gone!"

"Gone where?" Patsy asked.

"Gone off straight into de woods," Claude panted. "She broke away crazy-like when Jake tried to get her off de truck. I couldn't help him none."

"No," said Patsy. "I shouldn't think you could. That arm looks pretty well smashed up."

"Jake was driving de van and he didn't get hurt. So he go for help. He done tied Vixen and Dixie Boy, but Holiday go crazy. She awful stupid on de road, Miss Patsy," the man half sobbed, "and in de woods and de dark she sure to break her laig."

"Don't try to walk around," Patsy ordered. "You'll only make yourself worse.

Spike and I will have Holiday back by the time help gets here. Which way did she go?"

"Thataway, miss. Oh, Lordy, Lordy, she ain't used to nothin' but de practice ring. Miss Cecily don't nevah take her cross-country."

"Useful hack," Patsy sniffed, heading Spike into the woods. "Useful for what? Why, if she can't stand up on a rough trail and she's scared besides, she's sure to hurt herself." Spike broke into his steady canter. "Good boy," she encouraged him. "We've got to find her."

They soon came to a little clearing, and Patsy stopped to get her bearings. "Holiday must have turned right here and gone farther into the woods, or else she went left down to the river," Patsy mused. "Maybe she was what made that crackling noise at the top of the hill. Spike, we'd better go uphill as fast as we can. If it gets really dark, we'll never catch her."

The little horse made his way along the rough trail as though it were broad daylight. Patsy's back ached, but she was too excited to care. Branches cut her face, but she hardly knew it. "If only you don't stumble, Spike," she whispered to the tired pony, "I just know we'll get her."

In another five minutes Patsy heard a crackling of branches and a frightened whinny. There in the trail ahead of her was a black figure. Patsy could hear the quick breath and the pawing foot. Holiday hasn't hurt herself yet, she thought, but we mustn't frighten her by coming up too suddenly. Quickly she dismounted.

"Stand still, Spike," she ordered. "I'm going to walk up to her. Easy, pet, steady, girl," she crooned, approaching the excited horse.

The next minute she held the broken bit of rope that hung on to Holiday's halter and was leading her back to Spike. Now, she thought, if Spike'll stand still while I get on, we'll be all right. She mounted and, for the second time that day, was glad of all the afternoons she had trained Spike in the field at home. Even with an excited horse whinnying and balking at his side, Spike stood like a small statue.

At last they were back on the road leading to the bridge. If a car comes by and Holiday gets scared, we're lost, Patsy thought. If she tries to run, I'll never be able to hold on to this rope. Carefully Spike picked his way along the road, the frightened horse shying and stumbling at his side.

As they drew near to the bridge, Patsy saw from the number of headlights that help had come. But how was she ever to get Holiday over to that frightening array of cars? Holiday plunged and the rope tore through Patsy's blistered hands. She's gone, Patsy thought, and then nearly tumbled off as Spike with a catlike turn jumped to the startled animal's far side. Spike, his long ears laid back, was turning and twisting like one possessed. It was all Patsy could do to keep astride of him.

Why, he's riding herd, she suddenly realized, as the little cowpony urged the larger horse a few paces nearer the lights. Why, he's herding Holiday right up to the van.

Scared by the noise and confusion, Holiday balked suddenly, but Spike was ready for her, and with bared teeth he urged her forward. "Hey, Claude," Patsy called, still clinging to the saddle. "Get somebody to hold this horse. Spike can't keep her here forever."

In another minute someone was holding on to Holiday's halter and Patsy had her arms around Spike's neck, telling him what a good horse he was.

The next morning, as Patsy came slowly down the stairs, she could hear her father and Jack in the dining room talking about the horse show. Jack was going over every detail of Tipperary's triumph in the hunter class. Patsy hated the thought of going in. Jack would be so patronizing about Spike.

But the moment she was in the room she caught sight of a package by her plate. She opened it with trembling fingers. Packages were always exciting.

"She had it hands down," Jack was saying.

"Look," interrupted Patsy, as she pulled a fluttering blue rosette out of the parcel. A card dropped to the table, and as Patsy stood speechless looking at the ribbon, Jack read the card out loud.

"Dear Patsy," it ran. "Since Spike proved himself so much the more useful horse last night, it seems only fair that he should share Holiday's honors. So she is sending him the ribbon which she won in the useful road-hack class with thanks for his wonderful help. Gratefully, Cecily Prentice."

"It's Spike's very own ribbon," said Patsy, when she could say anything at all. "And he'll have it hanging right by his stall so that Tipperary'll never laugh at him again."

DESERT

The Three Travellers

by Joan Aiken

Must life be so boring?
It was worth a trip to find out.

There was once a little tiny station in the middle of a huge desert. On either side of it the sand stretched away as far as the eye could see, and beyond the sand lay prairie, and beyond the prairie were valleys and mountains, and through all these the railway ran in both directions, on and on.

The station's name was Desert. There was just one building, and in it lived Mr. Smith the signalman, Mr. Jones the porter, and Mr. Brown the ticket collector.

You may think it odd that there were three men to look after one tiny station, but the people who ran the railway knew that if you left two men together in a lonely place they would quarrel, but if you left three men, two of them could always grumble to each other about the third, and then they would be happy.

The men were happy enough, for they had no wives to worry about the desert dust, and no children to pester them for stories or piggybacks, but they weren't *completely* happy, and this is why.

Every day huge trains would thunder across the desert, from west to east and from east to west, getting bigger and bigger as they neared the station, and smaller and smaller as they rushed away from it, but they never stopped. Nobody wanted to get off at Desert.

"Oh, if only I could use my signals once in a while," mourned Mr. Smith. "I oil them and polish them every day, but not once in the last fifteen years have I had a chance to pull the lever and signal a train to stop. It breaks a man's heart!"

"Oh, if only I could clip a ticket once in a while," sighed Mr. Brown. "I keep my clippers shining and bright, but what's the use? Not once in fifteen years have I had a chance to punch with them. A man's talents rust in this place."

"Oh, if only I could carry someone's luggage once in a while," lamented Mr. Jones. "In the big city stations the porters are rich from the tips people give them, but how can anyone hope to get rich here? I do my push-ups every morning to keep me strong and supple, but not once in fifteen years have I had the chance to carry so much as a hatbox. There's no chance for a man here!"

There was another thing that fretted these three men. They had one day off every week—Sunday, when no trains ran either way—but there was nothing to do on it. Nowhere to go. The next stop along the line from Desert was more than a thousand miles away, and it would cost more than a week's wages to go so far. And even if you took the last train out on a Saturday night, you couldn't travel all that way and go to the cinema and be back by Monday morning. So on Sundays they just sat about on the station platform, and yawned, and wished it were Monday.

But one day Mr. Jones counted his savings and said, "Friends, your wishes are going to be granted. I have saved enough for a week's holiday. Mr. Smith can signal a train to stop, and Mr. Brown can clip my ticket, and I'm going to see the world, as far as the train can take me."

The other two men were wildly excited. Mr. Smith spent the whole night oiling his levers, and Mr. Brown polished his clippers. It was a splendid moment next morning when the train came hissing to a stop, all for Mr. Jones.

He put his own luggage on it, climbed up, waved good-by to his friends, and off he went to the east.

Halfway through the week they had a postcard, dropped from a passing train, to say he'd be back by the noon train on Saturday, so a couple of hours before it was due Mr. Smith pulled his signal to the "stop" position. He and Mr. Brown had spent all their spare time that week discussing what Mr. Jones would have to tell them when he came back, and what he would bring them.

As soon as the train stopped, Mr. Jones jumped off it, and Mr. Brown carefully took his ticket while Mr. Smith signaled the train on its way again. Then they made a pot of coffee and sat down to listen to the traveller's tale.

"Brothers!" said he. "The world is a big place! The train took me through more country than I could remember in a lifetime, and ended in a city bigger than the whole of this desert. Why, the station itself was as big as a town, with shops and theaters and hotels and restaurants in it. There was even a circus, right in the station! So I never bothered to go out into the city, just stayed in the station, and I had a fine time, I can tell you. I've brought you these things."

And he carefully brought out the presents—for Mr. Smith a paperweight shaped like a skyscraper, and for Mr. Brown a box with a picture of a huge, splendid station on its lid. They were very pleased.

Next week Mr. Smith counted his money and said, "Brothers, you're in luck again, for now I've saved enough money for my holiday and I'm going to catch the westbound train and go as far as it will go."

"But who will look after the signals?" objected Mr. Jones.

"Mr. Brown will; I've been teaching him all week."

So Mr. Brown got out a ticket for Mr. Smith and then hurried off to the signals. Mr. Jones took Mr. Smith's case and put it on the train (and Mr. Smith gave him a handsome tip). He climbed on board, and off he went.

Next Saturday, back he came with eyes like stars. As soon as they had made a pot of coffee, they sat down to listen to his story.

"My!" said Mr. Smith. "The world is even bigger than I thought! So much country we went through, I've already forgotten half of it. But at the end of the journey we went over a range of mountains so high I thought we'd graze the moon, with pine trees like needles, and snow like a shaking of salt. Then the train went rushing down, till I was sure the brakes would fail and we'd go over a precipice. At last we came to the sea, and there we stopped. Brothers, the sea is even bigger than this desert! I brought you these things."

He had brought for Mr. Brown a pearl-colored shell, and for Mr. Jones a big chunk of shining white crystal rock, and they thought these presents were very beautiful.

Then they began saying to Mr. Brown, "When are you going for your holiday?"

And Mr. Smith said, "Go to the mountains and the sea!"

But Mr. Jones said, "No, go to the city! The city is much more beautiful and fascinating."

And they began to argue and shout.

But Mr. Brown was a quiet man. He thought for a long time and said, "I don't fancy going for such a long train ride. I get trainsick. Besides, you've been to those places and told me what they're like. I want to go somewhere different."

"But there isn't anywhere else to go," they told him. "The railway only goes two ways, east and west."

"I shall go north," said Mr. Brown, and he packed a bag, just a little one, with some bread and cheese and a bottle of beer.

"How *can* you go north?"

"Walking, on my feet," said Mr. Brown, and when Sunday came he set off walking, very early in the morning.

Mr. Jones and Mr. Smith watched his figure getting smaller and smaller in the distance, until he was out of sight. At first his footprints were sharp and clear, while the dew lay on the sand, and then as the sun climbed higher up the sky they gradually crumbled and sank away, as if the sand were melting like snow in the heat.

"Shall we ever see him again?" Mr. Jones and Mr. Smith asked each other.

But in the evening when the sun was level and low they saw a tiny dot far away coming nearer and nearer, and when it was quite close they saw that it was Mr. Brown. And his eyes were shining and his face was full of joy.

"Well?" they said, when they had made a pot of coffee and sat down to drink it. "Where have you been and what have you seen?"

"Brothers," said Mr. Brown, "two hours away from this station I found an oasis. There's a spring of fresh water, and grass, and flowers, and orange and lemon trees. I've brought you these presents."

He gave to Mr. Jones an enormous juicy orange, and to Mr. Smith a bunch of feathery leaves and blue flowers.

If you should ever find yourself at Desert station on a Sunday, you won't be surprised to see that there is nobody at home. The three men are two hours' walk away, lying on the grass by the cool spring and listening to the birds.

On the station signboard, under DESERT, the words FOR OASIS have been added.

Alphonse, That Bearded One

by Natalie Savage Carlson

Alphonse marched proudly and fought bravely for New France. But who was he? A man? Or a bear?

In a forgotten time when Canada was New France, a settler named Jeannot Vallar went hunting in the wilderness that lay around his cabin. He did not have to go far to find an old she-bear digging at a rotted stump.

"*Bien!*" exclaimed Jeannot to himself. "This fat one will keep me in grease until next winter."

He shot the bear, pinched her fat sides, then lifted her over his shoulders with many a puff and a grunt. As he started away, almost bent double under her weight, he heard a whining sound in a nearby tree.

He looked up and saw a little bear cub clinging to a branch and trembling with fright. "The old one can wait here for a time," said Jeannot. "She is in no hurry anyhow."

He dropped the dead bear to the ground and pulled the cub from the tree.

"Game can be shot any day," said the settler to the cub, "but it is not every day that I can catch such a pet as you. I will call you Alphonse."

He took the cub back to his cabin. All the way there the little bear cuddled close to him, for here was something warm and living even if it had a strange smell.

Alphonse soon became used to this smell. It belonged to the rude cabin to which Jeannot brought him and to the Indians and trappers who dropped in for short visits.

It was especially strong when the grizzled woodsman, Arsine Jolicoeur, crossed the threshold one day and squatted by the hearth to mold some lead balls for his long, long gun.

"So-ho!" said Arsine to Jeannot. "You may not have much longer to live in this snug cabin. The Iroquois are beginning to cause trouble again. The governor's men will be looking for strong ones like you who have seen service with the army. Your gray hairs will be no excuse."

After the visitor had left, Jeannot climbed to the loft. He whistled to Alphonse to follow. Then he pulled the cobwebs away from the old chest in the corner and lifted the lid. He peered at the contents.

He pulled out a musketeer's jacket and looked back and forth from it to the bear. He held up a dented helmet and looked first at it, then at the bear's furry head. Next he laid a rusty sword across his knees. He stared from it to the bear's long claws. Then he neatly returned all these things to the chest and closed the lid tightly.

He smiled slowly and thoughtfully.

"Alphonse," he told the cub, "you have many things to learn."

Jeannot made a little suit of tanned hides for Alphonse and taught him to dress himself and to understand a great many things. Alphonse learned quickly. When there were things that he could not understand, he would swing his head and roll his eyes, *çà* and *là*, *çà* and *là*, for that is the spirit of a bear.

When Alphonse was as big as he was going to get, Jeannot opened the chest again. He took out the helmet, the jacket and the sword. The jacket was too small for Alphonse, so Jeannot let out a tuck here and put in a gusset there until it would go all the way around him. He cobbled a sturdy pair of jackboots, and these boots were the only part of the outfit that fitted Alphonse properly.

The bear was taught to march to the beat of a drum, to shoulder a gun and to handle the sword well. And of all these things, Alphonse was best at marching and never lost a chance to show off before strangers. For that is the spirit of bears as well as of men.

On a late afternoon, Jeannot had him dress in battle array and gave him his last lesson.

"Alphonse," he said, "this is the oldest and most important rule for a soldier: keep your eyes open, your mouth shut, your powder dry and do not volunteer for anything."

The bear listened intently. He rolled his head and his eyes a little, *çà* and *là*.

There was a sudden rat-a-tat on the cabin door. Jeannot put his finger to his lips. He motioned Alphonse to climb up and hide in the loft. The bear quickly obeyed, but he crouched close to the landing above the top rung and peeked down, for it is the spirit of a bear to be as curious as a boy.

Jeannot opened the door. There stood a corporal with a document in his hands. He was a great moose of a man with a pulled-out chin and a squashlike nose flattened over his mustache. Beside him stood a leftover piece of a fellow with pale blue eyes and a bouquet of hair on his chin. Both carried knapsacks on their backs and long, long guns.

"Duty calls, Jeannot Vallar," said the big man. "I am Corporal Pagot and this is the common soldier Genest."

Jeannot bowed and invited them in.

"I have always wanted to fight the Iroquois and become a hero," he said, "but I am no longer young. I suffer from ague and I see spots in front of my eyes. Sometimes my ears ring, and I get mad spells when I believe that I am the king of France. Perhaps it is better that I send my brother in my place. He is a big, strapping fellow—not unlike yourself, my corporal, although shy of talk—and he has had some military training."

The corporal studied the document in his hands.

"That should be agreeable with my captain," he said. "Better a strong wife than a weak ox to pull the plow. Where is your brother?"

Jeannot walked to the ladder leading to the loft and whistled through his fingers. In no time at all, Alphonse came lumbering down.

The soldiers stared in amazement at his long, furry nose and fiery little eyes. Pagot's eyes were pulling from their sockets. At last he found his voice—such a weak, little one for a man his size.

"But, m'sieu," he protested, "your brother looks like a bear to me."

Jeannot Vallar turned an insulted look on his visitor.

"Is that politeness, my corporal?" he asked. "Does my brother say that you look like a moose?"

"Many of his men do," offered the little soldier, speaking for the first time.

Pagot glowered at him.

"If your long ears listened to orders instead of gossip, my little one," he said, "you would be something more than a common soldier in the ranks."

"You see," said Jeannot, "everyone has a right to his own opinions, but it is not politeness to carry this thing too far."

"But he has fur all over his face, and paws instead of hands," insisted Corporal Pagot. "And just now he growled."

Jeannot clucked his tongue.

"*Hélas!*" he sighed. "It was a great tragedy for us that time the bears stole little Alphonse from his cradle. You have heard of such things, surely, my corporal—a baby carried off by a she-wolf or a lynx and raised as its own. Is it any wonder our Alphonse still carries the mark of his life with the bears? It was only two years ago that I found him in a trap and dragged him back home, snarling and biting. Poor Alphonse!"

The corporal was not sure of this.

"I think that you made a mistake, Jeannot Vallar," he said. "I fear that it is one of the bears that you brought home. Your Alphonse must still be in the woods. Perhaps we might search for him a bit. I am in no hurry to get back to the war and my captain."

Jeannot shook his head.

"There can be no mistake about this being my brother," he declared. "About-face, Alphonse. Bend over." Jeannot flipped out the stub of a tail. "You see! A pompom on the end of his backbone. Our Alphonse was so marked. This is absolute proof, my corporal. Have you any more questions?"

Corporal Pagot doubled up his fist and beat it against his forehead as if to stir up his brains.

"It is most extraordinary," he admitted. "You must be correct, m'sieu. But it will take quite a bit of explaining to put this thing in the right light before my captain. Luckily he is nearsighted."

"Then there will be nothing to explain," said Jeannot, "and I can promise you that Alphonse will keep his silence about the whole matter."

Still the corporal had a doubt left.

"Don't bears have pompoms on the end of their backbones?" he asked.

As the corporal spoke, Jeannot's whole appearance changed. He haughtily stretched to his full height, raised his chin in the air and tossed his long gray hair over his shoulders. He pulled a greasy rag from his pocket and daintily flicked it at the soldier.

"And who questions the king of France?" he demanded. "Away, peasants, varlets, knaves! And take this bearded one with you. My Majesty will have no more of this insolence."

The two soldiers turned limp. The little Genest made a tight bow to Jeannot Vallar, and Corporal Pagot fell on his knees.

"Forth to battle!" shouted Jeannot. "The enemy is at the palace gates!"

Alphonse marked time in his tall boots. Pagot rose to his feet. Both soldiers fell into step with Alphonse. Left, right, left, right, left, right, the trio marched out the door and down the trail that led to the fort.

So in this way, a bear from the wilderness marched forth to join the army of New France.

Left, right, left, right, left, right, the soldiers marched down the trail as if in step to the beat of a drum. Alphonse was in the lead because neither man wanted to walk in front of him.

The sun shone on his breastplate and helmet. His short legs seemed all boots as he plodded on. The same sun shone on Corporal Pagot and the little Genest. It drew beads of sweat out of their smooth-shaven cheeks.

Deeper into the forest wriggled the trail. The trees hid the three soldiers. On they marched and marched and marched. The men were beginning to weary, but Alphonse pushed tirelessly on.

"I'm hungry," Genest complained.

Alphonse turned and looked at him. He licked his chops.

"It isn't time yet," replied the corporal. "The shadows are still short. Let us talk about something that will take our minds off food. The wild boar forgets acorns when the huntsman's horn fills his mind with other thoughts."

"*Bon!*" agreed Genest. "Let us talk about what we will do when we leave the army. What are your plans, my corporal?"

Pagot fell into a jaunty swagger. Alphonse kept on licking his chops as if the conversation had not been changed.

"I shall return to Normandy and seek an easier life," said the corporal. "Perhaps some fine nobleman will take me into service as his lackey. I will have nothing to do all day long but open and close carriage doors. What are your plans?"

"I am going to become a cook in some prosperous inn," said the other. "I shall cook pigs' feet and hare smothered in butter and—"

"Enough of that," scolded Pagot. "Perhaps we should give the subject a turn. Think of the village fetes and fairs! I saw my first juggler at one, and a little white pig that danced to a pipe."

Alphonse began to drool over his breastplate.

"And once I climbed the greased pole to the very top," boasted the corporal. "What did you do at the fairs, Genest?"

"I sat under a tree and ate sausages and cheese."

"Think of the puppet shows," urged Pagot, "and dancing on the grass with the pretty maidens in their ruffled white bonnets. Did you dance much, Genest?"

"No," confessed the soldier. "I was afraid that if I set my sausages and cheese down, somebody might steal them."

Alphonse stopped and turned around. He pointed appealingly to his mouth, for it is the spirit of bears to get very hungry—as any woodsman knows.

"So, so, Alphonse, we will eat right away," promised Pagot. Under his breath he said to Genest, "This wild man looks as if he is ready to make a meal of us."

"There is a stream at the next turn of the trail, if I remember rightly," said

Genest. "Let us stop there and catch some nice fish for supper."

The path turned from the woods, and there was the stream.

"Halt!" ordered the corporal. "Here is our supper waiting to be caught."

The men made themselves busy fashioning three fishing poles from willow branches and knotting bits of string. Alphonse watched them closely.

"Dig some worms for us, Alphonse," ordered Pagot. "Your long nails should be good for that."

Alphonse dug worms out of the wet bank, as he had so often done for Jeannot Vallar. Pagot baited three hooks. He held one pole out to Alphonse, but the bear pushed it away.

"All right, my fine friend," said Pagot. "Those who won't hold a pole get no fish for supper. You can go hungry."

Pagot and Genest squatted on the bank and flipped their lines into the water. Alphonse lumbered over and sat down beside the corporal.

The sun sank low as the men waited for a bite. But the fish did not seem to be as hungry as they. Nothing nibbled at the bait. Then, to their astonishment, Alphonse plunged his paw into the water and splashed a big fish onto the bank. He swallowed it—bones, tail and all.

The men kept on fishing but had no luck. Alphonse frisked a second fish out of the water, then a third and a fourth. The men watched the fishtails disappear into his big mouth.

Genest leaned over to Pagot.

"Let me put a flea in your ear, my corporal," he whispered. "I'm sure this bearded fellow is a bear. And that pompom on the end of the backbone doesn't prove anything to me."

"*Chut!*" warned Pagot, finger to lip. "This Alphonse must be a man when we get back to the fort, or it is the pillory for both of us."

When it began to grow dark, they gave up the fishing and scattered to collect wood. Soon they had a cheery bonfire going. Alphonse pulled up a big log and the three sat on it. Pagot and Genest munched the cold, dried, salted army food from their knapsacks.

As the little Genest buckled his knapsack, he remembered something.

"We have only two blankets among us," he said. "Someone will have to sleep with 'Phonse."

"I appoint you to sleep with the bearded one," said Pagot.

"No, no," refused Genest. "You sleep with him."

"Not I," said the corporal.

"Nor I," added the other. "I'll sleep on the bare ground by myself."

The black night crept closer about them, brightening the flames of the fire. Across the stream an eerie light played over the marshland.

"Look!" Genest pointed at it. "The *feu follet!*"

Pagot stiffened, but Alphonse sleepily dropped his head between his knees.

"It is truly the wicked goblin with his little light, out to make mischief," said little Genest, moving closer to Pagot.

The forest seemed to come to life. From its depths a wolf howled. An owl hooted among the treetops. This chorus was swelled by the wild cry of a loon.

Alphonse lifted his head and wriggled about restlessly.

Then a sudden gust of wind shrieked through the trees.

"Hark!" cried Pagot, hand to ear. "It is the *chasse galerie.*"

"Y-yes," Genest whispered through chattering teeth. "The ghostly hunter rides through the sky tonight. Hear the baying of the hound and the cries of the hunter? It means bad luck."

Alphonse smelled the wind. He growled deep down in his chest.

The strange cries came closer. A circle of hostile, shining eyes surrounded the little group by the fire.

"Indians!" cried Genest. "Put out the fire, 'Phonse."

"Wolves!" bawled Pagot. "Build up the fire, Alphonse."

Alphonse did neither. He growled furiously. He rose in his boots and strode toward the eyes.

"Gr-r-r-r-r-r-r-r! Gr-r-r-r-r-r-r-r!" he growled.

The eyes disappeared and furry paws ran away in all directions.

Alphonse gave a last mighty growl, then returned to the log. For it is not the spirit of a bear to fear any other beast in the forest.

The two men sat in silence for several minutes. Genest spoke first.

"I have changed my mind," he said. "I will sleep with 'Phonse after all."

"Ho-ho!" exclaimed Pagot. "You are too late. I changed mine before you did. *I* will sleep with Alphonse."

The dispute was settled by the three

sleeping together, with Alphonse in the middle.

So in this way, the bear from the wilderness gained the respect of his two fellow soldiers.

The left, right, left, right of the soldiers covered their boots with dust by the time they reached the fort in the woods.

Pagot was now in the lead, with Alphonse last, because an armed column should have strong protection from the rear. Between them was little Genest, like a fly crawling between two beetles.

The high palisade of the fort rose before them. It was made of great logs turned on end. Over it flew the white flag of France with its golden lilies.

A guard peered out of a loophole over the gate. He pointed the muzzle of his long, long gun at the approaching party.

"Halt!" shouted the guard. "Who goes there?"

"Corporal Pagot and party," answered the big man.

"Advance and give the password."

Pagot stepped nearer the gate.

"Harquebuses and brassards," the corporal replied.

There was a pause.

"That was the password last week," retorted the guard. "You can't come in unless you know this week's password."

Pagot clenched his long, long gun.

"Charlot Bonnet," he bellowed, "you know me well. Open the gate and let us in."

"Not without the password, my corporal," grinned Bonnet. "Those are my orders."

Pagot's nose grew purple. Alphonse's head began to sway and his eyes to roll, *çà* and *là*.

"Bonnet," shouted Pagot. "I will have you put in the pillory. I will have you thrown in irons."

"You will have to get in first," the guard saucily reminded him. "And you need the password for that."

Then Alphonse stepped forward and pulled back his nose.

"Gr-r-r-r!" he growled angrily, for it is the spirit of bears to get cross when they are tired and hungry.

"Ah, now that's it," said the guard. "*Gruau!* Groats. We had them for breakfast. Open the gate, you Henri down there."

The heavy gate swung open. The three soldiers marched through.

There were log cabins along the inner sides of the fence. Soldiers were loitering about in the square. They wore shiny new shoulder belts, and some of them made fine style with their big hats dripping with plumes.

"*Pouah!*" snorted Pagot. "The new lace-cuffed soldiers with their frills and froufrou have arrived from France. Perhaps this explaining about Alphonse won't be so hard after all, eh, my little friend?"

"We are in luck," agreed Genest. "These fellows straight from France will believe anything."

The soldiers quickly gathered around the newcomers.

"Why is this bear dressed up so funny?" asked one of them, a foppish lad with golden curls and round blue eyes. "Is bearbaiting the latest sport in New France?"

"This is no bear, my simpleton," retorted Pagot. "Have you never seen a man from the wilderness?"

"But he has fur all over him," said another mincing soldier.

"Ha-ha! Wait until you have spent as many winters in New France as this fellow," said Pagot. "You will grow fur all over you too."

"With that long snout, he looks like a bear," insisted the first.

"Is that what passes for manners in the king's guard now?" demanded the corporal. "Does my comrade say that you look like a pussycat?"

And all the while they talked about him, Alphonse rocked his head *çà* and *là*.

A third soldier found his tongue.

"I have heard the stories told by my father, whose grandfather sailed with Jacques Cartier," he offered. "He said that to the west of New France is the kingdom of Saguenay. In it are great lakes full of sea serpents so large they can swallow a canoe. The land is covered with gold and rubies. Strange men live there, some of them having only one leg—unipeds he called them."

"This bearded one is from there," said Pagot. "He is one of the long-nosed men covered with fur."

The soldier with the curls sneered.

"The kingdom of Saguenay was a myth," he scoffed. "There is no such place."

Pagot saw that Alphonse was growing impatient with the spirit of a bear that wants to be somewhere else.

"Stand aside, my fine lace cuffs," he said. "We must report to the captain."

The elegant new soldiers opened an aisle for them. But as Alphonse marched past, the pussycat of a soldier blew his lips out with a disrespectful sound like a cow pulling its hoof from mud.

"That fancy young truffle needs salting," remarked Pagot to Genest.

He stalked manfully to the captain's desk and made a deep flourish. The captain squinted at him.

"Corporal Pagot reporting with the new conscript," said the corporal.

"Where is the conscript?" asked the officer, blinking his eyes and turning his head from side to side like an inquiring rooster.

Pagot pulled at Alphonse.

"Here he is, sir," he said. "Alphonse Vallar, sharp of wit and sound of body."

The captain blinked and squinted more than ever.

"Alphonse Vallar," he repeated. "He looks like a bear to me."

Then Pagot forced a loud laugh.

"Ha-ha!" came out Pagot's false laugh. "What a wit you are, my captain! Now that you mention it, this conscript *has* the look of a bear. Let us hope that he can fight like one. Ha-ha!"

The captain laughed too. He tossed his gray hair. Then he swallowed his laugh.

"We have quite a score to settle with the Iroquois," he said, "but we don't have to wait much longer, now that reinforcements have arrived from France. You may go."

The three soldiers turned on their heels and walked out.

"Genest," said Pagot as they crossed the square. "I have a little matter to settle with Charlot Bonnet. He is not a featherhead like these new soldiers. I think it best to enter into a little plot with him. I will not punish him for his waggishness if he will keep his mouth shut about our new conscript."

Corporal Pagot hurried to the gate and climbed the ladder that led to the landing near the top of the palisade.

"You might as well come into the barracks and get rid of those tortoiseshells," Genest said, pointing to Alphonse's armor. "None but pikemen and cannoneers wear them anymore."

As they were about to enter one of the log cabins, their path was blocked by the pussycat soldier and his companions.

"Regard the man from the Saguenay kingdom," taunted the youth. "He has the outmoded armor of a soldier and the nose of a bear."

The becurled soldier pulled a small jeweled box from his pocket. He daintily flipped the lid and took a pinch of snuff. He sniffed it first into one side of his nose, then into the other.

Sniff! Sniff!

Alphonse leaned over and looked into the little box.

"Have a sniff, my bearded gentleman," invited the soldier. He pushed the box under the bear's nose. "Take a deep breath. It will clear that big furry head of yours."

"Don't do it, 'Phonse," warned Genest. "You will be sorry."

Alphonse took a deep breath. *Sno-o-o-o-of!* His head cleared like an exploding blunderbuss. *Ahchoo-o-o-o-o!*

The bear shook his stinging nose. Then he let out a terrible roar. He stepped forward and gave the owner of the snuff-box such a cuff on the right cheek that the man fell to his knees. As he tried to rise, Alphonse gave him a cuff on the left cheek that sent him sprawling in the dust.

The soldier sprang up angrily. He whipped out his sword. Alphonse pulled out the rusty blade that Jeannot had given him.

Bong! Cling! Clank! There was a flash of steel in the sunlight. The two figures jumped this way and that way, with toes turned out. They furiously struck at each other.

Bang! Cling! The fighters stepped forward and sideways. Twice the French soldier's blade struck Alphonse, but the steel of his breastplate blocked it. The bear fought like a hero, but it was easy to see that he was no match for this swordsman from France.

Corporal Pagot came sliding down the ladder.

"Stop!" he shouted. "Stop this instant!"

No one heard him. All the soldiers were busy watching the duel. Backward, backward stepped Alphonse's boots until they were against the logs of the palisade. Then his enemy lunged forward. With a twist of the wrist, the man sent the bear's sword spinning through the air.

Alphonse snarled furiously. He reached out and grabbed the man's blade in his tough paw. He pulled it away from the soldier and threw it over the palisade.

With a thundering roar, he seized the frightened soldier in his paws. He pulled him into the grip of his powerful arms and began to squeeze him to his chest. For it is the spirit of a bear to fight to win, not to uphold honor.

The man's eyes started to bulge. Pagot grabbed Alphonse's shoulder and shook it roughly with his own powerful arm.

"Enough, Alphonse! *Attention!*" he cried.

Alphonse released his victim. He dropped his paws to his sides and raised his nose in the air.

The defeated swordsman slunk away to the jeers of his comrades.

"At ease!" Pagot ordered Alphonse. "Company dispersed!"

The bear gave one final loud sneeze. *Ahchoo-o-o-o-o!*

Wild cheering rose from the crowd.

"Hurrah for Alphonse!"

"Long live Alphonse, that bearded one!"

The hero lumbered over to where he had so recently had his back to the palisade. He slowly scratched his back against the logs.

So in this way, the bear from the wilderness gained the respect of all his comrades-in-arms.

Next morning a great *fla* and *ra* of drums awoke Alphonse. He sat up in the narrow bunk and scratched his ears.

Pagot, wearing all his equipment, came dashing over to him.

"The croak-notes are playing the tune that calls everyone out for something important," he cried. "Into your clothes and don't forget your sword."

Alphonse dressed slowly, shaking his head *çà* and *là* from time to time. Genest tried to stop him when he clamped the breastplate over his chest.

But Alphonse pushed him away and finished his dressing by donning the dented helmet. Jeannot Vallar had always demanded that this armor be worn when the drum sounded, and it is not the spirit of a trained bear to change the routine of his tricks.

The soldiers were drawn up in long lines in the square. The captain saluted them with his sword.

"Brave soldiers of New France," he began, "we are ready to march against our Iroquois enemies. All we need is some knowledge of their strength and their plans. Who will volunteer to get this information? Step forward two paces, brave volunteer."

No one stepped forward. Rather, each man stepped back two paces. Each *man*, that is, but not Alphonse. He did not move one way or the other. He just stood in his best at-attention pose, his nose high in the air.

Looking back and forth, the nearsighted captain caught sight of the blurred form of Alphonse two paces ahead of the line.

"The new conscript!" exclaimed the officer. "What a brave one!"

At this, Genest jumped out of the ranks and pulled at the bear.

"Back, 'Phonse," he warned. "Back up. You are stepping into a trap."

Then Pagot must join Genest to help save Alphonse.

The captain was full of admiration.

"*Three* volunteers!" he cried. "This is a proud day for New France. Company dispersed. Brave volunteers, come with me."

In his office, the captain began thumbing through maps and drawings. Pagot peered over his shoulder fearfully.

"Just what is our mission, my captain?" he asked.

"You are to be spies," answered the officer. "Sergeant Besette here will help you with your disguises. You are to pose as Indian warriors. Go to the Iroquois village. Mingle with the Indians and learn all you can."

Sweat broke out on Pagot's heavy face. Genest grew pale. Only Alphonse showed no fear.

"You will leave immediately," said the officer. "There is no time to lose."

Sergeant Besette went to work on the disguises. He helped Pagot and Genest take off their clothing. He handed them breechcloths and blankets and moccasins.

He cut off Pagot's mustache and Genest's chin whiskers. He shaved their heads, leaving only one short scalp lock on each, which had something of the look of the pompom on the end of Alphonse's backbone. Then he fastened an eagle feather to each pompom.

He mixed little pots of paint and slopped and daubed like an inspired artist, for he had been a sign painter in Paris before he joined the army.

First he gave each man a blue nose. He smeared black over their eyelids and cheeks, and red over the rest of their faces. The upper parts of their bodies he painted with stripes of every color in the pots. Then he jumped back and looked at them with pride.

"Ah, I am a great artist!" He kissed his fingers. "Regard my masterpieces."

He turned to the bear.

"Now," said Sergeant Besette, "it is Alphonse's turn. What shall we do with Alphonse?"

For any third-rank fool could see that Alphonse was going to be a difficult subject for this painter. The bear had taken off his armor and clothes and stood in his own fur coat, waiting to be made into an Iroquois.

The three men studied him from every angle. They scratched their heads. They bit their fingernails. They beat their foreheads.

"I fear that I do not have enough talent for this," sighed the painter. "But I will paint his nose and nails red just to show that I am not one to shirk his duty."

Sergeant Besette made Alphonse's nose into a beautiful red strawberry and daintily painted his nails.

"Perhaps we will think of something on the way," said Pagot. "Come, Alphonse,

let us get this unpleasant business over as soon as possible."

All the way out of the fort and through the woods, the two men argued about what to do to make Alphonse into an Iroquois.

"I have it!" exclaimed Genest as they crossed the last ravine. "We will pretend that 'Phonse is a bear."

Pagot beamed upon him.

"Sometimes I think that you have something in your head other than sausages and cheese, my little soldier," he glowed. "That is perfect. I have seen Indians carrying a deer home from the hunt. It was tied to a pole by its hoofs. Just before we reach the Iroquois village, we will fix Alphonse so."

"With those red nails and that nose," added Genest, "it will look as if we had a fierce struggle with him. We shall play the brave hunters."

"Don't let us try to make this thing too good," warned Pagot. "A few herbs flavor the soup, but too many turn it bitter."

When they came to the edge of the Indian cornfields, Alphonse was told to play dead. They tied his paws together with buckskin thongs and lashed them to a long pole. Then the two false Iroquois bravely strode toward the gate of the Indian palisade. Between them hung the limp form of Alphonse, so cleverly disguised as a bear.

The gate of the Iroquois village was open because many Indians were returning. As they entered, they saw the longhouses fanned around an open yard.

An Iroquois painted like the Frenchmen stepped beside them. On his head were elk antlers and the unlucky elk's teeth hung in a necklace around his neck. He pushed his blue nose within a few inches of Pagot's.

"Ough," grunted the Indian.

"Ough," Pagot returned.

"Ough, ough," croaked Genest.

Pagot glared back at him.

"Don't be so talkative," he warned out of the corner of his mouth. "You will give us away."

The Indian seemed satisfied. He led the men toward a big pot steaming over a fire and motioned them to lay Alphonse down. As they did so, Pagot untied the thongs binding him to the pole.

"You are in a ticklish situation," he whispered into the bear's ear, "but stay dead as long as you can."

Alphonse did not understand him, but he was sleepy and the fire felt warm. He lay quietly with his eyes closed.

Then a terrific racket broke out behind one of the bark houses. A group of Indian warriors in full war paint and feathers came dancing into the yard. They waved gourd rattles and tomahawks. Deer hoofs dangled from their knees and kicked into the air. Tom-toms thumped.

The dancers formed a circle, stamping along on their heels and raising and lowering their bodies in time to the tom-toms. As they danced, they chanted and made hideous faces.

"Ough?" invited Pagot as he pulled Genest into the dancing circle.

The two soldiers fell into step with the Indians. They stamped, howled and flung their arms about in imitation of their fellow dancers.

Hi-yah! Hi-yah! Stomp, stomp, stomp! Boom, boom, boom!

From his place by the fire, Alphonse opened one eye. His little ears raised. One hind paw began twitching to the beat of the tom-toms. Then both hind paws began kicking in rhythm.

He stood up and started marching

toward the dancers, left, right, left, right. For it is the spirit of a trained bear to want to show off every time he gets the chance.

At sight of what they had supposed to be a dead bear coming to life, the dancing Indians froze in their steps.

"Oh, *là, là!*" cried Pagot. "This ends the fete."

Both men ran toward Alphonse. Pagot grabbed his paw and spun him around.

"Come, Alphonse," he cried. "Run for your life!"

The sudden turn of affairs threw the Indians into confusion. They went running into their houses and into each other. All was spill and tumble. By the time they had recovered from the shock, the three spies were out the gate and halfway across the cornfields. A delayed whistle of arrows blew them into the woods.

Moccasins and paws went so fast they hardly touched the ground. Huh, huh, huh, panted Pagot and Genest. But Alphonse was fresh as a moosebird because he had had a nice rest by the fire.

Pagot thought that it was better not to take a straight cut to the fort, or the Iroquois might overtake them. So they broke away from the trail and went into the thick underbrush.

Night found them hopelessly lost in the woods. They slept on the ground, and this time the two blankets shared were the ones that Pagot and Genest had worn as part of their costumes.

All the next day they wandered through the forest. Pagot and Genest were full of despair. But Alphonse was happy as a finch, because it is the spirit of a bear to feel more at home in the forest than under a roof.

It was he who finally led them to a cave among the rocks. It was getting dark again and the men were overjoyed to find shelter.

They went into the cave, stumbling over rocks in the darkness. Weary and footsore, they huddled together and fell fast asleep. The cave was filled with snore echoes.

So in this way, Alphonse learned that a soldier's life is not all drums and marching and cheers.

When Pagot woke up, he had to go outside to find out if it was morning yet. The sun was shining and the birds twittering.

The corporal gathered an armful of brush and twigs. He carried them into the cave and started a fire with his flint.

Soon the flames were crackling cheerily. They showed an irregular chamber strewn with rocks. Roots hung down from the ceiling and water slowly dripped from them. *Three* bears were sleeping in a row.

Pagot let out a shriek that loosed new echoes in the cave. He reached for his sword, but his hand touched only skin garments.

"Genest! Alphonse!" he cried. "Wake up!"

The little soldier sat up and rubbed his eyes. Alphonse sat up and scratched his ears. The two strange bears rose to their haunches and bared their long fangs.

Genest squealed and ran to Pagot. The two bears got to their paws and shuffled toward the men, snarling and growling. Then Alphonse added his own growls to the uproar and the whole cave was turned into a bear garden.

The bears began grunting and rubbing noses. For Alphonse realized that he was among those of his own spirit. What one bear tells another no one knows, but soon the two wild bears stopped growling at the men. One of them even licked Genest's cold white face.

When he was able to speak, Genest pointed to the new companions.

"Look!" he cried. "Those pompoms on the end of the backbone. They have those birthmarks too."

"Genest," said Pagot. "I have had a flea in the ear about this Alphonse from the very first. There is no longer any reason for us to make the dunces about him. What is more, it looks as if we are now bears also."

Genest's face brightened. "Why can't 'Phonse and his countrymen catch some fish for us?" he suggested.

Pagot ordered Alphonse to do this very thing. The bear shook his head *çà* and *là*. Then Pagot gave him a push toward the entrance of the cave. Alphonse grunted to the other bears to follow him.

Outside the cave, he stood and shook his head some more, *çà* and *là*. He did not know what the men wanted him to do. Then his little eyes brightened. He broke three branches off a willow tree.

He nudged the other bears to rise on their hind legs. He gave each one a branch and showed him how to carry it over his shoulder.

Then he started marching back and forth, for this seemed to be the thing that men expected of bears.

"Ouf, wouf, ouf, wouf," Alphonse grunted.

The other bears fell into step behind him. Ouf, wouf, ouf, wouf, they marched back and forth.

Alphonse was the only one out of step when Pagot and Genest came from the cave to see if the bears had caught any fish yet.

"That is what comes of sending a bear to do a man's job," said Pagot. "Oh, well, perhaps we can help with this."

Pagot joined in the lesson. He taught the wild bears to mark time and stand at attention. He even taught them how to not volunteer. He lined them up with Genest.

"Now who will volunteer to go to the Iroquois village and steal a haunch of venison?" he asked. "No, no, you in front. Do not look me straight in the eye. Never look me straight in the eye when I ask for volunteers. It draws my attention to you. Alphonse—" But Alphonse had already stepped back two paces, because it is not the spirit of a bear to be caught in the same trap twice. "And you, Genest, stop scratching your neck."

"I can't help it," replied Genest. "I feel like somebody is watching us. I can feel eyes crawling all over the back of my neck."

The bears began looking over their shoulders. They sniffed the air and growled. The hair on their shoulders stood on end. For through the leaves of the bushes appeared hideously painted faces.

Alphonse and the bears dropped on all fours and streaked for the cave. The two men almost beat them there.

"Close the entrance," directed Pagot. "Alphonse, you and your bears push that great boulder into it."

Alphonse grunted and pushed with all his might, but the wild bears were no help at all. They crouched in the back of the cave with an I-told-you-so look gleaming in their eyes.

As the boulder shivered and slowly moved under the force of the Indian onslaught, the men and Alphonse piled more and more rocks against it. Genest even tried to outpush the Iroquois.

"Now we have made a snug fort," announced the corporal at last. "It is a poor badger that can't dig some kind of a hole."

They sank to the ground, panting and exhausted.

"Huck! Huck! Our fire is making a lot of smoke," coughed Genest.

Shuddering, Pagot pointed toward their wall of rocks.

"It isn't coming from the fire," he groaned. "Look!"

The smoke was pouring in through the cracks.

"*Hélas!*" he moaned. "The Iroquois are trying to smoke us out. Ba-hup! Ba-hup!"

"I'm not—huck, huck, huck—going out," choked Genest.

"Huck, gr-r-r-r-huck, huck," coughed the bears.

At last they had to pull the stones away from their doorway. They staggered out into the fresh, biting air. And as they came out, one by one, the Iroquois seized them.

When the captives reached the Indian village, they were greeted by a noisy and curious crowd. They were led into one of the longhouses and securely bound. The wild bears snarled and bit at the thongs that held them. Alphonse whined and shook his great head *çà* and *là*.

Then the boom, boom of drums shook the smoky air in the house. The Indian warriors left.

"We are cuckoo eggs hatching in a hawk's nest," sighed Pagot. "A council is being called. Our fate will be decided."

Alphonse showed no interest in their talk. All of his attention was given to the beating drums.

"I wonder what will happen to 'Phonse," mused Genest.

Pagot looked at the bear sadly.

"Good old Alphonse," he said. "They will surely get him into the cookpots this time, peace be to his broth!"

As the soldiers brooded over the possible fate of the bearded one in order to forget their own, the Iroquois men returned from the council.

The captives were roughly dragged out before a screaming, scowling mob. Pagot and Genest were fastened to two stakes set in the middle of the square.

Alphonse and the wild bears were carried to the edge of a blazing fire where the cookpots waited. But the Iroquois women were too excited about the doomed men to waste any time on bears at the moment.

All the Indians were intently watching the hapless Pagot and Genest. Some were piling firewood around them. Others shook tomahawks at them and made horrible faces. All the while the drums beat impatiently. *Boom, boom, boom.*

Only one little Indian boy took any interest in the bears. He stood staring at Alphonse, a small tomahawk held in his brown hand. The bear's paws were twitching to the beat of the drums. His head was straining from side to side, *çà* and *là*.

Alphonse stared back at the boy. He lifted his shackled paws to him in a beseeching manner.

The little Indian looked at the sharp edge on his tomahawk. Then he pressed his tongue between his teeth and began cutting the leather thongs that held Alphonse. At last the bear was free.

He rose to his hind legs and shook his fur coat. Again he held his paws out beggingly. Delighted with these antics, the boy handed him the tomahawk.

Alphonse swung it over his head and let out a roar that drowned all the other noises and sent the little Indian crawling

under a wolfskin. Clumsily he hopped upon one hind paw, then the other.

"Gr-r-r-r-r-rh-rh! Yee-ai-ai-ai-ai!"

Alphonse was doing the war dance which he had been kept from performing at the last Indian fete.

"Gr-r-r-r-r-rh-rh! Yee-ai-ai-ai-ai!"

Alphonse growled and squealed as he raised and lowered his furry body on his stamping hind paws. He waved the tomahawk wildly and bared his long, sharp fangs in a terrible snarl.

The Indians were rooted to the ground like the trees of their own forest. Only their black eyes moved as they watched Alphonse's war dance.

Around the stakes he danced four times.

"Gr-r-r-r-r-rh-rh! Yee-ai-ai-ai-ai!"

Then he sat down on his haunches with his nose in the air and waited for cheers of "Long live Alphonse, that bearded one!" But the Iroquois were struck dumb with astonishment and Genest had fainted.

At last the chief broke the spell. He was so old that his skin was brown and wrinkled as a dried tobacco leaf, but his step was as sure as that of a lynx. He walked to Alphonse with savage grace. He put his hand on the bear's head.

"Friends and relatives," shouted the chief to his tribe, "it is a sign. The bear chief warns us that all the bears of the forest will war against us if we kill these white men."

The Indians started murmuring and shifting about uneasily.

"This is no ordinary bear," agreed one. "With our own eyes we saw him teaching his brothers the white man's walking war dance."

"Yai! Yai!" remembered another. "Our own eyes have also seen him come to life beside our campfire once before."

"Through magic he has broken his strong bonds this time," added yet another. And it did not seem likely that the Indian boy hiding under the wolfskin would dispute his words.

"The Frenchmen have outwitted us again," shouted the first speaker. "They have made allies of the bear tribe. The very forests will be peopled with our enemies. This war is bad medicine for the red man."

"Another council," demanded the chief. "A peace council! Build up the fire under the great oak. Release the captives."

Pagot and Genest, who had come out of his faint by this time, were cut loose from the stakes. But as soon as the wild bears were freed, they raced for the palisade and quickly scrambled over it. Alphonse longingly watched their pompoms disappear from sight.

The old chief stretched his arm out to Alphonse.

"Chief Dancing Bear shall have the place of honor at the council," he decreed. "Through him, we shall make peace with the white men."

So in this way, a bear from the wilderness ended a war before it was well begun.

Alphonse might have become a great general, but it is not the spirit of a bear to want to command armies. He received high honor, it is true. Even the king of France rewarded him.

"For great bravery, Alphonse Vallar is granted fifty square miles of land. In return he must build a mill, gather dependents, level forests, clear fields and make two blades of grass grow where only one grew before," wrote the king of France in his own fancy hand.

Alphonse yawned when this grant was read to him, for it is not the spirit of a bear to turn forests into fields. But Pagot and Genest were full of plans.

"Let us stay in the New World," Pagot urged Genest. "We shall become the dependents of this new seigneur."

When they returned to the cabin in the wilderness, Jeannot Vallar approved of this plan. He grabbed the axe from the corner and pressed it into Pagot's big hand. A mad light came into his eyes.

"Off to the battle of the trees!" he commanded. "And take Genest with you."

When the dependents had left, he turned to Alphonse with a laugh.

"Ha-ha! My heroic brother," he said. "With these stupid servants to work for us, we shall live like noblemen."

Alphonse unbuckled his breastplate and threw it into a corner. The helmet was banged on top of it. He tore off his ill-fitting garments and threw them on top of the breastplate. Lastly he kicked off his worn boots.

Then dropping on all fours he marched down the trail, one, two, three, four, one, two, three, four, to join the other bears. For it is not the spirit of a bear to want servants and the life of a nobleman.

The Snail and the Rosebush

by Hans Christian Andersen

Translated by Erik Christian Haugaard

Have you ever wondered what a snail is thinking as he goes so cautiously on his way?

Around the garden ran a hedge of hazelnuts, beyond it there were fields and meadows, where cows and sheep grazed; but in the center of the garden there was a rosebush in full bloom. Under it lay a snail, who was very satisfied with the company he kept: his own.

"Wait till my time comes," he would say, "and see what I shall accomplish. I am not going to be satisfied with merely blossoming into flowers, or bearing nuts, or giving milk as the cows and sheep do."

"Oh, I do expect a lot of you. Won't you tell me when it's going to happen?" asked the rosebush very humbly.

"I must take my time," said the snail. "Do you think anyone would expect much of me if I hurried the way you do?"

The following year the snail lay in the same sunny place, under the rosebush. The plant was full of buds and flowers, and there were always fresh roses on it, and each and every one was a tiny bit different from all the others. The snail crept halfway out of his house and stretched his horns upward; then he pulled them back in again.

"Everything looks exactly as it did last year. No change and no advancement. The rosebush is still producing roses; it will never be able to do anything else."

Summer was past and autumn was past. Until the first snow, the rosebush continued to bloom. The weather became raw and cold. The rosebush bent its branches toward the ground and the snail crawled down into the earth.

Another spring came. The rosebush

blossomed and the snail stuck his head out of his house. "You are getting old," he said to the rosebush. "It is about time you withered and died. You have given the world everything you could. Whether what you gave was worth anything or not is another question, and I don't have time to think about it. But one thing is certain and that is that you have never developed your inner self, or something more would have become of you. Soon you will be only a wizened stick. What have you got to say for yourself? . . . Aren't you listening? . . . Can you understand what I am saying?"

"You frighten me so." The rosebush trembled. "You have asked me about things I have never thought about."

"I don't think you've ever thought about anything. Have you ever contemplated your own existence? Have you ever asked yourself why you are here? Why you blossom? Why you are what you are, and not something else?"

"No," the rosebush said. "My flowers spring forth out of joy! I cannot stop them from coming. The sun is warm, the air refreshing. I drink the dew and the rain. From the soil and the air I draw my strength. I feel so happy that I have to flower. I cannot do anything else."

"You have lived a very comfortable and indolent life," said the snail severely.

"How true! I have never lacked anything. But you have been given much more than I. You are a thinker. You can think deeply and clearly. You are gifted. You will astound the world."

"Astound the world! Not I!" The snail drew in his horns and then stretched them out again. "The world means nothing to me. Why should I care about the world? I have enough within myself. I don't need anything from the outside."

"But isn't it the duty of all of us here on earth to do our best for each other, to give what we can? I know I have given only roses. But you who have received so much, what have you given? What will you give?"

"What have I given! What shall I give!" snarled the snail. "I spit on the whole world. It is not worth anything and means nothing to me. Go on creating your roses, since you cannot stop anyway. Let the bushes go on bearing their nuts, and the cows and the sheep giving their milk. Each of them has his own public; and I have mine in myself. I am going to withdraw from the world; nothing that happens there is any concern of mine." And the snail went into his house and puttied up the entrance.

"It is so sad," said the rosebush. "No matter how much I wanted to, I couldn't withdraw into myself. My branches are always stretching outward, my leaves unfolding, my flowers blooming. My petals are carried away by the wind. But one of my roses was pressed in a mother's psalmbook, another was pinned on a young girl's breast, and one was kissed by a child to show his joy in being alive. Those are my remembrances: my life."

The rosebush went on blooming innocently, and the snail withdrew from the world, which meant nothing to him, by hibernating in his house.

The years passed. The rosebush had become earth and the snail had become earth; even the rose that had been pressed in the psalmbook was no more. But in the garden, rosebushes bloomed, and there were snails who retreated into their houses: the world meant nothing to them.

Should I tell the story from the beginning again? I could, but it would be no different.

The Professor and the Flea

by Hans Christian Andersen

Translated by Erik Christian Haugaard

The performing flea was wonderfully well trained. His master knew a few tricks, too.

There once was a balloonist—that is, a captain of a balloon—who came to a bad end; his balloon ripped and he fell straight to the ground and was smashed. His son, who had been along on the trip, had parachuted down two minutes before the tragedy. That was the young man's good luck. He landed safe and sound, with invaluable experience in ballooning and a great desire to make use of it; but he didn't have a balloon or any money to buy one with.

He had to make a living, so he taught himself how to talk with his stomach; that is called being a ventriloquist. He was young and handsome, and when he had bought new clothes and grown a mustache, he had such a noble look that he might have been mistaken for the younger son of a count. All the ladies found him handsome; and one of them so much so that she ran away from home to follow him. They traveled to distant towns and foreign lands, and there he called himself professor, no less would do.

His greatest desire was still to get a balloon and then ascend into the sky with his wife, but balloons are expensive.

"Our day will come," he declared.

"I hope it will be soon," said his wife.

"We can wait; we are young. Now I am a professor. Crumbs are not slices, but they are bread," he said, quoting an old proverb.

His wife helped him. She sat at the door and sold tickets, which was no fun in the winter when it was cold. She also took part in the act. She climbed into a chest and then vanished. The chest had a double bottom; it was a matter of agility, and was called an optical illusion.

One evening after the performance, when he opened the false bottom, she wasn't there. He looked everywhere, but she was gone. Too much dexterity. She never came back. She had been sorry and now he was sorry. He lost his spirit, couldn't laugh or clown, and then he lost his audience. His earnings went from bad to worse and so did his clothes. At last the only thing he owned was a big flea. He had inherited the animal from his wife and therefore was fond of it. He trained the flea, taught it the art of dexterity: how to present arms and to shoot off a cannon; the latter was very small.

The professor was proud of the flea and the flea was proud of himself. After all, he had human blood in his stomach, if not in his veins. He had visited the grand capitals of Europe and performed before kings and queens—at least that was what was printed in the playbill and the newspapers. He knew he was famous and could support a professor, or a whole family if he had had one.

The flea was proud and famous; and yet, when he and the professor traveled, they always went fourth class—it gets you to your destination just as quickly as first. They had a silent agreement that they would never part; the flea would remain a bachelor and the professor a widower, which amounts to the same thing.

"A place where one has had a great success one should never revisit," said the professor. For he knew human nature, and that is not the poorest sort of knowledge.

At last they had traveled in all the civilized parts of the world; only the lands of the savages were left. The professor knew that there were cannibals who ate Christian human beings. But he was not a real Christian and the flea not a human being, so he thought that there was no reason not to go there, and he expected it to be a profitable trip.

They traveled by steamer and sailing ship. The flea performed and that paid for their passage.

At last they came to the land of the savages. Here a little princess reigned. She had overthrown her own parents, for though she was only eight years old, she had a will of her own and was marvelously charming and naughty.

As soon as she had seen the flea present arms and shoot off his little cannon, she fell wildly in love with him. As love can make a civilized man into a savage, imagine what it can do to one who is already a savage. She screamed, stamped her feet, and said, "It is him or no one!"

"My sweet little sensible girl, we shall have to make him into a human first," said her father.

"You leave that to me, old man," she answered, and that was not a very nice way to speak to her own father, but she was a savage.

The professor put the flea in her little hand.

"Now you are a human being," declared the princess. "You shall reign together with me, but you will have to obey, or I shall kill you and eat the professor."

The professor got a room for himself. The walls were made of sugarcane; if he had had a sweet tooth, he could have licked them; but he didn't. He got a hammock for a bed, and lying in that was almost like being in the balloon he still dreamed about.

The flea stayed with the princess, sat on her hand and on her sweet neck. She pulled a long hair out of her head and made the professor tie one end around the leg of the flea; the other end was fastened to her coral earring.

The princess was happy, and she thought

that if she was happy, then the flea ought to be happy too. But the one who was not happy was the professor. He was used to traveling, sleeping one night in one town and the next in another. He loved reading in the newspaper about himself, how clever he was at teaching a flea human accomplishments; but there were no newspapers among the savages. Day after day he lay in his hammock, lazy and idle. He was well fed. He was given fresh bird's eggs, stewed elephant's eyes, and roasted leg of giraffe, for the cannibals did not eat human flesh every day; it was a delicacy.

The professor was bored. He wanted to leave the land of the savages, but he had to take the flea along; it was his protégé and the supplier of his daily bread.

He strained his power of thought as much as he could, and then he jumped out of the hammock and exclaimed, "I've got it!"

He went to the princess' father and said, "Please allow me to work. I want to introduce your people to what we, in the great world, call culture."

"And what can you teach me?" asked the father of the princess.

"My greatest accomplishment," answered the professor, "is a cannon which when fired makes such a bang that the earth trembles and all the birds in the air fall down roasted and ready to eat."

"Bring on that cannon," said the king.

But the only cannon in the whole country was the little one the flea could fire, and that was much too small.

"I will make a bigger one," said the professor. "I need lots of silk material, ropes, strings, needles, and thread. Besides some oil of camphor, which is good against airsickness."

All he asked for, he got. Not until the balloon was finished and ready to be filled with hot air and sent up did he call the people together to see his cannon.

The flea was sitting on the princess' hand, watching the balloon being blown up. And the balloon stretched itself and grew fatter and swelled. It was so wild it was difficult to hold.

"I have to take the cannon up in the air to cool it off. Alone, I cannot manage it; I have to have someone who knows something about cannons along to help me, and here only the flea will do."

"I hate giving him permission to go," said the princess as she held out the flea to the professor, who took it on his hand.

"Let go of the ropes, up goes the balloon!" he cried.

The savages thought he said "up goes the cannon," and the balloon rose up into the air above the clouds and flew away from the land of the savages.

The little princess, her father and her mother, and all their people stood and waited. They are waiting still, and if you don't believe me, you can travel to the land of the savages. Every child there will tell you the story of the flea and the professor. They are expecting him back as soon as the "cannon" has cooled off. But he will never return, he is back home. When he travels on the railroad he always goes first class, not fourth. He has done well for himself, with the help of the balloon, and nobody asks him where or how he got it. The flea and the professor are wealthy and respectable, and that kind of people are never asked embarrassing questions.

A Lemon and a Star

by E. C. Spykman

Jane never would have dreamed that one birthday could hold so many scares—and so much joy.

On her tenth birthday Jane Cares was walking up the west end of the Summerton Village road back to the red house. She was taking slow and careful steps so that her new sneakers would make clear, complete patterns in the soft gray dust. All the way from the old gate of the big field, where she had slipped out onto the road, they were perfect, and she was praying—lightly and without much hope—that the watering cart would not come by this afternoon and spoil them. Craning her neck to admire a trail that even a tenderfoot could have followed through the wilderness, she shifted the small suitcase she was carrying from one hand to the other and stumbled over a stone. Darn, she thought crossly, and stopped a minute to punish the stone by kicking it violently into the gutter. Oh well, she thought, I'm almost home.

Two hours before, she had run away, with the thought of living in a tree, because Theodore had said he was going to kill her. "If he caught you, I guess he'd do it too, Jane," Hubert had said. Hubert was only eight, but he knew a thing or two. And Jane agreed with him. Theodore, who was thirteen and had red hair, green eyes, and freckles, would do anything when he was in a temper, especially if someone had managed to hit him squarely in the neck with a mud pie. Jane had decided to run, and her neat new sneakers had carried her like wings. She had escaped into the house and upstairs, where she had packed a few clothes, and by jumping into the soft loam of the geranium bed while Ted was banging at her locked door, had got off across the fields.

Her intention had been to climb up the old maple at the lower end of the barn field, unpack, and set up housekeeping in a place of peace and quiet, where she could concentrate on hating Theodore. It had seemed a good idea. The maple stood alone and the approach of enemies could be seen from all sides. The brook ran along one side for water, and a vegetable garden stretched away on the other side for food. But now she was on her way home, because it had not worked. Living in a tree was impractical. Nothing would stay where you put it.

After a few more cautious steps the whole of the red house and its landscape came in sight. It sat quiet and serene enough in the summer sun. It was a stylish house with deep piazzas and a porte cochere, with a great red barn a little to the right and back. It was low and white-trimmed, and in the middle of the two halves was a bow window with plants, some green and some bright-colored. Around it was a lawn held back from the road by a good stone wall, and there were lots of trees.

The Cares children thought it a wonderful place to live. It had no mother in it, but only Theodore could tell if that mattered or not, because of her dying so long ago when Edie was born. They did know that the vine on the side wall was just right for high jumping, the circular drive could be used for bicycle races, and all the roofs could be climbed. At the back was a sandpile for Edie, rabbit hutches for Jane and Hubert, ponies for everyone, and bees—for nobody. Not even Theodore dared go near them.

Besides all this there were flowering shrubs in the corners of walls, yards, and fences. Lilacs hid the barn corners, privet blocked off the dank manure pit, and a great syringa bush stood by the kitchen door. By the circular drive stood a horse-chestnut tree, which in the spring was a mass of small white Christmas trees. Jane did not like being exiled from all these things. And as she stood looking at them she remembered it had all been on account of that silly Hubert.

On this seventeenth of June, 1907, Hubert had gotten up early, stolen Theodore's new steam-making machine, and tried to run it himself. As a result, warfare had broken out as soon as Father had left to take his train. Jane had wondered what she could do for Hubert, who had seemed in great danger, and what she had done had been to fire one of Edie's mud pies. She had been more than successful. Hubert had gotten completely away, and so had she, but still it was not much of a beginning for a birthday, and she was contemplating gloomily the time to come.

She stood a minute to listen and look. The red house seemed to be deserted. She could not see or hear Edie, who, because she was five, could usually be seen or heard. She sauntered from behind the horse chestnut out into the open, keeping herself well balanced on the balls of her feet, and finally walked casually up to the steps of the piazza under the porte cochere. Somebody moved behind them. It was Edie, looking like a blue and gold frog amid her slough of mud pies.

"Hello," said Jane, sitting down on the steps.

Edie paid no attention. With great intensity she was scooping out a hole and putting the dirt through a sieve.

"Where are the boys?" Jane asked.

"Out in the backyard," said Edie, and added without emotion, "They have a wild animal out there."

"What sort of wild animal?"

"I don't know," said Edie, mixing a pie. "It might be a wolf."

"A wolf. Pooh," said Jane.

Edie stopped stirring with a little jerk and looked at her sideways. "It bites," she said tentatively. "It bit Hubert badly."

"I guess I better go and see," said Jane, slipping off the steps.

She strolled out of the drive and along the wide gravel stretch that led to the backyard. There was Hubert, and there was Theodore too! They were so interested in something that they had quite forgotten her. Their hands were clutched around the opening of a tumbling, jerking burlap bag, and Mike Daley, the boy who worked for Pat, the coachman, was trying to catch and hold the thing they had inside. Ted's and Hubert's faces were red as fire, their hair was matted down on their foreheads, and Mike was purple. Jane came very near and her brothers looked up.

"Hi," said Hubert breathlessly. "Want to help?"

"Sure," said Jane, looking at Theodore warily. "What is it?"

"It's a fox," said Hubert. "I caught him. We've got to get the trap off his paw."

Theodore looked at Jane with a half smile. "We were looking for you, old girl," he said, "but we found this fox. He's almost as hard to handle."

Jane considered a minute what she would do about this fighting speech, but she could see that the mud was still on Theodore's neck so she let it go. She watched silently, her hands on her hips and her braids tucked behind her ears.

Mike flung himself on the bag and began to wrestle with it. The fox made small wiry sounds under his weight.

"Make him stop that," Jane said to Theodore, taking a step nearer and jerking her head at Mike.

"All right, old lady," Ted said, nodding at her. "Try it yourself, then."

Jane looked at the plunging bag a minute. She thought very likely the fox could bite, his teeth could go through that bag as easy as butter, and animal bites, Nurse said, were poisonous.

"Hurry up, confound you," Theodore said.

The mud, she could see, had trickled down inside his shirt. It must be good and sticky by this time.

Jane got down on her knees beside the bag and began to feel along it with quick desperate hands. Suddenly she made a dart and caught two sides of something furry and held on.

"I've got him," she said, wondering how such a miracle could happen. But the fox did not like it and she did not either. "Hurry up, yourself," she said to Theodore.

Both boys scrambled for the opening of the bag. For one infinitesimal second the fox lay still and there was a tiny crack of light between the trap jaws. Hubert was ready and he slipped the neat little paw quickly out and held it limp and soft against his hand. It did not look broken or damaged, Jane could see with relief, only limp, and the hair was out of place. Ted gave Hubert a shove with his knee to get him out of the way and gathered up the end of the bag's mouth again.

"Good girl," he said to Jane. "Let him go."

Jane would have liked to say something about the way Ted had got that trap to open. He always did what was impossible. For the thousandth time in her life she examined him, almost sure for the thousandth time that he had changed and was some sort of hero, or at least a boy that you could like.

"What are you staring at?" said Theodore, embarrassed. "Don't be too proud. I'll get you yet."

Jiminy, she had forgotten the mud pie. Well, he was not going to get her if she could help it, but she would have to be watchful.

After the fox had been dragged to the woodshed, tipped gently out of the bag, and gone to hide between the logs, Hubert wanted to know how it was going to eat. They all went back to the porte cochere to have a talk about it, sitting down.

Jane slid onto the third step. "Foxes eat meat," she said. "Raw meat. We'll have to get some from the kitchen. I saw some on the table this morning."

"So easy," said Theodore. "How are you going to get rid of Cook? I never saw that woman in a good temper in my life."

It was just yesterday that Cook had put Theodore out of the kitchen with the broom, when all he had wanted was to borrow one of her thousands of dishrags to wipe up a little mess his bleeding toe had made in the hall. Hubert had had "the best part of her tongue" several days ago because he had tried to get one cookie when he was dying of hunger, and Jane had left the cat's dish where Cook had stepped in it. "God's mercy it was too that she had a foot left on her at all." She did though, and the milk had scattered far and wide from its enormousness. No, they were stumped. Theodore took out his knife, opened the big blade, and began cutting slices out of the steps; Hubert played his fingers on his round face; and Jane made a mustache for herself with her braids, remembering all the time that hunger was gnawing the fox's vitals.

"We've got to get her out of the kitchen somehow," said Hubert finally. "What do you think would happen if she saw a rat?"

"You can't make a rat walk into the kitchen," said Jane.

"I know where there is one," said Hubert thoughtfully.

"A live one? So do I. Heaps."

"No, a dead one, and we could put him on the end of a pitchfork and hold him up when she's washing dishes at the sink."

"It's the best idea anyone ever had, Hubert," said Jane appreciatively. "But where is it? I bet you can't find him."

They all knew that although Father barked at Hubert continually to make him accurate, he sometimes wasn't. But Hubert really did have a dead rat. He had buried it in one of the geranium beds only yesterday, and all they had to do was steal a spade from the toolhouse and dig it up. A few geraniums got dug up too, but they were careful to set them back again, and before anyone came along to interfere, they did find Hubert's monster rat, slightly damaged by a dog bite and with dirt filling its eyes, ears, and mouth. This they brushed off with handfuls of grass and it was in perfect condition to get Cook out of the kitchen. Jane got the pitchfork. Theodore took it out of her hand, but for once Hubert was aware of his rights.

"You give it to me," he said. "It's my rat, and my idea, and my fox."

Ted had to give in; even Edie was ready to stand up for Hubert.

Hubert walked off on his tiptoes in the direction of the laundry yard, where he could stand on the clothespin box and be high enough so that the rat would look right into Cook's face when she might raise her head.

"You go and hide in the syringa bush by the door," Theodore directed Jane. "I bet she'll run for miles."

"Suppose she comes out this way?"

"She won't. She'll go and get in bed somewhere."

"What are *you* going to do?" Jane asked, but she did not wait for an answer. She raced off to the syringa bush and got behind it. Peeking cautiously through the window, she could just see the rat appear waveringly in the opposite one, above the back edge of the kitchen sink. She could hear Cook, unaware of its awful presence, serenely banging saucepans to pieces almost in its face.

To Jane the rat seemed to stay hung up in the air a long time, and it wavered so badly she wondered if Hubert's marvelous plan was going to work. But then it steadied; Ted had got there to help, and she willed passionately for Cook to look. She was hardly able to believe her eyes, but her willing did it. The saucepans made a louder clatter than ever and then stopped. Cook shrieked three times like the Summerton fire whistle and after that there was a peaceful silence. She had

evidently gone off to bed, as Theodore had said.

Jane crawled onto the top step and spied through the lower half of the screen door. There was no one in sight. She got to her feet, opened the door carefully and swiftly, and with fast noiseless steps got across the kitchen to the icebox. She grabbed two enormous handfuls of meat and, sticking it deep in her pinafore pockets, turned to escape and was almost away and out the door before she realized that after all she *had* seen Cook under the kitchen sink—a horrid bony sight with her face the color of green skim milk. Theodore was waiting just outside the kitchen door.

"Here," said Jane, shoving two fists at him. "Take it."

Theodore fled to the woodshed while Jane followed mechanically. When he came out, Jane took him by the arm. "Hey, stop pinching me," he said.

"Ted, listen," she said. "We're murderers. We've scared Cook to death. What shall we do?"

She told him how she had seen Cook under the sink looking like pea soup.

"Gosh," said Theodore, getting white in the face. "I suppose people do die of fright. I've read it in the newspapers."

They got Hubert out of the woodshed, where he had been trying to coax the fox to like his dinner. He turned even whiter than Theodore.

"Let's run," said Jane suddenly, turning as if she meant to start.

"We can't do that," said Theodore.

"We've murdered somebody," said Jane excitedly. "We *have* to."

"Don't be a fool," Theodore said. "I'm going to see." He took her arm. "And you're coming with me, old girl," he said. "See!"

Because it was Jane's birthday, and because Theodore was so brave, and because Hubert and Edie had cried and Jane had said she was sorry over and over again, and because the parlormaid had thrown a saucepan of water over Cook to bring her out of her faint and had then brought tea and a bottle of Father's whiskey, and because Father himself didn't get home till after it was all over, the only punishment for the attempted murder was that no one got lunch. Cook said she was "that unsthrung" she couldn't lift her hand.

The children did not want any lunch; they did not want anything except to go away separately to their rooms. And when Father got home—a little early because he had invited them all to drive as a part of Jane's birthday present—they were ready for him, washed and brushed as he liked them to be.

Driving like this, with the pair of horses, and the backboard of the wagon down, was one of the things they liked best to do. There were turns for who should sit in front, and even in the back there was no end to the privileges they had today because it was Jane's birthday. While the white dust steamed up on either side, slightly warmed and smelling of the stables, and while they watched the way it settled cloudlike at the farther end of the road, they swung their legs in a quick even time to the trot, trot, trot of the horses. Jane had brought a stick, and she let one end scrape along behind so that it made a fine clear wiggling mark on the plain surface of the road and sent up spurts and showers of dirt when she pressed it down with both hands. Sometimes she let it hop loosely, and then it bounced from the tops of stones and uneven places. Hubert asked to try and she gave it to him. He used it to lay against one of the wheels and make a fountain of earth fly out.

When it was Jane's turn to sit in front, she was allowed to touch the horses lightly now and then with the whip and feel them answer instantly to this infinitesimal flick of the lash, and when it was Theodore's turn to sit in back, he had brought with him two pocketfuls of stones and they flung them at the passing trees. Occasionally Father let the horses out, which meant that they flew and the children saw the country only as a sea of melted green.

On the way home they settled themselves into limp attitudes of content. Jane lay back along the length of the wagon and watched the white radiant blobs of cloud. Theodore took her stick and made it jump tremendously. Hubert, in front, let the whip down at one side and caught the tongue around a daisy head. Father only calmly told him not to. Jane wished it could be like this forever. She had fallen in love with the sun and the light it made on the trees and grass; with the reservoir basins that ran through the middle of Summerton; and with their sedgy edges, where there were muskrats working in the water; with the pink stone walls; and even with the dust that had settled on the roadside bushes.

They were a little late getting home, so that they had to rush to wash again for Jane's birthday party. When she came down the stairs into the hall, Father was there waiting, and the screen that had been put up in the dining room to hide her birthday table had been taken down. The boys were there before her and shone with the water on their plastered hair. Edie had on a pink dress with a sash and was parading up and down to show it off. Jane saw things from the stairs. She couldn't help it. The whole dining room was square in front of her and open to the plainest view. At her seat was a small mountain of white packages done up with colored ribbons, and the best of all, with an enormous pink and white striped bow, was perched at the top. This was a wonderful birthday after all.

"All ready, Jane?" said Father. "Happy birthday. Come, boys, let's go in, the feast's waiting."

Jane headed the procession to the table, wondering about the largest parcel. It was probably from Father, and this year it might be something really *good.* Last year it had been a set of Dickens bound in calf, so beautiful Father had taken the books away again and put them with his own. Jane approached her chair gingerly and looked things over.

"Hurry up, Jane," said Edie. "I want to see what's inside."

But Jane had a right to take her time. First she moved the big box to one side. It shone with promise and its ribbon dripped on all four sides. It must be a brand new bridle at the very least.

"I'll open that last," she said.

Underneath was something flat in tissue paper, a little smudged.

"That's mine," said Edie, wriggling in her chair. "It's a good present, but the paper got dirty."

Jane pulled off the ribbon and slipped the good present out. It was a flat thick piece of licorice.

"It cost five cents," said Edie. "If you give me a taste, I'll only take the tiniest lick." She nodded violently.

"It's wonderful," said Jane. "I'll eat it after supper."

Hubert was sitting with his hands tightly pinched between his knees. He could see that the next package was his. Jane picked it up with great deliberation. Hubert, when he was short of cash, had been known to give a colored stone or two, and once a tattered muskrat skin he thought was wonderful. This was round and hard and had some bumps along one side.

"What can it be?" Jane said, looking consideringly at Hubert.

Hubert grinned bashfully. "Not much," he said. "I was broke."

Out of a crumpled paper came a china bird's nest, and there were two birds, one red and one blue, perched on its edge, about to go and sit on it. Jane thought it ravishing. It almost made her eyes water.

"I don't know what you use it for," said Hubert apologetically, while he waited. "But I liked the birds."

"That's the best present I ever had," said Jane. "Gee, Hubert." She put it very gently down beside the licorice. "Thanks."

Cook had given her a puzzle, and the picture was exciting; a bear was going to eat a man, if the man did not hurry up and shoot.

"Now Father's," Jane said, turning to the big box.

"That's not mine," said Father. "Look again, there's something left beside the paper."

Jane shoved the mess to one side and found a small square box. She opened it slowly. Up from the bottom, where it rested on a piece of cotton, looked a sort of eye. It must be one of Father's "ancient" presents, she decided, the kind he gave them sometimes to keep them in touch with history and the lore of man.

"What is it, Jane?" asked Edie impatiently. "Why don't you show us?"

Jane put her finger under the eye and pulled it out. It dangled cold and frightful from a fat gold chain. It looked as if it might be a bracelet, but it was much too big for her bony wrist.

"That, young lady," said Father importantly, "came out of a tomb."

They stared at it silently and hard.

"Was the person *dead?*" asked Edie in a whisper.

"Thousands of years," said Father.

"Nothing but bones?" asked Edie.

"Nothing but dust, Edith."

"Don't wear it, Jane," said Edie hoarsely. "It'll hant you."

Edie, who never did anything for anybody when she was asked, sometimes saved them just the same. Jane kissed Father and thanked him while they were all laughing. "It's a very valuable present," she said. "I'll keep it carefully."

"Perhaps after you've looked at it enough," said Father, "you'll let me keep it for you."

And now for the handsome box! Jane's heart lifted. But she hesitated just a minute. Where was Ted's present? He could not be giving her anything that looked like that. Ted was willing to spend his money all right, but not on her. Jane was again entangled in the puzzle of Ted's curious ways. Perhaps he had, this once, she thought. Perhaps like his crazy courage, his generosity was crazy too, and he had spent it all on her.

She brought the box squarely in front of her and undid its splendid bow. She folded the ribbon neatly, taking good care of it. If Ted could be generous, so could she. Taking off the beautiful cover, she found tissue paper, new crushed tissue paper that never came out of Nurse's rag-bag but could only have come from some good store. There was a heap of it, so

much it made a great tumbled mound beside her plate. She took more out, and there was more, and still more. She stopped and looked at Ted sideways. There might be nothing! She had better be ready for that. But she was not ready. She found a white card, a regular card, like those florists use, which said, "Many Happy Returns. I got this just for you. Ted." Under it was something round like Hubert's bird's nest. It was done up in sheaths of paper. Jane unwound and unwound. Everyone else was watching eagerly. Finally a bright yellow sphere was in her hand; it tumbled out bare and in plain sight. She held it, shocked, for one second and then dropped it, as if burned, back into the handsome box.

Her feeling was that someone had shot her through the stomach and she must sit and die as quietly as she could for sheer protection's sake. The boys were keeping their heads down and their mouths tight closed across the table, dying themselves of laughter. But Edie was not going to allow any quiet dying while she was still alive.

"What *is* it, Jane? You didn't show us what it was."

"A lemon," said Jane, though her mouth was almost too stiff to talk. "Te-o-tadpole has given me a lemon. See?" She took it out of the box and held it up by both ends. She wished she were a bull at a bullfight and could drop down dead.

How to get through her birthday dinner with Father on one side, his ancient present in front, and the lemon at her feet was the thing Jane's muscles had to think about hard. Potato soup—hot and flavored with onion—seemed to run into the hole where she had been shot and dam it up a little. Steak went down harder, but once down there, made a sort of padding. Rice, peas, and little red beets seemed like wedges going in to stop the bleeding. And then came ice cream—a cold, damp, lovely bandage. Jane could look up now and put on an interested face while Father told about the ancient stone.

First she looked across the table at Ted.

"You got me just the way you said," she admitted, and then sent down some more ice cream.

Ted yawned. "For heaven's sake," he said uncomfortably.

Finally Father put his napkin on the table. "Come on, kids, have you finished? Jane, you? Edith, go up to bed in a hurry. Jane, clear up your mess and come along. Give me the stone and you shall have it again when you're old enough. In the meantime you can think of it as safe and sound. Quite a silent old girl you are tonight on your birthday night. Not sick I hope, or eaten too much?"

"Oh *no*," said Jane.

Hubert was so pleased with his cleverness about Jane's present that he went out of the dining room backward with his hands in his pockets, making bigger and better suggestions all the way.

"I know what she needs. A little shaking up. I tell you, let's go up to the Main Dairy and play hide-and-seek with the kids up there. Let's walk the whole way up there on the walls."

It was surprising how much all this activity could do for a wound. Stuffed with food and limbered up by running, it was still sore, but the pain was going. Then the hide-and-seek at the Main Dairy was like a drink that cured you of everything. Lying on the earth behind a vine, crouching in last year's leaves under the veranda, getting the breath of cows when you hid in the cow pen, racing like a streak of light to goal. Coming down the hill through the dark blue early night on the way home, Jane and Hubert bumped each other's shoulders and even fell carelessly into Ted as they skittered and fooled along the road.

It was the memory of this dark blueness of the night that made Jane look at it again as soon as she got to her room. The air that came to the window in little gusts against her face smelled of lilies and roses. Kneeling down with her arms on the sill, she watched the fireflies beginning in the pool of darkness—shooting like sparks from shrubs and hedges. They made her think that what she suddenly saw was a gigantic firefly that had somehow pitched itself into the sky and was coming down again. And then she realized it was not.

A star—big, bright, and yellow—had got loose and was falling slowly, leaving a trail of light behind it, right before her eyes, into the garden. It was so clear, so near, and so big, her whole body waited to hear the hiss as it went out against the earth. But although it fell just across the backyard behind the wall, the night did not make an extra sound. The tree toads sang, the trees moved, a dog barked, nothing paid attention to the wonder—except herself. Excitedly she felt that she must go at once and search for it. A star had fallen almost at her feet; she was the only one to see it, or know where it was. Of course she must go and look for it. But she sat bound and held by the tremendousness of what had happened. Slowly the blaze of light around her faded and she felt the night come back.

She remembered gradually what she had heard about falling stars. It was probably a million miles away—more. She did not believe it, she would never believe it. That, she thought, was my birthday star. But she knew at least that it would be no use looking for it in the garden. Just the same, feeling as if she had been there and had found it, she was willing to go to bed. She lay a long time without going to sleep. She was tired—tireder than she could ever remember—but who would care about that, or who would care about *anything*, if they had caught a falling star?

Pecos Bill

by Leigh Peck

A tall tale about the early days of a Texas hero.

Pecos Bill lived in Texas when he was little. One day his mother heard that a new neighbor had moved in only fifty miles away. She decided, "This part of Texas is getting too crowded. We must move out where we will have more room."

So Pecos Bill's father hitched the old spotted cow and the old red mule to the covered wagon. The father and mother put their eighteen children into the wagon, and they started over the prairie. Their son Bill was four years old then. He sat in the very end of the wagon, with his feet hanging out.

When they were driving through the low waters of the Pecos River, one wheel of the wagon hit a rock, and the jolt threw Bill right out of the wagon and onto the sand of the river. No one saw him fall or heard him call, "Wait for me!" After Bill saw that the wagon was going on without him, he got up and ran after it. But his short little legs could not go so fast as the wagon. Soon it was gone, and Bill was left all alone. There were still seventeen children in the wagon, and no one noticed that little Bill was gone until his mother counted the children at dinnertime.

"Where is Bill?" she asked.

No one had seen him since they had crossed the river. So the family hurried back to the river and hunted for little Bill. They looked and looked, but they could not find him. Because they had lost him at the Pecos River, they always spoke of him after that as their little lost Pecos Bill.

Little Pecos Bill was not lost for long. His father and mother never did find him, but he was found by an old grandfather coyote named Grampy. Grampy showed little Pecos Bill berries to eat, dug up roots for him, and found mesquite beans for him, too. At night Grampy led Pecos Bill to his cave in the mountain, where he could sleep safe and warm. Grampy showed his man-child to each of the other hunting animals and asked them not to hurt little Pecos Bill.

The bear grunted, "*W-f-f-f!* I will not hurt your man-child. I will show him where to find wild honey in the bee trees."

The wolf yelped, "I will not hurt your man-child. Let him come play with my cubs."

But the rattlesnake shook his rattles, "*Th-r-r-r!*" and hissed, "*S-s-s-s!* Keep him out of my way! I bite anybody that crosses my path, but I give fair warning first. *Th-r-r-r! S-s-s-s!*"

The mountain lion yowled, "Get your child out of my way before I eat him up! A nice fat man-child is what I like to eat best of all!"

But all the other animals except the rattlesnake and the mountain lion promised to be good to little Pecos Bill. He learned to talk to all the animals and birds in their own languages.

But the coyotes liked Pecos Bill best of all. They taught him how to hunt. When he grew older, he was able to run so fast that he could catch the long-eared jackrabbit and the long-tailed roadrunner. Finally he grew big enough to catch the deer, and even the antelope, which runs fastest of any animal. He grew strong enough to pull down a buffalo for his brother coyotes. He climbed the mountaintops and jumped about from crag to crag to catch the mountain sheep.

When one of the coyotes got a cactus thorn in his foot or a porcupine quill in his nose, Pecos Bill pulled it out. The coyotes were all very proud of their brother and very fond of him. At night he went out on the prairie with the coyotes and howled at the moon. He thought he was a coyote.

In all the years while Pecos Bill was living with the coyotes, he had never seen a human being. Then one day Bill's brother Chuck came riding along on his cow pony and found Bill. Bill was a tall young man now, his skin was a dark brown color, and his black hair hung long and tangled. But Chuck knew him at once, and cried, "Why, you are my long-lost brother, Pecos Bill!"

Bill replied, "I'm not your brother! I am the brother of the coyotes. Why, I even have fleas!"

But Chuck replied, "That doesn't prove you are a coyote. Why, all cowboys have a few fleas!"

"But I howl at the moon at night," Bill insisted, and he sang a little song:

"I'm wild and woolly and full of fleas,
Never been curried below the knees,
And this is my night to howl—
Yippe-e-e-e!"

Chuck repeated, "That doesn't prove a thing. All cowboys howl sometimes!" Then he added, "Look in the spring with me here, and see yourself and me in the water. You are no brother of the coyotes—you are my brother, for you look like me."

Bill looked in the spring and saw Chuck and himself in the water. He agreed. "We do look alike. Perhaps I am your brother!"

Chuck said, "Brother, you must put on some clothes and come with me to the ranch where I work and be a cowboy, too. But I don't have any extra clothes with me. I don't know what we can do!"

Pecos Bill laughed. "If anything has to

be done, I can do it! Just a minute and I'll have some clothes!"

He looked around until he found a big old steer with horns measuring six feet from tip to tip. He grabbed it by the tail, yelled loudly, and scared it so badly that it jumped right out of its skin! (That didn't hurt the old steer; it wanted to grow a new hide anyhow.) From the hide Pecos Bill made himself a leather jacket, using a yucca thorn for a needle. He made some boots, too.

Then he made himself a pair of leather pants, the kind that are now called chaps. Other cowboys wear them now, to keep from getting scratched when riding through thorny bushes. They learned that from Pecos Bill.

When Bill had put on his clothes, Chuck told him, "Get up behind me on my cow pony, and he will carry both of us to the ranch."

But Pecos Bill laughed. "Ride your pony, and I'll go afoot, and I'll beat you to the ranch."

Sure enough, Bill galloped along easily, faster than Chuck's cow pony could run.

Chuck argued, though, "You really must not go up to the ranch on foot. Nobody walks in the ranch country. We must find you some old pony to ride, and a whip to urge him along with."

Just then Pecos Bill nearly stepped on the rattlesnake that lay in the trail. It was fifteen feet long and had thirty rattles on the end of its tail.

"Get out of my way," hissed Pecos in snake language.

"I won't," the snake hissed back. "I told Grampy long ago to teach you to stay out of my way."

The snake spit poison at Pecos Bill, hitting him right between the eyes. Bill said, "I'll give you three chances at me before I even begin to fight."

The three shots of poison didn't even blister Pecos Bill's skin. Next, Bill spit back at the snake, right on the top of the snake's head, and the snake fell over, unable to move for a moment.

Bill jumped on the snake and stamped it before it had time to bite him. He caught the snake up by the throat and asked, "Had enough yet?"

The snake cried, "I give up!" Pecos Bill wrapped it around his arm and galloped on ahead of Chuck's pony.

Soon they met the mountain lion. He was the largest mountain lion in all the world, twice as large as Chuck's cow pony. The mountain lion growled, "I said I would eat you up if ever you got in my way, and now I will!"

He jumped at Pecos Bill, but Bill dodged and pulled out a handful of the mountain lion's fur as he went by. The fight lasted for two hours. Every time the mountain lion tried to jump on Pecos Bill, Bill pulled out some more of his hair. The sky was so full of the mountain lion's hair that it was almost as dark as night.

Finally the lion lost all of his hair except just a little on the tips of his ears and under his chin. Then he begged, "Please, Pecos Bill, don't hurt me anymore."

"Very well," agreed Pecos Bill, "but you must let me ride you for a cow pony."

So Pecos Bill jumped on the mountain lion's back, and using the rattlesnake for a whip, rode on to the ranch with Chuck.

Just at sundown, Pecos Bill rode up to the cowboys' camp on the mountain lion, twice as big as a cow pony, and he was still using the rattlesnake fifteen feet long for a whip. The cowboys around the campfire were too surprised to say a word.

Chuck announced proudly, "Boys, this is my brother Pecos Bill."

Pecos Bill asked, "Who is the boss here?"

A big man seven feet tall and wearing three guns stepped forward. "I was," he said, "but you be now, Pecos Bill. Anybody that can ride a mountain lion and use a rattlesnake for a whip is boss here as long as he wants to be."

Pecos Bill soon tired of riding the mountain lion. It did not make a very good cow pony, because all the cattle were afraid of it. So Pecos Bill decided to get a real cow pony, and he asked the cowboys, "What's the very best horse in these parts?"

They answered, "The best horse in all the world is running loose in these very hills. He runs fast as the lightning, so we call him Lightning. Others call him the Pacing White Mustang, and some even say that his real name is Pegasus. We have all tried to catch him, but no one

has ever got close enough to him to put a rope on him or even to see him clearly. We have chased him for days, riding our very best ponies and changing horses every two hours, but he outran all our best ponies put together."

But Pecos Bill told them, "I'll not ride a cow pony when I chase this horse. I can run faster than any of your ponies can."

So Pecos Bill threw his saddle and bridle over his shoulder and set out on foot to look for the famous wild white horse. When he got close enough to take a good look at Lightning, he saw that only the horse's mane and tail were a pure white. The beautiful animal was really a light cream or pale gold color—the color of lightning itself.

Pecos Bill chased Lightning five days and four nights, all the way from Mexico across Texas and New Mexico and Arizona and Utah and Colorado and Wyoming and Montana, clear up to Canada, and then down to Mexico again. He had to throw away his saddle and bridle as they leaped across cactus-covered plains, down steep cliffs, and across canyons.

Finally Lightning got tired of running from Pecos Bill and stopped and snorted, "Very well, I'll let you try to ride me if you think you can! Say your prayers and jump on!"

Pecos Bill smiled. "I say my prayers every night and every morning." And he jumped on Lightning's back, gripping the horse's ribs with his knees and clutching the mane with his hands.

First, Lightning tried to run out from under Pecos Bill. He ran ten miles in twenty seconds! Next, he jumped a mile forward and two miles backward. Then he jumped so high in the air that Pecos Bill's head was up among the stars. Next, Lightning tried to push Pecos Bill off his back by running through clumps of mesquite trees. The thorns tore poor Bill's face and left his skin torn and bleeding.

When that failed, too, Lightning reared up on his hind legs and threw himself over backward. But Pecos Bill jumped off quickly, and before Lightning could get on his feet again, Bill sat down on his shoulders and held him firmly on the ground.

"Lightning," Pecos Bill explained, "you are the best horse in all the world, and I am the best cowboy in all the world. If you'll let me ride you, we will become famous together, and cowboys everywhere forever and forever will praise the deeds of Pecos Bill and Lightning." Then Pecos Bill turned Lightning loose and said to him, "You may decide. You are free to go or to stay with me."

The beautiful horse put his nose in Pecos Bill's hand and said, "I want to stay with you and be your cow pony—the greatest cow pony in all the world."

Pecos Bill and Lightning went back and found the saddle and bridle where Bill had thrown them. Lightning let Pecos Bill put the saddle on him, but he didn't want to take the bit of the bridle into his mouth. So Pecos Bill just put a halter on him and guided him by pressure of the knees and by pulling on the reins of the halter.

Lightning would not let anybody but Pecos Bill ride him. Three-Gun Gibbs tried once, while Bill was not looking, but Lightning threw him so hard that he cracked the ground open where he fell. After that, the cowboys used to call Lightning Widow-maker.

The Bear in the Pear Tree

by Alice Geer Kelsey

Nasr-ed-Din knew one story that was better left untold.
A Turkish tale.

The ring of Nasr-ed-Din's axe sounded through the woods of the lonely mountainside. There was silence as the hodja—or teacher—rested. It was very still on that mountainside—no noise but the twitter and call of birds, the hum and chirp of insects, and the rustle and whir of the leaves of the forest.

Suddenly the hodja jumped to his feet. What was that tramping through the twigs on the forest floor? Crackle—crunch—crackle. Those were not the footsteps of a squirrel, a rabbit, or a fox. Nasr-ed-Din stood frozen to attention, his eyes fixed on the place from which the sound came, crunch—crackle—crunch, steadily nearer and nearer, steadily louder and louder. A glimpse of moving black fur! Four stiff legs swinging awkwardly toward him! A shiny black nose between two sharp eyes! The biggest bear the hodja had seen in all his wood-chopping days!

For once Nasr-ed-Din did not stop to argue. He ran for the nearest tree, a wild pear tree, and scrambled up it more nimbly than he had moved since he was a boy.

Crackle—crunch—crackle. Straight for the pear tree, looking neither to right nor to left, plodded the enormous black bear. The nearer it came, the bigger it seemed. Crunch—crackle—crunch. It was directly under the very tree where the hodja was hiding. The bear yawned. It stretched. It yawned again. It lay down on the ground under the pear tree, gave a drowsy grunt, and closed its eyes.

You don't fool me that way! thought the hodja. You pretend to sleep, but you are just waiting to pounce on me. Nasr-ed-Din still clung to the branch, his eyes fixed wildly on the big bear. He expected it any minute to jump at him. He wanted to climb higher in the tree but was afraid of the telltale sounds he might make.

He saw the bear's muscles tighten. He thought of all the mistakes of his life—of all the times he had been cross to his wife, of all the times he had played tricks on people. He looked down at his home valley, perhaps for the last time. Then the bear shivered. It relaxed. Its breathing lengthened into a loud snore.

"You are asleep!" whispered the hodja, not quite sure that he dared believe what he saw. He wriggled about, trying to find a comfortable place on his high perch. A magpie scolded to find such a clumsy stranger in her favorite tree. An inquisitive bee buzzed about the hodja. The bear below the tree snored cozily. The hodja squirmed from one position to another, making little showers of leaves and twigs fall around the heavily sleeping bear.

From far down in the valley floated dimly the musical chant of muezzins in many minarets, singing forth the call to prayer, "*Allah eekbar, Allah eekbar.*"

That means that it is two hours till sunset, thought the hodja, wondering how long this could last.

Lower and lower marched the sun. Stiffer and stiffer grew the hodja's poor cramped body. The sun touched the horizon and the melodious call to prayer, "*Allah eekbar, Allah eekbar,*" wafted up from the valley.

The sun was down and the moon shining so brightly that the hodja could peer through his leafy screen and see the huge black bulk below him rise and fall regularly as the big bear snored. Once more the lilting sweetness of the call to prayer floated up from the valley.

"That means two hours after sunset!" groaned the hodja as he looked pleadingly toward Mecca, the sacred city in the east.

At last there was a stirring in the black mass below him. The big bear stretched, rose stiffly to its feet, and sniffed hungrily. Then, to the hodja's horror, it stuck its great claws into the very pear tree where the hodja was clinging. Up the tree it came, while the poor hodja trembled so that he could scarcely hang on to the branches. Sniff went the great nose, until the bear found just what it wanted—a juicy wild pear. Eating and climbing, eating and climbing, up the tree came the bear. Shivering and shaking, shivering and shaking, up the tree went the hodja. Finally the hodja was on the highest branch that could possibly hold his weight. Oh, if only the bear would be content to climb no higher! Smack, smack went the bear's great lips until every wild pear within reach was gone. Then up it came, so close that the hodja could feel its hot breath. Out went one big paw, scooping up a pear, and swinging around so that it almost touched the hodja's mouth. Was it trying to share the pears?

"Oh, no, thank you!" screamed the hodja, trying to be polite even at such a time. "I do not care for pears. I never eat them. No, never, never, never!"

Now, the bear was really a gentle and shy old fellow, not at all prepared to have sudden screams pop out at it from behind a leafy branch. With a terrified howl, the bear lost its balance and toppled crashing through the branches. There was a thud as it hit the ground. Then there was silence—welcome silence.

The hodja spent the rest of the night edging slowly down the tree, his eyes warily on the black heap that lay motionless in a patch of moonlight below him. After each move, the hodja would wait to be sure that the bear still lay lifeless. By morning the hodja had reached the lowest branch of the wild pear tree. As the first rays of daylight shone through the woods, even the cautious hodja was certain that the bear would never frighten anyone again. Never again would it climb trees to eat wild pears in the moonlight.

Nasr-ed-Din jumped clumsily from the lowest branch, a million needles pricking his numb arms and legs. He started limping toward home and breakfast, thinking what a story he would have to tell. However, the more he pictured himself telling of his harrowing night, the more he felt there would not be much glory in the telling for him. Something was wrong with a story that showed him up to be so shaky a hero.

Suddenly his old grin burst over his tired face. He ran back to the pear tree, whipped out his knife, and skinned the big bear. With the thick black fur slung over his shoulders, he strode singing down the mountainside and across the plain toward Ak Shehir. He did not enter the city by the small gate nearest his home, but walked around the city wall to enter by the main gate near the marketplace. He did not take the shortest path through the market to his house, but walked through one busy street after another, until all Ak Shehir knew—or thought it knew—that Nasr-ed-Din was a mighty hunter.

He did not need to say a word about his experiences of the night. Other people were talking for him, talking about the brave and wonderful hodja who had killed the huge and ferocious black bear, single-handed.

Donkey, Mind Your Mother!

by Alice Geer Kelsey

Was he an excellent donkey, or a bad, bad boy? Or both? A tale of ancient Persia.

"Hee-haw! Hee-haw!" sounded on every side of the mullah as he stood in the donkey bazaar of a long-ago Persian city. The donkey dealers crowded about him, each one trying to outshout the others. Every man had a different way of saying, "In all the world there is no better donkey than the one I am selling. And what a bargain!"

The mullah stroked his gray beard and thought about the donkeys. His own small white donkey still served him well, but she was growing old. A young donkey could do some of her work now and be ready to take her place when she grew too old to work.

The mullah looked most important standing there, among the braying donkeys, in the turban and long dark coat that marked him for priest, teacher, and judge of his village. The men in the donkey bazaar were eager to sell to him. Finally a white donkey pleased him. It had such a wise way of waggling its long, velvety ears, even though it was very young. Its bray told such a long, long story. The beast was pretty—white with a zigzag gray saddle mark on its back.

The mullah bargained with the trader for a jolly half hour. All the good points of the donkey were made bigger and better as the dealer talked. All the bad points were made bigger and worse as the mullah talked. Down a dinar at a time went the price the dealer demanded. Up a dinar at a time went the price the mullah offered. At last the price met halfway. The seller, who was well pleased, beat his chest and vowed he had been robbed. The mullah, who was delighted with his bargain, wrung his hands and groaned that *he* had been robbed. But both men were happy as the mullah passed over the money and took the rope that was tied around the donkey's neck.

Throwing one leg over the back of his old donkey and slipping his arm through a loop of the new donkey's rope, the mullah started off on the long ride to his own village. There was nothing new for him to see in the hot and treeless countryside—the same waving wheat fields, the same sheep and goats in their stubbly pasture, the same distant mountains with their traces of last winter's snow. The day was hot and growing hotter. The mullah knew he could trust his faithful old donkey to jog home unguided toward her supper of straw. He tested the knots of the rope about the new donkey's neck. Then he did not even try to keep awake.

As he jounced along, fast asleep, he was joined by two rascals, an old man named Massoud and a boy named Suleiman. Both were strangers to the mullah. They were riding their donkeys toward the city, looking for some mischief to do. They noticed how the mullah's head bobbed in his sleep. They turned their donkeys' heads away from the city.

"That's a fine donkey the old mullah is leading," whispered Massoud.

"It would bring a good price in the bazaar," young Suleiman whispered back.

"The mullah is dozing," said Massoud. "He would not notice if you and the young donkey changed places. You could slip your head through the rope and keep it taut. You could walk behind that old donkey, going *clip-clip* just like the young donkey. I could take the young donkey to the bazaar to sell."

"How about *you* and the donkey changing places," suggested the boy.

"Remember my lame foot!" Massoud was glad to think of such a good excuse. "An old man like me should not try to walk from here to the next village."

After a bit more of argument, Suleiman slipped the rope off the donkey's neck and tied it with a rope old Massoud carried. Then the boy stuck his own head through the rope held by the sleeping mullah. Massoud rode his own donkey to the bazaar, leading Suleiman's gray donkey and the mullah's young donkey with its zigzag gray saddle mark on its white coat. And Suleiman trudged along the road, the donkey's rope around his neck, breathing the chalky white dust stirred up by the small hoofs of the mullah's old donkey.

Once in a while the mullah's neck would stiffen as he wakened for a minute. He would feel the rope taut around his arm. He would hear steady footsteps behind him, *clip-clip, clip-clip*. All was well. Too sleepy to turn his head, the mullah would doze off again.

It was when his old donkey stopped at his own street gate that the mullah woke up. His wife lifted the latch in answer to his call. He rode inside with the proud air of a man who knows he has made a good bargain.

"See the fine donkey I bought in the

bazaar in Isfahan," he said to his wife.

"What donkey?" she asked, and stared at Suleiman.

Seeing her surprise, the mullah turned. For the first time he saw there was a boy where his new donkey had been. Suleiman was standing behind the old donkey, the rope still around his neck. He was wondering whether it would be a good idea to try to bray.

"Who are you?" shouted the mullah. "And where is the fine young donkey I bought?"

"I am that donkey." Suleiman could think quickly when necessary, and he had a story to tell. "I was a boy once before. I was changed into a donkey because I was always disobeying my mother. Belonging to such a good master as you, I was changed back to a boy again. Thank you, good mullah, for doing this wonderful thing for me."

The mullah stroked his beard. He did not know whether to be glad for the boy's good luck or sorry at the loss of the fine young donkey. "I paid many good dinars for you," he said at last, "but you are of no use to me. You may go free—on one condition."

"I will do anything for my freedom," promised Suleiman.

"You must promise to mind your mother. Go back to her as quickly as you can, and do whatever she tells you." The mullah pointed his finger at Suleiman in his best teacher-judge manner. "Always obey your mother. Then you will keep out of trouble."

"I promise," vowed Suleiman solemnly. Then the mullah slipped the rope from the boy's neck.

"Go," said the mullah, "and may Allah bless you."

The next day the mullah had to go back to the bazaar to buy a new donkey to take the place of the one that had turned into a boy. Once again he stood in the donkey bazaar, stroking his gray beard and comparing donkeys. There were old donkeys and young donkeys, gray donkeys, black donkeys, white donkeys.

Suddenly the mullah saw one that gave him quite a start. It waggled its long, velvety ears wisely in his direction. It brayed as though it had an especially long and interesting story to tell. And it was white with a zigzag gray saddle mark. It was the very donkey that he had bought yesterday, the donkey that had turned back into a boy. Now it was a donkey again.

In a whirl of flowing sleeves and streaming coat, the mullah strode over to the donkey. He shook his finger at the little animal in his best teacher-judge manner.

"You bad boy!" he scolded. "You promised me that you would mind your mother! You disobeyed her again! Now see what has happened to you! You bad, bad boy!"

But the white donkey with the zigzag gray saddle mark only waggled its ears wisely and brayed.

Handy Sandy

by Jed F. Shaw

Sandy was still a boy. But he solved a problem that baffled the U.S. Army.

It was a long, cold ride from the MacLeod farm to Burnsville. Even with hot bricks for their feet and three buffalo robes, Mr. MacLeod and the two boys, Sandy and Angie, had to huddle close together on the wagon seat, and still they were cold. When they finally reached Burnsville, the three stamped their feet on the ground to get their blood circulating again. Mr. MacLeod went straight to the bank, where he hoped to borrow money for fodder for the stock. This left Sandy and Angie on their own.

It was Angie's eleventh birthday, and the trip to town was really his birthday present. It was a small town, but to Angie it was an exciting place, and his first move was toward the show window of the big store. He stuck his nose against the frost-covered glass. Soon his warm breath had melted a hole in the frost and he could peep through to the wonders beyond. Right before his eyes was a Barlow knife with five blades, such as he had been dreaming of for weeks.

"Gosh all fishhooks, Sandy. Ain't it a beauty!"

"What's a beauty?" asked Sandy. He pushed Angie away from the hole and peeped in. "Oh! The knife." Sandy paused. "Wish Father could buy it for your birthday, Angie, but you know he can't." The two boys turned away from the window.

Ever since they had stepped from the wagon, Sandy had had eyes for only one thing. Down at the other end of Main Street was a group of buildings. Black, sooty soft-coal smoke poured from many chimneys. These buildings were the main industry of Burnsville, the iron foundry.

Sandy took Angie's hand and, almost as though drawn by a magnet, he walked toward the foundry. In those days foundries were not guarded as they are now.

So when Sandy and Angie walked in the door of the big molding loft, no one paid them any attention.

Sandy was his father's son. Mr. MacLeod had been an engineer before he had become a farmer; it was only natural that Sandy took to mechanics as a duck takes to water. To him the trip through the iron foundry was pure happiness. To Angie it was just a nice warm place. But out in a storage yard Sandy found something he couldn't figure out. There, piled in mound after mound, were round iron shells with small holes in them.

"Why, these are cannonballs!" exclaimed Sandy.

"What's cannonballs?" asked Angie.

"All these shells you see. There must be thousands of them, Angie. They must have been here a long time. Look how dirty they are."

"Come on in, Sandy. It's cold out here." Angie shivered. He didn't care what the shells were.

It suddenly occurred to Sandy that his father might be through at the bank. "Come on, Angie. We'd better get back to the wagon. Father might be looking for us." After considerable search, Sandy reached a hall that promised a way out, but the boys stopped at the sound of loud voices.

"You haven't been of much help, Captain Bragg!" said one of the men, whom Sandy recognized as Mr. Holmes, the owner of the foundry. It was he who had bought from a United States arsenal the five thousand shells that Sandy had seen. They were a type discarded by the army soon after the Civil War.

"I have told you that the only way I can think of to break them, Mr. Holmes, is to explode them," answered Captain Bragg. The captain was an army officer who had come, at Mr. Holmes's request, to help solve the problem of melting down the iron shells.

"We did explode them. But they blew pieces all over the place!" Mr. Holmes was groaning now.

Sandy and Angie had gradually drawn nearer as this talk was going on. Sandy was interested.

"And you can't use them until they are broken?" continued Captain Bragg.

"Too dangerous. There is still powder left in some of them," answered Mr. Holmes.

"And you had no luck in breaking them?"

"No, Captain, no luck," Mr. Holmes said bitterly. "A five-hundred-pound skull cracker wouldn't break them." Mr. Holmes went on. "There they lie, nearly five thousand shells; a lot of money tied up in them until they are used."

"I'm sorry, Mr. Holmes, but I don't see what I, or the government, can do about it—"

Sandy had forgotten all about having to get back to the wagon. *He had an idea!* He stepped to the door of the room. "Mr. Holmes," he piped up, "how much will you give me if I can break 'em? How much?"

"What? Who the dickens are you? How did you get in here?" Mr. Holmes's eyes were big with astonishment.

"I'll bet I can break those shells. How much will you pay?" Sandy was afire with his idea.

"Run along, boy. Don't bother me now. I'm busy," said Mr. Holmes shortly.

But Sandy was not to be put off. "If I can't break 'em, it won't cost you anything to let me try. How much will you pay a shell?"

Angie was scared. He kept pulling at

Sandy's coat, but his brother pushed his hand away. Sandy was in earnest.

Mr. Holmes caught a wink from Captain Bragg. He searched through his pockets and pulled out a nickel.

"I'll pay you a nickel apiece, son, for all you can break." Mr. Holmes grinned. "And here's a down payment on the first shell you break. Now get busy, and don't you dare come back until you bring me a sample. Get along with you, now."

Mr. Holmes and Captain Bragg were chuckling.

Sandy wasn't at all flustered. "Can I have a shell to work on, Mr. Holmes?" he asked.

"A shell? Oh! Sure. Take as many as you need. As many as you can carry." And again the two men chuckled.

"I'll be back, Mr. Holmes. It's a bargain!" Sandy said. He took Angie by the hand and they were off.

A half hour later Mr. Holmes walked over to the office window. What he saw caused him to break into a broad grin. "Come here, Captain Bragg. I want to show you something."

The captain joined Mr. Holmes. At a shell heap they saw two boys with a grain sack. The small figures were slowly pulling the sack over the snow and away from the foundry. The men looked at each other and laughed. Then a foreman came into the office and joined them at the window.

"Who are those kids?" asked Mr. Holmes.

"Looks like the MacLeod kids. They farm out north about fifteen miles. Nice kids. Sandy, the oldest, is smart as a whip."

Mr. Holmes told him about Sandy and his bargain. The foreman didn't laugh. "Maybe he can do it. The Scotch are a tough race to beat, once they get an idea," answered the foreman.

Mr. Holmes was serious now. "I wish you were right. More power to the boy if he can do it. I would double the price I offered him if he could."

That evening the MacLeod family were gathered around the kitchen stove. Sandy was busy poring over one of his father's books.

The idea he'd had at the foundry was still just an idea. While the captain and Mr. Holmes had been talking, two things had flashed into Sandy's quick mind. One was a book chapter heading. It read, "The forces of nature, properly directed, can accomplish almost any task man may set them to."

The second was another chapter in the same book. It was headed, "The forces of expansion and contraction. Their application and practical uses."

"What are you reading about, Sandy?" asked Mr. MacLeod.

"Water, Father. It's the most wonderful stuff!"

"It's bonnie, all right!" answered his father.

Sandy continued studying the book.

"Hurrah!" shouted Sandy. "Here's what I have been looking for!" He read, " 'Freezing water expands its physical body by one eleventh. If you put eleven pints of water in a twelve-pint measure, the measure will be full when the water is frozen.' "

"That's right, Sandy." Mr. MacLeod nodded.

"And, Father," continued Sandy, "it says, 'This expansion of freezing water is of great force.' "

"That's right, it is," said Mr. MacLeod.

"Then if you put water in something,

and it freezes, that will break it?" asked Sandy.

"Yes," answered his father, "freezing will break it. That is, if the water can't get out any other way. Then it will break its way out. I don't know of anything it won't break."

"That's what I figured, Father! And that's the reason I told Mr. Holmes I could do it!"

"You could do what, Sandy?" asked Mr. MacLeod.

Sandy told his father of his bargain with Mr. Holmes to break the shells. Mr. MacLeod thought this over.

"That's a large order, Sandy," he said. "But I've an idea it might work. Anyway, try it out, and luck to you, lad."

The next day Sandy, with Angie's help, started on his experiment. Sandy was going to try hard for that money—two hundred and fifty dollars.

First they hunted all over the place for a metal plug for the fuse hole. It was cold hunting. Finally they found an old harrow tooth, which, after a little grinding, fitted snugly.

Then Angie and Sandy pulled the forty-four-pound shell into the toolshed. A few blows would set the plug hard. Now to fill the shell, plug it, and let it freeze. Suddenly Sandy heard water dripping. He looked out the shed door and up at the roof. A trickle of water spattered on his nose.

"Angie!" cried Sandy. "The snow is melting. The water in the shell can't freeze, and it won't break!"

For three days it held warm; for three days Sandy fretted.

"It won't do any good, Sandy, to fever yourself. Weather is just something you have to wait on." Mr. MacLeod cocked his eye up at the sky. "It will be cold enough—and soon now," he told his son.

On the fourth day it started to turn cold.

Then Angie had an idea. " 'Tain't hardly cold enough to freeze. Why don't we give her a head start? Let's cover the shell with snow. That'll get it cold and it won't take so long to freeze."

"S-a-y! Angie," replied Sandy, "you're smart." Sandy filled the shell with water, drove the plug in, covered it with snow, and all was ready for the freezing.

That night it was fairly cold. When Sandy got up in the morning, he dashed out to the shell. Angie was right at his heels. The two hacked away at the snow pile. There was an ice crust about three inches thick, but below the crust the snow was soft.

Just then Mr. MacLeod passed on his way to the barn. "What are you two doing?" he asked.

"It's the shell. We piled snow on it so it would freeze faster," answered Sandy. He dug down and uncovered the shell.

"Father!" cried Sandy. "It isn't broken!" And it wasn't. It lay there as sound as a nut. Sandy was near to tears.

"Wait a minute, boys!" Mr. MacLeod stooped down and examined the snow pile. Then he grinned. He saw the three-inch crust and the soft snow beneath.

"Sandy and Angie," he said, "you two have outsmarted yourselves. When you piled that snow on the shell, you might as well have covered it with a blanket. Because that's what you really did. See that crust? That is how deep your snow pile froze last night. Below the crust the snow is soft. It didn't freeze there. Your shell was buried deep, so it couldn't freeze."

The shine came back into Sandy's eyes. "Then I'm not licked yet, am I, Father?"

"No, Sandy, you're not licked. Leave the shell as it is. It will be cold tonight. Tomorrow will tell the tale, son."

Early the next morning Angie was routed out of his warm bed by Sandy. "Come on, Angie, you lazybones. Get up!"

Angie crawled out, rubbing his eyes with his fists. "W-h-a-z-e the matter?" he mumbled, half asleep.

"Get dressed, you dummy! We're going out to see if the shell is broken!" roared Sandy.

When they got to the kitchen, they found their mother standing at the window trying to look out.

"What's the matter, Mother?" asked Sandy.

"It's a terrible blizzard, Sandy! You never saw the like."

Sandy started for the door. "But, Mother, I've got to go out. I must see my shell."

"You'll not move an inch out of this house today, young man. Nor Angie, either. Nor your father, when he gets back."

For two days the blizzard held, and Sandy writhed. On the third morning the storm was over.

"Hurrah!" shouted Sandy. "The sun is out again. Come on, Angie. We'll dig the shell out. Oh! I know it's broken. It must be broken!"

Bundled to their ears, they were out in the yard punching with sticks in the snow that lay three feet deep. They worked in a circle. Then Sandy shouted, "I've got it, Angie!" and he burrowed down into the snow like a badger going into his hole. When Sandy came to light again, he was struggling to lift a ragged half of a forty-four-pound shell.

The shell was broken!

Angie whooped, and tumbled about like a small puppy. "Now I can have my knife! Remember, Sandy, you promised!"

Sandy struggled to his feet. Hugging the jagged piece of iron, he ran to the barn as fast as he could. As he ran he called, "Father! Father! Father!"

At the barn door, Sandy stumbled and skidded to a stop at the feet of an astonished Mr. MacLeod.

"What the dickens—" exclaimed Mr. MacLeod. Sandy put the broken shell into his father's outstretched hands.

"It worked, Father, it worked! It's broken! Two hundred and fifty dollars, Father. You can pay the bank."

"By jingo! Lad, you've really done it!" Mr. MacLeod was turning the piece of shell over and over.

Sandy went on. "Angie can have his knife! Mother can have a new dress! And you, Father, you are going to have a warm new coat!"

"Wait a minute, Sandy. What are *you* going to get out of it?" asked Mr. MacLeod quietly.

"I'm going to be very busy," he said importantly. "I'll have to show them just how to do it at the iron foundry. Can we go to town tomorrow, Father?"

"Tomorrow, Sandy, we will go to town. Patience, boy!"

The next morning Mr. Holmes was sitting at his desk. When someone knocked, he didn't even look up. "Come in!" he called. When he did look up, a man and a boy were standing before him. The boy laid on his desk a rusty, jagged piece of iron. The man laid another piece beside the first.

"There you are, Mr. Holmes!" said Sandy.

Mr. Holmes looked first at Sandy and then at Mr. MacLeod. Then he took the two pieces of iron and fitted them together. They fitted perfectly.

Mr. Holmes finally found his voice. "Well, I'll be melted, molded, and forged! You've done it!" Mr. Holmes patted the shell pieces. "But how, son, how?"

"Water and—" started Sandy.

"Water? Water and what?" asked Mr. Holmes.

"Water and cold, Mr. Holmes," answered Sandy.

Mr. Holmes looked closely at the shell halves. "I have it! You filled them with water and plugged the fuse holes tight. When they froze, they burst. It's as simple as all that," murmured Mr. Holmes. "By the way, what is your name?"

"Sandy, sir. Sandy MacLeod," answered Sandy.

Mr. Holmes yelled out into the factory for his foreman. When the foreman came in, Mr. Holmes said to him, "Here is the new boss of the shell-breaking department. He'll work under you, but the men he needs will work under him. He's found a way to break the shells! He freezes them open. What do you think of that? And he gets ten cents a shell for every one he breaks, and that's a pretty penny for a small lad."

The foreman grinned. "Remember, I told you the Scotch were a tough race to stop when they got an idea. Come on, Sandy. You're the youngest boss on a job the foundry ever had. And it's my guess you'll hold that record."

The Tale of Godfrey Malbone

by M. Jagendorf

"There's nothing my money won't buy," bragged Godfrey Malbone. But Peleg knew better.

In those days, in the early days, there lived in Newport by the sea the merchant prince Godfrey Malbone. He was a big man, this Godfrey Malbone, and a proud man, and a rich man.

"Big!" he'd roar. "I'm as big as the faith for which this plantation stands, the first settlement in America that truly carried out the great ideal of freedom for all. Any man can worship God as he wills, and he's welcome in Rhode Island as a brother.

"Proud! I've a right to be proud," he'd cry. "I've built a merchant empire with my own hands and brain, and now there's no man in the world I fear.

"Rich! I'm the richest merchant in Rhode Island by the sea," he'd shout. "Two hundred trading and privateering ships cover the ocean wide with my name and bring me wealth I cannot count. There's nothing, nothing in this big world, my money can't buy."

Those were his words, and to show that he meant it, he wrote them down and posted them publicly for all to read.

"There's nothing in the world my money won't buy," the poster said.

Now there lived in Newport young Peleg, who carved beautiful figureheads for brave ships that sailed the ocean wide. He was not a big fellow, but he was big in understanding. So, quietly one day, when no one was near, he put right underneath Godfrey Malbone's challenging words, "There's nothing in the world my money won't buy," these lines:

All the money in the place,
Will not buy Malbone a handsome face.

For you must know that old Malbone had a face homely enough to stop a clock. When Godfrey Malbone saw Peleg's words, he ranted and swore and threatened and roared: "I can't put horns on hares, but I can outsmart, outeat, outdrink, outtrick any merchant alive. My face is the face of a man and not that of a whining ninny. Any man who'll tell me the name of the scoundrel who wrote these dastardly words, I'll give ten new golden guineas. I'll make that scoundrel look like a jellyfish pounded in a hard gumwood mortar."

The next day there was a grand feast in Malbone's rich, large home, built like a courthouse for human justice. There were present: captains from ships come from long voyages, merchants, judges, soldiers, and friends, big as Godfrey Malbone and almost as rich.

Twenty-seven courses were served, cooked with rare spices. Every kind of wine graced the table. And in between the eating and drinking there was big talk of great deeds, with tales of feats of strength on the wild ocean.

Now the wine was served in silver goblets, but the food was served on plain white plates. When a course was done, Godfrey Malbone would sing a song in a roaring voice and at the end would break the plate from which he had eaten. Captains and guests joined the chorus and smashed the plates as well.

"Ha!" cried the jolly host with red steaming face. "It saves washing in the kitchen and gives the poor plate makers of old England a chance to earn a little more money from me. What won't money buy? Again I cry, ten shiny guineas for the one who tells me the name of the dog who wrote the scurvy rhyme under my words."

Right then there came a cry of "Fire! Fire in the kitchen!" Cooks and servants rushed out wildly while big flames began leaping from the fifty-foot-long room where Godfrey Malbone's food was cooked.

Guests and host rushed out, too. They took along two big red-running roasts, three sweet-smelling hams, seven bronze-breasted turkeys, a calf's leg, a mountain of corn bread and mince pies, with buckets and bottles of rich wines.

There were crying and screaming and a wild to-do, but all to no avail. The fine white-pillared house was burning high, yellow, and smoky. The brisk west wind made the flames dance in the air like ragged autumn leaves.

Roared Godfrey Malbone, "What a fine sight! Nero saw no better when Rome was burning. But while the heathen king could only think of fiddling, I would rather think of good eating. Come, captains and gentlemen, come, all of ye. Let us sit under this old buttonwood tree and eat and drink and be merry. Ho, there! Serve the meal under the tree," he said to his servants.

Soon they sat around the old tree as if nothing were amiss. It was a wondrous sight to see. There amid dark green boxwood, red roses, larkspur, yellow flag, pinks, and other flowers arranged in fine design near a little pond of silver fish, sat this grand company of big Rhode Islanders. They sat eating, drinking, and singing in the light of the red sun and the yellow leaping flames of the burning house.

People came from far and from near, drawn by the high flames and the smoke, wanting to help, but Godfrey Malbone shouted, "Don't disturb us at our meal. Let my house burn to cinders. My money'll build me a new one soon enough. Ha! What won't money buy! Remember, captains, gentlemen, and people of the town, ten fine golden guineas to the one who tells me who wrote the slandering rhyme about me."

A young fellow, smiling pleasantly, stepped forth from the crowd. It was Peleg, the carver. He said quietly, "Master Malbone, I claim the ten golden guineas."

"But first I want to know the name of the rascal who wrote the scurrilous rhyme," said Malbone.

"Why, it was none other than me, sir," replied Peleg.

There was a dead silence among the grand company and among the townspeople. Godfrey Malbone's face turned purple. The knuckles of his balled fists were white. Rising from his seat, he walked up to where Peleg stood smiling and quiet. He raised his heavy fists high and then . . . his hands dropped slowly to his sides. On his big, ugly face there came first a twitching at the corners of his mouth, then a slow grin, then a big, hearty, roaring laugh. The company looked at this first in speechless surprise and then joined in the good laughter.

Shouted Godfrey Malbone, "By God! It's only a little man who can't laugh when the joke's on him. Peleg, you young scamp, sure as the Lord made little apples, you're right and deserve the ten golden guineas. Here they are, and come join us in our feast. Only, remember, 'twas the good Lord gave me my face, and so it can't be ugly altogether."

Peleg sat down, and all the people cheered Godfrey Malbone so that the angels heard it in the sky. For there was a real man—a big man, a generous man, one who loved happy laughter so much he could laugh at himself!

From that day on, Peleg, the carver, and Godfrey Malbone, the merchant prince, became the best of friends, and never again did the latter brag that money could buy everything.

The Dog of Pompeii

by Louis Untermeyer

Bimbo took loving care of his young master—
even on that terrifying day when Mount Vesuvius erupted.

Tito and his dog Bimbo lived (if you could call it living) under the wall where it joined the inner gate. They really didn't live there; they just slept there. They lived anywhere. Pompeii was one of the gayest of the old Roman towns, but although Tito was never an unhappy boy, he was not exactly a merry one. The streets were always lively with shining chariots and bright red trappings; the open-air theaters rocked with laughing crowds; sham battles and sports were free for the asking in the great stadium. Once a year the Caesar visited the pleasure city and the fireworks lasted for days; the sacrifices in the Forum were better than a show. But Tito saw none of these things. He was blind—had been blind from birth. He was known to everyone in the poorer quarters. But no one could say how old he was, no one remembered his parents, no one could tell where he came from. Bimbo was another mystery. As long as people could remember seeing Tito—about twelve or thirteen years—they had seen Bimbo. Bimbo had never left his side. He was not only dog, but nurse, pillow, playmate, mother and father to Tito.

Did I say Bimbo never left his master? (Perhaps I had better say comrade, for if anyone was the master, it was Bimbo.) I was wrong. Bimbo did trust Tito alone exactly three times a day. It was a fixed routine, a custom understood between boy and dog since the beginning of their friendship, and the way it worked was this. Early in the morning, shortly after dawn, while Tito was still dreaming, Bimbo would disappear. When Tito awoke, Bimbo would be sitting quietly at his side, his ears cocked, his stump of a tail tapping the ground, and a fresh-baked bread—more like a large round roll—at his feet. Tito would stretch himself; Bimbo would yawn; then they would breakfast. At noon, no matter where they happened to be, Bimbo would put his paw on Tito's knee and the two of them would return to the inner gate. Tito would curl up in the corner and go to sleep, while Bimbo, looking quite important, would disappear again. In half an hour he'd be back with their lunch. Sometimes it would be a piece of fruit or a scrap of meat, often it was nothing but a dry crust. But sometimes there would be one of those flat rich cakes, sprinkled with raisins and sugar, that Tito liked so much. At suppertime the same thing happened, although there was a little less of everything, for things were hard to snatch in the evening with the streets full of people. Besides, Bimbo didn't approve of too much food before going to sleep. A heavy supper made boys too restless and dogs too stodgy—and it was the business of a dog to sleep lightly, with one ear open and muscles ready for action.

But, whether there was much or little, hot or cold, fresh or dry, food was always there. Tito never asked where it came from and Bimbo never told him. There was plenty of rainwater in the hollows of soft stones; the old egg woman at the corner sometimes gave Tito a cupful of strong goat's milk; in the grape season the fat wine maker let him have drippings of the mild juice. So there was no danger of going hungry or thirsty. There was plenty of everything in Pompeii—if you had a dog like Bimbo.

As I said before, Tito was not the merriest boy in Pompeii. He could not romp with the other youngsters and play hare and hounds and I spy. But that did not make him sorry for himself. If he could not see the sights that delighted the lads of Pompeii, he could hear and smell things they never noticed. He could really see more with his ears and nose than they could with their eyes. When he and Bimbo went out walking, he knew just where they were going and exactly what was happening.

"Ah," he'd sniff, and say, as they passed a handsome villa, "Glaucus Pansa is giving a grand dinner tonight. They're going to have three kinds of bread, and roast pigling, and stuffed goose, and a great stew—I think bear stew—and a fig pie." And Bimbo would note that this would be a good place to visit tomorrow.

Or, "Hm," Tito would murmur, half through his lips, half through his nostrils. "The wife of Marcus Lucretius is expecting her mother. She's shaking out every piece of goods in the house; she's going to use the best clothes—the ones she's been keeping in pine needles and camphor—and there's an extra girl in the kitchen."

Or, as they passed a small but elegant dwelling opposite the public baths, "Too bad! The tragic poet is ill again. It must be a bad fever this time, for they're trying smoke fumes instead of medicine. Whew! I'm glad I'm not a tragic poet!"

Or, as they neared the Forum, "Mm-m! What good things they have in the Macellum today!" (It really was a sort of butcher-grocer-marketplace, but Tito called it the Macellum.) "Dates from Africa, and salt oysters from sea caves, and cuttlefish, and new honey, and sweet onions, and—ugh!—water-buffalo steaks. Come, Bimbo, let's see what's what in the Forum." And so the two of them entered the center of Pompeii.

The Forum was the part of the town to which everybody came at least once during each day. It was the central square, and everything happened here. There were no private houses; all was public—the chief temples, the gold and red bazaars, the silk shops, the town hall, the booths belonging to the weavers and jewel merchants, the woolen market, the shrine of the household gods. Everything glittered here. The buildings looked as if they were new—which, in a sense, they were. The earthquake of twelve years ago had brought down all the old structures, and since the citizens of Pompeii were ambitious to rival Naples and even Rome, they had seized the opportunity to rebuild the whole town. And they had done it all within a dozen years. There was scarcely a building that was older than Tito.

Tito had heard a great deal about the earthquake—a light one, as earthquakes go. The weaker houses had been shaken down, parts of the outworn wall had been wrecked; but there was little loss of life, and the brilliant new Pompeii had taken the place of the old. No one knew what caused these earthquakes. Records showed they had happened in the neighborhood since the beginning of time. Sailors said that it was to teach the lazy city folk a lesson and make them appreciate those who risked the dangers of the sea to bring them luxuries and protect their town from invaders. The priests said that the gods took this way of showing their anger to those who refused to worship properly and who failed to bring enough sacrifices to the altars and (though they didn't say it in so many words) presents to the priests. The tradesmen said that the foreign merchants had corrupted the ground and it was no longer safe to traffic in imported goods that came from strange places and carried a curse with them. Everyone had a different explanation—and everyone's explanation was louder and sillier than his neighbor's.

They were talking about it this afternoon as Tito and Bimbo came out of the side street into the public square. The Forum was the favorite promenade for rich and poor. What with the priests arguing with the politicians, servants doing the day's shopping, tradesmen crying their wares, women displaying the latest fashions from Greece and Egypt, children playing hide-and-seek among the marble columns, knots of soldiers, sailors, peasants from the provinces—to say nothing of those who merely came to lounge and look on—the square was crowded to its last inch. His ears guided Tito to the place where the talk was loudest. It was in front of the shrine of the household gods that, naturally enough, the householders were arguing.

"I tell you," rumbled a voice that Tito recognized as bath master Rufus', "there won't be another earthquake in my lifetime or yours. There may be a tremble or two, but earthquakes, like lightnings, never strike twice in the same place."

"Do they not?" asked a thin voice Tito had never heard. It had a high, sharp ring to it and Tito knew it as the accent of a stranger. "How about the two towns of Sicily that have been ruined three times within fifteen years by the eruptions of Mount Etna? And were they not warned? And does that column of smoke above Vesuvius mean nothing?"

"That?" Tito could hear the grunt with which one question answered another. "That's always there. We use it for our weather guide. When the smoke stands up straight, we know we'll have fair weather; when it flattens out, it's sure to be foggy; when it drifts to the east—"

"Yes, yes," cut in the edged voice. "I've heard about your mountain barometer. But the column of smoke seems hundreds of feet higher than usual and it's thickening and spreading like a shadowy tree. They say in Naples—"

"Oh, Naples!" Tito knew this voice by the little squeak that went with it. It was Attilio, the cameo cutter. "*They* talk while we suffer. Little help we got from them last time. Naples commits the crimes and Pompeii pays the price. It's become a proverb with us. Let them mind their own business."

"Yes," grumbled Rufus, "and others, too."

"Very well, my confident friends," responded the thin voice, which now sounded curiously flat. "We also have a proverb—and it is this: Those who will not listen to men must be taught by the gods. I say no more. But I leave a last warning. Remember the holy ones. Look to your temples. And when the smoke tree above Vesuvius grows to the shape of an umbrella pine, look to your lives."

Tito could hear the air whistle as the speaker drew his toga about him, and the quick shuffle of feet told him the stranger had gone.

"Now what," said the cameo cutter, "did he mean by that?"

"I wonder," grunted Rufus. "I wonder what he meant."

Tito wondered, too. And Bimbo, his head at a thoughtful angle, looked as if he had been doing a heavy piece of pondering. By nightfall the argument had been forgotten. If the smoke had increased, no one saw it in the dark. Besides, it was the Caesar's birthday, and the town was in holiday mood. Tito and Bimbo were among the merrymakers, dodging the charioteers who shouted at them. A dozen times they almost upset baskets of sweets and jars of Vesuvian wine, said to be as fiery as the streams inside the volcano, and a dozen times they were cursed and cuffed. But Tito never missed his footing. He was thankful for his keen ears and quick instinct—most thankful of all for Bimbo.

They visited the uncovered theater, and though Tito could not see the faces of the actors, he could follow the play better than most of the audience, for their attention wandered—they were distracted by the scenery, the costumes, the byplay, even by themselves—while Tito's whole attention was centered in what he heard. Then to the city walls, where the people of Pompeii watched a mock naval battle, in which the city was attacked by the sea and saved after thousands of flaming arrows had been exchanged and countless colored torches had been burned. Though the thrill of flaring ships and lighted skies was lost to Tito, the shouts and cheers excited him as much as any, and he cried out with the loudest of them.

The next morning there were *two* of the beloved raisin-and-sugar cakes for his breakfast. Bimbo was unusually active and thumped his bit of a tail until Tito was afraid he would wear it out. The boy could not imagine whether Bimbo was urging him to some sort of game or was trying to tell something. After a while he ceased to notice Bimbo. He felt drowsy. Last night's late hours had tired him. Besides, there was a heavy mist in the air—no, a thick fog rather than a mist—a fog that got into his throat and scraped it and made him cough. He walked as far as the marine gate to get a breath of the sea. But the blanket of haze had spread all over the bay, and even the salt air seemed smoky.

He went to bed before dusk and slept. But he did not sleep well. He had too many dreams—dreams of ships lurching in the Forum, of losing his way in a screaming crowd, of armies marching across his chest, of being pulled over every rough pavement of Pompeii.

He woke early. Or, rather, he was pulled awake. Bimbo was doing the pulling. The dog had dragged Tito to his feet and was urging the boy along. Somewhere. Where, Tito did not know. His feet stumbled uncertainly; he was still half asleep. For a while he noticed nothing except the fact that it was hard to breathe. The air was hot. And heavy. So heavy that he could taste it. The air, it seemed, had turned to powder, a warm powder that stung his nostrils and burned his sightless eyes.

Then he began to hear sounds. Peculiar sounds. Like animals under the earth.

Hissings and groanings and muffled cries that a dying creature might make dislodging the stones of his underground cave. There was no doubt of it now. The noises came from underneath. He not only heard them—he could feel them. The earth twitched; the twitching changed to an uneven shrugging of the soil. Then, as Bimbo half pulled, half coaxed him along, the ground jerked away from his feet and he was thrown against a stone fountain.

The water—hot water—splashing in his face revived him. He got to his feet, Bimbo steadying him, helping him on again. The noises grew louder; they came closer. The cries were even more animal-like than before, but now they came from human throats. A few people, quicker of foot and more hurried by fear, began to rush by. A family or two—then, it seemed, an army broken out of bounds. Tito, bewildered though he was, could recognize Rufus as he bellowed past him, like a water buffalo gone mad. Time was lost in a nightmare.

It was then the crashing began. First a sharp crackling, like a monstrous snapping of twigs; then a roar like the fall of a whole forest of trees; then an explosion that tore earth and sky. The heavens, though Tito could not see them, were shot through with continual flickerings of fire. Lightnings above were answered by thunders beneath. A house fell. Then another. By a miracle the two companions had escaped the dangerous side streets and were in a more open space. It was the Forum. They rested here awhile—how long he did not know.

Tito had no idea of the time of day. He could *feel* it was black—an unnatural blackness. Something inside—perhaps the lack of breakfast and lunch—told him it was past noon. But it didn't matter. Nothing seemed to matter. He was getting drowsy, too drowsy to walk. But walk he must. He knew it. And Bimbo knew it; his sharp tugs told Tito so. Nor was it a moment too soon. The sacred ground of the Forum was safe no longer. It was beginning to rock, then to pitch, then to split. As they stumbled out of the square, the earth wriggled like a caught snake, and all the columns of the big temple, the Capitolium, came down. It was the end of the world—or so it seemed. To walk was not enough now. They must run. Tito was too frightened to know what to do or where to go. He had lost all sense of direction. He started to go back to the inner gate; but Bimbo, straining his back to the last inch, almost pulled his clothes from him. What did the creature want? Had the dog gone mad?

Then, suddenly, he understood. Bimbo was telling him the way out—urging him there. The sea gate of course. The sea gate—and then the sea. Far from falling buildings, heaving ground. He turned, Bimbo guiding him around open pits and dangerous pools of bubbling mud, away from buildings that had caught fire and were dropping their burning beams. Tito could no longer tell whether the noises were made by the shrieking sky or the agonized people. He and Bimbo ran on—the only silent beings in a howling world.

New dangers threatened. All Pompeii seemed to be thronging toward the marine gate, and squeezing among the crowds, there was the chance of being trampled to death. But the chance had to be taken. It was growing harder and harder to breathe. What air there was choked him. It was all dust now—dust and pebbles, pebbles as large as beans. They fell on his head, his hands—pumice stones from the black heart of Vesuvius. The mountain was turning itself inside out. Tito remembered a phrase that the stranger had said in the Forum two days ago: "Those who will not listen to men must be taught by the gods." The people of Pompeii had refused to heed the warnings; they were being taught now—if it was not too late.

Suddenly it seemed too late for Tito. The red-hot ashes blistered his skin, the stinging vapors tore his throat. He could not go on. He staggered toward a small tree at the side of the road and fell. In a moment Bimbo was beside him. He coaxed. But there was no answer. He licked Tito's hands, his feet, his face. The boy did not stir. Then Bimbo did the last thing he could—the last thing he wanted to do. He bit his comrade, bit him deep in the arm. With a cry of pain, Tito jumped to his feet, Bimbo after him. Tito was in despair, but Bimbo was determined. He drove the boy on, snapping at his heels, worrying his way through the crowd; barking, baring his teeth, heedless of kicks or falling stones. Sick with hunger, half dead with fear and sulfur fumes, Tito pounded on, pursued by Bimbo. How long he never knew. At last he staggered through the marine gate and felt soft sand under him. Then Tito fainted. . . .

Someone was dashing seawater over him. Someone was carrying him toward a boat.

"Bimbo," he called. And then louder, "Bimbo!" But Bimbo had disappeared.

Voices jarred against each other. "Hurry—hurry!" "To the boats!" "Can't you see the child's frightened and starving!" "He keeps calling for someone!" "Poor boy, he's out of his mind." "Here, child—take this!"

They tucked him in among them. The oarlocks creaked; the oars splashed; the boat rode over toppling waves. Tito was safe. But he wept continually.

"Bimbo!" he wailed. "Bimbo! Bimbo!" He could not be comforted.

Eighteen hundred years passed. Scientists were restoring the ancient city; excavators were working their way through the stones and trash that had buried the entire town. Much had already been brought to light—statues, bronze instruments, bright mosaics, household articles; even delicate paintings had been preserved by the fall of ashes that had taken more than two thousand lives. Columns were dug up and the Forum was beginning to emerge.

It was at a place where the ruins lay deepest that the director paused.

"Come here," he called to his assistant. "I think we've discovered the remains of a building in good shape. Here are four huge millstones that were most likely turned by slaves or mules—and here is a whole wall standing with shelves inside it. Why! It must have been a bakery. And here's a curious thing. What do you think I found under this heap where the ashes were thickest? The skeleton of a dog!"

"Amazing!" gasped his assistant. "You'd think a dog would have had sense enough to run away at the time. And what is that flat thing he's holding between his teeth? It can't be a stone."

"No. It must have come from this bakery. You know, it looks to me like some sort of cake hardened with the years. And, bless me, if those little black pebbles aren't raisins. A raisin cake almost two thousand years old! I wonder what made him want it at such a moment?"

"I wonder," murmured the assistant.

Call This Land Home

by Ernest Haycox

In the Oregon Territory, land was free to settlers.
But it wasn't easy for a family to make a home there.

One at a time, the emigrant families fell out where the land most pleased them, and at last only two wagons of the overland caravan moved southward along the great green valley of Oregon. Then the Potters discovered their fair place and John Mercy drove on with his lone wagon, his wife in unhappy silence beside him, and Caroline and young Tom under the canvas cover behind. Through the puckered opening at the wagon's rear young Tom saw the Potters grow dim in the steaming haze of this wet day. Rain lightly drummed on the canvas as he listened to the talk of his people.

"Have we got to live so far from everybody?" his mother asked.

In his father's voice was that fixed mildness which young Tom knew so well. "The heart of a valley's always better than foot or head. I want two things—the falls of a creek for my mill and plenty of open land round about," he told his wife.

She said, "Rough riding won't do for me much longer."

"I know," he said, and drove on.

In middle afternoon two days later the wagon stopped, and his father said, "I believe we're here." Crawling over the tailgate, young Tom—Thomas Jackson Mercy, age eight—saw the place on which he was to spend the rest of his long life. In three directions the fall-cast green earth ran off in the gentle meadow vistas, here and there interrupted by low knobs and little islands of timber, and cross-hatched by the brushy willow borders of creeks. On the fourth side a hill covered by fir and cedar ran down upon the wagon. A stream smaller than a river, but bigger than a branch, came across the meadows, dropped over a two-foot rock ledge like a bent sheet of glittering glass, and sharply curved to avoid the foot of the hill, running on toward some larger stream beyond view.

John Mercy turned toward the wagon to give his wife a hand, and young Tom noted that she came down with a careful awkwardness. Then his father stamped the spongy earth with his feet and bent over and plunged his tough fingers into the soil and brought up a sample, squeezing and crumbling it, and considering it closely. He was a very tall man, a very powerful man, and all his motions were governed by a willful regularity. A short curly beard covered his face as far as the cheekbones; a big nose, scarred white at the bridge, stood over a mouth held firm by constant habit. He seemed to be smiling, but it was less a smile than a moment of keen interest that forced little creases around mouth and eyes. To young Tom, his father, at twenty-eight, was an old man.

John Mercy said, "It will take a week of clear weather to dry this ground for plowing." He turned, looking at the timber close by and at the rising slope of the hill; he put his hands on his hips, and young Tom knew his father was searching out a place for the cabin. A moment later Mercy swung to face his wife with a slightly changed expression. She had not moved since leaving the wagon; she stood round-shouldered and dejected in the soft rain, reflecting on her face the effect of the gray day, the dampness and the emptiness that lay all around them. Young Tom had never seen her so long idle, for she was brisk in everything she did, always moving from chore to chore.

Mercy said, "In another two years you'll see neighbors wherever you look."

"That's not now," she said.

"The Willamette River's beyond this hill somewhere. There's settlers on it."

She said, "I long for back home," and turned from him and stood still again, facing the blind distance.

John Mercy stepped to the wagon and lifted the axe from its bracket. He said to young Tom, "Go cut a small saplin' for a pole, and some uprights," and handed over the axe. Then he got into the wagon and swung it around to drive it under the trees. When Tom came out of the deeper timber with his saplings, the oxen were unyoked and a fire burned beneath the massive spread of a cedar. The tailgate was down, and his father had reversed an empty tub to make a step from wagon to ground. They made a frame for the extra tarpaulin to rest on, thereby creating a shelter. His mother stood by, still with her unusual helplessness on her, and he knew, from his father's silence, that there was trouble between them.

His father said, "Water, Tom," and went on working. When Tom came back with the big camp kettle filled, his father had driven uprights at either side of the fire, connected by a crosspiece on which the hook hung. Tom lifted the camp kettle to the hook and listened a moment to the fire hissing against the kettle's wet bottom. The grub box was let down from the wagon box, and his mother was idle at the fire, one arm around Caroline, who stood by her. His father was at the edge of the timber, facing the meadow. He went over.

"Now, then," his father said, "it's sickly weather and we've got to get up a cabin. It'll go here. We'll cut the small trees yonder, for that's where the good house will stand someday. So we'll be doing two things at the same time—making the cabin and clearing the yard." His eyes, gray to their bottommost depths, swung around, and their effect was like a heavy weight on young Tom. It was seldom that he gave young Tom this undivided attention. "We've got everything to do here, and nothing to do it with but our hands. Never waste a lick, and make every lick work twice for you if you can. No man lives long enough to get done all he wants to do, but if he works slipshod and has got to do it over, then he wastes his life. I'll start on that tree. You trim and cut."

The blows of the axe went through the woods in dull echoing, not hurried—for his father never hurried—but with the even tempo of a clock's ticking. His mother worked around the grub box with her disheartened slowness. First shadows were sooty in the timber, and mist moved in from the meadows. He listened to the sounds of the empty land with tight fascination; he watched the corridors of the timber for moving things, and he waited for the tree to fall.

The rains quit. Warmed by a mild winter sun, the meadows exhaled fleecy wisps of steam, which in young Tom's imagination became the smoke of underground fires breaking through. They dropped trees of matched size, cut and notched and fitted them. When the walls were waist high, Mercy rigged an incline and a block and tackle; but even with that aid his body took much of the weight of each log, his boots sank into the spongy soil, and his teeth showed in white flashes when hard effort pulled back his lips.

After supper, with a fire blazing by the cabin, he adzed out the rough boards for door and window frames and inner furniture; and late at night young Tom woke to hear his father's froe and mallet splitting the cedar roof shakes, and sometimes heard his mother calling fretfully, "Mercy, come now! It's late enough!" Lying awake, he listened to his father come into the wagon and settle down upon the mattress with a groaning sigh and fall asleep at once. The dying yellow of the firelight flickered against the wagon canvas; strange sounds rustled in the windy woods, and far off was the baying of timber wolves. Caroline, disturbed by that wild sound, stirred against him.

The meadows dried before the roof of the cabin was on. John Mercy said, "It might be the last clear spell all winter. I have got to stop the cabin and break that meadow and get the wheat in." He looked at his wife. "Maybe you won't mind living in the wagon a week longer."

"I mind nothing," she said, "except being here."

John Mercy turned to his son. "Go round up the animals."

The two brindle oxen were deep in the meadow. Driving them back to the cabin, young Tom saw his people at the campfire; they were saying things not meant for him, his mother with her arms tight across her breasts and her head flung up. Presently his father turned away to yoke the oxen, hitch on the breaking plow, and go into the meadow.

The ancient turf became coiled, gloss-brown strips. John Mercy watched the sky as he plowed, and plowed until the furrows grew ragged in the fading day; and ate and built his fire and hewed out the cabin rafters. And by morning's first light he was at work again, harrowing the meadow into its rough clods, into its pebbled smoothness. The gray clouds thickened in the southwest and the wind broke and whirled them on. With the wheat sack strapped before him like an apron, John Mercy sowed his grain, reaching for the seed, casting with an even sweep, pacing on, and reaching and casting again. Young Tom sawed out the top logs, shortening and angling each cut meant for the cabin's peak; and at night, by the bonfire's swaying glow, he laid his weight against the block-and-tackle rope while his father heaved the logs up the incline into place.

On Sunday his father said, "Take the gun, Tom, and go over this hill and keep on till you find the Willamette. See what you can see. Come back around the side of the hill and tell me which is the short way."

Within a hundred yards the cabin vanished behind the great bark-ribbed firs whose trunks were thicker through than the new cabin. They ran far to the sky and an easy cry came out of them as they swayed to the wind. Pearly shafts of light slanted down into this still wilderness place. Fern and hazel stood head high to him, and giant deadfalls lay with their red-brown rotted wood crumbling away.

Tom climbed steadily, now and then crossing short ravines; and down a long vista he saw a buck deer poised alertly at a pool. His gun rose, but then he heard the cool advice of his father, "Never shoot meat far from home," and he slapped his hand against the gun stalk and watched the deer go bounding into the deeper forest gloom.

A long two miles brought him to the crest of the hill, from which he saw the surface of a big river in smooth patches between the lower trees. Another half mile, very rough, brought him down to the river's margin; he turned to the right, and presently the timber and the hill rolled out into the meadowlands. Directly over the river he saw a cabin in a clearing, and saw a girl at the break of the bluff, watching him.

At such a distance he could not clearly see her face; she was about his size, and she stared at him with a motionless interest. He stirred his feet in the soft earth, and he raised his hand and waved, but she continued to look at him, not answering. And in a little while he turned and followed the open meadows as they bent around the toe of the dark hill, and reached home before noon.

His father said, "What did you see?"

"The river's on the other side of the hill, but it's easier to go around the hill. I saw a deer."

"That's all?"

"And a cabin across the river," said Tom. "There was a girl in the yard."

John Mercy looked at his wife. "Now,"

he said quietly, "there's one neighbor," and waited for her answer.

She looked at him, reluctant to be pleased. "How far away?"

Young Tom said, "More than an hour, I guess."

His mother said, "If they saw you, they'll come to visit . . . and it's a terrible camp they'll see. . . . Caroline, go scrub and change your dress. I've got to fix your hair." Suddenly she was irritably energetic, moving around to put away the scattered pans and the loose things lying under the canvas shelter.

John Mercy went toward a pile of saplings roughly cut into rafters; he cast a secret glance of benevolence at young Tom. Something had pleased him. He said, "We'll get these on in short order."

The saplings went up and poles were set across them. The first row of shakes was laid when a man's strong hallo came ringing in from the meadow and a family moved through the trees, man and wife, two tall boys carrying sacks, and the girl young Tom had noticed across the river.

The man said in a great grumbling voice, "Neighbor, by the Lord, we could of saved you sweat on that cabin if we'd known you were here. Teal's my name. Iowa."

Talk broke through the quiet like a sudden storm. The two women moved beyond the wagon, and young Tom heard their voices rush back and forth in tumbling eagerness. The men were at the cabin.

Teal said, "Boys, you're idle. This man needs shakes for his roof. Go split 'em. . . . It's agoing to rain, Mercy, and when it rains here, it's the world drowned out. The drops are big as banty eggs. They bust like ripe watermelons, they splatter, they splash. You're soaked, your shoes squash, you steam like a kettle on the fire. . . . Boys, don't stand there. Mercy and me will lay on what shakes that's cut."

The Teal girl stood in front of young Tom and stared at him with direct curiosity. She was not quite his height; she was berry brown, with small freckles on her nose, and her hair hung down behind in one single braid. Caroline cautiously moved forward and looked up to her, and suddenly put out a hand and touched her dress. The Teal girl took Caroline's hand, but she kept her eyes on young Tom.

"I saw you," she said.

"What's your name?"

"Mary," said the girl, and turned with the quickest motion and walked toward the older women.

The Teal boys worked on shakes, one splitting, one drawing the cedar panels down with the knife; the men talked steadily as they worked. The smell of frying steak—brought by the Teals—was in the air to tantalize young Tom.

He leaned against a tree and watched Mary Teal from the corner of his eye, then turned and walked away from the trees to the falls of the creek and squatted at the edge of the pool, his shadow sending the loafing trout into violent crisscross flight. Gray clouds ran low over the land. He hunched himself together like a savage over a fire; he listened into the wind and waited for the scurrying shapes of the enemy to come trotting in war file out of the misty willow clumps. He sat there a long while, the day growing dull around him. The wind increased and the pool's silver surface showed the pocking of rain. His mother's voice called him back to mealtime.

He ate by the fire, listening to the voices of the older people go on and on. His mother's face was red from the heat of the fire, and her eyes were bright, and she was smiling; his father sat comfortably under the cedar tree, thawed by the company. It was suddenly half-dark, the rain increasing, and the Teals rose and spoke their farewells and filed off through the trees. Silence returned; loneliness deepened.

His mother said, "It was good to see people."

"They'll be fine neighbors," his father said.

His mother's face tightened. She looked over the flames and suddenly seemed to remember her fears. "Four miles away," she said, and turned to the dishes on the camp table. She grew brisk. "Tom, I want water. . . . Stack these dishes, Caroline, and come out of the rain."

John Mercy went into the darkness beyond the cabin and built his work fire; lying awake in bed, young Tom heard his father's mallet steadily splitting out shakes, and he continued to hear the sound in his sleep.

By morning a great wind cried across the world. John Mercy lighted the campfire and cooked breakfast for the women within the wagon. He laid on heavy logs for the fire's long burning and took up a piece of rope and the axe and hammer and nails. "We have got a chore to do at the river," he said to young Tom. "You pack the gun."

They skirted the foot of the hill, trailing beside a creek, and the southwest wind roughly shoved them forward through sheets of fat raindrops sparkling in the mealy light. When they reached the river, they saw a lamp burning in the window of the Teal house, but John Mercy swung to a place where the hill's timber met the bluff of the stream.

"There will come a time," he said, "when I'll have to send you to the Teals' for help. You'll need a raft to cross."

They cut down and trimmed six saplings for a raft bed, bound them with two crosspieces nailed in. A pole, chipped flat at one end, made an oar. Then John Mercy tied the rope to the raft and towed it upstream a hundred yards beyond the Teal house. He drew it half from the water and secured the rope to an overhanging tree, and laid the oar in the brush. "You'll drift as you paddle," he said.

Homeward bound, the wind came at them face on. Young Tom bent against it, hearing his father's half-shouted words: "It ought to be a month or more before the baby's due. But we're alone out here, and accidents come along. We've got to expect those things. No sensible man watches his feet hit ground. He looks ahead to see what kind of ground they'll hit next."

They came around a bend of the creek and heard a massive cannon crack of sound in the hills above them, and the ripping fall of a tree; its jarring collision with the earth ran out to them. They pressed on, John Mercy's pace quickening as though a new thought disturbed him. High in the air was an echo like the crying of a bird, lasting only a moment and afterward shredded apart by the storm; but it rose again, thinner and wilder, and became a woman's voice screaming.

John Mercy rushed around the last bend of the hill, past the pool of the falls, and into the cabin clearing. Young Tom followed, the gun across his chest. Through the trees he saw a figure by the campfire, not his mother's form, but a dark head and a dark face above some kind of cloak. His father stopped at the fire before the stranger; reaching the scene, young Tom discovered that the stranger was an Indian. His mother stood back against the wagon with a butcher knife in her hand; her face shocked him, white and strange-stretched as it was.

He lifted the gun, waiting. The Indian was old and his cheeks were round holes rimmed by jawbone and temple. His eyes were sick. His hand, stretched through the blanket, was like the foot of a bird, nothing but bone and wrinkled dark flesh. He spoke something, he pointed at the food locker. For a moment—for a time-stopped space in which the acid clarity of this scene ate its way so deeply into young Tom's memory that ninety years of living neither changed nor dimmed a detail of it—he watched the latent danger rise around his father's mouth and flash his eyes; unexpectedly his father turned to the grub box, found half a loaf of bread, and gave it to the savage. Then his father pointed at the gun in young Tom's hand and pointed back to the Indian, snapping down his thumb as though firing; he seized the Indian at the hips, lifting him like a half-emptied sack, walked a few steps and dropped him, and gave an onward push. The Indian went away without looking behind him, his shoulders bent.

His mother's voice, high-pitched and breathless, drew young Tom's attention. She was shaking, and in her eyes was a great wildness. "I don't want to be here! I didn't want to come! Mercy, you've got to take me home! I want my old house back! I want my people! I'll die here!"

John Mercy said, "Tom, take your sister for a walk." Caroline stood in the doorway of the cabin, frightened by the scene. Young Tom went over to catch her hand. The half-finished roof kept Caroline dry, and he stood indecisively under this shelter, disliking to leave it, yet compelled by his father's order.

John Mercy lifted his wife into his arms, speaking: "The creature was harmless. There are no bad Indians around here. I know the weather's poor and there's no comfort, but I'll have the roof on the cabin by tonight." He carried her into the wagon, still talking.

Young Tom heard his mother's voice rising again, and his father's patient answering. He clung to Caroline's hand and watched the rain-swept world beyond the cabin and saw no other shelter to which he might go. He was hard pressed to make up his mind, and when his father came out of the wagon, he said in self-defense, "Caroline would get awfully wet if I took her for a walk."

"You did right," John Mercy said. "Caroline, go keep your mother company." He looked up at the unfinished roof, he drew a hand down across his water-crusted beard, and for a moment he remained stone-still, his whole body sagged down with its accumulation of weariness. He drew a long breath and straightened. "Soon as I finish the roof, Tom, we'll line the fireplace with clay. I'll need some straw to mix with the clay. You go along the creek where the old hay's rotted down. Bring me several swatches of it."

The rain walked over the earth in constant sheets, beating down grass and weeds and running vines; the creek grew violent between its banks and the increased falls dropped roaring into its pool. Bearing his loads of dead grass to the cabin, young Tom watched his father lay the last rows of shakes on the roof and cap the ridge with boards hewn out earlier, by the late firelight; afterward John Mercy, working faster against the fading day, went beside the creek to an undercut bank and shoveled out its clay soil, carrying it back to the cabin by bucket. He cooked a quick supper and returned to the cabin, mixing clay and dead-grass stems, and coated the wood fireplace and its chimney with this mortar. He built a small fire, which, by drying the mud, would slowly season it to a brick-hard lining.

Throughout the night, fitfully waking, young Tom heard the dull thumping of a hammer and twice heard his mother call out, "Mercy, come to bed!" At daybreak young Tom found a canvas door at the cabin; inside, a fire burned on the dirt hearth and a kettle steamed from the crane. The crevices between logs were mud-sealed, the table and grub box and benches had been brought in. Standing before the fire, young Tom heard the wind search the outer wall and fall away, and suddenly the warmth of the place thawed the coldness that lay beneath his skin. He heard his mother come in, and he turned to see his parents standing face to face, almost like strangers.

His mother said, "Mercy, did you sleep at all?"

His father's answer was somehow embarrassed. "I had to keep the fire alive, so the mud would dry right. Today I'll get the puncheons on the floor and we can move the beds in." In a still gentler voice, the uncertainness of apology in it, his father added, "Maybe, if you shut your eyes and think how all this will look five years from now—"

She cut him off with the curt swing of her body and walked to the fire. Stooping with a slowness so unlike her, she laid the Dutch oven against the flame and went to the grub box. She put her yellow mixing bowl on the table; she got her flour and her shortening and her salt. She stood a moment over the mixing bowl, not looking at John Mercy. "As long as I can do my share, I'll do it. . . . Tom, fetch me the pail of water."

He stood with his father at the break of the trees, viewing the yellow-gray ground beyond it, and the valley floor running away to the great condensed wall of mist. He knew, from the dead gentleness of tone, that his father was very tired; it was not like him to waste time speaking of the future. "The orchard will go right in front of this spot," his father said. "That will be pretty to look at from the house. The house will stand where we're standing. These firs will go down." He was silent, drawing the future forward and finding comfort in it. "All this is free—all this land. But it's up to a man to make something out of it. So there's nothing free. There never is. We'll earn every acre we get. Don't trust that word *free*. Don't believe it. You'll never own anything you didn't pay for. But what you pay for is yours. You've got it while other men wait around for something free and die with nothing. Now, then, we have to cut down some small firs, about eight inches through. We'll split them in half for floor puncheons."

He turned, walking slower than usual; he searched the trees, nodding at one or the other, and stopped at a thin fir starved by the greater firs around it; its trunk ran twenty feet without a branch. "That one," he said, and went to the cabin wall for his axe. "Tom," he said, "I want you to go up in the hills and see how close you can find a ledge of rock. That's for the fireplace floor." He faced the tree, watching the wind whip its top; he made an undercut on the side toward which he wished the tree to fall, and squared himself away to a steady chopping.

Young Tom passed the cabin, upward bound into the semidarkness of the hill; the great trees groaned in their swaying, and their shaken branches let down ropy spirals of rain. It was like walking into a tunnel full of sound. His overcoat grew heavy with water, which, dripping on his trouser legs, turned them into ice-cold bands; his shoes were mushy. Behind him he heard the first crackling of the tree going down, and he turned and saw his father running. The tree, caught by the wind, was falling the wrong way. He shouted against the wind; his father looked behind, saw the danger, and jumped aside. The tree, striking a larger fir, bounced off, and young Tom saw its top branches whip out and strike his father to the ground. His father shouted, buried somewhere beneath that green covering.

His mother came crying out of the cabin. "Mercy! Mercy!" She stumbled and caught herself, and rushed on, fighting the branches away as she reached the tree.

When he got there, he saw his father lying with both legs beneath the trunk. The branches, first striking, had broken the force of the trunk's fall; and then they had shattered, to let the trunk down upon his father, who lay on an elbow with his lips the color of gray flour paste. Young Tom never knew until then how piercing a gray his father's eyes were.

His mother cried, "Your legs! Oh, God, Mercy!" She bent over him, she seized the trunk of the tree, and she stiffened under her straining.

John Mercy's voice was a vast shout of warning: "Nancy, don't do that!" His arms reached out and struck her on the hip. "Let go!"

She drew back and laid both arms over her stomach, a shock of pain pressing her face into its sharp angles. "Oh, Mercy," she said, "it's too late!" and stared down at him in terror.

Young Tom raced to the cabin wall, got the shovel and rushed back; a branch interfered with his digging. He found the axe, thrown ten yards away by Mercy in his flight; he returned to cut the limb away. Mercy lay still, as though he were listening. He watched his wife, and he put a hand over his eyes and seemed to be thinking; the impact of the axe on the trunk threw twinges of pain through him, but he said nothing until young Tom had finished.

"Give me the shovel," he said. "Now go get Mrs. Teal."

Young Tom stood irresolute. "You got to get out of there."

"Those legs," said John Mercy, and spoke of them as though they didn't belong to him, "are pinched. If they were broken, I'd know it . . . and they're not." He paused and a dead gray curtain of pain came down on his face; he suffered it and waited for it to pass. "Do as I tell you." Young Tom whirled and started away at a hard run, and was almost instantly checked and swung by his father's command. "You've got a long way to go, and you'll not do it starting that fast. Steady now. I've told you before . . . think ahead."

Young Tom began again, trotting out upon the meadow; he looked back and saw his father awkwardly working with the shovel, sheltered by the outstretched apron of his mother. But even before young Tom ceased to look, she dropped the apron, put both hands before her face and walked toward the wagon.

The scene frightened him, and he broke into a dead run along the margin of the creek; he ran with his fists doubled, his arms lunging back and forth across his chest. A pain caught him in the side, and he remembered his father's advice and slowed to a dogtrot. He grew hot and stopped once to crawl down the bank of a creek for a drink, and was soon chilled by the wet ground against his stomach and the rain beating on his back.

After a rest of a minute he went on, stiffened by that short pause. The river willows at last broke through the rain mist forward, and he saw the low shape of the Teal cabin. He crossed the last meadow and came to the bank; he hadn't forgotten the raft, but he wanted to save time. The wind was with him, carrying his call over the water. He repeated it twice before the cabin door opened and Mrs. Teal stepped into the yard. Tom raised his arm, pointing behind him toward his home. Mrs. Teal waved back at him immediately and ran into the house.

Squatted on the bank, young Tom saw the three Teal men come out, lift a boat and carry it to the water; in a moment Mrs. Teal joined them, and the four came over the river. Mrs. Teal had a covered basket in her hand. She said, "Your mother, Tom?"

"My father's caught under a fir that fell on him. That made Mother sick."

Teal turned on his lank, Indian-dark sons. "Git ahead and help him."

"Oh, Lord, Lord," said Mrs. Teal. "Take the basket, Nate. We've got to go fast. It's going to come early."

Young Tom started after the Teal boys, they running away with a loose and ranging ease. "No," said Teal, "you stay with us. You've had runnin' enough. The boys are a pair of hounds; let 'em go."

They went forward, Mrs. Teal now and then speaking to herself with a soft exclamation of impatience. Otherwise there was no talk. The wind was against them and the rain beat down. Young Tom opened his mouth to let the great drops loosen his dry throat, and silently suffered the slow pace. The coming baby never entered his mind; it was of his father lying under the tree that he thought with dread, and when the creek began to bend around the toe of the hills, close by the falls, he ran ahead and reached the cabin.

His father had dug himself out from the trap; there was a little tunnel of earth where he had been. The two boys stood silently at the fire, and one of them motioned toward the cabin. Young Tom drew the doorway canvas back from the logs to look in: his father had moved the bedstead from the wagon and had set it up near the cabin's fireplace. His mother was on it, groaning, and his father knelt at the bedside and held her hands. Young Tom retreated to the fire, watching the Teals come through the trees. Mrs. Teal seized the basket from her husband and went at once into the cabin; a moment later his father came out.

John Mercy said to Teal, "It's a good thing to have neighbors. I'm sorry I can't offer you coffee at this minute." He let his head drop, and he spread his hands before the fire and gravely watched it. The sockets of his eyes seemed deep and blackened; his mouth was a line straight and narrow across his skin.

"My friend," said Teal, "the first winter's always a bad one. Don't work so hard or you'll be twenty years older by spring." He turned to the taller of his two sons. "Jack, take Mercy's gun and go fetch in a deer."

Young Tom heard his mother's sharp cry from the cabin. He moved away; he stood by the tree and stared at the trench in which his father had been, and noticed the marks scrubbed into the soft ground by his father's elbows. He walked along the tree and gave it a kick with his foot, and continued to the millpond. There he squatted, watching the steamy mists pack tighter along the willows of the creek. In the distance, a mile or so, a little timbered butte stood half concealed by the fog, seeming to ride free in the low sky. He tightened his muscles, waiting for the enemy to come single file through the brush; but then he thought of the old savage, so bony and stooped and unclean, who had seized the half loaf of bread, and his picture of a row of glistening copper giants was destroyed. He heard voices by the cabin, and rose and saw Mrs. Teal by the fire. He went back.

Mrs. Teal looked at him with her kindness. "Your mother's all right, Tom. You had a brother, but he wasn't meant to stay. You understand, Tom? It's meant that way and you oughtn't sorrow."

She was telling him the baby boy was dead. He thought about it and waited to feel like crying, but he hadn't seen this boy and he didn't know anything about him, and didn't know what to cry for. It embarrassed him not to feel sad. He stood with his eyes on the fire.

Teal said to his second son, "That Methodist preacher is probably down at Mission Bottom, Pete. You go home, get the horse, and go for him." He walked a little distance onward, speaking in a lower tone to his son. Then the boy went on, and Teal turned back to the cabin and got the saw standing by the wall and went over to the fallen log. He called to young Tom. "Now then, let's not be idle. Puncheons he wanted, wasn't it? We'll just get 'em ready while we wait."

A shot sounded deeper in the forest—one and no more. "There's your meat," said Teal. "You've seen the trout in the creek, ain't you? Mighty fat. Next summer there'll be quail all through those meadow thickets. What you've got to have is a horse for ridin'. Just a plain ten-dollar horse. I know where there's one."

The minister arrived around noon the next day, and out of this wet and empty land the neighbors began to come, riding or walking in from all quarters of the mist-hidden valley, destroying forever young

Tom's illusion of wilderness. They came from the scattered claims along the river, from French Prairie, from the upper part of La Creole, from the strangely named creeks and valleys as far as twenty miles away; the yard was filled with men, and women worked in the cabin and at the fire outside the cabin. Young Tom stared at strange boys running through the timber, and resented their trespassing; he heard girls giggling in the shelter of the wagon. It was a big meeting. A heavy man in buckskins, light of eye and powerfully voiced, strolled through the crowd and had a word for everyone. People visited, and the talk was of the days of the wagon-train crossing, of land here and land there, of politics and the Hudson's Bay Company. A group of men walked along the break of the hill until they reached a knoll a hundred yards from the cabin. Tom watched them digging.

In a little while they returned, bringing quietness to the people. The minister came from the cabin, bareheaded in the rain. Mr. Teal followed, carrying a small bundle wrapped within a sheet and covered by a shawl; they went on toward the grave, and young Tom, every sense sharpened, heard the knocking of a hammer and the calling of a voice. The crowd moved over, and his father walked from the cabin carrying his mother. Young Tom saw Caroline alone at the cabin's doorway, crying; he went to her and got her hand and followed his father.

A little box stood at the grave, the minister by it; he had a book in his hand, which he watched while the rain dripped down his long face. Young Tom's mother was on her feet, but she wasn't crying, though all the women around her were. The minister spoke a long while, it seemed to Tom. He held Caroline's hand and grew cold, waiting for the minister's words to end. Somebody said, "Amen," and the minister began a song, all the people joining.

Looking at his feet, young Tom felt the coldness run up his legs, and his chest was heavy and he, too, cried. As soon as the song was done, his father carried his mother back to the house, and the crowd returned to the fire. A woman dumped venison steaks into a big kettle on the table, and cups and plates went around, and the talk grew brisker than it had been before.

Young Tom said, "Caroline, you go into the wagon." From the corner of his eye he saw men shoveling dirt into the grave; he thought about the grave and imagined

the rains filling it with water, and the shawl and the white sheet growing black in the mud. He went over to the fallen log and sat on it.

He remained there, wholly lost in the forest of his imagination while the roundabout neighbors, finished with eating and finished with visiting, started homeward through the dulling day. They went in scattered groups, as they had come, their strong calling running back and forth in the windy rain; and at last only the Teals remained. He saw Caroline and Mary Teal watching him through the front opening of the wagon. He rose and went around to the cabin, hearing the older Teals talking.

Mrs. Teal said, "I'm needed. We'll stay tonight."

Teal looked at his two tall sons. "You had best get at those puncheons. Mercy's legs will trouble him for a while. Tomorrow we are agoin' to knock down some trees for a barn lean-to."

Young Tom quietly drew back the canvas covering of the cabin's doorway. He was troubled about his mother and wanted to see her, and meant to go in. But what he saw suddenly shut him out and brought great embarrassment to him.

His father stood beside the bed, looking down, and young Tom heard him say, "I can't stay here when your heart's not in it. There is no pleasure in this work, and no point in looking ahead to what it'll be someday, if you don't feel it too. Well, you don't. We'll go home . . . in the spring when it's possible to travel. That's what you want, I clearly know."

She was pale and her eyes were stretched perfectly round; her head rolled slightly, her voice was very small. "I couldn't leave now. I've got a baby buried here. It's a mighty hard way to come to love a country . . . to lose something in it. Mercy, put a railing around that grave. I have not been of much use, I know, and it's hurt me to see you work the way you've done. It will be better when I can get up and do what I can do."

John Mercy bent down and kissed his wife, and suddenly in young Tom the embarrassment became intolerable, for this was a thing he had never seen his people do before, and a thing he was to see again only twice so long as they lived. He pulled back and let the canvas fall into place; he thought he heard his father crying. He walked by the big kettle with its remaining chunks of fried venison steak. He took one, eating it like a piece of bread. Caroline and Mary Teal were now at the back end of the wagon, looking at him.

He said, "I know a big cave up on the hill."

Mary Teal came from the wagon, Caroline following; and the three walked into the woods, into the great sea swells of sound poured out by the rolling timber crowns. Mary gave Tom a sharp sideways glance and smiled, destroying the strangeness between them and giving him a mighty feeling of comfort. The long, long years were beginning for Tom Mercy, and he was to see that smile so many times again in the course of his life, to be warmed and drawn on by it, to see tears shining through it, and broken thoughts hidden by it. To the last day of his life far out in another century, that smile—real or long after remembered—was his star, but like a star, there was a greater heat within it than he was ever to feel or to know.

The Four Brothers

by Walter de la Mare

In this, the first of two old tales retold by a famous poet, four farm boys go into the great world to seek their fortunes.

In the days of long ago, there was a farmer who had four sons. His was not a big farm; he had only a small flock of sheep, a few cows, and not much plow- or meadowland. But he was well content. His sons had always been with him on his farm or near about, and he had grown to love them more and more. Never man had better sons than he had.

For this reason he grew ill at ease at the thought of what they were giving up for his sake; and at last one day he called them together and said to them, "There will be little left, when I am gone, to divide up among four. Journey off, then, my dear sons, into the great world; seek your fortunes, and see what you can do for yourselves. Find each of you as honest and profitable a trade as he can; come back to me in four years' time, and we shall see how you have all prospered. And God's blessing go with you!"

So his four sons cut themselves cudgels out of the hedge, made up their bundles, and off they went. After waving their father good-by at the gate, they trudged along the highroad together till they came to crossroads, where four ways met. Here they parted one from another, and each went off, whistling into the morning.

After he had gone a few miles, the first and eldest of them met a stranger, who asked him where he was bound for. He told him he was off to try his luck in the world.

"Well," said the stranger, "come along with me, and I will teach you to be nimble with your fingers. Nimble of fingers is nimble of wits. And I'll warrant when I've done with you, you'll be able to snipple-snupple away any mortal thing you have an eye to, and nobody so much as guess it's gone."

"Not me," said the other. "That's thieving. Old Master Take-What-He-Wanted was hanged on a gallows. And there, for all I care, he hangs still."

"Aye," said the old man, "that he were. But that old Master Take-What-He-Wanted you are talking of was a villainous rogue and a rascal. But supposing you're only after borrowing its lamp from a glowworm or a loaf of bread from a busy bee, what then? Follow along now; you shall see!" So off they went together. And very well they did.

The second son had not gone far when he chanced on an old man sitting under a flowering bush and eating bread and cheese and an onion with a jackknife. The old man said to him, "Good morning, my friend. What makes you so happy?"

He said, "I am off to seek my fortune."

"Ah," said the old man, "then come along with me; for one's fortune is with the stars, and I am an astronomer and a stargazer." In a bag beside him, this old pilgrim showed the young man a set of glasses for spying out the stars. After looking through the glasses, the young man needed no persuasion and went along with him. And very well they did.

The third brother, having turned off into the greenwood, soon met a jolly huntsman with a horn and a quiver full of arrows on his shoulder. The huntsman liked the fine fresh look of the lad. He promised to teach him his ancient art and skill with the bow; so they went along together. And very well they did.

The youngest brother tramped on many a mile before he met anybody, and he was resting under a tree, listening to the birds and enjoying a morsel of food out of his bundle, when a tailor came along, with crooked legs and one eye. And the tailor said to him, "Plenty to do, but nothing doing!"

The boy laughed and said, "I have been walking all morning, having just left my dear old father for the first time. Now I am resting a moment, for I am off into the world to get my living and to see if I can bring him back something worth having."

And the tailor, taken by his way of speaking, said, "If you are wishful to learn a craft, young man, come along with me." So off they went together. And very well they did.

Now, after four years to the very day, the four brothers met again at the crossroads and returned to their father. A pleasant meeting it was. For though their old father was getting on in years, he had worked on alone at the farm with a good heart, feeling sure that his sons were doing well in the world. That night when they were all sitting together at supper—two of his sons on either side of him, and himself in the middle—he said to them, "Now, good sons all, tell me your adventures, and what you've been doing these long years past."

The four brothers looked at one another, and the eldest said, "Aye, so we will, Father, if you'll wait till tomorrow. Then we will do whatever you ask us, to show we have learned our trades and not been idle. Think over tonight what you'd like us to do in the morning, and we'll all be ready."

The old man's one fear that night as he lay in bed thinking of the morrow was lest he might give his sons too hard a thing to do. But before he could think of anything that seemed not too hard yet not too easy, he fell asleep.

The next morning, after the five of them had gobbled up their breakfast, they went out into the fields together.

Then the old man said, "Up in the branches of that tree, my sons, is a chaffinch's nest, and there the little hen is sitting. Now could any one of you tell me how many eggs she has under her?" For he thought the youngest would climb into the tree, scare off the bird, and count them.

But nothing so simple as that. "Why, yes, Father," said the second son, and taking out of his pocket a certain optic glass his master had given him as a parting present, he put it to his best eye, looked up, squinnied through it, and said, "Five."

At this the old man was exceedingly pleased, for he knew his son told him the truth.

"Now," says he, "could one of you *get* those eggs for me, and maybe without alarming the mother bird overmuch? Eh? What about that?"

There and then the eldest son, who had been taught by his master every trick there is for nimble fingers, shinned up into the tree and dealt with the little bird so gently that he took all her five eggs into the hollow of his hand without disturbing even the littlest and downiest of her feathers in the nest.

The old man marveled and said, "Better and better! But now, see here," he went on, gently laying the five eggs on a flat patch of mossy turf, and turning to the son who had gone off with the huntsman. "Now, shoot me all these, my son, with one arrow. My faith, 'twould be a masterstroke!"

His son went off a full fifty paces, and drawing the little black bow made of sinew (which his master had bought from the Tartars), with a tiny twang of its string he loosed a needle-sharp arrow that, one after the other, pierced all five eggs as neatly as a squirrel cracks nuts.

"Ha, ha!" cried the old man, almost dumbfounded, and prouder than ever of them all, then turned to his youngest son. "Aye, and can *you*, my son, put them together again?" But this he meant only in jest.

With that, the youngest son sat down at the foot of the tree, and there and then, and they all watching, with the needle and thread that had once been his master's, he sewed the shells together so deftly that even with his second son's magic glass his old father could scarcely see the stitches. This being done, the eggs were put back into the nest again, and the mother bird sat out her time. Moreover, the only thing strange in her five nestlings when they were all safely hatched out of their shells was that each had a fine crimson thread of silk neatly stitched around its neck—which made her as vain and proud of her brood as the old father was of his four sons.

"Now stay with me for a time," he entreated them. "There is plenty to eat and drink, and there are a few little odd jobs you might do for me. Never man had better sons, and a joy it is beyond words to have you all safely home again."

So they said they would stay with their old father as long as he wished.

However, they had scarcely been a week at home when news came that a dragon that had been prowling near one of the King's castles at the edge of a vast fen, or bogland, had carried off the Princess, his only daughter. The whole realm was in grief and dread at this news, and the King in despair had decreed that anyone who should discover the dragon and bring back the Princess should have her for wife. After pondering this news awhile the old farmer said to his sons, "Now, my lads, here's a chance indeed. Not that I'm saying it's good for a man, as I think, to marry anybody he has no mind to. But to save any manner of human creature from a cruel foul dragon—who wouldn't have a try?"

So the four brothers set out at once to the castle, and were taken before the King. They asked the King where the dragon was. And the King groaned. "Who knows?"

So the stargazer put up his spyglass to his eye and peered long through its tube—north, east, south, then west. And he said at last, "*I* see him, Sire, a full day's sailing away. He is coiled up grisly on a rock with his wings folded, at least a league to sea, and his hooked great clanking tail curled around him. Aye, and I see the Princess too, no bigger than my little finger in size, beside him. She's been crying, by the looks of her. And the dragon is keeping mighty sly guard over her, for one of his eyes is an inch ajar."

The King greatly wondered, and sent word to the Queen, who was in a chamber apart; and he gave the four brothers a ship, and they sailed away in the King's ship until they neared the island and the rock. In great caution they then took in sail, drifting slowly in. When they were come near, they saw that the Princess was now asleep, worn out with grief and despair, and that her head lay so close to the dragon that her hair was spread out like yellow silk upon its horny scales.

"Shoot I dare not," said the huntsman, "for, by Nimrod, I might pierce the heart of the Princess."

So first the nimble-fingered brother swam ashore, and creeping up behind the dragon, stole and withdrew the Princess away with such ease and cunning that the monster thought only a gentle breeze had wafted upon its coils with its wings. Stealthy as a seal the brother slipped into the sea again and swam back to the ship, the Princess lying cradled in the water nearby him, for, though she could not swim herself, she rode almost as light on the water as a seabird. Then the four brothers hoisted sail and with all haste sailed away.

But the ship had hardly sailed a league and a league when the dragon, turning softly in his drowsiness, became aware that a fragrance had gone out of the morning. And when he found that his captive was lost to him, he raised his head with so lamentable a cry the very rocks resounded beneath the screaming of the seabirds; then writhing his neck this way and that, he descried the white sails of the ship on the horizon. Whereupon he spread his vast, batlike wings and, soaring into the heavens, pursued the ship across the sea.

The four brothers heard from afar the dreadful clanging of his scales, but waited till he was near at hand. When at last he was circling overhead, his hooked and horny wings darkening the very light of the sun, the huntsman, with one mighty twang of his bowstring, let fly an arrow, and the arrow sped clean through the dragon from tip of snout to utmost barb of tail, and he fell like a millstone. So close, however, in his flight had he approached the ship, that his huge carcass crashed flat upon it in the sea and shattered it to pieces.

But by marvelous good fortune the dragon fell on that half of the ship which is between the bowsprit and mainmast, so that neither the Princess nor the four brothers came to any harm (for they were in the parts abaft the mainmast), except that one and all were flung helter-skelter into the sea. There they would certainly have drowned but for the tailor son, who at once straddled a balk of timber and, drawing in every plank within reach as it came floating by, speedily stitched up a raft with his magic needle. Soon all the other three brothers had clambered up out of the sea onto the raft, and having lifted the Princess as gently as might be after them, they came at last safely ashore.

There, sitting on the sunny shingle of the beach, they dried their clothes in the sun, and the Princess sleeked her hair, and when she had refreshed herself with a morsel of honeycomb which the stargazer found in the heart of a hollow tree, the four brothers led her safely back to the palace; and great were the rejoicings.

The King, having listened to their story, marveled, and bade that a great feast should be prepared. A little before the hour fixed for this feast, he sent for these brothers, and they stood beside his chair.

"Now, which of you," he said, "is to have the Princess to wife? For each did wondrous well: the spying out, the stealing away, the death wound, and the rafting. Her life is yours, but she cannot be cut into quarters." And he smiled. "Still, a king is as good as his word; and no man can do better. Do you decide."

Then the four brothers withdrew a little and talked together in a corner of the great hall. Then they came back to the King, and the eldest thanked the King for them all, and said, "We are, Liege, sons of one dear father, who is a farmer. If of your graciousness Your Majesty would see that he is never in want, and that he prospers howsoever long he lives, even though he live to be an old, old man and can work no more, we shall be your happy and contented subjects to the end of our days. You see, we might die, Your Majesty, and then our poor old father would have to live alone with none to help him."

The King stroked his beard and smiled.

"Besides, Your Majesty," the eldest son went on, "never was Princess more beautiful than she we have brought back in safety, but a dragon dead is dead forever, and no pretty maid we ever heard of, high or low, but wished to choose a husband for herself, whatever dragons there might be to prevent her."

At this the King laughed aloud, and the Queen bade the four brothers come and sit on either side of her at the banquet, two by two, and the Princess kissed each of them on the cheek. Then they showed their marvels and their skill; and there was music and delight until the stars in the heavens showed it to be two in the morning.

Next day the four brothers set out together for home, with twelve fen horses, which have long manes and tails and are of a rusty red, and each of these horses was laden with two sacks, one on either side, and each sack was bulging full of gifts for the four brothers and for their old father. And a pleasant journey home that was.

The Hare and the Hedgehog

by Walter de la Mare

For a race, the hare had better legs, but the hedgehog had better brains.

Early one Sunday morning, when the cowslips or paigles were showing their first honey-sweet buds in the meadows and the broom was in bloom, a hedgehog came to his little door to look out at the weather. He stood with arms akimbo, whistling a tune to himself—a tune no better and no worse than the tunes hedgehogs usually whistle to themselves on fine Sunday mornings. And as he whistled, the notion came into his head that, before turning in and while his wife was washing the children, he might take a little walk into the fields and see how his young nettles were getting on. For there was a tasty beetle lived among the nettles; and no nettles—no beetles.

Off he went, taking his own little private path into the field. And as he came stepping along around a bush of blackthorn, its leaves now showing green, he met a hare; and the hare had come out to look at his spring cabbages.

The hedgehog smiled and bade him a polite good-morning. But the hare, who felt himself a particularly fine sleek gentleman in this Sunday sunshine, merely sneered at his greeting.

"And how is it," he said, "*you* happen to be out so early?"

"I am taking a walk, sir," said the hedgehog.

"A walk!" sniffed the hare. "I should have thought you might use those bandy little legs of yours to far better purpose."

This angered the hedgehog, for as his legs were crooked by nature, he couldn't bear to have bad made worse by any talk about them.

"You seem to suppose, sir," he said, bristling all over, "that you can do more with your legs than I can with mine."

"Well, perhaps," said the hare airily.

"See here, then," said the hedgehog, his beady eyes fixed on the hare. "I say you *can't*. Start fair, and I'd beat you nowt to ninepence. Aye, every time."

"A race, my dear Master Hedgehog!" said the hare, laying back his whiskers. "You must be beside yourself. It's *childish*. But still, what will you wager?"

"I'll lay a golden guinea to a bottle of brandy," said the hedgehog.

"Done!" said the hare. "Shake hands on it, and we'll start at once."

"Aye, but not quite so fast," said the hedgehog. "I have had no breakfast yet. But if you will be here in half an hour's time, so will I."

The hare agreed, and at once took a little frisky practice along the dewy green border of the field, while the hedgehog went shuffling home.

He thinks a mighty deal of himself, thought the hedgehog on his way. But we shall see what we *shall* see.

When he reached home, he bustled in and, looking solemnly at his wife, said, "My dear, I have need of you. In all haste. Leave everything and follow me at once into the fields."

"Why, what's going on?" says she.

"Why," said her husband, "I have bet the hare a guinea to a bottle of brandy that I'll beat him in a race, and you must come and see it."

"Heavens, husband!" Mrs. Hedgehog cried. "Are you daft? Are you gone crazy? You! Run a race with a hare!"

"Hold your tongue, woman," said the hedgehog. "There are things simple brains cannot understand. Leave all this fussing and titivating. The children can dry themselves; and you come along at once with me." So they went together.

"Now," said the hedgehog, when they reached the plowed field beyond the field that was sprouting with young green wheat, "listen to me, my dear. This is where the race is going to be. The hare is over there at the other end of the field. I am going to arrange that he shall start in that deep furrow, and I shall start in this. But as soon as I have scrambled along a few inches and he can't see me, I shall turn back. And what *you*, my dear, must do is this: when he comes out of his furrow *there*, you must be sitting puffing like a porpoise *here*. And when you see him, you will say, 'Aha! So you've come at last?' Do you follow me, my dear?" At first Mrs. Hedgehog was a little nervous, but she smiled at her husband's cunning and gladly agreed to do what he said.

The hedgehog then went back to where he had promised to meet the hare, and he said, "Here I am, you see; and very much the better, sir, for eating a good breakfast."

"How shall we run?" simpered the hare scornfully. "Down or over; sideways, longways; three legs or altogether? It's all one to me."

"Well, to be honest with you," said the hedgehog, "let me say this. I have now and then watched you taking a gambol and disporting yourself with your friends in the evening, and a pretty runner you are. But you never keep straight. You all go round and round, and round and round, scampering now this way, now that and chasing one another's tails as if you were crazy. And as often as not you run uphill! But you can't run *races* like that. You must keep straight; you must begin in one place, go steadily on, and end in another."

"I could have told you that," said the hare angrily.

"Very well, then," said the hedgehog. "You shall keep to that furrow, and I'll keep to this."

And the hare, being a good deal quicker on his feet than he was in his wits, agreed.

"*One! Two! Three! and AWAY!*" he shouted, and off he went like a little whirlwind up the field. But the hedgehog, after scuttling along a few paces, turned back and stayed quietly where he was.

When the hare came out of his furrow at the upper end of the field, the hedgehog's wife sat panting there as if she would never be able to recover her breath, and at sight of him she sighed out, "Aha, sir! So you've come at last?"

The hare was utterly shocked. His ears trembled. His eyes bulged in his head. "You've run it! You've run it!" he cried in astonishment. For she being so exactly like her husband, he never for a moment doubted that her husband she actually was.

"Aye," said she, "but I was afraid you had gone lame."

"Lame!" said the hare. "Lame! But there, what's one furrow? 'Every time' was what you said. We'll try again."

Away once more he went, and he had never run faster. Yet when he came out of his furrow at the bottom of the field, there was the hedgehog! And the hedgehog laughed and said, "Aha! So here you are again! At last!" At this the hare could hardly speak for rage.

"Not enough! Not enough!" he said. "Three for luck! Again, again!"

"As often as you please, my dear friend," said the hedgehog. "It's the long run that really counts."

Again, and again, and yet again the hare raced up and down the long furrow of the field, and every time he reached the top, and every time he reached the bottom, there was the hedgehog, as he thought, with his mocking "Aha! So here you are again! At last!"

But at length the hare could run no more. He lay panting and speechless; he was dead beat. Stretched out there, limp on the grass, his fur bedraggled, his eyes dim, his legs quaking, it looked as if he might fetch his last breath at any moment.

So Mrs. Hedgehog went off to the hare's house to fetch the bottle of brandy; and if it had not been the best brandy, the hare might never have run again.

News of the contest spread far and wide. From that day to this, never has there been a race to compare with it. And lucky it was for the hedgehog he had the good sense to marry a wife like himself, and not a weasel, or a wombat, or a whale!

The Doughnuts

by Robert McCloskey

The new doughnut-making machine was
the hit of the lunchroom. Homer knew how to start it.
But stopping it was another story.

One Friday night in November Homer Price overheard his mother talking on the telephone to Aunt Agnes over in Centerburg. "I'll stop by with the car in about half an hour and we can go to the meeting together," she said, because tonight was the night the Ladies' Club was meeting to discuss plans for a box social and to knit and sew for the Red Cross.

"I think I'll come along and keep Uncle Ulysses company while you and Aunt Agnes are at the meeting," said Homer.

So after Homer had combed his hair and his mother had looked to see if she had her knitting instructions and the right size needles, they started for town.

Homer's uncle Ulysses and aunt Agnes have a very up-and-coming lunchroom over in Centerburg, just across from the courthouse on the town square. Uncle Ulysses is a man with advanced ideas and a weakness for laborsaving devices. He equipped the lunchroom with automatic toasters, automatic coffee maker, automatic dishwasher, and an automatic doughnut maker. All the latest thing in laborsaving devices. Aunt Agnes would throw up her hands and sigh every time

Uncle Ulysses bought a new laborsaving device. Sometimes she became unkindly disposed toward him for days and days. She was of the opinion that Uncle Ulysses just frittered away his spare time over at the barbershop with the sheriff and the boys, so what was the good of a laborsaving device that gave you more time to fritter?

When Homer and his mother got to Centerburg they stopped at the lunchroom, and after Aunt Agnes had come out and said, "My, how that boy does grow!" which was what she always said, she went off with Homer's mother in the car. Homer went into the lunchroom and said, "Howdy, Uncle Ulysses!"

"Oh, hello, Homer. You're just in time," said Uncle Ulysses. "I've been going over this automatic doughnut machine, oiling the machinery and cleaning the works. . . . Wonderful things, these laborsaving devices."

"Yep," agreed Homer, and he picked up a cloth and started polishing the metal trimmings while Uncle Ulysses tinkered with the inside workings.

"Opfwo-oof!" sighed Uncle Ulysses. And, "Look here, Homer, you've got a mechanical mind. See if you can find where these two pieces fit in. I'm going across to the barbershop for a spell, 'cause there's somethin' I've got to talk to the sheriff about. There won't be much business here until the double feature is over, and I'll be back before then."

Then as Uncle Ulysses went out the door he said, "Uh, Homer, after you get the pieces in place, would you mind mixing up a batch of doughnut batter and putting it in the machine? You could turn the switch and make a few doughnuts to have on hand for the crowd after the movie . . . if you don't mind."

"Okay," said Homer. "I'll take care of everything."

A few minutes later a customer came in and said, "Good evening, bud."

Homer looked up from putting the last piece in the doughnut machine and said, "Good evening, sir. What can I do for you?"

"Well, young feller, I'd like a cup o' coffee and some doughnuts," said the customer.

"I'm sorry, mister, but we won't have any doughnuts for about half an hour, until I can mix some dough and start this machine. I could give you some very fine sugar rolls instead."

"Well, bud, I'm in no real hurry, so I'll just have a cup o' coffee and wait around a bit for the doughnuts. Fresh doughnuts are always worth waiting for is what I always say."

"Okay," said Homer, and he drew a cup of coffee from Uncle Ulysses' automatic coffee maker.

"Nice place you've got here," said the customer.

"Oh, yes," replied Homer. "This is a very up-and-coming lunchroom, with all the latest improvements."

"Yes," said the stranger. "Must be a good business. I'm in business too. A traveling man in outdoor advertising. I'm a sandwich man. Mr. Gabby's my name."

"My name is Homer. I'm glad to meet you, Mr. Gabby. It must be a fine profession, traveling around and advertising sandwiches."

"Oh, no," said Mr. Gabby. "I don't advertise sandwiches. I just wear any kind of an ad, one sign on front and one sign on behind, this way. . . . Like a sandwich. Ya know what I mean?"

"Oh, I see. That must be fun. And you travel too?" asked Homer as he got out the flour and the baking powder.

"Yeah. I ride the rods between jobs, on freight trains, ya know what I mean?"

"Yes, but isn't that dangerous?" asked Homer.

"Of course there's a certain amount a risk, but you take any method a travel these days, it's all dangerous. Ya know what I mean? Now take airplanes . . ."

Just then a large shiny black car stopped in front of the lunchroom and a chauffeur helped a lady out the rear door. They both came inside, and the lady smiled at Homer and said, "We've stopped for a light snack. Some doughnuts and coffee would be simply marvelous."

Then Homer said, "I'm sorry, ma'am, but the doughnuts won't be ready until I make this batter and start Uncle Ulysses' doughnut machine."

"Well, now aren't *you* a clever young man to know how to make *doughnuts!*"

"Well"—Homer blushed—"I've really never done it before, but I've got a recipe to follow."

"Now, young man, you simply must allow me to help. You know, I haven't made doughnuts for years, but I know the best recipe for doughnuts. It's marvelous, and we really must use it."

"But, ma'am . . ." said Homer.

"Now just *wait* till you taste these doughnuts," said the lady. "Do you have an apron?" she asked as she took off her fur coat and her rings and her jewelry and rolled up her sleeves. "Charles," she said to the chauffeur, "hand me that baking powder, that's right, and, young man, we'll need some nutmeg."

So Homer and the chauffeur stood by and handed things and cracked the eggs while the lady mixed and stirred. Mr. Gabby sat on his stool, sipped his coffee, and looked on with great interest.

"There!" said the lady when all of the ingredients were mixed. "Just *wait* till you taste these doughnuts!"

"It looks like an awful lot of batter," said Homer as he stood on a chair and poured it into the doughnut machine with the help of the chauffeur. "It's about *ten* times as much as Uncle Ulysses ever makes."

"But you wait till you taste them!" said the lady, with an eager look and a smile.

Homer got down from the chair and pushed a button on the machine marked START. Rings of batter started dropping into the hot fat. After a ring of batter was cooked on one side, an automatic gadget turned it over and the other side would cook. Then another automatic gadget gave the doughnut a little push and it rolled neatly down a little chute, all ready to eat.

"That's a simply *fascinating* machine," said the lady as she waited for the first doughnut to roll out. "Here, young man, *you* must have the first one. Now isn't that just *too* delicious!? Isn't it simply marvelous?"

"Yes, ma'am, it's very good," replied Homer as the lady handed doughnuts to Charles and to Mr. Gabby and asked if they didn't think they were simply divine doughnuts.

"It's an old family recipe!" said the lady with pride.

Homer poured some coffee for the lady and her chauffeur and for Mr. Gabby, and a glass of milk for himself. Then they all sat down at the lunch counter to enjoy another few doughnuts apiece.

"I'm so glad you enjoy my doughnuts," said the lady. "But now, Charles, we really must be going. If you will just take this apron, Homer, and put two dozen doughnuts in a bag to take along, we'll be on our way. And, Charles, don't forget to pay the young man." She rolled down her sleeves and put on her jewelry; then Charles managed to get her into her big fur coat.

"Good night, young man. I haven't had so much fun in years. I *really* haven't!" said the lady as she went out the door and into the big shiny car.

"Those are sure good doughnuts," said Mr. Gabby as the car moved off.

"You bet!" said Homer. Then he and Mr. Gabby watched the automatic doughnut machine make doughnuts.

After a few dozen more doughnuts had rolled down the little chute, Homer said, "I guess that's about enough doughnuts to sell to the after-theater customers. I'd better turn the machine off for a while."

Homer pushed the button marked STOP and there was a little click, but nothing happened. The rings of batter kept right on dropping into the hot fat, and an automatic gadget kept right on turning them over, and another automatic gadget kept right on giving them a little push, and the doughnuts kept right on rolling down the little chute, all ready to eat.

"That's funny," said Homer. "I'm sure that's the right button!" He pushed it again, but the automatic doughnut maker kept right on making doughnuts.

"Well, I guess I must have put one of those pieces in backward," said Homer.

"Then it might stop if you pushed the button marked START," said Mr. Gabby.

Homer did, and the doughnuts still kept rolling down the little chute, just as regular as a clock can tick.

"I guess we could sell a few more doughnuts," said Homer, "but I'd better telephone Uncle Ulysses over at the barbershop." Homer gave the number, and while he waited for someone to answer he counted thirty-seven doughnuts roll down the little chute.

Finally someone answered, "Hello! Hello! This is the sarberbhop, I mean the barbershop."

"Oh, hello, Sheriff. This is Homer. Could I speak to Uncle Ulysses?"

"Well, he's playing pinochle right now," said the sheriff. "Anythin' I can tell 'im?"

"Yes," said Homer. "I pushed the button marked STOP on the doughnut machine, but the rings of batter keep right on dropping into the hot fat, and an automatic gadget keeps right on turning them over, and another automatic gadget keeps giving them a little push, and the doughnuts keep right on rolling down the little chute! It won't stop!"

"Okay. Wold the hire, I mean, hold the wire and I'll tell 'im." Then Homer looked over his shoulder and counted another twenty-one doughnuts roll down the little chute, all ready to eat. Then the sheriff said, "He'll be right over. . . . Just gotta finish this hand."

"That's good," said Homer. "G'by, Sheriff."

The window was full of doughnuts by now, so Homer and Mr. Gabby had to hustle around and start stacking them on plates and trays and lining them up on the counter.

"Sure are a lot of doughnuts!" said Homer.

"You bet!" said Mr. Gabby. "I lost count at twelve hundred and two, and that was quite a while back."

People had begun to gather outside the lunchroom window, and someone was saying, "There are almost as many doughnuts as there are people in Centerburg, and I wonder how in tarnation Ulysses thinks he can sell all of 'em!"

Every once in a while somebody would

come inside and buy some, but while somebody bought two to eat and a dozen to take home, the machine made three dozen more.

By the time Uncle Ulysses and the sheriff arrived and pushed their way through the crowd, the lunchroom was a calamity of doughnuts! Doughnuts in the window, doughnuts piled high on the shelves, doughnuts stacked on plates, doughnuts lined up twelve deep all along the counter, and doughnuts still rolling down the little chute, just as regular as a clock can tick.

"Hello, Sheriff, hello, Uncle Ulysses. We're having a little trouble here," said Homer.

"Well, I'll be dunked!!" said Uncle Ulysses.

"Durned ef you won't be when Aggy gits home," said the sheriff. "Mighty fine doughnuts, though. What'll you do with 'em all, Ulysses?"

Uncle Ulysses groaned and said, "What will Aggy say? We'll never sell 'em all."

Then Mr. Gabby, who hadn't said anything for a long time, stopped piling doughnuts and said, "What you need is an advertising man. Ya know what I mean? You got the doughnuts, ya gotta create a market. . . . Understand? . . . It's balancing the demand with the supply . . . that sort of thing."

"Mr. Gabby's right," said Homer. "We have to enlarge our market. He's an advertising sandwich man, so if we hire him, he can walk up and down in front of the theater and get customers."

"You're hired, Mr. Gabby!" said Uncle Ulysses.

Then everybody pitched in to paint the signs and to get Mr. Gabby sandwiched between. They painted SALE ON DOUGHNUTS in big letters on the window too.

Meanwhile the rings of batter kept right on dropping into the hot fat, and an automatic gadget kept right on turning them over, and another automatic gadget kept right on giving them a little push, and the doughnuts kept right on rolling down the little chute, just as regular as a clock can tick.

"I certainly hope this advertising works," said Uncle Ulysses, wagging his head. "Aggy'll throw a fit if it don't."

The sheriff went outside to keep order, because there was quite a crowd by now—all looking at the doughnuts and guessing how many thousand there were, and watching new ones roll down the little chute, just as regular as a clock can tick. Homer and Uncle Ulysses kept stacking doughnuts. Once in a while somebody bought a few, but not very often.

Then Mr. Gabby came back and said, "Say, you know there's not much use o' me advertisin' at the theater. The show's all over, and besides, almost everybody in town is out front watching that machine make doughnuts!"

"Zeus!" said Uncle Ulysses. "We must get rid of these doughnuts before Aggy gets here!"

"Looks like you will have ta hire a truck ta waul 'em ahay, I mean haul 'em away!!" said the sheriff, who had just come in. Just then there was a noise and a shoving out front, and the lady from the shiny black car and her chauffeur came pushing through the crowd and into the lunchroom.

"Oh, gracious!" she gasped, ignoring the doughnuts. "I've lost my diamond bracelet, and I know I left it here on the counter," she said, pointing to a place where the doughnuts were piled in stacks of two dozen.

"Yes, ma'am, I guess you forgot it when you helped make the batter," said Homer.

Then they moved all the doughnuts around and looked for the diamond bracelet, but they couldn't find it anywhere. Meanwhile the doughnuts kept rolling down the little chute, just as regular as a clock can tick.

After they had looked all around, the sheriff cast a suspicious eye on Mr. Gabby, but Homer said, "He's all right, Sheriff. He didn't take it. He's a friend of mine."

Then the lady said, "I'll offer a reward of one hundred dollars for that bracelet! It really *must* be found! . . . It *really* must!"

"Now don't you worry, lady," said the sheriff. "I'll get your bracelet back!"

"Zeus! This is terrible!" said Uncle Ulysses. "First all of these doughnuts and then on top of all that, a lost diamond bracelet . . ."

Mr. Gabby tried to comfort him, and he said, "There's always a bright side. That machine'll probably run outta batter in an hour or two."

If Mr. Gabby hadn't been quick on his feet, Uncle Ulysses would have knocked him down, sure as fate.

Then while the lady wrung her hands and said, "We must find it, we *must!*" and Uncle Ulysses was moaning about what Aunt Agnes would say, and the sheriff was eyeing Mr. Gabby, Homer sat down and thought hard.

Before twenty more doughnuts could roll down the little chute he shouted,

"Say! I know where the bracelet is! It was lying here on the counter and got mixed up in the batter by mistake! The bracelet is cooked inside one of these doughnuts!"

"Why . . . I really believe you're right," said the lady through her tears. "Isn't that *amazing?* Simply *amazing!*"

"I'll be durned!" said the sheriff.

"Ohh!" moaned Uncle Ulysses. "Now we have to break up all of these doughnuts to find it. Think of the *pieces!* Think of the *crumbs!* Think of what *Aggy* will say!"

"Nope," said Homer. "We won't have to break them up. I've got a plan."

So Homer and the advertising man took some cardboard and some paint and printed another sign. They put this sign in the window, and the sandwich man wore two more signs that said the same thing and he walked around in the crowd out front.

Then . . . the doughnuts began to sell! *Everybody* wanted to buy doughnuts, *dozens* of doughnuts!

And that's not all. Everybody bought coffee to dunk the doughnuts in. Those who didn't buy coffee bought milk or soda. It kept Homer and the lady and the chauffeur and Uncle Ulysses and the sheriff busy waiting on the people who wanted to buy doughnuts.

When all but the last couple of hundred doughnuts had been sold, Rupert Black shouted, "I gawt it!!" and sure enough . . . there was the diamond bracelet inside of his doughnut!

Then Rupert went home with a hundred dollars, the citizens of Centerburg went home full of doughnuts, the lady and her chauffeur drove off with the diamond bracelet, and Homer went home with his mother when she stopped by with Aunt Aggy.

As Homer went out the door he heard Mr. Gabby say, "Neatest trick of merchandising I ever seen." Aunt Aggy was looking skeptical, while Uncle Ulysses was saying, "The rings of batter kept right on dropping into the hot fat, and the automatic gadget kept right on turning them over, and the other automatic gadget kept right on giving them a little push, and the doughnuts kept right on rolling down the little chute, just as regular as a clock can tick—they just kept right on acomin', an' acomin', an' acomin', an' acomin'."

A Hero by Mistake

by Anita Brenner

A man who runs when nothing's there may stand his ground when something is.

There was once a man named Dionisio who was very much afraid. He happened to be an Indian.

Grown men of course are not supposed to be afraid, and especially not Indians.

This Dionisio lived in a hut near the woods, in Mexico. He had a few neighbors who lived in a village near him. Others were scattered around the valley in huts like his own, except some huts were bigger because their owners were rich.

There were also the mountains. They made Dionisio feel very safe, because they were so big and lovely and peaceful. But when he was afraid, even the mountains seemed dark and full of evil things.

Sometimes it seemed as if almost anything made him feel *uuuuh!* and like rocks inside him, and like running away and hiding all at once. You know how it is.

For instance, one morning he felt something behind him. A shape! Something following him! He began to run. The shape ran too. He saw it running and he ran harder, and the more he ran the more afraid he was . . . and this shape right behind him.

Yes, of course, it was his own shadow. Dionisio realized it when he had to stop for breath.

"Oh, what a silly I am!" he said, and hit himself on the head with his hands.

The people who lived in the village all knew that Dionisio was not a brave man. Sometimes he was so afraid he ran lickety-split like a cat, and they laughed at him.

And afterward he would laugh too, and say, "How silly!" Then there was a happy feeling of "There is nothing so much, after all, to be afraid of in this world."

Dionisio was a woodchopper. Once he was chopping up on the mountain, and heard another axe far away. Another woodcutter, he thought, and yelled, "I'm Dionisio!"

A faraway hoarse voice answered, "*Dionisio.*"

"He knows me." And he began to worry. "I'm alone here," and . . . "What if he isn't my friend?"

He worried and wondered and wondered and worried; then he yelled, "Who are you? Friend or enemy?" The voice came back very shrill, "*Enemy!*"

Oh, dear, Dionisio thought, I've just *got* to be brave. So he shouted fiercely, "If you bother me, I'll kill you!" And the voice yelled even more ferociously, "*I'll kill you!*"

And then Dionisio, terrified, began to run. He ran to the village for help.

So ten brave men came back with him. At the place where Dionisio had heard the ferocious voice they started to yell, and ten brave voices yelled right back. Then they laughed and laughed because, of course, it was just an echo. "Oh, what a silly I am!" said Dionisio, and hit himself on the head and laughed too.

Dionisio was a frightened man all right, but he was a hard worker. He worked so hard that finally he had chopped all the wood the people in his valley needed, and so nobody would buy any more.

So Dionisio loaded his burro and went out to look for a market. He traveled and traveled until, way ahead there, he saw a town. When he was almost there, *Crash! Crash! Crash!* he heard.

"Oh me, oh my!" said Dionisio. "Shooting!"

How could he run away and leave his burro?

Crash! Crash! Crash!

So Dionisio got under his burro. There he was, shaking and trembling, when along the road came a little old woman. She was surprised to see a man all curled up in a ball under his burro.

"What are you doing there, good neighbor?" the old woman asked. "Are you ill?"

"Oh, madam," Dionisio said to her, "you'd better get under here too. You might be killed."

"But who would kill us, good sir? We're all peaceful folks here," she said.

"Who knows what wicked souls are shooting up the town?" Dionisio said. "Come quickly, before you're killed!"

Then the old woman began to laugh. "Oh, goodness," she said, laughing and laughing, "it's firecrackers."

"Firecrackers? But what for? It isn't a holiday today!"

"Well, it is here. It's the christening of the baby daughter of Don Gedovius. Oh, poor you," said the old lady, laughing like anything. "How frightened you must have been. Come on out now. You look very strange under that burro."

"Oh," said Dionisio, hitting himself on the head. "But . . . what a silly I am!"

Now, you can't sell wood in a town where everybody is busy celebrating, so Dionisio went on. After a while he met a man who had musical instruments for sale: guitars, violins, and bugles.

He was so pleased that nothing had happened to him that he bought a bugle, and the man taught him then and there to play it, *Ta-ta-ta-ta-ta-ta-ta-taaaaaa!* the way soldiers blow.

So along went Dionisio again, with his bugle and his burro and all the load of wood that he wanted to sell. Pretty soon there were more wheel tracks in the road.

He was near another town when again, of all things, he heard *Crash! Crash!* And louder, *CRASH-CRASH-CRASH!*

This time, Dionisio said to himself, "I'm not going to be such a silly. I shall blow my bugle so I'll be invited to the party. I'm getting hungry, and where there's a christening there ought to be a turkey dinner." And Dionisio blew his bugle the way the soldiers do.

And what do you think? Five men on horseback galloped *cloppity-clop* furiously out of the town, in a great big cloud of dust. They had handkerchiefs tied around their faces.

And who would they be? Dionisio thought as he watched them disappear down the road. They certainly need those handkerchiefs around their noses, in all that dust.

He was still standing looking at the dust when a lot of people came running out of town—men, women, and children. They hugged him and said, "Oh, sir, you have saved us!"

"Me?" said Dionisio. "But from what?"

"Why, from those bad men who rode in on horseback and wanted to rob us! When you blew your bugle they thought it was soldiers, and how they ran!"

"What a brave man you are!"

"Me?" said Dionisio.

Well, they just *had* to give him a party. They wouldn't take no for an answer.

And they gave him so many presents he could hardly get them all loaded onto his burro. It was nighttime when he said good-by . . . and no way to tell them he was afraid to leave . . . that he was such a frightened man he had never gone anywhere alone at night.

So there went Dionisio along the dark road, holding on to his burro and feeling like rocks in his stomach, he was so afraid. Suddenly, ahead of him he saw two great big glowing eyes coming toward him, fast.

They came along closer and closer. "Help! Help! Save me from this monster!" yelled Dionisio, and jumped into the bushes, pulling his burro after him.

Then *whooosh!* Something raced past in a flood of light. The monster was just a truck.

"Oh!" said Dionisio. "Silly, silly me!"

And so, sillying himself along, he reached the dirt road to his village. He was going up a slope, very pleased to be so near home, when almost right ahead of him he saw two lights that looked like eyes, again. They were smaller than the others had been, and they glowed in a very ugly way.

"I'm *not* going to be such a silly this time," said Dionisio sternly to himself, and kept straight on.

But then his burro wouldn't budge. He planted his forelegs stiff and just would not go on, and shook as if frightened.

"Arreh! Giddyap, giddyap. Arreh!" Dionisio scolded and tugged and pulled. But the burro, instead of going forward, started to back up.

Dionisio was so busy struggling with

his animal that he forgot about the ugly lights on the road, and then *whish!* Something jumped.

It was a wildcat! Dionisio saw it scrambling away among the bushes, running from him.

"Then wildcats are afraid too?" Dionisio marveled. "How strange. A wildcat afraid of *me!*"

He was still thinking about that when he got home and lay down to sleep.

He was fast asleep when suddenly he awoke. There seemed to be something making a noise. Something outside. Walking softly, softly.

"Oh, dear!" said Dionisio. "Some robber surely saw me leave that town all loaded with presents and followed me. And here, sure enough, is the end of me."

He didn't know what to do. He just rolled up in a little ball in a corner of his hut, shaking and trembling so hard his teeth went *tat-tat* in his head.

Then he heard those steps again, closer. Softly, softly, the door was being pushed open. He couldn't stand it then. He jumped up and yelled. And what does he see?

His burro, which had gotten loose from its stall!

"Oh," said Dionisio, "is there anyone in the whole world like me? What a silly I *am!*" And he hit himself on the head like anything, and then went back to sleep.

A little while later he woke up again. Again he heard, softly, softly, something moving out there. Like steps.

"Oh, you stupid burro!" Dionisio yelled. "Wait till you see what I'll do to you, waking me up like that!"

And he jumped up and grabbed his lasso and rushed out.

Outside everything was dark. All he could see was something running in the dark near the cactus patch. So he grabbed a hunk of firewood and he threw it as hard as he could, he was so angry.

"That will teach you to run away."

Then, gripping his lasso, he ran to the cactus patch. He was running hard when he tripped over something big and soft and almost fell over it.

He looked to see what it was and it was a man, fallen among the cactus, unconscious and bleeding. Dionisio had hit him square on the head when he threw that wood.

Well, naturally, Dionisio tied him up. Then he went to call the authorities to come and see who that man was and find out what he was doing in Dionisio's cactus patch.

So the authorities came to look into this matter. And they took the man away.

And the next day a telegram arrived. It said that there was a very wicked and dangerous man in the neighborhood, that there was fifty thousand pesos for whoever brought him in, and sixty thousand if they brought him in alive.

"Uuum," said the authorities. "Wonder if that is the fellow Dionisio caught?"

And he was. He was the very same bandit that they were searching for. So they gave Dionisio the sixty thousand. The municipal president made a speech, and the band played a victory march.

From then on, Dionisio wasn't called Dionisio anymore. As he was rich, everybody called him *Don* Dionisio, which is the same as, respectfully, mister.

And every time he said, "Oh, what a silly I am!" they all said to him, "Oh, no, sir, you are the most intelligent and bravest man in the whole region. You are a hero!"

Gluck
Hans
Schwartz

The King of the Golden River

by John Ruskin

A classic tale of golden treasures and greedy men.

CHAPTER ONE

How the Agricultural System of the Black Brothers Was Interfered With by South-West Wind, Esquire

In a secluded and mountainous part of Stiria, there was, in old time, a valley of the most surprising and luxuriant fertility. It was surrounded on all sides by steep and rocky mountains, rising into peaks, which were always covered with snow, and from which a number of torrents descended in constant cataracts. One of these fell westward, over the face of a crag so high that when the sun had set to everything else, and all below was darkness, his beams still shone full upon this waterfall, so that it looked like a shower of gold. It was, therefore, called by the people of the neighborhood the Golden River.

It was strange that none of these streams fell into the valley itself. They all descended on the other side of the mountains, and wound away through broad plains and by populous cities. But the clouds were drawn so constantly to the snowy hills, and rested so softly in the circular hollow, that in time of drought and heat, when all the country around was burned up, there was still rain in the little valley; and its crops were so heavy, and its hay so high, and its apples so red, and its grapes so blue, and its wine so rich, and its honey so sweet, that it was a marvel to everyone who beheld it, and was commonly called the Treasure Valley.

The whole of this little valley belonged to three brothers, called Schwartz, Hans, and Gluck. Schwartz and Hans, the two elder brothers, were very ugly men, with overhanging eyebrows and small, dull eyes, which were always half shut, so that you couldn't see into *them*, and always fancied they saw very far into *you*. They lived by farming the Treasure Valley, and very good farmers they were. They killed everything that did not pay for its eating. They shot the blackbirds, because they pecked the fruit, and killed the hedgehogs, lest they should suck the cows; they poisoned the crickets for eating the crumbs in the kitchen, and smothered the cicadas, which used to sing all summer in the lime trees. They worked their servants without any wages, till they would not work anymore, and then quarreled with them, and turned them out of doors without paying them.

It would have been very odd if, with such a farm and such a system of farming, they hadn't got very rich; and very rich they *did* get. They generally contrived to keep their corn by them till it was very dear, and then sell it for twice its value; they had heaps of gold lying about on their floors, yet it was never known that they had given so much as a penny or a crust in charity; they never went to Mass, grumbled perpetually at paying tithes, and were, in a word, of so cruel and grinding a temper as to receive from all those with whom they had any dealings the nickname of the "Black Brothers."

The youngest brother, Gluck, was as completely opposed, in both appearance and character, to his seniors as could possibly be imagined or desired. He was not above twelve years old, fair, blue-eyed, and kind in temper to every living thing. He did not, of course, agree particularly well with his brothers, or rather, they did not agree with *him*. He was usually appointed to the honorable office of turnspit, when there was anything to roast, which was not often; for, to do the brothers justice, they were hardly less sparing upon themselves than upon other people. At other times he used to clean the shoes, floors, and sometimes the plates, occasionally getting what was left on them, by way of encouragement, and a wholesome quantity of dry blows, by way of education.

Things went on in this manner for a long time. At last came a very wet summer, and everything went wrong in the country around. The hay had hardly been got in when the haystacks were floated bodily down to the sea by an inundation; the vines were cut to pieces with the hail; the corn was all killed by a black blight; only in the Treasure Valley, as usual, all was safe. As it had rain when there was rain nowhere else, so it had sun when there was sun nowhere else. Everybody came to buy corn at the farm, and went away pouring maledictions on the Black Brothers. They asked what they liked and got it, except from poor people, who could only beg, and several of whom were starved at their very door, without the slightest regard or notice.

It was drawing toward winter, and very cold weather, when one day the two elder brothers had gone out, with their usual warning to little Gluck, who was left to mind the roast, that he was to let nobody in and give nothing out. Gluck sat down quite close to the fire, for it was raining very hard and the kitchen walls were by no means dry or comfortable-looking. He turned and turned, and the roast got nice and brown. What a pity, thought Gluck, my brothers never ask anybody to dinner. I'm sure, when they've got such a nice piece of mutton as this, and nobody else has got so much as a piece of dry bread, it would do their hearts good to have somebody to eat it with them.

Just then there came a double knock

at the house door, yet heavy and dull, as though the door knocker had been tied up—more like a puff than a knock.

"It must be the wind," said Gluck. "Nobody else would venture to knock double knocks at our door."

No, it wasn't the wind. There it came again very hard, and what was particularly astounding, the knocker seemed to be in a hurry, and not to be in the least afraid of the consequences. Gluck went to the window, opened it, and put his head out to see who it was.

It was the most extraordinary-looking little gentleman that he had ever seen in his life. He had a very large nose, slightly brass-colored; his cheeks were very round and very red, and might have warranted a supposition that he had been blowing a refractory fire for the last eight-and-forty hours; his eyes twinkled merrily through long, silky eyelashes, his mustaches curled twice around like a corkscrew on each side of his mouth, and his hair, of a curious mixed pepper-and-salt color, descended far over his shoulders. He was about four feet six in height, and wore a conical-pointed cap of nearly the same altitude, decorated with a black feather some three feet long. His doublet was prolonged behind into something resembling a violent exaggeration of what is now termed a swallowtail, but was much obscured by the swelling folds of an enormous black glossy-looking cloak, which must have been very much too long in calm weather, as the wind, whistling around the old house, carried it clear out from the wearer's shoulders to about four times his own length.

Gluck was so perfectly paralyzed by the singular appearance of his visitor that he remained fixed without uttering a word, until the old gentleman, having performed another, and a more energetic concerto on the door knocker, turned to look after his flyaway cloak. In so doing he caught sight of Gluck's little yellow head jammed in the window, with his mouth and eyes very wide open indeed.

"Hollo!" said the little gentleman. "That's not the way to answer the door. I'm wet; let me in."

He *was* wet. His feather hung down between his legs like a beaten puppy's tail, dripping like an umbrella; and from the ends of his mustaches the water was running into his waistcoat pockets, and out again like a millstream.

"I beg pardon, sir," said Gluck. "I'm very sorry, but I really can't."

"Can't what?" said the old gentleman.

"I can't let you in, sir—I can't indeed; my brothers would beat me to death, sir, if I thought of such a thing. What do you want, sir?"

"Want?" said the old gentleman petulantly. "I want fire and shelter; and there's your great fire there blazing, crackling, and dancing on the wall, with nobody to feel it. Let me in, I say. I only want to warm myself."

Gluck had had his head so long out the window that he began to feel it was really unpleasantly cold; and when he turned and saw the beautiful fire rustling and roaring and throwing long bright tongues up the chimney, as if it were licking its chops at the savory smell of the leg of mutton, his heart melted within him that it should be burning away for nothing. "He does look *very* wet," said little Gluck. "I'll just let him in for a quarter of an hour." Around he went to the door and opened it; and as the little gentleman walked in, there came a gust of wind through the house that made the old chimneys totter.

"That's a good boy," said the little gentleman. "Never mind your brothers. I'll talk to them."

"Pray, sir, don't do any such thing," said Gluck. "I can't let you stay till they come; they'd be the death of me."

"Dear me," said the old gentleman. "I'm very sorry to hear that. How long may I stay?"

"Only till the mutton's done, sir," replied Gluck, "and it's very brown."

Then the old gentleman walked into the kitchen and sat himself down on the hob, with the top of his cap accommodated up the chimney, for it was a great deal too high for the roof.

"You'll soon dry there, sir," said Gluck, and sat down again to turn the mutton. But the old gentleman did *not* dry there, but went on drip, drip, dripping among the cinders, and the fire fizzed and sputtered and began to look very black and uncomfortable. Never was such a cloak; every fold in it ran like a gutter.

"I beg pardon, sir," said Gluck at length, after watching the water spreading in long, quicksilverlike streams over the floor for a quarter of an hour. "Mayn't I take your cloak?"

"No, thank you," replied the little gentleman.

"Your cap, sir?"

"I am all right, thank you," said the old gentleman rather gruffly.

"But—sir—I'm very sorry," said Gluck hesitatingly. "But—really, sir—you're putting the fire out."

"It'll take longer to do the mutton, then," replied his visitor dryly.

Gluck was very much puzzled by the behavior of his guest; it was such a strange mixture of coolness and humility. He turned away at the spit meditatively for another five minutes.

"That mutton looks very nice," said the old gentleman at length. "Can't you give me a little bit?"

"Impossible, sir," said Gluck.

"I'm very hungry," continued the old gentleman. "I've had nothing to eat yesterday, nor today. They surely couldn't miss a bit from the knuckle!"

He spoke in so very melancholy a tone that it quite melted Gluck's heart. "They promised me one slice today, sir," said he. "I can give you that, but not a bit more."

"That's a good boy," said the old gentleman again.

Then Gluck warmed a plate and sharpened a knife. I don't care if I do get beaten for it, thought he. Just as he had cut a large slice out of the mutton, there came a tremendous rap at the door. The old gentleman jumped off the hob, as if it had suddenly become inconveniently warm. Gluck fitted the slice into the mutton again, with desperate efforts at exactitude, and ran to open the door.

"What did you keep us waiting in the rain for?" said Schwartz as he walked in, throwing his umbrella in Gluck's face.

"Aye! What for, indeed, you little vagabond?" said Hans, administering an educational box on the ear as he followed his brother into the kitchen.

"Bless my soul!" said Schwartz when he saw the old gentleman.

"Amen!" said the little gentleman, who had taken his cap off and was standing in the middle of the kitchen, bowing with the utmost possible velocity.

"Who's that?" said Schwartz, catching up a rolling pin and turning to Gluck with a fierce frown.

"I don't know, indeed, brother," said Gluck in great terror.

"How did he get in?" roared Schwartz.

"My dear brother," said Gluck deprecatingly, "he was so *very* wet!"

The rolling pin was descending on Gluck's head, but at the instant, the old gentleman interposed his conical cap, on which it crashed with a shock that shook the water out of it all over the room. What was very odd, the rolling pin no sooner touched the cap than it flew out of Schwartz's hand, spinning like a straw in a high wind, and fell into the corner at the farther end of the room.

"Who are you, sir?" demanded Schwartz, turning upon him.

"What's your business?" snarled Hans.

"I'm a poor old man, sir," the little gentleman began very modestly, "and I saw your fire through the window, and begged shelter for a quarter of an hour."

"Have the goodness to walk out again, then," said Schwartz. "We've quite enough water in our kitchen without making it a drying house."

"It is a cold day to turn an old man out,

sir; look at my gray hairs." They hung far over his shoulders, as I told you before.

"Aye!" said Hans. "There are enough of them to keep you warm. Walk!"

"I'm very, very hungry, sir; couldn't you spare me a bit of bread before I go?"

"Bread indeed!" said Schwartz. "Do you suppose we've nothing to do with our bread but to give it to such red-nosed fellows as you?"

"Why don't you sell your feather?" said Hans sneeringly. "Out with you!"

"A little bit," said the old gentleman.

"Be off!" said Schwartz.

"Pray, gentlemen."

"Off, and be hanged!" cried Hans, seizing him by the collar. But he had no sooner touched the old gentleman's collar than away he went after the rolling pin, spinning around and around till he fell into the corner on top of it. Then Schwartz was very angry and ran at the old gentleman to turn him out; but he also had hardly touched him when away he went after Hans and the rolling pin, and hit his head against the wall as he tumbled into the corner. And so there they lay, all three.

Then the old gentleman spun himself around with velocity in the opposite direction; continued to spin until his long cloak was all wound neatly about him; clapped his cap on his head, very much on one side (for it could not stand upright without going through the ceiling), gave an additional twist to his corkscrew mustaches, and replied with perfect coolness, "Gentlemen, I wish you a very good morning. At twelve o'clock tonight I'll call again; after such a refusal of hospitality as I have just experienced, you will not be surprised if that visit is the last I ever pay you."

"If ever I catch you here again—" muttered Schwartz, coming, half frightened, out of his corner. But before he could finish his sentence, the old gentleman had shut the house door behind him with a great bang; and there drove past the window, at the same instant, a wreath of ragged cloud that whirled and rolled away down the valley in all manner of shapes, turning over and over in the air, and melting away at last in a gush of rain.

"A very pretty business indeed, Mr. Gluck!" said Schwartz. "Dish the mutton, sir. If ever I catch you at such a trick again— Bless me, why, the mutton's been cut!"

"You promised me one slice, brother, you know," said Gluck.

"Oh! And you were cutting it hot, I suppose, and going to catch all the gravy. It'll be long before I promise you such a thing again. Leave the room, sir, and have the kindness to wait in the coal cellar till I call you."

Gluck left the room, melancholy enough. The brothers ate as much mutton as they could, locked the rest in the cupboard, and proceeded to get very drunk after dinner.

Such a night as it was! Howling wind and rushing rain, without intermission. The brothers had just sense enough left to put up all the shutters and double-bar the door before they went to bed. They usually slept in the same room. As the clock struck twelve, they were both awakened by a tremendous crash. Their door burst open with a violence that shook the house from top to bottom.

"What's that?" cried Schwartz, starting up in his bed.

"Only I," said the little gentleman.

The two brothers sat up on their bolster and stared into the darkness. The room was full of water, and by a misty moonbeam, which found its way through a hole in the shutter, they could see in the midst of it an enormous foam globe, spinning around and bobbing up and down like a cork, on which, as on a most luxurious cushion, reclined the little old gentleman, cap and all. There was plenty of room for it now, for the roof was off.

"Sorry to incommode you," said their visitor ironically. "'I'm afraid your beds are dampish; perhaps you had better go to your brother's room; I've left the ceiling on there."

They required no second admonition, but rushed into Gluck's room, wet through and in an agony of terror.

"You'll find my card on the kitchen table," the old gentleman called after them. "Remember, the *last* visit."

"Pray heaven it may be!" said Schwartz, shuddering. And the huge foam globe disappeared.

Dawn came at last, and the two brothers looked out of Gluck's little window in the morning. The Treasure Valley was one mass of ruin and desolation. The inundation had swept away trees, crops, and cattle, and left, in their stead, a waste of red sand and gray mud. The two brothers crept, shivering and horror-struck, into the kitchen. The water had gutted the whole first floor; corn, money, almost every movable thing had been swept away, and there was left only a small white card on the kitchen table. On it, in large, breezy, long-legged letters, were engraved the words:

South-West Wind, Esquire

CHAPTER TWO

Of the Proceedings of the Three Brothers After the Visit of South-West Wind, Esquire; and How Little Gluck Had an Interview With the King of the Golden River

South-West Wind, Esquire, was as good as his word. After the momentous visit above related, he entered the Treasure Valley no more; and what was worse, he had so much influence with his relations, the West Winds in general, and used it so effectually that they all adopted a similar line of conduct. So no rain fell in the valley from one year's end to another. Though everything remained green and flourishing in the plains below, the inheritance of the three brothers was a desert. What had once been the richest soil in the kingdom became a shifting heap of red sand; and the brothers, unable longer to contend with the adverse skies, abandoned their valueless patrimony in despair, to seek some means of gaining a livelihood among the cities and people of the plains. All their money was gone, and they had nothing left but some curious, old-fashioned vessels of gold, the last remnants of their ill-gotten wealth.

"Suppose we turn goldsmiths?" said Schwartz to Hans as they entered the large city. "It is a good knave's trade; we can put a great deal of copper into the gold, without anyone's finding it out."

The thought was agreed to be a very good one; they hired a furnace, and turned goldsmiths. But two slight circumstances affected their trade: the first, that people did not approve of the coppered gold; the second, that the two elder brothers, whenever they had sold anything, used to leave little Gluck to mind the furnace, and go and drink out the money in the alehouse next door. So they melted all their gold, without making money enough to buy more, and were at last reduced to one large drinking mug, which an uncle had given to little Gluck, and which he was very fond of and would not have parted with for the world, though he never drank anything out of it but milk and water.

The mug was a very odd mug to look at. The handle was formed of two wreaths of flowing golden hair, so finely spun that it looked more like silk than metal; and these wreaths descended into and mixed with a beard and whiskers of the same exquisite workmanship that surrounded and decorated a very fierce little face, of the reddest gold imaginable, right in the front of the mug, with a pair of eyes that seemed to command its whole circumference. It was impossible to drink out of the mug without being subjected to an intense gaze out of these eyes; and Schwartz positively averred that once, after emptying it full of Rhenish seventeen times, he had seen them wink! When it came to the mug's turn to be made into spoons, it half broke poor little Gluck's heart; but the brothers only laughed at him, tossed the mug into the melting pot, and staggered out to the alehouse, leaving him, as usual, to pour the gold into bars when it was all ready.

When they were gone, Gluck took a farewell look at his old friend in the melting pot. The flowing hair was all gone; nothing remained but the red nose, and the sparkling eyes, which looked more malicious than ever. And no wonder, thought Gluck, after being treated in that way. He sauntered disconsolately to the window and sat himself down to catch the fresh evening air and escape the hot breath of the furnace.

Now this window commanded a direct view of the range of mountains, which, as I told you before, overhung the Treasure Valley, and more especially, of the peak from which fell the Golden River. It was just at the close of the day, and when Gluck sat down at the window, he saw the rocks of the mountaintops, all crimson and purple with the sunset; and there were bright tongues of fiery cloud burning and quivering about them; and the river, brighter than all, fell in a waving column of pure gold from precipice to precipice, with the double arch of a broad purple rainbow stretched across it, flushing and fading alternately in the wreaths of spray.

"Ah!" said Gluck aloud, after he had looked at it for a little while. "If that river were really all gold, what a nice thing it would be."

"No, it wouldn't, Gluck," said a clear metallic voice close at his ear.

"Bless me! What's that?" exclaimed Gluck, jumping up. There was nobody there. He looked around the room, and under the table, and a great many times behind him, but there was certainly nobody there, and he sat down again at the window. This time he didn't speak, but he couldn't help thinking again that it would be very convenient if the river were really all gold.

"Not at all, my boy," said the same voice, louder than before.

"Bless me!" said Gluck again. "What *is* that?" He got up and looked again into all the corners and cupboards, and then began turning around and around, as fast as he could, in the middle of the room, thinking there was somebody behind him, when the same voice struck again on his ear. It was singing now very merrily, *"Lala-lira-la";* no words, only a soft running effervescent melody, something like that of a kettle on the boil.

Gluck looked out the window. No, it was certainly in the house. Upstairs, and downstairs. No, it was certainly in that very room, coming in quicker time, and clearer notes, every moment: "*Lala-lira-la.*" All at once it struck Gluck that it sounded louder near the furnace. He ran to the opening and looked in; yes, it seemed to be coming not only out of the furnace but out of the pot. He uncovered it and ran back in a great fright, for the pot was certainly singing. He stood in the farthest corner of the room, with his hands up and his mouth wide open, for a minute or two, when the singing stopped and the voice became clear and pronunciative.

"Hollo!" said the voice.

Gluck made no answer.

"Hollo! Gluck, my boy," said the pot again.

Gluck summoned all his energies, walked straight up to the crucible, drew

it out of the furnace, and looked in. The gold was all melted and its surface as smooth and polished as a river; but instead of a reflection of his own head, Gluck saw, meeting his glance from beneath the gold, the red nose and sharp eyes of his old friend of the mug, a thousand times redder and sharper than ever he had seen them in his life.

"Come, Gluck, my boy," said the voice out of the pot again. "I'm all right; pour me out."

But Gluck was too much astonished to do anything of the kind.

"Pour me out, I say," said the voice, rather gruffly.

Still Gluck couldn't move.

"*Will* you pour me out?" said the voice, passionately. "I'm too hot."

By a violent effort, Gluck recovered the use of his limbs, took hold of the crucible, and sloped it, so as to pour out the gold. But instead of a liquid stream, there came out, first, a pair of pretty little yellow legs, then some coattails, then a pair of arms stuck akimbo, and, finally, the well-known head of his friend the mug; all which articles, uniting as they rolled out, stood up energetically on the floor in the shape of a little golden dwarf, about a foot and a half high.

"That's right!" said the dwarf, stretching out first his legs, and then his arms, and then shaking his head up and down, and as far around as it would go, for five minutes, without stopping, apparently with the view of ascertaining if he were quite correctly put together, while Gluck stood contemplating him in speechless amazement. He was dressed in a slashed doublet of spun gold, so fine in its texture that the prismatic colors gleamed over it, as if on a surface of mother-of-pearl; and over this brilliant doublet his hair and beard fell full halfway to the ground, in waving curls so exquisitely delicate that Gluck could hardly tell where they ended; they seemed to melt into air. The features of the face, however, were by no means finished with the same delicacy; they were rather coarse, slightly inclining to coppery in complexion, and indicative, in expression, of a very pertinacious and intractable disposition in their small proprietor.

When the dwarf had finished his self-examination, he turned his small sharp eyes full on Gluck and stared at him deliberately for a minute or two. "No, it wouldn't, Gluck, my boy," said the little man.

This was certainly rather an abrupt and unconnected mode of commencing conversation. It might indeed be supposed to refer to the course of Gluck's thoughts, which had first produced the dwarf's observations out of the pot; but whatever it referred to, Gluck had no inclination to dispute the dictum.

"Wouldn't it, sir?" said Gluck, very mildly and submissively indeed.

"No," said the dwarf conclusively. "No, it wouldn't." And with that the dwarf pulled his cap hard over his brows and took two turns of three feet long up and down the room, lifting his legs up very high and setting them down very hard. This pause gave time for Gluck to collect his thoughts a little, and seeing no great reason to view his diminutive visitor with dread, and feeling his curiosity overcome his amazement, he ventured on a question of peculiar delicacy.

"Pray, sir," said Gluck, rather hesitatingly, "were you my mug?"

On which the little man turned sharp around, walked straight up to Gluck, and drew himself up to his full height. "I," said the little man, "am the King of the Golden River." Whereupon he turned about again and took two more turns, some six feet long, in order to allow time for the consternation that this announcement produced in his auditor to evaporate. After which he again walked up to Gluck and stood still, as if expecting some comment on his communication.

Gluck determined to say something at all events. "I hope Your Majesty is very well," said Gluck.

"Listen!" said the little man, deigning no reply to this polite inquiry. "I am the King of what you mortals call the Golden River. The shape you saw me in was owing to the malice of a stronger king, from whose enchantments you have this instant freed me. What I have seen of you, and your conduct to your wicked brothers, renders me willing to serve you; therefore attend to what I tell you. Whoever shall climb to the top of that mountain from which you see the Golden River issue, and shall cast into the stream at its source three drops of holy water, for him, and for him only, the river shall turn to gold. But no one failing in his first can succeed in a second attempt; and if anyone shall cast unholy water into the river, it will overwhelm him, and he will become a black stone."

So saying, the King of the Golden River turned away and deliberately walked into the center of the hottest flame of the furnace. His figure became red, white, transparent, dazzling—a blaze of intense light—rose, trembled, and disappeared. The King of the Golden River had evaporated.

"Oh!" cried poor Gluck, running to look up the chimney after him. "Oh, dear, dear, dear me! My mug! My mug! My mug!"

CHAPTER THREE

How Mr. Hans Set Off
on an Expedition to the Golden River,
and How He Prospered Therein

The King of the Golden River had hardly made the extraordinary exit related in the last chapter before Hans and Schwartz came roaring into the house savagely drunk. The discovery of the total loss of their last piece of gold had the effect of sobering them just enough to enable them to stand over Gluck, beating him very steadily for a quarter of an hour, at the expiration of which period they dropped into a couple of chairs and requested to know what he had to say for himself.

Gluck told them his story. Of course they did not believe a word. They beat him again, till their arms were tired, and staggered to bed. In the morning, however, the steadiness with which he adhered to his story obtained him some degree of credence; the immediate consequence was that the two brothers, after wrangling a long time on the knotty question, which of them should try his fortune first, drew their swords and began fighting. The noise of the fray alarmed the neighbors, who, finding they could not pacify the combatants, sent for the constable.

Hans, on hearing this, contrived to escape, and hid himself; but Schwartz was taken before the magistrate, fined for breaking the peace, and, having drunk out his last penny the evening before, was thrown into prison till he should pay.

When Hans heard this, he was much delighted, and determined to set out immediately for the Golden River. How to get the holy water was the question. He went to the priest, but the priest could not give any holy water to so abandoned a character. So Hans went to vespers in the evening for the first time in his life, and, under pretense of crossing himself, stole a cupful, and returned home in triumph.

Next morning he got up before the sun rose, put the holy water into a strong flask, and two bottles of wine and some meat in a basket, slung them over his back, took his alpine staff in his hand, and set off for the mountains.

On his way out of the town he had to pass the prison, and as he looked in at the windows, whom should he see but Schwartz himself peeping out of the bars and looking very disconsolate.

"Good morning, brother," said Hans. "Have you any message for the King of the Golden River?"

Schwartz gnashed his teeth with rage and shook the bars with all his strength; but Hans only laughed at him and advised him to make himself comfortable till he came back again; he shouldered his basket, shook the bottle of holy water in Schwartz's face, and marched off in the highest spirits in the world.

It was, indeed, a morning that might have made anyone happy, even with no Golden River to seek for. Level lines of dewy mist lay stretched along the valley, out of which rose the massy mountains—their lower cliffs in pale gray shadow, hardly distinguishable from the floating vapor, but gradually ascending till they caught the sunlight, which ran in sharp touches of ruddy color along the angular crags, and pierced, in long level rays, through their fringes of spearlike pine. Far above shot up red splintered masses of castellated rock, jagged and shivered into myriads of fantastic forms, with here and there a streak of sunlit snow, traced down their chasms like a line of forked lightning; and far beyond, and far above all these, fainter than the morning cloud but purer and changeless, slept, in the blue sky, the utmost peaks of the eternal snow.

The Golden River, which sprang from one of the lower and snowless elevations, was still mostly in shadow—all but the uppermost jets of spray, which rose like slow smoke above the undulating line of the cataract and floated away in feeble wreaths upon the morning wind.

On this object, and on this alone, Hans's eyes and thought were fixed; forgetting the distance he had to traverse, he set off at an imprudent rate of walking, which greatly exhausted him before he had scaled the first range of the green and low hills. He was, moreover, surprised, on surmounting them, to find that a large glacier, of whose existence, notwithstanding his previous knowledge of the mountains, he had been absolutely ignorant, lay between him and the source of the Golden River. He entered on it with the boldness of a practiced mountaineer; yet he thought he had never traversed so strange or so dangerous a glacier in his life. The ice was excessively slippery; and out of all its chasms came wild sounds of gushing water, not monotonous or low, but changeful and loud, rising occasionally into drifting passages of wild melody, then breaking off into short melancholy tones, or sudden shrieks, resembling those of human voices in distress or pain. The ice was broken into thousands of confused shapes, but none, Hans thought, like the ordinary forms of splintered ice. There seemed a curious *expression* about all their outlines—a perpetual resemblance to living features, distorted and scornful. Myriads of de-

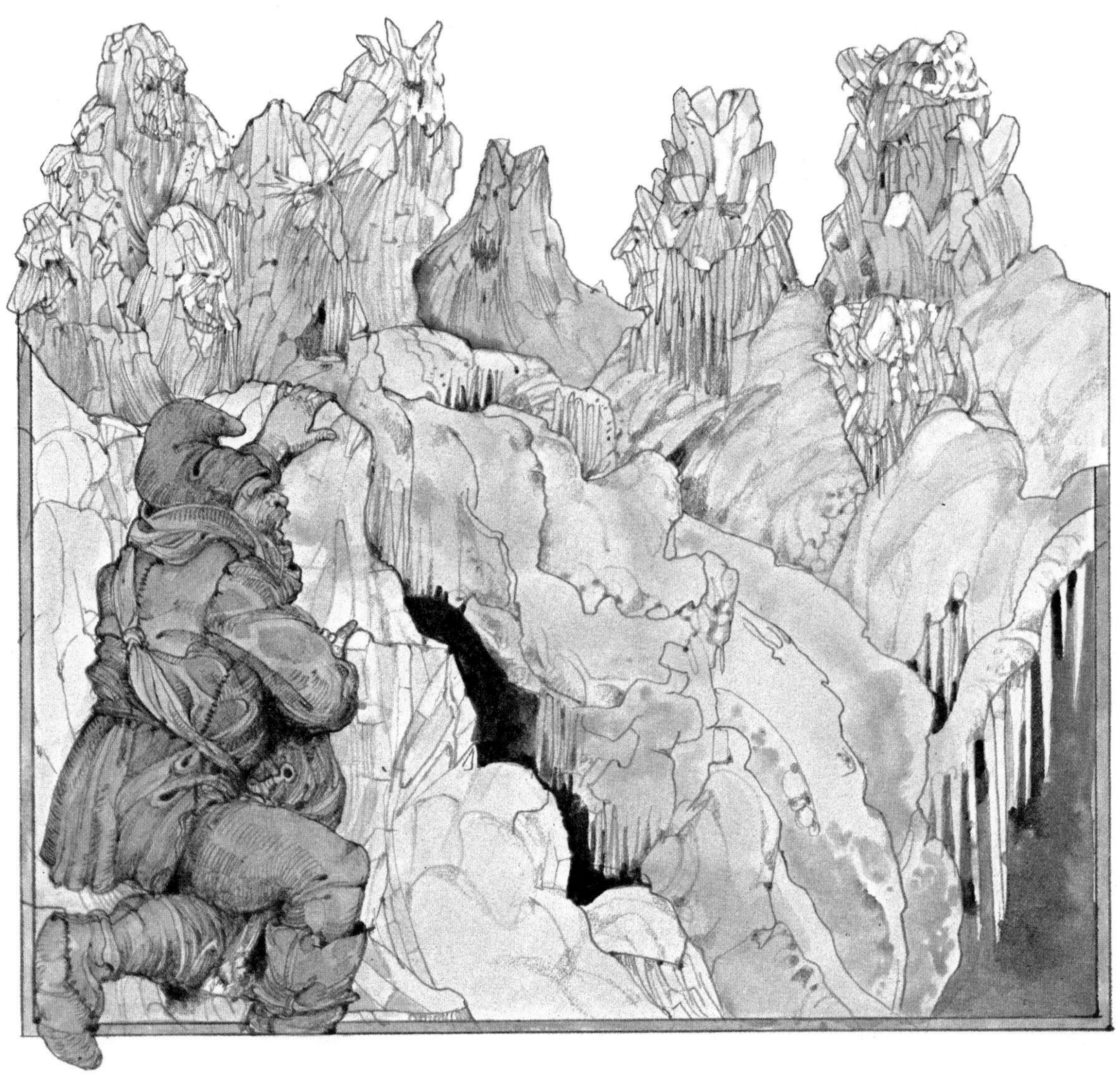

ceitful shadows and lurid lights played and floated about and through the pale blue pinnacles, dazzling and confusing the sight of the traveler; while his ears grew dull and his head giddy with the constant roar of the concealed waters.

These painful circumstances increased upon him as he advanced; the ice crashed and yawned into fresh chasms at his feet, tottering spires nodded around him and fell thundering across his path; and though he had repeatedly faced these dangers on the most terrific glaciers, and in the wildest weather, it was with a new and oppressive feeling of panic terror that he leaped the last chasm and flung himself, exhausted and shuddering, on the firm turf of the mountain.

He had been compelled to abandon his basket of food, which became a perilous encumbrance on the glacier, and had no means of refreshing himself but by breaking off and eating some of the pieces of ice. This, however, relieved his thirst; an hour's repose recruited his hardy frame, and with the indomitable spirit of avarice he resumed his laborious journey.

His way now lay straight up a ridge of bare red rocks, without a blade of grass to ease the foot or a projecting angle to afford an inch of shade from the south sun. It was past noon, and the rays beat intensely upon the steep path, while the whole atmosphere was motionless and penetrated with heat. Intense thirst was soon added to the bodily fatigue with which Hans was now afflicted; glance after glance he cast on the flask of water that hung at his belt. Three drops are enough, at last thought he. I may at least cool my lips with it.

He opened the flask, and was raising it to his lips when his eyes fell on an object lying on the rock beside him; he thought it moved. It was a small dog, apparently in the last agony of death from thirst. Its tongue was out, its jaws dry, its limbs extended lifelessly, and a swarm of black ants were crawling about its lips and throat. Its eye moved to the bottle that Hans held in his hand. He raised it, drank, spurned the animal with his foot, and passed on. And he did not know how it was, but he thought that a strange shadow had suddenly come across the blue sky.

The path became steeper and more rugged every moment; and the high hill air, instead of refreshing him, seemed to throw his blood into a fever. The noise of the hill cataracts sounded like mockery in his ears; they were all distant, and his thirst increased every moment. Another hour passed, and he again looked down to the flask at his side; it was half empty, but there was much more than three drops in it. He stopped to open it, and again, as he did so, something moved in the path above him. It was a fair child, stretched nearly lifeless on the rock, its breast heaving with thirst, its eyes closed, and its lips parched and burning. Hans eyed it deliberately, drank, and passed on. And a dark gray cloud came over the sun, and long, snakelike shadows crept up along the mountainsides.

Hans struggled on. The sun was sinking, but its descent seemed to bring no coolness; the leaden weight of the dead air pressed upon his brow and heart, but the goal was near. He saw the cataract of the Golden River springing from the hillside, scarcely five hundred feet above him. He paused for a moment to breathe, and sprang on to complete his task.

At this instant a faint cry fell on his ear. He turned, and saw a gray-haired old man extended on the rocks. His eyes were sunk, his features deadly pale and gathered into an expression of despair. "Water!" He stretched his arms to Hans and cried feebly, "Water! I am dying."

"I have none," replied Hans. "Thou hast had thy share of life." He strode over the prostrate body and darted on. And a flash of blue lightning rose out of the east, shaped like a sword; it shook thrice over the whole heaven and left it dark with one heavy, impenetrable shade. The sun was setting; it plunged toward the horizon like a red-hot ball.

The roar of the Golden River rose on Hans's ear. He stood at the brink of the chasm through which it ran. Its waves were filled with the red glory of the sunset; they shook their crests like tongues of fire, and flashes of bloody light gleamed along their foam. Their sound came mightier and mightier on his senses; his brain grew giddy with the prolonged thunder. Shuddering, he drew the flask from his girdle and hurled it into the center of the torrent. As he did so, an icy chill shot through his limbs; he staggered, shrieked, and fell. The waters closed over his cry. And the moaning of the river rose wildly into the night as it gushed over

THE BLACK STONE.

CHAPTER FOUR

How Mr. Schwartz Set Off on an Expedition to the Golden River, and How He Prospered Therein

Poor little Gluck waited very anxiously alone in the house for Hans's return. Finding he did not come back, he was terribly frightened, and went and told Schwartz in the prison. Then Schwartz was very much pleased, and said that Hans must certainly have been turned into a black stone, and he should have all the gold to himself. But Gluck was very sorry and cried all night.

When he got up in the morning, there was no bread in the house, nor any money, so Gluck went and hired himself to another goldsmith; and he worked so hard, and so neatly, and so long every day, that he soon got money enough together to pay his brother's fine, and he went and gave it to Schwartz, and Schwartz got out of prison. Then Schwartz was quite pleased, and said he should have some of the gold of the river. But Gluck only begged he would go and see what had become of Hans.

Now when Schwartz had heard that Hans had stolen the holy water, he thought to himself that such a proceeding might not be considered altogether correct by the King of the Golden River, and determined to manage matters better. So he took some more of Gluck's money and went to a bad priest, who gave him some holy water very readily for it. Then Schwartz was sure it was all quite right.

So Schwartz got up early in the morning before the sun rose, and took some bread and wine in a basket, and put his holy water in a flask, and set off for the mountains. Like his brother, he was much surprised at the sight of the glacier and had great difficulty in crossing it, even after leaving his basket behind him. The day was cloudless but not bright; there was a heavy purple haze hanging over the sky, and the hills looked lowering and gloomy. And as Schwartz climbed the steep rock path, the thirst came upon him, as it had upon his brother, until he lifted his flask to his lips to drink. Then he saw the fair child lying near him on the rocks, and it cried to him and moaned for water.

"Water, indeed," said Schwartz. "I haven't half enough for myself," and passed on. And as he went he thought the sunbeams grew more dim, and he saw a low bank of black cloud rising out of the west; and when he had climbed for another hour, the thirst overcame him again, and he would have drunk. Then he saw the old man lying before him on the path, and heard him cry out for water. "Water, indeed," said Schwartz once more. "I haven't half enough for myself," and on he went.

Then again the light seemed to fade from before his eyes, and he looked up, and behold, a mist of the color of blood had come over the sun; and the bank of black cloud had risen very high, and its edges were tossing and tumbling like the waves of an angry sea. And they cast long shadows, which flickered over Schwartz's path.

Then Schwartz climbed for another hour, and again his thirst returned; and as he lifted his flask to his lips, he thought he saw his brother Hans lying exhausted on the path before him, and as he gazed, the figure stretched its arms to him and cried for water. Schwartz laughed. "Are you there? Remember the prison bars, my boy. Water, indeed! Do you suppose I carried it all the way up here for *you?*" And he strode over the figure; yet as he passed, he thought he saw a strange expression of mockery about its lips. And when he had gone a few yards farther, he looked back; but the figure was not there.

And a sudden horror came over Schwartz, he knew not why; but the thirst for gold prevailed over his fear, and he rushed on. And the bank of black cloud rose to the zenith, and out of it came bursts of spiry lightning, and waves of darkness seemed to heave and float between their flashes over the whole heavens. And the sky where the sun was setting was all level and like a lake of blood; and a strong wind came out of that sky, tearing its crimson clouds into frag-

ments and scattering them far into the darkness. And when Schwartz stood by the brink of the Golden River, its waves were black, like thunderclouds, but their foam was like fire; and the roar of the waters below and the thunder above met as he cast the flask into the stream. And as he did so, the lightning glared in his eyes, and the earth gave way beneath him, and the waters closed over his cry. And the moaning of the river rose wildly into the night, as it gushed over the

TWO BLACK STONES.

CHAPTER FIVE

How Little Gluck Set Off on an Expedition to the Golden River, and How He Prospered Therein; with Other Matters of Interest

When Gluck found that Schwartz did not come back, he was very sorry and did not know what to do. He had no money and was obliged to go and hire himself again to the goldsmith, who worked him very hard and gave him very little money. So, after a month or two, Gluck grew tired and made up his mind to go and try his fortune with the Golden River. The little king looked very kind, thought he. I don't think he will turn me into a black stone. So he went to the priest, and the priest gave him some holy water as soon as he asked for it. Then Gluck took some bread in his basket, and the bottle of water, and set off for the mountains.

If the glacier had occasioned a great deal of fatigue to his brothers, it was twenty times worse for him, who was neither so strong nor so practiced on the mountains. He had several very bad falls, lost his basket and bread, and was very much frightened at the strange noises under the ice. He lay a long time to rest on the grass after he had got over, and began to climb the hill just in the hottest part of the day.

When he had climbed for an hour he got dreadfully thirsty, and was going to drink, like his brothers, when he saw an old man coming down the path above him, looking very feeble and leaning on a staff. "My son," said the old man, "I am faint with thirst. Give me some of that water."

Gluck looked at him, and when he saw that he was pale and weary, he gave him the water. "Only pray don't drink it all," said Gluck. But the old man drank a great deal, and gave him back the bottle two thirds empty. Then he bade him good speed, and Gluck went on again merrily. And the path became easier to his feet, and two or three blades of grass appeared upon it, and some grasshoppers began singing on the bank beside it; and Gluck thought he had never heard such merry singing.

He went on for another hour, and the thirst increased on him so that he thought he should be forced to drink. But as he raised the flask, he saw a little child lying panting by the roadside, and it cried out piteously for water. Gluck struggled with himself and determined to bear the thirst a little longer; and he put the bottle to the child's lips, and it drank it all but a few drops. Then it smiled on him, and got up, and ran down the hill; and Gluck looked after it till it became as small as a little star.

Gluck turned and began climbing again. And then there were all kinds of sweet flowers growing on the rocks, bright green moss, with pale pink starry flowers, and soft belled gentians more blue than the sky at its deepest, and pure white transparent lilies. And crimson and purple butterflies darted hither and thither, and the sky sent down such pure light that Gluck had never felt so happy in his life.

Yet when he had climbed for another hour, his thirst became intolerable again; and when he looked at his bottle he saw that there were only five or six drops left in it, and he could not venture to drink. As he was hanging the flask to his belt again, he saw a little dog lying on the rocks, gasping for breath—just as Hans had seen it on the day of his ascent. And Gluck stopped and looked at it, and then at the Golden River, not five hundred yards above him; and he thought of the dwarf's words, that no one could succeed, except in his first attempt; and he tried to pass the dog, but it whined piteously, and Gluck stopped again.

"Poor beastie," said Gluck. "It'll be dead when I come down again if I don't help it." Then he looked closer and closer at it, and its eye turned on him so mournfully that he could not stand it. "Confound the king and his gold too," said Gluck; and he opened the flask and poured all the water into the dog's mouth.

The dog sprang up and stood on its hind legs. Its tail disappeared, its ears became long, longer, silky, golden; its nose became very red; its eyes became very twinkling; in three seconds the dog was gone, and before Gluck stood his old acquaintance, the King of the Golden River.

"Thank you," said the monarch. "But don't be frightened, it's all right"; for Gluck showed manifest symptoms of consternation at this unlooked-for reply to his last observation. "Why didn't you come before," continued the dwarf, "instead of sending me those rascally brothers of yours, for me to have the trouble of turning into stones? Very hard stones they make too."

"Oh, dear me!" said Gluck. "Have you really been so cruel?"

"Cruel!" said the dwarf. "They poured unholy water into my stream; do you suppose I'm going to allow that?"

"Why," said Gluck, "I am sure, sir—Your Majesty, I mean—they got the water out of the church font."

"Very probably," replied the dwarf. "But"—and his countenance grew stern as he spoke—"the water that has been refused to the cry of the weary and dying is unholy, though it had been blessed by every saint in heaven; and the water that is found in the vessel of mercy is holy, though it had been defiled with corpses."

So saying, the dwarf stooped and plucked a lily that grew at his feet. On its white leaves there hung three drops of clear dew. And the dwarf shook them into the flask, which Gluck held in his hand. "Cast these into the river," he said, "and descend on the other side of the mountains into the Treasure Valley. And so good speed."

As he spoke, the figure of the dwarf became indistinct. The playing colors of his robe formed themselves into a prismatic mist of dewy light; he stood for an instant veiled with them as with the belt of a broad rainbow. The colors grew faint, the mist rose into the air; the monarch had evaporated.

And Gluck climbed to the brink of the Golden River, and its waves were as clear as crystal and as brilliant as the sun. And when he cast the three drops of dew into the stream, there opened where they fell a small circular whirlpool, into which the waters descended with a musical noise.

Gluck stood watching it for some time, very much disappointed, because not only was the river not turned into gold, but its waters seemed much diminished in quantity. Yet he obeyed his friend the dwarf and descended the other side of the mountains, toward the Treasure Valley; and as he went, he thought he heard the noise of water working its way under the ground. And when he came in sight of the Treasure Valley, behold, a river like the Golden River was springing from a new cleft of the rocks above it and was flowing in innumerable streams among the dry heaps of red sand.

And as Gluck gazed, fresh grass sprang beside the new streams, and creeping plants grew and climbed among the moistening soil. Young flowers opened suddenly along the riversides, as stars leap out when twilight is deepening; and thickets of myrtle and tendrils of vine cast lengthening shadows over the valley as they grew. And thus the Treasure Valley became a garden again, and the inheritance, which had been lost by cruelty, was regained by love.

And Gluck went and dwelt in the valley, and the poor were never driven from his door; so that his barns became full of corn and his house of treasure. And for him, the river had, according to the dwarf's promise, become a River of Gold.

And to this day, the inhabitants of the valley point out the place where the three drops of holy dew were cast into the stream, and trace the course of the Golden River under the ground until it emerges in the Treasure Valley.

And at the top of the cataract of the Golden River are still to be seen two black stones, around which the waters howl mournfully every day at sunset; and these stones are still called by the people of the valley

THE BLACK BROTHERS.

The Lady Who Put Salt in Her Coffee

by Lucretia P. Hale

For the irrepressible Peterkin family, remedies were many, but cures were few.

Mrs. Peterkin had poured out a delicious cup of coffee, and just as she was helping herself to cream, she found she had put in salt instead of sugar! It tasted bad. What should she do? Of course she couldn't drink the coffee; so she called in the family, for she was sitting at a late breakfast all alone. The family came in; they all tasted, and looked, and all sat down to think.

At last Agamemnon, who had been to college, said, "Why don't we go ask the advice of the chemist?" (For the chemist lived over the way, and was a very wise man.)

Mrs. Peterkin said, "Yes," and Mr. Peterkin said, "Very well," and all the children said they would go too. So the little boys put on their boots, and over they went.

Now, the chemist was just trying to find out something that should turn everything it touched into gold; and he had a large glass bottle into which he put all kinds of gold and silver, and many other valuable things, and melted them all up over the fire till he had almost found what he wanted. He could turn things into almost gold. But just now he had used up all the gold that he had around the house, and gold was high. He had used up his wife's gold thimble and his great-grandfather's gold-bowed spectacles; and he had melted up the gold head of his great-great-grandfather's cane. Just as the Peterkin family came in, he was down on his knees before his wife, asking her to let him have her wedding ring to melt up with all the rest, because this time he knew he should succeed, and should be able to turn everything into gold. Then she could have a new wedding ring of diamonds, all set in emeralds and rubies and topazes, and all the furniture could be turned into the finest of gold.

Now, his wife was just consenting when the Peterkin family burst in. You can imagine how mad the chemist was! He came near throwing his crucible—that was the name of his melting pot—at their heads. But he didn't. He listened as calmly as he could to the story of how Mrs. Peterkin had put salt in her coffee.

At first he said he couldn't do anything about it; but when Agamemnon said they would pay in gold if he would only come, he packed up his bottles in a leather case and went back with them all.

First he looked at the coffee, and then stirred it. Then he put in a little chlorate of potassium, and the family tried it all around; but it tasted no better. Then he stirred in a little bichlorate of magnesia. But Mrs. Peterkin didn't like that. Then he added some tartaric acid and some hypersulfate of lime. But no; it was no better. "I have it!" exclaimed the chemist. "A little ammonia is just the thing!" No, it wasn't the thing at all.

Then he tried, each in turn, some oxalic, cyanic, acetic, phosphoric, chloric, hyperchloric, sulfuric, boracic, silicic, nitric, formic, nitrous nitric, and carbonic acids. Mrs. Peterkin tasted each, and said the flavor was pleasant, but not precisely that of coffee. So then he tried a little calcium, aluminum, barium, and strontium, a little clear bitumen, and a half of a third of a sixteenth of a grain of arsenic. This gave rather a pretty color; but still Mrs. Peterkin ungratefully said it tasted of anything but coffee. The chemist was not discouraged. He put in a little belladonna and atropine, some granulated hydrogen, some potash, and a very little antimony, finishing off with a little pure carbon. But still Mrs. Peterkin was not satisfied.

The chemist said that all he had done ought to have taken out the salt. Perhaps a little starch would have some effect. If not, that was all the time he could give. He should like to be paid, and go. They were all much obliged to him, and willing to give him $1.37½ in gold. Gold was now selling at 2.69¾, so Mr. Peterkin found in the newspaper. This gave Agamemnon a pretty little sum. He sat down to do it. But there was the coffee! All sat and thought awhile, till Elizabeth Eliza said, "Why don't we go to the herb woman?"

Now, the herb woman was an old woman who came around to sell herbs, and knew a great deal. They all shouted with joy at the idea of asking her, and Solomon John and the younger children agreed to go and find her too. The herb woman lived down at the very end of the street; so the boys put on their boots again, and they set off. It was a long walk through the village, but they came at last to the herb woman's house, at the foot of a high hill. They went through her little garden. Here she had marigolds and hollyhocks and tall sunflowers, and all kinds of sweet-smelling herbs. Over the porch grew a hop vine, and a brandy-cherry tree shaded the door, and a luxuriant cranberry vine flung its delicious fruit across the window. They went into a small parlor, which smelled very spicy. All around hung little bags full of catnip and peppermint and all kinds of herbs; and dried stalks hung from the ceiling; and on the shelves were jars of rhubarb, senna, manna, and the like.

But there was no little old woman. She had gone up into the woods to get some more wild herbs, so they all thought they would follow her—Elizabeth Eliza, Solomon John, and the little boys. They had to climb up over high rocks, and in among huckleberry bushes and blackberry vines.

At last they discovered the little old woman. They knew her by her hat. It was steeple-crowned, without any vane. They saw her digging with her trowel around a sassafras bush. They told her their story—how their mother had put salt in her coffee, and how the chemist had made it worse instead of better, and how their mother couldn't drink it, and wouldn't she come and see what she could do? And she said she would, and took up her little old apron, with pockets all around, all filled with everlasting and pennyroyal, and went back to her house.

There she stopped, and stuffed her huge pockets with some of all kinds of herbs. She took some tansy and peppermint, caraway seed and dill, spearmint and cloves, pennyroyal and sweet marjoram, basil and rosemary, wild thyme and some of the other time—such as you have in clocks—sappermint and oppermint, catnip, valerian, and hop; indeed, there isn't a kind of herb you can think of that the little old woman didn't have done up in her little paper bags, that had all been dried in her little Dutch oven. She packed these all up, and then went back with the children, taking her stick.

Meanwhile Mrs. Peterkin was getting quite impatient for her coffee.

As soon as the little old woman came she had it set over the fire, and began to stir in the different herbs. First she put in a little hop for the bitter. Mrs. Peterkin said it tasted like hop tea, and not at all like coffee. Then she tried a little flagroot and snakeroot, then some spruce gum, and some caraway and some dill, some rue and rosemary, some sweet marjoram and sour, some oppermint and sappermint, a little spearmint and peppermint, some wild thyme, and some of the other tame time, some tansy and basil, and catnip and valerian, and sassafras, ginger, and pennyroyal. The children tasted after each mixture, but made up dreadful faces. Mrs. Peterkin tasted, and did the same. The more the old woman stirred, and the more she put in, the worse it all seemed to taste.

So the old woman shook her head, and muttered a few words, and said she must go. She believed the coffee was bewitched. She bundled up her packets of herbs, and took her trowel, and her basket, and her stick, and went back to her root of sassafras, that she had left half in the air and half out. And all she would take for pay was five cents in currency.

Then the family were in despair, and all sat and thought a great while. It was growing late in the day, and Mrs. Peterkin hadn't had her cup of coffee. At last Elizabeth Eliza said, "They say that the lady from Philadelphia, who is staying in town, is very wise. Suppose I go and ask her what is best to be done." To this they all agreed, it was a great thought, and off Elizabeth Eliza went.

She told the lady from Philadelphia the whole story—how her mother had put salt in the coffee; how the chemist had been called in; how he tried everything but could make it no better; and how they went for the little old herb woman, and how she had tried in vain, for her mother couldn't drink the coffee. The lady from Philadelphia listened very attentively, and then said, "Why doesn't your mother make a fresh cup of coffee?"

Elizabeth Eliza started with surprise. Solomon John shouted with joy; so did Agamemnon, who had just finished his sum; so did the little boys, who had followed on. "Why didn't we think of that?" said Elizabeth Eliza; and they all went back to their mother, and she had her cup of coffee.

Four Fables by Aesop

For twenty-five hundred years, storytellers have repeated the fables credited to a Greek slave named Aesop. Here are four of the best.

The Lion and the Mouse

Once when a Lion was asleep a little Mouse began running up and down upon him. This soon wakened the Lion, who placed his huge paw upon him and opened his big jaws to swallow him. "Pardon, O King," cried the little Mouse. "Forgive me this time, I shall never forget it. Who knows but what I may be able to do you a turn some of these days?" The Lion was so tickled at the idea of the Mouse being able to help him that he raised his paw and let him go. Some time after, the Lion was caught in a trap, and the hunters, who desired to carry him alive to the king, tied him to a tree while they went in search of a wagon to carry him on. Just then the little Mouse happened to pass by, and seeing the sad plight in which the Lion was, went up to him and soon gnawed away the ropes that bound the King of the Beasts. "Was I not right?" said the little Mouse.

Little friends may prove great friends.

The Ant and the Grasshopper

In a field one summer's day a Grasshopper was hopping about, chirping and singing to its heart's content. An Ant came by, bearing with great toil an ear of corn it was taking to the nest.

"Why not come and chat with me," said the Grasshopper, "instead of toiling in that way?"

"I am helping to lay up food for winter," said the Ant, "and recommend you do the same."

"Why bother about winter?" said the Grasshopper. "We have got plenty of food at present." But the Ant went on its way and continued its toil. When the winter came the Grasshopper had no food and found itself dying of hunger, while it saw the ants distributing every day corn and grain from the stores they had collected in summer. Then the Grasshopper knew.

It is best to prepare for the days of need.

The Frog and the Ox

"Oh, Father," said a little Frog to the big one sitting by the side of a pool, "I have seen such a terrible monster! It was as big as a mountain, with horns on its head, and a long tail, and it had hoofs divided in two."

"Tush, child, tush," said the old Frog, "that was only Farmer White's Ox. It isn't so big either. He may be a little bit taller than I, but I could easily make myself quite as broad; just you see." So he blew himself out, and blew himself out, and blew himself out. "Was he as big as that?" asked the old frog.

"Oh, much bigger than that," said the young Frog.

Again the old one blew himself out, and asked if the Ox was as big as that.

"Bigger, Father, bigger."

So the Frog took a deep breath, and blew and blew and blew, and swelled and swelled and swelled. And then he said, "I'm sure the Ox is not as big as—" But at this moment he burst.

Self-conceit may lead to self-destruction.

The Crow and the Pitcher

A Crow, half dead with thirst, came upon a Pitcher which had once been full of water; but when the Crow put its beak into the mouth of the Pitcher he found that only very little water was left in it, and that he could not reach far enough down to get at it. He tried, and he tried, but at last had to give up in despair. Then a thought came to him, and he took a pebble and dropped it into the Pitcher. Then he took another pebble and dropped it into the Pitcher. Then he took another pebble and dropped that into the Pitcher. Then he took another pebble and dropped that into the Pitcher. Then he took another pebble and dropped that into the Pitcher. Then he took another pebble and dropped that into the Pitcher. At last he saw the water mount up near him; and after casting in a few more pebbles he was able to quench his thirst and save his life.

Little by little does the trick.

DRUG

Being a Public Character

by Don Marquis

For a dog and his boy,
fame has both advantages and disadvantages.

Ever since I bit a circus lion, believing him to be another dog like myself, only larger, I have been what Doc Watson calls a Public Character in our town.

Freckles, my boy, was a kind of Public Character, too. He went around bragging about my noble blood and bravery, and all the other boys and dogs in town sort of looked up to him and thought how lucky he was to belong to a dog like me. And he deserved whatever glory he got out of it. For, if I do say it myself, there's not a dog in town got a better boy than my boy Freckles. I'll back him against any dog's boy that is anywhere near his size, for fighting, swimming, climbing, footracing, or throwing stones farthest and straightest. Or I'll back him against any stray boy, either.

Becoming a Public Character happened to me all in a flash, and it was sort of hard for me to get used to it. One day I was just a private kind of a dog, eating my meals at the Watsons' back door, and pretending to hunt rats when requested, and not scratching off too many fleas in Doc Watson's drugstore, and standing out from underfoot when told, and other unremarkable things like that. And the next day I had bit that lion and was a Public Character, and fame came so sudden I scarcely knew how to act.

People would come tooting up to the store in their little cars, and get out and look me over and say, "Well, Doc, what'll you take for him?"

Doc would wink and say, "He's Harold's dog. You ask Harold."

Which Harold is Freckles' other name. But any boy that calls him Harold outside of the schoolhouse has got a fight on his hands, if that boy is anywhere near Freckles' size. Harry goes, or Hal goes, but Harold is a fighting word with Freckles. Except, of course, with grown people. I heard him say one day to Tom Mulligan, his parents thought Harold was a name, or he guessed they wouldn't have given it to him; but it wasn't a name, it was a handicap.

Freckles would always say, "Spot ain't for sale."

And even Heinie Hassenyager, the butcher, got stuck on me after I got to be a Public Character. Heinie would come two blocks up Main Street with lumps of hamburger steak and give them to me. Steak, mind you, not old gristly scraps. And before I became a Public Character, Heinie even begrudged me the bones I would drag out of the box under his counter when he wasn't looking.

My daily hope was that I could live up to it all. I had always tried, before I happened to bite that lion, to be a friendly kind of a dog toward boys and humans and dogs, all three. I'd always been expected to do a certain amount of tail wagging and be friendly. But as soon as I got to be a Public Character, I saw right away that I wasn't expected to be *too* friendly anymore. So, every now and then, I'd growl a little, for no reason at all. A dog that has bit a lion is naturally expected to have fierce thoughts inside of him; I could see that. And you have got to act the way humans expect you to act if you want to slide along through the world without too much trouble.

When Heinie would bring me the steak I'd growl at him. And then I'd bolt and gobble the steak like I didn't think so derned much of it, after all, and was doing Heinie a big personal favor to eat it.

That way of acting made a big hit with Heinie, too. I could see that he was honored and flattered because I didn't go any further than just a growl. It gave him a chance to say he knew how to manage animals. And the more I growled, the more steak he brought. Everybody in town fed me. I pretty near ate myself to death for a while there, besides all the meat I buried back of Doc Watson's store to dig up later.

The worst of it was that people, after a week or so, began to expect me to pull something else remarkable. Freckles, he got up a circus, and charged pins and marbles, or cents, to get into it, and I was the principal part of that circus. I was in a cage, and the sign over me read:

SPOT, THE DOG THAT LICKED A LION
TEN PINS ADMITION

To feed the lion-eater, one cent or two white chiney marbles extry but bring your own meat.
Pat him once on the head twinty pins, kids under five not allowed to.
For shaking hands with Spot the lion-eater, girls not allowed, gents three white chinies, or one aggie marble.
Lead him two blocks down the street and back, one cent before starting, no marbles or pins taken for leading him.
For sicking him on the cats three cents or one red cornelian marble if you furnish the cat. Five cents to use Watson's cat. Watson's biggest Tom-cat six cents must be paid before sicking. Small kids and girls not allowed to sick him on cats.

Well, we didn't take in any cat-sicking money. And it was just as well. You never can tell what a cat will do. But Freckles put it in because it sounded sort of fierce. I didn't care for being caged and circused that way myself. And it was right at that circus that considerable trouble started.

Seeing me in a cage like that, all famoused-up, with more meat poked through the slats than two dogs could eat, made Mutt Mulligan and some of my old friends jealous.

Mutt, he nosed by the cage and sniffed. I nosed a piece of meat out of the cage to him. Mutt grabbed it and gobbled it down, but he didn't thank me any. Mutt, he says, "There's a new dog downtown that says he blew in from Chicago. He says he used to be a Blind Man's Dog on a street corner there. He's a pretty wise dog, and he's a right ornery-looking dog, too. He's peeled considerably where he has been bit in fights."

"Well, Mutt," says I, "as far as that goes I'm peeled considerably myself where I've been in fights."

"I know you are, Spot," says Mutt. "You don't need to tell me that. I've peeled you some myself from time to time."

"Yes," I says, "you did peel me some, Mutt. And I've peeled you some, too. More'n that, I notice that right leg of yours is a little stiff yet where I got to it about three weeks ago."

"Well, then, Spot," says Mutt, "maybe you want to come down here and see what you can do to my other three legs. I never saw the day I wouldn't give you a free bite at one leg and still be able to lick you on the other three."

"You wouldn't talk that way if I was out of this cage," I says, getting riled.

"What did you ever let yourself be put into that fool cage for?" says Mutt. "You didn't have to. You got such a swellhead on you the last week or so that you gotta be licked. You can fool boys and humans all you want to about that accidental old lion, but us dogs got your number, all right. What that Blind Man's Dog from Chicago would do to you would be aplenty!"

"Well, then," I says, "I'll be out of this cage along about suppertime. Suppose you bring that Blind Man's Dog around here. And if he ain't got a spiked collar onto him, I'll fight him. I won't fight a spike-collared dog to please anybody."

And I wouldn't, neither, without I had one on myself. If you can't get a dog by the throat or the back of his neck, what's the use of fighting him?

"Hey, there!" Freckles yelled at Tom Mulligan, who is Mutt Mulligan's boy. "You get your fool dog away from the lion-eater's cage!"

Tom, he hissed Mutt away. But he says to Freckles, being jealous himself, "Don't be scared, Freck. I won't let my dog hurt yours any. Spot, he's safe. He's in a cage where Mutt can't get to him."

Freckles got riled. He says, "I ain't in any cage, Tom."

Tom, he didn't want to fight very bad. But all the other boys and dogs was looking on. And he'd sort of started it. He didn't figure that he could shut up that easy. And there was some girls there, too. "If I was to make a pass at you," says Tom, "you'd wish you was in a cage."

Freckles, he didn't want to fight so bad, either. But he was running this circus, and he didn't feel he could afford to pass by what Tom said too easy. So he says, "Maybe you think you're big enough to put me into a cage."

"If I was to make a pass at you," says Tom, "there wouldn't be enough left of you to put in a cage."

"Well, then," says Freckles, "why don't you make a pass at me?"

"Maybe you figure I don't dast to," says Tom.

"I didn't say you didn't dast to," says Freckles. "Anyone that says I said you didn't dast to is a liar, and so's his aunt Mariar."

Tom, he says, "I ain't got any Aunt Mariar. And you're another and dasn't back it."

Then some of the other kids put chips onto Freckles' and Tom's shoulders. And each dared the other to knock his chip off. And the other kids pushed and jostled them into each other till both chips fell off, and they went at it then. Once they got started they got really mad and each did all he knew how.

And right in the midst of it Mutt run in and bit Freckles on the calf of his leg. Any dog will fight for his boy when his boy is getting the worst of it. But when Mutt did that, I gave a budge against the wooden slats on the cage and two of them came off, and I was on top of Mutt. The circus was in the barn, and the hens began to scream and the horses began to

stomp, and all the boys yelled, "Sick 'im!" and "Go to it!" and danced around and hollered, and the little girls yelled, and all the other dogs began to bark, and it was a right lively and enjoyable time. But Mrs. Watson, Freckles' mother, and the hired girl ran out from the house and broke the fight up.

Grown women are like that. They don't want to fight themselves, and they don't seem to want anyone else to have fun. You got to be a hypocrite around a grown woman to get along with her at all. And then she'll feed you and make a lot of fuss over you. But the minute you start anything with real enjoyment in it she's surprised to see you acting that way. Nobody was licked satisfactory in that fight, or licked anyone else satisfactory.

Well, that night after supper, along comes that Blind Man's Dog. Never did I see a Blind Man's Dog that was as tight-skinned. I ain't a dog that brags, myself, and I don't say I would have licked that heavy a dog right easy, even if he had been a loose-skinned dog. What I do say is that I had been used to fighting loose-skinned dogs that you can get some sort of a reasonable hold on to while you are working around for position. And running into a tight-skinned dog that way, all of a sudden and all unprepared for it, would make anybody nervous. How are you going to get a purchase on a tight-skinned dog when you've been fighting loose-skinned dogs for so long that your teeth and jaws just naturally set themselves for a loose-skinned dog without thinking of it?

Lots of dogs wouldn't have fought him at all when they realized how tight-skinned he was. But I was a Public Character now, and I had to fight him. More than that, I ain't ready to say yet that that dog actually licked me. Freckles, he hit him in the ribs with a lump of soft coal, and he got off of me and run away before I could get my second wind. There's no telling what I would have done to that Blind Man's Dog, tight-skinned as he was, if he hadn't run away before I got my second wind.

Well, the word got around town that that Blind Man's Dog, so called, had licked me! Every time Freckles and me went down the street someone would say, "Well, the dog that licked the lion got licked himself, did he?"

And if it was a lady said it, Freckles would spit on the sidewalk through the place where his front teeth are out and pass on politely as if he hadn't heard, and say nothing. And if it was a man that said it, Freckles would thumb his nose at him. And if it was a girl that said it, he would rub a handful of sand into her hair. And if it was a boy anywhere near his size, there would be a fight.

For a week or so it looked like Freckles and I were fighting all the time. On the way to school, and all through recess times, and after school, and every time we went onto the street. I got so chewed and he got so busted up that we didn't hardly enjoy life. I didn't care so awful much for myself, but I hated it for Freckles. For when they got us pretty well hacked, all the boys began to call him Harold again.

And after they had called him Harold for a week he must have begun to think of himself as Harold. For one Saturday afternoon when there wasn't any school, instead of going swimming with the other kids or playing baseball, or anything, he went and played with girls. He must have felt himself pretty much of an outcast, or he wouldn't have done that. Any boy will play with girls when all the boys and girls are playing together, and some girls are nearly as good as boys; but no boy is going off alone to look up a bunch of girls and play with them unless he has had considerable of a downfall.

Right next to the side of our yard was the Wilkinses. They had a bigger house and a bigger yard than ours. Freckles was sitting on the top of the fence looking into their orchard when the three Wilkins girls came out to play. There was only two boys in the Wilkins family, and they was twins; but they were only year-old babies and didn't amount to anything. The two oldest Wilkins girls, the one with taffy-colored hair and the squint-eyed one, each had one of the twins, taking care of it. And the other Wilkins girl, the pretty one, she had one of those big dolls made as big as a baby. They were rolling those babies and the doll around the grass in a wheelbarrow, and the wheel came off, and that's how Freckles happened to go over.

"Up in the attic," says the taffy-haired one, when he had fixed up the wheelbarrow, "there's a little old express wagon with one wheel off that would be better'n this wheelbarrow. Maybe you could fix that wheel on, too, Harold."

Freckles, he fell for it. After he got the wagon fixed, they got to playing charades and fool girl games like that. Pretty soon Mrs. Wilkins hollered up the stairs that she was going to be gone for an hour, and to take good care of the twins, and then we were alone in the place.

Well, it wasn't much fun for me. They played and they played, and I stuck to Freckles—though his name was called nothing but Harold all that afternoon. But after a while I got pretty tired and lay down on a rug, and a new kind of flea struck me. After I had chased him down and cracked him with my teeth I went to sleep.

I must have slept pretty sound and pretty long. All of a sudden I waked up with a start, and almost choking, for the place was smoky. I barked and no one answered.

I ran out to the landing, and the whole house was full of smoke. The house was on fire, and it looked like I was alone in it. I went down the back stairway, which didn't seem so full of smoke, but the door that led out onto the first-floor landing was locked, and I had to go back up again.

By the time I got back up, the front stairway was a great deal fuller of smoke, and I could see glints of flame winking through it way down below. But it was my only way out of that place. On the top step I stumbled over a gray wool bunch of something or other, and I picked it up in my mouth. Think I, "That is Freckles' gray sweater, that he is so stuck on. I might as well take it down to him."

It wasn't so hard for a lively dog to get out of a place like that, I thought. But I got kind of confused and excited, too. And it struck me all of a sudden, by the time I was down to the second floor, that that sweater weighed an awful lot.

I dropped it on the second floor and ran into one of the front bedrooms and looked out.

By jings! The whole town was in the front yard and in the street.

And in the midst of the crowd was Mrs. Wilkins, carrying on like mad.

"My baby!" she yelled. "Save my baby. Let me loose! I'm going after my baby!"

I stood up on my hind legs, with my head just out of that bedroom window, and the flame and smoke licking up all around me, and barked.

"My doggie! My doggie!" yells Freckles, who was in the crowd. "I must save my doggie!" And he made a run for the house, but someone grabbed him and slung him back.

And Mrs. Wilkins made a run, but they held her, too. The front of the house was one sheet of flame. Old Pop Wilkins, Mrs. Wilkins' husband, was jumping up and down in front of Mrs. Wilkins yelling, here was her baby. He had a real baby in one arm and that big doll in the other, and was so excited he thought he had both babies. Later I heard what had happened. The kids had thought that they were getting out with both twins, but one of them had saved the doll and left a twin behind.

The squint-eyed girl and the taffy-haired girl and the pretty girl was howling as loud as their mother. And every now and then some man would make a rush for the front door, but the fire would drive him back. And everyone was yelling advice to everyone else, except one man who was calling on the whole town to get him an axe. The volunteer fire engine was there, but there wasn't any water to squirt through it, and it had been backed up too near the house and had caught fire and was burning up.

Well, I thinks, that baby will likely turn up in the crowd somewhere, after all, and I'd better get out of there myself while the getting was good. I ran out of the bedroom, and run into that bunched-up gray bundle again.

I ain't saying that I knew it was the missing twin in a gray shawl when I picked it up the second time. And I ain't saying that I didn't know it. But the fact is that I did pick it up. I don't make any brag that I would have risked my life to save Freckles' sweater. It may be I was so rattled I just picked it up because I had had it in my mouth before and didn't quite know what I was doing.

But the *record* is something you can't go behind, and the record is that I got out the back way and into the backyard with that bundle swinging from my mouth, and walked around into the front yard and laid that bundle down—*and it was the twin!*

"My baby!" yells Mrs. Wilkins. And she kissed me. I rubbed it off with my paw. And then the taffy-haired one kissed me. But when I saw the squint-eyed one coming I got behind Freckles and barked.

"Three cheers for Spot!" yelled the whole town. And they give them.

And then I saw what the lay of the land was, so I wagged my tail and barked.

It called for that hero stuff, and I throwed my head up and looked noble—and pulled it.

An hour before, Freckles and me had been outcasts. And now we was Public Characters again. We walked down Main Street and we owned it. And we hadn't any more than got to Doc Watson's drugstore than in rushed Heinie Hassenyager with a lump of hamburger steak, and with tears in his eyes.

"It's got chicken livers mixed in it, too!" says Heinie.

I ate it. But while I ate it, I growled at him.

The Claws of the Cat

by Stuart Cloete

Was Jappie old enough to be left alone on the South African farm? His father thought so. But no one foresaw the dangers he would have to face.

"I am old enough," the boy said.

"He is old enough," his father said from the bed.

"He's only twelve," the woman said.

"And I'm not afraid," the boy said.

"That's it," his mother said, putting her hand on his shoulder. "It makes me afraid that you are afraid of nothing."

"It's his Boer blood," his father said. "He has bold blood from both sides."

"*Ja*, Jan!" the woman said. "And look where our boldness has got us. Because of it you are crippled."

"I shall get well," the man said. "The doctor has promised it. Besides, how could I refuse to ride the horse? If there had been no rain, he would not have slipped and fallen on me."

"I have Moskou!" the boy said, pointing to the big hound, half foxhound and half collie, lying at his feet. "And I have the gun."

"He's young to leave alone on the farm," the woman said.

She looked around the kitchen. She looked at the door of the great oven where she baked bread, where her mother had baked bread before her. At the wood-burning stove, at the clay floors so carefully tended each day. She looked at the wall recess that held the crockery. This was reality to her. All that was real in the world. Her home, her husband, her son. She had been born here and had never slept away from the place, except when they went camping each year by the sea, till she was grown up.

And now she must leave all this and go with her husband to Cape Town, to the hospital. The doctor had said she must be there, just in case. Besides, she knew that Jan would not be happy if she was not near him. Like a big black-bearded baby was this bold husband of hers.

"Cape Town," she said to herself. "And in a motorcar." She had never been in a car. But it would get them there in a day, and it would take five with horses. Besides, the horses had never been in a town any more than she had. And though she could drive them in the open veld and over the mountains, she would be as frightened as they in a great town.

A bed had been moved into the kitchen, because it was easier to take care of her husband there. A man put his head in and said, "It is here." That was the motorcar.

"I do not hear it," she said.

"It's a new one," he said. "It moves very quietly."

"You have the gun," the man in bed said.

"*Ja,* Pa, I have the gun."

The man and the boy stared at the old Mauser hanging from a nail on the wall. The nail was as old as the house, hand forged.

"And the dog," the man said.

"*Ja,* and the dog."

"And your blood that knows no fear," the man said. "The blood of the Swarts and the de Wets. A good cross," he said. "*Ja,* a good mixture like Moskou."

Two men came in, followed by the doctor, who said, "We'll take you now, Jan, if you're ready."

"I'm ready," he said.

The two men picked Jan Swart up. He was a big man and they staggered under his weight. His wife followed them to the car, and the boy followed his mother.

The doctor propped the sick man up, wedging him in one corner of the back seat. "Get in, wife," he said.

Jappie pushed past her to kiss his father.

"Do not fear for me," his father said. "I cannot die. I can only be killed. It is not reasonable to think that I shall be the first of my race to die in bed. Fear nothing," he said. "And do what your heart prompts you, for through it courses the wild blood of your people."

"I shall fear nothing," the boy said. He backed out of the car, and his mother held him to her.

"Be good," she said, "and take care of yourself." She got in beside his father and wiped her eyes on a blue cotton handkerchief.

The doctor took the wheel. The car started.

The boy shouted, "Good-by, *tot siens,* till I see you."

"*Tot siens,*" shouted his father.

The car got smaller. In a few minutes it stopped being a real car and became a toy. Then it stopped being even a toy. It disappeared behind a shoulder of the hill and was gone.

Then Herman Smit, the bigger of the two men, said, "It's gone. If you have any trouble, Jappie, come over to us."

His brother said, "Yes, come. And one of us will ride over every now and again to see how you are doing."

"*Baie dankie,*" the boy said, "very thank you, but I shall be all right."

"*Ja,*" Herman said, "but all the same we shall come, for we are neighbors. And now we must go. It's a long walk back." The brothers laughed, because a walk of six miles over the mountains was nothing to them.

"*Tot siens*, Jappie," they said.

"*Tot siens,*" the boy said. He watched them go up the face of the hill. At the top they turned and waved to him. Then their legs disappeared, their bodies, their heads. For a moment Hendrik's hat was visible; then that, too, fell below the ridge.

Now he was really alone. Moskou pushed his head into his hand. He reached a little higher than his hand, because without bending, the boy could hold his collar.

Moskou was yellow all over, a pale golden chestnut, lemon, as it is called, with a thick smooth coat, and eyes like yellow, black-centered agates. The only other black things about him were his wet nose and the short, hard nails of his round, catlike feet. He stood twenty-seven inches at the shoulder and had the legs of a foxhound. They were strong and straight, set on at the corners of his body. He appeared to have no hocks or pasterns, and his body was deep and thick. Around his neck he had a ruffle of thicker hair from his collie mother, but for the rest of him he resembled a great golden foxhound. As a matter of fact, his grandfather had come to Africa from a famous English pack, so there was good blood in Moskou. The blood that had hunted the fox and the buck for centuries, and before that had hunted the wild boar, the wolf, and the bear, when such hounds had been called Saint Huberts, and England was still a forest.

His dam, the collie, was guardian of sheep, swift and vigilant, the servant and companion of man. And Moskou combined the qualities of his parents—the great speed, weight, and nose of his sire and grandsire, and the wisdom and affectionate nature of his dam.

Moskou was in his prime, four years old. His tail was slightly feathered and fastened strongly onto his back. When he was hunting, it lashed back and forth like a golden plume. When he got a hot scent, he gave tongue, first whimpering, and then as the scent grew hotter giving his deep, bell-like bay, which in still weather would carry a mile or more over the mountains.

It seemed as if he knew his responsibility—as if he knew they were alone on the farm, the sole protectors of the homestead and the stock—because he came closer to the boy, his great shoulders rubbing against Jappie's thigh.

Alone, the boy thought, as he stroked the dog's head and gently pulled his ears. He was not afraid, but he was uneasy. It was a new experience and a great responsibility.

He had been alone with his mother before, once when his father had been gone a week seeking a lost heifer. But quite alone like this he had never been, and the silence of the hills and their mystery fell upon him, covering him like a cloak. A green-and-scarlet sugarbird flew into the pomegranate tree by the orchard gate. It was like a jewel, he thought, that shone and sparkled in the light. Then it, too, flew away and the world seemed quite empty.

Jappie thought of his mother and tears came into his eyes. He thought of how she had married his father. She had told him the tale many times. Of how he had come courting her on the strong wild horses he was breaking, and how her heart had fluttered like a bird in her breast when she saw this great bearded man on a big wild horse. Breaking and training horses and oxen for draft and saddle was his business and his pleasure. He was also a kind of vet, attending animals when they were sick and curing many of them with simple country remedies. He had a great way with dumb things, and his wife often laughed about it, saying, "I was as tame as a cow with that man from the first."

People paid him for his work in cash and in kind, but mostly in kind, so that he had effects of all sorts on his place. Crippled animals that had been given to him, broken plows and carts, poultry, and the like, that he doctored up or mended and sold. People said, "If you can do anything with that, you can have it." And he took it, the plow or the mare. And he mended them, or fattened them, or tamed them, and out of them made enough to buy himself food and clothing; and what was more important to him, he had the friendship of all, for they sent for him only when they needed help and were always glad to see him when he came.

At first, though his coming had made his mother's heart flutter, she had not wished to marry him because of his wildness and his lack of education. But when she had inherited the farm, and he had said, "My heart, let us go into the mountains together and farm the place," she had agreed. Because otherwise she would have had to sell it, and big as it was—it was eight thousand acres—it was worth little, being all mountain, bush, and forest. A place only half tamed. But as he said, it was not right to sell the home of one's ancestors, the house where one had been born, when there was a man like him ready to help her with it.

His argument and the beating of her heart, which was never stilled when he was near, had convinced her. And for thirteen years they had lived in Baviaansfontein, Baboon Spring, and he had tamed it a little, building dams, clearing bush, and plowing patches of arable land that they had discovered among the trees and rocks. Little lands like big handkerchiefs dropped into the mountains from the sky.

And now all this was in Jappie's hands—the stock, four horses, six cows, four calves, eight oxen, one mule, a flock of twenty sheep, and the poultry. This was all they owned in the world. It was their capital and income. It had been won hardly. Bred, worked for, suffered for, it was, if lost, irreplaceable. It took nine months to make a calf. It took three more years to turn it into a cow, or four into a marketable ox. A horse could be worked at two, but was not at its best until five. And sheep, if they bred more quickly, died more easily. So that the flock they were trying to breed grew more slowly than they had hoped.

Now, until his parents came back, he was the master of all this. The master, but also the servant. For man is the slave of the land and the beasts that require tending upon it. All must be watered and fed, cows must be milked, eggs picked up, sheep herded into their kraals at night, fences kept in order, and the weeds in the lands kept in check, before becoming so strong that they overwhelmed it. All, now, looked to him. It seemed to him that even the wheat in the land below the house swung in the breeze toward him, saying, "Keep the beasts from eating us up." And the chickens walking on the short grass near the house said, "Protect us at night from the wild prowling things." A cow lowed in a field and her calf answered. And it was he who must bring the cow's overflowing udder to the calf's hungry mouth.

His father had said he was old enough, and he was. But only just. His father had said he must not be afraid, and he was not afraid. Not much afraid. His father had said he could count on the bold blood that ran in his veins, and his father never lied. But his blood and his nerve were

untested, like a young soldier going into battle for the first time. What he feared was fear; what he was most afraid of was being afraid.

His work he knew. All of it, feeding, milking, herding, weeding. There was no work he could not do, save the heaviest, and that was not because of lack of knowledge but because of lack of strength. All of it he had done many times before, but never with no one to talk to about it. This was the first thing he noticed. When he found that the black hen, sitting in a barrel, had hatched ten chicks, and he had put her in the big barn and given her water and mealies and bread crumbs, there was no one to whom he could say, "The black hen has ten chicks, and I have put her in the barn and watered and fed them."

He told Moskou, and Moskou wagged his yellow tail, and smiled up at him with open jaws. And so the first day went by, with all the work well done, and after cooking his mealie porridge and making coffee, he went to bed in his father's bed in the kitchen. The comfortable smell of the man still lingered in it, and he lay with the dog stretched out beside him, and the Mauser leaning against the wall in the corner, and matches and a homemade candle on a shelf behind his head.

The next day passed quickly. There was no time for Jappie to think till evening when all the work was done, and then he was too tired. All he could do was go over the day's work in his mind. Yes, everything was done. The cows milked, the calves shut in their hock, the horses watered and fed, the chickens shut up, the sheep counted and safely kraaled. He had cut wood for the fire in the morning. He had drawn a bucket of water from the fountain, bailing it out with a dipper from the cleft in the rocks that was worn with the steps of his ancestors' comings and goings, and the scraping of their vessels, as they had for a hundred years bailed the sweet fresh water from the rocky pool, into the buckets they carried into the house. The little path was worn deep with footprints so that it was a green, sunken ribbon that led from the house, past the banana clumps, to the hillside.

"Everything is done," he said aloud, and Moskou wagged his tail so that it thumped on the floor. Jappie was proud of himself. He had accomplished the work of a man this day. I am, he thought, a boy no longer, since I can do a man's work. The responsibility that had weighed him down disappeared, canceled by his ability to meet the demands that had been put upon him. He dreamed, half awake and half asleep, of the time when the twenty sheep would number a hundred, five hundred. When the six cows would be a herd of fifty, when . . . And then he slept, his arm thrown out and hanging beside his dog's head. The dog licked his hand and then curled up beside him on the floor.

The next day Herman Smit rode over to see if he was all right.

"*Ja,*" the boy said. "I am all right."

"That is good," Herman said.

The boy put the coffee on the fire, and when he had drunk, Herman mounted and rode away.

When he had gone, Jappie almost wished he hadn't come, because a loneliness he had not felt before now descended upon him. Five more days went by, days filled with the work of the farm, the ministering to the beasts and birds that depended upon him, and upon which his welfare and that of his parents depended.

Then Herman rode over again. He said, "I have had news from the *dorp*. A man passed, Piet Fourie, with a message from your pa."

"My pa?" Jappie said. His heart almost stopped as he spoke. "He is well?" he asked.

"*Ja*, he is well. It is all over. They cut something in him. He has it in a bottle and is bringing it to show you."

"When are they coming?" Jappie asked.

"That is the message," Herman said. "They will be here Tuesday, if God is willing and all goes well."

"I will pray that all goes well," Jappie said. "I have prayed it every night and morning since they went away, but now I will pray more strongly." In his heart he had prayed already: Dear God, let nothing happen. Let them come back, for this burden is too great for a small son like me.

For though he was bold enough and unafraid with one part of him, the other part cried for the presence of his mother in the kitchen and the sight of his tall father working on the lands. The world was empty without them. Without the clatter of his mother's pans and the sound of her singing as she worked, and the shouts of his father to the horses as he plowed. They were sounds that were a part of his life, as much a part as the cry of the plover in the moonlight, the bark of the baboons in the hills, and the clattering cry of a bush pheasant when it got up in front of him with whirring wings. The sounds of his parents at work were a part of what his ears were accustomed to hearing, and the sight of them about the house and in the lands and fields helped to fill his eyes, rounding off, as it were, the landscape, giving it cause and reason.

"Today is Saturday," Herman said.

"*Ja*," Jappie said.

"There is Sunday," Herman said, "and Monday, and then they will be here, if God is willing."

"*Ja*," Jappie said, "if God is willing." To himself he said, "The day after tomorrow, I will be able to say tomorrow."

"If there is more news, good or bad," Herman said, "I will bring it."

Then he mounted and rode away, leaving a space behind him. A space that was filled by the thought that the day after tomorrow he could say, "Tomorrow."

Sunday passed, also a working day for a boy alone, for the beasts must be tended. But he read from the Gospel of Saint John, which was where his father had left off. Each Sunday he read a chapter aloud, reading the Bible through from end to end. In that Bible were the names of his forebears, the dates of their births, marriages, and deaths. It belonged to his mother, and he saw her birthday. She was thirty-one, and then he began working out the dates on the calendar that his father had been given by the storekeeper. Tuesday was the twelfth of September. It was his mother's birthday. That was a good omen.

He wished he could bake her a cake or give her some gift. He generally managed to buy something. His father used to take him to the store, ten miles away, for the purpose. But now there was nothing he could do. He could not leave the farm to ride twenty miles. It would take too long. And then the violets came to his mind. Some were in bloom by the pomegranate trees. His mother loved flowers, and if he picked them now, they would last.

He went out to get them and arranged them in a glass, with a border of their own leaves. Their perfume filled the room. He set them on the little table by his parents' bed, and he closed the door to hold in the scent. Then he went to skim the cream from the milk he had set in pans in the dairy that morning, and from there to the stableyards and kraals to shut up for the night. It was a still evening. Very beautiful, and all was well. He watched the last bees coming home to the box hives. How late some of them worked. And tomorrow he could say, "Tomorrow."

He was up before dawn saying it, "Tomorrow, tomorrow." He said it to himself, and then he saw Herman coming on his black horse. News, he thought. "Good or bad," Herman had said.

And the news he brought was bad. His father was wonderfully well, but they were not coming until Thursday, not for three days. Well, three days would pass, as the others had, but it was a blow to him. His mother would not be home for her birthday and the violets would not last. Still, there had been plenty of buds, and on Wednesday he would pick more. The days had gone quickly enough, because there was so much work. And the few days that separated him from his parents would go quickly too.

"You are a good boy," Herman said. "Your father will be proud of you, for it is not every young son who could have done what you have done. And many would be afraid."

"I have Moskou and the gun," the boy said.

"Nevertheless," Herman said, "many would be afraid. Why, many men would fear to be alone in so wild a place."

"It's my *woonplek*, my living place," Jappie said. "I know no other place, and I am not lonely with the animals and birds about me."

And again Herman rode away, but this time he left no space behind him; Jappie was getting used to being left alone. As he watched him go he saw the sheep coming in, led by Wit Booi, the big white *kapater*, the gelded goat. He had a bell fastened to a strap around his neck, and each evening he got a handful of mealies as a reward for leading the flock home. Behind him came the ram and, strung out behind them, the ewes and lambs. That night Moskou was uneasy. He barked once and growled.

Jappie got up and, taking the gun from its nail, went out with the dog. But they saw nothing. All was still.

Wednesday morning, when he went to the sheep kraal, one ewe lay dead. There was no mark on her, no blood. Perhaps she had died of illness, a sickness, but when they had come in last night, all had been well. They had moved quickly and their eyes had been bright.

While he wondered, Moskou began to whimper. He went to the dog, and there on the soft ground outside the kraal was a spoor. It was big and round, a cat spoor, but nearly three inches across. "*Rooikat,*" he said—lynx—and then, calling the dog to him, he went back into the kraal and, parting the heavy wool around the ewe's neck under the yellow yolk that waterproofed her white skin, he found two tooth marks.

He dragged the sheep to the back veranda and, fastening a strap about its hocks, hoisted it onto a beam and made the strap fast. Later he would skin it and the meat would be good. But now he must make a plan. He worked quickly, milking, watering, feeding, and turning out the stock.

Plan? Before God, there was only one plan. He must do as his pa would have done. He must kill the lynx, for it would be back. There had been a shower in the night. The scent would be good and the spoor easy to see. He went into the house for the gun.

The boy went back to the kraal, patted Moskou and pointed to the spoor, saying, "Now go and find him and we will kill him, before he kills more of our sheep."

The dog put his nose to the ground. His tail lashed furiously, and then he was off at a canter. He went up the mountain, giving tongue.

Jappie ran behind him. The gun was heavy in his hand, and the bandolier bumped up and down against his hip. He could hear Moskou, the bell-like note of his cry coming from not more than a hundred yards ahead, and then he came up to him. The hound had checked. Marking the place where he had lost the scent on a rocky flat, Jappie cast around in a circle with the dog and picked it up again. This time it was hotter and the hound went faster. The note of his voice deepened to a bay.

He is near, Jappie thought, and ran hard. Then in some heavy milkbush he heard Moskou barking loudly. He's treed him, he thought. Then came savage yelps and deep bays, as the lynx broke cover with the dog close behind him.

Jappie thought, He's seen me and he knows I can shoot him down from a tree. With the dog alone he would have stayed up there. The lynx ran up a steep cliff and turned into a small cave in the limestone. Now we've got him, Jappie thought, because Moskou was barking at the entrance and looking back at him as he climbed.

The cave gave onto a ledge, and as he reached it he saw the lynx crouched on the floor, glaring at him. Its great yellow eyes were narrowed slits, and its lips were drawn back over its bared fangs. Its red body was flat on the ground, its short tail raised. Its black tufted ears were laid back against its neck.

Jappie put up his gun and pulled the trigger. Nothing happened. He opened the bolt, reloaded, and fired again. This time the cartridge exploded, but as he shot, the animal charged. The boy warded it off with the barrel, but the lynx bit him in the arm and scratched him from neck to belt with its sharp claws. He felt its breath on his face.

Dropping the rifle he gripped its throat, trying to keep it away from his face, and felt with his other hand for the knife in his belt.

As the lynx jumped at Jappie, Moskou had sprung at it, seizing it in the loin. The lynx turned away from the boy as he stabbed it in the side, and swung back on the dog. As it turned, Jappie passed his hand over its back and drove the hunting knife in again behind its shoulder blade.

Dropping him completely, the lynx fell on its back and, reaching upward, seized Moskou by the throat from below. The hound and the lynx became an indistinguishable blur of red fur and yellow skin. A spitting, snarling, growling, bloody mass.

Moskou shook himself free and stood over the lynx, his ruff covered with thick dark blood. With a savage roar he closed in again, his jaws on the lynx's throat. It was dead now, limp but twitching still. The hound stood over it for an instant, and then staggered and fell. Half skinned alive, the great muscles of his side exposed, one cheek torn out, he lay and, turning his golden eyes to Jappie, he died on top of the lynx. His eyes never closed, they simply lost expression, glazing slowly as death came to him.

Jappie sat down on the bloody floor of the cave. They had done it. The lynx was finished, but Moskou was dead, and without Moskou the lynx might have killed him. The dog had died so that he might live. He looked at his arm. It was badly torn and bleeding. He took off his shirt and cut it into strips with his knife and bandaged himself as well as he could. When he got home, he would put turpentine on it from the bottle on the shelf and cover it with cobwebs.

He was very cool now. He must fix up his wounds, and then fetch the dog and the lynx. He must come back with a horse. He went over the horses in his mind. There was only one, old Meisie, that was tame enough for the job. Horses did not like the smell of blood.

Jappie sat a little longer and then took off his bandolier. It was badly scratched and had helped to save him. He laid it in a corner of the cave and stood the rifle beside it. His pa had said, "You have the dog and the gun and your blood." Now he had neither the dog nor the gun, but his blood had saved him, the fury of it that had boiled over when the lynx's fangs had broken the skin and muscles of his arm.

He went slowly home, his arm in a rough sling made from the rest of his shirt. At the house he took the brandy bottle from the cupboard and drank half a cup. He had never tasted brandy before, and it burned him, but made him feel better. Then he poured turpentine on his wounds. It bit him, stung like a hot iron. He walked up and down until the pain was less severe, and then, poking some cobwebs from the thatch, he covered the wound and bandaged his arm with the strips of old linen that his mother kept rolled and ready for accidents.

Now for Meisie. She was near the house and easy to catch. He bridled and saddled her. He got two *riems*, thongs, from the wagon shed and led her up the mountain. Twice he had to rest. When he got near the cave, he tied the mare to a tree and dragged out the dead dog and the lynx. He succeeded in getting them onto a flat rock that was almost as high as the saddle. Then he took off his coat, covered the old mare's head with it, crossed the stirrup leathers, and hoisted the lynx from the rock onto the mare's back, tied it, passing the *riem* from its legs through the stirrup irons. Now for the dog.

As he tied Moskou beside the lynx he could hardly see for his tears. Then, taking his coat off the mare, he led her back. His mind was very clear. He knew what he must do. He knew he must do it quickly, because as soon as he stopped he knew he could not go on. The cows. The cows must be allowed to run with their calves. He would not be able to milk. The horses could run. If the kraal was left open, Wit Booi would bring in the sheep. The poultry he would feed heavily, and then they must manage for themselves.

He offsaddled the mare, letting the saddle fall to the ground with its burden. Then he washed her back and flanks free of blood, because blood would cause her hair to come out. Then, running a *riem* through a pulley on one of the beams of the barn, he hoisted the body of the lynx and tied the end of the *riem*. It could hang there, beside the sheep it had killed, till tomorrow when his father came.

The grave for Moskou was another matter. It was hard to dig with one hand. He drove in the spade, pressed it home with his foot, and then scooped out the earth, levering the spade shaft against his knee. It was not a proper grave. It was more of a scraping in the black ground that ended, when he had dragged Moskou into it, as a mound beside the violet bed. That had been the only place to bury him. That he had been certain of since the beginning. There he would be remembered and safe.

With the grave finished, and the dog covered under a soft blanket of rich brown earth, Jappie dropped the spade and went into the house. He did not undress. He took off his shoes and fell on his father's bed. His father would be back tomorrow. Until tomorrow everything must take care of itself. He had done what he could and could do no more.

Not even with his blood could he do more. For a while he tossed about. Then he slept. Then he dreamed of his fight again, saw the blazing eyes so near his own. Once more he saw the bared fangs, the white cheeks, the black whiskers, the tufted ears laid back, heard the snarls, and flung himself about in the frenzy of battle. Then he slept again.

His father looked about the room. The boy had not heard them come. "Where's Moskou?" he said.

His father looked pale and much thinner, Jappie thought.

His mother said, "What happened, Jappie?"

"Nothing," he said. "The *rooikat* scratched me."

"Lynx?" his father said.

"*Ja,*" the boy said. "The lynx. We killed it. All is well but one sheep. He killed the sheep, Pa."

"And Moskou?" his father said again.

"Moskou is dead," he said. "I buried him. *Ja*, I buried him by the violets."

"A brave dog," his father said. "*Ja*, a brave dog."

"A brave boy," his mother said, stroking Jappie's forehead.

"*Ja*, he is brave," his father said, "but what else could he be with his blood? How did you kill him, Jappie?"

"With my knife," Jappie said.

"But the gun? Surely you took the gun."

"I took the gun. But the shells are old, Pa. It misfired, and he charged. Moskou took him from behind, but he turned on him . . . and then I drove home the knife."

"I should not have left him," his mother said.

"He was big enough," his father said. "To kill a lynx with a dog and a knife is big enough."

"Moskou is dead," the boy said again, and turned his face to the wall.

"*Groot genoeg,*" his father said. "Big enough."

The Giant Who Sucked His Thumb

by Adrien Stoutenburg

A great giant was Fingal,
but his wife Oonagh was the winner this day.

Everybody in Ireland, from Bantry Bay to Ballycastle and back again, knows about the great Irish giant, Fingal. Just how large Fingal was isn't certain, but it would seem that he wasn't much more than a hundred feet or so tall. It is true that he was big enough to pull a fair-sized tree up by the roots, knock off its branches, and use it for a walking stick. But he was not mighty enough to be able to leap across the Irish Sea to England; not even across the North Channel to Scotland at the channel's narrowest point, which is only thirteen miles. This is known for a fact, because a bridge that he and his giant neighbors started to build across the channel still exists today. It is called the Giant's Causeway and it is right there at the tip of County Antrim for all to see.

Fingal and his friends were not engineers, of course. They were just big, ordinary, hardworking giants dressed in regular work clothes, and their idea of a bridge was simply to lug slabs of rock to the water and stand them on end to make huge stepping-stones. And for all that they were very strong and had hammers to break up mountains for the rock slabs, it took them many years before they had filled in the channel almost the whole way to the other shore. Of course, they took time off now and then to go home and see their wives, or to have wrestling matches with each other to test who was the strongest. Fingal didn't take part in such games. Being much stronger than all the others, he was afraid he might injure them so that they wouldn't be able to continue work on the bridge.

One day Fingal was sitting watching the other giants playing a game of leapfrog during the lunch hour, when his right thumb began to itch. Now, there was something very special about Fingal's right thumb. Long ago, when he had been a boy, a much older giant had come to Killyclogher, where Fingal was born, and kidnapped him. This giant, called Blacksod, forced Fingal to be his slave. Young though he was, Fingal had to cook and clean and haul wood—and dig for worms every minute he could. For Blacksod spent all his time fishing in a lough—the Irish word for lake. Actually, Blacksod did not care for fish at all, and didn't even like fishing. But what he did want was to catch one particular fish, a certain magical salmon with a silver mark on its forehead. Anyone who caught the salmon and ate the first piece of it would, thereafter, be able to see into the future.

For seven years Blacksod fished, and for seven years young Fingal dug for worms. On the very last day of the seventh year, Blacksod hauled in the magical salmon. At once he ordered Fingal to roast it, bellowing, "If you let anything happen to it, I'll put you on to boil for soup!"

Fingal's hands shook as he laid wood for a fire. His eyebrows shook when he hung the salmon by a strong rope over the blaze. His knees shook all the while the fish was cooking. When the fire began to die down, he ran on shaking legs for more wood. And then, when he returned, his heart shook, for there was a mammoth heat blister on the side of the salmon closest to the fire. Blacksod, he knew, would go into a rage over that. Terrified, Fingal reached out and tried to press the blister down with his thumb. It was like touching hot iron. He yanked back and thrust his thumb into his mouth to ease the smart. A piece of steaming fish had stuck to his thumb, and so Fingal accidentally was the first person to swallow a piece of the magical fish. With that he gained the power of prophecy that Blacksod had been seeking. So, even before he heard the old giant's footsteps as Blacksod returned from his evening bath in the lough, Fingal knew the giant was coming.

He fled in terror and kept running for days. Blacksod roared after him, but Fingal always managed to escape, because every time he thrust his thumb into his mouth he was able to know the best way to run. His thumb even told him how to get rid of the mean old giant forever. Fingal raced to the edge of a towering cliff, with Blacksod at his heels. Just at the edge, Fingal changed course. Blacksod was running too swiftly to stop—and over he went with a crash that made the earth shake.

Fingal headed north until he reached the causeway country, and there he settled down with a yellow-haired giantess called Oonagh. Oonagh had a cousin in Scotland whom she yearned to visit and she began pestering Fingal about building a bridge across the channel.

So that was how it began, and now, as Fingal watched the other workmen playing leapfrog, there was that sudden pricking of his thumb. He put his thumb in his mouth. As he sucked it he grew pale and his hands, eyebrows, and knees began to shake. From his thumb he learned that a giant greater than any that had ever been in Ireland before was on his way to challenge Fingal to a duel. That giant, called Cucullin, was so powerful that one stamp of his foot shook the whole country around him. With one blow of his fist he could flatten a thunderbolt and keep it in his pocket in the shape of a pancake.

"Arrah!" Fingal exclaimed to himself in fear. "What shall I do? Faith, and I'm no match for the likes of Cucullin." He pronounced it "Cahoolin," for his thumb had told him that was the proper way.

He sucked his thumb again, seeking advice. *Go home to Oonagh* was the message his thumb gave him.

So Fingal stood up and called his men together. He told them that he was not feeling very well—for he did not want to admit that he was afraid of anything or anybody—and that he had decided to go home and rest his bones a bit.

He set off for his house on the very tiptop of Knockmany Hill, the windiest and wettest place for miles around. But it was also the highest and gave Fingal a fine view of the countryside so that he could watch out for enemies. Also, from there he could look out at all the other green hills of the Emerald Isle and watch the comings and goings of the small earth people with their little donkey carts and herds of tiny sheep or cattle. He would smoke his big clay pipe, sending up enormous clouds to blot out the sun—though the sun didn't shine often on Knockmany—and think how dreadful it would be to be as small as those other earth dwellers.

Right now he wished that he were even smaller, so tiny that Cucullin couldn't even see him. There was a brisk peat fire going in the hearth, he saw, as he strode toward his house and flung the door open.

Oonagh dropped a kettle in her surprise and ran to him. "Fingal!" she cried out happily. "And you're welcome home to your own house, you darling bully!"

They hugged each other with giant hugs, and though Fingal tried to look as happy as Oonagh, she saw at once that something was bothering him. "You've trouble in your mind, my hero," she said. "And won't you be telling of it?"

"Yerra, I will that," he said with a sigh, and told her about Cucullin's searching for him. He had scarcely finished when his thumb began to itch. He thrust it into his mouth and shuddered.

"What now, then?" Oonagh asked.

"He's coming!" Fingal cried. "He's tramping along, bigger than a round tower, below Dungannon."

"When will he get here?" Oonagh questioned, her voice surprisingly calm.

"Tomorrow at two o'clock," Fingal groaned. "If I run away, I'm disgraced. And in any case, I know that sooner or later I must meet him, for my thumb tells me so."

"Don't be cast down," said his wife. "Depend on me and maybe I'll bring you better out of this scrape than you could by the rule of your thumb."

Fingal only gave a deeper groan, for he had little faith in Oonagh's being able to protect him. She was a mere woman, after all, and only about ninety feet tall. How could she hope to save him from a mountain on legs like the fierce Cucullin?

"Rest now and sup your tea," his wife said, "while I go about getting ready for our guest."

Nervously Fingal watched her as she tromped around gathering fagots and peat for a fire on a knob of rock outside. Once the fire was going well, she tossed green grass and leaves on it to make a smoke that rose high in the air. Then she put two fingers in her mouth and gave a whistle so loud it carried across ten counties.

Fingal leaped up, more scared than before. Oonagh was giving the signal that the Irish always used to tell any stranger in the neighborhood that he was welcome. She was actually inviting Cucullin to come!

"Have you said farewell to your wits, woman?" he shouted at her. "Am I to be skivered like a rabbit before your eyes and have my name disgraced forever in the sight of all my tribe, and me the best man among them? How am I to fight this man-mountain, this cross between an earthquake and a thunderbolt? Him who carries a pancake in his pocket that was once lightning. Answer me that!"

It was the nearest they had ever come to having a real quarrel, and a few tears leaked out of Oonagh's eyes. "Be easy, Fingal. Troth, I'm ashamed of you. Talking of pancakes, maybe we will give him as good as he brings with him, thunderbolt or otherwise."

Fingal felt a bit calmer, for in spite of his doubts, he did have confidence in his wife. She had helped him out of many a quandary before. And since he had no answer to the present problem, there was nothing to do but hope that she did have. So he lit his pipe, nibbled on a griddle cake she had baked the week before, and drank more tea while she went about her own affairs.

Panting up and down the surrounding mountains, Oonagh went to all the neighbor giantesses within a hundred-mile area. From them she borrowed every round iron baking platter she could get until she had twenty-one. Back home, she stirred up a batch of batter for twenty-two griddle cakes. Then she covered with batter the twenty-one platters she had borrowed. In spite of the iron platters inside, they looked like ordinary cakes. She added the one other griddle cake that did not have a platter hidden in it and left the whole lot to bake.

Next, she put a large kettle of milk on the hearth and let it bubble until it turned into curds and whey. The curds were the thickened, solid part of the milk, which separated from the watery part, the whey. She placed the kettle on a shelf beside the twenty-two freshly baked griddle cakes and then sat down to knit calmly before going to bed.

"What has all this cooking to do with saving my skin?" Fingal asked her. "Or do you plan to fatten Cucullin up so that he will be bigger than ever?"

"Never you fear, my darling bruiser," she said, her huge knitting needles clacking away.

Fingal, having nothing better to do, sucked his thumb. And he learned something further about Cucullin. "Wife," he said, "I've found out something else about that monster villain hurrying here. All of his strength is bound up in the middle finger of his right hand."

"Faith, and is that the truth?" she said, and she stopped knitting long enough to look very thoughtful, though not at all worried.

When Fingal and Oonagh got up in the morning, Fingal tested his thumb and then gazed through the mist floating around Knockmany Hill. "He's reached Londonderry by now, wife. He'll be here by two o'clock, as I said."

"Thank goodness, then, he'll be on time," she answered cheerfully.

It was impossible for Fingal to be cheerful. He paced back and forth, smoking more than was good for him, clouding up the place so much that Oonagh got a coughing fit.

"Fin, my darling," she said, "when we have a little one to raise, you must do your smoking outdoors." She glanced at the great cradle that Fingal had already built for the day when they would have a baby giant of their own.

"Yerra, that I will, my dear," Fingal promised, and looked at the big cradle as fondly as she had. For a moment he almost forgot his fear over Cucullin's coming, until he noticed that the dim sun was directly overhead. "He'll be here soon!" he cried.

"Aye, and I am ready," said Oonagh. "Now, this is what you must do, my boy. Put on the nightgown and the nightcap that I have made for the baby. Then you must squeeze yourself into the cradle and pretend that you are Baby Fingal."

Fingal blinked and stared at her, not knowing what to think.

"Do as I say, my burly dove," Oonagh commanded.

"Ah!" Fingal exclaimed, suddenly realizing what she was up to. He gave her a great hug, telling her that never had there been a smarter giantess in Ireland. Then he hurriedly stripped off his working clothes and pulled on the baby's nightgown. Since baby giants are very large, this was no difficult problem for Fingal—and it so happened that Oonagh had made the gown extra large, by mistake. In the same way, Fingal had made the cradle extra large, for he was not a very skillful carpenter. Even so, it was something of a squeeze, and his bare feet stuck out over the footboard.

Oonagh gave his cheek a pat and pulled the baby bonnet down a bit farther around his face. "Now, then, big baby, just lie there snug and say nothing. Be guided by me."

Fingal nodded, but what could be seen of his face was decidedly pale.

There was a distant rumbling sound. The sound grew louder by the minute. It was the steady stomp of Cucullin's feet.

While Fingal shivered in silence, Oonagh ran to the window. "Yerra," she said, "it's his own self marching up over the horizon. Faith, he is a mountain of a man!"

Fingal felt a hot stab of jealousy at the admiration in her tone.

The ground shook as the mammoth giant stomped up Knockmany Hill. Then, from the yard, he roared out, "Is this where the great Fingal lives?"

Oonagh opened the door. "Indeed it is, honest man," she answered. "Save you kindly—won't you be coming in and setting yourself down now?"

"Thank you, ma'am," said Cucullin, and he took off the round cap he wore and dusted the travel stains from his knickers. Even though the kitchen doorway was over a hundred feet high, he had to duck down to enter, and when he sat in Fingal's chair, Oonagh feared it might break. "You are Mrs. Fingal, I suppose?" he said to her.

"I am," she replied, "and I have no reason, I hope, to be ashamed of my husband."

"No, he has the name of being the strongest and bravest in Ireland. But, for all that, there's a man not far from you that's very eager of taking a shake with him. Is he at home?"

"Why, then, no. If ever a man left his house in a fury, it was Fingal. It appears that someone told him of a big basthoon of a giant called Cucullin being down at the causeway to look for him, and so he set out there to try if he could catch him. Troth, I hope for that poor giant's sake he won't meet with him, for if he does, Fin will make a paste of him at once."

"Well," said the other, "I myself am Cucullin and I have been seeking him these twelve months, but he always kept clear of me. I will never rest night or day until I lay my hands on him."

Oonagh gave a loud laugh and looked at the giant as if he were a mere handful of a man. "Did you never see my strapping Fingal?"

"No, I have not. He always took care to keep his distance."

"For fear of hurting you, then. If you take my advice, you poor-looking creature, you'll pray you never see him, for it will be a black day for you." She paused as the moist Knockmany wind rattled the door and sent a chill draft through the room. "Alas," she said, "as you can perceive, the wind is on the door. Since Fingal is not home, maybe you would be kind enough to turn the house around, as he always does."

Cucullin blinked twice, looking as if he had not heard right.

"But as you turn the house away from the wind," she added, "kindly do it as gently as possible so as not to wake the baby there in the cradle."

Cucullin looked toward the cradle for the first time and blinked again. Seeing the enormous size of "the baby," he glanced toward the rattling door as if he would like to leave in a hurry. But he had boasted so much that he knew he had to prove his strength. So he stood up, pulling at the middle finger of his right hand, where all his strength was, until it cracked three times. Then he went outside, wrapped his arms around the house, and turned it as Oonagh had asked.

When Fingal saw this, the sweat ran down his face like a waterfall.

"I'm much obliged," said Oonagh, joining the giant outside. "As you are so helpful, maybe you would do another small favor. Our present water supply is getting very low. Fin says there is a fine spring well under the rocks behind the hill here. It was his intention to pull the rocks asunder, but having heard of you, he left the place in such a fury he forgot to do it. Now, if you will open the spring, I'd think it a kindness."

Cucullin stared at her with his mouth agape.

"You look nervous," said Oonagh. "Well, now, if you are afraid you are not strong enough . . ."

"Blasts of lightning!" he roared. "I'm a thousand times stronger than that feeble Fingal!"

"Very well," she said, and led him down the slope to where there was nothing but solid rock in every direction. Yet under the rock there was a sound of gurgling water. "If you would open up the ground here so that the springwater can flow out, it would be a blessing."

Cucullin took a deep breath and cracked his middle finger nine times. He got a grip on two rocky spires standing up above all the other rock. Then, with a grunt and a groan, he pressed against each spire until the rock under his feet split open with a fearful, rending sound. (Fingal, in his cradle, heard it, and the sweat ran down his face like two waterfalls.) The cleft that Cucullin opened up was four hundred feet wide and a quarter of a mile long, now called Lumford's Glen.

"Thank you most kindly," Oonagh said. "You must be hungry after your work—small jobs though they were. Won't you come in and have a bite?"

"To tell the truth," Cucullin admitted, "I'm as hungry as a hurricane, for I have scarcely eaten on my way here, being so eager to have a go with your husband."

Back in the kitchen, Oonagh set the table and put before the giant half a dozen of the griddle cakes, a couple of jars of butter, a side of boiled bacon, and a big pile of cabbages—this was before the invention of Irish potatoes.

Cucullin gobbled down half of the bacon and cabbages, and then he buttered a griddle cake. He bit into the cake, his teeth clashing against the iron platter buried inside it. He gave a yell and spat out two broken teeth.

"What is the matter?" Oonagh asked coolly, and then clapped her hand to her mouth. "Oh, dear! I gave you Fin's bread that I bake special for him, for he cannot tolerate it if it is too soft. Nobody can eat it but himself and that little child there in the cradle. Still and all, I thought that as you were reported to be a rather stout fellow you could manage it, and I did not wish to affront a man who thinks he can fight Fingal. Here's another—maybe it's not so hard."

Cucullin was so ravenous he made a second try, then gave a yell louder than the first, spitting out two more broken teeth. "Thunder and gibbets!" he roared. "I'll not have a tooth left."

"Well, please be more quiet," Oonagh ordered. "You've wakened the baby."

Fingal gave a loud wail that made the other giant start as if the roof had fallen in. "Mother mine," Fingal blubbered, "I'm hungry."

Oonagh hurried over to the cradle with a griddle cake—the one that had no iron in it—and handed it to Fingal. He took it and chewed merrily away, making loud, gurgling noises of contentment.

Cucullin stared, his face pale. "I'd like to get a better glimpse of that lad," he said, "for I can tell you that the infant who can manage that nutriment is no joke to look at, or to feed of a scarce summer."

"I agree, with all the veins of my heart," Oonagh said proudly, and walked to the cradle. "Get up, acushla," she murmured, her voice tender. Over her shoulder, she told the visiting giant, "He has only begun to take his first steps."

Fingal struggled out of the cradle, then crawled in baby fashion to the headboard. There he reached out and pulled himself up to his feet, the infant's nightgown falling to his ankles, the baby bonnet frilling his face. He asked Cucullin, "Are you strong?" Even though he tried to make his voice low and lisping, it boomed.

"What a voice in so young a chap!" said Cucullin.

"Are you strong, mister man?" Fingal asked again. "Are you able to squeeze water out of a stone? Mother mine, where is my boulder I use for a plaything?"

Oonagh brought a boulder from beside the hearth and handed it to the giant guest, even though he did not look eager to take it. But he had no choice. He clenched his mighty hands around the boulder and squeezed and squeezed until the veins stood out on his forehead. It was no use. The boulder did not give out even one drop of water.

"Now, acushla," Oonagh spoke up, "show what Fingal's infant son can do." She walked in front of Cucullin, blocking his view, saying, "Excuse me, but I see the baby needs me to wipe his little nose." At the same time, she picked the boulder up in her apron and then, on the sly, managed to seize a clump of milk curds, which she placed on top of the boulder.

Fingal grasped the boulder, and when he squeezed, the whey that still remained in the curd trickled down from his hands like clear water.

Cucullin's huge jaw dropped and his knees trembled.

Fingal looked pityingly at Cucullin. "I'll go back to my cradle now, for I scorn to lose my time watching somebody so weak. You had better leave before my daddy returns, for if he catches you, he will mop the floor with your hair."

"That is so," Oonagh agreed as Fingal climbed back into the cradle. "It is well for you, Cucullin, that Fin doesn't happen to be here, for he would make hawk's meat out of you."

Cucullin seized his round cap from the table, his knees knocking together. "Faith, and I'll be taking my leave, assuredly. But before I go, will you let me feel what kind of teeth the lad has got that they can eat a griddle cake like that?"

"With all pleasure in life," Mrs. Fingal said. "Only, as his teeth are so far back in his head, you must put your finger a good way in."

Cucullin thrust his right middle finger into Fingal's mouth. There was a crunch, and when the giant fellow removed his hand, the powerful finger was missing. He gave a groan of terror and weakness, for his strength was now completely gone.

Fingal sprang out of his cradle, ready

to swing his enemy across the sea to Scotland. But Oonagh held him back.

"It would be a disgrace, my darling brute," she said, "to waste your strength on such a poor, weak creature as him. Let him go, for I am certain in my mind that he will never come near this house again."

Oonagh was right. Poor, trembling Cucullin streaked out of the house and down Knockmany Hill as if a lightning bolt were chasing him, and Fingal and his good wife never saw the mountain-sized giant again.

There was only one bad thing about it. As Cucullin pounded across the causeway, fleeing toward Scotland, his thrashing feet pushed many of the rock slabs down, ruining the bridge that Fingal and his friends had built. In fact, for the last ten miles his feet pushed so hard that the rocks sank completely underwater. And that is why today only three miles of the Giant's Causeway remain.

When Fingal went back to the causeway and saw what had happened, he was so discouraged he could not bring himself to start building the bridge all over again. As a result, Oonagh never did get to see her cousin in Scotland. But she didn't mind too much, for not long after Cucullin's visit there was a real Baby Fingal in the house on the windy hill, and she tromped around singing to the baby, and cooing at it, from sunrise to sunset, as happy as could be.

Fingal had to puff his big pipe outside, of course, but that was all right with him, for he was as happy as Oonagh. As for the baby—even though his nightgown and cap and cradle were all a bit large—he was as happy as both of them.

The Winner Who Did Not Play

by Devereux Robinson

Eastgate High's big basketball game against Mapleton is tomorrow. And their star player has disappeared.

It was the first time I had ever seen "Chunky" Potter run. He came bounding in from the gymnasium, his balloon cheeks flushed and his breath coming in a series of rapid chugs, and began talking to the air.

"Gone—disappeared!" he wailed, falling on me like a young hippopotamus.

"What's gone—what's disappeared?" I demanded.

"It's Boots!" Chunky panted. "He's missing—vanished!" I began to catch some of Chunky's excitement. "Boots" Ryan was the best center who ever dribbled a ball for Eastgate High. All season we had been counting on him to turn the trick against Mapleton, the school that had defeated us five years straight. We were invading Mapleton Saturday—tomorrow—and here was Chunky telling me that Boots had disappeared.

"Talk sense, will you?" I snorted, shaking Chunky's well-upholstered shoulder. "Where has Boots disappeared?"

"Let go of me and talk sense yourself, Badger," replied Chunky. "How could he be disappeared *anywhere?* If he were anywhere, he wouldn't be disappeared, would he? He's gone, that's all, and out in all this snow, too. He hasn't been to school today, wasn't home last night, and there isn't a trace of him anyplace. If he doesn't turn up in time to go to Mapleton tomorrow, we're sunk."

"What's going to be done?" I asked.

"Why, we're going to find him!" Chunky declared. "Police have been notified, and the sheriff, but it's really up to us. About all the rural phones went dead in last night's blizzard, so they won't help. Some of the fellows are over at the gym now getting ready to scour the river bottoms. Another bunch in cars is going to hunt through the country in every direction. Now if you can get your dad's car—"

"You'll ride with me," I put in the words for him. "You animated medicine ball, you won't come out for sports and do something for your school yourself, but when the school's one real athlete gets lost, you will help hunt for him—if you can ride."

Chunky grinned good-naturedly. "Someone has to ride!" he argued.

"A big walrus like you should be hiking through the river bottoms," I complained as we crawled into our overcoats. "But come on."

We were whipped by an arctic wind as we threaded our way through the snowdrifts that the late February storm had heaped into Eastgate. Bitter cold had set in after the snow, and we were thankful for the big coat collars that came up around our ears.

"Where do you suppose he could be in weather like this?" Chunky remarked, shivering.

"If we only knew." I shrugged. "I can't believe he is in any danger. That boy Boots can take care of himself. Still, it must be something pretty serious, for he knows as well as you or I that we're playing Mapleton tomorrow."

We stopped at Boots's house on our way to mine. His mother was a woman with a large family and many worries. She refused to be greatly concerned about her son's overnight absence.

"Dear me, boys," she said, smiling. "You're not going out in all this cold to look for Hubert, are you? He's been away like this before. He's probably sitting by the stove in some warm farmhouse waiting for the weather to break so he can get home without chilling his nose."

"You haven't any idea where he went?" Chunky questioned.

"Land's sake, no!" she answered, throwing up her hands. "I never could keep track of that boy. He got a letter yesterday and went off on his bicycle the minute he read it. I suppose he rode out into the country and got caught in the storm. Didn't it turn cold quickly, though? He knows a lot of farmers. Some of them took him in for the night and he is staying there today to work out his board."

"Do you have that letter, Mrs. Ryan?" Chunky asked.

"No," she replied. "He must have stuffed it into his pocket when he left. I found the envelope it came in on the table today."

"May we see the envelope, please?" requested Chunky. She pointed it out on the table and he took it up eagerly.

"Keep it if you want it," she told him.

Chunky's face fell as he scanned the envelope, first on one side, then on the other. "No return address," he grumbled, slipping it into his pocket. "Not even a hint as to who sent it."

When we left the house, I said to Chunky, "Wish I could be as cheerful about Boots as his mother is."

"Me, too," he mumbled from the depths of his huge coat. "Boots isn't loafing around any farmhouse fire with the Mapleton game coming off. He'd be here if he had to freeze his eyebrows to make it. There's something wrong."

Dad let me have the roadster the minute I told him why we wanted it. For miles we bucked the deep snow on the country roads, the cold biting through the lap robes. The only life we saw was an occasional farmer, who shook his head when asked about Boots and went hurrying about his chores.

It was long after dark when we returned to the city. Other search parties were straggling in, half frozen and discouraged. Boots had not been found. We all agreed that nothing more could be done that night.

"Boots is still missing" was the message that ran through town Saturday morning. The search parties took the field again, braving the bitter cold, which still continued. I rolled the roadster out of the garage and drove over to pick up Chunky. He stuck his nose out of his nice warm house when I honked. "I'm not going," he called. "Please come in a minute."

I went, ripping mad, ready to drag him out by his lazy legs.

"What do you mean, you're not going?" I demanded. "Are you going to sit here over a radiator while Boots is out freezing somewhere and we are playing Mapleton with a sub center?"

Chunky grinned and waited for me to calm down. "See this envelope?" he said, holding up the one in which the letter to Boots had come. "I believe we can find out about Boots at the place from which this was sent. He started out immediately after reading the letter it contained. It looks as if that letter was a message asking him to go somewhere. Evidently he went, and he hasn't come back."

"But how can we find who sent the letter?" I asked.

"I don't know." Chunky shrugged. "But we can try. It's better than going out and freezing ourselves to death on another wild-goose chase. The only marks on the envelope, aside from it being sort of dirty, are Boots's address, scrawled in pencil, and the postmark, which shows Eastgate post office, four ten Wednesday afternoon. Let's go down to the post office and see if we can tell anything by that."

Mr. Grimes, the postmaster, took us into his office when we told him we were trying to trace the missing Boots through an envelope.

"Is there any way we can tell where this came from?" Chunky questioned, producing the envelope.

The postmaster examined it a moment, then shook his head. "It might have come from most anywhere, boys," he said. "It might have been dropped in the mailbox here at the post office Wednesday afternoon by someone living in town, or it might have been brought in from the country by the rural carriers, whose mail is canceled about four o'clock."

"I have an idea it came from the country," Chunky piped up. "If we knew which rural carrier brought it in, we'd know from what part of the country it came, at least. Which of the rural carriers gets in at four o'clock?"

"Oh, half a dozen of them," replied the postmaster, handing back the envelope. "You can't tell anything from that."

Chunky looked crestfallen.

"You had a fine idea, only it wouldn't work," I remarked. "Come on, let's get out and hunt."

"You just hold your horses," he growled, turning the envelope over and over and studying it intently. After a minute he asked, "What time does the carrier whose route goes through Boone township get in, Mr. Grimes?"

"He is one of those who come in about four," the postmaster replied.

"Then he's the man who brought in this letter," Chunky declared.

"I'm afraid you're just guessing, aren't you, son?" Mr. Grimes smiled.

"There's no guesswork about it," Chunky vowed. "This letter could have come from just one place in Eastgate County—Boone township—and just the western part of that. How do I know?" he went on, seeing doubting looks on our faces. "Well, Wednesday was warm and the ground was thawing, you remember. Consequently, when this envelope was dropped by the person mailing it, it fell in the mud. The mud was cleaned off, but not very carefully, and a little remained along this edge."

He showed us a tiny streak of dried mud near one corner, and continued. "If you remember what we studied in the agriculture class, Badger, you know that the soil of Eastgate County is largely of three types, black loam, sandy loam, and sandy clay. In just one place in the county, the western half of Boone township, there is an area of red clay. That mud on the envelope is red."

We looked closer, and sure enough, the mark of mud had a reddish tinge.

"Sam Walters carries the Boone township route," said the postmaster. "He hasn't been able to get through the hills out there since the storm; but he will be in this morning, and perhaps he can remember where he picked up this particular envelope."

We waited and waited. Finally Mr. Walters arrived.

"I might have brought that in, boys," he said when shown the envelope, "but I handle scores of letters every day, and of course I can't remember any certain one."

"There's just one thing for us to do," Chunky told me as we left the post office, "and that is to go out to Boone township as quickly as that old boat of yours will take us."

We had lost a lot of time at the post office, and it was nearly noon when we got started. Not a trace of Boots had been found, and the team, accompanied by a small band of rooters, was taking the noon train for the fifty-mile trip to Mapleton without him.

The locality for which we were headed was ten miles straight back into the hills. The going became almost impossible as the hills closed in around us, deep drifts choking the valley through which the road wound. Finally I stopped the car and said, "Look here, Chunky, it has taken an hour to make the last three miles. We haven't passed a farmhouse since I don't know when. We must be in the center of your red clay district, but we haven't seen a chipmunk, let alone anything that looks like Boots. He couldn't be out here."

Chunky didn't answer. He was staring at a lane that opened on the road a little way ahead.

"Badger!" he exclaimed. "Do you know that lane?"

"Yes," I told him, recognizing a landmark. "It's the lane leading back to Uncle Jack's greenhouses."

Uncle Jack was a queer old botanist who lived back in the hills and experimented with strange plants. We fellows often visited him in the summer on our hikes into the hills. He was a friendly old chap, to us boys at least, and we always called him Uncle Jack.

"I've got a hunch!" Chunky shouted, slapping my shoulder. "Boots is at Uncle Jack's."

He sprang from the car, I after him. We wallowed up the lane, the smooth snow showing that not a person had gone that way since the storm. We walked a quarter of a mile before we topped a hill and looked down on Uncle Jack's greenhouses, nestling in a little valley. Smoke was pouring from the chimney of the furnace room, as if someone were heaping on fresh coal.

We waded on and hammered at the door of the living quarters. There was no answer. We tried the door, found it open, and stepped inside.

"Hello!" I called. "Anyone here?" Only the echo of my voice answered. We advanced to the door of Uncle Jack's bedroom and peered inside. On the bed lay the old man, breathing heavily in a deep sleep.

The sound of shoveling came from the furnace room. We made our way toward the noise. The glow from the open furnace door fell on the figure of a tall fellow who was heaving a scoopful of coal into the fiery depths.

"Boots!"

The exclamation from both of us came in a gasp of relief. Boots turned, surprised, while Chunky burst out excitedly, "What are you doing out here? Man, man, all Eastgate has been combing the country for you! And we're playing Mapleton tonight. The team has gone without you!"

"He's sick." Boots motioned toward Uncle Jack's room. "I have to stay here to keep up the fires and keep his plants from freezing. It's been a night-and-day fight against this cold. I couldn't leave long enough to call help or to tell anyone where I was. Thank goodness you've come!"

"How on earth—" I began, but Chunky cut me short.

"No time for talk now," he chirped. "Get going, you two." He glanced at his watch. "It's ten minutes to four. The last train's gone, but if you drive your best, you may make it. You can call a doctor on your way."

Chunky peeled off his big overcoat and held it for Boots. "Get into this!" he commanded. "I'm going to take care of things here while Badger takes you to Mapleton to win that game." His white, fat hand took the shovel from Boots's hard, coal-begrimed one.

"You can't do this, Chunky," Boots protested. "It's a man-killing job. If those thermometers fall below fifty, years of Uncle Jack's work will be wiped out."

"Can't I?" snapped Chunky. "I can't play basketball, but I can shovel as well as you can. Make tracks before it's too late."

Boots looked at me for advice.

"It's all you can do," I told him.

A few directions about the heating plant and the care of Uncle Jack, and we were off.

"Good old Chunky!" Boots remarked as we went out into the frigid afternoon.

"Say, tell me," I asked. "How did it all happen?"

"Well," he explained, "I got a letter from Uncle Jack on Thursday. You know I worked for him some last summer. He said his helpers had left him suddenly and he was all alone. He wasn't feeling very

well and needed some medicine. He couldn't leave the place, so he asked if I couldn't bring it to him.

"I jumped on my bike, got his medicine, and pedaled out here with it. When I arrived, I found Uncle Jack in bed, helpless, and the snowstorm beginning. There wasn't anything else to do but stay."

I sent the roadster flying back to Eastgate in the tracks we had broken on the way out. Boots dozed in the seat beside me. Darkness had fallen when we drove into town. Pulling up at a filling station, I ordered gasoline and ran to a drugstore across the street.

"A hot malted milk, with two eggs in it, as fast as you can make it," I called to the soda-fountain boy, and grabbed up the telephone. In a few seconds I had Police Chief Carter on the wire.

"We've found Ryan," I sang into the transmitter. "He's all right. Get the word to his mother and rush a doctor out to Uncle Jack's greenhouse. He's sick. By the way," I added, "you can tell the world Eastgate is going to win tonight."

I rushed the steaming malted milk across the street to Boots and made him sip it as we got under way again. The courthouse clock showed six sharp when we passed. The game was to be called at eight, and fifty miles of snow-heaped roads separated us from the playing floor.

Boots settled deep into the lap robes, and the roaring of the motor soon sang him back to sleep. I clung to the wheel and pushed the accelerator as far down as I dared. Speed was impossible. On windswept stretches where only a thin crust of white clung to the road, I was able to open up a little, but in dips of the road where previously passing cars had left deep ruts through drifts, I had to drop into second gear.

Hours passed, it seemed. Finally a glow of light in the sky ahead told me we were nearing the city. In a few minutes more we were shooting through the streets of Mapleton.

A bump jolted Boots into consciousness. "Where are we?" he asked, yawning and rubbing his eyes.

"Almost there," I answered. "If we're only on time!"

We heard cheering when we were two blocks from the school. The game was on. It was the Mapleton crowd cheering, of course, and we knew well enough what that meant.

I jerked the car to a stop in front of the gym. Boots dashed for the building, I at his heels. As we bounded up the steps, a revolver cracked and the Mapleton cheering broke out with renewed frenzy.

"It's over," I groaned. "They've won."

We stopped midway on the steps. I became suddenly tired all over, and Boots wilted completely. A wildly excited Mapleton student who burst out the door nearly knocked us over.

"Whoopee!" the fellow shouted. "Twenty to seven at the end of the half!"

"End of the half!" we both echoed, and came to life like a flash.

You should have seen the Eastgate rooters when we walked down the floor. They were sitting as solemn as judges in the midst of hundreds of hilarious Mapleton rooters, who packed the gym. One of our fellows noticed Boots and let out a whoop. Then they all saw him and were turned into wild men, standing on their seats, waving hats, and howling with joy.

The Mapleton crowd was puzzled by this sudden demonstration. They had heard about the missing Eastgate star, but it took a few moments for them to understand. When they did, they burst out into applause, and their cheerleader led them in nine good big ones for Boots. I squeezed in among the Eastgaters and told them about Uncle Jack as we waited for play to begin again.

Eastgate took the offensive with a rush that swept Mapleton off its feet when the second half opened. With Boots in the pivot position, our fellows were always a hard bunch to stop, but never had they shown the stuff they displayed that second period against Mapleton. Boots seemed to have thrown off the fatigue of his night-and-day work at Uncle Jack's. He led every play and his pep inspired every player on the team.

Eastgate goals swished through the basket in a stream. The Mapleton lead was cut in half in the first five minutes. Our little group of rooters yelled themselves hoarse while the big Mapleton crowd looked on glumly.

The Mapleton five rallied determinedly when they saw their overwhelming lead vanishing. They scored once on a long shot and added a couple more points from the foul line. Eastgate came back with a display of pretty passing that carried the ball close under the basket, where Boots threw short sure shots again and again. We were right on Mapleton's heels, the score standing twenty-four to twenty-two.

But time was on Mapleton's side. Signals from the bench told the players that only one minute of play remained. Mapleton flung a five-man defense across the floor, determined to hang on to that two-point advantage until the final gun. Things looked desperate. Boots took the ball and dribbled full speed at the Mapleton formation. Down the floor he went, straight for the basket, Mapleton guards all over him. The play was almost too fast to follow. I saw the ball shoot upward and, without touching the ring, fall swishing through the net.

Before the groan that ran through the Mapleton rooters had died away, he had done it again—dribbled through the entire team and hit the basket. Mapleton was beaten for the first time in six years!

After the game, Boots fell exhausted in the dressing room. We carried him to a hotel and put him to bed. I discovered I was too tired to drive back to Eastgate that night, and also hit the hay.

We didn't come to until after nine o'clock the next morning. We were dressing leisurely—when we both remembered at the same instant!

"Chunky!" we gasped, staring at each other openmouthed and guilty-faced.

We flung on the rest of our clothes like a couple of firemen answering an alarm, and were off in the roadster in less than no time. I put the old car over the road, and by eleven o'clock we were roaring into Eastgate. We stopped just long enough to pick up Hank Woods, a laborer, and crowding him into the car, we set out for Uncle Jack's.

When we arrived, Uncle Jack was sitting up in bed, much improved. "Go stop that boy." He smiled, indicating the furnace room. "He's roasting me out."

Chunky was dozing against the corner of the coalbin when we reached him. Great black circles were under his eyes. His hands, still holding a shovel, were grimy and swollen. When he saw us, he grinned weakly and pointed to one of the thermometers.

"They got down to fifty-five once," he said, "but I won. How did you come out?"

"Twenty-six to twenty-four!" we told him, and he got up and led a three-man snake dance through the greenhouses, leaving Hank to take over the work.

Spring came in a few weeks, and Eastgate High closed its most successful basketball season in years with a big celebration in the school auditorium. The players were called to the front, one by one, by Superintendent Craig and presented with sweaters bearing the big *E* of Eastgate. When the last of the athletes had been honored, Mr. Craig still had one sweater left. It was a huge thing. He held it up, saying, "This is for a lad who was never seen on the basketball floor, yet who won the season's finest victory—Cecil Potter."

The whole school burst into deafening applause. As an embarrassed fat boy came forward, our cheerleader called for a yell, and we roared:

"Chunky! Chunky! Chunky!"

Nonsense

by Edward Lear

There was an Old Man of the Coast,
Who placidly sat on a post;
But when it was cold he relinquished his
 hold,
And called for some hot buttered toast.

There was an Old Man with a beard,
Who said, "It is just as I feared!—
Two Owls and a Hen, four Larks and a
 Wren,
Have all built their nests in my beard."

There was a Young Lady of Ryde,
Whose shoestrings were seldom untied;
She purchased some clogs, and some
 small spotty Dogs,
And frequently walked about Ryde.

There was an Old Person of Minety,
Who purchased five hundred and ninety
Large apples and pears, which he threw
 unawares
At the heads of the people of Minety.

There was a Young Lady whose chin
Resembled the point of a pin;
So she had it made sharp, and purchased
  a harp,
And played several tunes with her chin.

There was an Old Man, who when little,
Fell casually into a kettle;
But growing too stout, he could never get
  out,
So he passed all his life in that kettle.

There was an Old Man in a tree,
Who was horribly bored by a Bee;
When they said, "Does it buzz?" he
  replied, "Yes, it does!
It's a regular brute of a Bee."

There was an Old Man of the Nile,
Who sharpened his nails with a file,
Till he cut off his thumbs, and said calmly,
  "This comes
Of sharpening one's nails with a file!"

Tom and the Dude

by John D. Fitzgerald

In just three months, it seemed Tom's brother had turned into a real sissy. Could The Great Brain help?

Christmas was coming up, and my oldest brother, Sweyn, was coming home for the holidays. We all went down to the depot to meet him.

When Sweyn had gone back east to live with relatives in Boylestown, Pennsylvania, for his first year of high school, he had worn a blue serge suit with knee-length breeches and a cap, like all boys in Adenville wore until they were sixteen. A fellow didn't get a pair of long pants until he was sixteen. But when Sweyn, who was only fifteen, returned home, he had blossomed out into a full-blown dude. He was wearing a light gray checkered wool suit with long pants, shoes without laces that you pulled on, a derby, a blue-and-white striped shirt, and a purple necktie with a handkerchief to match in the breast pocket of the suit, all the likes of which had never been seen in Adenville, and maybe not even in all of Utah.

You can bet that my other two brothers, Tom and Frankie, and I held our heads down with shame as we walked toward home. People on the street turned around to stare at my oldest brother. Folks peeked out of windows and came out of stores to watch a full-blown dude walking down Main Street. I had never felt so humiliated.

Sweyn had arrived on the morning train, Monday, December 19. He would be home for ten days. Boy, oh, boy, the thought of having the fellows see my big sissy dude brother with his fancy duds for ten days was enough to make me want to run away from home. It was bad enough when Sweyn had disgraced us by starting to go with a girl at the age of thirteen. And now at fifteen he had turned into a sissy dude.

Sweyn was in such a hurry to show off his fancy duds to his girl, Marie Vinson, that he excused himself from the table as soon as we finished lunch. He got his derby from the hallway hat rack and came back into the dining room.

"Adieu and toodle-oo," he said with a wave of the derby.

Tom stood up. "And a cockle-doodle-doo to you," he said, flapping his arms as if they were the wings of a rooster.

That made everybody but Sweyn laugh.

"Enfant," he said, and then left.

Tom sat back down at the table and looked at Papa. "What is that 'adieu' and '*enfant*' business?" he asked.

"Your brother is just showing off some of the French he learned in high school," Papa replied. "Adieu means good-by and *enfant* is French for infant."

"I'll infant him," Tom said, frowning. "And what about that 'toodle-oo'? What kind of an insult is that?"

"It isn't an insult," Papa said, chuckling. "It is a rather common expression back east, like we say so long out west."

Tom shook his head. "Are you going to let Sweyn run around Adenville wearing those fancy duds and giving people that 'adieu' and 'toodle-oo' business?"

"Why not?" Papa asked.

"I'll tell you why not," Tom said. "People will think he has turned into an eighteen-karat sissy for sure."

"Don't be too hard on your brother," Papa said. "It is a phase every boy goes through during his first year of high school."

"Not me," Tom said. "If I have to wear fancy duds to go to high school in Pennsylvania next year, I'm not going."

"You will change your mind when you get there," Papa said. "All things, including clothing, are relative to time and place."

"What do you mean?" Tom asked.

"Well," Papa said, smiling, "I wouldn't walk down Main Street and go to work at the *Advocate* office wearing my nightshirt, because it is the wrong time and place to wear a nightshirt. But it is perfectly proper to wear my nightshirt to bed, because that is the time and place for it."

That made us all laugh.

"Seriously, Tom," Papa said, "you would be just as much out of place wearing clothing suitable for Adenville at high school back in Boylestown, Pennsylvania, as your brother is wearing his eastern clothing here."

"Then why don't you make him stop wearing those fancy duds while he is home?" Tom asked.

"Let him enjoy himself by showing off his new wardrobe to his girl," Papa said.

"Maybe Sweyn will enjoy himself," Tom said, "but J.D., Frankie, and I sure won't. The fellows will really make fun of us for having a sissy dude for a brother."

After lunch Eddie Huddle came over to play with Frankie. I sat on the railing of our corral fence with Tom. "Why are we sitting here?" I asked. "It's Christmas vacation. Let's go to Smith's vacant lot and play with the fellows."

"No, J.D., I don't feel like listening to the fellows rub salt in our wounds because we've got a sissy dude brother," Tom said. "I'm going up to my loft and put my great brain to work on how to make Sweyn stop wearing those fancy duds while he is home."

I didn't want to just sit on our corral fence for my Christmas vacation, so I went to Smith's vacant lot. Tom was sure right. All the fellows stopped playing and crowded around me.

Parley pushed his coonskin cap to the back of his head. "Who was that fancy pants your family met at the train this morning?" he asked.

"You know darn well it was my brother Sweyn," I said.

Danny Forester grinned. "I'll bet he uses perfume," he said.

Seth Smith nodded. "And pomade on his hair," he said.

Hal Evans got in his licks. "If I had a sissy dude brother like that," he said, "I'd go hide in the mountains and become a hermit."

Seth patted my shoulder. "I feel sorry for you and Tom," he said. "It must run in the family. That means both you and Tom will become sissies and dudes when you are fifteen."

"We will not," I said. "Tom is up in his loft right now putting his great brain to work on how to make Sweyn get rid of all those fancy duds."

I thought they would leave me alone after that, but they kept making disparaging remarks about Sweyn until I got disgusted and went home. I waited for Tom until he came down from his loft to help with the evening chores.

"Boy, oh, boy," I said. "You were sure right. The fellows let me have it with both barrels. Did your great brain figure anything out yet?"

"Not yet," Tom said. "But it will. I'm not going to let Sweyn spoil our Christmas vacation."

"If your great brain doesn't do something," I said, "I'm going to pretend I'm sick and stay in bed for the whole Christmas vacation."

That evening Sweyn went up to his room. He didn't come down until Mama and Aunt Bertha, who lived with us, had finished the supper dishes. He had on a brand-new dude outfit. He was wearing white flannel trousers, a thing he called a blazer that was like a coat only it was made from light material that had big red and white stripes on it, and he was carrying a straw hat in one hand and a tennis racket in the other.

Tom stared at him. "Have you gone plumb loco?" he asked. "There aren't any tennis courts in Adenville, and you can't play tennis in the dark anyway."

"I promised Marie that I'd show her my tennis outfit," Sweyn said. "And if I do say so myself, I learned to play a very good game of tennis back east. And next summer I'm going to get some young fellows together and build us a tennis court here in Adenville."

"But you can't go walking down Main Street in that outfit," Tom said. "People will think you are crazy wearing white flannel trousers and a straw hat and carrying a tennis racket in the middle of winter."

"You're just jealous of my outfit," Sweyn said.

"How can I be jealous of a jackass?" Tom asked. Then he turned to Papa. "Please stop him. He'll make us the laughingstock of Adenville."

But Papa just smiled. "I think you are making a mountain lion out of a kitten," he said.

Mama agreed. "So do I," she said. "And Sweyn, you do look very nice."

Sweyn gave us a wave with his straw hat. "Toodle-oo, everybody," he said as he left.

Right on the spot I decided not to show my face outside the house until Sweyn went back to high school. Some of the fellows were sure to see him, and boy, oh, boy, would they rub it in. I continued playing checkers with Frankie, but he beat me because I didn't have my mind on the game. Tom was reading a book, but I knew his mind wasn't on what he was doing either.

Then Mama spoke. "The ragbag is almost full, Bertha," she said. "I think we should start making another patch quilt."

Aunt Bertha looked up from her darning. "Can't start tomorrow," she said. "The Ladies Sewing Circle meets."

"Then we will start the day after tomorrow," Mama said.

I was surprised to see how interested Tom had become in the conversation. He stopped reading and just sat there. I knew his great brain was working on something because of the furrows in his forehead.

I couldn't see why the ragbag would interest Tom. Mama never threw anything away. When our clothes wore out, she laundered them and put them in the ragbag in the bathroom closet. When she needed a rag, she always took out something white, like a worn-out suit of underwear. All the colored pieces in the ragbag she kept to make patch quilts. I was so curious as to why the ragbag interested Tom that I stayed awake that night until he came up to bed.

"Why were you so interested in the ragbag?" I asked, sitting up in bed.

"My great brain has come up with a plan to make Sweyn stop wearing those fancy duds," Tom said. "We'll put the plan into action tomorrow afternoon when Mama and Aunt Bertha leave for the Ladies Sewing Circle. Don't ask me any more questions. There are a few details my great brain has to figure out."

I was curious as all get-out, but I didn't learn any more until the next afternoon. I was sitting on the back porch steps with Tom and Frankie. Mama opened the kitchen door. She was all dressed up.

"Bertha and I are leaving now," she said.

We walked to the side of the house and waited until we saw Mama and Aunt Bertha going down the street.

"Everything is working out perfect," Tom said. "Mama and Aunt Bertha are gone. Papa has Sweyn helping him at the *Advocate*. Let's go."

He got the ragbag and dumped its contents on the floor.

"What's the idea?" I asked.

"Yeah, what?" Frankie said.

"Sweyn's girl, Marie Vinson, has been at Saint Mary's Academy in Salt Lake City since school started," Tom said. "She hasn't seen any of us since last summer. Now do as I tell you and stop asking questions. Strip down to your underwear and take off your shoes and socks."

Tom began looking through the pile of stuff from the ragbag. Mama had a system. When we got a new suit, it became our Sunday best, which we wore to church. When it became too worn for church, we wore the suit to school. When it became too worn for school, we wore the suit for playclothes, and it remained playclothes as long as Mama could mend and patch it. Then it was fit only for the ragbag.

Tom picked out an old suit of Frankie's that was worn and patched. Then he picked out a worn-out suit for himself and one for me. He found us all worn and patched shirts, and he tore a few of the patches off before he handed them to us. All the clothes were too small for us because we'd grown. When we got dressed, we looked like three ragamuffins from the poorest family in town.

"Now here is the plan," Tom said. "I

want Marie Vinson to think Papa and Mama are spending so much money buying Sweyn fancy duds that the three of us have to wear rags. Let's go."

"But no kid goes barefoot this time of the year," I protested.

"I want her to think we don't even have shoes and socks to wear," Tom said.

We sneaked down alleys without being seen until we reached the Vinson home.

"We know Mr. Vinson is at work," Tom said, "and Mrs. Vinson is at the Ladies Sewing Circle meeting. That means Marie must be alone in the house. Follow me."

He led us to the back porch and knocked on the kitchen door. A moment later Marie opened it.

"We didn't want to disgrace you by going to the front door," Tom said. "But I've got to see my brother Sweyn. Is he here?"

Marie stood bug-eyed and tongue-tied for about a minute before she could speak.

"You . . . you . . . you can't be," she finally said. "No, I know you are Sweyn's brothers. Why are you dressed like that? Are you going to a masquerade party?"

"No," Tom said, sadly shaking his head. "These are the clothes we wear to school and all the time now. You see, it has cost Papa and Mama so much money to send Sweyn back east to school and buy him all those fancy clothes, there just isn't any money left to buy clothes for us."

"But that isn't fair," Marie said.

"Papa and Mama can't help it," Tom

said. "Sweyn is their pet. They give him everything he wants, even if it means we have to wear rags. I guess he isn't here. I wonder where he could be?"

"He told me that he had to help your father at the *Advocate* this afternoon," Marie said.

"Thank you," Tom said. "I'll see him there."

"And when you do," Marie said, "just tell him that I never want to see him again, the selfish thing."

She shut the door. Tom winked at Frankie and me. We had a hard time not laughing until we reached the alley. Then we laughed all the way home. We put the old clothes back in the ragbag and got dressed in our regular clothes.

"She went for it hook, line, and sinker," Tom said, grinning broadly. "The first part of my great brain's plan was a complete success."

Frankie looked up at Tom. "But won't Sweyn be mad?" he asked.

"If my plan works," Tom said, "he will not only be angry but also heartbroken. We can't take a chance of Marie Vinson seeing us dressed like this. We'll have to play in our backyard the rest of the day."

That evening after supper Sweyn got all dressed up in another new suit, new shirt, and new necktie. He sat in the parlor staring at the clock on the mantelpiece.

Papa noticed. "Calling on your girl again tonight?" he asked.

"At seven o'clock," Sweyn said.

"Time moves slowly for lovers when they are apart," Papa said.

That made Sweyn blush.

Mama and Aunt Bertha finished the supper dishes and came into the parlor. Mama looked at Sweyn. "Aren't you going to spend one evening at home during your Christmas vacation?" she asked.

"I'll stay home Christmas Eve and Christmas night and of course the night before I go back east," Sweyn said.

Papa took a puff on his after-dinner cigar. "You'll do better than that," he said. "We do not mind sharing you with Marie Vinson, but we don't want her monopolizing all of your time. I think seeing her every other night is enough."

Sweyn looked as disappointed as a dog would if you took away its bone.

"All right, Dad," he said as he stood up. Then he gave us a wave of his derby and that "toodle-oo" business and left.

About twenty minutes later Sweyn returned. Papa was reading a farm magazine. Aunt Bertha was knitting. Mama was crocheting a doily. Tom was reading a book. Frankie and I were playing dominoes on the floor. We all stopped what we were doing and stared at Sweyn. He walked—no, he staggered, as if he were drunk—to a chair and slumped down in it. His face was pale. He looked positively sick.

"Are you ill?" Mama asked.

Sweyn pressed his hand to his heart. "Only here," he said. "You won't have to worry about Marie monopolizing any more of my time."

Mama was the first to speak. "What happened between you and Marie?" she asked.

"I rang the front doorbell," Sweyn said, as if he were reading a funeral service over a grave. "She opened the door. She gave me a nasty look and said she never wanted to see me again because I was the most selfish person in the world."

"Selfish?" Mama asked.

Sweyn nodded sadly. "That is what she called me just before she slammed the door in my face," he said.

"Are you sure she wasn't just teasing you?" Mama asked. "Young girls do that, you know."

"I'm sure," Sweyn said. "I rang the doorbell again. This time her mother answered it. She told me that Marie never wanted to see me again. I just don't understand it. We've been going together since I was thirteen. We wrote to each other every week while she was at Saint Mary's Academy and I was in Boylestown. We had a sort of understanding that someday . . ." He didn't finish the sentence as he stood up. "I think I'll go up to my room," he said.

We watched him leave and heard him go upstairs.

Mama looked very concerned. "I'm going to phone Ida Vinson and find out what this is all about," she said.

I thought for sure Mama was going to blow Tom's plan sky-high, but Papa saved the day.

"People who interfere in young lovers' quarrels are asking for trouble," he said.

"But I don't understand the selfish part," Mama said.

"I think I do," Papa said. "Sweyn had promised to go horseback riding with Marie this afternoon. He was quite upset when I told him I needed him at the *Advocate*. He phoned Marie from the office. And I guess, being so young, she considered it selfish of him not to keep his promise and go riding with her."

Later Tom surprised me by going upstairs with Frankie and me when it was our bedtime. He could stay up an hour later if he wanted.

"Now to carry out the second part of my plan," Tom said. "You two wait for me here."

"No," I said. "We want to listen."

"All right," Tom said, "but take off your shoes."

Frankie and I took off our shoes. We followed Tom to the door of Sweyn's bedroom. The transom was open. We could hear Sweyn sort of crying and groaning at the same time.

"Got him," Tom whispered. Then he motioned for Frankie and me to stand to the side, so we wouldn't be seen when the door was opened. Tom knocked.

"Just a minute," Sweyn called.

It was more than a minute before he opened the door. Tom entered the bedroom and closed the door behind him.

"I heard you crying," he said. "You really must be stuck on Marie Vinson."

Frankie and I could hear perfectly through the open transom.

"I know I'm only fifteen," Sweyn said, "but I've been in love with Marie for two years. And now it is all over. I think I'll run away to sea."

"It's too bad you aren't old enough to join the French Foreign Legion," Tom said. "But I guess you are old enough to become a cabin boy on a ship."

"I don't care what happens to me," Sweyn cried out. "Without Marie life has lost all meaning."

"You've really got it bad," Tom said. "I guess you would do just about anything to fix things like they were before tonight."

"I'll say I would," Sweyn said.

"Would you stop wearing all those fancy eastern duds and just wear your old blue serge suit until you go back to school?"

"What has the clothing I wear got to do with Marie?" Sweyn asked.

"Do you want my great brain to fix things between you and Marie or not?" Tom demanded.

"Sure, if you can," Sweyn said.

"I can. But first you will have to give me your word of honor you will never mention it to Papa or Mama."

"I'm beginning to smell something," Sweyn said.

"Smell all you want," Tom said. "I came here to help you make up with your girl. But you don't want my help. So go back to your bawling and groaning."

"Wait," Sweyn said. "I'll do anything you say if you get me back my girl. I give you my word I won't say anything to Papa or Mama."

"And will you also give me your word that you will stop wearing all those fancy duds you bought back east?" Tom asked.

"I don't know what my clothing has to do with it, but I give you my word."

"All right," Tom said. "Tomorrow morning after breakfast we'll straighten this whole thing out. And remember to wear your old blue serge suit with the knee breeches."

The next morning Tom, Frankie, and I all got dressed in our Sunday-best suits. Sweyn wore his old blue serge. Mama was goggle-eyed when she saw us enter the kitchen for breakfast.

"Why are you three boys all dressed up?" she asked. "And Sweyn, why are you wearing your old suit?"

"We'll do the chores later," Tom said. "But first we have to call on Marie Vinson and convince her that Sweyn isn't a selfish person."

Papa wasn't fooled. "I have a feeling," he said to Tom, "that this is another one of your great brain schemes."

Sweyn spoke before Tom could. "I don't care what it is as long as Marie and I make up," he said.

After breakfast the four of us went to the Vinson home. Mrs. Vinson opened the front door.

"We must talk to Marie," Tom said.

"She is up in her room," Mrs. Vinson said. "I'll call her."

In a couple of minutes Marie came to the front door. She looked at Sweyn and then stared at Tom, Frankie, and me.

"I'm sorry," Tom said, "but we played a mean joke on you and Sweyn yesterday. We dug those old clothes out of our rag-bag. We have plenty of clothes to wear. Our father is quite well off and can afford to send Sweyn back east to school and buy him the latest fashions in clothing."

"I don't understand," Marie said. "Why did you let me think you had to dress like ragamuffins because of Sweyn?"

"To make him stop wearing those fancy duds in Adenville," Tom said. "Being a girl maybe you won't understand. But all the fellows are making fun of us because they say we've got a sissy dude for a brother. We'll be getting into fights every day as long as Sweyn wears those fancy clothes. Anyway, if you love him, it won't make any difference what kind of clothes he wears."

Marie stepped out on the porch. She took hold of Sweyn's hand and smiled at him. "I wouldn't care if you called on me wearing overalls," she said. "I cried all night."

"So did I," Sweyn said.

And that is how The Great Brain got rid of a dude. And for my money, if being in love can make you stay awake and cry all night, I hope I never fall in love.

As Hai Low Kept House

by Arthur Bowie Chrisman

Somehow yesterday's rule never fitted today's situation.
A Chinese tale.

After weary years of saving, a few coins each calendar, Hai Lee moved from the mountains, where nothing ever happens, and bought a tiny house that stood near Ying Ling toll road, which is the king's road, and where strange sights are seen. In that region the people have a saying, "He who lives on the king's road has seen the whole world."

With him the newcomer brought his little brother, Hai Low. Hai Low was to keep house, while Hai Lee worked in field and forest. The new house was no larger than two by twice, and poorly furnished. Nevertheless, Hai Lee and Hai Low imagined it to be grand. For they had always lived in a mountain cave.

Many times Hai Lee cautioned his brother to take good care that no harm came to their magnificent house. And Hai Low promised faithfully to guard. His eyes would be unblinkingly open. Have no fear.

Upon the very first day, as Hai Low kept house, a fox dashed under the flooring. A band of hunters soon appeared. The hunters said, "We hope you enjoyed a tasty dinner." That by way of greeting.

"Our fox has hidden beneath your house. He is a very damage-doing fox, and we desire his ears. For permission to dig we will thank you a thousand times—and more if the fur be of good quality."

Hai Low thought of his brother's warning. Whereupon he replied to the hunters, "Your digging might injure the house, and my honorable brother has told me to keep all harm away. Therefore, excellent huntsmen, I must, in sorrow, give you no. Dig you cannot, for the house might fall."

With soft voices the hunters wheedled. Hai Low said no. With harsh voices the hunters blustered and threatened. Hai Low said no. Money the hunters offered. Hai Low said no. His mind was fixed, and nothing could move it. No once. No twice. No thrice. And again no. The hunters departed. The fox remained. And Hai Low believed he had done well for his first day of housekeeping. He imagined that his brother would praise him.

The opposite came to pass. Hai Lee frowned. "That was wrong and stupidly done, small brother. A little digging could have given no hurt. The fox is an evil enemy. He will catch all of our fowls, even to the last speckled hen. We must get rid of that scamp. If any more hunters come—tell them to dig."

Upon the next day, as Hai Low kept house, he beheld two men with crossbows. In joy he rushed to greet them. With much bowing and scraping he said, "I hope that your rice was well cooked, and you had plenty of it. Will you not come to the house and dig?"

One of the men said, "This fellow reminds me of the way Wu Ta Lang got out of the cherry tree—it was quite simple."

But the other, who was more crafty, squinted an eye to say, Be quiet. Then, using his tongue, he spoke to Hai Low. "For nothing else we came. With all our hearts will we dig. Only open the door. Our rice was well cooked." The hunters entered the house and began to tear up stones from the hearth.

Hai Low said, "Do you not think the fox will be alarmed and try to escape through the hole by which he entered?"

The elder hunter replied, "A wise question, truly. What shall we do? Can you not sit with your back to the entrance? Then the fox will be unable to depart."

Hai Low readily agreed to aid. He went outside and sat with his back to the wall.

The hunters struck many blows upon the hearth, laughing all the while. Soon each said, "Oh," and stopped digging.

"Have you got it?" asked Hai Low.

"We have," the elder huntsman answered. "We have it in a sack. How fortunate that you invited us in! Our digging was most successful." He was greatly pleased. The other hunter seemed equally pleased.

Hai Low, too, was delighted. A very fine thing he thought it that the fox had been captured. He felt sure that his brother would speak words of praise.

But such was far from being. Hai Lee tossed a sack upon the table and said, "Oh, my little brother, a sad mistake you made this day. Not hunters, but thieves were those men. Not a fox, but all of our money they carried off in the sack. By chance alone I regained it. But such good luck rarely happens a second time. Now heed my words. Never again permit strangers to enter the house. Never."

Next day, as Hai Low kept house, the door shook with a great knocking. The boy peeped from a window. He beheld an old man, beating the door. Said Hai Low, "I hope you relished your dinner—but you must go away. My brother says that I am to admit no strangers. Go away. You cannot enter."

The old man remarked, in a loud tone, that Hai Low spoke nonsense. "Open the door that I may enter, you who deserve a bamboo upon your back. Is this any way to treat your own flesh and blood?"

Hai Low repeated his command. "You cannot enter. Go away hurriedly—else I shall pour hot water." He tilted a kettle and began to pour. Whereupon the old man took to his heels, for the water steamed, hot from a fire. Hai Low was well pleased with himself. Beyond doubt, he would receive great praise from his brother.

But Hai Lee came home in a huff. Angry, dismayed, was the big brother. "Oh, you wrongdoing little brother, you have ruined our future. The man whom you chased away was Grandfather Hai Ho, wealthy and about to make us his heirs. Now he says he will leave us not so much as one coin, not one. For pity's sake, small brother, be more tactful. We have another rich grandfather. When the next stranger comes, ask him if he is your grandfather, before you pour heated water."

Next day, as Hai Low kept house, the door rattled and banged. Someone wished to come in. At least, it seemed probable. Hai Low peered from a window. He beheld a man, well dressed and round, at the door. Behind the impatient one were many slaves. At once Hai Low thought of his other rich grandfather. Said he, "I hope your rice was served on a golden dish. Are you my grandfather?"

"What?" roared the stranger. "What? What impudence were you saying?"

Hai Low used a full breath to shout, "I asked, Are you my grandfather? *My grandfather.*"

At that the large stranger tottered. His slaves made a tremendous breeze with fans, seeking to revive him. Still fanning, they carried him away. Hai Low was somewhat puzzled. And puzzled he remained until his brother came home.

The brother was frightened, likewise angry. "Oh, dear me, small brother, why were you so rude to the governor? You have insulted the governor and will be lucky if you escape with your life. Even if you are not beheaded, you will have to pay a fine of a thousand large coins. All because of your foolish questions. I beseech you, don't ask visitors any more questions. Don't open your mouth to a stranger."

Next day, as Hai Low kept house, he chanced to glance at the stable. The stable door was open. Before the boy could close it, a stranger came out, leading Hai Lee's fine donkey. Hai Low began to imagine that mischief was being done. Thrice he opened his mouth, but each time he remembered his brother's instruction to ask no questions. So he remained silent. The donkey was soon saddled. Away it went, with the stranger astride.

When big brother returned home for evening rice, he spoke harshly to Hai Low. "Goodness, gracious me, very small brother, you will ruin us yet. Now you've let a rogue take my trotting donkey, and only by a lucky accident was I able to recover the beast. Really, your housekeeping is a bad thing altogether. Never let another stranger approach the stable. He might take our milking cow. If another stranger goes near the stable—shoot him."

Next day, as Hai Low kept house, he sat upon the doorstep. In his hand he clenched a bow. Again and again he glanced toward the stable. No person should take the milking cow. Not without regret. Beware, rogues, or suffer.

A traveler came down the road. He was a rich man and wore a hat that was high and covered with feathers. It was such a hat as the wind demons love for a toy. A sudden breeze lifted the traveler's hat and whirled it fast and far. It came to earth in front of the stable. Of course the stranger followed it, running, to the stable door.

Hai Low remembered his brother's command. He made a V of the bowstring. His hurried arrow went seeking a mark. The traveler gave up all thought of recovering his hat. Down the road he dashed madly, shouting that he had been killed. However, he was a traveler, and travelers are noted for stories hard to believe. Hai Low sat on the steps and had practice with his bow. No man should take the milking cow without taking an arrow also. A thief had best wear clothes of iron.

When big brother Hai Lee came home, his voice was doleful. "Oh, brother, my brother, you have put us into vast trouble. Why on earth did you shoot an arrow into the traveler's quilted coat? He is a foreign ambassador and says that his country will instantly declare war upon us. Think of the sadness your act will cause. I beg of you be not so rash in future. The next time you see a stranger lose his hat, don't shoot. Instead, be polite and chase the hat."

Next day, as Hai Low kept house, he noticed a great company of men approaching. Gong beaters led. Behind them came carriers of banners, tablet men, keepers of the large umbrellas, warriors, more gong musicians, fan carriers, incense swingers—a long procession it was. Hai Low knew that it must be the marching train of a truly great man. He hoped that he might behold the high and mighty one. And so he did. As the gilded sedan chair was borne past, a breeze threshed its curtains. A hat soared out of the sedan. Carried by the wind demons, it rolled across turnip patch and radish. Hai Low dashed away in chase. He thought himself being polite and useful—to rescue the great one's hat.

Alas, a hundred bludgeon men and spear wavers rushed after him. They shouted that he must stop and be killed for his sin. Hai Low had no idea why they wished to slay him. Neither had he the faintest idea of stopping. He lifted his heels with such rapidity that he gained a thicket three leaps ahead of the foremost warrior men. In the heavy growth of briers and bushes he was safe, for he knew the tangle in all its winding ways. To follow was folly.

When late the boy reached home, he found his brother waiting. Hai Lee's despair was shown in tears and quavering words. "Oh, brother of mine, I fear that your life is worth less than a withered carrot. Why did you lay hands upon His Majesty's right royal hat? Do you not know that death is the penalty for so doing? Soldiers have sought you high and low. If they find you—I cannot bear to say what will happen. Now please have regard for my words, little brother. Go into the house and crawl under a bed—and stay there. Stay there."

Next day, as Hai Low kept house, he kept it beneath a bed. So still he lay that a mouse took a nap at his side. Soldiers came and emptied the pantry, eating and drinking as only king's men can. None of them thought to glance under the bed. And that was just as well—just as well for Hai Low. It was for him that they had come to search.

Soon after the soldiers had departed, an odor of burning filled the air. The house was afire. Hai Low coughed, but he dared not crawl from his shielding bed. He had no doubt the fire had been set in an effort to rout him from hiding.

The door flew open and in rushed big brother Hai Lee. Hai Lee flung water upon the flames, then pulled little brother from beneath the bed. He was greatly exasperated. "My word and all, not very large brother, would you let the house

burn and not fling a bucket? The soldiers were gone. Why didn't you arise and douse the flames? Now hear what I speak, little brother. The next time you see flames—pour on water. Pour on water."

Next day, as Hai Low kept house, he chanced to gaze down the road. A brisk fire burned in the open. With two filled buckets the boy hastened to obey his brother's order. In no time he wet the fire out of burning.

Scarce had he entered the house when big brother Hai Lee entered. Hai Lee had his tongue on edge for scolding. "My very own brother, why must you be always at mischief? What in all the green earth and the blue sky made you throw water upon that fire? A traveler was boiling his rice—and you with water put out his fire. It was outrageous. Now then, to atone for your impishness, take this stick of dry wood to the traveler so that he can boil his rice. And as you give him the stick, be sure to apologize. Ask for pardon."

Away went Hai Low at his fastest, bearing a huge bamboo. The traveler beheld him and promptly mounted a horse. Many robbers made misery in that region. The traveler had gained saddening experience of them. He imagined that Hai Low must be a robber—else why did the fellow wave a long bamboo? So the traveler put heels to his horse and galloped. But Hai Low was not to be left far behind. He followed swiftly, shouting words that mean stop, wait, hold on, tarry. And the more he shouted, the more determined grew the traveler never to stop until he had found protection in a camp of soldiers.

Several young men let curiosity lead them to follow Hai Low. They wished to discover why he pursued the traveler. As they raced through a village, other men joined. Another village gave a dozen more. A town furnished twice as many. Soon Hai Low had an enormous crowd at his heels. Dust hung above in a blinding curtain. The trample of feet and the excited shouts could be heard for distant miles. More dust and more, more men and more. At first they asked, "What's it all about?" Later, "Catch him," and "Kill him," they cried.

Hai Low had long since lost sight of the fast-fleeing horseman. But he reasoned that the traveler would enter Ying Ling, the capital city. Hence he, too, leading his curious host, entered Ying Ling. He was determined to do as his brother had bidden.

Now it chanced that King How Wang was a most unpopular ruler. Threats had been made against him. A prince from the north was said to be raising an army of rebels. When King How Wang beheld Hai Low's approach at the head of a vast army, he imagined Hai Low to be the northern prince. Hai Low's curious rabble he thought a rebel army. So thinking, he called for his horse. . . . And what became of him no one can say. He vanished, for good and all.

The royal generals, instead of ordering a fight, promptly knelt before Hai Low and bumped their heads in the dust. Said they, "We bow unto our new king." The palace soldiers said, "Hail to our new king." And the breathless mob shouted, "Long live our new king." The crown was placed upon astonished Hai Low's head. The mace of authority was placed in his hand. And "Hail," and "Hail," and "Hail."

Thus did Hai Low, in chase of an unknown traveler, become king upon a throne. His days of housekeeping were ended. And so is the story . . . ended.

Mama and the Graduation Present

by Kathryn Forbes

"It's practically the most important time in a girl's life—when she graduates," Katrin told Mama.

The year I graduated from the Winford public school for girls, we lived in a big house on Steiner Street in San Francisco. My family there included Mama, Papa, and my only brother, Nels. There was also my sister Christine, closest to me in age, and the littlest sister, Dagmar.

The aunts came there too—Mama's four sisters—and their husbands.

The aunts' old bachelor uncle, my great-uncle Chris, also came, with his great impatience, his shouting and stamping. And brought mystery and excitement to our humdrum days. Papa called him a "black Norwegian"—because of his swarthiness and dark mustache.

In those days, if anyone had asked Mama unexpectedly, "What nationality are you?" I believe she would have answered without hesitation, "I am a San Franciscan."

Then quickly she would add, "I mean Norvegian. American citizen."

But her first statement would be the true one. Because from the moment she had arrived, confused and lonely in a strange land, San Francisco had become suddenly and uniquely her own.

"Is like Norvay," the aunts said Mama had declared.

And straightway she'd taken the city to her heart.

I remember so many things about Mama. There was the time Papa had to go to the hospital for a serious operation connected with an old head injury. The day he came home, it was like a party. We all stayed home from school, and Mama let Dagmar decorate the table real fancy.

Papa walked into the kitchen and sat down in the rocking chair. His face was white, and he looked thinner, but his smile was the same. He had a bandage on his head, and he made little jokes about how they shaved off his hair when he wasn't looking.

It was strange having Papa about the house during the day, but it was nice too. He would be there in the kitchen when I came home from school, and I would tell him all that had happened.

Winford school was the most important thing in life to me. I was friends with all the girls and was invited to their parties. Every other Wednesday they came to my house, and we would sit up in my room, drink chocolate, eat cookies, and make plans about our graduation.

We discussed "high" and vowed to stay together all through the next four years. We were enthralled with our superiority. *We* were going to be the first class at Winford to have evening graduation exercises; *we* were having a graduation play; *we* were making our own graduation dresses in sewing class.

And when I was given the second lead in the play—the part of the Grecian boy—I found my own importance hard to bear. I alone of all the girls had to go downtown to the costumer's to rent a wig, a coarse black wig that smelled of disinfectant. At every opportunity I would put it on and have Papa listen to my part.

Then the girls started talking about graduation presents. Madeline said she was getting an onyx ring with a small diamond. Hester was getting a real honest-to-goodness wristwatch, and Thyra's family was going to add seven pearls to the necklace they had started for her when she was a baby. Carmelita was getting something special: her sister Rosė was putting a dollar every payday onto an ivory manicure set.

I was intrigued, and wondered what great surprise my family had in store for me. I talked about it endlessly, hoping for some clue. It would be terrible if my present were not as nice as the rest.

"It is the custom, then," Mama asked, "the giving of gifts when one graduates?"

"My goodness, Mama," I said, "it's practically the most important time in a girl's life—when she graduates."

I had seen a beautiful pink celluloid dresser set at Mr. Schiller's drugstore, and I set my heart upon it. I dropped hint after hint, until Nels took me aside and reminded me that we did not have money for that sort of thing. Had I forgotten that the hospital must be paid up?

"I don't care," I cried recklessly. "I *must* have a graduation present. Why, Nels, think how I will feel if I don't get any. When the girls ask me—"

Nels said he thought I was turning into a spoiled brat. And I retorted that since he was a boy he naturally couldn't be expected to understand certain things.

When Mama and I were alone one day, she asked me how I would like her silver brooch for a graduation present. Mama thought a lot of that brooch—it had been her mother's.

"Mama," I said, "what in the world would I want an old brooch for?"

"It would be like a—an heirloom, Katrin. It was your grandmother's."

"No, thank you, Mama."

"I could polish it up, Katrin."

I shook my head. "Look, Mama, a graduation present is something like—well, like that beautiful dresser set in Mr. Schiller's window."

There now, I had told. Surely, with such a hint—

Mama looked worried, but she didn't say anything. Just pinned the silver brooch back on her dress.

I was so sure that Mama would find some way to get me the dresser set, I bragged to the girls as if it were a sure thing. I even took them by Schiller's window to admire it. They agreed that it was wonderful. There was a comb, a brush, a mirror, a pincushion, a clothes brush, and even something called a hair receiver.

Graduation night was a flurry of excitement. I didn't forget a single word of my part in the play. Flushed and triumphant, I heard the teacher say that I was every bit as good as Hester, who had taken elocution lessons for years. And when I went up to the platform for my diploma, the applause for me was long and loud. Of course the aunts and uncles

were all there, but I pretended that it was because I was so popular.

And when I got home—there was the pink celluloid dresser set!

Mama and Papa beamed at my delight, but Nels and Christine didn't say anything. I decided that they were jealous.

I carried the box up to my room and placed the comb and brush carefully on my dresser. It took me a long while to arrange everything to my satisfaction. The mirror, so. The pincushion, here. The hair receiver, there.

Mama let me sleep late the next morning. When I got down for breakfast, she had already gone to do her shopping. Nels was reading the want-ad section of the paper. Since it was vacation, he was going to try to get a job.

After my breakfast, Christine and I went upstairs to make the beds. I made her wait while I ran to my room to look again at my wonderful present. Dagmar came with me, and when she touched the mirror, I scolded her so hard she started to cry.

Christine came up then and wiped Dagmar's tears and sent her down to Papa. She looked at me for a long time.

"Why do you look at me like that, Christine?"

"What do you care? You got what you wanted, didn't you?" She pointed to the dresser set. "Trash," she said, "cheap trash."

"Don't you *dare* talk about my lovely present like that! You're jealous, that's what. I'll tell Mama on you."

"And while you're telling her," Christine said, "ask her what she did with her silver brooch. The one her very own mother gave her. Ask her that."

I looked at Christine with horror. "What? You mean— Did Mama—"

Christine walked away.

I grabbed up the dresser set and ran down the stairs to the kitchen. Papa was drinking his second cup of coffee, and Dagmar was playing with her doll in front of the stove. Nels had left.

"Papa, oh, Papa!" I cried. "Did Mama—Christine says—" I started to cry then, and Papa had me sit on his lap.

"There now," he said, and patted my shoulder. "There now."

And he dipped a cube of sugar into his coffee and fed it to me. We were not allowed to drink coffee—even with lots of milk in it—until we were considered grown up, but all of us children loved that occasional lump of sugar dipped in coffee.

After my hiccuping and sobbing had stopped, Papa talked to me very seriously. It was like this, he said. I had wanted the graduation present. Mama had wanted my happiness more than she had wanted the silver brooch. So she had traded it to Mr. Schiller for the dresser set.

"But I never wanted her to do that, Papa. If I had known—"

"It was what Mama wanted to do."

"But she *loved* it so. It was all she had of Grandmother's."

"She always meant it for you, Katrin."

I stood up slowly. I knew what I must do. And all the way up to Mr. Schiller's drugstore, the graduation present in my arms, I thought of how hard it must have been for Mama to ask Mr. Schiller to take the brooch as payment. It was never easy for Mama to talk to strangers.

Mr. Schiller examined the dresser set with care. He didn't know, he said, about taking it back. A bargain was a bargain, and he had been thinking of giving the brooch to his wife for her birthday next month.

Recklessly I mortgaged my vacation.

If he would take back the dresser set, if he would give me back the brooch, I would come in and work for him every single day, even Saturdays.

"I'll shine the showcases," I begged. "I'll sweep the floor for you."

Mr. Schiller said that would not be necessary. Since I wanted the brooch back so badly, he would call the deal off. But if I was serious about working during vacation, he might be able to use me.

So I walked out of Mr. Schiller's drugstore not only with Mama's brooch but with a job that started the next morning. I felt very proud. The dresser set suddenly seemed a childish and silly thing.

I put the brooch on the table in front of Papa. He looked at me proudly. "Was it so hard to do, daughter?"

"Not so hard as I thought." I pinned the brooch on my dress. "I'll wear it always," I said. "I'll keep it forever."

"Mama will be glad, Katrin."

Papa dipped a lump of sugar and held it out to me. I shook my head. "Somehow," I said, "I just don't feel like it, Papa."

"So?" Papa said. "So?"

And he stood up and poured out a cup of coffee and handed it to me.

"For me?" I asked wonderingly.

Papa smiled and nodded. "For my grown-up daughter," he said.

I sat up straight in my chair. And felt very proud as I drank my first cup of coffee.

Stormy Place

by Sara and Fred Machetanz

Can a young newcomer to Alaska
help save three Eskimos stranded in a blizzard?

Barney had been living with his uncle Charlie in the small Eskimo village of Unalakleet in western Alaska just six weeks when the great blizzard came. That day Barney had stayed late at school, and by the time he started for the trading post in which he and his uncle lived, the blizzard had become a blinding terror. If his dog, Seegoo, hadn't known the way, Barney might not have reached home.

When at last Barney did get to the post, Uncle Charlie met him at the door.

"You gave me a scare, boy!" he said. "Where have you been?"

Barney explained what had happened. Then he asked, "Is it all right if Seegoo stays inside tonight, Uncle Charlie?"

"It surely is. You can chain him right here beside the door," Uncle Charlie said. "Well, Barney, I guess you found out this afternoon what the name Unalakleet means."

"What's that?" Barney asked as he gave Seegoo a final pat for the night.

"Why, Unalakleet is an Eskimo word meaning stormy place," his uncle said.

"Then I'd say it's well named," Barney replied as they started upstairs to the living quarters.

"We're having two guests tonight, Barney," Uncle Charlie said.

Barney stopped with one foot in the air. "We are? Who?" he asked.

"An airplane pilot and an old friend of mine who has done a lot of prospecting for gold around here," Uncle Charlie said as he led Barney into the front room. "Barney, I want you to meet Slim Dickson. We've hit a lot of trails together and have been partners in prospecting on and off for many years."

Barney shook hands with a man about as old as Uncle Charlie. The man had a brown, leathery, kind-looking face.

"And this is Johnny Quinn," Uncle Charlie continued, "one of the best bush pilots in Alaska."

Johnny was a tall young man with a nice smile and bright blue eyes.

"What kind of pilot did Uncle Charlie say you were?" Barney asked as they shook hands.

"Bush pilot," Johnny said, and smiled. "That means I fly in the bush country, where there aren't many landing fields."

"Where do you land?" asked Barney.

"Oh—" Johnny shrugged his shoulders. "In the best place that I can find. I land on a frozen lake, or a sandspit, or on the tundra."

A big gust of wind hit so hard it shook the building and made the windows rattle. Just then Velik, Uncle Charlie's Eskimo cook, came into the room and announced supper.

I'm not going to mind this blizzard at all, Barney thought as they all went into the kitchen. Not with such interesting company.

While they were eating, Slim told about his prospecting. "Charlie," Slim said, "you remember that claim I staked inland from the Hot Springs about eleven years ago?"

Uncle Charlie nodded, and Slim went on with his story.

A bit later, Seegoo started barking.

"I'll go see what the matter is," said Barney. He excused himself and went downstairs. Seegoo jumped up and barked and wagged his tail when he saw his master. There didn't seem to be anything wrong.

"What's the matter, Seegoo?" said Barney. "Were you lonesome?"

Right at that moment Barney heard a pounding on the front door. So that was what Seegoo had been trying to tell him! He hurried to the door and pulled it open.

An Eskimo woman stumbled in out of the blizzard. "Charlie here?" she asked, shaking the snow from her parka. She looked very worried.

"Yes, he is," said Barney, and invited her to follow him upstairs.

"Why, hello, Miowak," Uncle Charlie said, rising to meet her. "What brings you out on a night like this? Is something wrong?"

The woman nodded. "Ongan not come home. Dog team come back home. Broken towline. No sled. No Ongan. Two sons with him," she said.

Uncle Charlie's face grew serious. "You mean the dogs broke their towline, came home, and left Ongan and your two sons out in this storm?" he asked.

Miowak nodded again.

"Where were Ongan and the boys going?" Uncle Charlie asked. "Do you know how far away they are?"

"Ongan go toward Yukon. Two days away. Dogs tired, hungry," she said.

Johnny Quinn looked up. "What's the matter?" he asked.

"Something serious, Johnny," Uncle Charlie told him. "Ongan and his two boys are stranded about sixty miles inland in this blizzard. We could look for them by dog team when the storm's over, but all signs of their trail would be covered and they'd be pretty hard to find."

Johnny listened closely. Then he walked over to Miowak. "I'll go look for them," he promised, "just as soon as the wind dies down and it's light."

Miowak clasped her hands together. "Thank you. Thank you," she said.

"I'll need somebody to lend a hand digging my plane out of the snow,"

Johnny told Uncle Charlie. "And it would be a good idea if someone flew with me and helped look."

Barney turned toward his uncle. Oh, how he'd like to go along on the rescue trip!

"Well," Uncle Charlie said. "Well . . ."

Barney dug his hands deep into his pockets and bit his lip, he was hoping so hard that Uncle Charlie would think of him.

"I don't think I could leave the post," Uncle Charlie said. "Slim would probably go with you—but he can't see well enough to be of much help." Uncle Charlie rubbed his chin. "Panpok's been sick with a cold for two days, and Tagiak can't leave the post office. How about Barney here?"

Johnny looked pleased. "Barney? He'd be just fine. I have to be careful not to overload my plane anyway. How about it, Barney? What do you say?"

Barney felt like jumping up and down, but he tried not to show how anxious he was to go. He was still afraid Uncle Charlie might think he was too young.

"I'll be glad to go along and help in any way I can," he told Johnny, man-to-man fashion.

The bush pilot nodded. "Good!" he exclaimed. "Then I'll tell you what we'd better do. We'd better go to bed right away, because the minute the storm dies down, we'll start digging out the plane so we can leave when it's daylight."

Barney was disappointed. He would have liked to stay up and hear more about prospecting for gold from Slim and about Johnny's flying adventures. Then Barney realized that three lives were at stake. It was no time to think of what he would like to do instead of what he should do.

"Okay," he said cheerfully. "Good night, everyone!"

"I stay by window and watch for wind to stop," Miowak said.

"Now, Miowak, you'd better try to get some sleep. I'll watch for the storm to pass," Uncle Charlie offered.

"Miowak no sleep tonight," Miowak said as she shook her head. She walked over to the window and looked out into the wild night.

Barney felt very sorry for her. He hoped he could help Johnny find her family. But the best way to help now is to get some sleep, he told himself as he walked into his room. He undressed quickly and crawled into bed.

The next thing Barney knew, Johnny was shaking him by the shoulder. "Come on, Barney," he said. "The wind's died down. It'll be light by the time we dig out. Let's go!"

When they stepped outside the post, the air was clear but so cold that each breath seemed to burn their noses and throats. A faint gray light marked the place in the sky where the sun would come up.

Barney could hardly believe what he saw. It looked as if he'd stepped out into a different world. The village was half buried in snowdrifts. Snow was jammed up against all the cabins, and a great long bank, ten feet high, jutted out from the front of the trading post.

"Come on, Barney. There's no time to waste," called Johnny.

Barney took one more look at the magic the blizzard had left and ran toward the pilot.

They found the plane surrounded by snow three feet deep. Johnny gave a long whistle. "That'll take a lot of digging," he said, handing Barney one of the shovels he was carrying.

As the sky grew light, several boys Barney knew at school came down to see what was going on. When they found that Barney and Johnny were going to look for Ongan, they brought shovels and helped too. It wasn't very long before the plane was free. Barney was surprised to see it had skis instead of wheels.

Just as he and Johnny laid down their shovels, Miowak came up, pushing a sled with a can of gasoline on it. "For you," she said to Johnny.

"You shouldn't have bought this, Miowak!" Johnny exclaimed.

"Village buy it," she said. "Everybody help."

Johnny quickly emptied the can of gasoline into his tank, put one foot on the strut, and vaulted into the plane. Barney followed.

Johnny gunned the motor several times, rocking the plane to shake the frozen skis loose. Some of the Eskimos helped by pushing. Barney felt the plane start forward. He turned and waved good-by as they skimmed down the frozen river and took off.

"I'm heading toward the Yukon River," Johnny said. "We'll follow the trail that Miowak says her husband usually takes. Unless he and the boys have had an accident, they'll be walking—probably on a frozen stream."

As the plane cruised along, Barney tried to look over every foot of land. Soon Johnny spoke again. "We're coming to the mountains, so keep a sharp eye out. I'll look ahead and you watch directly below for any sign of something moving."

Johnny twisted the plane over a winding creek bed through a mountain pass. Once or twice Barney thought he saw something, but it turned out to be only logs or rocks.

"The weather's beginning to look bad," Johnny said after a while. "Maybe we'd better turn back and—"

Before he could finish, Barney broke in. "No, wait! I think I see someone!" he said excitedly.

"Where?" Johnny asked, and he leaned forward.

"Just below on the right!"

Johnny squinted his eyes and looked harder. Yes, it was a man, sure enough! He was struggling toward the center of the frozen creek and waving his arms. Two other figures came out from the trees.

"There they are! Good boy, Barney!" Johnny exclaimed as he dived over the waving figures to let them know they'd been seen. Then he climbed again.

"Now, to land this plane," Johnny continued. "We just passed a frozen lake that looked like a good landing place."

He started the plane back and circled over the lake.

"Yes," he said. "We won't have any trouble landing."

Barney looked at the flat, white, round place. It looked dangerously small for a landing field. Trees began to come closer. Barney shut his eyes as he saw them almost brush against the plane. When he opened his eyes again, the plane was taxiing to a stop and Miowak's husband was coming toward them, waving his arms.

As soon as the plane stopped, Johnny pushed the door open. "Everyone safe?" he called.

Ongan began shouting. "Glad you come! Glad you come! Dogs run away. Bad storm!"

"Yes, we know," Johnny said as he

jumped out of the plane. "Say, your face is frostbitten." The skin on the Eskimo's cheeks, chin, and forehead was as white as snow.

"We have accident," Ongan explained as his two sons came up. One of them was limping. "His foot frozen," he added.

"Then we'd better get you back right away," Johnny said.

He and Barney helped the three Eskimos into the plane. A few minutes later they were in the air on their way back to Unalakleet.

During the trip Ongan told how he and his sons had been going up the frozen creek when their sled and all their supplies went through the ice.

"Spring in river make water warm, ice thin," Ongan said.

The sharp ice had broken the towline, and his dogs had run away. After that, Ongan and his sons had started walking toward the village. Then they were caught in the blizzard. They had made a shelter out of branches to keep warm through the night and had started out again when morning came. Today had been bad, for they were tired and hungry and it was very cold.

"Maybe we not get home if you not come," Ongan finished.

"I'm glad I could come," Johnny said.

"Me too," Barney echoed.

Back at the village, a big crowd was out to meet them. A dogsled was waiting to take Ongan and his sons home.

There was a low murmur of relief as Barney and Johnny helped Ongan and his two sons from the plane. Miowak stepped out from the others and went up to her husband. Ongan said something to her in Eskimo. She nodded and looked down at the ground. Then, waving the dogsled driver aside, Ongan turned and started for home on foot. Miowak came over to Barney and Johnny. Her eyes were full of tears.

"You save my husband and sons," she said to Johnny. Then she turned to Barney. "You save them too. I never forget. From now on my home, your home. You be son like my own."

Barney swallowed hard to keep the tears out of his own eyes. Miowak was thinking of him as one of her family. From now on Barney would have an Eskimo foster mother.

The Dragon in the Clock Box

by M. Jean Craig

A very short story about a very small boy
who had a very secret secret.

On Tuesday afternoon Joshua's mother went shopping and bought a new alarm clock. When she unwrapped it, Joshua asked if he might have the box it came in.

"Of course, Josh, if you like. What are you going to do with it?"

"Something," answered Joshua, but politely.

On Wednesday Joshua's mother saw that he had taken some paper tape and sealed the clock box closed again. Every slit and every corner was tightly covered. And wherever Joshua went and whatever he did, he kept the clock box with him. When he played with his soldiers on the side porch, he put the clock box on the porch step, in the sun. When he ate supper, he set it under his chair. When he went to bed, he laid it next to his pillow.

"Can you tell me what you have in the clock box?" asked Joshua's mother when she was tucking him in.

"Yes. I can."

"Well—what?"

"It's a dragon's egg," said Joshua.

"I see. . . . Joshua—is it really?"

"Yes, it is. Really," said Joshua, and went to sleep.

On Thursday, at breakfast time, Joshua's father asked him, "How is your dragon's egg doing this morning, Josh?"

"It isn't *doing*. It's just waiting."

"What on earth is it waiting for?" asked Joshua's big sister.

"For it to be time," answered Joshua. "I would like some toast, please."

"Time to hatch, I suppose?" And Joshua's big sister giggled as she passed him the toast.

"Yes, time to hatch," said Joshua, without smiling even a little bit. "I would like some jam on it, please."

"I hear you have a dragon's egg in that box of yours," said Joshua's big brother when he came home from high school late in the afternoon. "How did it get there?"

"The mother dragon laid it there," said Joshua. "Before."

"Before? What do you mean, before? Before what?" asked Joshua's big brother.

"Before I sealed it up. Of course," Joshua answered him, and he picked up the clock box and went out of the room with it.

That evening Joshua's father wanted to know how any air could get into the box when it was taped shut.

"It doesn't need air yet," explained Joshua. "It just needs to be warm and quiet. Until it's hatched."

"When is it going to hatch?" asked Joshua's big brother.

"When it's ready to," Joshua told him.

"But how will you know when it's ready to?" Joshua's big sister asked him, not laughing this time.

Joshua looked at her for a minute before he spoke again.

"*I* don't have to know. *It* will know." And then in a whisper, to himself, he added, "Silly."

On Friday morning Joshua came down to breakfast a little bit late. He put the clock box on the table close to his plate, instead of under his chair. There was a small, neat hole cut in one corner of it.

"He's a boy dragon," Joshua told his mother as he sat down. "He hatched. Last night. Very late."

Joshua's mother spoke softly. "How can you tell?"

"It was time."

"Did you hear it?"

"*Him*, not *it*. No, he was very quiet. But it was time, and he was ready, so I knew. So I made a hole just now. Because now he needs air."

"And now you can peek through the hole to see what he's like," said Joshua's big sister.

"I know what he's like. He's like a baby dragon. Just hatched."

"But you could look, just to be sure, couldn't you?"

"I am sure," said Joshua. "And he doesn't want me to look yet. Because he's very young. He wants to be all alone for a while."

On Saturday Joshua's mother and his father and his big sister and his big brother all happened to be rather busy all day. It wasn't until nearly bedtime that anyone spoke to him again about the clock box.

"Do you still have a baby dragon in that box, Josh?" his brother asked him.

"Yes," said Joshua.

"Have you seen him yet?"

"Yes," said Joshua. "Now I have."

"Say, that's wonderful! What does he look like?"

"He's pink, a little. His wings are still soft. With goldy edges. I think. Because it's dark in there."

"Then make the hole bigger, so you can see him better."

"No, I can't. He wants it dark. While his wings are so soft, it has to be dark."

"How do you know that, Joshua?" his mother asked him.

"It's always that way with dragons," said Joshua. "With baby boy dragons."

On Sunday morning, just before lunch-time, Joshua told his big sister, "His name is Emmeline."

"But Josh, that's a girl's name!"

"I know, but he's a Chinese dragon. And Chinese boy dragons like to have girls' names. His eyes are purple. And his wings are hardly soft at all now."

"May I see him?"

"No. He's too shy."

"But *you* look at him now, don't you?"

"He's used to me," said Joshua.

Monday evening Joshua's father asked him what he had been feeding the dragon.

"They don't eat when they're little," said Joshua. "Not baby dragons. Not while their wings are still even a little bit soft."

"Well, then, what are you going to feed him when his wings get strong?"

"I won't have to feed him then," answered Joshua, and he laid his hand gently on the clock box.

And then it was Tuesday again, and Joshua came to the breakfast table without the clock box. But everyone was in a hurry to start the day, and no one noticed.

It was later, when Joshua's mother was making his bed, that she saw the clock box on the floor. The tape had been torn off and the box was open wide. It was empty.

"Joshua! Your dragon's gone!"

Joshua was busy taking his marbles out of a bag, and he didn't turn around when he answered her. "He was big enough last night. And his wings were strong. He flew away."

"Did he really? But, Josh, where could he fly to?"

Joshua turned around, then, and walked over to where the empty clock box was, and picked it up.

"Where dragons go," he said. "This is a very good box to keep marbles in, I think. I'm going to put my marbles in it now."

And he did.

The Dancing Fox

Translated by John Bierhorst

All the girls wanted to dance with such a charming partner.
A Peruvian tale.

Foxes love to dance. They dance in the dark with young women who slip quietly from their beds and come running out into the night. But the fox must wear a disguise. He must hide his long, bushy tail. He must wrap it around him and stuff it inside his trousers, though when he does he is really too warm. He perspires. Yet still he is able to dance.

Now, one of these foxes was young and amorous, and he never missed the nightly dancing. Toward morning, however, as the cock began to crow, he would always hurry away.

This fine fox was a subtle flatterer, a favorite with all the young women. Each of them wanted to dance with him. And as it happened, one or another would sometimes feel slighted and then grow resentful.

One of them once, in a fit of pique, drew her companions aside and pointed out that the fox always left before dawn. Who was he? And why did he run away?

The young women wondered. Then they made up their minds to catch him and hold him until it was daylight.

The next night, when it was fully dark,

they made their circle and began to dance. Soon the fox appeared, as usual disguised as a young man in shirt and trousers. Suspecting nothing, he danced and sang. The girls made him heady with their caresses, and he became more spirited and more flattering than ever.

As soon as the cock crowed, he started to leave. "No, no," they all cried, "don't go! Not yet! The cock crows six times. You can stay till the fifth."

The dancing continued, and there were more caresses. The fox forgot that he had to leave, and at last the white light of dawn appeared. Frightened, he tried to flee. But the young women held him. They entangled him in their arms. Then suddenly, with a growl, he bit their hands, leaped over their heads, and ran.

As he leaped, his trousers ripped open and out flew his tail. The girls all shrieked with laughter. They called after him and mocked him as he ran out of sight, his long, bushy tail waving between his legs. Then he disappeared and was seen no more. He never came back again.

A Pair of Lovers

by Elsie Singmaster Lewars

James and the beautiful collie loved each other, but the boy knew that eventually the dog would be taken from him.

The first shadows from the western mountains fell upon the little farm at their foot. Often they seemed to chase James down the road. He had gone for the cows alone since he was six years old, but he had never grown accustomed to the queer shapes of the alder bushes in the evenings and to the dark masses that filled the fence corners. Even familiar Mooley and Daisy and Bess took on vast and unfamiliar proportions. James did not often run, and having safely crossed the bridge over the stream that made his mother's land such fine pasture, he grew bold. From there he could see the kitchen light, darkened sometimes as his mother passed before it, or he could hear the great tin pails rattling on her arm as she swung open the barnyard gate.

This evening James could not see the kitchen light or hear the pleasant clink of his mother's pails. Already the loud "Gee, Mooley! Haw, Bess!" with which he expressed his return to confidence in himself and in the reasonable structure of the world was on his lips. But the shout died soundlessly away.

The light of his mother's lamp was lost

in a brilliant glare that came from the road. A round, still, white light—or, rather, two round, still, white lights—illuminated the road to the bridge. James could count every nail in the railing, every knot in the floor. He could see also, as he looked down to gauge the astonishing power of the fiery eyes, his own bare feet, released today from their winter bondage of shoes. He could see the smooth, beautifully colored bodies of the Alderneys, moving placidly up the road in the face of the great light as though they were indifferent to the strange phenomenon.

James stopped so long in amazed contemplation that the cows were halfway to the barn. Then he ran at furious speed.

"It is one of *them!*" he cried, divided between fright and rapture.

At the gate of the house yard he stopped, breathless. The automobile lights were now behind him; he could see that the kitchen lamp was burning and that his mother stood in the doorway, her pails, one inside the other, in one hand, her lantern in the other. Facing her on the step was a stranger, a tall young man with an eager, commanding voice.

"The dairyman told me about you. He said that you loved animals and were kind to them. Robin should be on a farm while we are away. I wouldn't have bought him if I had known we were going so soon. He won't be any trouble, and I will pay you well."

Mrs. Schelling set the lantern on the sill beside her. She was a Pennsylvania German and spoke English with difficulty. She braced herself by putting her hand against the door.

"I could not say his name, to call him."

"Robin! Call him Bob, Bobby; anything you like!"

"I could not talk to him in English."

The young man laughed. "Then talk to him in German!"

Mrs. Schelling answered with a slow "Well." Two dollars a week would be a desirable addition to her income. Suddenly her face brightened. "The little one can talk to him!"

At this mention of himself, James withdrew to the shadows. But it was not at him that the stranger turned to look. The stranger gave a signal, a sharp stroke of middle finger against palm. In answer, a creature leaped in a single, startling curve through the air. It hurled itself from the seat of the automobile and landed on the step between the stranger and James's mother. It was a collie dog, brown as a chestnut.

"Isn't he a beauty?" The young man did not wait for an answer. While James's mother gasped at the suddenness with which the dog had hurled himself at her, his master put him through a series of tricks. He said one word and the collie sat up on his hind legs, another and he leaped higher than his master's head.

"You will keep him?" said he, like one who is accustomed to obedience. "Robin, you are to stay here till I come."

Without another word, the young man stepped into his car. There was a whirring noise, a jolt of wheels, and the car moved. The ribbon of light rolled itself up until it vanished like the gloves of a magician. Loneliness and darkness descended once more upon the little farm. The spring evening seemed like a dark winter night.

"James!" called Mrs. Schelling.

James came out of his hiding place into the pale light by the door. His blue eyes almost popped from his head. He looked up at his mother, and she looked down at him. Between them, the collie turned warm brown eyes from one to the other. Neither mother nor son was given to speech, not because their minds traveled with especial slowness but because their thoughts were alike.

"It is a dog!" said James's mother slowly in German, as though she could not believe in his presence.

"Will he stay all the time here?" asked James in the English that his mother required.

"Till winter. This was young Harmon from town."

"Will he bite?" asked James in dread.

"No, he is kind." Mrs. Schelling started with pails and lantern toward the barn. "You are to sit with him till I come back."

"He might run away from me!" objected James.

"Then call him! He will come if you call him."

James sat on the doorsill and the dog lay on the step.

James was in an ecstasy compounded of delight and terror. If he had ever desired a dog, he had not asked for one. He was a person who accepted the existent as the inevitable. Now he was afraid, not so much that the dog would bite him as that the beautiful creature would scorn him. This was a rich dog, a proud dog. The Harmons lived in a great and wonderful house. James looked down embarrassed at his soiled bare feet, then solemnly back at the brown eyes.

For a long time he did not move. He could hear the sound of the milk streaming between his mother's strong fingers into the pails; he could hear an owl hoot in the distance and a whippoorwill call nearby. At the latter dismal sound, accustomed as he was to it, he moved a little on the step, as though, under pressure of loneliness, he dared seek acquaintance with his proud companion.

"Robin!" said little James. "You—you doggy!"

Then the dog did a strange thing. James recounted it shyly to his mother when she came from the barn. Though speech was difficult, this pleasant experience must be imparted.

"Mother," said he. "I spoke to him by name and he licked me!"

James's mother looked down at the pair. The collie sat with his head on the little boy's knee, and James's arm was around his neck. The tears gathered in her eyes as she carried her heavy pails into the kitchen. Perhaps she thought of the human playmates whom James might have had if life had been different.

For a week the collie was not allowed to leave the yard. When James started for the cows, the dog accompanied him to the gate and waited there till he came back. He did not seem to miss his master, to whom he had belonged only a short time. When James came in sight, he barked like mad.

One evening James started later than usual. The shadow of the mountain lay already on the farm; to go toward it was like entering a darkening cave. Mrs. Schelling came twice to the door to bid him go.

"Take him with you!" She never ventured the dog's name. The collie had become "him," as all masters of Pennsylvania German households are "him."

The little boy leaped and shouted. "Dare I?"

"Why, yes. He knows enough now to come back."

Then was the gate of paradise opened. The two went down the lane with the speed of greyhounds, but with the erratic course of june bugs. They advanced and they receded, retracing their steps from pure joy. They screamed and barked together. The little boy was transformed; he behaved as though he had become insane. His mother called to him to drive the cows carefully, and as though to make up for the soberness of the return, the two behaved all the more crazily. The collie sprang over fences; he sprang over the little boy's head. The little boy, a week ago so sober and quiet, danced like a maenad or like a fakir of India. He drowned out the cry of the whippoorwill with his wild clamor, his shrieks and song.

The cows walked home slowly, but behind them were strange doings. The little boy danced into the shadows, challenging them scornfully.

"Oh, you nix nutz under the tree! Oh, you fat pig in the corner!" He shrieked with laughter, as though his sentiments were the wittiest in the world. He beat at the shadows and kicked them. There was nothing in the universe that he feared.

All the summer, paradise continued. The little boy explored the mountain upon which he had hitherto never dared to set foot. He went far from home along the country roads. When a man spoke to him roughly, the collie leaped at the stranger with the same curving swiftness with which he had leaped from his master's automobile.

When school opened, the dog went with the little boy to the schoolhouse and lay in the corner of the room, being often used as an example by the teacher. The teacher regarded James with astonishment. From the most quiet of her pupils he had become the noisiest.

When September changed to October, the cows were once more fetched at twilight. The progress to the pasture was still as wild as a june bug's flight. The evenings were cool; the two would have moved swiftly even if life had not danced within them.

The little boy had for some time crossed the bridge by walking on the handrail, with the dog barking in admiration or fright below him. The night of the first frost his foot slipped, and he plunged headfirst into the dark pool. He could swim, but the icy water bound him with fetters. He sank and rose and sank again in spite of all his frantic efforts to strike out with feet and hands. Then, beside him, he felt a support at which he could clutch; his fingers sank into a shaggy coat, and in an instant his feet touched the rising bank.

Foolishly, he went on for the cows, not dashing about and shaking himself as the collie did, but walking slowly, trying to choke back his sobs. He could scarcely pull the pasture bars out of their sockets or follow the slow pace of the cows. They had crossed the bridge before he had left the shadows of the alders.

When he reached the bridge, he gave a sharp cry. Again the light in his mother's kitchen was invisible; again there stretched to his feet a broad, shining ribbon up which Daisy and Mooley and Bess were making their placid way. He called the dog in terror, but he did not come. Already four flying feet had carried the collie up the lane to the side of the young man on the step. Mrs. Schelling faced him, her lantern in one hand, a roll of money in the other.

"I do not like to take it," said she. "He was like a person to us." She could see the little boy creeping along the edge of the lighted road.

"I'm much obliged to you," said the

young man. "There is something there for your little boy too." He gave a brisk command, and the dog hurled himself into the car. There was a whir, a jolt of wheels, and the ribbon of light rolled itself up once more.

Mrs. Schelling waited for the little boy on the doorstep.

"Come in, little James." She laid her hand on his shoulder. "My child, you are wet!"

The little boy could make no answer, but stood with contorted face, trembling. His mother felt his clothes, questioning him wildly.

"What has happened? You were in the water? What ails you?"

At last the little boy found his voice. "I fell in the creek. He pulled me to the bank! Oh, Mother, Mother, Mother!"

Mrs. Schelling stripped off his clothes and began to rub the shivering body. Then she wrapped him in a blanket and took him in her arms. Daisy and Mooley and Bess waited long to be milked.

In the frosty morning the little boy went for the cows. His icy plunge had not hurt him, but he moved slowly. In the evening he cried softly all the way to the pasture and all the way home, too smitten with grief to observe the threatening shadows.

But the next evening the shadows were in their places, darker, more terrible than ever. They seemed like sentient beings who would remember that he had mocked this one, had thrust that one with a sword of wood. They had grown larger; he could scarcely find a path between them and the fence. When he came to the house, his face was so white that his mother was frightened.

"I could get you a dog," said she.

"Oh, no!" cried James. "Oh, no, Mother!"

By November, darkness had fallen completely when the little boy came home with the cows. There was still green pasturage in sheltered places, but it was far away. The little boy had to go around the enormous, rustling crown of a fallen tree; he had to encircle a pile of huge boulders. The wind made crackling noises in the underbrush; the shadows thrust out arms to seize him. He dared not run and he was afraid to walk slowly.

One evening the cows were restless. James was late, having postponed his journey as long as he dared. The sky was black and the air was full of threatening sounds. When James thought he heard padding feet and panting breath, he stood still and screamed. Then his cry changed to a shout.

"Is it thou!" laughed he. "Thou! Thou!"

His mother waited for him at the barn gate and did not see his shining eyes till she came into the kitchen.

"What ails you?" she asked.

"He was here," answered the little boy.

"He? Who?"

"*He*, Mother! He brought me till over the bridge, then he went home."

"It cannot be!"

"He was here," insisted the little boy.

The next evening James came home again with shining eyes. His mother looked at him in terror.

"He was here again," said James quietly. "He was here with me till the bridge. He remembers about the bridge."

In the morning Mrs. Schelling went out in the starlight to talk to the dairyman who fetched her milk cans.

"Do you think I could buy this dog?" she asked. "My little one is—is—" She could not say the dreadful thing she feared.

The dairyman shook his head.

"That dog cost two hundred dollars. If that young fellow wanted the moon, he could have it. All his life he has had everything."

Mrs. Schelling was now terrified because she had had in her house so valuable a creature. She wished that she had never seen the young man and his dog.

That afternoon the young man himself rode up the lane and beckoned Mrs. Schelling to the gate.

"My dog runs away every day. Does he come here?"

"The little one says he does."

"Where is the boy?"

"At school."

"Tell him to drive the dog home." The young man spoke angrily. It was easy to see that he had always had everything. "Tell him to throw a stick at him. He's cunning as a fox about getting off."

Having issued his commands, the young man pulled a lever and the car slid down the hill.

Mrs. Schelling gave James the young man's order.

"You are to throw a stick at him and drive him off."

James laughed. "He would only fetch the stick!"

"I will drive him off. The man talked as if we would steal him!"

The next evening Mrs. Schelling crossed the bridge to meet the returning procession. The cows moved placidly along, behind them the little boy laughed and waved his arms, beside him leaped the collie. The dog ran forward and took Mrs. Schelling by her apron and skirt. When he could release her for an instant, he barked for joy.

"You lump!" cried Mrs. Schelling in a furious tone. "You bad dog!" Mrs. Schelling's voice weakened a little. "You rascal! You scoundrel! Go home!" The last words were as weak as the chirp of a sparrow. "Oh, *please* go home!" she cried.

At the end of another week the young man came again. This time he waited until James came from school.

"You must drive him home," he commanded sternly. "I can't keep him penned up night and day. He's getting to be a tramp dog. Do you feed him?"

"No," answered Mrs. Schelling.

"I save him sometimes a little something from dinner," confessed James.

"You're ruining him. He'll have to be beaten if he doesn't stay at home. I'm determined to conquer him."

That evening the collie waited at the bars.

"Tomorrow I will chase him," said the little boy. The next day he said again, "Tomorrow," and the next. When six days had passed, he still had done nothing. Then the collie came, walking heavily, with welts from a whip on his back.

"Oh, you must stay home!" wailed the little boy.

To his terror the collie would not leave him at the bridge. But if he did not go home, he might be killed. James picked up the end of a fence rail and threw it with all his strength, and the collie dropped as though he had been shot.

Somehow the little boy and his mother got the dog to the kitchen. His eyes were open and he breathed; otherwise he gave no sign of life. James sat beside him on the kitchen floor, speechless with woe. Suddenly he began to cry.

"The man is coming!"

Mrs. Schelling met the stranger at the door in the glare of light from the automobile lamps.

"The little boy threw a stick at him," said she.

The young man crossed the room and knelt down and passed his hand over the thick coat and the sleek legs. The cruel welts were still there; it was not the little boy who had hurt the dog.

"He's not badly hurt; he's only tired out."

Then the young man moved his hand quickly away from a wet, warm, forgiving touch and got to his feet. He looked about the simple room, bare of everything but the necessities of life, at the hardworking woman and at the little boy in his homemade clothes. He was himself not much more than a boy, and indulgence and prosperity had not yet so hardened him that his heart could not be touched. Now, if he conquered anything, it was a creature much harder to conquer than a dog.

"You may keep him," said he in his clear, sharp way.

The little boy gave a startled cry. "For always?"

"Yes," replied the young man, "for always."

ABE

The Boy Who Voted for Abe Lincoln

by Milton Richards

Sam was only twelve, but he had good reasons to pick Lincoln for President.

Sam Adams climbed to the wagon seat and spoke to the yoke of oxen. His father was out of sight now, over the hill, heading for the wheat field. Jolting on the hard plank, Sam looked back and waved to his mother. She was standing in the middle of the farmyard, her yellow hair and gray calico skirt blowing in the brisk wind.

She waved anxiously. "Hurry, Sam!" she called. "You know how much that wheat means to your pa. If those cattle get in before he gets the fence up . . . !" She left the sentence unfinished.

"I'll get there, Ma," he called back reassuringly. "Don't worry."

But he couldn't help worrying himself. A herd of cattle roving over the hills had already destroyed the Hillis cornfield and the Moores' oats. It was Mr. Moore who had ridden over to warn Sam's father that the cattle were headed that way.

Sam gritted his teeth. That wheat field meant everything to his father, to the whole family. If anything happened to it, next winter would be a barren one. Food scarce. Money scarcer. Sam could remember two years ago, when he had been only ten. All winter long there had been an empty ache where his stomach should have been. No. He didn't want another winter like that. He tried to get the oxen to move faster.

But the road was narrow and full of deep ruts. It was muddy, too, from yesterday's rain.

Bumping and sliding, the wagon, with its burden of fence rails, came finally within sight of the field.

Sam gave a glad shout. He was almost there, and the wheat was rippling in the wind, still untrampled. He could see his father riding along the far edge.

But Sam's shout had stopped the oxen. To them it had sounded like a call to halt.

Too late, Sam tried to urge them forward. The right wheels were sunk deep, up to the hubs, in the sticky mud.

"Giddap," cried Sam desperately. It was no use. The wagon was stuck, glued to the slimy ruts. He lifted his head, opened his mouth to call for his father to come and help. The shout died in his throat. Thronging the hill beyond the wheat field were moving cattle, a hundred head or more. They were coming steadily on toward the precious wheat field.

No use now to call his father. They would never get the wagon out in time, nor the fence up. Could his father head the cattle off alone? If he did, it would be a miracle.

Sam choked. He had tried to be brave, but now tears came to his eyes. It was no use. The cattle would ruin the wheat. Eyes blinded, he slid from the wagon seat. As he did so, he heard the beat of a horse's hoofs behind. Someone was coming down the road!

Shouting hoarsely, Sam waved his arms and pointed to the wheat field. Tears blurred his vision so that he could not tell if the man approaching were friend or stranger.

He backed against the wagon as the horse galloped forward, spurting mud toward him.

"Don't worry, son! Block up your wheels and put rails under them. I'll help head off the cattle."

Sam hadn't had time to see what the man looked like. Now, brushing the tears from his eyes, he stared after him in relief. Help for his father. The wheat field had a chance now, maybe.

The man on the horse was long and lanky, Sam saw. But in heading off cattle, he was clever and successful. Soon he and Sam's father had managed to herd the steers away from the wheat. They thundered off, bellowing, in the direction they had come.

His heart hammering gratefully, Sam watched the stranger dismount and talk with his father. Then he remembered the horseman's instructions for getting the wagon out of the mud. Busily he started to work.

The cattle had been headed off for the time being, but no telling how soon they might come back. The sooner he got the fence rails to the field, the better.

When he looked up again, the stranger was riding off down the road at a canter, his lean form swaying awkwardly.

Mr. Adams crossed the field toward his son. He was mopping his brow with a large handkerchief.

"That was sure a close shave, son," he said, coming up to the wagon. "If it hadn't been for Abe, we'd have lost the wheat, sure. I never coulda headed them steers off alone."

"Abe who?" asked Sam. "A friend of yours, Pa?"

"Why, that was Abe Lincoln, son. He was on his way back to Springfield after making a speech someplace. As for being a friend of mine, I guess Abe's just about everybody's friend."

"He sure was our friend, all right," said Sam gratefully. "What does this Abe Lincoln do, Pa? Is he a-farming, like us?"

"He's a lawyer, son; in politics, too. In fact, he's just been nominated for the presidency of the United States. On the new Republican Party ticket. Don't know as he's got much of a chance, though."

"Why not?" asked Sam loyally. "I guess we'd be lucky, wouldn't we, Pa, to get a man as good as him?"

"You bet we would. But, you see, he's

up against some pretty smart fellows. Men that makes a business of being smart. Educated folk. Stephen Douglas, for instance."

"But you're going to vote for Mr. Lincoln, aren't you, Pa?"

"You bet I'll vote for him, Sam. Nothing can stop me from polling my vote for Abraham Lincoln, come November."

But something did stop Hank Adams from voting for Abraham Lincoln. In early July he was thrown from a horse and seriously injured. Judith, his young wife, and his son, Sam, were beside him when he died.

"Don't—forget—about—the wheat, Sam. Take—it—into—Springfield." He sighed, closed his eyes. "I—meant—to—take—it—in—Election Day. When—I—voted—for Abe."

Two weeks later Sam answered a knock at the door. Two men stood outside.

"This the Adams farm?" asked one.

"Yes, sir. Will you come in?"

"Who is it, Sam?" called his mother. She came in, wiping her red, roughened hands on her apron.

"I'm Joe Winship, mum," said the taller of the two strangers. "And this is my pardner, Jerry Hogan. We've brought you a letter from Mr. Abe Lincoln."

"From Abe Lincoln?" She took it wonderingly. "Why, it's addressed to both of us, Sammy."

"To me, too?" asked Sam eagerly. "Open it, Ma. What does it say?"

She looked up at the two men, whom, in the excitement of the letter, she had almost forgotten. "Oh, I'm sorry. I—I guess I've clean forgot my manners, gentlemen. Sammy, push up some chairs for Mr. Winship and Mr. Hogan."

"Oh, don't mind us, mum. We're just—just part of the letter, you might say." Mr. Hogan flushed.

But Sam ran for some chairs. When he came back, his mother had the letter open. She looked up from it, her face glowing.

"God bless Abe Lincoln," she said softly. "It's a beautiful letter."

"He's a kind man, mum," said Mr. Winship fervently. "There ain't many lawyers would let Jerry and me work out a debt like this, instead of paying straight cash."

"What does it say, Ma?" asked Sam eagerly.

"It says," replied his mother gently, "that Mr. Lincoln is deeply sorry to learn of your pa's going. And he hopes we'll be kind enough to let these two friends of his, Mr. Winship and Mr. Hogan, work out their debt to him for legal work by helping us with the farm for a spell."

"Glory, Ma!" breathed Sam. "That means we'll have help threshing the wheat."

"You sure will," said Mr. Hogan, grinning widely. "All the help you need."

"I—I don't know what to say," said Mrs. Adams, choking. "It—it just seems like help from heaven. Sam's doing fine, but he's a long way from being a man grown. How can I thank Mr. Lincoln?"

"We'll just tell him about the look on your face when you read the letter, Miz Adams. That'll be thanks enough for Abe."

"Is that all the letter, Ma?" asked Sam. "Didn't he say anything about me? You said the letter was addressed to me, too."

"Why, yes, Sam. There is a note for you."

The boy took the page eagerly. It read, "Sam, I used to hear your father talk about what a fine, good boy you were.

He was very proud of you. I know he's glad you're there to take care of your mother. Don't ever give up if you should get stuck in the mud again. There's always a way out. Something or someone will come along to help if you just keep trusting the Almighty."

Sam put the letter down. "Glory, Ma! Abe Lincoln's just got to be elected President. Why, I reckon he must be the best man in the whole world."

In November Sam Adams took the wheat into Springfield to sell. It was fine wheat, he thought proudly, and he ought to get a fine price for it. Before they had left to go back to town, Joe Winship and Jerry Hogan had told him where to take it in order to get the best price.

It was good to know that his mother wouldn't have to worry about money all winter long. They'd have enough to eat now. He wished he could keep her from missing Pa too much. Maybe if he bought her something . . . something with the money she'd said he could have for his very own.

It was still early morning when he rolled into Springfield. There were a lot of people going to town. The streets hummed with excitement. There was something in the air, something in the way women laughed and whispered, in the way men gathered in groups on street corners, that set young Sam Adams' pulses throbbing.

Then a group of men marched down the street bearing banners. A band played blaring music. The banners said, "Elect Stephen Douglas President."

Sam sat bolt upright, shocked. Elect Mr. Douglas? Why, it was Abe Lincoln they should be electing. His own pa had been going to vote for Lincoln.

He knew then why there were so many people here in Springfield today. It was Election Day—the day the people voted for President of the United States. He wondered why his mother hadn't told him. But they'd been working so hard lately that she must have clean forgot.

Well, he was here now, luckily. He'd go sell the wheat first, then come back.

He got an even better price for it than he'd expected. The man who bought it, Mr. Salford, said he'd been expecting him. Joe Winship had told him about Sam.

"Too bad your mother couldn't come into town, too," said Mr. Salford, helping Sam unload the bags of wheat.

"I reckon she'll be mighty sorry, too, when she hears it's Election Day," said Sam. "But someone had to stay and take care of the farm. There's only us two now."

"Well, you're a fine, strong lad," complimented Mr. Salford. "I'm sure your mother depends on you a good deal."

Sam asked the way to the nearest polling place. The town hall was closest, Mr. Salford said, waving good-by.

The street outside the town hall was crowded. The sidewalks were clotted with groups of gesticulating men, all talking in loud voices or speaking in low, confidential asides. Sam nudged a man with a very red nose and fierce black beard.

"Where do folks go to vote?" he asked timidly.

"Just follow the crowd," answered the man, waving a hand. Then, getting a good look at Sam for the first time, he stared. "Are you figgering to vote, son?" He burst into loud laughter. "Well, if you do, don't vote for that scarecrow, Abe Lincoln!" A group of men nearby also laughed uproariously.

Sam felt his ears get hot. He hurried past them. There were little booths in the room where people voted. As soon as one man left one of the booths, another man went in. Sam waited patiently for his chance. At the first opportunity he went into a booth.

"Hey!" said a voice. "A kid went in that booth! Yank him out."

They did yank him out. "But—but I want to vote," pleaded Sam. "I want to vote for Mr. Lincoln."

A man laughed. "But you're not old enough to vote, kid. You have to be twenty-one in order to vote. On your way, son!"

"But please, mister—I'm voting for my pa. He aimed to cast his ballot for Lincoln."

"Well, he'll have to come himself," said the man impatiently. "Now go on—get out of here."

"But my pa can't come himself," pleaded Sam. "Honest, mister, why ain't it all right for me to—"

The man beckoned two burly-looking

men. "The youngster's stubborn, boys. I reckon you'd better show him the way out."

The two men took hold of Sam and lifted him squirming from the floor.

Two minutes later he picked himself up from the street outside. His best pants were torn. His hat had fallen into the gutter. But worst of all was the way he felt inside. He'd failed. Failed both his pa and Mr. Lincoln.

He got up and picked his hat out of the gutter. It was crumpled and muddy. His eyes filled with tears. He tried to choke back sobs.

A heavy hand fell on his shoulder. Sam looked up, startled. "Please, mister. I ain't doing anything. I'm going now."

"What's the trouble, son?"

Sam saw the face of a man so homely that, despite the kindness of his tone, the boy's fright returned. Maybe they'd sent this man to come and put Sam in jail. Maybe they put folks in jail for trying to vote when they hadn't ought to.

"Please, mister," he sobbed. "I didn't know it was wrong. I was just trying to help make Mr. Lincoln President."

"Were you now? And what makes you think he ought to be President?"

"Because he's so good," said Sam tearfully. "That's why I wanted to vote for him."

The long arm went around his shoulder, tightened. "You mean—you tried to cast a vote for him, son?"

Sam nodded. "I was going to vote for my pa, mister. He can't vote for Mr. Lincoln like he said he wanted to, because—because—he's dead, mister." He shook the tears from his eyes and looked up proudly. "You see, my pa, he knew Mr. Lincoln."

The eyes that looked down at him were warm and pitying. All at once the man's face didn't look homely to Sam anymore. It was the kindest face he had ever seen.

"What was your father's name, son?"

"Henry Adams, mister. We live out by Apple Creek. There's just my ma and me now, though. But Mr. Lincoln sent some men out to help us thresh our wheat, and so we won't have to worry all winter about having enough," he said earnestly. "My pa said Mr. Lincoln was always doing nice things. He was everybody's friend, he said."

"I knew your father, son. He was a fine man. I'm glad you got the wheat crop threshed all right."

"I'm glad, too," said Sam. But his face clouded again. "But my pa's going to feel awful bad up there in heaven, on account of not casting his vote for Mr. Lincoln."

"Is he?" said the man softly. "I reckon we ought to do something about that. You know, I haven't voted yet myself. I was kind of debating about the matter. You see, I'm not completely convinced that Abe Lincoln is the man for President."

"But he is, mister. Pa said so."

"Well," the tall man drawled, rubbing his chin, "I don't know that I can sincerely cast my vote for Abe on my own account. But I'll tell you what I'll do. I'll go in and vote for Lincoln for your father's sake."

"Glory, mister!" Sam's face glowed. "That's sure fine of you. Me and my pa and ma'll be mighty grateful to you."

He watched the tall, thin figure mount the steps. He seemed to know a great many people, for he spoke to nearly everyone, nodding and smiling.

I wonder who he is, thought Sam. He's a mighty nice man, even if he wasn't quite sure about voting for Mr. Lincoln. I reckon that since he knew my pa, I should have asked his name to tell Ma.

It was getting late. He'd have to hurry if he wanted to get that present for Ma. He hastened along the street to the general store. The store was crowded. It took a long time to get waited on. He came out, his arms full of packages, and went to the team and wagon.

He climbed to the seat and clucked to the horses. It was getting late. He'd have to hurry to get home before Ma began to worry about him. As he started up, there was a commotion on the street. People were cheering and shouting. Towering above the crowd was the man Sam had persuaded to cast his father's vote.

Quickly he leaned down and called to a boy his own age, who was standing near the wagon. "Say, can you tell me what that man's name is there? That tall one?"

The boy stared. "You must be from the country. Everybody in Springfield knows Abe Lincoln!"

The Clever Gretel

by The Brothers Grimm

A hilarious tale of a cook
who liked her own cooking—too much.

There was once a cook named Gretel who wore shoes with red knots, and when she went out with them on, she used to turn about this way and that way, and then say to herself quite contentedly, "Ah, you are a very pretty girl!" And when she came home, she drank a glass of wine for joy. And as the wine made her wish to eat, she used to taste of the best that she had and excuse herself by saying, "The cook ought to know how her cooking tastes."

One day it happened that her master said to her, "Gretel, this evening a guest is coming. So cook me two fowl very nicely."

"I will do it directly, master," replied Gretel. She soon killed the fowl, plucked, dressed, and spitted them, and as evening came on, she put them before the fire to roast. They began to turn brown and to cook through, but still the guest had not come. Then Gretel said to the master, "If your guest does not come soon, I shall have to take the fowl from the fire, but it will be a great shame not to eat them while they are very juicy."

The master said, "I will run out myself and bring the guest home." And as soon as he had turned his back, Gretel took the spit with its two fowl off the fire, and thought to herself, Ah, I have stood so long before the fire that I am quite hot and thirsty. Who knows when he will come? Meanwhile I will run down into the cellar and have a draft.

Gretel ran down the stairs and set down a jug, and saying, "God bless you, Gretel!" she took a good pull at the beer. And when that was down, she had another draft.

Then she went up again and placed the fowl before the fire, and turned the spit around quite merrily, first spreading some butter over their skins.

But the roasting fowl smelled so good that Gretel thought, They had better be tasted now. And so she dipped her finger into the gravy and said, "Ah, how good these fowl are! It is a sin and shame that they should not be eaten at once."

She ran to the window, therefore, to see if her master was yet coming with his guest, but there was nobody, and she turned again to the fowl. "Ah, one wing is burned!" said she. "I had better eat that." And cutting it off, she ate it. But then she thought, I had better take the other, too, or master will see that something is wanting.

When she had finished the two wings, she went again to see whether her master was coming, but without success. "Who knows," said she, "whether they will come or not? Perhaps they have stopped along the way. Well, Gretel, be of good courage. The one fowl is begun. Have another drink and then eat it up completely, for when it is eaten, you will be at rest. And besides, why should good things be allowed to spoil?"

So thinking, Gretel ran once more into the cellar, took a hearty drink, and then ate up one fowl with great pleasure. As soon as it was down, and the master still had not returned, Gretel looked at the other fowl and said, "Where the one is, the other ought to be also. The two belong with one another. What is right for the one is right for the other. I believe that another draft would not harm me." So saying, she took another hearty drink and let the second fowl slip down after the other.

Just as she was enjoying the eating, the master came running up and called, "Make haste, Gretel! The guest is coming directly."

"Yes, master," said she. "It will soon be ready."

The master went in to see if the table was properly laid, and taking up the great knife wherewith he was to carve the fowl, he began to sharpen it on the stones. Meantime the guest came and knocked politely at the door.

Gretel ran to see who it was, and when she perceived the guest, she held her finger to her mouth to enjoin silence and said, "Hasten quickly away! If my master discovers you, you are lost. He certainly did invite you here to supper, but he has it in his mind to cut off your ears. Just listen how he is sharpening his knife!"

The guest listened to the sound and then hurried down the steps as fast as he could, while Gretel ran screaming to her master and said to him, "You have invited a fine guest!"

"What?" said he. "What do you mean?"

"Why," replied Gretel, "just as I was about to serve them up, your guest took the two fowl off the dish and bolted away with them."

"That is fine manners, certainly!" said the master, grieved for his fine fowl. "He might have left me one of them, at least, so that I might have had something to eat." He called after his guest to stop, but the man pretended not to hear. Then he ran after him, knife in hand, calling out, "Only one! Only one!" meaning that his guest should leave one fowl behind him and not take both. But the latter supposed that his host meant that he would cut off only one ear, and so he ran on as if fire were at his heels, so that he might take both ears home with him.

The Straw, the Coal, and the Bean

by The Brothers Grimm

The surprising adventures of an unlikely trio.

Once there was a poor old woman who lived in a village. She had collected a bundle of beans and was going to cook them. So she prepared a fire on her hearth, and to make it burn up quickly she lighted it with a handful of straw. When she threw the beans into the pot, one escaped her unnoticed and slipped onto the floor, where it lay close to a straw. Soon afterward a glowing coal jumped out of the fire and joined the others.

Then the straw began and said, "Little friends, how did you come here?"

The coal answered, "I have happily escaped the fire, and if I had not done so by force of will, my death would certainly have been a most cruel one. I should have been burned to a cinder."

The bean said, "I also have escaped so far with a whole skin. But if the old woman had put me into the pot, I should have been pitilessly boiled down to broth like my comrades."

"Would a better fate have befallen me, then?" asked the straw. "The old woman packed all my brothers into the fire and smoke. Sixty of them were all done for at once. Fortunately I slipped through her fingers."

"What are we to do now, though?" asked the coal.

"My opinion is," said the bean, "that as we have escaped death, we must all keep together like good comrades. And so that we may run no further risks, we had better quit the country."

This proposal pleased both the others, and they set out together. Before long they came to a little stream where there was neither path nor bridge, and they did not know how to get over.

The straw at last had an idea and said, "I will throw myself over, and then you can walk across upon me like a bridge."

So the straw stretched itself across from one side to the other, and the coal, which was of a fiery nature, tripped gaily over the newly built bridge. But when it got to the middle and heard the water rushing below, it was frightened and remained speechless, not daring to go any farther. The straw, beginning to burn, broke in two and fell into the stream. The coal, falling with it, fizzled out in the water.

The bean, who had cautiously remained on the bank, could not help laughing over the whole business, and having begun, could not stop, but laughed till it split its sides. Now all would have been over for it had not, fortunately, a wandering tailor been taking a rest by the stream. As he had a sympathetic heart, he brought out a needle and thread and stitched it up again, but as he used black thread, all beans have a black seam to this day.

Blue Willow

by Doris Gates

For Janey, the daughter of a migrant worker, the plate with its Chinese scene had the power to change a hard, drab life.

Janey Larkin paused on the top step of the shack and looked down at her shadow. Just now it was a very short shadow even for a ten-year-old girl who wasn't nearly as tall as she should be. The squatty dark blotch running out from under Janey's feet didn't reach to the edge of the cracked boards. It was noon, and the sun hung white and fierce almost directly overhead. It beat down upon Janey, the shack, and all the wide, flat country stretching away for miles and miles in every direction. It was hot, so terribly hot that when Janey cupped her hands and blew into her sweaty palms, her warm breath seemed cooler than the air she was breathing.

But it was better here on the steps than inside the stifling one-room shack where the heat of a wood stove added its bit to the best that the sun could do. Besides, here you could look out across the shimmering heat waves to the west, where the mountains were supposed to be. And somewhere on the other side of the mountains was a blue ocean. At this season the heat hid the mountains, which were far off anyway, and not even a breath from the ocean could find a way through the hidden ranges into this wide and scorching San Joaquin Valley. But earlier in the day, while they were driving here, Janey's father had told her there was an ocean to the west. So, lowering herself onto the top step, she sat humped and listless while she tried to find comfort in thinking about it. She looked very small and very lonely sitting there. Even her shadow, now she had seated herself, had shrunk almost to the vanishing point, abandoning her to the heat.

Across the road was another board shack, a little larger and more substantial-looking than the one in which the Larkin family had found shelter. Already Janey had learned that a Mexican family named Romero lived there. Dad had gone over to talk with them soon after the Larkins had arrived here this morning. Janey wondered without much interest what their neighbors were like. Dad hadn't said whether there were any children or not. Of course there would be, though. Every family had children. Every family except the Larkins, that is. Sometimes, as now, Janey regretted her lack of brothers and sisters. Big families always seemed to have a better time of it than she did. Even when they were fighting.

Of course she might scrape acquaintance with the family across the road. Janey considered this possibility for a moment before she discarded it. No, it wouldn't be any use. She wouldn't be here long enough to make it worth her while. Besides, it was just as well not to get too thick with strangers. Saved you a lot of trouble.

"Takes two to make a quarrel," Mom always said. "Mind your own business and the other fellow won't have to mind it for you."

Mom was right, Janey supposed. Mom was nearly always right. Still, there were times when this standoffishness seemed vaguely wrong. It was at best a lonesome business. Right at this particular moment, for instance, she would have welcomed a quarrel as a pleasant break in the monotony of sitting here on the front step staring listlessly at a house across the road.

Suddenly her sagging shoulders straightened a little, and an expectant look widened her blue eyes. A little girl with a baby in her arms had just come out of the Romero house and was starting across the road toward the Larkin shack. For a moment Janey intently watched her approach, and when she was sure the girl and baby were really coming her way, she called a warning over her shoulder.

"Here comes one of the Romeros with a baby."

There was no answer from inside, only the sound of a garment being rubbed along a washboard. Mrs. Larkin was taking advantage of the present halt to do the washing. It wasn't a very big job, since the Larkins didn't possess a great quantity of clothes. But it takes a little time to rub out even one tubful, and this was the first real chance she had had to do it in many days.

With some surprise, Janey watched the Mexican girl pick her way among the greasewood and tumbleweed. It hadn't occurred to her that one of the Romeros might seek her out. When the stranger was within easy hailing distance, Janey called, "Hello," with careful indifference. But her eyes were alert.

"Hello," came the answer, rather shyly given. The newcomer stopped in front of the steps as if she were awaiting judgment and shifted the baby in her arms.

"My name is Lupe Romero," she said. "This is Betty"—giving the baby another bounce. "She's kind of bashful, so I brought her over. It's good for her to see people."

Janey had expected the girl to offer an excuse for her visit. You didn't go out of your way to meet strangers without good reason. Betty seemed a satisfactory one.

"I'm Janey Larkin. Why don't you sit down?"

Lupe lowered herself onto the bottom step and deposited Betty beside her.

For a moment neither of them could think of anything to say. Then, "It's sure hot, isn't it?" Lupe ventured.

"Yes," said Janey. "Awful hot."

"I saw you when you got here this morning," said Lupe. "I would have come over right away, but my mother said to wait. How long are you going to stay?"

Janey was used to this question. She had answered it many times in the past five years, and always she gave the same answer as she now gave to Lupe.

"As long as we can," said Janey.

"Did they say you could move in here?"

"No," Janey replied. "Dad said it didn't look as if anyone had been staying here for a long time, so we thought maybe it wouldn't matter if we did."

"My father says this house belongs to the man who owns that herd in the next field where the windmill is," Lupe explained. "No one has lived in this house for a long time."

"How long have you lived over there?" Janey nodded toward the house across the road.

"A little over a year."

Janey's cloak of indifference fell away from her.

"Have you been staying in that place for a whole year?" she asked in astonishment. It was a wonderful thing for a family to remain put for so long a time.

"Sure," said Lupe, making a grab for Betty, who had wiggled off the step. Then, "Where did you come from?" she asked, when Betty was safe again.

"Do you mean in the beginning or just lately?" asked Janey. It made a difference in the length of the answer, for the whole story of the wanderings of the Larkin family since they had left northern Texas to come to California would have taken longer than Lupe might have cared to listen.

"I mean where did you stay last before you came here?"

"We camped down by Porterville last night. Dad came up here to work in the cotton."

"Have you any brothers or sisters?" Lupe asked pleasantly.

Janey shook her head and tried to look as if she didn't care.

"I have a brother"—Lupe's voice was smug— "and of course Betty. It is a good thing to have brothers and sisters," she added importantly. "It is too bad you have none." This last was in a tone of exaggerated regret.

Lupe was, of course, merely trying to make a teasing brother and a bothersome baby sound attractive. But Janey didn't know that and decided at once that Lupe was giving herself airs. Since it was a part of Janey's code never to feel inferior to anyone, something began to stir in her. Something that was a mixture of resentment and pride. She began to wonder if perhaps Lupe, though a stranger, already sensed her loneliness. Perhaps Lupe was even feeling sorry for her. Well, she didn't need to! Janey would make that clear once and for all. Lifting her chin, she sent her words as from a great height to Lupe.

"I have a willow plate," she said. "A willow plate is better than brothers or sisters or anything."

Lupe's interest was caught on the instant. She was even impressed. But not in the way Janey had intended.

"You mean a plate made of willows? I have not heard of that before."

Janey gave her a pitying look and felt much better for it. Lupe might have a brother and a sister. She might even have stayed in one house for a whole year. But she didn't even know what a willow plate looked like!

"Come inside," said Janey, tolerantly but with an eagerness that rather spoiled the effect. "I'll show it to you."

Lupe rose quickly, her dark eyes bright with curiosity. She picked up Betty and followed close on Janey's heels.

As they entered the house, a tall, thin woman with a tired face glanced up at them over a tub of steaming suds. The odor of soap and wet clothes in the stifling little room made the air seem too heavy to breathe.

"Mom, this is Lupe Romero, and her sister, Betty."

Embarrassed, Lupe pressed her face against the baby in her arms.

"There's quite a family of you Romeros, isn't there?" Mrs. Larkin gave Lupe the ghost of a smile. "How old is the baby?"

"Six months," replied Lupe, answering the last question first, and daring to look at the grown-up. "I have a brother, but I'm the oldest. I'm ten."

"Janey's all the child we've got, and she's a runty little thing. Skinny as a June shad." There were worry lines between her eyes as Mrs. Larkin studied Janey's blue-overalled figure. "It's moving about from pillar to post does it," she continued. " 'Tisn't any way to raise a young one, but a family's got to live somehow."

Janey acted as if she hadn't heard. She knew the words weren't really meant for her and Lupe anyway. She knew Mom was just talking to herself, as she did every now and then.

Lupe seemed to understand, too, and covered the awkward moment by looking curiously all about her. No detail of the room escaped her soft eyes.

The shack was not much to look at, either for itself or for its furnishings. The sides were rough, unfinished boards. Every crack and seam and knothole was there in plain view. It was exactly like the inside of a chicken coop, and not much larger.

In one corner was an iron bedstead

with more rust than paint on it. The mattress, which spent most of its time traveling on the top of the Larkin car, had been dumped onto it along with a mixed heap of household things, including a roll of bedding. Across the room was a small stove as rusty as the bed. Two chairs placed facing each other were doing duty just now as a rest for the washtub. A wobbly table was the only other piece of furniture.

"You can hang these things over the fence pretty soon," Mrs. Larkin said to Janey. "I'll be needing another bucket of water, too." She wrung the last garment. "Help me dump this tub," she said, and Janey sprang to take hold of a handle.

Together they carried the tub to the back door and poured its contents out onto the parched ground.

"Do you want me to hang out the clothes right now, or can I show Lupe the plate first?" Janey asked.

"No, I'll save the last tub of suds for scrubbing up, and I'll rinse after that. Then they'll be ready to hang out."

There would be plenty of time to show Lupe the plate, Janey decided thankfully. She needed a lot of time to show anyone the plate. Indeed, she never hurried in showing it to herself, for it was no ordinary plate. It meant to her what a doll might have meant if she had had one. Or brothers and sisters. And it meant much more, besides.

To begin with, it had belonged to Janey's great-great-grandmother, so it was very old. Then it had belonged to Janey's mother. But that was a long, long time ago, before that mother had died and Mom had come to take her place. The memory of her mother was so shadowy to Janey that if she tried to hold it even for a second, it faded away altogether. It was like a bit of music you can hear within yourself, but which leaves you when you try to make it heard. Mixed up with this faint memory were Mother Goose rhymes and gay laughter and a home of their own. And because the willow plate had once been a part of all this, it had seemed actually to become these things to Janey. It was the hub of her universe, a solid rock in the midst of shifting sands.

In addition to everything else, the willow plate was the only beautiful thing the Larkins owned. It was a blue willow plate, and in its pattern of birds and willows and human figures it held a story that for Janey never grew old. Its color, deep and unchanging, brought to her the promise of blue skies even on the grayest days and of blue oceans even in an arid wasteland. She never grew tired of looking at it.

But, strangely enough, not once since the drought and dust storm had driven them out of Texas had the blue plate ever been used as a dish or for any other purpose. Never had it been unpacked except for brief moments. And never, Mrs. Larkin had declared long ago, would it be put out as a household ornament until they had a decent home in which to display it. In the meantime it was kept safely tucked away, a reminder of happier days before its owners had become wanderers in search of a livelihood.

Janey rummaged among the heap of things on the bed and succeeded finally in hauling forth a scarred and battered suitcase. She worked it to one side of the roll of bedding, leaving a cleared space on the springs.

"You two sit there," she directed Lupe, who still held Betty in her arms. She tried to keep her voice matter-of-fact in spite of her growing excitement. She couldn't remember when she had ever been more eager to exhibit her treasure than on this occasion. Lupe would be dazzled. Never again would she boast of brothers and sisters in Janey's presence. Of course she couldn't be expected to appreciate the plate's whole significance. Nobody could except Janey herself. But no one could be indifferent to its great beauty. Not even Lupe Romero.

While Lupe and Betty made themselves as comfortable as possible on the wobbly bedsprings, Janey opened the suitcase and carefully rolled back a top layer of folded things. Reaching in, she slowly lifted up the blue willow plate.

For an instant she held it at arm's length, her head tilted a little to one side, so that the ends of her slightly wavy tow-colored hair bent against her shoulder. Then she drew the plate up level with her pointed chin and blew an imaginary speck of dust off it. Still holding it in her two hands, she placed it on the bed beside Lupe and slowly let go of it. Not saying a word, she stood back, her eyes still feasting on the treasure, and something in her rapt face cast a silence over Lupe, too.

As a matter of fact, so interested was Lupe in watching Janey's strange conduct that she didn't so much as glance at the thing responsible for it. She was a little bothered by the way Janey was acting. Never outside of church had Lupe seen just such a look on anybody's face. It made her feel uneasy, and clutching Betty to her, she at last slid her eyes toward the plate, half fearful of what she might see there.

But it was just a plate, after all, Lupe discovered. A pretty enough plate, to be sure, but certainly nothing to make such a fuss about. Its color she found distinctly disappointing. Why couldn't it have been red with a yellow pattern and perhaps a touch of green? But the gentle Lupe did not reveal her thoughts. Something in Janey's face forbade it. At the same time she was too disappointed to be able to say anything fitting. She had expected something marvelous, and she had been shown what to her was a very ordinary plate.

Only to Janey did the willow plate seem perfect. Only for her did it have the power to make drab things beautiful, and to a life of dreary emptiness bring a feeling of wonder and delight.

Bending over it now, she could feel the cool shade of willows, she could hear the tinkling of the little stream as it passed under the arched bridge, and all the quiet beauty of a Chinese garden was hers to enjoy. It was as if she had stepped inside the plate's blue borders, into another world as real as her own and much more desirable.

For the moment she had quite forgotten Lupe, and it was only when a grimy finger descended upon the arched bridge and a small voice said doubtfully, "It's pretty," that Janey was jerked back to her real world of heat and soapsuds and poverty.

Lupe's questioning dark eyes were lifted to Janey's blue ones, as deeply blue now in their excitement as the plate itself. "But why does it have such funny-looking houses and people on it?" Lupe was trying to be polite.

"They all mean something," Janey explained. "You see, the plate has a story. Dad has told me about it lots of times." Then eagerly, "Would you like to hear it?"

Lupe nodded without much interest, but Janey didn't notice. Had Lupe been so cruel as to shout No! it is more than likely that Janey would have insisted on telling the story anyway. It was nice, of course, that Lupe had nodded, but not absolutely necessary so far as Janey was concerned.

"Once upon a time over in China there was a rich man who had a beautiful daughter," she began.

"Were they Chinamen?" asked Lupe incredulously.

"Sure. They lived in China, didn't they?" Janey was annoyed at the interruption. She scowled at her listener, who looked apologetic and was silent as Janey went on.

"Well, this rich old man had promised another rich man to let him marry the beautiful daughter. But the daughter was already in love with a poor man who was very handsome. And when the father found it out, he shut his daughter up in a tower. See, here it is in the picture. But the handsome man stole her away, and they ran across the bridge to an island, and there they lived for quite a while. But the father found out about it and went to the island to kill them."

At this point Lupe furtively looked in the direction of Mrs. Larkin. But Mom wasn't listening to Janey's chatter. She was too busy with her own affairs.

Janey, noting that Lupe's interest had wavered for the moment, paused until her visitor's round dark eyes should be once more directed at the plate. Lupe misunderstood the pause and, eager to know the outcome, asked breathlessly, "Did he kill them?"

Janey ignored the question. This was the great moment in the story; she couldn't think of giving it away with a paltry yes or no.

"He went to the island to kill them,"

she repeated, relishing the suspense, "and he would have done it, too, but just as he got to their house, something changed the lovers into two white birds, and so they escaped and lived happily ever after."

"What changed them?" asked Lupe as soon as Janey had finished.

"I don't know, but something did."

"It was a miracle," Lupe announced awesomely.

"I don't know much about miracles," Janey confessed. "But Mom says things just happen and you have to make the best of it, so I guess that's what the lovers did. Anyway, it would be sort of fun to be a bird," she added dreamily, bending over the plate.

"What kind of trees are those?" Lupe pointed to some waving, frondlike branches that swept almost across one side of the plate.

"Willows. That's why it's called a willow plate."

"I know what willows are; there's lots of them along the river, but they don't look anything like those on that dish," declared Lupe stoutly, defending her ignorance.

Janey chose not to argue the matter. "Whereabouts is the river?" she asked instead.

Lupe slid off the bed and took Betty into her arms again.

"Right over there," she said, balancing the baby on one hip in order to point out the back door with her free arm.

Janey came and stood beside her in the doorway. Away to the east she could see a billowy line of foliage that distance had shrouded in a misty blue. It seemed to begin nowhere and to end in nothing. That was because one curve of the river swept it within her sight and another drew it away again.

"That's the river," Lupe informed her, adding with a wistful sigh, "I wish it was closer."

"How far away is it?" Janey asked.

"About a mile."

"We must have come by there this morning," said Janey, speaking more to herself than to Lupe. "It's nice to know there are willows here just as there are in the plate."

Lupe turned on Janey dark eyes in which there lay a mild hint of vexation. "But they aren't anything like those in the plate," she said reprovingly.

Janey didn't answer for a moment. A wise smile played at the corners of her mouth as she continued to gaze dreamily toward the river, indifferent to Lupe's troubled glances.

"From here they are exactly the same," she said at last, her voice almost a whisper. "They're even blue like the plate. Maybe there's a little arched bridge near them, too."

Lupe's face brightened. "Yes," she said, relieved that Janey was beginning to talk sense. "There's a bridge where the highway crosses the river, only it hasn't got any arch."

Janey looked at her with heavy scorn. "Can't you ever make believe about things?" she asked. "I don't mean an old highway bridge. I mean a little bridge with a house by it, like there is in the plate."

Lupe shook her head slowly. "I don't know about that. Maybe there's a house there. I can ask my father."

"No, don't." Janey spoke quickly. "I'd rather not know if there isn't one. And if I don't know for sure, I can keep on playing there's one."

Lupe surveyed Janey with real interest. It was funny the way this strange girl talked almost as if she saw things other people couldn't see. Lupe wasn't altogether certain that it was safe to be too friendly with that kind of person. Maybe she was just queer and therefore to be avoided. But she didn't look queer, and it was sort of fun to hear her talk. You couldn't tell what she would say next. She sounded like somebody out of a storybook or a movie. Lupe had never been around anyone like this before, and she found the experience rather pleasantly exciting. In Janey, thoughtful now over something that Lupe was at a loss to understand, she could sense a difference that set this newcomer apart from all other people. Weighing the matter slowly and carefully, Lupe decided at last that she liked Janey in spite of her difference. On the heels of that decision came the hope that the Larkins wouldn't soon move away.

A tired voice behind them put an end to Lupe's thoughts and recalled Janey from her daydreams.

"You can hang these clothes out along the fence now, Janey."

Lupe hesitated for a moment, undecided what her position as visitor demanded in such a situation. Then her natural courtesy came to the rescue. "I'd help you, Janey, only, if I put Betty down, she'll start to cry."

"That's all right," said Janey absently. Her eyes were still on the river.

Lupe edged out the back door. "Come over to my house when you get through," she said, adding, "The plate is real pretty, and I hope you stay here for a long time."

Janey didn't reply immediately, but continued to stand quietly gazing out the back door. Puzzled, Lupe began to move away, wondering if her polite little speech had been heard at all.

At length, with a start, Janey became aware of her guest's departure and turned to Lupe like someone just awakened from sleep. The little Mexican girl with Betty in her arms had already covered half the distance to the corner of the house, the baby looking back owlishly over her sister's shoulder.

"Thanks, Lupe. I hope we stay here, too," Janey called to her just as Lupe rounded the corner and disappeared from sight.

Then Janey went over to the tub of clean clothes, picked it up, and started with it to the back door. But she didn't go directly outside. Instead, she halted in the doorway and stood there musing, while the tub pulled her thin arms straight. At that very instant there had come over her the distinct feeling that something fine had happened. Not just the feeling she always had when looking at the willow plate that something fine was about to happen. This time it actually had. Lupe had said she hoped they would stay! It was the first time anyone had ever said that to Janey. A new warmth was encircling her heart, the kind of warmth that comes there only when one has found a friend. She stood perfectly still to let the full joy of the discovery travel all through her. It didn't really matter now that Lupe had thought the river willows different from those in the plate. Lupe had actually said she hoped they would stay! At that moment Janey would have forgiven her anything.

She turned back into the room. "Lupe's nice, isn't she?" She sounded almost fearful. Everything depended on Mom's answer.

"She's a very well mannered child," said Mrs. Larkin without enthusiasm.

But Janey was more than satisfied. She started away with the tub, a smile on her lips. While the Larkins remained in this place, Janey would have a friend. No longer would she have to feel lonely. There would be Lupe as well as the willow plate. And with that thought, Janey walked out into the blazing sunlight, her step as light as the washtub would permit.

The Tale of the Lazy People

by Charles J. Finger

Have you ever wondered how the jungle got so many monkeys?

In Colombia, it seems, there were always monkeys, at least as far as the memory of man goes. An old historian named Oviedo noted, "When the Christians make an expedition to the interior and have to pass by woods, they ought to cover themselves well with their shields . . . for the monkeys throw down nuts and branches at them. . . . I knew one, a servant. This man threw a stone at a monkey, who caught it and returned it with such force that it knocked out four or five of Francisco's teeth, and I know this to be true for I often saw the said Francisco, always without his teeth."

Now one day a man told me the tale of the monkeys, and he talked and talked until the stars came out and shone clear and steady and the air was heavy with perfume, and owls and bats floated strangely, as they will do, and when he had finished he still talked, making a long affair of a short matter, picking out a piece here and another there. But here is the meat of the story.

Long, long ago there were no monkeys, and the trees were so full of fruit, and the vines of grapes, that the people became lazy. At last they did little but eat and sleep, being too idle to carry away the rinds and skins of the fruit they lived on, and too lazy to clean their thatched houses.

It was very pleasant at first, but soon winged things that bit and stung came in thousands to feed on the things thrown aside, and they, too, grew lazy, finding so much to eat ready at hand; and when people tried to brush them away, there was a loud and angry buzz and much irritated stinging, so that soon no one knew what to do. For a time it seemed easier to move the village to a new spot and to build new houses, for the dwellings were light affairs and in a day or less a good house could be built. But then they lived by a lake from which the water for drinking was taken, and as it was but a little body of water, it was not long before the people had built right around it and so were back again at the starting place. The stinging flies were soon worse than the mosquitoes, while a great wasp was worst of all. So there was much talk and much argument, and the people agreed that something had to be done, and that very soon.

One day there came to the village a queer and rather faded kind of man, ragged and tattered and torn, as though he had scrambled for miles through the thornbush forest. He had rough yellow hair, and queer wrinkles at the corners of his eyes, which made him look as if he were smiling. It was late in the afternoon when he came and the people were still taking their rest after the noon meal, so no one took much notice of him, although he went here and there, looking at things, and so walked around the lake. But the curiosity of everyone was excited when he was seen to make a basket and then commence to gather up the fruit skins and rinds in one place. Now and then someone or other raised himself in his hammock, with a mind to talk to him, but it seemed almost too much trouble, and when some great blue-winged butterfly fluttered past or some golden-throated hummingbird flashed in the sunlight, his eyes wandered away from the old man and he forgot him again. So the sunlight died and the forest was a velvet blackness and everyone slept, except the old man. The next morning he was still working diligently, though he had but a small place cleared.

The headman was very curious to know why the stranger went to so much trouble, seeing that he neither lived there nor was of the lake men. So Tera, the headman, called to Cuco, who was his servant, telling him to bring the stranger to him, and Cuco did his part by calling Yana and delivering the message to him. And Yana in turn told his servant, Mata, who told his servant, Pera, who told his servant, Racas, who told a boy, so that at last the message reached the old man. Then back went the old man, handed by the boy to Racas, by Racas to Pera, by Pera to Mata, by Mata to Yana, and by Yana to Cuco, so that at last he stood before Tera, the headman; and the others, being curious to know what was afoot, gathered about.

"What is your name, from where do you come, and what do you want?" asked Tera, putting his three questions at once, to save trouble. Then the headman looked at those about him with a little frown, as much as to say, Note how wisely I act; and each man nodded at his neighbor. But the little old man was quite unimpressed with the greatness of the great man.

"I want to work," he answered. "I want to be told what you want done and to see that it is done."

The language that he spoke was one new to those who listened, but somehow they seemed to understand. But the thing that he said they found truly astonishing. The headman, though as astonished as anyone there, quickly regained his composure and asked, "What is your trade?"

"I have no trade," said the old man. "But I get things done."

"What kind of things?"

"All kinds of things."

"Do you mean big things, like housebuilding and all that?" asked the headman.

"Yes. And little things, too, which are really big things when you come to consider," said the old man, but that seemed an odd thing to say, the headman thought.

"Little things left undone soon become big things," explained the old man, and waved his hand in the direction of a heap of fruit skins and husks nearby.

"Yes. Yes. But you must not preach to us, you know," said Tera a little testily. "Tell me the names of your trades."

So the little old man began to tell, naming big things and very little things, things important and things not important at all, and having finished, asked politely whether anyone there had anything to be done.

Then Pera said, "If you work for me, I will let you have one fish out of every ten that you catch, for I am a fisherman."

And Racas pushed him aside, saying, "But I will do better, for I am supposed to be a fruit gatherer and will give you two things for every ten you gather."

And so it went, each bidding higher than his neighbor, until it came to the turn of the man whose duty it was to gather the rinds and fruit skins. He said, "I will let you have ten out of ten if you will work for me." At that the old man said quite positively that he would take no pay at all.

No more was said then, and the little old man turned away without so much as bowing to the headman; seeing which, the headman waved his hand and said, "You may go, and so that you will lose no time, you need not bow to me."

And all the rest gathered there said very hastily, "Nor to me, either."

The old man went away singing, for he had a gay, lighthearted disposition; and having reached the place he had cleared, he took flat pieces of wood and began cutting out figures like little men, and each figure had a kind of handle that looked like a long tail. Nor did he cease whittling until he had made at least twenty wooden figures for each man and woman in the village. Being finished, he stood up to stretch his legs and straighten his back, and when the people asked him what the little figures were for, he shrugged his shoulders but spoke never a word. Then he lifted the figures that he had made, one by one, and set them upright in the sand until there was a long row of them, and took his place in front of them like a general before his army. It was beautiful to look at, for one figure was as like another as one pin is like another. After a moment the old man waved his hand in a peculiar way, spoke some magic word, and waved his hand again, at which each of the figures came to life and nodded its head; seeing which, all the people laughed and clapped their hands. The ragged man bade them make no noise, but watch.

"Since you do not like to work," he said, "I have made twenty figures for each of you, and they will work for you without pay, doing what you require them to do; only you must not give any figure more than one particular job. Now let each man or woman clap three times, then call out the name of the thing to be done."

When he had said this, the figures started running, twenty gathering in a circle about each man and woman there, bowing from the hips and straightening themselves again, so that their tails of wood went up and down like pump handles.

"Now see," said the ragged man, "you have things to work for you, and as I call out, the figures will stand forth, each ready to do his task." And he began calling, thus: "Armadillo hunters, stand forth!" and a hundred and more active figures ran together like soldiers.

So he named others in order as

Breadmakers
Cassava gatherers
Despolvadores, who would gather up dust
Esquiladores, who would shear the goats
Farsantes, whose work was to amuse tired people
Guardas, to keep order about the place
Horneros, or bakers
Industriosos, who were to do odd jobs
Jumentos, who were to carry burdens
Labradores, to do heavy work and clear away garbage
Moledores, to grind the corn
Narradores, who told stories, related gossip, and so on
Olleros, or potmakers
Pocilga figures, to attend to the pigs
Queseros, to make cheese from goat's milk
Rumbosos, or proud-looking things to walk in parades
Servidores, or food carriers
Trotadores, to run errands
Vaqueros, to attend to the cows

So everyone was well pleased, and each one had his twenty figures to do all that needed to be done, and all that day there was a great scraping and cleaning and carrying and currying and hurrying and scurrying. Silently the little figures worked, never stopping, never tiring, never getting in one another's way, and all that the living people had to do was to rest and watch the men of wood and keep their brains free for higher things. For it must be understood that before the old man came there with his wonderful gift, the people had complained that there was so much to be done that they had no time to write poems or to make songs or to create music; and they had said that with the daily tasks abolished their brains would be more active.

Not two days had passed before the children of the place complained that they had so much to do, what with hunting for things lost, looking after their small brothers and sisters, keeping things in order, trying to remember things they were told, cleaning things, and a dozen other tasks, that they really had no time to play, much less to study. So they went in a body to the old man and asked him to give each child twenty figures to do odd things. So the old man whittled out many, many more figures, and in another twenty-four hours each and every boy and girl had his own

Abaniquero, or fanmaker, so that none had to pluck a palm leaf
Baliquero figure, to carry messages
Cabrero, to look after the goats
Desalumbrado, to hunt for things in the dark
Enseñador, or private teacher, who was never to scold
Florista, to save them the trouble of gathering flowers
Guasón figure, to amuse them
Hojaldrista, to make cakes
Juego figure, to arrange games
Keeper of things
Lector, to read and tell stories
Mimo, to act as clown
Niñera, to look after younger children
Obediencia figure, to make others obey
Postor, to buy things for them
Quitar figure, to take things away when children tired
Recordación figure, or rememberer
Solfeador, to sing to them
Tortada man, to make pies
Volante, as servant

Before a month had passed, in all that place there was not a thing out of order, soiled, broken, bent, lost, misplaced, undone, unclean, or disorderly. Neither man nor woman nor child had to worry. Dinners were always prepared, fruits gathered, beds made, houses in perfect order, and all was spick-and-span. All that the grown-up people had to do was to look on, and no one was proud of the order in his house because every other house in the place was as orderly. As for the children, they had nothing at all to do but to eat, drink, rest, and sleep. Then, presently, more figures were called for as this one or that wanted a larger house, a finer garden, or grander clothes.

But as the wooden figures became more numerous, and as no figure could do more than one task, the ragged man had to make figures for the figures and servants for the servants; for as things went on, there had to be more fruit gatherers, more water carriers, more scavengers, more cooks, because the figures had to eat and drink. Thus it came to pass that before long, instead of there being twenty figures for each person, there were sixty or seventy, with new ones coming from the old man's knife every day. Soon the lively manikins were everywhere, inside houses as well as outside, thick as flies in summer and certainly a great deal more persistent, for there could be no closing of doors against the manikins. Indeed, had anything like that been attempted, there would have been a great cry for special door openers. So, many houses were quite cluttered with wooden men, those who were on duty rushing about until it made the head swim to look at them, and those who were resting or sleeping; for soon they learned to rest and to sleep, lying about the floors, piled up in corners, or hanging from rafters by their tails. All that increase in help had made for the production of a thousand or more *guardas,* whose task it was to keep order; and they were everywhere, alert and watchful and officious, and the real people had to step about very gingerly sometimes, to avoid treading on them and annoying them.

At last there came a day when the people began to grow a little tired of doing nothing, and they told one another that a little help was a very good thing, but help in excess was too much of a good thing altogether. So there was a meeting and much talk, and the manikin *narradores*, whose duty it was to carry gossip and the news, were very busy rushing from here to there with their scraps of information.

"It is very clear that something must be done," said Tera, the headman.

"But everything *is* being done," answered the little old man.

"You see, the days are so very long, so very dull," said the man who had wished to have time that he might become a poet. "At the shut of day we are not weary."

"We do not want to be petted," said another.

"The trouble is," sighed a fat man, "you can't be happy when everything is done for you."

Another said very mournfully, "It seems to me that when these wooden things do things with our things, then the things that they do and make and care for are not our things."

"Too many 'things' in that speech," said the fat man.

"Well, there are too many things," answered the other. "Look at me. I used to be gardener and now I'm nothing. When my garden is dug and planted and tended and watered and the very flowers plucked by these wooden things, then my garden does not seem to be mine." He added after a while, "I hope you know what I mean, because it is not very clear to me, yet it is so. I remember—"

At that the little old man put up his hand and said, "You must not try to remember, really you must not, because there are manikins to do all the remembering, if you please."

"Well, but I think—" began the man.

"Please do not think," said the little old man. "We have things to do the thinking, if you please." He thought for a moment, his bent forefinger on his lips, then he said, "I'll see what can be done. It is clear that you are not satisfied, although you have everything that you asked for and certainly all the time that you want."

"Let us do something," murmured Tera.

"I'm afraid there is nothing that you can do," said the little old man, "because, as you see, everything is done, and when everything is done it is quite clear that something cannot be left to be done. The only thing that is clear is that there is nothing to be done."

At that the meeting broke up and each went to his own hammock to think things over, and soon the general cry was, "We must have elbowroom." And hearing that, the little old man went to work and whittled more figures of wood, a whole army of them, ten for each living man, woman, and child, and in voices that creaked like wooden machinery they marched hither and thither, crying, "Elbowroom. Elbowroom!"

Soon there was confusion. It was manikin against manikin for a time, the elbowroomers thrusting and pushing the other working manikins, some going about their work with frantic haste, others interfering with them, clutching at them and at the things they carried, a tangled knot of them sometimes staggering, to go down with a crash. Soon in every house was a jangling tumult, manikins and men running about inside and dashing out into the open spaces outside; the noise of slamming doors and breaking pots; the clamor of animals. Above all could be heard everywhere cries of "We want elbowroom! We want elbowroom!"

Soon men were running away from the houses, with those strange swift manikins hanging on to them, sometimes beating them, while other manikins threw things out the doors and through the windows, food and household things. And excited children fled, too, while their manikins ran at their sides, some chattering, some acting the clown as was their duty, some telling stories as they ran, while other strange little figures of wood ran bearing heavy burdens.

Everywhere the manikins who were *guardas*, or order keepers, ran about, tripping people and manikins alike in the effort to stop the rush. But when the day was near its end, there were no people in the houses, and the hammocks swung idly, for all the men and women and children had fled to the farther side of the lake, where they could have elbowroom, leaving the houses and all that was in them to the manikins.

The next day, the people plucked their fruit for themselves, and it seemed as though fruit was never sweeter. The water that they carried from the lake tasted better and cooler than water had for many a long day, and when night came they were happily tired and slept well, without any manikin to swing their hammocks and sing to them. And in the morning they woke early to discover the pink and gold of the sunrise most wonderful to see, and there was music in the sound of the wind among the grasses.

So, as the day passed, they were both amazed and astonished at the wonderful and beautiful things that they had almost forgotten, the sight of butterflies fluttering from flower to flower, the shadows chasing across the hills, the richness of the green earth and the blueness of the sky, the gold of sunlight on the leaves, the rippling water, and the bending trees; indeed the memory of the manikin days was like a fearful nightmare. Very lighthearted then they grew, and the world was full of the music of their laughter and song; and briskly they worked, enjoying it all, building new houses and making things to put in them.

Meanwhile in the village things had gone queerly. For one thing the elbowroomers kept up their crowding and pushing, so that the manikins trying to work at their old tasks were sadly hindered. There were other figures of wood with nothing to do, since the people they served were gone, and these fell to quarreling among themselves and grew mischievous. For instance, the potmakers and the pot cleaners fell out, and the pot cleaners started to break the pots so that the potmakers would have more work to do. That meant that the clay gatherers and the clay diggers had to work harder; then, because they worked harder, they grew hungrier and wanted more to eat. Because of all that, the fruit gatherers had more to do and the breadmakers had to bake as they had never baked before. That meant the wood gatherers also had to work harder and to eat more, so still more work came on the food bringers. And all the time the elbowroomers rushed about, always in groups of ten, driving and commanding, rushing on workers and sweeping them aside. So everywhere were little figures hurrying one after the other, busy about nothing, fighting about nothing.

The trouble came when the elbowroomers interfered with the dogs and the cats, the goats and the hens, pushing and hustling them. For the animals, disliking all the disorder and clatter, fell upon the manikins, workers and idlers alike. Seeing that, the household utensils took a hand, and the very pots and kettles ran or rolled or fell, spilling hot water over the wooden things with pump-handle tails. The very embers from the fires leaped into the fray. All the while from the grinding stones in which the corn had been ground came a low growling, and the growling formed itself into words:

"Day by day you tortured us—
Grind, grind, grind.

Bring to us the torturers—
Grind, grind, grind.

Let them feel our power now—
Grind. Grind. GRIND!"

So the stones turned and turned, going around and around without hands, and presently an elbowroomer that was struggling with a corn grinder stumbled, and both fell between the grinding stones and in a moment were crushed to powder. In a flash, house utensils and animals learned the new trick, and in every house manikins were pushed into the grinding stones. Then sparks began to fly and roofs to catch on fire, and manikins bolted here and there in confusion, sometimes jamming in doorways, there were so many and all in such disorder. Then came dazzling, flickering lightning and a great rain, so that for safety the manikins fled to the forest and climbed the trees. And there they have lived ever since, for they grew hair and became monkeys.

But the remembrance of all that passed stayed with them, and in their hearts to this very day is no love for man. For that very reason, when a Christian passes through a forest he must look well to himself, lest the manikins in revenge try to hurt him by casting nuts and branches at his head.

A Look at the Grand Champ

by Harold Webster Perry

Three hundred pounds of bucking calf is a lot to capture. Sammy was sure it was worth the fight.

Sammy Bledsoe never took his keen brown eyes off the livestock judges as they walked slowly around the sleek steer he was holding by the halter. Having examined it carefully, the judges moved toward the center of the arena for a whispered conference. Sammy tried to calm his restless charge by running one hand soothingly along the animal's neck. This was his first entry in the 4-H Club exhibit at the Farview Fair, and he was intensely proud of it.

Standing beside the red steer, his round, freckled face appearing just above the fat animal's back, Sammy tried not to show his nervous eagerness as the conference proceeded.

"Gee whillikers, but they sure take their time!" he groaned. This crucial pause was almost too much for his fourteen years. He tried to control himself by gazing about at the spectators in the stands surrounding the huge arena but saw only a blurred sea of faces.

At this moment the steer unaccountably threw up its head and snorted and tried to start away. Pulling hard on the halter rope with both hands, Sammy dug his heels into the ground to try to hold back the animal. The steer's excitement seemed to die away almost immediately, and it became docile again. Unnoticed, and without intending it, Sammy had come quite near to the whispering judges. As he placed a gentling hand upon the steer, he heard part of the judges' conference—but that one fragment was enough to dull his spirits: "Seems a shame to have put such expert care and feeding on an inferior animal."

When the judging was over, Sammy found his way out of the arena and led his losing steer back to the allotted stall. There the tears could be held back no longer, and he sank upon a bale of hay in utter abandonment to his grief.

It wasn't that he hadn't done his best, thought Sammy. What an argument he'd had with Dad a year ago about fattening a calf for this exhibit! He'd saved the money earned from chores done for Mr. Lander, a mile down the road, and wanted to use it to purchase a calf from the father of his chum Phil Roberts. Mr. Roberts raised highbred stock. But Dad wouldn't stand for it. Dad wasn't sympathetic toward the idea of well-bred stock. To him, a critter was a critter.

His father had finally given Sammy a likely-looking calf from his own herd. How proud the boy had been! A calf of his own to feed! He recalled how surprised Dad had been when, wanting to feel the calf was fully his, Sammy had insisted on paying his father for it from the chore money. Dad had met the proposal with a sputtering refusal but in the end reluctantly agreed to accept half the animal's value. Dad was really swell!

From his chore money, Sammy had bought all the feed for the calf during the year, though between school and the chores at Mr. Lander's he had been hard pressed to find daylight hours to give the animal attention. But he had stuck to it and had gradually fed and fattened the calf until even Dad had shown a reluctant enthusiasm when he entered the steer in the 4-H Club exhibit at the fair.

And now that calf had failed to win because of its inferior quality. If Dad had only let him get one of Mr. Roberts' calves. What was it the judges had said about expert care and feeding? The recollection served somewhat to soothe his aching heart.

There was a commotion at the end of the big barn as the door swung open, and Sammy sat up to learn its cause. Down the aisle by the stalls came Phil Roberts, leading his steer and surrounded by an enthusiastic group of boys and men. Phil was beaming and fairly strutting as he led the fat animal up to its stall just next to Sammy's.

"Hi, Sammy," he called proudly. "Look!" He held forth a purple ribbon.

"Four-H Grand Champion!" yelled an admirer.

"Congratulations!" cried Sammy sincerely, rushing over to shake Phil's hand.

"Your dad sure must have swell stock," said a boyish bystander.

"Ha-ha!" Phil laughed. "This wasn't a calf from his herd. I won this animal here last year in the boys' calf contest. Those are real highbred calves they give away."

Then, noticing Sammy's face, which still showed traces of the tears, Phil quickly slipped an arm about his chum's shoulders as they walked along. "Buck up, Sammy," he said. "Those judges said you'd fed your steer like an expert."

Sammy struggled to subdue his own feelings in his effort to be glad for his friend's success.

"They said you were pretty good yourself," he replied. "And they nailed their words fast with a purple ribbon. Jeepers, I'm sure glad you won, Phil!"

"It was nothin'. I got the swellest calf in the contest last year. . . . Listen, Sammy! You're eligible for the calf contest this year. You get one of those calves and then show 'em what you can do!"

In his disappointment Sammy had forgotten about that. The boys' calf contest was to be held in the arena during the rodeo performance the following afternoon. Every year the businessmen of Farview contributed money for the purchase of twenty purebred steer calves. These were released in the arena, and the 4-H boys tried to capture them. Those who won calves would take them home, feed them according to 4-H Club instruction, and then exhibit them the following year. The purpose was to stimulate in these potential stockmen the desire for better-bred stock. The contest was open to all 4-H Club boys under sixteen who were exhibitors of cattle at the fair.

Sammy's disappointment was forgotten. He'd get a calf! See if he didn't! And next year those old judges wouldn't get together and whisper that he had brought a scrub to the fair. He'd show them!

Sitting in the truck with his father, Sammy could hardly wait for the ten-mile ride out to the farm to end. He wanted to practice on some of the calves at home—practice throwing them and slipping a halter over their heads. He was in a more cheerful mood. His own steer had been purchased at a good price by a packer-buyer who knew properly fed, solid flesh when he saw it.

"That buyer knows more than all those judges," said Mr. Bledsoe as they drove along, eager to console the boy for his loss.

"No, he doesn't, Dad," replied Sammy. "He knew the steer had been well fed, but I know it didn't have the"—he struggled to master the word—"the conformation. I was just hopeful," he added bravely. They drove on in silence.

As they neared the farm, Sammy said, "I've learned a lot about feeding this past year, from the Four-H Club lessons and practicing on the steer. If I can get one of those calves in the contest tomorrow, I'll bring 'em back a steer next year that will make the judges' eyes pop out!"

The remainder of the afternoon was a trying one for the two four-month-old calves that Sammy drove into the corral. He practiced on them alternately, chasing each about the corral, grabbing it around the neck, struggling sometimes to throw the calf down and at other times merely to put a halter on the reluctant animal while it was still standing. Then he would lead it, haltingly and much against its will, first to one corner of the corral and then another, experimenting with different methods of making the stubborn beast move forward each time it balked.

Mr. Bledsoe paused by the corral fence from time to time to observe the progress being made. After watching his son fairly drag one of the calves into each of the four corners of the corral in turn, he asked, "What do you want to spend so much time leading them around for? Isn't the calf in the contest yours when you get a halter on him?"

"No, he isn't," Sammy answered. "You also have to lead the calf out of the arena. He isn't yours till you've got him through the gate. Lots of the fellows lose theirs when they've led them almost out." He slipped the halter from the calf, and it bounded to the far corner of the corral.

"Those contest calves," Sammy continued, "are wild critters. They walk along quietly for a ways, and then all of a sudden they'll give a wild plunge and yank the halter right out of your hands."

"Well, son," said Mr. Bledsoe as he turned away, "it's nearly dark. I guess you had better call it a day."

The band on its platform at one end of the big arena struck up a march, and the rodeo performance of the afternoon was on. Every seat was filled, and hundreds of spectators jostled each other in the space between the seats and the fence encircling the arena. Then the gate at the far end swung wide, and the parade of prizewinning cattle began.

Sammy, sitting beside his father near the center, fidgeted uneasily. He would have to leave his seat soon to be ready with the other boys in the calf contest. After the parade of prizewinning cattle came the steer wrestling, followed by the trick and fancy riding, and then the calf contest.

The huge arena seemed to be full of fat cattle now, winding in and out as they trudged along on their short legs, some snorting and tugging at their halter ropes, but most of them peacefully following the men who led them.

Sammy watched the bulldogging with a critical eye, noting how the cowboys leaped from their horses to the steers' necks and then twisted the heads of the animals until they fell to their sides with their feet out.

"They're lucky to have those long horns to hold on to," said Sammy. "Those calves don't have much horns."

As the steer-wrestling event ended, Sammy hurried out to the place appointed for the 4-H contestants to assemble. He was surprised to find nearly fifty boys were there. Competition was going to be keen. Phil was there, too, hoping to have another turn of good fortune. A good deal of boasting was going on.

But all talk was ended by the appearance of an official to summon the boys to the arena. Sammy clenched his halter tightly as he crowded with the young mob through the gate at one end. He saw a big cattle truck pull into the far end of the arena. From its rear, men led down a chute twenty frisky, three-hundred-pound Hereford calves, wild critters just off the range, who kept two horsemen busy to keep them marshaled against the end fence as the truck drove away.

From the loudspeaker boomed a voice explaining the rules of the contest: "While a boy has a hold on a calf, no other boy is allowed to interfere. Should the calf get away from the boy, any other boy may then try to capture it. Remember, it is not sufficient merely to get the halter on the calf; the boy must lead him from the arena."

The boys lined up on a tape stretched across the ground; the whistle blew, and they all surged forward. The horsemen rode quickly away from the calves, and the wild young animals, seeing the yelling mob of boys charging down upon them, scattered in all directions. Some of the larger boys were swifter than Sammy and reached the first calves ahead of him, but he hurried on.

Suddenly a heavy body struck him from the rear, knocking him to the ground. It fell upon him, driving the wind out of him. As he turned his head to get his face out of the dirt, a hoof shot across his shoulder and to the ground right before

his nose. "Hot doggie!" he gasped as, with what little strength he had left, he quickly grasped the leg, and held on for dear life.

The animal had jerked backward to free itself from another boy and in doing so had knocked Sammy down, the impact causing it to lose its balance and fall upon him. Now, regaining its feet, it struggled to free itself from its new captor. Sammy, pretty well winded, managed to swing around enough to throw his other arm about the calf's neck, but he did not have the strength to rise to his feet. Jiminy, but a three-hundred-pound calf is strong, he thought, as the beast, backing around in circles in its efforts to extricate its head, dragged him along the ground.

Suddenly the calf gave one lunge forward and immediately jerked back again and, wresting itself free from the still winded lad, went bucking and bounding away, leaving Sammy sprawled in the dirt. He raised himself to his knees, much chagrined, to see a dozen other boys chasing the calf about the center of the arena.

Slowly Sammy got to his feet, clenching wads of dirt in both hands, trying not to show the disappointment that was almost overwhelming him. There was not another calf he could see that did not have a boy attached to it. Most of the contests were still in the wrestling stage; in some instances both calf and boy were down, struggling on the ground, while in others the boy was on the ground, merely holding on, and the animal was on its feet, doing all the wrestling. A few boys had got their halters on their calves and, with varying degrees of success, were leading them toward the gate. Some had given in easily and were consenting to be led; others balked with all the art of a disconsolate mule.

Then Sammy noticed Phil wrestling with a calf almost in the center.

"Them that has, gits!" muttered Sammy bitterly. He had read that somewhere. Then, realizing Phil was in no way to blame for his own misfortune, Sammy rebuked himself. Phil had as much right as he to try to get a calf. He walked slowly toward his chum.

There seemed to be no love lost between Phil and his calf. Both were down, rolling in the dirt. Phil had one arm around the animal's neck and was holding a foreleg with the other hand. Whenever he tried to let go of the leg to reach for his halter, the calf pawed him vigorously in the chest with the free hoof.

Suddenly, when Phil seemed to have the damaging hoof blocked and reached for the halter, the calf jerked back abruptly and caught the boy off-balance. Its head slipped from Phil's arm, and it plunged away.

"Gee!" exclaimed Sammy. "He's lost his calf, too!"

Instantly he realized that the animal was charging straight toward him. It was almost upon him! But it swerved sharply and galloped in a new direction.

Sammy did not hesitate. Taking a few swift strides, he made a flying tackle. He threw both arms about the calf's neck as he struck it. The force of the impact brought both boy and calf to the ground.

The crowd roared. Loud applause, mingled with yells of "Attaboy!" "Hold him, cowboy!" and similar expressions of enthusiasm, rolled out across the arena, but Sammy was too busy to hear. He and the calf were enveloped in a rising cloud of dust, and it was difficult for a moment to tell what was occurring.

The wily critter quickly regained its feet and began backing, trying to draw its head from the locked arms. But this time Sammy was not winded, and he held on. If he could just regain his feet and still keep both arms tightly about the calf's neck! Boy! He'd made it! Now where was that halter? He'd dropped it when he made his flying tackle.

Fortunately it was not far away, and with a little tugging he got the calf over where he might stoop down and pick it up. With one arm tightly locked around the beast's neck, he bent slowly down and reached for the halter. The calf did not budge. It even stood contentedly while Sammy slipped the halter over its head and fastened it. A roar of applause went up from the audience, and Sammy realized for the first time that he had for the moment been the center of attraction.

That was easy, Sammy assured himself. Mister calf seems to like me, so getting him through the gate will be a cinch.

As they neared the gate of triumph, the calf gave one wild, sudden lunge and started off to the side. It took Sammy completely by surprise, and the halter rope slipped through his fingers. Terrified, he gripped the rope tightly just as the knot at the end reached his hand.

The sudden jerk had the effect of a cracking whip, with Sammy the end of the whip. The calf had the advantage of a running start when the rope became taut, and Sammy did a complete somersault followed by a headlong dive into the dirt, his face acting as a sort of plow, and his two arms stretched out ahead of him—but still holding the rope.

The tense silence that had spread over the audience at the unexpected upset turned quickly into a sigh of relief, grew into a murmur of gratification, and finally rose into a combined cheer.

The calf began kicking up its heels, bucking and circling around Sammy as a hub. After several efforts and new tumbles into the dirt, Sammy managed to regain his feet, but the calf continued its antics.

"Well! You're sure a regular buster bronco!" Sammy gasped as he tried to haul in on the halter rope.

In a moment the crafty beast suddenly stopped bucking and set into a dead run, gaining speed as it circled around and around the boy. The increased whirling made Sammy dizzy, and he fell again. In rising, he gave a little slack to the rope, and the calf, feeling this, swerved suddenly and made a dash directly toward the fence, yanking Sammy, who had not yet braced himself, stumbling after it.

But the animal's goal wasn't just the fence; it was the big gate! As this suddenly swung wide, calf and boy shot through, while the crowd roared!

Beyond the gate were friendly hands to help, and laughing men held the bucking calf while Sammy wiped some of the dirt out of his eyes and felt of himself carefully to see what bones were broken. It appeared that except for dirt and bruises he was intact.

"You sure earned this calf, buddy," said one of the men holding it. "It's a fine one, too. You can tell that even through the dirt."

The calf was nearly black with dirt, but Sammy didn't mind. He slipped both arms about the animal's neck—lovingly now. The calf was his—his!

"You bet your boots he's a fine calf," he said proudly. "He's a regular buster. . . . That's it! I'll call him Buster!"

Phil came running up. "Swell work, Sammy! Did you hear the crowd roar? You sure put on a star performance!"

Sammy felt a little embarrassed. "Phil," he said hesitatingly, "I'm sorry I got your calf."

"Aw, bugs!" said Phil. "It wasn't your fault he got away from me. And if I couldn't have him, I'm glad you could."

Together the chums guided the calf across the lot and into the barn toward Sammy's allotted stall. There in the stall adjoining was Phil's Grand Champion—nine hundred pounds of fat steer, standing contentedly on its short legs as it calmly chewed its cud and regarded them with soft eyes.

"Whoa, Buster!" said Sammy, pulling on his calf's halter. "Wait a minute!" He shoved the calf around until it faced the Grand Champion.

"Look, Buster," he said. "See that big fat steer? Take a good long look! I just want you to see what can be done!"

Tony Beaver

by Anne Malcolmson

Tony was tall, all right. But not so tall as this tale.

Tony Beaver, the great lumberjack of the South, lived "up Eel River." You won't find Eel River on any maps. The geographers haven't decided where to put it. The people of Louisiana and Arkansas are sure that it's in the cypress swamps. Georgians are just as sure that it's in the turpentine hills. North Carolinians insist that it's in the Smoky Mountains. But West Virginians, who know most about Tony, say that Eel River is high up in their own Alleghenies.

It's not hard to visit the camp, however, if you really wish to see it. Just send word to the lumberjack himself by the next jaybird you see, and Tony will send his path after you.

By the way, this path has an interesting story. One autumn day long ago, as Tony Beaver walked through the woods, something tickled his legs. It felt smooth and ribbony, like a snake. He tried to brush it off, but it clung to his boots and licked at his laces. Glancing down, he saw a baby path, dancing, frisking, romping around him. Tony searched the bushes, expecting to find a mother road nearby. But the path was all alone.

From the way the little fellow wagged its tail and jumped up and down, Tony guessed that it must be lonely. From the looks of its stones and weeds, which hadn't been brushed in a long time, he knew it lacked a mother's care. It was obviously an orphan, just a poor little orphan path that led from Somewhere to Nowhere.

Tony took a fancy to it and carried it gently back to Eel River. Here he gave it food and brushed the cockleburs out of its grasses. He let it sleep in front of the fire. In time it became the camp pet. The boys were fond of the clever little thing and taught it a number of tricks. When it became old enough and strong enough, Tony made it his special messenger.

The path still has one bad habit, which Tony has never been able to cure. It likes speed. It skims over the hills and down the valleys like a runaway roller coaster. Some timid people who have visited Eel River say they'd rather spend the rest of their lives at camp than ride home on that streak of greased lightning.

If you aren't too shaken up when you get there, you will find Eel River an unusual logging camp. It's very large, in the first place. After all, Tony and his jacks are big men.

In the second place, the bunkhouses look like overgrown watermelons. Instead of the square log buildings you find in Minnesota and Maine, these are shaped like footballs. Their outer walls are smooth and green, their inner walls soft and pink. The bunks and chairs are carved from the same hard black material as the fireplaces. In case you think your eyes are spoofing you, the bunkhouses really are watermelons.

Before Tony became interested in logging, he had a melon farm. He grew fruit so huge that the hands had to use bucksaws to cut them from the vines. The only trouble with them was they were too big to haul to market. Tony had to think about that problem for several days. While he was thinking, he sat by his fire and smoked his pipe. The clouds of black smoke rising from his corncob made the people of Arkansas hide in their cellars. They thought a tornado was blowing up.

Finally Tony figured it out. He built a railroad right up to the melon patch. Three flatcars were hitched together. The smallest melon was rolled aboard. The engine chugged off with Tony Beaver sitting on top of his prize, as proud as you please.

Unfortunately, the tracks ran up a steep grade and down again in a hairpin turn. The engineer forgot to be careful. The cars lurched against the hillside. The cargo wobbled unsteadily. Then, whang! The melon, Tony and all, rolled off the flatcars, down the hill, and splashed into Eel River with a kerplunk that caused a flood as far away as New Orleans.

The force with which it hit the water broke the melon into a thousand pieces. For hours the river churned red. It looked as though Tony had been drowned. But, no! He simply pulled himself up on one of the seeds and paddled ashore.

As the other seeds floated downstream they caught against the dam by the sawmill. The jam there gave Tony an idea. He made a bargain with the miller, who cut them up into planks and sold them for hardwood. Thus Tony Beaver became interested in the logging business.

He didn't want to waste the rest of those melons. He had his boys roll them to the edge of the field. They dug out the red meat, cut doors and windows, and put in chimneys. Then they built fireplaces of some seeds and carved others into furniture. Lo and behold! There stood as fine a set of bunkhouses as ever was!

The most interesting person at the Eel River Camp is, of course, Tony Beaver himself. He's too great a person to describe. You'll have to see him for yourselves. And until you do, you'll have to be satisfied with stories of some of the wonderful things he's done.

Some years after he'd given up farming and gone into the lumber business, Tony was brought again into the public eye. He still kept a small garden of a few thousand acres, on which he raised peanuts. His "goobers," as he called them, were sold at circuses and baseball games all over the United States. He had also a stand of molasses maple trees, which produced the sweetest, most delicious syrup you ever poured over a flapjack.

Tony Beaver never could learn to do things in a small way. One season he produced so many goobers and so much molasses that even he was swamped. The Eel River warehouses were bursting with unsold goods.

Then it began to rain. It rained for days and nights without stopping, until the hill country above Tony's private town of Eel River Landing was flooded. At first the townsfolk didn't mind. They found it entertaining to be able to sit on their own front porches and watch hen houses and church steeples sweeping past them downstream.

Still it poured. They began to be alarmed. Their own levees were about to break. It looked as though Eel River Landing itself might be washed out into the Gulf of Mexico.

A committee was elected and sent to ask Tony if he could do something to stop the flood. He shook hands with all the members and sat down in front of the bunkhouse fire to smoke his pipe and think. Soon a big idea came to him.

The members were sent home to bring all their friends and relations to the peanut warehouses. The loggers were sent to the molasses stores. Big Henry and

Sawdust Sam, his foreman, hitched the big oxen to the vinegar cruet and the salt box, and drove them to the riverside. Tony himself borrowed a wooden spoon from the cookhouse and followed after.

As soon as everyone had met, Tony gave his directions. The townsfolk shelled the peanuts as fast as they could and tossed the nuts into the river. The lumberjacks emptied the molasses barrels into the water from the other side. Sam dumped in the salt. Big Henry poured in the vinegar. Great Tony Beaver straddled the flood, one foot on one side, one on the other, and stirred that river for all he was worth.

The goobers and molasses stuck to the reeds. They clogged the riverbed. The current began to slacken. Eel River was oozing, not racing, toward the town.

Then the sun came out, the hot noonday sun. A sweet-smelling mist arose as its rays heated the mixture. Still Tony swished his spoon from bank to bank. Bubbles appeared gradually along the shores, little pearl bubbles at first, then big balloon bubbles. Finally the whole river boiled up. The steam rose higher than the mountains. The odor was delicious!

Tony's spoon churned faster and faster. As the river bubbled and hissed and spouted, its brown speckled waters thickened. From time to time the big lumberjack lifted his ladle and let it drip. Each time the drops fell more slowly, until at last one spun out into a fine hard thread.

With that, Tony Beaver tossed the spoon aside and jumped to the bank. With a jerk he yanked a cloud across the sun. Immediately the river cooled. The thick, sticky mass stopped seething and began to harden. The current had stopped completely. There above Eel River Landing stretched a dam and a broad lake, as brown and quiet and hard as a rock. Except for the white pebbly specks made by the goobers, it was as smooth as a skating rink.

The townsfolk cheered. A holiday was declared, and the committee gave Tony a vote of thanks for saving the village. The kids ran home for their ice skates. Soon everyone was gliding in and out among the peanut bumps. People for miles around came to help celebrate.

It was the best party West Virginia ever had, except that there were no refreshments. These were easily supplied, however. "Break yourself off a piece of the dam," Tony suggested to a hungry-looking youngster. "It tastes mighty good."

The boy thought Tony was joking. But when the big logger reached down and broke off a hunk, he agreed to try it. M-m-m-m! It certainly did taste good. One or two other brave fellows tried it. Soon there was a scramble for the sweet nutty stuff.

Tony had not only saved the town. He had invented peanut brittle.

Spurs for Antonia

by K. W. Eyre

Could the young girl from Boston earn a place on the cattle ranch? With help from her horse, Lucky, she hoped she could.

Down at the barn, the milk cows were beginning to stir and rustle in the sweet-smelling hay. Manuela's black hens were pulling their heads out from under their wings, but at the ranch house everyone was still asleep when Romero opened the kitchen door and tiptoed across the floor. He lighted the lamp on the shelf above the sink and looked quickly at the woodbox.

Good! Full to the top with oak chunks and fine, dry kindling. A hot blaze under the frying pan and coffeepot would be only a matter of seconds. Breakfast would be ready in a wink, in spite of Manuela's scoffing boast that she was the only one on the Aguas Vivas rancho who could cook a respectable meal. Better walk softly! She would take a rolling pin to him if he spoiled her sleep, that fat, lazy sister of his!

Coffee, eggs, warmed-over tortillas, and honey to spread on them, amber brown, from the hives in Sage Canyon. Romero nodded with satisfaction. He set the waxy honeycomb on the table, licked his sticky fingers, and poured milk in a glass. His little Antonia liked milk when the cream floated on top, thick and lumpy. While he smiled affectionately, thinking about her, the hall door opened and Antonia Rawlins ran in with an excited, whispered good-morning.

"*Buenos días!* Am I on time, Romero? I was scared the clock wouldn't go off! Manuela's still asleep. She didn't hear a thing, even when my boots dropped on the floor!"

She giggled at the thought of Manuela deep in her blankets. Sitting down at the table, she began to eat as fast as she could get her fork to her mouth.

Spring roundup time had come at last. Though it was only four o'clock and still dark, she and Romero would soon be riding out of the corral to catch up with the Aguas Vivas outfit and her father, the boss. They had been in the hills for more than a week, rounding up the four thousand head of cattle that were scattered from the wide, oak-shaded valleys of the flatlands to the rough, brushy wild country that lay far to the north and west, almost in sound of the sea.

Antonia sighed blissfully, thinking of the day ahead. Only a few short months ago she had never even been on a horse. She had never done anything more exciting than take stupid walks along Boston's prim streets with Grandaunt Alicia; nothing more interesting than sitting in the parlor on winter afternoons, close to the stuffy little coal grate, her face burning hot as she learned to stitch wool roses on a piece of scratchy canvas. And now, today, she and Lucky were going to be part of a rodeo!

When breakfast was over and the kitchen left tidy enough to meet Manuela's sharp eyes, Antonia and Romero saddled their horses and rode out of the corral. With a quick slap of her knotted reins on Lucky's sorrel flanks, Antonia hurried ahead to swing open the wide heavy gate.

"I can do it myself," she insisted importantly, leaning out of the saddle and struggling with the bars. "You don't have to help me at all." Romero's black eyes under their scraggly brows were bright with approval as she sidled her horse handily against the gate.

The grass was high, brushing their stirrups as they took the river trail. After the long, late rains the feed had grown magically, tall and sweet and full of strength, and Antonia knew, confidently and happily, that a good year lay ahead for the boss of the Aguas Vivas rancho. A good year, too, for Joe Sloane's family, who lived up the road.

Humming a contented, wordless little song, she let Lucky carry her along through the poppies and purple lupine, his head tossing in time with the quick step of his newly shod hoofs and the jingle of bit and bridle. A smart cow pony knew what to expect on a fine spring morning like this. When the long line of bawling, white-faced cattle wound off the hills with the Aguas Vivas outfit riding herd behind them, he would have his eager, sweating, flying-hoofed share in the important business of driving them to the holding corral to wait their turn for parting out and vaccination and branding.

"How much longer will the rodeo last, Romero?" Antonia asked, leaning out of the saddle to pick a yellow poppy for her hatband. "Till the end of the week?"

"Yes," the old Californio answered, "and don't forget, Tonita, when the hard work is over, when the riatas have been thrown in the last loops, when the branding irons have cooled, then will come the barbecue down by the willows."

"Will it be fun?"

"More than you can imagine, *amigacita.*" Romero nodded, his eyes sparkling. "This year, because you have brought us luck, because the grass is high, your father has invited all the neighbors. There will be steaks from a fat steer, and frijoles to feed a hundred people! *El patrón* considers it proper that the countryside meet his daughter."

"I can't wait! Will you play your guitar, Romero? Will you sing, the way you do down at the bunkhouse? We can hear you every night after supper. Pops likes the song about the jumping flea, but I like the one about the star best."

" 'Estrellita'? *Sí,* that is a song you shall have at the barbecue, I promise."

Two hours later Antonia reined in Lucky and looked anxiously along the high ridge that led to Moon Valley. "Isn't this where Pops said to wait, Romero? You don't think he could have driven the cattle around the other way? I'd hate to miss anything." Her face clouded as she spoke, and her gray eyes were sulky. "I wish I could have gone along and stayed all week with him! Camping out would be wonderful. Joe Sloane went—I don't see why I couldn't!"

Romero raised his eyebrows. "Oh, so life is very hard for you, my little owl? You think things are not fair?"

Antonia's face reddened. "Well, just the same, if I were a boy, like Joe, I'd be lucky. I could ride right alongside of Pops. He'd teach me to rope! He'd let me practice on the calves! He wouldn't say, No, you can't have a riata to throw, you might get a finger pulled off."

She looked down resentfully at her small sunbrowned hands and then went on in a burst of self-pity. "I'd get a chance to sleep out on the hills, with the stars right on top of my head! Joe says you can reach up and touch them. He says here on the ranch they're bigger and brighter and closer than anywhere else in the whole world."

Romero shook his head, his eyes wise and kind. "Poor Tonita *mía!* Fighting so hard against the way God made you! Tell me—to be a boy, is that truly so fine a thing? No, no, little one! Be patient. When the right time comes, you will ride every year to the roundup with *el patrón.* But now you are only a small one, and rodeos are for men." He sighed and smiled as he looked down at the little, slim, straight-backed girl riding next to him.

"Remember, Tonita, what I once told you? That poor old Romero would have nothing to do all day but sit in the sun and dream the hours away if your legs grew too long—if your eyes too wise? Be kind to me, amiga! Do not grow up too fast. Let me ride by your side for a long time to come."

Antonia stared at him. "Why, of course, we'll always ride together. Always and always!"

Romero smiled again, gravely. "Every day, Tonita *mía,* until the last leaf is blown from the tree. But now, we have talked enough, you think? Let us ride fast, vaquero. The cattle will top the ridge in another half hour."

He touched his horse, Pronto, with his spurs, and as the big gray shot ahead, Antonia slapped the sorrel on his red rump, and they circled out into a wide loop that would bring them to the rear of the oncoming cattle's downhill swing. Antonia suddenly pulled up with an excited shout. "There they are!"

Sitting straight and eager in her saddle, she waved her hat wildly as the vanguard of the great lurching, pushing, bellowing herd topped the ridge and wound down the trail in an unending line.

Shading her eyes against the glare, she stared impatiently. Oh, there was Pops! And there was Mr. Sloane, riding his bay colt. What a beauty! Look at it dance! When Mr. Sloane got through breaking it, when there was a real bit in its mouth instead of a hackamore around its nose, you would see a fine cow horse, almost as good as any in her father's string. And look—there was Joe, following along on Whitey.

"Hi, Joe. Did you have a good time?" Antonia's excited greeting was lost in the pound of horses' hoofs and the bawling, grunting rush of cattle as the outfit, yelling and halloing, herded the cows and calves down the steep trail. Joe grinned through the dust and sweat on his face and waved his hat as he galloped past.

"Hi, Tony! You sure missed it, not comin' along. Oh boy!"

Antonia glanced at Romero out of the corner of her eye, and then she shouted to Joe, with her nose in the air. "Camping isn't so much; I'd rather ride with Romero any day!" She dug her heels into Lucky, then, and rode forward to meet her father, her yellow head high.

The boss, unshaven and grimy, his eyes bloodshot from sun and wind and dust, smiled as she loped next to him. "Good work, cowpuncher—you must have started early to catch up with us. I've got a job ready for you. Want to ride along while I bring in those yearling calves up there in that gulch—see, up there to the left, in the brush? They think they're hiding out on us, the little devils! Well, when we get them rounded up, we'll be through for the day. The men won't be sorry, and neither will I. It's been a tough week." He pulled a handkerchief out of his pocket and wiped the sweat that stood in beads on his forehead and blinked the dust from his strained, tired eyes.

Then, while Antonia stared open-mouthed, he gave a quick exclamation, spurred his horse abruptly, and whirled down the trail at top speed. Oh! Oh! The colt! Bucking wildly, Mr. Sloane's young, green horse was lunging through the cattle, scattering them in every direction as he reared and snorted and whirled.

The bellow of hundreds of terrified animals and the din of cowboy yells told the tale. By the time Joe's father got his bay colt gentled down, the herd would be spread from here to China! While Antonia stared horrified, Romero wheeled past her, galloping at top speed, with Joe close behind, spurring Whitey.

All along the line the outfit closed in, shouting and yelling and prodding. Completely bewildered by the sudden confusion, her heart pounding hard, Antonia hung on to the reins and tried her best to quiet Lucky's excited prancing. What was the best thing to do when you found yourself alone on a hillside, with outfit and cattle floundering down below you in a choking cloud of dust? One thing was sure—you had sense enough to keep out of the way. Nobody wanted a girl around when cattle were on the rampage. She would just have to sit and wait until the excitement died down. It would be at least an hour before anyone got around to giving her the slightest thought.

She stared down the trail, coughing away the gritty dust that burned her throat and hanging on to the reins as tight as she could. Maybe Lucky wouldn't jump around so much, maybe he wouldn't pull so hard, if he had something interesting to do—if his mind were taken off that milling, bawling mix-up down below.

What was it her father had said about a little bunch of calves up there in the brush? Why, of course! It would help a lot if she brought them down and headed them toward the holding corral. Poor Pops. He was so tired already that he would be glad to have the job done for him. This was a chance to help.

Reining Lucky toward the brushy gulch that split a deep gash in the hillside, Antonia took the trail that climbed steeply through yellow mustard plants and tall grass. Far below she could hear the outfit shouting as the men rode hard on the heels of the scattered herd, and turning in the saddle, she saw the dim shapes of cattle and horses moving through the brown dust of the river flat.

Now, what would be the first thing to do? How should she go about the business of rounding up those yearling calves? Perhaps she could not manage it all alone, but at least she could try. Without practice, no one could expect to turn into a real vaquero. What a golden opportunity!

She let Lucky stop for a breathing spell and began to count the calves huddled ahead of her, under the shelter of a scrub-oak thicket. Ten of them. They needn't think they could hide. Didn't they know the boss wanted them at the corral? And that was where they were going.

She snatched off her hat and waved it wildly as she kicked her heels into the sorrel and sent him along the trail on a run. "Get going, Lucky boy! Yahoo—yippee! Yahoo!" In sturdy imitation of Joe Sloane's cowboy yells, Antonia shouted at the top of her lungs. "Attaboy, Lucky! Chase 'em out of there! Yahoo! Yippee!" The white-faced yearlings fixed astonished eyes on her for a moment and then turned and broke into a run for the thick brush.

The grass and the mustard stalks had disappeared now, and rough sage and chaparral scratched Antonia's face and arms as she ducked from thicket to thicket, trying to be in ten places at once. The calves thoroughly understood that this business of being a vaquero was something quite new to her. Here and there, everywhere, they ran from one brushy cover to another.

No sooner did Lucky have them covered and headed downhill than they broke away and scattered again in ten separate directions.

The little sorrel did his best. Gallantly he worked with all the heart and intelligence of a seasoned cow horse. This way and that he turned, with Antonia half out of the saddle as he whirled to head off a calf. With her yellow hair blowing in streamers, she jammed her sombrero down over her ears and caught her breath grimly.

Grabbing the horn of the saddle, she held on for dear life. Pulling leather was a big help—as long as no one was around to see you. Whew—Joe would have to admit that Lucky could turn on a dime! She clenched her blue-jeaned legs against the sorrel's sweating flanks and laughed aloud, half frightened to death, half crazy with glorious excitement.

If she could only hang on long enough, she and Lucky would have those calves just where they wanted them! Pops and the outfit, way, way down below, looked like little black ants. There wasn't time to notice how they were getting along. She had troubles of her own. Things were looking better, though—if she could only manage to circle around that pesky scrub oak and keep the calves on the run. Good old Lucky boy. Beautiful, darling Lucky. There wasn't a horse in the whole world who knew more about working cattle.

At last, one by one, the calves gave up their losing fight for freedom and dropped into line along the trail that led to the holding corral and the river. Lucky kept close to their heels. The sorrel horse was not taking any chances, and at the first sign of bolting, he was off again at a run, heading them back with a quick turn, or a lightning jump that would throw Antonia out of the saddle onto his neck with squeals of surprise and small, choked-back gasps of fright.

"It's all right with me, Lucky, whatever you want to do." She giggled meekly, her hands aching from their grip on the reins, her knees rubbed sore as they clamped desperately. "You know lots more about roundups than I do."

When at last the steep, narrow trail lay behind them and the flat, oak-dotted fields stretched ahead, Antonia, with a tremendous, panting sigh of relief, took off her hat and wiped the perspiration from her forehead. The worst was over. The calves could see the other cattle ahead of them now, and they could smell the river. They would not try to break back to the brushy gulch again. All they wanted was to run to the willows and join the herd that was wallowing and snuffing and bellowing in the cool, deep stream.

At the gate of the holding corral, meanwhile, the boss turned to Romero with an anxious frown. "What do you suppose is keeping Antonia? I lost track of her in all the excitement, but I took for granted she was riding right behind us. I knew she'd have sense enough to keep out of the way. Do you suppose she circled back and rode on home?"

Romero shook his head, his black eyes worried. "She was on the hillside safely, holding Lucky quiet, senor, when I looked back the last time to make sure all was well. Because the little sorrel is so gentle, because he has a head full of sense, I was not afraid to leave her alone. But now, if you have no more need of me, *patrón*, Pronto and I will ride back and look for her."

Joe Sloane, perched on top of the fence rail where he had climbed while Whitey had a rest and a drink, broke into the conversation, his blue eyes popping. "Guess you don't have to worry about Tony any longer, Boss. Take a look at what's heading across the field, sir! The crazy kid—I'll be doggoned!"

Almost knocked off the fence by surprise, Joe pointed. By golly! The Boston Bean herself, riding herd on ten yearling calves, and that little old sorrel of hers holding 'em in line like a veteran. The darn little cayuse—look at him lope along—and look at that half-pint in the saddle, sitting there as uppity and cool as all get-out! Talk about your old-timers! A fella could sure spot the makings of a real cowhand when he saw one!

Mr. Rawlins, speechless, stared unbelievingly at the dusty, hot, disheveled little rider astride her sweat-stained horse, and Romero nudged him, chuckling and beaming, his eyes shining with pride. "*Sí*, senor, it is truly our Tonita. You like a little yellow-head vaquero on the Aguas Vivas, eh? I agree, *patrón!*"

Joe, still gawking, scrambled off the fence and untied Whitey from the rails. Halloing at the top of his lungs, he galloped off across the field to open the lower gate of the holding corral, and Antonia and Lucky drove their calves through to the riverbank and watched them lurch over the side into the water.

Antonia took off her hat again and fanned herself, the noonday sun beating hotly on her tangled hair and dirty face. Her black eyelashes were gray with dust, and her blue cotton shirt was ripped on the right side in a long, brush-torn slit from shoulder to cuff. From her right eye to her chin a jagged red scratch made a bright path through the dust and perspiration.

The boss rode alongside of her and put out his big hand, his eyes warm with approval and pride.

"Shake, cowpuncher! You handled those cattle like a top hand. The outfit says you're hired! You've moved right in! But tell me something— Whatever made you chase up the canyon after those yearlings, Antonia? What put the idea in your head?"

Antonia, with her grimy small hand in his, looked up at her father with surprised eyes.

"Well," she said simply, "you said you had a job for me. You said you wanted them in the corral, didn't you, Pops?"

Reggie's No-Good Bird

by Nellie Burchardt

All blue jays were no good, Reggie thought—
until he held one in his hand.

The three-o'clock bell clanged inside the school on First Avenue. Almost at once the boys of Mrs. Sullivan's fourth grade, which was nearest the door, burst out onto the sidewalk. As usual, Reggie Thompson was in the lead. He blinked and shaded his eyes with his hand as he came out into the dazzling June sunlight.

"Hey, Reggie," yelled a boy behind him. Reggie turned his head just in time to be hit in the face with a baseball cap.

"I'll get you for that, Joey," he yelled.

He snatched the cap from the ground and flung it back at Joey. Joey ducked when he saw it coming, and the cap hit a girl behind him.

She shrieked. "You awful Reggie Thompson! I'm going to tell Mrs. Sullivan on you."

"I should worry, I should care," chanted Reggie. "Come on, Joey. Last one to the corner is teacher's pet."

The two boys raced off.

At the corner, the sixth-grade crossing guard stood on the curb. His arms were outspread to keep anyone from crossing the street before the light changed, but

Reggie was going too fast to stop. He ran full force into the guard's back.

"Okay. Who's the wise guy?" the boy demanded as he turned around. His face was flushed with anger. "Oh, it's *you* again," he said as he caught sight of Reggie. "I warned you the last time, if you got funny just once more, I'd report you. Now, what's your name?" He grabbed a handful of Reggie's shirt.

"Puddintane," jeered Reggie.

"*Very* funny. What's your real name?"

The light changed and the heavy traffic screeched to a halt. The stream of children following Reggie divided and went around him and the guard, who glanced both ways to be sure the street was safe to cross. In that instant, Reggie yanked away from his hold and dashed across to the other side.

"Hey, you, come back here," shouted the guard. "I didn't say you could go."

But Reggie was lost in the crowd of children. Joey caught up with him.

"Boy! Are you going to be in trouble!" said Joey.

"Aw, he's too bossy. He thinks he knows it all just because he's a sixth grader," grumbled Reggie. "I didn't mean to bump into him. I just couldn't stop in time. Why should he report me for that?"

"He'll get you the next time he sees you, anyhow," said Joey.

Three other boys came running across the street to join Reggie and Joey.

"What'll we do today, Reg?" one of the boys asked.

"How about seeing what we can find in those buildings they're tearing down? My brother found some real good junk there the other day," said Reggie.

"Yeah!"

"Great!"

"Let's go!"

The boys tore off at top speed along the crowded sidewalk. A group of girls scattered before them with little shrieks.

"It's that awful Reggie Thompson," said one of the girls.

"He's the worst pest in the whole school," another added.

By now, Reggie and his friends had reached the next block. Down at the other end a big metal ball swung back and forth from a crane as the wreckers turned the buildings into piles of rubble. At this end of the block the houses were still standing, with all their windows marked by big white x's.

Reggie grabbed a broken brick from the sidewalk and heaved it at a window. The glass gave a satisfying crash.

"Ya-ay!" yelled Reggie. "Bull's-eye!"

"Anyone can hit a target that big," said Joey. He picked up another brick and was just about to throw it when a man's head appeared in the broken window.

The man shook his fist at the boys. "Go on. Get out of here," he shouted.

Joey dropped the brick and ran.

"How do you like that?" said Reggie. "They've even got a watchman for this dump. A guy can't have any fun at all around here."

He ran after Joey, leaving the other boys behind. "Joey, wait," he yelled.

In the next block they slowed down.

"What'll we do now?" asked Joey.

Across the street was the city housing project where they both lived. They started to take a shortcut through the playground.

At the entrance was a sign that read,

NO
BALL PLAYING
ROLLER SKATING
BICYCLE RIDING
DOGS

Reggie read the sign out loud. "How do they expect a guy to live around here?" he grumbled. "It's a wonder they don't make a rule against breathing."

"Yeah," agreed Joey. "What do they want us to do? Play with dolls like girls? Or play in the sandbox with the little kids there?"

They hurried past the sandbox. The nearby benches were lined solidly with mothers keeping an eye on their younger children.

Beyond the playground was Reggie's building, and there the project trees began—the only trees within blocks. In one of them was a nestful of blue jay fledglings. Two of them had just pulled themselves up to the edge of the nest, where they teetered and clutched the rim fearfully with their still weak claws. They stretched their half-grown wings. It would be some time yet before they were strong enough to fly.

"I'll bet I can hit that no-good old blue jay there," said Reggie. He picked up a crushed tin can lying beside a wastebasket and threw it at the birds.

"Missed," shrieked Joey. "Is your aim rotten!"

One baby jay fluttered unsteadily back into the nest. The other one flapped its wings wildly, then lost its balance and fell to the ground.

Several girls walking behind the boys screamed.

"Ha!" said Reggie. "I did not miss. I got him, all right, all right."

The bird lay on the ground at the base of the tree, its eyes closed.

"I got him. I got him," gloated Reggie. He did a triumphant hunter's dance around the trunk of the tree.

"Aw-w-w. It's a *baby* bird," cried one of the girls.

"Reggie Thompson, you're the meanest boy in the whole school," said another.

It was that silly Diane from his class, Reggie noticed. She was always screaming. He couldn't stand her.

He stopped prancing around the tree. "I sure am," he said, grinning proudly. "And I've got the best aim in the whole school, too," he boasted.

"Is the bird dead?" asked Diane.

Reggie shrugged. "I guess so," he said.

"Why don't you pick it up and find out?"

Reggie nudged the jay with the toe of his sneaker. The bird's eyes remained closed.

"He's dead, all right," said Reggie.

"How can you be sure, unless you pick it up?" asked Diane.

Reggie hesitated. He had never touched anything dead before—except bugs and worms, and they didn't count.

"You're scared to touch it," said Diane.

"I am not."

"You are too. I dare you to pick it up."

Reggie bent down and gingerly scooped up the bird in his hands. Its head wobbled loosely on its neck. Reggie shifted one hand to keep the bird's neck steady. Its body felt warm in his hands. Dark gray feathers were just breaking out of their sheaths on the bird's chest, and the bright blue tail feathers with clear white adult markings were partly grown out.

The jay lifted its head weakly for a fraction of an inch. Its eyes remained closed.

Reggie was so shocked when it moved that he almost dropped it.

"It's alive! It's alive!" screamed Diane in his ear.

He winced. "It's alive," he repeated in amazement.

The bird's head sank down onto his

hand again. Suddenly Reggie felt sick to his stomach. Up until now he hadn't thought of the bird as something alive. It had been only a target up in a tree.

"What are you going to do with it now?" asked Diane.

"Maybe put it back in the nest," said Reggie, looking up and measuring the climb to the limb that held the nest.

"Do you think the mother will know how to take care of it when it's hurt like that?" asked Diane.

"How should I know?" asked Reggie. He was feeling sicker by the minute. Holding this warm bird was a lot different from picking up dead bugs.

The bird raised its head again. This time it tried to open its eyes. Reggie could see its sides heaving up and down with the effort of breathing.

"It'll be your fault if it dies," said Diane.

By then Reggie wished he had never heard of tin cans or blue jays—or girls either, for that matter. Why did the silly girls have to make such a fuss over an old blue jay? Blue jays were no good, anyhow. Reggie had heard his father say so time and again. "Noisy, thieving, no-good varmints," his father called them. He had lived on a farm when he was a boy, and he ought to know.

"Well, what are you going to do about it?" asked Diane.

Reggie looked around for help from Joey, but Joey had disappeared. A fine pal he was.

"Oh, leave me alone," he muttered.

"I'll take it home and take care of it," said Diane, reaching out her hand for the bird.

"You keep your hands off him. He's my bird," Reggie said.

He undid the top two buttons of his shirt and tucked the blue jay inside.

"What are you going to do with it?" asked Diane.

"Mind your own business," said Reggie. He turned and started to walk toward his own building. He felt the bird stir inside his shirt. Now what on earth had he taken the bird for, and what was he going to do with it? he wondered. He didn't even know what to feed a blue jay. He just knew he wasn't going to let any girl have his bird.

Reggie found Joey waiting for him in the hallway of their building.

"A fine pal you are," he said, "leaving me with all those girls."

"I thought you were right behind me," Joey answered. "Why did you stay there talking to them?"

"You don't think I was going to let them get my bird, do you?" asked Reggie.

"What's the difference? It's dead, isn't it?"

"No. I've got it here inside my shirt."

"You're kidding! What do you want to keep it for?"

"Because—" Reggie couldn't have explained it. He just knew that the bird was his now.

He got the apartment key from Mrs. Lomax next door, as he always did. His mother would not be home from work until five o'clock.

"Sh-h-h!" he warned Joey as he unlocked the door. "Pop's asleep."

"Is he on night shift again?"

Reggie nodded. The boys tiptoed back to the room Reggie shared with his big brother, Hank. There Reggie took out the bird and laid it carefully on his bed.

The jay seemed to be breathing a little more easily, but its eyes were still closed.

"He doesn't look so good," said Joey.

Reggie knelt down beside the bed and looked at the bird closely. Joey was looking right over his shoulder. It made Reggie nervous. "Give me room, will you?" he said.

Joey backed up a step. "Is he hurt bad?" he asked.

"No, he's just stunned from the fall," said Reggie, trying to sound more sure of himself than he really felt. "I think I'll get him some water." He got to his feet again.

"How's he going to drink it when he's unconscious?" asked Joey. "That's dumb."

"Not to drink, stupid. To put on his head. Don't you know that's what they do with people when they faint?" said Reggie. Who did Joey think he was, telling him how to take care of his own bird?

Reggie went into the bathroom and got a glassful of water.

A sleepy voice came from behind the closed door of his parents' room. "That you, Reg?"

"Yes, Pop." His father mustn't see the bird. Reggie knew well enough what his father thought of blue jays. Pop would make him get rid of it, for sure.

"What are you doing, Reg?" came his father's sleepy voice again.

"Nothing, Pop."

"Well—do it more quietly."

"All right, Pop."

Reggie tiptoed back to his room with the water. The bird still lay motionless.

Joey watched as Reggie dipped up a few drops of water with his fingertips and sprinkled them on the bird's head. The blue jay stirred slightly.

"Hey, how about that!" exclaimed Joey. "It worked. He's coming to."

"Nothing to it," said Reggie. "Didn't I tell you I knew what to do? I've been thinking of being a doctor when I grow up." He hadn't been thinking of it for more than ten seconds, but there was no need to tell Joey that.

"You?" said Joey. "With your marks? That's a laugh."

Reggie ignored him. What was the matter with everyone? No one—not even his own best pal—gave him credit for being able to do anything. He'd show Joey. He'd get this bird well if it was the last thing he did.

Now the jay's beak was slightly open, and Reggie held a drop of water on his forefinger and let it drip into the bird's mouth. The jay closed its beak and tilted its head up a bit. It seemed to be considering the taste of the water. Then its beak opened a shade wider than before.

"Will you look at that?" said Joey. "He wants more."

Reggie let another drop of water run into the bird's beak. Again the jay tilted its head up.

There was a noise at the front door.

"That must be Hank already," said Reggie. "I didn't think he'd be home yet from delivering his papers. Quick! We've got to hide the bird."

"How about this?" asked Joey. He picked up Reggie's pajama top from the floor, where Reggie had dropped it that morning.

"It'll have to do," said Reggie. He spread the pajama top carefully over the bird.

His big brother came into the room, went straight to his own bed, and flung himself down onto it without a word.

"Hi," said Reggie.

Hank looked over at the two younger boys in surprise.

"Hi, infants," he said. "I didn't see you sitting there on the floor." He closed his eyes and sighed. "If anyone ever offers you a paper route," he added, "just laugh in his face."

"Hard work, huh?" said Reggie, trying to put a lot of sympathy into his voice. Maybe if he put Hank in a good mood, he wouldn't object to the bird.

Hank opened his eyes and looked sharply at Reggie. "How come you're so sympathetic all of a sudden?" he asked.

Reggie looked down. Hank always saw through him.

Hank rose on one elbow. "What have you got there?" he asked.

"Got? Got where?" asked Reggie innocently.

"There on your bed. What are you trying to hide?"

"Hide? We're not hiding anything."

"Oh, yes, you are," said Hank. "What's on your bed there?"

"That? Oh, that's just my pajamas. I forgot to hang them up this morning."

"What's under them?"

"Nothing," said Reggie, trying to get between Hank and the pajama top.

"Come on, infant," said Hank. "Let me see what you've got."

Reggie gave up, afraid that Hank might

try to grab the pajama top and in doing so would hurt the bird.

"It's just a blue jay," he said, lifting the covering.

"For Pete's sake!" exclaimed Hank. "What'll you drag home next?" He stood up and came over to Reggie's bed to look at the bird more closely. "What do you want with a dead bird? Don't you know they're full of germs and stuff? Maybe he died of rabies."

"He's not dead," said Reggie.

"Well, if he isn't now, he's going to be soon," said Hank. "And you'd better get him out of my room."

"It's my room, too. And he's not going to die!" exclaimed Reggie.

Suddenly the bird's living seemed the most important thing in all the world. If it lived, that decided it. He'd be a doctor when he grew up—maybe a famous surgeon. Then they'd all laugh out of the other side of their faces—Diane and Joey and Hank and all of them.

"Pipe down," warned Hank. "You'll wake up Pop."

"He's *not* going to die," repeated Reggie in a softer voice. "He's better already."

As if to back up his words, the jay lifted its head.

Hank looked at the bird in disgust. "What do you want with a no-good old blue jay, anyhow?" he asked. "All they ever do is squawk."

That was just like Hank, thought Reggie—always running down anything that belonged to him.

"Don't you dare call him no good!" Reggie clenched his fists in rage, forgetting that he had been calling blue jays the same thing only a short while before. "He's just as good as the dumb old turtle you had last year."

"Okay—okay!" said Hank. "Keep your shirt on! But you'd better not let Mom or Pop see him."

"You won't tell them, will you, Hank?" asked Reggie.

"That all depends," said Hank, sitting down on his own bed again. "If I do you a favor, what will you do for me?"

"I don't know, " said Reggie.

"Let me see now," said Hank. He leaned back on the bed again, with his arms clasped behind his head, and looked up at the ceiling with a pleased smile. "You might make my bed for me every morning—or polish my shoes every day. No, those aren't things I really *have* to do. I've got it!" Hank sat up straight. "My paper route! It's too long and takes up too much of my time. You can help me with it. And if you don't make any mistakes, I just *might* consider keeping quiet about the bird. Though why anyone would want to keep a no-good bird like that, I can't imagine."

"That's not fair!" exclaimed Reggie. "Why should I do your work for you?"

"Oh, well," said Hank, "if you're not interested, I'll have to speak to Mom about it when she gets home. I think she might like to know how the bird got hurt, too. Mothers don't approve of that sort of thing, you know."

"How did you know I—" Reggie started to speak before he realized Hank had trapped him.

"Aha!" said Hank. "Got you that time! Now I think you'll be interested in those papers, won't you?"

"Oh—all right," said Reggie.

Behind him the bird gave a faint peep. Reggie hurried back to look at his patient.

It stretched out its neck and opened its beak wide, making a bright pink diamond shape.

"Peep!" said the bird again, more firmly.

"Look! He's okay now!" exclaimed Joey.

"Maybe he's hungry," said Reggie.

"Maybe he thinks you're his father," said Joey.

"Why would he think a dumb thing like that?"

"All right. He thinks you're his mother, then," said Hank.

"Ha-ha!" said Reggie. "Aren't we funny today!"

"Watch your lip, junior," said Hank, "or somebody might just happen to hear about that bird."

"What do you suppose he eats?" asked Reggie, quickly changing the subject.

"Birdseed or bugs, I guess," said Joey. "My grandmother's canary eats birdseed and lettuce."

"But he's not a canary," said Reggie. "Maybe what a canary eats would make him sick."

"All I can say is you'd better feed him soon and shut him up, or he won't be a secret any longer," said Hank.

Now the bird was keeping up a steady peep-peep-peep.

"But where am I going to get something to feed him?" said Reggie.

"Why don't you ask Mrs. Lomax's canary to lend you some birdseed?" asked Hank.

"It's worth trying, at least," answered Reggie.

He went next door and begged some birdseed from Mrs. Lomax. But when he put some in a little dish in front of the bird, it kept on peeping. Reggie tried pushing its head down into the dish, but the bird struggled to get free and peeped louder. Even dropping the seed into the bird's wide-open mouth did not work. The jay merely let the seed roll out of the side of its beak.

"Maybe he's too young for birdseed," said Reggie at last. "How am I going to find out what to feed him?"

"They invented something for people like you," said Hank.

"What?"

"Libraries."

"Of course! Sometimes I think you're a genius, Hank!" exclaimed Reggie.

"Well, not quite, but I'm getting there," answered Hank. "I'm glad you noticed, though."

"Oh—shut up!" Reggie knelt down and fished an old shoe box from under his bed. He dumped out the collection of marbles, baseball cards, and string that it contained and put the bird in it. Terrified, the jay threshed around, banging its wings against the hard sides of the box.

"He's going to hurt himself that way," said Joey.

Reggie picked up the bird again, stuffed his pajama top into the box, then put the bird back. It settled down and seemed to be more comfortable.

"Come on, Joey," said Reggie. "Let's hurry and get this information from the library before Charley starts peeping again."

"Charley, is it?" said Hank. "What makes you so sure it's a he?"

"Of course it's a he," said Reggie. "You don't think I'd have any old *girl* bird, do you?"

The Trout

by Sean O'Faolain

Nobody knew how the trout got in the tiny woodland pool. Or if he could survive.

One of the first places Julia always ran to when they arrived in G—— was The Dark Walk. It is a laurel walk, very old, almost gone wild; a lofty midnight tunnel of smooth, sinewy branches. Underfoot the tough brown leaves are never dry enough to crackle; there is always a suggestion of damp and cool trickle.

She raced right into it. For the first few yards she always had the memory of the sun behind her, then she felt the dusk closing swiftly down on her so that she screamed with pleasure and raced on to reach the light at the far end; and it was always just a little too long in coming so that she emerged gasping, clasping her hands, laughing, drinking in the sun. When she was filled with the heat and glare she would turn and consider the ordeal again.

This year she had the extra joy of showing it to her small brother, and of terrifying him as well as herself. And for him the fear lasted longer because his legs were so short and she had gone out at the far end while he was still screaming and racing.

When they had done this many times

they came back to the house to tell everybody that they had done it. He boasted. She mocked. They squabbled.

"Crybaby!"

"You were afraid yourself, so there!"

"I won't take you anymore."

"You're a big pig."

"I hate you."

Tears were threatening, so somebody said, "Did you see the well?"

She opened her eyes at that and held up her long, lovely neck suspiciously and decided to be incredulous. She was twelve, and at that age little girls are beginning to suspect most stories; they have already found out too many, from Santa Claus to the stork. How could there be a well! In The Dark Walk? That she had visited year after year? Haughtily she said, "Nonsense."

But she went back, pretending to be going somewhere else, and she found a hole scooped in the rock at the side of the walk, choked with damp leaves, so shrouded by ferns that she uncovered it only after much searching. At the back of this little cavern there was about a quart of water. In the water she suddenly perceived a panting trout. She rushed for Stephen and dragged him to see, and they were both so excited that they were no longer afraid of the darkness as they hunched down and peered in at the fish panting in his tiny prison, his silver stomach going up and down like an engine.

Nobody knew how the trout got there. Even old Martin in the kitchen garden laughed and refused to believe that it was there, or pretended not to believe, until she forced him to come down and see. Kneeling and pushing back his tattered old cap, he peered in.

"Be cripes, you're right. How the divil did that fella get there?"

She stared at him suspiciously. "You knew?" she accused.

But he said, "The divil a' knew," and reached down to lift it out. Convinced, she hauled him back. If she had found it, then it was her trout.

Her mother suggested that a bird had carried the spawn. Her father thought that in the winter a small streamlet might have carried it down there as a baby, and it had been safe until the summer came and the water began to dry up. She said, "I see," and went back to look again and consider the matter in private.

Her brother remained behind, wanting to hear the whole story of the trout, not really interested in the actual trout but much interested in the story his mummy began to make up for him on the lines of "So one day Daddy Trout and Mummy Trout . . ."

When he retailed it to Julia she said, "Pooh."

It troubled her that the trout was always in the same position; he had no room to turn; all the time the silver belly went up and down; otherwise he was motionless. She wondered what he ate, and in between visits to Joey Pony and the boat, and a bathe to get cool, she thought of his hunger.

She brought him down bits of dough; once she brought him a worm. He ignored the food. He just went on panting. Hunched over him, she thought how all the winter, while she was at school, he had been in there. All the winter, in The Dark Walk, all day, all night, floating around alone. She drew the leaf of her hat down around her ears and chin and stared. She was still thinking of it as she lay in bed.

It was late June, the longest day of the year. The sun had sat still for a week, burning up the world. Although it was after ten o'clock, it was still bright and still hot. She lay on her back under a single sheet, with her long legs spread, trying to keep cool. She could see the half-moon through the fir tree—they slept on the ground floor. Before they went to bed her mummy had told Stephen the story of the trout again, and she, in her bed, had resolutely presented her back to them and read her book. But she had kept one ear cocked.

"And so, in the end, this naughty fish who would not stay at home got bigger and bigger and bigger, and the water got smaller and smaller. . . ."

Passionately she had whirled and cried, "Mummy, don't make it a horrible old moral story!" Her mummy had brought in a fairy godmother then, who sent lots of rain, and filled the well, and a stream poured out and the trout floated away down to the river below. Staring at the moon, she knew that there are no such things as fairy godmothers and that the trout, down in The Dark Walk, was panting like an engine. She heard somebody unwind a fishing reel. Would the *beasts* fish him out?

She sat up. Stephen was a hot lump of sleep, lazy thing. The Dark Walk would be full of little scraps of moon. She leaped up and looked out the window, and somehow it was not so lightsome now that she saw the dim mountains far away and the black firs against the breathing land and heard a dog say *bark-bark*. Quietly she lifted the ewer of water and climbed out the window and scuttled along the cool but cruel gravel down to the maw of the tunnel. Her pajamas were very short so that when she splashed water it wet her ankles. She peered into the tunnel. Something alive rustled inside there. She raced in, and up and down she raced, and flurried, and cried aloud, "Oh, gosh, I can't find it," and then at last she did. Kneeling down in the damp, she put her hand into the slimy hole. When the body lashed they were both mad with fright. But she gripped him and shoved him into the ewer and raced, with her teeth ground, out to the other end of the tunnel and down the steep paths to the river's edge.

All the time she could feel him lashing his tail against the side of the ewer. She was afraid he would jump right out. The gravel cut into her soles until she came to the cool ooze of the riverbank, where the moon mice on the water crept into her feet. She poured out, watching until he plopped. For a second he was visible in the water. She hoped he was not dizzy. Then all she saw was the glimmer of the moon in the silent-flowing river, the dark firs, the dim mountains, and the radiant pointed face laughing down at her out of the empty sky.

She scuttled up the hill, in the window, plonked down the ewer, and flew through the air like a bird into bed. The dog said *bark-bark*. She heard the fishing reel whirring. She hugged herself and giggled. Like a river of joy her holiday spread before her.

In the morning Stephen rushed to her, shouting that "he" was gone, and asking where and how. Lifting her nose in the air, she said superciliously, "Fairy godmother, I suppose?" and strolled away patting the palms of her hands.

Byng Takes a Hand

by S. P. Meek

Howell was sure the men were poachers. But where were the birds they had shot?

As the game warden, Corporal Jimmy Howell, left the building, a big springer spaniel who had been sitting patiently on the porch rose and came eagerly toward him, his stump of a tail wagging.

"Hello, Byng," the corporal said as he stooped to stroke the sleek liver-and-white head. "Did you get lonesome?"

The spaniel jumped up and rested his paws against Howell's leg, striving in his best dog language to express the joy he felt at seeing his master after the long separation of fully five minutes.

"Yes, sir, you're a fine dog," Howell went on, "but right now you're going back to barracks. I've got to ride patrol, and bird dogs aren't allowed on the range this time of year. Back to barracks, Byng, understand?"

He mounted his motorcycle, which stood by the curb. Byng dropped to a crouch on the sidewalk, his big hazel eyes looking longingly at his master, and whimpered mournfully. Howell cast a swift glance around.

"Oh, all right," he said, "if you feel that way about it. If you're right with me, you can't do any harm. I'll take a chance. I'm in trouble now and a little more won't matter. Hop in."

The dog sprang to his feet, expressing joy in every movement. He rose in a clean leap that landed him in the seat of the sidecar. Then he scrambled up and licked his master's face in gratitude. As the motorcycle started, he dropped to the floor of the sidecar and crouched low, with his nose thrust out to test every passing breeze.

Howell drove through the post and out onto the artillery range, a vast area of over thirty thousand acres, partly wooded and dotted with numerous ponds and lakes, in most of which the wild mallard ducks were now breeding. It was Corporal Howell's duty to patrol this area daily, assuring himself that the nesting birds were not disturbed, and keeping down, as well as he could, those birds and animals that, if allowed to multiply unchecked, would make game on the reservation a thing of the past.

Presently he left the road and turned into a little-used trail leading through dense pine thickets. After half a mile he stopped his machine. Byng bounded out and looked at his master with his head cocked inquiringly, asking whether he was at liberty to range.

"Heel this time, Byng," Howell said as he slipped his rifle from its boot and started through the brush toward a little unnamed pond where he knew five mallard hens were setting. The springer followed closely at his master's heels, his keen nose testing the air, hoping to find the scent of some animal he would be allowed to chase.

The corporal pushed his way through a fringe of brush and stood on the edge of the lake. There was an excited quacking as half a dozen mallards rose from the water and winged rapidly away. Howell watched them, a puzzled expression on his face.

"Now why did they take off like that?" he asked himself. "They aren't usually so wild."

Instead of swinging around in a circle and settling again on the water, as was their usual practice, the birds went straight away, heading for another lake several miles distant. The frown grew deeper on Howell's face as he watched. He was certain that those ducks had been disturbed very recently.

"Probably a skunk or weasel," he decided. "Byng, search!"

At the word the springer bounded away and started going over the ground, his keen nose close to the earth and his tail wagging vigorously. Rifle in hand, Howell started around the little lake.

Byng stiffened a moment, then approached the water, his head held high, evidently working on a high body scent, instead of the ground scent that a springer usually follows. Howell followed the dog, his rifle held ready.

The springer dashed forward into the water and swam toward a point of land projecting out into the pond. Howell watched him closely, for he knew that a mallard hen was nesting on that point.

The dog swam on to the point and started through the rushes. Suddenly Howell's voice rang out. "Byng, come back here! Stop it, dog, stop it! You mustn't disturb a nesting duck."

Byng cast a look back over his shoulder, then pressed on, as though he had not heard his master's commands. Presently he put his nose to the ground and gently picked up a brown body, which fluttered feebly. With it in his mouth he reentered the water and swam toward his master.

Howell's cries had died away as Byng picked up the duck. It was evident that something was the matter with her, or she would have sprung off the nest in full flight at the dog's near approach. Byng swam up and sat down before his master, offering him the duck. Howell took it from his jaws and examined it. His face grew dark as a thundercloud. The hen had one wing broken and on her body were half a dozen wounds made by bird shot. She moved her head feebly, but it was evident that she had at best only a few minutes to live.

Howell ground his teeth as he thought of the nest of eggs, almost ready to hatch.

"That bird was shot not more than an hour ago," he said to himself as he examined the wounds, from some of which the blood was still flowing. "She was knocked down, crippled, and not found. She had just strength enough to make her nest before she gave out. Come, Byng, search!"

He laid the dying duck gently down on the grass and started around the lake, his keen eyes searching the ground intently. Suddenly he gave an exclamation and picked up a bright green shotgun shell.

"Fresh!" he said as he sniffed the end. "Here, Byng, smell. Now search!"

Byng sniffed at the shell, then started through the grass. In a moment he was back with a second shell in his mouth.

"Good work, Byng," the corporal praised as he compared the two shells, then pocketed them. "Search again."

In ten minutes he and Byng had found eight shells of the same size and pattern, all carrying the smell of freshly fired powder. Howell pocketed them and scanned the ground closely. To his trained eyes, the marks were easy to read. Two men had been there, wearing boots. He found the place where the poachers had crawled on their hands and knees to the water's edge, and later where they had left, walking upright.

"Here's their trail, Byng," he said with satisfaction. "Now if we can just follow it when we get on harder ground! It's too bad you aren't a bloodhound."

Foot by foot he followed the rapidly dimming trail. Just as it left the woods there were marks showing where an automobile had been standing. The two men had evidently entered it and driven away.

"Stay here, Byng," Howell commanded. "I'll get the chug-chug."

He struck off through the woods toward the spot where he had left his motorcycle. He knew every foot of the range, and made a wide swing back around the marsh to where the dog waited.

"Hop in," he commanded. When Byng obeyed, Howell leaned over his handlebars and began to follow the car tracks carefully. Luckily no other machine had passed over the trail that morning, and although he lost the tracks on spots of hard ground, he was always able to pick them up again. Presently he stopped and surveyed the country.

"They're heading for Nisqually Lake," he declared. "Well, they're going to the right place, all right. There are more ducks nesting there than in any other spot on the reservation."

He turned his motorcycle away from the road and started cross-country, heading directly for his goal. He was still a mile from the lake when Byng gave a sudden yelp and stiffened into attention. Howell stopped his machine instantly and listened. From the direction of Nisqually Lake came the sound of two shots. Above the timber surrounding the lake he could see ducks rising.

"Good work, Byng, I think we've got them. Hold on, old boy!" he cried as he drove across the prairie as rapidly as he dared. Byng braced himself against the seat, but even so he was nearly thrown from the sidecar a dozen times.

Back on the road, as Howell approached the lake he heard the sound of a car starting. He drove even more recklessly, but when he topped the rise that had hidden the lake from him, he saw a car four hundred yards away, headed for town. He opened his throttle and sped after it, Byng barking excitedly and leaning forward, as though he were about to leap from the swaying machine and give independent chase.

When Howell neared the car, it stopped. He noted with satisfaction, as he drew up alongside, that its tires had the same tread as those whose marks he had been following. In the automobile were two men, and the corporal felt a glow of excitement when he recognized the driver as Tony Alvous, a man he had long suspected of breaking the game laws.

"Hello, Corporal!" Alvous exclaimed jovially. "What's your hurry?"

"Were you shooting on Nisqually Lake?" Howell snapped, ignoring the question.

"Yeah, sure," Alvous replied. "Me and my cousin, Al Dorset. We shot four times at a big duck hawk, but he was too far away. We didn't get him."

"What did you get?"

"We got nothing. I said he was too far away."

"Were you at the pond back of Shannon Marsh this morning?" Howell went on.

"Sure thing. That's where we got this big fellow." Alvous reached into the rear of his car and held up a big hawk.

"How many shots did you fire?"

"Oh, quite a bunch, six or eight, maybe ten. I broke his wing the first shot, but he went over the ground so fast that we had to chase him and shoot a lot of times before we killed him."

Howell ground his teeth. The story fitted with what he had found, almost too well, but he knew that he was helpless. A quick glance into the rear of Alvous' car had already told him that, except for the hawk, it was empty. Yet, in his heart, he was certain that Alvous or his companion had shot the mallard hen he had found dying.

"I'm going to search your car," he announced suddenly.

Alvous' eyes narrowed.

"Where's your search warrant?" he demanded.

"I don't need one. This is a military reservation."

"Without a search warrant you don't search my car!" Alvous declared hotly. For a moment the two men glared at one another, then a smile broke over Alvous' face. "Say, Corporal, there's no use in anyone getting hard here. Take a look into the car if you want to. You can see there's nothing there."

"I want to look into that trunk on the rear."

Alvous hesitated a moment, then laughed.

"All right," he said. "I'll open it. I don't want any argument with you fellows. I've always got along fine with the range guards."

He climbed out of the car and went to the rear, Howell following him. The trunk was opened, but it proved to be empty. There was not even a telltale feather to be seen.

Alvous chuckled and started toward the front of his car. Howell remained in the rear, biting his lips and wondering just what to do next. To be frank with himself, he had no evidence that the other's smoothly told story did not explain. He was roused from thought by a sharp yelp. Striding around the car, he saw Byng standing a few feet from Alvous, his teeth bared and the hair along his back raised. On the ground lay the dead hawk that had been in the car a moment before.

"What happened?" Howell demanded.

Alvous turned a face distorted with rage. "That dog got too fresh!" he said. "I'll teach him to keep his nose out of my car!"

He stepped toward Byng. The springer

stood his ground and growled, a deep, warning note. Alvous launched a kick at him. Byng sprang back to avoid the kick, but stood regarding his enemy in a puzzled manner, as if undecided whether to attack or not. Kicking was a new experience to him.

Howell's blood boiled at the sight. He stepped forward and grasped Alvous by the shoulder, whirling him about.

"You coward!" he cried furiously.

Alvous glared at him, his fists clenched. It seemed certain there would be a fight. Then a cry came from Al Dorset, Alvous' companion. Byng had leaped into the car and was sniffing and scratching at the rear cushion.

Alvous sprang for the dog, but before he could touch Byng, Howell had him again by the shoulder. Mad with rage, Alvous swung his fist at the corporal's face. Howell dodged the blow, and in a moment the two men were wrestling with all their strength.

They were fairly evenly matched, but Howell had been trained in the army to use his strength to the best advantage. The fight would soon have ended had there been but the two of them, but aid was coming to Alvous. Dorset leaped from the car, a shotgun in his hand. He grasped it by the barrel and advanced cautiously, looking for a chance to hit Howell's head.

He stepped in and swung the gun. Howell tried to duck, but the gun butt came relentlessly at him. Just before it landed, Dorset gave a shriek of pain and swung about so that the blow fell only glancingly on Howell's shoulder. Byng had taken a hand and had seized Dorset by the leg with his powerful jaws.

Dorset swung the gun at the dog, but before the blow could land, Byng released his grip and sprang back, facing the onset with bared fangs. Dorset snapped open the breech of the gun and inserted two shells.

Desperation gave Howell strength. With a mighty effort he lifted Alvous from his feet and hurled him heavily to the ground. So fast that it almost seemed a part of the same movement, his fist swung in a long arc and struck Dorset on the neck. The shot aimed at Byng buried itself harmlessly in the ground. Dorset turned, but Howell had leaped back and drawn his automatic.

"Drop that gun!" he snapped.

Dorset hesitated. Howell deliberately shifted his aim until his gun was pointed at Dorset's leg. As he tightened his grip on the trigger, the shotgun clattered to the ground.

"Stand over there, both of you!" Howell ordered. "Backs to me and hands up. Way up."

Alvous got to his feet, and the two men obeyed. Howell went over and searched them rapidly, but effectively, for hidden weapons.

"Now stand right where you are," he directed. "If you make a false move, I'll shoot. Come, Byng, show me where those ducks are. Search, boy."

The springer jumped into the car and scratched eagerly at the rear cushion. Howell lifted up the seat and gave an exclamation of dismay. There was nothing under it but a few tools. "Gosh, Byng, if you're wrong, we're done for!" he muttered.

The dog was now scratching at the back of the seat, whining with excitement. Howell studied it for a moment, then grasped it by the top. There was no movement. He hesitated a moment, then exerted his strength. There was a tearing sound and the back cushion came forward. Byng gave a yelp of triumph and dived behind it, to come out with a mallard drake in his mouth.

"Good boy!" Howell cried. A quick glance showed him a dozen ducks and pheasants behind the cleverly made removable cushion.

"All right, you two would-be hard guys," he said. "Climb in your car and head for the post. You're going to get a chance to explain these birds to your Uncle Samuel. I'll be right behind you on my motorcycle, so don't try any funny business. I'd be glad of an excuse to expend a little government ammunition on you. That's what it was given to me for—to kill vermin with."

"Fine work, Corporal!" Captain Rae exclaimed as Howell laid eight ducks and five pheasants on his desk and reported the capture of the two poachers. "Tell me what happened."

Howell related his movements of the morning, laying the empty shells down on the provost marshal's desk and telling the part Byng had played.

"So Alvous had a secret place in the

back of his car to carry game? He's probably been poaching for years, under the guise of vermin hunting. Was it a hard place to find?"

"Very hard, sir. The cushion was made so it would tilt forward, then lock back in place without any looseness. You could search the car twenty times if you didn't know the secret, and never suspect it. But it couldn't fool Byng's nose. He knew there was game there."

"It's lucky for you that you had him along with you—against orders," Captain Rae said dryly.

"Yes, it sure was, sir. And please, sir, couldn't he go out on patrol with me, sir? He's very useful, and—he loves to get out, sir."

"Oh, he does, does he?" The provost marshal chuckled as he looked down into the spaniel's pleading eyes. "Well, I guess he's earned some special consideration," he said, pulling Byng's long ears. "Hunting dogs aren't allowed on the range during breeding season, but I guess I can get around that order by assigning Byng as assistant game warden or something of the sort. Go ahead and take him with you."

"Thanks, sir."

"That's all. You may go. But, Byng, mind you don't chase any birds!"

Caddie Woodlawn and the Indians

by Carol Ryrie Brink

In a bad hour, which was stronger—fear or trust?

In 1864 Caddie Woodlawn was eleven, and as wild a little tomboy as ever ran the woods of western Wisconsin. She was the despair of her mother and of her elder sister, Clara. But her father watched her with a little shine of pride in his eyes, and her brothers accepted her as one of themselves without a question. Indeed, Tom, who was two years older, and Warren, who was two years younger than Caddie, needed Caddie to link them together into an inseparable trio. Together they got in and out of more scrapes and adventures than any one of them could have imagined alone. And in those pioneer days Wisconsin offered plenty of opportunities for adventure to three wide-eyed redheaded youngsters.

In those days, too, the word massacre filled the white settlers with terror. Only two years before, the Indians of Minnesota had killed a thousand white people, burning their houses and destroying their crops. The town of New Ulm had been almost entirely destroyed. Other smaller uprisings flared up from time to time, and only a breath of rumor was needed to throw the settlers of Wisconsin into a panic of apprehension.

"The Indians are coming! The Indians are coming!" Without waiting to hear more, people packed what belongings they could carry and started the long journey back east. Others armed themselves as best they could for the attack and gathered together in groups, knowing that there was strength in numbers. Sometimes, leaving the women and children at home, the men went out to attack the Indians, preferring to strike first, rather than be scalped in their beds later. The fear spread like a disease, nourished on rumors and race hatred. For many years now the whites had lived at peace with the Indians of western Wisconsin, but so great was this disease of fear that even a tavern rumor could spread it like an epidemic throughout the country.

One night after the other children had gone to bed, Caddie sat beside the fire with Father and Mother. There was no sound but the ticking of clocks and the occasional crackling of the fire. But something warm and peaceful seemed to flow through the quiet room.

Then suddenly Caddie heard another sound—distant hoofbeats on the road. Father and Mother had heard it, too. Father went to the window and looked out. Mother sat still, listening, her face turned toward the road from Dunnville. In those days people did not ride abroad at night in February without some good reason. The hoofbeats were more distinct now. Someone was riding rapidly in spite of the darkness.

"They're coming here," said Mrs. Woodlawn, jumping up. "One of the neighbors is sick, perhaps. I must get my shawl and bonnet."

The hoofs sounded to the very door and stopped. Then someone was knocking, loudly and urgently, on the door. Father went and opened it. A cold wind blew in and Caddie could see the pale face of a man beyond Father's shoulder. She brought the lamp to light them. The man was Melvin Kent, from the other side of Dunnville.

"I don't want to alarm you, Woodlawn," he said, "but there's a serious rumor going around. The Indians—"

"Just a moment, Kent," said Father, and he stepped outside and closed the door behind him.

Caddie replaced the lamp on the table. Mother had come back with her shawl and bonnet. She and Caddie looked at each other silently, their eyes frightened and questioning. They stood together near the table, listening to the rumble of men's voices outside. All the peace and friendly security of the quiet room had flown out into the February darkness when Father had opened the door.

It seemed a very long time before Father came back. His face was grave, but outwardly he was calm.

"What is it, Johnny? What is it?" cried Mrs. Woodlawn, unable to bear the suspense any longer.

"Nothing serious, I hope," said her husband, laying his hand absently along Caddie's shoulder as he spoke. "A man from the country west of here came into the tavern tonight and told the men that the Indians are gathering for an uprising against us."

"*Massacre!*" breathed Mother, laying her hands against her heart. Her face had gone quite white.

"No, Harriet, not that word," said Father quietly. "Not yet. I hope that this is only a tavern rumor and nothing more. Many a fool who has had too much to drink will start a rumor. I am willing to stake my farm, and a good deal that I hold dear besides, on the honor and friendliness of the Indians hereabouts. Still, we must keep clear heads and be ready for emergencies. Whatever happens, the white settlers must stand together. I have told Kent that the neighbors may gather here."

"Yes, yes!" said Mrs. Woodlawn. "We can house them better than anyone. We can put down pallet beds in the parlor for the women and children. The men can bunk in the hay, if those wicked redskins don't fire it before they have a chance to bunk. I'll need to begin baking. Fetch me six strings of dried apples from the storeroom, Johnny, and a bucket of water from the spring. What, Caddie! Are you still here? Get to bed as fast as you can, child. I'll call you at daybreak."

Early the next morning people began arriving from all directions. They came bringing what food and bedding they could carry. They did not know how soon they would dare return to their homes, nor whether they would find anything but a heap of charred sticks when they did return. Of course, school was not to be thought of, and in spite of the general fear, the children were delighted with the unexpected holiday.

With shouts of joy the young Woodlawns greeted the other children. They played I Spy around the barn and farmyard, their pleasure keenly edged by the nearness of danger. An exciting game became much more exciting when, on coming out of hiding, one felt that he might find himself face to face with a redskin.

Mrs. Woodlawn loved a gathering of people, and one of her great griefs in Wisconsin was that she saw so few outside her own family. Now she had all the neighbors here and could herself serve them beans such as none but she, outside of Boston, knew how to bake. Happy in the necessity of the moment, she did not let her mind dwell on the danger from the Indians.

Clara worked beside her mother, her thin cheeks red with excitement, her capable hands doing as much as a woman's. Caddie helped, too, but after she had broken a dish and spilled applesauce over the kitchen floor, her mother told her that she had better run and play, and Caddie ran. Flinging her arms over her head, she let out an Indian war whoop that set the whole farm in an uproar for a moment. Women screamed. Men ran for guns.

"Aw, it's only Caddie," said Tom, "letting off steam."

"Put a clothespin on her mouth," suggested Warren.

But Caddie did not need a clothespin now. The men with their guns looked too grim to risk another war whoop on them.

The day wore slowly on, and nothing unusual happened. The children tired of their games and sat together in the barn, huddled in the hay for warmth, talking together in low voices.

"You 'member the time the sun got dark, eclipse Father called it, and we were so scared? We thought the world had come to an end, and we fell down on our faces. You 'member?"

"Yah. We saw a bear in a tree that day, too. Remember?"

"Golly! Do you think the Indians'll come tonight?"

"Maybe they will."

"I don't dast to go to sleep."

Their voices trailed off, lower and lower, almost to whispers.

The night came, gray and quiet, slipping uneventfully into darkness. The February air had a hint of spring in it. Would the promise of spring ever be fulfilled for them? Or would the Indians come?

Mr. Woodlawn's calm voice sounded among the excited people. "I believe that we are safe," he said. "I trust our Indians."

Caddie's heart felt warm and secure again when she heard him speak.

After dark, sentries were stationed about the farmhouse to keep watch during the night. Fires were kept burning in the kitchen and dining room for the men to warm by when they changed their sentry duty. Windows were shuttered and lanterns covered or shaded when carried outside. A deep silence settled over the farm. The settlers did not wish to draw the Indians' attention by needless noise or light.

The night passed as the day had passed, and nothing fearful happened. The children awoke stiff and aching and rubbed the sleep out of their eyes. But the good cows had not been frightened out of giving their milk, and Robert Ireton, the Woodlawns' hired man, brought in two foaming buckets of it for the children to eat with big bowls of meal mush.

But the second day people were fidgety and undecided. Should they go home or should they stay on? The food supplies they had brought with them were giving out. They could not let the Woodlawns exhaust all their supplies in feeding them. Yet the redskins might only be awaiting the moment when they would scatter again to their homes to begin the attack. It was a gray, dark day, not designed to lift anybody's spirits.

The women and little children, crowded into the farmhouse, and tired of confinement, were restless. The men paced back and forth in the farmyard, or stopped in groups beneath the four pine trees that sheltered the front of the house. They polished and cleaned and oiled their guns, and smoked their pipes. Everyone felt that the strain of waiting had become almost unbearable.

In the afternoon a few of the men went to get more supplies. Tom, Warren, and Father went with them. The others watched them go, fearful and yet somehow relieved to see any stir of life along the road.

Caddie felt the strain of waiting, too, and she was impatient with the people who had no faith in the Indians. The Indians had not yet come to kill. Why should they come at all? Indian John had never been anything but a friend, ever since she had first met the big Indian three years before in the store in the village. Why should he turn against them now? Why should his people wish to kill hers? It was against all reason. Good John, who had brought her so many gifts—bits of oddly carved wood and once a doll, its tiny head made of a pebble covered with calico, black horsehair braids, calico arms and legs, and a buckskin dress!

"Caddie," said Mrs. Woodlawn, "go fetch me a basket of turnips from the cellar, please." Caddie slipped on her coat, took up the basket, and went outside to the cellar door at the side of the house. She had to brush by a group of men to get into the cellar. They were talking earnestly together, their faces dark with anger and excitement.

"It is plagued irksome to wait," one of them was saying as Caddie brushed past.

She went into the cellar and filled her basket. "Yes, it's irksome to wait," she said to herself, "but I don't know what they mean to do about it. They'd be sorry enough if the Indians came."

But what they meant to do about it was suddenly plain to her as she came up the stairs again with the turnips.

"The thing to do is to attack the Indians first," one man was saying. It was the man Kent, who had ridden out on the first night to spread the alarm. Caddie stopped still in her tracks, listening unashamed.

"Yes," said a second man. "Before they come for us, let us strike hard. I know where John and his Indians are camped up the river. Let's wipe them out. Then

we can sleep peacefully in our beds."

"But the rumor came from the west. So killing John's tribe would not destroy the danger," objected a third man.

"It would be a beginning. If we kill or drive these Indians out, it will be a warning to the others that we deal hard with redskins here."

Caddie set her basket down upon a step. It suddenly seemed too heavy for her to hold. Massacre! Were the whites to massacre the Indians, then? A sick feeling swept across her heart. Surely this was worse than the other.

"Woodlawn will be against it," said the cautious third man.

"Woodlawn puts too much faith in the Indians. If we can get enough men to our way of thinking, we need not consult Woodlawn. Wipe the Indians out, is what I say. Don't wait for them to come and scalp us. Are you with me?"

White and trembling, Caddie slipped past them. The men paid no attention to the little girl, who had left her basket of turnips standing on the cellar step. They went on talking angrily among themselves, enjoying the sound of their boastful words. Caddie went to the barn and into the stalls. There she slipped a bridle over Betsy's head. She was trembling all over. She must warn John and his Indians, and she was afraid.

Oh, for Tom and Warren now! But they

were gone with the men for supplies. Oh, for Father, who was always so wise and brave! But she could not wait for him to come back. There was no use talking to Mother or Clara. They would only cry out in alarm and forbid her to go, and since Father and the boys were not here, she felt that she must go. She knew as well as Kent where Indian John and his tribe had built their winter huts of bark. Fortunately the barn was deserted. She must leave before anybody saw her. She led Betsy to the little door that opened toward the river.

Then she flung herself on Betsy's back and dug heels into her flanks. They were away across the field and into the dripping woods. The gray mist was turning into fine rain. There was still snow in the woods and there would still be ice on the river.

Clip-clop-clip sounded Betsy's hoofs across the field. There was a treacherous slime of mud on the surface, but underneath it the clods were still frozen as hard as iron. Then the bare branches of the trees were all around them, and Caddie had to duck and dodge to save her eyes and her hair. Here the February thaw had not succeeded in clearing the snow. It stretched gray and treacherously soft about the roots of big trees. Caddie slowed her mare's pace and guided her carefully now. She did not want to lose precious time floundering in melting snow. Straight for the river she went. Not a squirrel or a bird stirred in the woods. So silent! So silent! Only the *clip-clop-clip* of Betsy's hoofs.

Then the river stretched out before her, a long expanse of blue-gray ice under the gray sky.

"Carefully now, Betsy. Take it slowly, old girl." Caddie held a tight rein with one hand and stroked the horse's neck with the other. "That's a good girl. Take it slowly."

Down the bank they went, delicately onto the ice. Betsy flung up her head, her nostrils distended. Her hind legs slipped on the ice, and for a quivering instant she struggled for her balance. Then she found her pace. Slowly, cautiously, she went forward, picking her way, but with a snort of disapproval for the wisdom of her young mistress. The ice creaked, but it was still sound enough to bear their weight. They reached the other side and scrambled up the bank. Well, so much done! Now for more woods!

There was no proper sunset that day, only a sudden lemon-colored rift in the clouds in the west. Then the clouds closed together again and darkness began to fall. The ride was long, but at last it was over.

Blue with cold, Caddie rode into the clearing where the Indians had built their winter huts. Dogs ran at her, barking, and there was a warm smell of smoke in the air. A fire was blazing in the center of the clearing. Dark figures moved about it. Were they in war paint and feathers? Caddie's heart pounded as she drew Betsy to a stop. But, no, they were only old women bending over cooking pots. The running figures were children, coming now to swarm about her. There was no war paint! No feathers! Surely she and Father had been right! Tears began to trickle down Caddie's cold cheeks. Now the men were coming out of the bark huts. More and more Indians kept coming toward her. But they were not angry, only full of wonder.

"John," said Caddie in a strange little voice, which she hardly recognized as hers. "Where is John? I must see John."

"John," repeated the Indians, recognizing the name the white men had given to one of their braves. They spoke with strange sounds among themselves, then one of them went running. Caddie sat her horse, half dazed, cold to the bone, but happy inside. The Indians were not on the warpath, they were not preparing an attack. Whatever the tribes farther west might be plotting, these Indians, whom Father and she trusted, were going about their business peacefully. If they could only get away now in time, before the white men came to kill them! Or perhaps she could get home again in time to stop the white men from making the attack. Would those men whom she had heard talking by the cellar door believe a little girl when she told them that Indian John's tribe was at peace? She did not know. Savages were savages, but what could one expect of civilized men who plotted massacre?

Indian John's tall figure came toward her from one of the huts. His step was unhurried and his eyes were unsurprised.

"You lost, Missee Red Hair?" he inquired.

"No, no," said Caddie, "I am not lost, John. But I must tell you. Some white men are coming to kill you. You and your people must go away. You must not fight. You must go away. I have told you."

"You cold," said John. He lifted Caddie off her horse and led her to the fire. "No understan'," he said then, shaking his head in perplexity. "Speak too quick, Missee Red Hair."

Caddie tried again, speaking more slowly. "I came to tell you. Some bad men wish to kill you and your people. You must go away, John. My father is your friend. I came to warn you."

"Red Beard, he send?" asked John.

"No, my father did not send me," said Caddie. "No one knows that I have come. You must take your people and go away."

"You hungry?" John asked her, and mutely Caddie nodded her head. Tears were running again and her teeth were chattering. John spoke to the squaws, standing motionless about the fire. Instantly they moved to do his bidding. One spread a buffalo skin for her to sit on. Another ladled something hot and tasty into a cup without a handle.

Caddie grasped the hot cup between her cold hands and drank. A little trickle of warmth seemed to go all through her body. She stretched her hands to the fire. Her tears stopped running and her teeth stopped chattering. She let the Indian children, who had come up behind her, touch her hair without flicking it away from them. John's dog came and lay down near her, wagging his tail.

"You tell John 'gain," said John, squatting beside her in the firelight.

Caddie explained, slowly, how the whites had heard that the Indians were coming to kill, how her father had not believed, but how some of the people planned to attack the Indians first. She begged John to go away with his tribe while there was still time. When she had finished, John grunted and continued to sit looking into the fire. All about the fire were row upon row of dark faces, staring at her with wonder but no understanding. John knew more English than any of them, and still, it seemed, he did not yet understand. Patiently she began again to explain.

But now John shook his head. He rose and stood tall in the firelight above the little white girl. "You come," he said.

Caddie rose uncertainly. She saw that

it was quite dark now outside the ring of firelight, and a fine, sharp sleet was hissing down into the fire. John spoke in his own tongue to the Indians. What he was telling them she could not say, but their faces did not change. One ran to lead Betsy to the fire and another brought a spotted Indian pony that had been tethered at the edge of the clearing.

"Now we go," said the Indian.

"I will go back alone," said Caddie, speaking distinctly. "You and your people must make ready to travel westward."

"Red Hair has spoken," said John. "John's people go tomorrow." He lifted her onto her horse's back, and himself sprang onto the pony. Caddie was frightened again, frightened of the dark and cold, and uncertain of what John meant to do.

"I can go alone, John," she said.

"John go, too," said the Indian.

He turned his pony into the faint woods trail by which she had come. Betsy, her head drooping under a slack rein, followed the spotted pony among the dark trees. Farther and farther behind they left the warm, bright glow of fire. Looking back, Caddie saw it twinkling like a bright star. It was something warm and friendly in a world of darkness and sleet and sudden icy branches. From the bright star of the Indian fire Caddie's mind leaped forward to the bright warmth of home. They would have missed her by now.

She bent forward against Betsy's neck, hiding her face from the sharp needles of sleet. It seemed a very long way back. But at last the branches no longer caught at her skirts. Caddie raised her head and saw that they had come out on the open riverbank. She urged Betsy forward beside the Indian pony.

"John, you must go back now. I can find my way home. They would kill you if they saw you."

John only grunted. He set his moccasined heels into the pony's flanks and led the way onto the ice. Betsy shook herself with a kind of shiver all through her body, as if she were saying, No! No! No! But Caddie's stiff fingers held the rein tight and made her go. The wind came down the bare sweep of the river with tremendous force, cutting and lashing them with the sleet. Betsy slipped and went to her knees, but she was up again at once and on her way across the ice. Caddie had lost the feeling of her own discomfort in fear for John. If a white man saw him riding toward the farm tonight, he would probably shoot without a moment's warning. Did John understand that? Was it courage or ignorance that kept John's figure so straight, riding erect in the blowing weather?

Up the bank, through the woods, to the edge of the clearing they rode, Indian file. Then the pony stopped.

Caddie drew Betsy in beside him. "Thank you!" she panted. "Thank you, John, for bringing me home. Go, now. Go quickly." Her frightened eyes swept the farmstead. It was not dark and silent, as it had been the night before. Lanterns were flashing here and there, people were moving about, voices were calling.

They're starting out after the Indians! thought Caddie. Father hasn't been able to stop them. They're going to massacre.

She laid her cold hand on the spotted pony's neck. "John!" she cried. "John, you must go quickly now!"

"John go," said the Indian, turning his horse.

But before the Indian could turn back into the woods, a man had sprung out of the darkness and caught his bridle rein.

"Stop! Who are you? Where are you going?" The words snapped out like the cracking of a whip, but Caddie knew the voice.

"Father!" she said. "Father! It's me. It's Caddie!"

"You, Caddie? Thank God!" His voice was full of warm relief. "Hey, Robert, bring the lantern. We've found her. Caddie! My little girl!"

Suddenly Father was holding her close in his arms, his beard prickling her cheek, and over his shoulder she could see Robert Ireton, the hired man, with a bobbing lantern that threw odd shafts of moving light among the trees. John, too, had dismounted from his pony, and stood straight and still, his arms folded across his chest.

"Oh, Father," cried Caddie, remembering again her mission and the last uncomfortable hours. "Father, don't let them kill John! Don't let them do anything bad to the Indians. The Indians are our friends, Father. I've been to the camp and seen them. They mean us no harm."

"You went to the Indian camp, Caddie?"

"Yes, Father."

"That was a dangerous thing to do, my child."

"Yes, Father, but Mr. Kent and some of the other men meant to go and kill them. I heard them say so. They said they wouldn't tell you they were going, and

you weren't there. Oh, Father, what else could I do?"

He was silent for a moment, and Caddie stood beside him, shivering, and oppressed by the weight of his disapproval. In the swaying lantern light she searched the faces of the three men—Robert's mouth open in astonishment, Father's brows knit in thought, John's dark face impassive and remote, with no one knew what thoughts passing behind it.

Caddie could bear the silence no longer. "Father, the Indians are our friends," she repeated.

"Is this true, John?" asked Father.

"Yes, true, Red Beard," answered John gravely.

"My people fear yours, John. Many times I have told them that you are our friends. They do not always believe."

"My people foolish sometime, too," said John. "Not now. They no kill white. Red Beard my friend."

"He brought me home, Father," said Caddie. "You must not let them kill him."

"No, no, Caddie. There shall be no killing tonight, nor any more, I hope, forever."

Over her head the white man and the red man clasped hands.

"I keep the peace, John," said Father. "The white men shall be your brothers."

"Red Beard has spoken. John's people keep the peace."

For a moment they stood silent, their hands still in the clasp of friendship, their heads held high like two proud chieftains. Then John turned to his pony. He gathered the slack reins, sprang on the pony's back, and rode away into the darkness.

"Oh, my little girl," said Father. "You have given us a bad four hours. But it was worth it. Yes, it was worth it, for now we have John's word that there will be peace."

"But, Father, what about our own men? They meant to kill the Indians. I heard them."

"Those men are cowards at heart, Caddie. Their plans reached my ears when I got home, and I made short work of such notions. Well, well, you are shivering, my dear. We must get you home to a fire. I don't know what your mother will have to say to you, Caddie."

When they reached the farmhouse, there was great excitement over Caddie's return.

"Caddie, my dear," said Mrs. Woodlawn. "You ought to be spanked. But there's a bowl of hot soup for you on the back of the stove."

In the kitchen, all the children crowded around Caddie as she ate, gazing at her in silent admiration, as at a stranger from a far country.

"Golly, Caddie, didn't they try to scalp you?"

"Did they have on their war paint?"

"Did they wave their tomahawks at you?"

Caddie shook her head and smiled. She was so warm, so happy to be at home, so sleepy. . . .

Not Driving and Not Riding

by P. C. Asbjørnsen and Jørgen Moe

Translated by Pat Shaw Iversen and Carl Norman

A tale from Norway of a fickle prince and a clever maiden.

There was once a king's son who had wooed a maiden. But when they had come to an understanding and were on good terms, he lost all interest in the girl. Now he didn't want to marry her because she wasn't good enough for him. And so he thought he would try to be quit of her. But he said he would take her all the same, if she could come to him

> not driving and not riding,
> not walking and not sliding,
> not hungry and not full,
> not naked and not clad,
> not by day, and not by night.

For he believed she could never manage that.

She took three barleycorns and bit them in two, so she was not full, but she was not fasting either. And then she draped a net over herself, so that she was

> not naked and not clad.

She then took a ram and seated herself on its back, so her feet dragged along the ground. Thus shuffling forward she was

> not driving and not riding,
> not walking and not sliding.

And it was in the twilight between night and day.

When she reached the guards outside his palace, she asked to be allowed to talk with the prince, but they would not let her in because she looked such a sight. But the prince, awakened by the commotion, came to the window. She shuffled across and wrung off one of the ram's horns; standing up on the ram's back, she knocked on the window with it. So they had to open up and make her a princess.

The Husband Who Was to Mind the House

by P. C. Asbjørnsen and Jørgen Moe
Translated by Sir George Webbe Dasent

Who works harder, husband or wife? A Norwegian folktale.

Once upon a time there was a man so surly and cross he never thought his wife did anything right in the house. One evening, in haymaking time, he came home scolding and swearing, and showing his teeth and making a dust.

"Dear love, don't be so angry; there's a good man," said his wife. "Tomorrow let's change our work. I'll go out with the mowers and mow, and you shall mind the house at home."

Yes! the husband thought that would do very well. He was quite willing to mind the house, he said.

So, early next morning his wife took a scythe over her neck and went out into the hayfield with the mowers and began to mow; but the man was to mind the house and do the work at home.

First of all, he wanted to churn the butter; but when he had churned awhile, he got thirsty and went down to the cellar to tap a barrel of ale. Just when he had knocked in the bung and was putting the tap into the cask, he heard the pig come into the kitchen overhead. Then off the man ran up the cellar steps, with the tap in his hand, as fast as he could, to look after the pig, lest it should upset the churn. But when he got up and saw the pig had already knocked the churn over and stood there, routing and grunting in the cream, which was running all over the floor, he got so wild with rage that he quite forgot the ale barrel and ran at the pig as hard as he could. He caught it, too, just as it ran out of doors, and gave it such a kick that piggy lay for dead on the spot. Then all at once he remembered he had the tap in his hand; but when he got down to the cellar, every drop of ale had run out of the cask.

Then he went into the dairy and found enough cream left to fill the churn again, and so he began to churn, for butter they must have at dinner. When he had churned a bit, he remembered that their milking cow was still shut up in the barn and hadn't had a bit to eat or a drop to drink all the morning, though the sun was high. Then all at once he thought 'twas too far to take her down to the meadow, so he'd just get her up on the housetop—for the house was thatched with sod, and a fine crop of grass was growing there. Now their house lay close up against a steep hill, and he thought if he laid a plank from the hill to the back of the roof, he'd easily get the cow up.

But still he couldn't leave the churn, for there was his little babe crawling about on the floor, and if I leave it, he thought, the child is sure to upset it. So he took the churn on his back and went out with it; but then he thought he'd better first water the cow before he turned her out on the thatch. He took up a bucket to draw water out of the well; but as he stooped down at the well's brink, all the cream ran out of the churn over his shoulders and down into the well.

Now it was near dinnertime, and he hadn't even got the butter made yet; so he thought he'd best boil the porridge. He filled the pot with water and hung it over the fire. When he had done that, he thought the cow might perhaps fall off the thatch and break her legs or her neck. He got up on the house to tie her up. One end of the rope he made fast to the cow's neck and the other he slipped down the chimney and tied around his own thigh. He had to make haste, for the water now began to boil in the pot, and he had still to grind the oatmeal.

So he began to grind away; but while he was hard at it, down fell the cow off the housetop after all, and as she fell, she dragged the man up the chimney by the rope. There he stuck fast. As for the cow, she hung halfway down the wall, swinging between heaven and earth, for she could neither get down nor up.

And now the wife had waited seven lengths and seven breadths for her husband to come and call her home to dinner; but never a call she had. At last she thought she'd waited long enough and went home. When she got there and saw the cow hanging in such an ugly place, she ran up and cut the rope in two with her scythe. But as she did this, down came her husband out of the chimney; and so when his old dame came inside the kitchen, there she found him standing on his head in the porridge pot.

The Chimaera

by Nathaniel Hawthorne

A master storyteller gives fresh excitement to a classic tale of a three-headed monster, a hero, and a winged horse.

Once, in the old, old times, a fountain gushed out of a hillside in the marvelous land of Greece. There it was, welling freshly forth and sparkling down the hill-side in the golden sunset, when a handsome young man named Bellerophon drew near its margin. In his hand he held a bridle studded with gems and adorned with a golden bit. Seeing an old man and another of middle age and a little boy near the fountain, and a maiden who was dipping up some of the water in a pitcher, he begged that he might refresh himself with a draft.

"This is delicious water," he said to the maiden as he rinsed and filled her pitcher after drinking out of it. "Will you tell me whether the fountain has a name?"

"Yes; it is called the Fountain of Pirene," answered the maiden. "My grandmother has told me that it was once a beautiful woman; and when her son was killed by the arrows of the huntress Diana, she melted away into tears. And so the water, which you find so cool and sweet, is the sorrow of that poor mother's heart!"

"This, then, is Pirene?" said the stranger. "I have come from far away to find this very spot."

The middle-aged country fellow (he had driven his cow to drink out of the spring) stared hard at Bellerophon.

"The watercourses must be getting low, friend, in your part of the world," remarked he, "if you come so far only to find the Fountain of Pirene. But, pray, have you lost a horse? I see you carry the bridle in your hand; and a very pretty one it is. If the horse was as fine as the bridle, you are much to be pitied for losing him."

"I have lost no horse," said Bellerophon with a smile. "But I am seeking a very famous one, which wise people have informed me must be found hereabouts, if anywhere. Do you know whether the winged horse, Pegasus, still haunts the Fountain of Pirene, as he used to do in your forefathers' days?"

But then the country fellow laughed.

Some of you have probably heard that this Pegasus was a snow-white steed with silvery wings, who spent most of his time on the summit of Mount Helicon. He was as wild, and as swift, and as buoyant in his flight through the air, as any eagle. There was nothing else like him in the world. He had no mate; he never had been backed or bridled by a master; and, for many a long year, he had led a solitary and a happy life.

Oh, how fine a thing it is to be a winged horse! Sleeping at night, as he did, on a lofty mountaintop, and passing the greater part of the day in the air, Pegasus seemed hardly to be a creature of the earth. Whenever he was seen, up very high above people's heads, with the sunshine on his silvery wings, you would have thought that he belonged to the sky, and that, skimming a little too low, he had got astray among our mists and vapors and was seeking his way back again. It was very pretty to behold him plunge into the fleecy bosom of a bright cloud, and be lost in it for a moment or two, and then break forth from the other side. Or, in a sullen rainstorm, when there was a gray pavement of clouds over the whole sky, the winged horse sometimes would descend right through it, and the glad light of the upper region would gleam after him.

In the summertime, Pegasus often alighted on the earth and, closing his wings, would gallop over hill and dale for pastime, as fleetly as the wind. Oftener than in any other place, he had been seen near the Fountain of Pirene, drinking the delicious water or rolling himself upon the soft grass of the margin. Sometimes, too, he would crop a few of the sweetest clover blossoms.

To the Fountain of Pirene, therefore, people's great-grandfathers had been in the habit of going in hopes of getting a glimpse of the beautiful Pegasus. But of late years he had been very seldom seen. Indeed, many of the countryfolk dwelling within half an hour's walk of the fountain did not believe that any such creature existed. The country fellow to whom Bellerophon was speaking chanced to be one of them. And that was why he laughed.

"Pegasus, indeed!" cried he. "A winged horse, truly! Why, friend, are you in your senses? Of what use would wings be to a horse? Could he drag the plow so well, think you? To be sure, there might be a little saving in the expense of shoes; but then, how would a man like to see his horse flying out of the stable window—yes, or whisking him up above the clouds, when he only wanted to ride to mill? No, no! I don't believe in Pegasus."

"I have some reason to think otherwise," said Bellerophon quietly.

And then he turned to the old man, who was leaning on a staff and listening very attentively, with his head stretched forward and one hand at his ear, because he was rather deaf.

"And what say you, venerable sir?" inquired he. "In your younger days you must have seen the winged steed!"

"Ah, young stranger, my memory is very poor!" said the aged man. "If I ever saw the creature, it was a long, long while ago; and, to tell you the truth, I doubt whether I ever did see him."

"And have you never seen him?" asked Bellerophon of the girl, who stood with the pitcher on her head while this talk went on.

"Once I thought I saw him," replied the maiden. "It was either Pegasus or a large white bird, a very great way up in the air. And one other time, as I was coming to the fountain with my pitcher, I heard a neigh. Oh, such a melodious neigh that was! My heart leaped with delight at the sound. But it startled me, nevertheless, so that I ran home without filling my pitcher!"

"That was truly a pity!" said Bellerophon.

And he turned to the child. "Well, my little fellow," cried Bellerophon, playfully pulling one of his curls, "I suppose you have seen the winged horse."

"That I have," answered the child very readily. "I saw him yesterday, and many times before."

"Come, tell me all about it," said Bellerophon, drawing the child closer.

"Why," replied the child, "I often come here to sail little boats in the fountain. And sometimes, when I look down into the water, I see the image of the winged horse in the picture of the sky that is there. I wish he would come down and take me on his back and let me ride him up to the moon! But if I so much as stir to look at him, he flies far away out of sight."

And Bellerophon put his faith in the child, who had seen the image of Pegasus in the water, and in the maiden, who had heard him neigh so melodiously, rather than in the middle-aged clown, who believed only in cart horses, or in the old man, who had forgotten the beautiful things of his youth.

Therefore he haunted the Fountain of Pirene for many days. He kept continually on the watch, looking upward at the sky or else down into the water, hoping to see either the reflected image of the winged horse or the marvelous reality. He held the bridle, with its bright gems and golden bit, always ready in his hand. The rustic people who dwelt in the neighborhood and drove their cattle to the fountain to drink would often laugh at poor Bellerophon, and sometimes take him pretty severely to task. They told him that an able-bodied young man like himself ought to have better business than to be wasting his time in such an idle pursuit. They offered to sell him a horse, if he wanted one; and when Bellerophon declined the purchase, they tried to drive a bargain with him for his fine bridle.

But the gentle child who had seen the picture of Pegasus in the water often sat down beside the stranger and, without speaking a word, would look down into the fountain and up toward the sky with so innocent a faith that Bellerophon could not help feeling encouraged.

Now you will, perhaps, wish to be told why it was that Bellerophon had undertaken to catch the winged horse. And we shall find no better opportunity to speak about this matter than while he is waiting for Pegasus to appear.

In a certain country of Asia, a terrible monster, called a Chimaera, had made its appearance and was doing more mischief than could be talked about between now and sunset. This Chimaera was the ugliest and most poisonous creature, and the strangest and most unaccountable, and the hardest to fight with, and the most difficult to run away from, that ever came out of the earth's inside. It had a tail like a boa constrictor; its body was like I do not know what; and it had three separate heads, one of which was a lion's, the second a goat's, and the third an abominably great snake's. And a hot blast of fire came flaming out of each of its three mouths! It ran like a goat and a lion, and wriggled along like a serpent, and thus contrived to make about as much speed as all the three together.

With its flaming breath it could set a forest on fire, or burn up a field of grain, or a village with all its fences and houses. It used to eat up people and animals alive and cook them afterward in the burning oven of its stomach.

While the hateful beast was doing all these horrible things, it so chanced that Bellerophon came to that part of the world on a visit to the king. The king's name was Iobates, and Lycia was the country that he ruled over. Bellerophon was one of the bravest youths in the world and desired nothing so much as to do some valiant and beneficent deed that would make all mankind admire and love him. King Iobates, perceiving the courage of his youthful visitor, proposed to him to go and fight the Chimaera, which everybody else was afraid of, and which, unless it should be soon killed, was likely to convert Lycia into a desert. Bellerophon assured the king that he would either slay this dreaded Chimaera, or perish in the attempt.

But as the monster was so prodigiously swift, he bethought himself that he should never win the victory by fighting on foot. The wisest thing he could do was to get the very fleetest horse that could anywhere be found. And what other horse was half so fleet as Pegasus, who had wings as well as legs and was even more active in the air than on the earth? To be sure, a great many people denied that there was any such horse. But Bellerophon believed that Pegasus was real, and hoped that he might be fortunate enough to find him.

And this was why he had traveled to Greece and had brought the beautifully ornamented bridle. It was an enchanted bridle. If he could only succeed in putting the golden bit into the mouth of Pegasus, the winged horse would be submissive and would acknowledge Bellerophon as his master.

It was a weary and anxious time while Bellerophon waited and waited for Pegasus to come and drink at the Fountain of Pirene.

Well was it for him that the gentle child had grown so fond of him and was never weary of keeping him company.

"Dear Bellerophon," he would cry every morning, "I think we shall see Pegasus today!"

And at length, if it had not been for the little boy's unwavering faith, Bellerophon would have gone back to Lycia and would have done his best to slay the Chimaera without the help of the winged horse. And in that case he would most probably have been killed and devoured.

One morning the child spoke to Bellerophon even more hopefully than usual. "Dear, dear Bellerophon," cried he, "I know not why it is, but I feel as if we should certainly see Pegasus today!"

And all that day he would not stir a step from Bellerophon's side. In the afternoon, there they sat, and Bellerophon had thrown his arm around the child, who likewise had put one of his little hands into Bellerophon's. The child was gazing down into the water when suddenly Bellerophon heard a soft, almost breathless whisper.

"See there, dear Bellerophon! There is an image in the water!"

The young man looked down into the mirror of the fountain and saw what he took to be the reflection of a bird flying at a great height in the air, with a gleam of sunshine on its snowy or silvery wings.

"What a splendid bird it must be!" said he. "And how very large it looks."

"Do you not see that it is the winged horse, Pegasus?" whispered the child.

Bellerophon gazed keenly upward but could not see the winged creature, because just then it had plunged into the fleecy depths of a summer cloud. It was but a moment, however, before the object reappeared, sinking lightly down out of the cloud, although still at a vast distance from the earth. Bellerophon caught the child in his arms and shrank back with him, so that they were both hidden among the thick shrubbery that grew all around the fountain. Not that he was afraid of any harm, but he dreaded lest, if Pegasus caught a glimpse of them, he would fly far away again. For it was really the winged horse, coming to quench his thirst with the water of Pirene.

Downward came Pegasus, in wide, sweeping circles that grew narrower and narrower still as he gradually approached the earth. The nearer the view of him, the more beautiful he was. At last, with so light a pressure as hardly to bend the grass about the fountain or imprint a hoof-tramp in the sand of its margin, he alighted and, stooping his wild head, began to drink. He drew in the water with long and pleasant sighs. And when his thirst was slaked, he cropped a few of the honey blossoms of the clover.

Then the winged horse began to caper to and fro and dance, as it were, out of mere idleness and sport. Bellerophon, meanwhile, holding the child's hand, peeped forth from the shrubbery and thought that never was any sight so beautiful as this, nor ever a horse's eyes so wild and spirited as those of Pegasus.

At length Pegasus folded his wings and lay down on the soft green turf. But being too full of aerial life to remain quiet for many moments together, he soon rolled over on his back, with his four slender legs in the air. It was beautiful to see him, this one solitary creature, whose mate had never been created, but who needed no companion and, living a great many hundred years, was as happy as the centuries were long. The more he did such things as mortal horses are accustomed to do, the less earthly and the more wonderful he seemed. Finally Pegasus turned himself about and put out his forelegs in order to rise from the ground; and Bellerophon darted suddenly from the thicket and leaped astride his back.

Yes, there he sat, on the back of the winged horse!

But what a bound did Pegasus make when, for the first time, he felt the weight of a mortal man upon his loins! Before he had time to draw a breath, Bellerophon found himself five hundred feet aloft and still shooting upward, while the winged horse snorted and trembled with terror and anger. Upward he went, up, up, up, until he plunged into the cold misty bosom of a cloud. Then out of the cloud Pegasus shot down like a thunderbolt, as if he meant to dash both himself and his rider headlong against a rock.

I cannot tell you half that he did then. He skimmed straight forward, and sideways, and backward. He reared himself erect, with his forelegs on a wreath of mist and his hind legs on nothing at all. He flung out his heels behind and put down his head between his legs, with his wings pointing right upward. At about two miles' height above the earth, he turned a somersault, so that Bellerophon's heels were where his head should have been, and he seemed to look down into the sky instead of up. The steed twisted his head about and, looking Bellerophon in the face with fire flashing from his eyes, made a terrible attempt to bite him. He fluttered his pinions so wildly that one of the silver feathers was shaken out and, floating earthward, was picked up by the child, who kept it as long as he lived, in memory of Pegasus and Bellerophon.

But the latter had been watching his opportunity, and at last clapped the golden bit of the enchanted bridle between the winged steed's jaws. No sooner was this done than Pegasus became as manageable as if he had taken food all his life out of Bellerophon's hand. To speak what I really feel, it was almost a sadness to see so wild a creature grow suddenly so tame. And Pegasus seemed to feel it so, likewise. He looked around to Bellerophon with tears in his beautiful eyes, instead of the fire that so recently flashed from them. But when Bellerophon patted his head and spoke a few authoritative yet kind and soothing words, another look came into the eyes of Pegasus; for he was glad at heart, after so many lonely centuries, to have found a companion and a master.

While Pegasus had been doing his utmost to shake Bellerophon off his back, he had flown a very long distance; and they had come within sight of a lofty mountain by the time the bit was in his mouth. Bellerophon had seen this mountain before and knew it to be Helicon, on the summit of which was the winged horse's abode. Thither (after looking into his rider's face as if to ask leave) Pegasus now flew and, alighting, waited patiently until Bellerophon should please to dismount. The young man leaped from his steed's back, but still held him fast by the bridle. Meeting his eyes, however, he was so affected by the gentleness of his aspect and by the thought of the free life which Pegasus had heretofore lived, that he could not bear to keep him a prisoner if he really desired his liberty.

Obeying this generous impulse, he slipped the enchanted bridle off the head of Pegasus and took the bit from his mouth.

"Leave me, Pegasus!" said he. "Either leave me or love me."

In an instant, the winged horse shot straight upward from the summit of Mount Helicon. Being long after sunset, it was now twilight on the mountaintop and dusky evening over all the country round about. But Pegasus flew so high that he overtook the departed day and was bathed in the upper radiance of the sun. Ascending higher and higher, he looked like a bright speck and, at last, could no longer be seen. And Bellerophon was afraid that he should never behold him more. But while he was lamenting his own folly, the bright speck reappeared and drew nearer and nearer, until behold, Pegasus had come back! After this, he and Bellerophon were friends and put loving faith in one another.

That night they lay down and slept, with Bellerophon's arm about the neck of Pegasus, not as a caution but for kindness. And they awoke at peep of day and bade one another good morning, each in his own language.

In this manner Bellerophon and the wondrous steed spent several days, growing better acquainted. They went on long aerial journeys and visited distant countries, amazing the inhabitants. Bellerophon would have liked to live always in the same way, but he could not forget the horrible Chimaera, which he had promised to slay. So, at last, when he had become well accustomed to feats of horsemanship in the air and could manage Pegasus with the least motion of his hand, he determined to attempt this perilous adventure.

At daybreak, therefore, as soon as he unclosed his eyes, he gently pinched the winged horse's ear in order to arouse him. "Dear Pegasus! Today we are to fight the terrible Chimaera."

As soon as they had eaten their morning meal, Pegasus held out his head so that his master might put on the bridle. Then, with a great many airy caperings, he showed his impatience to be gone, while Bellerophon was girding on his sword and hanging his shield about his neck and preparing himself for battle. When everything was ready, the rider mounted, and they ascended five miles perpendicularly, so Bellerophon could better see whither he was directing his course. He then turned the head of Pegasus toward the east.

It was still early in the forenoon when they beheld the lofty mountains of Lycia, with their deep valleys, in one of which the Chimaera had taken up its abode.

Now the winged horse gradually descended with his rider, and they took advantage of some clouds that were floating over the mountaintops to conceal themselves. Hovering on the upper surface of a cloud and peeping over its edge, Bellerophon could look into all Lycia at once. There was a wild, savage, and rocky tract of high and precipitous hills. In the more level part of the country, there were the ruins of houses that had been burned and, here and there, the carcasses of dead cattle strewn about the pastures.

The Chimaera must have done this mischief, thought Bellerophon. But where can the monster be?

There was nothing remarkable to be detected at first sight, unless it was three spires of black smoke that issued from what seemed to be the mouth of a cavern and clambered sullenly into the atmosphere. Before reaching the mountaintop, these three black smoke wreaths mingled themselves into one. The cavern was almost directly beneath the winged horse and his rider, at the distance of about a thousand feet. The smoke, as it crept heavily upward, had an ugly, sulfurous, stifling scent that caused Pegasus to snort and Bellerophon to sneeze. So disagreeable was it to the steed (who was accustomed to breathing only the purest air), that he waved his wings and shot half a mile out of the range of this offensive vapor.

But on looking behind him, Bellerophon saw something that induced him to turn Pegasus about. He made a sign, which the winged horse understood. He sank slowly through the air until his hoofs were scarcely more than a man's height above the rocky bottom of the valley. In front, as far off as you could throw a stone, was the cavern's mouth, with the three smoke wreaths oozing out of it. And what else did Bellerophon behold there?

There seemed to be a heap of strange and terrible creatures curled up within the cavern. Judging by their heads, one was a huge snake, the second a fierce lion, and the third an ugly goat. The lion and the goat were asleep; the snake was wide awake, and kept staring around with a great pair of fiery eyes. The three spires of smoke issued from the nostrils of these three heads! So strange was the spectacle that, though Bellerophon had been expecting it, the truth did not immediately occur to him that here was the terrible three-headed Chimaera. The snake, the lion, and the goat were one monster! It held, in its abominable claws, the remnant of an unfortunate lamb, which its three mouths had been gnawing before two of them fell asleep!

All at once, Bellerophon started as if from a dream and knew it to be the Chimaera. Pegasus seemed to know it at the same instant and sent forth a neigh that sounded like the call of a trumpet to battle. At this sound, the three heads reared themselves erect and belched out great flashes of flame. Before Bellerophon had time to consider what to do next, the monster flung itself out of the cavern and sprang straight toward him, with its immense claws extended and its snaky tail twisting venomously behind. If Pegasus had not been as nimble as a bird, both he and his rider would have been overthrown by the Chimaera's headlong rush, and thus the battle have been ended before it was well begun. But in the twinkling of an eye, the winged horse was up aloft, halfway to the clouds, snorting with anger.

The Chimaera, on the other hand, raised itself up so as to stand absolutely on the tip end of its tail, with its talons pawing fiercely in the air and its three heads spluttering fire at Pegasus and his rider. How it roared and hissed and bellowed! Bellerophon, meanwhile, was fitting his shield on his arm and drawing his sword.

"Now, my beloved Pegasus," he whispered in the winged horse's ear, "you must help me to slay this insufferable monster, or else you shall fly back to your solitary mountain peak without your friend Bellerophon. For either the Chimaera dies, or its mouths shall gnaw this head of mine, which has slumbered upon your neck!"

Uttering these words, he shook the bridle; and Pegasus darted down aslant, as swift as the flight of an arrow, right toward the Chimaera's threefold head. As he came within arm's length, Bellerophon made a cut at the monster, but was

carried onward by his steed before he could see whether the blow had been successful. Pegasus continued his course, but soon wheeled around at about the same distance from the Chimaera as before. Bellerophon then perceived that he had cut the goat's head of the monster almost off, so that it dangled downward by the skin and seemed quite dead.

But to make amends, the snake's head and the lion's head had taken all the fierceness of the dead one into themselves and spit flame and hissed and roared with more fury than before.

"Never mind, my brave Pegasus!" cried Bellerophon. "With another stroke like that, we will stop either its hissing or its roaring."

And again he shook the bridle. Dashing aslant as before, the winged horse made another flight toward the Chimaera, and Bellerophon aimed another downward stroke at one of the two remaining heads as he shot by. But this time, neither he nor Pegasus escaped so well as at first. With one of its claws, the Chimaera gave the young man a deep scratch in his shoulder, and slightly damaged the left wing of the flying steed with the other. On his part, Bellerophon mortally wounded the lion's head of the monster, so that it hung down, with its fire almost extinguished and sending out gasps of thick black smoke. The snake's head was now twice as fierce and venomous as ever before. It belched forth shoots of fire five hundred yards long and emitted hisses so loud, so harsh, and so ear-piercing that King Iobates heard them fifty miles off.

Welladay! thought the poor king, the Chimaera is certainly coming to devour me!

Meanwhile Pegasus had again paused in the air and neighed angrily, while sparkles of a pure crystal flame darted out of his eyes.

"Do you bleed, my immortal horse?" cried Bellerophon, caring less for his own hurt than for the anguish of this glorious creature. "The execrable Chimaera shall pay for this mischief with its last head!"

Then he shouted loudly and guided Pegasus straight at the monster's hideous front. So rapid was the onset that it seemed but a dazzle and a flash before Bellerophon was at close grips with his enemy.

The Chimaera, after losing its second head, had got into a red-hot passion of pain and rage. It shot out a tremendous blast of its fiery breath and enveloped Bellerophon and his steed in flame, singeing the wings of Pegasus, scorching off one whole side of the young man's golden ringlets.

But this was nothing to what followed. When the winged horse had come within a hundred yards, the Chimaera gave a spring and flung its huge carcass right upon poor Pegasus, clung around him with might and main, and tied up its snaky tail into a knot! Up flew the aerial steed, higher, higher, higher, above the mountain peaks, above the clouds. But still the earthborn monster kept its hold and was carried upward, along with the creature of light and air. Bellerophon, meanwhile, turning about, found himself face to face with the ugly Chimaera and could only avoid being scorched to death, or bitten right in twain, by holding up his shield. Over the upper edge of the shield, he looked sternly into the savage eyes of the monster.

But the Chimaera was so wild with pain that it did not guard itself so well as might else have been the case. Perhaps, after all, the best way to fight a Chimaera is by getting as close to it as you can. In its efforts to stick its iron claws into its enemy, the creature left its own breast quite exposed; and Bellerophon thrust his sword up to the hilt into its cruel heart. Immediately the snaky tail untied its knot. The monster let go its hold of Pegasus and fell from that vast height downward; while the fire within its bosom, instead of being put out, burned fiercer than ever and quickly began to consume the dead carcass. Thus it fell out of the sky, all aflame, and (it being nightfall before it reached the earth) was mistaken for a shooting star or a comet. But at early sunrise, some cottagers were going to their day's labor and saw, to their astonishment, that several acres of ground were strewn with black ashes. In the middle of a field, there was a heap of whitened bones, a great deal higher than a haystack. Nothing else was ever seen of the dreadful Chimaera!

And when Bellerophon had won the victory, he bent forward and kissed Pegasus, while the tears stood in his eyes.

"Back now, my beloved steed!" said he. "Back to the Fountain of Pirene! To the gentle child who used to keep me company, and never lost his faith, and never was weary of gazing into the fountain."

Pegasus skimmed through the air, quicker than ever he did before, and reached the fountain in a very short time.

"You have won the victory," said the little boy joyfully, running to the knee of Bellerophon. "I knew you would."

"Yes, dear child!" replied Bellerophon, alighting from the winged horse. "But if your faith had not helped me, I should never have waited for Pegasus and never have conquered the terrible Chimaera. You, my little friend, have done it all. And now let us give Pegasus his liberty."

So he slipped off the enchanted bridle from the head of the marvelous steed. "Be free forevermore, my Pegasus!" cried he, with a shade of sadness in his tone. "Be as free as you are fleet!"

But Pegasus rested his head on Bellerophon's shoulder and would not be persuaded to take flight.

"Well then," said Bellerophon, caressing the airy horse, "you shall be with me as long as you will; and we will go together forthwith, and tell King Iobates that the Chimaera is destroyed."

Then Bellerophon embraced the child, and promised to come to him again, and departed. But in afteryears that child took higher flights upon the aerial steed than ever did Bellerophon, and achieved more honorable deeds than his friend's victory over the Chimaera. For, gentle and tender as he was, he grew to be a mighty poet!

Acknowledgments

THE GHOST IN THE ATTIC is slightly abridged and adapted from *The Moffats,* copyright 1941, copyright © renewed 1969 by Eleanor Estes. Reprinted by permission of Harcourt Brace Jovanovich, Inc., and The Bodley Head. HOW THE RHINOCEROS GOT HIS SKIN and THE CRAB THAT PLAYED WITH THE SEA are from *Just So Stories,* copyright 1912 by Rudyard Kipling. Reprinted by permission of Doubleday & Company, Inc., The National Trust and Macmillan London Limited. IMPUNITY JANE is from *Impunity Jane: The Story of a Pocket Doll,* copyright 1954 by Rumer Godden, published by Viking Press. Reprinted by permission of Viking Penguin Inc. and Curtis Brown, Ltd. KILDEE HOUSE is from *Kildee House,* copyright 1949 by Rutherford Montgomery. Reprinted by permission of Barthold Fles, Literary Agent. TWO LOGS CROSSING is from *Seven American Stories,* copyright 1943 by Walter D. Edmonds. Reprinted by permission of Little, Brown & Company and Harold Ober Associates Incorporated. HATS FOR HORSES is from *A Street of Little Shops,* copyright 1932 by Margery Williams Bianco. Reprinted by permission of Doubleday & Company, Inc., and the author's estate. THE MOST PRECIOUS POSSESSION and MARCH AND THE SHEPHERD are from *Old Italian Tales,* copyright © 1958 by Domenico Vittorini, published by David McKay Company, Inc. Reprinted by permission of Mrs. Helen W. Vittorini. JUG OF SILVER is from *A Tree of Night and Other Stories,* copyright 1945, copyright © renewed 1973 by Truman Capote. Reprinted by permission of Random House, Inc. WHEN SHLEMIEL WENT TO WARSAW and SHREWD TODIE & LYZER THE MISER are from *When Shlemiel Went to Warsaw & Other Stories,* copyright © 1968 by Isaac Bashevis Singer. Reprinted by permission of Farrar, Straus and Giroux, Inc., Longman Young Books and Laurence Pollinger Ltd. ROOF SITTER is from *There's One in Every Family,* copyright 1941 by Frances Eisenberg and Peggy Bacon, copyright © renewed 1968 by Peggy Bacon, published by J. B. Lippincott Company. Reprinted by permission of Harper & Row, Publishers, Inc. MIGHTY MIKKO, copyright 1922 by Parker Fillmore, copyright renewed 1950 by Louise Fillmore, is from *The Shepherd's Nosegay.* Reprinted by permission of Harcourt Brace Jovanovich, Inc. OSMO'S SHARE is from *Mighty Mikko: A Book of Finnish Fairy Tales and Folk Tales,* copyright 1922 by Parker Fillmore, copyright renewed 1950 by Louise Fillmore. Reprinted by permission of Harcourt Brace Jovanovich, Inc. THE PRINCESS AND THE VAGABONE, slightly abridged, is from *The Way of the Storyteller,* copyright 1942, copyright © 1962 by Ruth Sawyer, copyright © renewed 1970 by Ruth Sawyer. Reprinted by permission of Viking Penguin Inc. and The Bodley Head. THE SCOTTY WHO KNEW TOO MUCH, copyright 1940 by James Thurber, copyright © renewed 1968 by Helen Thurber, is from *Fables for Our Time,* published by Harper & Row, Publishers, Inc. Reprinted by permission of the estate and Hamish Hamilton Ltd. OLIVER AND THE OTHER OSTRICHES, copyright © 1956 by James Thurber, is from *Further Fables for Our Time,* published by Simon & Schuster. Reprinted by permission of the estate and Hamish Hamilton Ltd. COWPONY'S PRIZE, copyright 1935 by Lavinia R. Davis. Reprinted by permission of Samuel S. Walker. THE THREE TRAVELLERS is from *A Necklace of Raindrops and Other Stories,* copyright © 1968 by Joan Aiken. Reprinted by permission of Doubleday & Company, Inc., Jonathan Cape Ltd. and Brandt & Brandt Literary Agents, Inc. ALPHONSE, THAT BEARDED ONE by Natalie Savage Carlson, copyright 1954 by Harcourt Brace and Company. Reprinted by permission of Harcourt Brace Jovanovich, Inc. A LEMON AND A STAR is abridged and slightly adapted from *A Lemon and A Star,* copyright © 1955 by E. C. Spykman. Reprinted by permission of Harcourt Brace Jovanovich, Inc. PECOS BILL is from *Pecos Bill and Lightning,* copyright 1940, copyright © renewed

1968 by Leigh Peck. Reprinted by permission of Houghton Mifflin Company. THE BEAR IN THE PEAR TREE is from *Once the Hodja,* copyright 1943 by Alice Geer Kelsey, published by David McKay Company, Inc. Reprinted by permission of the author. DONKEY, MIND YOUR MOTHER! is from *Once the Mullah,* copyright 1954 by Alice Geer Kelsey, published by Longmans, Green and Co., Inc. Reprinted by permission of the author. THE TALE OF GODFREY MALBONE is from *New England Bean-Pot,* copyright 1948 by M. Jagendorf, copyright © renewed 1975 by Moritz Jagendorf. Reprinted by permission of Vanguard Press, Inc. THE DOG OF POMPEII, slightly abridged, is from *The Donkey of God* by Louis Untermeyer, copyright 1932 by Harcourt, Brace and Company, copyright © renewed 1960 by Louis Untermeyer. Reprinted by permission of Harcourt Brace Jovanovich, Inc. CALL THIS LAND HOME is from *Pioneer Loves* by Ernest Haycox, copyright 1947, 1948 by The Curtis Publishing Company, copyright © renewed 1976 by Jill Marie Haycox. Reprinted by permission of Jill Marie Haycox. THE FOUR BROTHERS and THE HARE AND THE HEDGEHOG are from *Tales Told Again,* copyright 1927 by Walter de la Mare, published by Alfred A. Knopf, Inc. Reprinted by permission of The Literary Trustees of Walter de la Mare and The Society of Authors as their representative. THE DOUGHNUTS is from *Homer Price,* copyright 1943, copyright © renewed 1971 by Robert McCloskey. Reprinted by permission of Viking Penguin Inc. A HERO BY MISTAKE, copyright 1953, copyright © renewed 1981 by Anita Brenner. A Young Scott Book, reprinted by permission of Addison-Wesley Publishing Company, Inc. BEING A PUBLIC CHARACTER is from *The Revolt of the Oyster* by Don Marquis, copyright 1917 by The Crowell Publishing Company, Inc. Reprinted by permission of Doubleday & Company, Inc. THE CLAWS OF THE CAT, copyright 1952 by Stuart Cloete. Reprinted by permission of William Morris Agency, Inc., on behalf of the author. THE GIANT WHO SUCKED HIS THUMB is from *Fee, Fi, Fo, Fum,* copyright © 1969 by Adrien Stoutenburg. Reprinted by permission of Viking Penguin Inc. and Curtis Brown, Ltd. TOM AND THE DUDE is from *The Great Brain Does It Again,* copyright © 1975 by John D. Fitzgerald. Reprinted by permission of The Dial Press and Ann Elmo Agency on behalf of the author. AS HAI LOW KEPT HOUSE is from *Shen of the Sea: Chinese Stories for Children* by Arthur Bowie Chrisman, copyright 1925 by E. P. Dutton & Co., Inc., copyright renewed 1953 by Arthur Bowie Chrisman. Reprinted by permission of E. P. Dutton. MAMA AND THE GRADUATION PRESENT is adapted from *Mama's Bank Account,* copyright 1943 by Kathryn Forbes, copyright © renewed 1971 by Richard E. McLean and Robert M. McLean. Reprinted by permission of Harcourt Brace Jovanovich, Inc., and Curtis Brown, Ltd. STORMY PLACE is from *Barney Hits the Trail,* copyright 1950 by Sara and Fred Machetanz. Reprinted by permission of Charles Scribner's Sons. THE DRAGON IN THE CLOCK BOX by M. Jean Craig, copyright © 1961 by The Curtis Publishing Company. Reprinted by permission of the author. THE DANCING FOX is from *Black Rainbow: Legends of the Incas and Myths of Ancient Peru,* translation copyright © 1976 by John Bierhorst. Reprinted by permission of Farrar, Straus and Giroux, Inc. THE BOY WHO VOTED FOR ABE LINCOLN by Milton Richards originally appeared in *The Catholic Boy,* copyright 1949 by Publications for Catholic Youth. Reprinted by permission of Winston Press. BLUE WILLOW is from *Blue Willow,* copyright 1940, copyright © renewed 1968 by Doris Gates. Reprinted by permission of Viking Penguin Inc. THE TALE OF THE LAZY PEOPLE is from *Tales from Silver Lands* by Charles J. Finger, copyright 1924 by Doubleday & Company, Inc. Reprinted by permission of Doubleday & Company, Inc. TONY BEAVER is from *Yankee Doodle's Cousins* by Anne Malcolmson, copyright 1941 by Anne Burnett Malcolmson, copyright © renewed 1969 by Anne Malcolmson von Storch. Reprinted by permission of Houghton Mifflin Company. SPURS FOR ANTONIA is from *Spurs for Antonia* by K. W. Eyre, copyright 1943 by Katherine Wigmore Eyre. Reprinted by permission of David McKay Company, Inc. REGGIE'S NO-GOOD BIRD is from *Reggie's No-Good Bird* by Nellie Burchardt, copyright © 1967 by Franklin Watts, Inc. Reprinted by permission of Franklin Watts, Inc. THE TROUT is from *The Man Who Invented Sin* by Sean O'Faolain, copyright 1948, copyright © renewed 1976 by The Devin-Adair Company. Reprinted by permission of the author and The Devin-Adair Company. BYNG TAKES A HAND is from *Dignity, a Springer Spaniel,* copyright 1937, copyright © renewed 1965 by S. P. Meek. Reprinted by permission of Alfred A. Knopf, Inc. CADDIE WOODLAWN AND THE INDIANS is from *Caddie Woodlawn,* copyright 1935 by Macmillan Publishing Co., Inc., copyright © renewed 1963 by Carol Ryrie Brink. Reprinted by permission of Macmillan Publishing Co., Inc. NOT DRIVING AND NOT RIDING is from *Norwegian Folk Tales* by Peter Christen Asbjørnsen and Jørgen Moe, published by Viking Penguin Inc. Reprinted by permission of Dreyers Forlag. The Reader's Digest Association, Inc., has attempted to clear permission with rights proprietors for HANDY SANDY by Jed F. Shaw, THE WINNER WHO DID NOT PLAY by Devereux Robinson, A PAIR OF LOVERS by Elsie Singmaster Lewars, and A LOOK AT THE GRAND CHAMP by Harold Webster Perry but, despite best efforts, has been unable to do so.